"An *immensely* entertaining novel." —Tor.com

"An extremely successful second-in-a-series book. . . . Wexler expands the cast in a smart and exciting fashion. It is a novel that, a week after finishing it, still has me thinking strongly about it." —SFFWorld

The Thousand Names

One of Buzzfeed's 12 Greatest Fantasy Books of the Year

"Wexler has produced something unusual in the fantasy line, with a setting reminiscent of the early Victorian period, out on the bleeding edge of Empire, a world of dust and bayonets and muskets . . . and magic. . . . I read it at a gulp and look forward to more." —S. M. Stirling

"I absolutely loved it. Wexler balances the actions of his very human characters with just the right amount of imaginative 'magic' to keep me wanting more."
—Taylor Anderson, *New York Times* bestselling author of the Destroyermen series

"Wexler's storytelling and characterization are top-notch, but he's really in command when the battles arrive . . . gritty, brutal, and yet wonderfully intimate . . . exceptional military fantasy."
—Jason M. Hough, *New York Times* bestselling author of *Zero World*

"Wexler's polished military fantasy . . . distinguishes itself from other epic doorstops with its unique setting, intricate plotting, and layered characters . . . for fans of Peter Brett, Daniel Abraham, and Joe Abercrombie." —*Booklist*

Also by Django Wexler

The Shadow Campaigns

The Thousand Names
The Shadow Throne
The Price of Valor
The Shadow of Elysium (a novella)

The Forbidden Library Novels

The Forbidden Library
The Mad Apprentice

THE
PRICE OF
VALOR

BOOK THREE OF THE SHADOW CAMPAIGNS

DJANGO WEXLER

A ROC BOOK

ROC
Published by New American Library,
an imprint of Penguin Random House LLC
375 Hudson Street, New York, New York 10014

This book is a publication of New American Library. Previously published in a Roc hardcover edition.

First Roc Mass Market Printing, June 2016

For more information about Penguin Random House, visit penguin.com.

ISBN 978-0-451-41809-8

Printed in the United States of America
10 9 8 7 6 5 4 3 2 1

Map illustration by Cortney Skinner

Penguin
Random
House

This one is for my friends,
who keep me sane (most of the time).

ACKNOWLEDGMENTS

This book was a new challenge for me. Since *The Shadow Throne* was largely completed before *The Thousand Names* was released, this was the first time I'd tried writing a book after having heard the response to the previous volumes. I've been lucky enough that the response has been largely positive, but it left me with a distinct feeling of pressure and the need to live up to everyone's expectations.

Fortunately, as always, I had plenty of help along the way. This time the first person to get her hands on a draft was Rhiannon Held. She took time away from her own writing to help me out, for which I'll be forever grateful; you should go read her books at once. Casey Blair *hadn't* read a draft, but she listened to me babble for an hour and then casually solved a plot problem I'd been worrying at for days, once again proving that she is the best. Lu Huan was kind enough to read several early versions and tip me off on where to go next.

My agent, Seth Fishman, was awesome as always, and as I was writing he gave me the welcome news that we'd gotten a contract for the fourth and fifth books in the Shadow Campaigns to close out the series. At the Gernert Company, I also owe thanks to Will Roberts, Rebecca Gardener, and Andy Kifer, and everyone else who helped bring these books around the world.

My editors, Jessica Wade at Roc and Michael Rowley at Del Rey UK, suffered through my bouts of angst and put up with my being late, and managed to do their usual excellent jobs in spite of my shenanigans. I owe Michael particular thanks for playing host and tour guide during my first visit to London; my thanks as well to all the Londoners who helped out the lost-looking, wrong-side-of-the-street-crossing American.

Once again, my final thanks to two really indispensable groups of people: first, everyone who works to make sure the book actually exists and turns up in stores, with a cover, not printed upside down or labeled as a Norwegian dictionary; second, everyone who read *The Thousand Names* and *The Shadow Throne* and thought they were worth talking about. Without you, I'd just be a guy telling stories to his cats. For the paperback edition, my thanks to Alan Wu for chasing down so many errors and typos.

THE PRICE OF VALOR

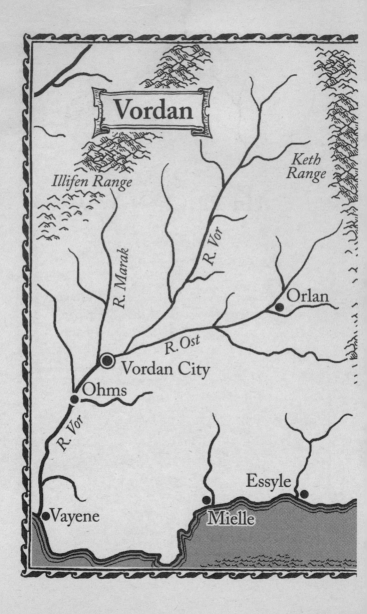

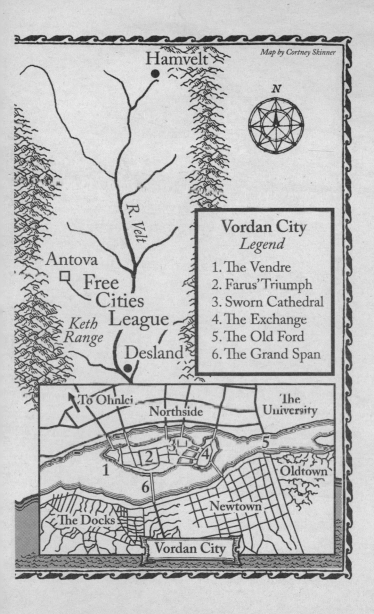

Hamvelt

N

R. Velt

Antova

Free
Cities
League

Keth
Range

Desland

Vordan City
Legend

1. The Vendre
2. Farus' Triumph
3. Sworn Cathedral
4. The Exchange
5. The Old Ford
6. The Grand Span

To Ohnlei

Northside

The
University

Oldtown

Newtown

The Docks

Vordan City

PROLOGUE

IGNAHTA SEMPRIA

Such pretty country, to be soaked in blood.

South of the city of Desland, the valley of the river Velt flattened out into a rolling carpet of fields, gridded by neat hedgerows and punctuated by tiny orderly hamlets, each with its tall-spired church tipped by a golden double circle. The river itself traced out a series of lazy curves, as though exhausted by its frantic descent from the highlands, and it flashed like molten silver in the warm autumn sun. Here and there, lone hills rose from the endless flat farmland like islands jutting out of the sea, crowned with gnarled, ancient trees, the last remaining strongholds of the great forests that had covered this land before the arrival of men.

Atop one of those hills, at the edge of one of those primeval woods, a man sat cross-legged on a boulder and stared down at the plain below. He was a young man, barely out of boyhood, with nut-brown hair and a wispy mustache. Dressed in leathers and homespun, he could have been mistaken for a native, the son of a peasant farmer come to trap or gather wood in the old forest.

In fact, he was a very long way from home, and he had no interest in firewood or game. His name was Wren. In his saddlebags, carefully folded and secured inside a lockbox, he carried a velvet mask sewn with a layer of glittering, clicking obsidian. It marked him as a servant of an order out of legend, one that was supposedly a hundred years dead: the Priests of the Black, fell agents of the Elysian Church, its spies and inquisitors.

Even within the hidden fraternity who carried out the will of the Black Priests, Wren was of a special breed. He had spoken the true name of a demon, and would play host to the creature until the end of his days. When his death came, he would be condemned to eternal torment for daring to traffic with the supernatural. He had accepted this burden, and the certainty of this ultimate fate, to serve the Church and save others from suffering similar punishment. He was one of the *Ignahta Sempria*, the Penitent Damned.

Wren stared down at the plain, across the miles, to a place where many campfires had lately burned like fireflies. At that distance, most men would have seen nothing but the fields and the rivers, but Wren's demon was with him. He could feel it in his eyes, a *tight* feeling like someone twisting knotted cords around his skull, and it sharpened his vision to excruciating precision. Tiny men in blue milled and marched and formed ranks, teams of horses were harnessed to cannon, and cavalrymen checked their saddles and mounted. An army, preparing for battle.

The brush beside him rustled. With his demon's strength wholly poured into his eyes, Wren's hearing was no better than a normal man's, and only the discipline of long training kept him from starting at the sound. Instead he let out a long breath and forced himself to relax, letting his demon return to its resting state. Between blinks, the clarity of his vision faded, though it still would have put any hawk to shame. Sound rushed back in, every tiny rustle and animal noise of the forest now as obvious as a fanfare. He could hear the heartbeats of the two men who now stood beside him, and their breathing was as loud as the rasp of a bellows.

"The Vordanai are breaking camp," he said. He spoke in Murnskai, the native tongue of those raised in the fortress-temple of Elysium. "But not to retreat. Vhalnich will offer battle to di Pfalen."

"Bold," said the man on his left.

He was much older than Wren, well into middle age, with a bald dome of skull sticking up from a ring of black and gray. His name, the only one that Wren had ever heard anyone use, was the Liar. Like Wren, he was dressed in simple peasant garb, but his hands might have invited comment: his nails were each at least an inch long, and painted with gleaming white resin.

"Di Pfalen has the numbers," Wren said. "He has broken his force into three columns to attempt to cut off Vhalnich's escape."

The Liar snorted. "I might not be so confident in his place, given Vhalnich's reputation."

Wren shrugged. The Liar liked to pass himself off as an expert in military matters, as in everything else, but the basic situation was simple enough. The revolution that had broken out after the death of King Farus VIII had shocked the civilized world, placing a sacred monarch in thrall to a mere elected parliament. With due encouragement from Elysium, the great powers of the west—Borel, Murnsk, and the Free Cities League—had gone to war to restore the rightful order. But declaration of war was one thing, and action another. Seafaring Borel preferred the slow weapons of blockade and economic warfare, while vast, backward Imperial Murnsk could take months to assemble her armies.

The League, on the other hand, was not a nation but a bickering, fractious collection of semi-independent polities. Vheed, Norel, and the more distant cities had sent only token contingents or empty promises to the supposedly common cause. Only Hamvelt and its close allies had leapt at the chance to defeat their longtime rival. So it was here, to familiar plains between Essyle and Desland, where the ever-shifting border between Vordan and the League ran, that the Vordanai had sent their newly minted hero. Janus bet Vhalnich. Conqueror of Khandar, vanquisher of the Last Duke, savior of Vordan. *Heretic. Sorcerer.*

"We will observe the result," the Liar said. "If Vhalnich falls, or is taken, our task is simplified. If not . . ."

The third man grunted. He stood with his arms crossed over his massive chest, more than a head taller than either of his companions. His craggy face was made ferocious by a thick, unkempt black beard like wild thornbush, and his small dark eyes glared out ferociously from deep, sunken sockets. While he was dressed like the other two, no one would ever take him for a simple laborer. Quite aside from his enormous frame, the air of menace he projected was unmistakable. His name was Twist. Wren had rarely heard him speak more than a single word at a time, and often he was not even that voluble.

"Either way," Wren said, "we'll need to get closer." They were still a solid day's ride from the place that would soon become a battlefield.

The Liar nodded. "We will seek another vantage. Ready the horses."

Wren got to his feet, legs aching from too long spent absolutely still, and suppressed a frown. The Penitent Damned had no formal hierarchy among themselves, no ranks or chain of command apart from their shared obedience to the Pontifex of the Black. On the rare occasions when they did not work alone, their orders made it explicit who was to lead. The Liar was an agent of many years' standing, and this was Wren's first mission outside Murnsk, so it made sense that the older man was in charge. But Wren occasionally suspected the Liar of harboring a taste for idleness and worldly pleasures that was inappropriate for his position, and it led him to treat Wren like a servant instead of an equal. It was something to raise with the pontifex on their return.

They had six horses, enough to carry their gear and provide remounts if they needed a burst of speed. Wren went through the familiar ritual of preparing saddles and tack, loading the camp supplies, and fixing each animal with his supernatural senses for a few moments, listening to their breathing and heartbeats. Satisfied that nothing was amiss, he led them one by one to the edge of the woods. Last in line was Twist's mount, a huge, stocky gelding matched to the big man's weight.

Twist took the reins from him with another grunt and heaved himself gracelessly into the saddle, provoking a snort of complaint from the animal. The Liar mounted more skillfully, a testament to half a lifetime spent in the saddle in the service of the order. Wren paused in front of his favorite mare, staring out to the north.

"Wren?" the Liar said. "Is something wrong?"

Wren closed his eyes and let the demon rush to his ears. The sounds that had been barely a shiver in the air a moment ago were now loud and distinct, low *crump*s and rumbles like distant thunder. In between, he could even hear the faint skirl of drums.

"Wren?" the Liar repeated, words booming in Wren's ears like the voice of God.

Wren opened his eyes and let the demon slither away inside his skull.

"It's begun," he said.

PART ONE

CHAPTER ONE

WINTER

"Keep it up! They're giving way!" Winter Ihernglass shouted.

The air was thick with acrid smoke, slashed by the brief brilliant flares of muzzle flashes. Musketry roared around Winter like a continuous crackling peal of thunder, and she had no way of knowing whether her soldiers could hear her. Her world had contracted to this small section of the line, where a dozen young women of the Girls' Own stood behind the shot-torn hedgerow, each going through the drill of loading her musket: ramming the ball home, priming the pan, and bringing the weapon back up to firing position.

The Hamveltai were unseen in the murk, visible only by the flash of their own muskets. But they were weakening—Winter could feel it—the return fire becoming more scattered and sporadic. *Just a minute more.* She walked along the line, shouting herself hoarse and slashing the air with her sword, while the constant din of the muskets rattled the teeth in her skull.

Ahead, she saw one of the casualty teams, made up of girls too young or too small to carry muskets. They worked in threes and fours, running up to the hedge whenever a soldier went down and dragging her back a few paces to assess the injury. As Winter watched, the team ahead of her abandoned a woman who'd taken a ball high in the chest and leaked a wide swath of blood into the muddy earth, and went back to retrieve a plump, matronly woman who'd fallen on her side, clutching a shattered hand. As they got her to her feet, one of the smaller girls suddenly doubled over, clutching at her gut with both hands. One of her companions looked her over, shook her head, and left her where she fell.

Brass Balls of the Beast. It was a scene Winter had witnessed before, but she couldn't get over how quickly girls who'd been selling flowers in Vordan not three months earlier had adapted to the brutal necessities of the battlefield. She thrust away a pang of guilt. There wasn't time for that. *No time for anything but survival.*

Winter hurried past the casualty team, stepping quickly around the dying girl, and continued down the line looking for Bobby. The young woman, who'd been a corporal in Winter's company on Janus' Khandarai campaign, now sported white lieutenant's stripes on her shoulder. A knot of women were gathered behind a dense spot in the hedge, loading awkwardly while crouched and then standing to loose another shot into the thickening bank of smoke.

"Bobby!" Winter said, grabbing her arm and pulling her close enough to hear over the din. "Go to Jane, tell her to move in!"

Bobby's pale skin was already grimed with powder residue. Like Winter, she was one of the few in the Girls' Own to have an honest-to-goodness regulation uniform; unlike Winter's, hers was no longer tailored to conceal the truth of her gender from prying eyes. When Janus had created the all-female Fifth Volunteer Battalion from the ragtag group of volunteers Winter and Jane had led into battle at Midvale, Bobby had elected to discard her disguise. She had been the one who'd taken the nickname "Girls' Own"— a play on the name old royal regiments, the King's Own, and the Boy's Own Guide series of books for children— and turned it from mockery into a badge of honor. Next to Winter and Jane, she was probably the most respected officer in the battalion.

She was also—cursed, enchanted, Winter didn't know what to call it—by the Khandarai *naath* that had saved her life. Winter knew that the scars of her wounds had healed, not in puckered skin, but as smooth, glittering stuff like living marble.

Bobby saluted to acknowledge the order, handed her musket to the nearest soldier, and hurried off to the right, bent double to keep her head from sticking above the hedge. *For all the good that will do.* A hedgerow might deflect a musket ball, but mostly it was good for hiding behind, and that only mattered against aimed fire. Nobody was aiming now; if not for their muzzle flashes and the accompanying noise, Winter wouldn't have been able to say whether the enemy was still there. She turned back in the other direction, keeping her eyes open for any signs of wavering or incipient panic, and was pleased to find her soldiers still firmly committed to their bloody work. The Hamveltai were laying down a hot, heavy fire, but for the moment the Girls' Own seemed to be standing up to the pressure.

As she moved toward the left, she could hear the deeper growl of artillery underneath the musketry. The hedge led to a small hamlet in that direction, no more than a dozen buildings, which was defended by a battalion of volunteers and half a battery of guns. Something was on fire—she could see the glow, even through the smoke—but the noise indicated the men there were still fighting hard.

On the right side of the line, the hedge took a dogleg forward a hundred yards before ending at a wide dirt path. Jane was waiting on the far side of that angle with another four companies, hunkered down and silent up until now, waiting to execute the trap. Winter didn't want her troops going toe-to-toe with a battalion of regulars longer than they had to.

Reaching the center of her line, Winter pressed herself against the hedge between a pair of soldiers and listened. *A couple of minutes for Bobby to run to Jane, a couple of minutes to get ready . . .*

A chorus of hoarse battle cries, identifiably feminine even through the rattle and bang musketry, rolled out of the smoke on the right. All along the line, Winter's soldiers echoed the cheer, which was followed in quick succession by a blaze of new firing. More flashes stabbed through the smoke, at right angles to the Hamveltai position, as Jane led her troops in a charge with fixed bayonets that took the enemy line end-on. As Winter had guessed, that convinced them that their position was untenable, and before another minute had passed there was no more shooting to her front. Along the hedgerow, the women of the Girls' Own were cheering themselves hoarse.

"Make sure those muskets are loaded!" Winter shouted, over the celebration. "They'll be back."

"You should have seen the looks on their faces," Jane said. "Bastards were so surprised they didn't even have a chance to shoot back."

"Nicely done," Winter said. Though rumors of the infamous female regiment had no doubt spread through the enemy camps by now, the League soldiers were always startled when they came into actual face-to-face contact with the Girls' Own. Winter was happy to use their hesitation to her advantage if it meant keeping her troops alive. "Any prisoners?"

"A few dozen," Jane said. "Plenty of wounded out there, but we didn't take any that couldn't walk."

They were squatting in the muddy dirt, a few yards back from the hedge. With the lull in the fighting, some of the Girls' Own were helping the casualty teams, carrying the wounded to a temporary station in the rear and dragging corpses clear of the firing line. Winter had cautioned them not to go too far. It was too easy to get caught up helping a wounded comrade and forget that the battle wasn't over yet.

To the left, artillery still growled, but the musketry had died away, indicating that the attack on the hamlet had tapered off while the League cannoneers continued the argument with their Vordanai counterparts at long range. The smoke was beginning to drift apart, torn into scraps by the late-morning breeze. Looking at the sun, Winter thought it was still at least an hour before noon; she already felt as if they'd been there for days. She closed her eyes for a moment, took a deep breath, and returned her mind to the matter at hand.

"See if any of the men you took speak Vordanai. I'd love to know what else they've got out there."

"You think they'll try it again?"

"I think they've got to. They want to push through here to take Janus from behind." It felt odd to her to casually refer to the general of the army—much less a count of Vordan—by his first name, but it had become a universal practice among the troops he commanded, as a demonstration of their affection for their strange commander. "They tried a narrow swing around the hamlet, and ran into us. So what's next?"

Jane shrugged. "You're the soldier."

Winter grimaced, but it was true, in a sense. While there were times when she still felt like a fraud—it was hard not to, when everyone but a select few thought she was a man—it was hard to deny that she had more military experience than anyone else in the Girls' Own, with the possible exception of her ex-corporals Graff and Folsom. For that matter, she had more combat experience than almost anyone in Janus' Army of the East, which was an awkward conglomeration of old Royal Army troops and scratch battalions of revolutionary volunteers.

Jane's experience was of a different sort. They'd been lovers, long ago, at Mrs. Wilmore's Prison for Young Ladies, before Jane had been dragged away into involuntary marriage to a brutal farmer and Winter had escaped to join the army. While Winter had spent three years in Khandar, lying low, Jane had escaped from servitude, freed the rest of the girls from the Prison, and brought them to Vordan City. There they'd fought criminals, tax farmers, and anyone else who got in their way, forming the core of the Leatherbacks and striving to provide a rough justice to the Docks. When Winter and Jane had been reunited in the chaos of the revolution—with a helping hand, Winter guessed, from Janus bet Vhalnich—Jane's girls joined the fight to save the city from Orlanko.

Now they made up almost half the Girls' Own, and Jane herself had accepted an officer's rank, but she didn't pretend to know anything much about tactics. Winter scratched a rough line in the earth with the toe of her boot. "If I were them, I'd feel us out to the right. If they've got another couple of battalions, they could throw one against us here and push another one down the road to get behind us."

"And if we run for it, they can surround the town," Jane said. She looked to the south, where only the occasional hedge broke the endless, open country. A lone wood-topped hill, miles distant, loomed like a distant gray monolith. "If they get us with horsemen in the open . . ."

Winter nodded. Jane might not have had a military education, but she had good instincts. The Girls' Own were brave, dedicated troops, but they didn't have the training to form square and stand off cavalry in the open. The volunteers who made up most of the rest of the force Janus had left to blunt the League advance were the same. They had only one regiment of "Royals"—professional soldiers of the old Royal Army—and a retreat under those circumstances could easily become a rout.

"I'll send Bobby to Colonel de Ferre," Winter said. "If he brings up the reserve before they get here, we can give them another nasty surprise. They've got to get sick of banging their heads against this wall eventually."

Jane nodded and got to her feet. "I'll get some of the girls out past the smoke to give us a bit of warning."

Winter stood a bit more slowly, her legs already aching. Her throat felt suddenly thick, in a way that had nothing to do with having spent the morning shouting at the top of her lungs.

"Be careful," she said.

Jane smiled her familiar, mischievous smile and gave a slapdash salute. Winter fought a sudden impulse to wrap her arms around her. Instead she nodded, stiffly, and watched Jane stride back toward the front line.

A passionate embrace between the commander of a battalion and his chief subordinate might have been a bit unorthodox, by old army standards, but Winter wasn't sure it would have made a difference if she'd given in to the temptation. Caution was an old, ingrained habit, though, and she tried to impress the importance of it on Jane. They lived in a weird fog of half-truths and lies—the fact that Captain Ihernglass was sleeping with Lieutenant "Mad Jane" Verity was an open secret, at least among the Girls' Own, who gossiped as badly as the old Colonials had. But only a small cadre among them, Jane's former Leatherback girls, knew the secret of Winter's gender. So far, they'd kept her confidence—Jane's girls were nothing if not loyal—but having that knowledge so widely spread made Winter intensely nervous.

Bobby hurried over and snapped a crisp salute. One of her sleeves was red with blood.

"Jane said you wanted to see me, sir?" she said.

"Are you all right?" A foolish question, Winter thought. Bobby was the one soldier on the field who was virtually guaranteed to live through the day's fighting, thanks to the ongoing legacy of her experience in Khandar.

"What?" Bobby caught sight of the blood and shook her head. "Oh, it's nothing. I was helping with the wounded."

Winter nodded. "I need you to ride to Colonel de Ferre. Tell him we need reinforcements here, at least a battalion, to extend the line on the right. We haven't got the strength to stretch that far, and if they get around us this whole position could come unstuck."

"Yes, sir!"

Bobby saluted again and hurried rearward. There was a small aid post there, where the battalion cutters did what they could for the casualties until they could be taken for proper care. Beside it was a string of horses, kept ready for couriers and other emergencies. Winter watched her mount up, then turned back to the front.

The corpses of the fallen had been removed from the line, and the injured helped to the rear. Now small parties vaulted the hedgerow, cautiously, and searched among the dissipating smoke for enemy wounded. Any who seemed likely to survive were taken prisoner and sent through the line for treatment.

The enemy was composed of Hamveltai regulars, called yellowjackets for their lemon-colored coats, striped with black and worn over black trousers. They wore tall black shakos with gold devices on the fronts and long red plumes fluttering from the peaks, the very image of professional soldiers. The contrast with the Vordanai, whose only uniform was a loose blue jacket worn over whatever each soldier had brought along, could not have been greater. But neat uniforms did not seem to provide any special protection from musket balls.

The prisoners were treated gently—orders on that subject had come down from Janus himself. The reasoning was not humanitarian, but brutally practical. The League commanders had made noises about treating Vordanai volunteers as partisans or bandits rather than soldiers due honorable captivity if captured, and the best defense against any abuses was for the Vordanai army to gather its own stock of prisoners against whom it could threaten retaliation, if necessary. That went double for the Girls' Own, who had no idea what to expect if they fell into enemy hands. Winter knew there was a quiet trend among her soldiers to carry small daggers in the inner pockets of their uniforms, to be used for self-destruction in the last resort. It wasn't something she encouraged, but she couldn't blame them for wanting the reassurance.

A certain amount of looting went along with the gathering of captives. Officially, they were only supposed to scavenge ammunition, food, and other military supplies, but Winter noted quite a few of the search parties returning with insignia, plumes, and other trophies. Another practice to which she felt she had to turn a blind eye. She didn't want her troops turning into ghouls, cutting off fingers to get at the rings, but pride in a hard-fought victory was something to encourage.

An outburst of laughter caught her attention. Over on the left, a knot of young women surrounded the stocky figure of Lieutenant Drake Graff, who was attempting to demonstrate the proper way to level a musket. It was hard to be sure under his thick beard, but Winter thought he was blushing. Another woman in a makeshift lieutenant's uniform was looking on, and Winter walked over to stand beside her.

"Sir," Cyte said, her salute almost as crisp as Bobby's.

Winter nodded her acknowledgment. "How is it?"

"We missed the worst on this side," Cyte said. "Anna got nicked by a splinter and bled a fair bit, but she'll be all right. No casualties in our company otherwise."

No wonder they're in the mood for laughing, Winter thought as another round of giggles came from the cluster around Graff.

Cyte, following Winter's gaze, heaved a sigh. "They like to tease him," she said. "I've tried to get them to stop, but . . ."

Winter shook her head. "Don't bother. You won't be able to." Soldiers would have their fun, regardless of what their officers wanted. "Just make sure it doesn't get out of hand."

"What's out of hand?" Cyte said. "Last week a gang of them found out where he was having a bath in the river and jumped in with him. They like to see him blush."

Winter had to work to stifle a giggle of her own, picturing the gruff, hard-bitten Graff frantically averting his eyes and muttering through his beard. When Janus had offered her the services of her former corporals to fill out her new regiment, Winter tried to make it clear to them what they were getting into. Folsom had fit right in, his quiet assurance off the battlefield and foulmouthed tirades on it provoking something like awe among his troops. Bobby, of course, had not been a problem. Graff had taken the longest to decide, grumbling about the impropriety of it all before finally agreeing on the grounds that someone had to take care of things. For an old soldier, he was surprisingly straitlaced, a fact that his women had discovered and exploited with gusto.

Cyte was another matter altogether. Winter had been surprised to find the University student among her early volunteers. She'd been among the revolutionaries whom the speeches of Danton Aurenne had mobilized, and she and Winter had fought together to free the prisoners of the Vendre. After the victory of the revolution and the ascent of the Deputies-General to power, Winter had expected

Cyte to take up a marginally safer life in politics. Instead she'd turned up not long after the declaration of war, with a copy of the *Regulations and Drill of the Royal Army of Vordan* under one arm and a quiet determination to master the military life that Winter found strangely familiar. Winter had quickly made her a staff lieutenant—recruited as it was mostly from the young women of the South Bank, the Girls' Own was desperately short of people with the basic education to perform an officer's duties.

"Someone's coming," Cyte said.

She pointed out across the field, where a lone figure was indeed sprinting through the remaining haze of smoke, headed for the hedgerow. Winter recognized Chris, one of Jane's Leatherback leaders, now wearing a sergeant's pips. Chris saw her at the same time and headed in her direction, coming up hard against the hedge.

"Winter!" she said without even an attempt at a salute. Military niceties were not the strong point of Jane's old cadre. "The yellowjackets are back."

"Hell," Winter said, looking over her shoulder. No sign yet of Bobby, much less of troops marching to their relief. "How many?"

"Looks like two groups," Chris said. "They're lining up just that way, on the other side of that little rise."

Two battalions, Winter translated, deploying into line for the attack. "One of them out by the road?"

Chris nodded, gulping air.

Winter grimaced. "Where's Jane?"

Chris pointed, and Winter hurried back along the line. Jane was helping hoist the returning scouts over the hedgerow, and Winter grabbed her by the shoulder and pulled her aside.

"You've heard?" Jane said.

Winter nodded. "Bobby's not back yet. De Ferre must be balking."

"Bastard." Jane smacked a fist against her palm. "Want me to go talk some sense into him?"

"I'll send Folsom," Winter said. "I need you here."

"You want to try and hold them off?"

Winter gritted her teeth. *If we fall back, the whole line could come unstuck.* But to stand and fight, against these odds, would mean serious losses even if the line held. *And if it breaks, they might run us all down.*

"I don't think we have a choice," she said.

Jane looked at her, an odd light in her green eyes. "You're in charge here," she said. "What's the plan?"

A few minutes later, the four companies Jane had led out of the angle onto the Hamveltai flank were forming up across the dirt road, a double line two hundred yards long. Jane and the other officers were still pushing the formation into shape—like most of the volunteer soldiers, the Girls' Own was more used to skirmishing than stand-up fighting. But someone had to block the yellowjackets' advance up the road, and until de Ferre brought up regulars from the reserve, these four companies were all Winter had.

Lieutenant James Folsom was tall and heavily muscled, with a long brown mustache and a quiet disposition that became animated only in the heat of battle. He listened carefully to Winter's orders, and shook his head.

"I should be here," he said in a quiet voice. "With my company."

"I know." The idea of leaving one's soldiers right as they were going into combat would grate on any officer. "But this is important. We can't hold this position if de Ferre doesn't bring up fresh troops. You're Royal Army. That'll carry some weight." *And you're a man,* she added silently. The tall, intimidating Folsom was more likely to impress an old aristocrat like de Ferre.

"What if he won't do it?"

"If he stalls, don't wait around for an answer. Come right back here and let me know, and we'll do our best to pull out." That would be quite a trick, with the enemy already on top of them, but Winter tried not to think about it.

Folsom nodded dolefully. "I'll be back soon, then." He turned and loped toward the aid station in the rear with long, easy strides.

With the line approximately formed, Winter took her

place behind the center. On her right, Jane and Abby waited with their respective companies. The two left-hand companies were commanded by Chris and another of Jane's old Leatherback leaders, a short, pale girl named Becca with an alarming fondness for knives. She had one out now, tossing it to whirl dangerously through the air before catching it smoothly in her off hand.

The women in the ranks were steady, Winter was pleased to see. They jostled and bumped one another somewhat while they loaded their weapons, but that was inevitable. Here and there, a ranker looked back over her shoulder, making sure the road behind them was open, but Winter didn't think they'd really run. *Not right away, at least.* Every band of soldiers, however brave, had a breaking point; there was only so much that flesh and blood could stand. She hoped very much that today wasn't the day she found out hers.

"Here they come!" someone shouted.

With the ground wet, there was no dust cloud to mark the advance, only a yellow line coming over the hill, sunlight flashing here and there on polished steel or silver. A moment later, the sound of the yellowjackets' drums reached them, the steady beat of the march pace. They were already deployed into their line, extending for some distance to either side of the road.

Time stretched like taffy. The Hamveltai troops seemed at once impossibly close and enormously distant, as though they were both right on top of Winter and her men and so far away they would never arrive. Each beat of the drum, accompanied by the synchronized tramp of a thousand boots, closed the gap further. When it was close enough, some of the women standing in front of Winter were going to die. Some of the men over there were, too. Winter wondered if they felt the same horrible anticipation—

The range closed to a hundred yards, and the yellowjackets showed no signs of stopping to fire. Winter raised her voice.

"Ready!"

Muskets came off shoulders, rattling up and down the line.

"Level!"

Four hundred barrels swung up into line. Winter gave them a heartbeat to steady.

"Fire!"

The volley crashed out with a roar. At a distance of perhaps eighty yards, it wasn't the most effective shooting—it was easy to over- or undershoot a target at that distance, even without the inherent inaccuracy of a smoothbore musket—but the smoke that puffed out over the Girls' Own was what Winter really wanted. They couldn't afford to let the Hamveltai get a really good look at what was in front of them; if they realized they outnumbered the defenders by better than two to one, they might charge at once, and Winter didn't think her troops would hold in the face of a thousand bayonets. Baiting the yellowjackets into a firefight would buy time.

Men dropped, all along the advancing line, and were swallowed by the formation as it closed up. The Hamveltai continued their march while the Girls' Own frantically reloaded, each woman ripping the top off a paper cartridge with her teeth and pouring the premeasured powder down her barrel, then spitting the ball in after. The fastest of them were just firing their second shot when the drums beat a new command, and the yellowjackets halted. Their first two ranks raised their weapons. Winter stared at the line of muskets, standing out like quills on a porcupine, and fought the instinct to curl into the fetal position. She was close enough to hear the officers on the other side scream in Hamveltai.

"Envir!"

The Hamveltai line lit up like a flash of lightning, swallowed immediately by a roil of smoke. Once again, Winter was surrounded by the *whir* of balls passing overhead and the *pock* of impacts on the dirt, accompanied by the wetter-sounding *thwack* of lead meeting flesh. Women toppled forward, or sagged against their neighbors, or stumbled back out of the line with screams and curses.

"Close up!" Winter shouted. She had to gasp for air; she'd been holding her breath. "Close up! Hold the line!"

Jane, Abby, and the other lieutenants took up the call, and the sergeants—chosen from volunteers Winter had hoped wouldn't panic under pressure—echoed them. The line contracted, rankers shuffling sideways to fill in gaps, pushing the fallen aside or stepping over them. More muskets banged, with the irregular rhythm of rain drumming on a window, each soldier firing as soon as she was ready. The second Hamveltai volley, when it came, was nearly as neat as the first, and another chorus of screams was added to the familiar sound of battle.

It was what Winter had wanted—a firefight, instead of a charge—but it was worse than she'd imagined. The yellow-jackets were good troops, well trained, and their volleys were as regular as the tolling of a clock. At every blast, more soldiers fell, the survivors pushing into the gaps, or being hit in their turn and collapsing atop dead or dying comrades. The banging of their own musketry started to sound pathetic by comparison, ragged and useless against the unwavering will of the Hamveltai elites.

"Close up!" Jane shouted on the right. "Hold the line!"

"Close up, you shit-stinking daughters of fucking goats!" Becca screamed, voice hoarse with excitement or terror. "Hold the *fucking* line!"

"Close u—" Chris said, then cut off. Winter glanced to her left, squinting against the smoke, and saw that a ball had gone right through her throat, producing a spectacular arterial spray. The big woman slapped a hand against the wound, bright red pulsing through her fingers, then crumpled in place.

They're going to break. They had to; there was no other way out. Stubborn pride and the unwillingness to show fear in front of their fellow soldiers would keep the rankers in the patently unequal firefight for a while, but it could have only one outcome. The Hamveltai certainly weren't going to give up, not with the return fire visibly slackening. When it had faded enough, they would fix bayonets and charge.

We have to fall back. But that would be as bad as a rout. *Maybe if we run for the village, some of us will make it.* They could barricade a building, hold out for a while. *Until de Ferre gets his head out of his ass.* Unless, of course, the colonel decided the day was lost and ordered a retreat. Then, cut off and surrounded, they would have no option but to surrender or fight to the death. Winter wasn't sure she was capable of giving either order. She felt paralyzed, watching her soldiers cut down by measured volleys, like the ticks of a funereal clock, unable to do *anything* to get them out of it—

Someone grabbed her arm, shouted in her ear. It took her a moment to parse the words over the blasts of musketry, and a moment longer to recognize Bobby.

"—coming up the road!" she was saying.

Winter blinked. She looked over her shoulder and saw a mass of men and horses behind them, working energetically around the low, deadly shapes of cannon. An officer was frantically clearing the teams and caissons out of the way, and artillerymen were already ramming home the first loads.

Bobby was still talking, but her words were distant and indistinct to Winter's abused ears. The sense behind them, though, was obvious.

"Fall back!" Winter shouted. "Back! Form behind the guns!"

Other voices took up the cry. She heard Jane's—*thank God, thank God*—and Folsom's bass roar. *He must have come back with Bobby.* The line had been leaking troops to the rear for some time, walking wounded making their escape, probably including some who weren't actually wounded at all. The shouts of their officers snapped the bonds of pride and duty that held the women of the Girls' Own in place, and they turned away from the firefight as one body, as though a mechanism had been suddenly tripped. Winter had to backpedal frantically to keep from being trampled by the mass of rankers; not screaming or throwing away their weapons, but shoving forward with a silent, earnest determination not to be the last in line.

One more volley stabbed out from the Hamveltai line, cutting down the rearmost stragglers and those whose wounds had made them slow to retreat. Winter heard the yellowjackets cheering, and their officers shouting orders. The drums thrilled faster, to the charge pace.

She turned away, running along with the rest. In a few moments she was among the guns, passing between the big, many-spoked wheels, and then into the clear space beyond. It took an effort of will to *stop* running, with the image of all those bayonets following close on her heels fresh in her mind, but Winter was pleased to see that most of her soldiers had managed it. They pulled up short, doubled over and breathing hard, fell to their knees or flopped to the ground. One girl caught Winter's eye, hands clasped in front of her face as she repeated a frantic prayer of thanks, over and over.

Behind them, the cannoneers were getting ready. Most of the Girls' Own were past, and only a few limping wounded were still on the road in front of the guns. As these last stragglers lurched past the muzzles of the artillery, the pall of smoke rippled, and the massed ranks of the yellow-jackets emerged, still marching in step. A ripple ran through their line at the sight of the guns, but it was too late to stop. They gave a hoarse cheer and broke into a charge.

A young lieutenant of artillery brought his hand down, a dismissive, peremptory gesture. Gunners brought their burning brands to the touchholes of their weapons. Winter had time to slam her hands over her ears, and a moment later a blaze of light and a crashing roar seemed to fill the world.

Winter could see that Colonel Broanne de Ferre was already sweating into his too-tight collar.

"My lord—" he began.

"As we are engaged in military service," General Janus bet Vhalnich said, his tone precise, "my social rank is not relevant." Seated behind his portable map table, one long-fingered hand resting on a stack of scouting reports, Janus eyed de Ferre coldly. The rigors of campaigning had thinned the general, Winter thought, and he hadn't had much flesh to lose. His young face was still dominated by those extraordinary eyes, huge and gray, but now they stared out from deep sockets in what was practically a death's head.

"Ah," de Ferre said. He looked unhappy—clearly he would have preferred to speak to Janus as a fellow peer, rather than as his military superior. "Yes. Of course, General."

"Go on."

De Ferre swallowed, trying to regain his lost momentum. He was a stocky man in his middle years, the bulge of his stomach not completely concealed by his exquisitely tailored uniform. The silver eagles on his shoulders that denoted his rank had tiny chips of ruby to give them glittering red eyes.

"Lieutenant Archer disobeyed my explicit orders," he said. "His actions might have endangered the survival of my entire force."

Janus looked down at the papers on his table for a moment. "This would be when he brought his battery forward to the support of the Fifth Volunteer Battalion?" That was the official designation for the Girls' Own. "Which by all accounts was thereby rescued from capture or annihilation."

"Yes, General." De Ferre drew himself up with all the stiffness of an old military man. "The fact that his action happened to be successful is no excuse for insubordination. If I had needed his battery in another position, the battle might have been lost by his rash action."

"Bullshit," said Jane, beside Winter. "If Archer hadn't brought those guns up—"

"Jane," Winter said, putting a restraining hand on her shoulder. Jane shrugged it off.

"*Fuck* that." She pointed at de Ferre. "My friends are *dead* because this bastard didn't have the balls for a fight, and now I have to stand here and listen while he blames the people who *did* help?"

De Ferre's round face was growing purple. "I object,"

he sputtered, "in the strongest terms. Why is this . . . this *female* even present?" He eyed Jane as though she were some strange specimen of an unknown species. "You are fortunate your gender protects you, *madam*, because if you were a man an accusation of cowardice would have to be settled with steel."

"If *you* were a man, I might bother to bring a sword," Jane shot back. "As it is, I'd be happy to settle you with my bare hands, if you'd care to join me outside, *sir*."

"Enough," Janus spit. "Lieutenant Verity is an officer in the Fifth Volunteers, and will be treated as such." He turned to lock eyes with Jane. "She will endeavor to restrain herself."

Winter had to give Jane credit. Most people, fixed with the full force of Janus' stare, would have flinched, but she matched him for a long moment before he grunted and looked away.

"General," de Ferre began again, "perhaps we could meet in private—"

"Colonel de Ferre," Janus snapped. "Please explain why, when you received Captain Ihernglass' message as delivered by Lieutenant Forester, you chose to ignore it?"

"As overall commander, it was my responsibility to assess overall threats to my force—"

Janus cut him off. "A regiment of Hamveltai regulars turning your right flank did not seem like a threat?"

De Ferre's eyes flicked from Janus to Winter, passing quickly over the fuming Jane. He cleared his throat. "I did not consider the information reliable, General."

"What were we supposed to do?" Jane burst out. "Send you a fucking engraved invitation?"

This time, Jane allowed Winter to quiet her. Janus remained focused on de Ferre.

"You doubted that Lieutenant Forester's message was the one entrusted to her by Captain Ihernglass?" he asked.

"No," de Ferre said. He was sweating. "But you know these volunteer officers. If—if you'll pardon the loose phrase, they're always convinced that the sky is falling. It is the responsibility of the senior officer to commit his reserve judiciously, and not fritter it away whenever some captain thinks the entire enemy army is descending on him."

"Some might say that a senior officer ought to place himself so that he can make such observations for himself," Janus said with the deadly calm of someone delivering a killing stroke.

"I . . . that is . . ." De Ferre wiped his forehead. "We *won* the battle, General. My force did everything you asked of it."

"Thanks largely to the efforts of Captain Ihernglass." Janus leaned back in his camp chair. "Colonel de Ferre, you are dismissed from command. Gather your baggage and report to the Directory in Vordan, and see if they have any further use for you. I do not."

"You can't do that," de Ferre snarled. "I hold a colonel's commission signed by the King of Vordan."

"I think you'll find that I can," Janus said. "My appointment as commander of the Army of the East was approved by both the deputies and the queen, and within its sphere my authority is unlimited. But if you think my actions are illegal, by all means make your case to the deputies. Sergeant!"

The tent flap opened, letting a gust of warm, smoke-scented air into the close confines of the command tent. A big man in a blue uniform poked his head through and said, "Sir?"

"Please escort Colonel de Ferre to his tent and assist him with gathering his baggage. He'll be leaving us in the morning."

The sergeant couldn't have failed to hear what was going on in the tent behind him, but he kept his expression wooden and his manner courteous as he turned to de Ferre. "Sir. If you'll come with me?"

"This is a mistake, Vhalnich," de Ferre said. "I have many friends—"

"Some of whom will be joining you on the road at daybreak," Janus said. "I hope you make for a merry company. Now go with the sergeant, please. I have work to do."

De Ferre stood stock-still a moment longer, his face increasingly resembling an overripe tomato. Just when Winter thought he might actually pop and shower them all in gore, he turned on his heel and stalked out with as much dignity as he could muster, with the sergeant escorting him at a respectful distance.

Winter knew that the concept of a general was not a popular one in the Royal Army, which had gotten along for centuries without any rank higher than colonel. Which regimental commander gave the orders to a larger force was determined by a complicated formula that took into account both the seniority of the man in question and the age and prestige of his unit. The effect was generally to give command to the oldest and most powerful noble families who led the oldest and most respected regiments.

In the frantic weeks after the declaration of war, the Deputies-General had improvised a number of new posts to coordinate the nationwide military effort, and it had been a given that one of them would go to the savior of the city. But while Janus was a count, his family was not among the most powerful, and he had commanded no storied regiment. Winter had heard that the Royal Army colonels were not taking his elevation well. *But I never thought I'd get to see one of them given the sack.* In the old Royal Army, a colonel served until he died, retired, or became embarrassingly senile; he was certainly never *dismissed* from his command, which was his by hereditary and financial right.

Janus gave a long sigh, and ran one hand through his hair. "Captain Ihernglass, may I speak with you privately?"

"Of course, sir. Give me a moment." Winter turned away, her heart hammering, and bent toward Jane. "Go back to the camp. I'll be there shortly."

"Are you going to be all right?" Jane said.

"I'll be fine. I'm sure it's . . . nothing serious. Go and check on the wounded."

Jane nodded, saluted raggedly toward Janus, and slipped out. Augustin, Janus' manservant, ghosted in through the open tent flap, acknowledging Winter with a respectful nod. He was an old man, silver-haired and dignified, but he'd served Janus steadfastly for years, even during the Khandarai campaign.

"Tea," Janus said. "And fetch something for the captain to sit on."

"Certainly, sir," Augustin said.

He bustled about, setting up a second camp chair for Winter and then busying himself at a kettle in the back of the tent. Winter sat, cautiously, and waited for Janus to speak, but the colonel seemed content to wait. After a few minutes, Augustin set two steaming bone-white cups and saucers on the table.

"Strong, with a bit of sugar, if I recall correctly," he said to Winter. "The blend is an indifferent one, I'm afraid."

Winter smiled. In spite of his complaints about the quality of food, tea, and furnishings, the old man was a wizard when it came to creating comfort for his master and his guests in the meanest surroundings, a valuable skill indeed in an army on the march.

Janus pursed his lips and blew across the surface of the tea, then took a cautious sip. "Perfect," he said. "Thank you, Augustin."

"Of course, my lord." The manservant bowed low and withdrew.

Winter reached for her own cup and took a deep breath, savoring the aroma, before tasting it. It was, as she'd expected, rather good.

Janus remained quiet, staring into his cup, and finally Winter felt it was incumbent on her to start the conversation. She cleared her throat, and the general looked up.

"I have to ask, sir," she said. "Was that wise?"

"What?" For a moment Janus looked as though he'd genuinely forgotten what he'd just done. "Oh, the business with de Ferre. Of course it was. The man is an oaf."

"And a count. The rest of the Royals aren't going to be happy."

"They're going to be even less happy in the morning." Janus set his cup down. "The performance of the army was, frankly, unacceptable."

"We did win the battle, sir. Didn't we?"

Janus waved a hand. "Only because Baron di Pfalen is an utter fool. A triple convergence, with no lateral communication, in a polyglot confederation army without a real chain of command?" He snorted. "We could have done nothing at all and watched the whole thing collapse under its own weight. I daresay *you* could have outgeneraled di Pfalen when you were still clinging to your mother's knees."

Winter, who had no memory of her mother, forbore to comment on that.

"Someday this army will go up against a real commander," Janus went on. "I know there are a few out there. The Duke of Brookspring, for one, and there must be others. Even a stiff-necked geriatric cabal like the Hamveltai High Council can't rid themselves of *every* man of talent. When that day comes, we need to be ready."

"You think we need more training, sir?"

"I'm afraid it goes beyond that. Yours was not the only set-to between Royals and volunteers, you know. The Second Infantry actually fired a volley into the Third Volunteers when some fool thought they'd changed sides."

Winter winced. "But you have a solution in mind?"

"I'm reorganizing the army. The royal regiments are too large, and the volunteers need to learn to work as part of a larger force. We'll break up all the old units and create new ones. Each new regiment will have one volunteer and one royal battalion. Getting to send all these thickheaded colonels packing is a side benefit."

"Some of those units are hundreds of years old," Winter said. "They're not—"

"Going to be happy. You mentioned that already." Janus smiled, just for a moment. "The colonels won't be, and some of the other noble officers. They're welcome to resign and take their case to the deputies. But I think the men in the ranks will be glad to be rid of them."

Winter nodded. There were two distinct classes of officer in the old Royal Army—those who'd bought or inherited their commissions like de Ferre, and those who'd come out of the War College like Captain Marcus d'Ivoire.

The former sort held the positions of command, but it was the latter who made the army work.

"Who'll command the new regiments?" she said, wondering what sort of new commanding officer she'd be saddled with.

"Whoever's most competent, regular or volunteer." He tapped the pile of papers again. "I'm giving you the Second Battalion of the Eighteenth Regiment, under Captain Sevran."

"I—you're—*what*, sir?"

"Your new unit will be designated the Third Regiment of the Line. You'll be bumped up to colonel, obviously."

"This is ridiculous," Winter said. "I'm a captain only because we needed someone to take charge of all girls who wanted to join up, and now—"

"You don't think you're up to the job?"

"Of course not!" Colonels were *lords*, often counts or their sons, men of power and consequence. You couldn't just *become* one, at the touch of a magic wand.

"Then our opinions differ on the subject. But, as this is an order, your options are either to obey it or to resign." Janus cocked his head. "Do you wish to resign?"

Winter pushed down the turmoil in her gut. "I . . . no, sir."

"Very good. Do you have any thoughts on who should command the Girls' Own?"

There was only one possible choice. "Lieutenant Verity, sir."

"Excellent. Please inform the lieutenant that she is hereby promoted to captain, and that she may have a free hand with her own junior officers. Under your supervision, of course."

"Sir . . ." Winter took a deep breath. "The Royals. This Captain Sevran. What if they won't obey my orders?" The idea of her, Winter Ihernglass, a girl run away from a home for unwanted children, giving *orders* to the proud regulars of Her Majesty's Royal Army seemed ridiculous on its face. "I'm not sure . . ."

Janus' expression darkened. "If they refuse to obey your

orders, then you are within your rights to hang them for insubordination and treason. Senior officers on an active campaign are permitted to make summary judgments on such affairs. I guarantee it will not take many examples to make your point."

"You're serious."

"Of course. Anyone who will not accept the chain of command is, at the root, failing to acknowledge my authority. I will not tolerate it."

"Yes, sir." Winter felt numb. "Understood."

"Official orders will be read to the entire camp tomorrow. Please keep this between you and your officers until then."

"Yes, sir."

"One more thing." Janus fixed her with his bottomless gray gaze. "My reports say that you were in the thick of the fighting today."

"I . . . yes, sir. I suppose I was."

"That is all well and good for a lieutenant, but you must take greater care in the future. God knows I have few enough officers of your promise, and I cannot afford to have your career ended early by a stray musket ball. And there are . . . other duties, to which you are uniquely suited. Do you understand?"

Winter thought she did, even the parts that Janus was reluctant to say out loud. "Other duties" had to refer to Infernivore, the demon she'd taken on herself in Khandar during the battle to secure the Thousand Names. For the most part, it lay quiescent in the darkest pits of her mind, but if she laid a hand on another demon-carrier, she could will it to come forth and devour the other creature. For Janus, that made her a weapon against what he called the true enemy: the Priests of the Black and their Penitent Damned. *And we can't have a weapon breaking too soon.* If Winter died on the field, Janus would have to find someone else to bear Infernivore, and from what he'd said the success rate for invoking the demon was not high. Failure, in that context, meant an agonizing death; when she thought about the risk she'd run, all unknowing, it still gave her the shivers.

"Yes, sir. I understand."

"Good." He straightened up and gave her his brief smile again. "Excellent work today, Colonel Ihernglass. Well done."

Winter paused, taken aback, then got to her feet and saluted. "Thank you, sir!"

As a captain, Winter rated a slightly larger tent than the usual, though it still wasn't tall enough that she could stand up inside. She peeked between the flaps and was not at all surprised to see Jane within, sitting cross-legged on a cushion beside the camp bed. Winter let out a long breath and resigned herself to talking Jane down from the raging fury she'd worked herself up to in Janus' command tent.

When she entered, though, Jane didn't explode. She didn't even look up. Her hands rested on her knees, and her eyes were fixed on the floor. Her soft red hair, reaching almost to her shoulders now, hung around her face in dirty tassels.

"Jane?" Winter said, slightly alarmed. "Are you all right?"

"No," Jane said. Her voice was thick.

"What happened?"

"I went to look in on . . ." She paused and took a deep breath. "On the injured."

"Oh."

Winter pulled off her boots and set them beside the door, then padded softly across the cloth-covered earth to Jane's side. She sat down, silently, and snaked one arm around the other woman's shoulders. Jane leaned against her, hunched and miserable. There were clear tracks on her face where tears had cut through the grime and powder residue.

"Chris died," Jane said in a whisper.

"I know," Winter said. "I was standing right next to her."

"Nobody told me. I didn't even notice she wasn't there."

Jane swallowed. "She'd been with me from the beginning. From Mrs. Wilmore's. A lot of the girls have."

"I know." Winter squeezed Jane's shoulder. "I'm sorry."

"I went over to the cutter's station. I thought I could . . . help, maybe. There was this girl, Forti. Short for Fortuna. You probably didn't know her."

Winter shook her head.

"We found her right after we came to Vordan City. When we were still living in the swamps. She just wandered into camp one day, a skinny little thing in rags, asking for food and cringing every time someone looked at her. Like she expected to be beaten."

Jane's hands tightened on her knees, until her knuckles were white. Winter said nothing.

"I let her come with us," Jane said. "Nobody knew how old she was, but she'd filled out once we gave her some proper food. She wanted to come so badly, and I told her she could."

"Is she . . ." Winter trailed off.

Jane pressed her head into Winter's shoulder. "When I got there, to the cutter's tent, they had her on the table. They had a . . . a saw, the kind of thing you'd use to chop the end off a log, and they were cutting through her arm." One of Jane's hands came up and closed around her own biceps, in unconscious sympathy. "She'd lost the gag they'd given her, and she was screaming, 'No, no, no, no,' over and over, even after they were through. One of the cutters picked up the arm and tossed it on a *pile*. All those hands . . . and . . ."

"God," Winter said softly. "Oh, Jane."

"I lost my lunch," Jane said. "Or yesterday's dinner, maybe, since I never got anything to eat today. Right in front of everyone. Then I ran for it, puke still dripping from my shirt."

"It's all right," Winter said. "They understand. Watching something like that . . ."

"I brought them here! I was supposed to be protecting them, and I brought them *here*. What the *fuck* am I doing?" Jane looked up at Winter, her eyes wide and frantic. "We should leave. Take them all and go home, back to the city, or out into the country, anywhere but *here*."

Winter stared at her. This was a Jane she hadn't seen before, the flip side of the fiery-tempered woman who'd wanted to kill the vicious tax farmer Bloody Cecil on the spot and had been ready to storm the Vendre in the face of cannon-fire. There was something childlike in her expression, a desperate need for reassurance that Winter felt ill-equipped to provide.

"Let's start with this," she said. "You didn't *bring* them here. They brought themselves, of their own free will. You know that. Everybody who came with us knew what could happen."

"I could have stopped them."

"Captain d'Ivoire wanted to stop *you*, but you didn't let him."

"I . . ." Jane took a deep breath. "I thought it would be over quickly. But this . . ." She shook her head. "Everyone who made it through today just gets to do it again tomorrow, and the next day, and the next. I can't just watch them all die. I can't."

Tears were welling in her eyes. Awkwardly, Winter pulled her close, and soon Jane's head rested in her lap. Jane pressed her face against the fabric of Winter's uniform, her back heaving with muffled sobs. They stayed like that a long time, Winter's hand resting on Jane's shoulder as she cried in near silence. Eventually, the sobs subsided, and Jane's breathing became slow and regular.

"Jane?" Winter said experimentally.

"Mm?" Jane looked up, then frowned at Winter's expression. "What are you looking at?"

"Sorry." Winter let the smallest smile appear. "One of my buttons has embossed a royal eagle on your forehead."

Jane touched the red spot and smiled weakly. Winter leaned down and kissed the mark, gently.

"I'm sorry," Jane said when she pulled back. "I didn't mean to fall apart on you like that. I just . . . I couldn't . . ."

"It's all right." Winter ran her fingers through Jane's hair, red and silky, even tangled and dirty as it was. "Listen. Anyone who wants to leave can go, you know that. It'd be my job to stop them, and I'm not going to. But they won't. They're here because they think Vordan needs defending."

"I know. I know! I didn't mean it. And I'd never leave you alone here, you know that, too."

"Thank God for that."

Jane's smile was stronger this time. Winter kissed her again, on the mouth this time, but drew back after a few moments.

"You," she said, "taste like puke and gunpowder."

Jane sighed, and pulled at a tangle in her hair. "Right. I should get cleaned up." She shook her head. "What did Janus want with you, anyway?"

"Nothing important," Winter said. "I'll fill you in in the morning."

CHAPTER TWO

RAESINIA

Claudia twirled her elegant umbrella and looked up at the gray autumn sky.

"Well," she said cheerfully, "at least the rain's held off!"

Oh yes, Queen Raesinia Orboan thought. It would be a shame if bad weather spoiled the executions.

She held her tongue, mindful of the watchful presence of Sothe at her shoulder. Claudia Nettalt sur Tasset was twenty-five, extremely wealthy, and beautiful. Raesinia found her fascinating to listen to, because everything that entered her head via her eyes or ears immediately left it again via her mouth, with no apparent processing in between. Since they'd been herded into the royal box, Claudia had offered her opinions on the number of people who'd gathered (quite a lot), Raesinia's dress (lovely), the color of the sky (gray), and of course the lack of rain. Now she looked around again with wide, guileless eyes.

"They're still working on the machine, Emil, look," she said, indicating the center of everyone's attention, where a black-robed scholar and a pair of assistants were indeed still working on a bulky machine.

Claudia's son, a boy of seven or eight, was dressed in a dark, sober suit, as appropriate for a noble still in mourning. He slumped with one shoulder against the railing of the box, immersed in a thick, leather-bound book that Raesinia recognized as the bloody adventure story *Heart of Khandar.* Claudia had introduced him when they first entered, but the Queen of Vordan was apparently a poor alternative to the exploits of Captain Merric and his men battling crocodiles and waterfalls.

On Raesinia's other side was a portly gentleman in gray, whom she recalled had something to do with the arms industry. He, thankfully, did not feel obligated to make conversation, and devoted his attention instead to scanning the crowd and occasionally muttering caustically. From the tone of his observations, it appeared that he was extremely satisfied to be placed beside the queen while his rivals were obliged to sit with the commons.

The center of Farus' Triumph, with its spectacular fountain and speaker's rostrum, was poorly suited to this kind of public spectacle. Instead a semicircle of bleachers had been constructed at the north end of the great square, in front of the Hotel Ancerre, where the new government had its headquarters. In the center of the arc was a fenced-off box for the queen and her guests, which made Raesinia feel a bit like a cow penned and awaiting slaughter.

The very ends of the arc of seats were occupied by the members of the Deputies-General, with the opposing factions pressed as far away from one another as it was physically possible to be. On the left were the Radicals, in the colorful, particolored coats and hats that had for some reason unfathomable to Raesinia become the fashion in their circle. On the right, Conservatives looked like a flock of crows in their black, high-collared coats. The no-man's-land between the feuding parties was taken up by other notables of Vordan, a mix of wealthy men of common stock and aristocrats who'd thrown in their lot with the new order.

On the open side of the semicircle, a long line of Patriot Guards in their blue and white sashes stood at attention, keeping back the mass of common folk who filled the rest of the square. The Guard carried halberds, but their vicious ax heads were shrouded in linen hoods as a symbol of goodwill.

In the empty space between the crowd and the bleachers, two wooden platforms had been erected. One was for the five members of the Directory of National Defense, flanked by more Patriot Guards. The other, larger platform, where Claudia had directed her attention, bore a solid-looking metal table big enough for a man to lie on. Beside the platform, eight wretched-looking men in gray rags huddled together, surrounded by a double ring of guards.

The royal box itself was filled with nobles and prominent citizens who'd been invited to share it with the queen, in thanks for their support. Claudia, for instance, was there because her father, Count Tasset, was one of the minority of noblemen who'd voiced his support for the new government. Most of the nobility had responded to the Directory's patriotic appeals by hunkering down in their country estates, determined to ride out the storm and survive, regardless of how matters ultimately fell out.

Sothe had arranged the invitations, of course. Until the Constitution was finalized by the wrangling deputies, Raesinia had no authority to speak of, but that didn't stop the cream of Vordanai society from preemptively trying to win her over. Sothe had been officially promoted from Raesinia's maid to her head of household, a position with vast if somewhat informal powers, and she'd proven surprisingly adept at managing the supplicants and favor-seekers who crowded the queen's door. When Raesinia had asked her about it, she commented that the only difference between working in the court and in the Concordat was that the courtiers didn't use knives.

She stood behind Raesinia now, along with a pair of blue-uniformed Grenadier Guards. Of the three organizations that had once protected the king, the Armsmen had been officially subsumed into the Patriot Guard while the Noreldrai Grays had been disbanded in disgrace, leaving only the elite army detachment on duty. The Patriot Guards, of course, were charged with the safety of all the citizens of Vordan, but they answered to the Deputies-General, and specifically to the Directory of National Defense. *Which means they answer to Maurisk.*

At that moment, one of the assistants waved to the men on the Directory platform and gave a thumbs-up. The pair of them scuttled out of sight, leaving only the black-robed scholar at the center of events. He bowed in the direction of the Directory, and one of five men sitting on their platform stood up and stepped forward to a low rostrum. Claudia looked down at Emil, frowned, and flicked him lightly on the side of the head.

"Put that book away and pay attention," she said. The boy sighed as he obeyed, scowling at the speaker.

Chairman of the Directory of National Defense Johann Maurisk did not cut an imposing figure. He was tall but painfully thin, the hanging folds of his dark coat making him look like a scarecrow, face pale under a gray bicorn hat. He did have a strong voice, though, strong enough to ring out across the square and quiet the murmuring of the crowd.

"Citizens of Vordan!" he said. "We are gathered here to bear witness to a great step forward. One more relic of the past, laden with superstition, is swept away by the miraculous products of the modern age!"

There was a cheer from the crowd, but not a loud one. Banners fluttered and whipped in the wind, held aloft on poles or in raised hands. Blue and white for the Radicals, black for the Conservatives. The factions in the deputies were mirrored among the common folk, and pockets of color were mixed with blobs of black. Bedsheets and pillowcases dyed with ink flapped as the Conservative supporters cheered for their hero, while the Radicals remained ominously silent.

"The genius responsible is Doctor-Professor Sarton," Maurisk went on. "I will let him explain the workings of the device."

Emil, who'd sagged with boredom as the de facto ruler of Vordan spoke, raised his head as the scholar beside the metal table straightened up. This was Doctor-Professor George Sarton, whose work the Directory had so enthusiastically embraced. Back before her father's death, when Raesinia had been sneaking out of the palace to organize the student radicals against the Last Duke, Maurisk and Sarton had been members of the inner circle of her conspiracy. He was an awkward, gangly man, with an unfortunate stutter that turned his face red with the effort of forcing out the words. He addressed Maurisk directly, leaving the rest of the assembled dignitaries to stare at the back of his head.

"I have made a s . . . s . . . study of the methods of execution used by the kings of Vordan," he said. It sounded like a rehearsed speech. "They have always been cruel and inhumane. A modern s . . . s . . . state may require men to die for their crimes, but it takes no pleasure in cruelty. I wanted to provide a means to end a life with an absolute minimum of pain."

Sarton turned to the metal table, running his hands across the steel with evident pleasure. "Hanging," he went on, "requires a great deal of s . . . s . . . skill on the part of the hangman to produce a quick death. Having one man who must fill the role of executioner is against the principles of equality embodied by the Deputies-General. A *mechanism* is much more s . . . s . . . suitable.

"As every man knows, it is the heart that is the seat of the emotions, including pain and suffering. Destruction of the heart, therefore, brings painless and instantaneous death. To achieve this, I have employed the power and precision of modern clockwork. No expertise is necessary. The condemned is positioned here"—he patted the center of the table—"and bound in place, and then it only remains to throw a s . . . s . . . switch."

He pressed something on the side of the table. Just left of the center, where a man's heart would be, a foot-long pointed steel piston slid straight up with the speed of a striking cobra and a *clank* of shivering metal.

"The procedure is utterly painless," Sarton said. "The heart is punctured before it has time to react. The limbs may twitch, but the s . . . s . . . soul has departed." He smiled beatifically, and for a moment his stutter vanished. "I call it the Spike."

There was a long moment of silence. Then the crowd

began to cheer, Radicals and Conservatives alike. Sarton dipped his head politely at Maurisk, and the chairman got to his feet again.

"These men," he boomed, gesturing at the huddled prisoners, "have confessed to their crimes! They are Borelgai spies. Paid to work against us, to spy and to sabotage, by a nation of shopkeepers and Sworn Church toadies. For years we have suffered the Borels to live among us, tolerated their poisonous words and let them work their malignant influence. All for a dangled purse of gold!"

Raesinia tensed. Maurisk was looking in her direction, and it seemed for a moment he was speaking to her directly. Her father, Farus VIII, had been responsible for much of the "tolerance" that the chairman so disliked. Some of it had indeed been for gold—loans from the great bankers of Borel had kept the Crown afloat—but there was also the little matter of the War of the Princes, which had ended with the death of her older brother Prince Dominic and Vordan's humiliating surrender.

"No longer," Maurisk said, his voice ringing off the flagstones. "The veil is torn. The enemies who have intrigued against us for years have been stung into action by the great steps forward we have taken, the establishment of the Deputies-General to ensure justice for all Vordanai. We are at war, my friends, and that means we do not need to abide this *treachery* in order to salve the feelings of merchants in Viadre! We can finally deal with such vile acts in the manner they fully deserve."

Cheers rose again, wild and uproarious, mixed with shouts of "Death to traitors!" and "Down with Elysian slaves!" A regular chant emerged, spreading and growing in volume, until it shook the square. "To the Spike! To the Spike!"

Emil joined in, enthusiastically, until his mother flicked him on the ear. "Emil! A gentleman does not *hoot* with a crowd. Applause will be sufficient." He subsided into clapping, and Claudia leaned closer to Raesinia. "He's a fine speaker, don't you think? Very loud. I could hear every word!"

"Oh yes," Raesinia muttered. "Very fine."

Maurisk gestured to the guards, who grabbed one of the prisoners and hauled him up onto the platform. Sarton's assistants reappeared, and with the guards' assistance they manhandled the man onto the Spike, lying facedown. Leather straps secured his arms, legs, and head, threaded through buckles built into the table, and a wide belt was cinched around his waist to keep him from arching his back.

When the prisoner was secured, the guards stepped back. Doctor-Professor Sarton looked to the Directory, and Maurisk gestured sharply downward. The black-robed scholar touched the switch, and the Spike gave a *clang*. A tiny steel point appeared, protruding from the prisoner's back like a strange metallic growth. The man jerked once, then lay still. Raesinia felt her gorge rise, and swallowed hard.

Underneath the Spike's platform, someone must have been working a mechanism to reset the clockwork. The steel piston withdrew, the machine *click-click-click*ing loudly as it was reset. When the guards untied the straps and lifted the corpse away, there was barely a stain on the steel surface.

"How lovely," Claudia said. "So much more *civilized* than a hanging. I always hate the way they kick and squirm."

"Mama, where does the blood go?" Emil said. "I thought it would spurt all over the place."

"I imagine there's a special drain," Raesinia said.

"A special drain," Claudia said, "of course! What a clever idea."

"Yes." Raesinia's voice was flat as she looked at the seven remaining prisoners. "Dr. Sarton has always been very . . . clever."

Confessed traitors, Maurisk had called the condemned. Huddled together, dressed in rags, they did not look terribly traitorous. Sothe had told her of the methods Duke Orlanko had employed to extract a confession, when one was required. She wondered if Maurisk had taken a page from the same book. She looked away, the pit of her stomach sour.

"Come on," Raesinia said to Sothe. "We're leaving."

"Leaving?" Sothe leaned close and lowered her voice

to a whisper. "We're here at the invitation of the Directory. Are you sure that's wise?"

The tone of Sothe's voice told Raesinia that she was sure that it was not, but Raesinia chose not to hear the rebuke. "We'll tell Maurisk my delicate digestion was upset by the spectacle. That ought to make him happy."

Sothe pursed her lips but didn't argue. Raesinia murmured something indistinct and polite-sounding in Claudia's direction, nodded at the fat arms merchant, and pushed her way back through the box. Her guards, after a moment of surprise, trailed behind her. Raesinia hopped down the two steps at the back of the box and onto the cobblestones as another cheer rose from the crowd, indicating that the Spike had claimed another traitorous victim.

Maurisk. The thought of him made her want to spit. When they'd worked together, she thought of him as an idealist, full of bold but impractical ideas. Once he'd gotten into the thick of the politics of the Deputies-General, though, he set some kind of speed record for selling out his high-minded ideals in pursuit of power. The complicated dance of parties, forming and re-forming like bits of foam in a bubbling soup pot, had somehow conspired to elevate Raesinia's old companion to the very height of power.

The war had done wonders for his authority, of course. The deputies had been content to endlessly debate the proper formula for a constitution when things had been going well. Once word got out that Vordan was at war with three of the great powers—including Imperial Murnsk, seat of the Sworn Church itself—the deputies had been running scared. They'd heaped powers on Maurisk's Directory of National Defense, and what they hadn't given him he'd taken for himself when he found that no one was willing to object. Only Durenne, new Minister of War and the one Radical member of the Directory, acted as a counterweight, and not a very effective one. While the war went on in the north, the east, and the west, Maurisk was busy trawling the capital for enemy spies, devising new methods of execution, and making sure every publisher and pamphleteer published only what was "appropriate and beneficial to a modern state."

"Well?" Raesinia said to Sothe as they walked toward the north end of the square where the royal carriage waited.

"Well what?"

"What do you think?" Raesinia jerked her head over her shoulder, at the spectacle unfolding behind them.

Sothe shrugged. "One way of killing a person is much like another."

"Maurisk's always hated the Borels. Now he's got people seeing them on every corner."

"I wouldn't be so certain he's wrong. The Concordat certainly intercepted quite a few Borelgai spies, and I can't imagine they've relaxed their efforts now that we're at war."

"I don't doubt that they're there. I question whether Maurisk's crowd could find them." The Directory had wasted no time building the Patriot Guard into a considerable force, much larger than the old Armsmen, but so far they seemed more interested in prestige than in fighting. Certainly Maurisk had no well-oiled intelligence service to match the peerless machine run by Duke Orlanko, the spymaster who'd so nearly seized the throne. Raesinia sighed. "Maybe we ought to rebuild the Ministry of Information."

Sothe raised an eyebrow. "I'm not sure that would go over well."

"We'd call it something else, of course. But we need *some* way of getting information without—"

For a moment, the world went white. A sound like a hundred-gun cannonade slammed into Raesinia with physical force, pulling at the lace of her dress before rushing on to shatter the glass in the shop windows ahead of her. The ground shook, a single pulse, as though a giant hammer had come slamming down.

Sothe reacted first, knives appearing in her hands as if by magic, stepping between Raesinia and the source of the blast. Her two guards belatedly began to fumble with their muskets, still disoriented from the concussion.

Raesinia, her own head ringing like a bell, turned and saw a tower of ugly black smoke rising into the sky.

"What—" she managed to say.

"This way," Sothe said, disappearing one of her daggers and grabbing Raesinia's arm. She pulled her to the edge of the square, into an alley between two shops, and shoved her up against the wall. The entrance was barely wide enough for one person to squeeze into, and Sothe stood athwart it, daring anyone to try and push past her.

The screams began, and the clatter of boots on flag-stones as the crowd gathered for the execution rushed to escape whatever had happened. Most of the commoners would flee south; here at the north end of the square, the fleeing mass was more distinguished, deputies and mer-chants, Conservatives and Radicals alike pushing and shoving in their haste to get away. There were a fair number of Patriot Guards mixed in as well, tossing their halberds aside to speed their flight.

"Could something have gone wrong with Sarton's machine?" Raesinia said.

"Not unless it was packed full of powder," Sothe said shortly, eyes never leaving the crowd. "That was a bomb."

"I thought so." Raesinia shook her head, trying to clear the daze that had swept over her. "I have to get out there."

"Don't be ridiculous," Sothe said. "That could be exactly what they're planning on. A bomb to panic the crowd, and another assassin ready to strike in the confu-sion. An old trick."

Raesinia lowered her voice. "*You* know we don't have to worry about that."

"*I* know that if you get shot in the head in public, and get back up again, people are going to *comment*." Sothe's tone was grim. "It'd be either a miracle or sorcery, and in my experience demonic intervention is usually more believable than divine."

Four years ago, Princess Raesinia Orboan had been on her deathbed, coughing her lungs to bloody pieces. With the king already suffering from the illness that would eventually kill him, and Prince Dominic dead two years previously at Vansfeldt, the Last Duke had acted to make certain the succession remained under his control. The Priests of the Black, the secret order of the Sworn Church that wielded sorcery in order to suppress knowledge of the supernatural, had guided Raesinia through the ritual of invoking the true name of a demon.

The creature had settled deep inside her, binding itself to her body and soul. Its power restored her to perfect health, repairing her flesh almost as soon as it was injured. As best Raesinia could tell, she couldn't be killed. She hadn't aged a day since something that was becoming increasingly problematic now that she was approaching her twentieth birthday—and she could no longer even sleep. While she was, technically, still alive, she had come to believe that she was no longer human.

Only a tiny handful of people knew the truth. Orlanko, of course, who'd once thought to use the knowledge to control her. His allies in the Priests of the Black, and Sothe, who'd once been his top agent. And Janus bet Vhalnich, who had been tasked by the king with finding a way to free his daughter from the supernatural trap.

The crowd was thinning out. There was no sign of the two Grenadier Guards, and Raesinia hoped they'd only been swept away in the confusion and not trampled underfoot. Screams and shouting continued near the base of the pillar of smoke, which she could now see rose from the where the royal box had been. A ring of Patriot Guards stood around it, halberds unshrouded, looking nervous as other men milled around behind them.

"I have to go," Raesinia said. "I have to see what's happening."

"Your Majesty," Sothe hissed, "please—"

But Raesinia was already squeezing past her, out the mouth of the alley and back into the square. Sothe swore softly and hurried after her as she dodged a few stragglers and reached the ring of guards. Clearly, no instructions had been issued, and the Patriot Guards were not clear on whether they were supposed to be keeping people out or protecting them, but in either case none of them were prepared to bar the queen's way.

Raesinia passed through their circle and nearly gagged at the thick stench of powder. Clouds of evil black smoke still billowed upward, but she could tell the explosion had indeed been centered on the royal box, where she'd been standing only minutes earlier. Guards and deputies rushed around in the murk, helping the injured or shouting unintelligible orders.

"Help!" The voice was high and terrified, a boy's. *Emil.* "Someone *help!*"

Raesinia darted forward and caught sight of him amid the billowing smoke. He was limping across the cratered flagstones, desperately tugging a limp body by one arm. Tears streamed from his eyes, cutting channels through a layer of soot.

"Please help," he said, voice going faint. "Mama won't get up. I think she's hurt."

Emil's right hand was fastened tight around his mother's, and a patter of blood dripped from a gash on his calf. His skin was milk white under the gray soot. Raesinia took one look at Claudia and averted her eyes; the ground beneath her was a slick of red, as though someone had spilled a bucket of paint.

"Your Majesty!"

Sothe appeared at Raesinia's side, with a trio of Patriot Guards behind her. *She's always had a gift for taking charge in desperate situations.* "Help the boy!" Raesinia barked.

Emil screamed as one of the guards pulled Claudia's limp hand from his grasp, then sagged into a dead faint. The guard caught him, looking uncertain.

"Up the street," Sothe said. "There's an aid station forming. He needs bandaging." The guard snapped to obey, and Sothe turned to Raesinia. "Your Majesty. You have to come with me."

"I should . . . help." Raesinia stared at the carnage, feeling hypnotized.

This was meant for me. If she hadn't decided to leave in a huff, she'd have been standing on the platform when the bomb went off. More people were dead because they had been standing next to her at the wrong time. *Like Ben. Like Faro.*

"Raesinia," Sothe hissed in her ear. "Come on. The guards can handle things now that I've given them a kick in the ass. We should get you somewhere safe."

Raesinia looked up at Sothe and felt things snap into focus. "Where's Maurisk?"

She kept her eyes on his face, from the moment she stepped into the café the Directory had commandeered as shelter from the disaster. Maurisk had always been better at flaunting his passions than concealing them. His reaction wasn't much—a brief indrawn breath, a narrowing of the eyes—but it was enough.

He knew this was coming. He didn't expect to see me alive.

"Your Majesty!" The President of the Directory stood up from the table where he and his colleagues had been arguing over an unrolled map of Vordan City. Patriot Guards were everywhere, standing beside the doorway and along the walls, armed with halberds and army muskets. Clearly, the Directory was taking no chances with its own safety.

"I can't tell you how comforting it is to see you unharmed," Maurisk went on, with an attempt at a smile. "I had heard reports that you'd left before the . . . event, but things are obviously very confused. We feared the worst."

"Her Majesty is fine," Sothe said. "No thanks to the efforts of the Patriot Guard, I might add. But many others are not."

"I've sent for help," Maurisk said. "Doctors are on the way from the University. And we've put the city on alert."

Raesinia kept her eyes on Maurisk, saying nothing. His smile flickered, just briefly.

"Do you think," she said after a moment, "the president and I could have a moment in private?"

Maurisk looked surprised, but he gestured sharply at the other Directory members. The speed with which they hurried out of the room spoke volumes about where the power in the Directory lay. Only Durenne, a tall, gangly man with a beak of a nose and a queue of long black hair, paused long enough to catch Raesinia's eye before leaving. The Patriot Guards followed, but Sothe lingered.

"Wait outside," Raesinia told her. "I won't be long."

Sothe hesitated briefly, then followed the guards out the front door. Maurisk and Raesinia were left alone in the café, its chairs scattered and overturned by fleeing patrons, its front windows shattered by the blast. Glass crunched under Raesinia's heel as she stepped forward.

"I'm not going to ask you if you were responsible for this," she said. "I'm sure you'd deny it, even just between us."

"I'm not sure I follow you, Your Majesty," Maurisk said.

His tone was polite, but there was acid hatred in his eyes. After the death of the king and the upheaval that had created the Deputies-General, he'd discovered Raesinia's double life as revolutionary conspirator and princess royal. He hated her for that, for using the idealistic fervor of his friends as a weapon to topple the Last Duke. The deaths that haunted Raesinia's conscience seemed to matter less to him than the fact that he'd been a tool of the very monarchy he so despised.

Unfortunately for Maurisk, even after the creation of the Deputies-General, the queen was still a potent symbol, and she had the support of the hero-general Janus bet Vhalnich. If he'd been in sole charge, she had no doubt he'd have had her arrested and executed by now, but the deputies and the mob would not allow it. *So now he's resorted to more direct measures, no matter who gets killed in the cross fire.*

She met his gaze and refused to flinch. "What do you want from me?"

Maurisk smiled. Not the fake grin he put on for public consumption, but his true smirk. It reminded Raesinia of a lizard.

"I think it would be best," he said, "if you retired to the

country for a time. Vordan City has obviously been heavily infiltrated by enemy agents. I will of course begin a vigorous campaign to root them out, but in the meantime I regret to say I cannot guarantee your safety. The Crown owns many small estates that would be suitable, and if the Grenadier Guards accompanied you, then I'm sure you would be perfectly secure."

"I see."

Maurisk spread his hands, as if nothing could be more reasonable. "I only have the state's interests in mind, of course. Your Majesty."

Raesinia blew out a long breath. "I'll consider your . . . suggestion."

The president's face hardened. "Please do. Every moment that you remain is another opportunity for the enemy to strike."

Raesinia turned on her heel and headed for the door, glass cracking and snapping under her shoes. The Patriot Guards had formed a cordon, with only Sothe and the other Directory members allowed within. On the outside were two blue-uniformed Grenadier Guards, who were engaged in a shouting match with the Patriot Guard sergeant. The men quieted as their queen emerged.

"Back to the carriage," Raesinia said, with a glance at Sothe.

The smoke was clearing, revealing a shallow crater in the once-smooth surface of Farus' Triumph. A broken pipe somewhere gushed water, forming a bloody mud puddle. The guards had taken the injured to a clear space, to await the arrival of the University contingent, and now were dragging the dead into neat rows. Claudia lay among them, stomach torn open to reveal glistening viscera. Raesinia looked away, her gorge rising.

She didn't say anything until she and Sothe were alone in the back of the carriage, with the guards taking their customary position on the top. Once Sothe shut the door, cutting off the cries and shouted orders from the outside, Raesinia said, "Maurisk was behind this."

Sothe's expression would never show anything as

human as surprise, but she raised an inquisitive eyebrow. "You're certain?"

Raesinia shook her head and swore. "I would swear he didn't expect me to walk out of here today. If he didn't plant the bomb, he at least knew about it."

"Someone in the government must have, at any rate," Sothe said. "An explosion that size would require quite a bit of powder stuffed under the floor of the box. That would be hard to sneak past the guards—"

"So the guards are in on it."

"At least some of them must be either complicit or suborned, yes. But that by itself doesn't implicate Maurisk."

Raesinia scowled. She had to admit her own bias; the dislike between her and her former companion had come to run both ways. *Still. The way he looked when I came in was as good as a confession.*

"The problem," Sothe went on, "is that we have something of a surplus of enemies."

"There's an understatement," Raesinia muttered. "Orlanko, for certain. Borelgai spies, the Hamveltai Komerzint, Murnskai fanatics. The older noble families hate me for surrendering royal powers to the Deputies-General, and the Radicals hate me for not abdicating in favor of a republic."

"Not to mention," Sothe said, "the Priests of the Black."

"You think they wouldn't bother with *bombs*," Raesinia said.

"Revealing your secret to the public would be just as effective as killing you, as far as Elysium is concerned." Sothe glared. "As I tried to explain earlier."

"So either Maurisk is trying to kill me, because he doesn't know he can't, or the Priests of the Black are trying to blow me to bits in front of witnesses so everyone can see what happens." Raesinia cocked her head. "If they did blow me to pieces, do you think the missing bits would grow back, or would you have to gather them up for me?"

"Your Majesty—"

"Sorry." Raesinia took a deep breath. "Maurisk told

me he wants me to leave the city. Hide out on a country estate until the danger's passed."

Sothe pursed her lips. "It *would* make it easier to keep you safe. There are too many unknowns in the city."

"No. I will not be run to ground like a frightened rabbit. Besides, if Maurisk *is* involved and I leave him alone in the city, I might as well hand him the crown and be done with it."

"Your Majesty . . ."

Raesinia looked at her, surprised. "You don't really think I should leave, do you?"

A frown creased Sothe's normally placid expression. She spoke slowly and deliberately. "If you do not, whoever was responsible for this attack will try again, and I am not confident in my ability to protect you."

That made Raesinia blink. For Sothe to be less than confident in her ability to do *anything* was as rare as a summer ice storm. "You've done a fine job so far."

"Only luck saved you this time, Your Majesty. You are too public a figure here. Your schedule is known, your routes of travel are known. Against assassins with swords or pistols, I can stand between you and harm, but this . . ." She shook her head. "Sooner or later, they will succeed."

"Then we have to track them down before they do."

"That's a race I'm not sure we can win," Sothe said. "And if Maurisk is involved, what then? He has the Patriot Guard in his pocket."

"If we could find proof, we could take it to the deputies." Raesinia knew that sounded weak, even as she said it. The Deputies-General had come more and more under the thumb of the Directory as the war had grown closer.

"Finding solid evidence could take weeks, maybe months. You'd be vulnerable the whole time."

Raesinia scowled. It *did* make sense, from a certain point of view. But it felt too much like abandoning her post. *Not to mention letting whoever planted the bomb get away scot-free.* Everyone who'd died for wanting to stand near their queen deserved better than that.

But Sothe is right. As long as I stay in the city . . .

An idea tickled the corner of her mind. *As long as the queen stays in the city . . .*

"You're right," she said slowly. "The queen should go to her country estates, to ensure her safety."

Sothe had spent enough time around Raesinia to know that it couldn't be *that* simple. "And?"

"The queen will go to the country," Raesinia said, "and *I* will stay here."

There was another long silence. Sothe stared thoughtfully at Raesinia, who shifted uncomfortably under the scrutiny.

"It's nothing we haven't done before," Raesinia said. "And if no one knows I'm here, they won't be looking for me."

"And if they try anything in the country, they won't get anywhere," Sothe said, considering the problem.

"It would also let me 'return' without taking the time for a round-trip. I imagine that would be quite a surprise to Maurisk."

"Not a bad card to have up our sleeves," Sothe said. "*Provided* we can fool them."

"You fooled Orlanko for more than a year. I'm sure you can manage it."

Sothe's eyes narrowed, and Raesinia felt her heart jump. "You mean for me to go?"

"I'm sorry," Raesinia said in a rush. "I can't think of any other way. We might be able to fake a ride to the country, but even if we tell people I'm closeted in mourning, someone will have to keep up the facade."

"Not to mention taking care of any spies that come poking around." It was logical, and Sothe knew it, but Raesinia could see the hesitation on her face. "But the last time I left you alone, you walked right into an ambush, and Orlanko nearly had you."

That had been the night Ben died, another stupid sacrifice for her sake. Raesinia's chest went tight for a moment, but she fought back the wave of guilt. "I'll be careful. And I still have contacts from the old days—"

"No one I trust." Sothe shook her head. "It's too dangerous. You'd have no backup if something went wrong."

Raesinia paused. "Do you trust Janus?"

"For the moment," Sothe said. "But he's with the Army
of the East, off in the League."

"Marcus d'Ivoire is here, and Janus trusts *him*."

"It's an idea," Sothe admitted. "You think he'd agree to
help?"

"I don't think he'll like it," Raesinia said. "But I *am*
the queen, and I don't plan to give him a choice."

"No," said Marcus. "Absolutely not. The whole idea is
ridiculous."

They sat in the drawing room at Twin Turrets, the
manor house that had served as Janus' command post
during his defense of Vordan City. Most of it had at one
point been converted into a barracks for Janus' personal
guard, a company of Mierantai Volunteers, expensive furniture dragged aside and stacked in the halls and polished
floorboards scuffed by the passage of many boots. This
room still had its original high-backed leather armchairs,
set in a half circle in front of the fire, but it was crowded
with tables, dressers, and other detritus.

Most of the Mierantai had gone with Janus on his campaign, but a few remained with Marcus. Since Raesinia
was proposing to place herself under their protection, she
was glad to see that they seemed reassuringly professional,
even if they often spoke with a gravelly mountain accent
so thick she could hardly understand them. Every man
carried a rifle as long as he was tall, and wore a dark red
uniform cut to the standard army pattern.

Marcus had received her courteously, but his expression
was grim. Raesinia hadn't spent much time with him since
the day he'd fought by her side, escaping from the traitorous
Noreldrai Grays. His face was more lined with care than she
remembered, and there were hints of gray in his close-
cropped beard. He wore crisp army blue, instead of the
Armsmen green uniform she remembered, and the silver of
a colonel's eagles sparkled on his shoulders.

Raesinia sat in one of the big chairs, which made her feel tiny. Sothe stood at her right hand, playing the dutiful servant. Marcus knew that Sothe was more than she seemed—he'd seen her cut down a half dozen Grays—but not the full extent of her service. Most important, Janus had told her that Marcus didn't know about Raesinia's own secret. That made sense—the fewer people who knew, the better—but it complicated the situation.

"You've heard what happened this afternoon?" Raesinia said.

"I had a report," Marcus said. "I was glad to hear you were safe."

"It was closer than I would have liked. Directory President Maurisk has asked me to retire to the country for my own safety."

"Which sounds like a fine idea," Marcus said. "Forgive me, Your Majesty, but—"

"I cannot leave the city," Raesinia said. "Not now, in the midst of the crisis. And there's the matter of discovering the identity of the bomber."

"Surely you can leave that to the Patriot Guard?" There was a hint in Marcus' voice that said he shared Raesinia's low opinion of that force.

"At least some of the Patriot Guard must have been compromised, or the bomb could not have been planted. I need to discover how deep the corruption goes." Raesinia looked him in the eye. "I'm asking for your help, Colonel."

Marcus shifted uncomfortably when she mentioned his rank, clearly still unaccustomed to it. "You're placing me in a very awkward position, Your Majesty. I have very clear instructions as to my mission here, and getting involved in politics is definitely not a part of it."

"You won't need to get involved, unless things go badly wrong," Raesinia said.

"That's not very reassuring," Marcus said. "In my experience, things *always* go badly wrong eventually. It would be impossible to ensure your safety."

Raesinia gritted her teeth. She was so, *so* sick of being treated like a fresh egg, to be wrapped in unspun wool and carried with bated breath. *If I'd known being queen was going to be like this, I wouldn't have worked so damned hard to get here.*

"No one expects you to withstand a siege here," she said. "But Sothe will maintain the illusion that I'm staying in the country, so my presence here should stay secret. That should be safe enough."

"We'd never be able to keep the truth from my own guards," Marcus said.

"I think we can count on their discretion." Janus' personal troops were from his home county, deep in the mountains. They were clannish, insular and suspicious of outsiders, and devoted to their beloved count. Janus had brought them to the capital specifically because it would be difficult for Concordat agents to infiltrate their ranks. "And all the servants are Mierantai as well?"

"Yes." Marcus sighed. "I'm going to have to ask for instructions."

"From Janus? That'll take weeks."

"We have . . . alternative channels," Marcus said. "I should have an answer by the day after tomorrow."

Raesinia glanced at Sothe, who gave a small nod. "It will take that long to make the preparations, Your Majesty."

"All right." Raesinia stood. "Until then, Colonel."

Marcus shot to his feet as soon as she did, and answered her nod with a bow. His expression was that of a man who'd been handed a bomb with a hissing fuse. "Of course, Your Majesty."

CHAPTER THREE

WINTER

Winter awoke to the soft sound of shuffling paper, and opened her eyes to find soft morning light filtering through the canvas of her tent.

"Sorry," Jane said. "I was looking for a drink."

"S'alright." Winter yawned and rolled sideways on her narrow sleeping pallet, which seemed much larger without another person crammed in beside her. Her body still felt warm and shivery from Jane's meticulous attentions, and the slight breeze from the tent flap was chilly. She pulled the thin sheet a bit tighter around herself. "It must be past dawn. Go ahead and light the lamp."

The flare of a match brightened the dimness of the tent for a moment, followed by the warmer glow of an oil lamp. Winter's eyes fixed on Jane, gloriously nude against the light, head tipped back as she drained a canteen. When it was empty, she tossed it aside and came back to the pallet, stepping carefully over the pile of papers she'd toppled. Winter lifted the blanket so she could wriggle underneath it, reveling in the warmth of Jane's skin pressing against her own. Jane kissed her, lips still wet.

"What is all that?" Jane said, prodding the fallen stack with one finger. "I thought Cyte was supposed to take care of the paperwork for you."

Winter sighed. "Official complaints. Have to be signed by the commander to show that she's seen them, then sent back to the archives."

"Complaints? From who?"

"Take a wild guess."

"The Royals."

"The Royals" was how everyone in the Girls' Own referred to the former Second Battalion of the Eighteenth Regiment of the Royal Army of Vordan, now the Second Battalion of the Third Regiment of the Line of the Army of the East and Winter's personal headache. Captain Sevran, their commander, had been relatively cooperative, but some of his subordinates were less willing.

"Specifically, Lieutenant Novus, the senior staff officer."

"Let me guess," Jane said. "He's the scion of a great and noble family."

"More or less."

Lieutenants in the Royal Army came in two flavors. Some were commoners who'd been recommended for aptitude to the War College and spent several years training there; captains like Marcus d'Ivoire did a tour as a junior officer before returning for further training. Others were granted their commissions on the spot by the Crown, either in recognition of their illustrious family names or in return for significant financial contributions to the royal coffers.

The revolution and the war had upset all that, of course, and Janus was upsetting it further, promoting commoners to the unheard-of rank of *colonel* based on nothing more than his personal judgment. *But some people are always willing to pretend nothing has changed.*

"What is he complaining about?" Jane said.

"Today? That the Second Battalion, in spite of its storied history, is placed behind the First in the marching order."

"Do the Royals really have a storied history?"

"Three hundred years' worth, apparently. Lieutenant Novus wrote about it in some detail. It seems that one of his ancestors was killed leading it to a glorious defeat during the reign of Farus the Fifth."

"So because some idiots got themselves slaughtered a

hundred years ago, we should eat their dust on the road all day?" Jane snorted. "That sounds like Royal Army thinking, all right. Janus should have sent the lot of them to the rear and let the volunteers do all the fighting."

"Janus needs every bayonet he can get his hands on," Winter said.

"Assuming they'll fight, which I doubt." Jane shook her head, rubbing her cheek against Winter's shoulder. "Did I tell you we caught another couple of Royals trying to sneak into our camp last night?"

"Oh God. Again?"

"They don't seem to learn."

"You didn't hurt them too badly, I hope."

"We may have pushed them around a bit. But we just sent them back where they'd come from." Jane grinned slyly. "Kept their pants and breeches, though. Only seemed fair."

"You really ought to file a report with their company commanders," Winter said, though she couldn't keep a broad grin off her own face.

"I think my way works better."

"Well. A good regimental commander leaves minor matters up to her subordinates." Winter put on her best pompous officer voice. "I'll leave things to your best judgment, Captain Verity."

"Is that out of that manual you borrowed from Janus?"

"Indeed. *A Comprehensive Guide to Regimental Command.* I hear it's a standard text at the War College."

"What does it have to say about kissing your captains?"

"Surprisingly little."

Their lips came together. Winter felt Jane's fingers running delicately up the inside of her thigh.

"Perhaps," Winter said when Jane pulled away for a moment, "I should submit a monograph to the College. To make sure their text is *truly* comprehensive."

"Sounds like an excellent plan to me."

Winter grinned wider. "Then, Captain Verity, I officially request that you assist me with my research."

"I don't know," Jane said, with mock seriousness. "I may have to run that up the chain of command."

She smothered Winter's mad giggles with another kiss, and for a while, rank was forgotten.

The Army of the East snaked along the road, a column of blue that stretched for miles through a country of brown, red, and gold. Autumn had come to the valley of the Velt, and the neat checkerboard of farms and orchards on either side of the road had gone from endless green to a ruddier palette. Here and there, a field of late grain still gleamed yellow in the sun, but most of the harvest was in, and the furrowed land left fallow or planted with winter crops. Breaking up the dark brown of bare earth were the fruit trees, apples, pears, and cherries, whose leaves had turned a riot of red and gold. Neat fenced-in orchards sported row after tidy row, their perfect order mocking the loose discipline of the soldiers marching past.

More surprising to Winter were the people, farmers and their families, who stood behind those fences to watch the army troop past as though on parade. Young boys yelled their approval and waved wildly, attracting waves in return from the bemused Vordanai troops. When they passed through villages—always laid out on perfect grids, with neat streets lined by half-timbered houses and the inevitable Sworn Church with its spire at the center—it seemed as though the entire population had turned out to line the route.

It was a far cry from the march through Khandar, where the civilian population had fled or hidden as the armies approached. Given what the Redeemers had done to anyone they suspected of disloyalty, Winter couldn't blame the Khandarai, nor could she wonder that they'd expected retribution from the Vordanai when they returned. But this was the Free Cities League, where war had for generations been a gentleman's pursuit, carried out with due attention to the sensibilities of the local inhabitants.

"They don't even seem angry with us," Winter said to Cyte as they rode down the length of the trudging infantry column.

"This is Deslandai territory," Cyte said. Winter had learned to consult the ex-University student when it came to matters of history or politics, which were usually perfectly opaque to her. "Desland has always been a shaky member of the League. There's a lot more Vordanai language and influence here than farther north, even if they are Elysian."

"It didn't stop their troops from fighting against us."

"I doubt the Grand Council in Hamvelt gave them a choice," Cyte said. "Hamvelt has been more or less running the League since the War of the Princes."

Winter went quiet a moment, guiding her horse over a tricky rut in the road. She'd been able to avoid riding much as a captain, but a colonel needed to be able to get from place to place quickly, and so she'd reluctantly taken to the saddle. The skill had come back to her surprisingly quickly. Riding had been on the syllabus at Mrs. Wilmore's, as an essential skill for a sturdy farmer's wife. Even in her earliest memories, just after her arrival at the institution as a little girl, she felt that she'd been familiar with horses. But rankers didn't ride, and so for three years in the army the closest she'd gotten to a horse was a pat on the nose.

All the best mounts had gone to the cavalry, which was desperately short of good horseflesh, so the quartermaster had issued her an aging plodder, a gelding named Edgar who exuded a sense of placid resignation. Winter wouldn't have wanted to push him to a gallop, but he served well enough for walking down a country road. When it came to actual fighting, she would be on her own two feet, colonel or not.

Cyte rode her mare with considerably less comfort, looking like someone with better grounding in the theory of horsemanship than the practice. Winter needed staff lieutenants, to deliver orders and handle the endless tide of paperwork, and she'd taken Cyte for the latter and Bobby for the former. She'd also requested Lieutenant John Marsh, Bobby's lover, from the Colonials, and given him a company in the Girls' Own.

Ahead, the column had come to a halt. Winter rode past the front ranks of the Royals and nodded to Captain Sevran, ahorse beside the battalion flag and drummers.

The Girls' Own stretched ahead in a loose march formation, small groups of young women standing around chatting in the road, and they waved genially at Winter as she passed rather than offering salutes. Quite a few, Winter saw, were carrying the tall plumed Hamveltai shakos.

Lieutenant Marsh, riding with the comfortable grace of an expert horseman, met them coming the other way. He was tall, blond, and handsome, with sparkling blue eyes and a ready smile. Winter could see why Bobby had fallen for him, and he'd proven himself unfailingly polite and competent, but she couldn't help maintaining a certain reserve around the man. He knew at least part of her secret—it was hard to hide the strange, marblelike discolorations that were gradually spreading across her skin—but Winter wasn't ready to bring him into her own confidence.

"Sir," he said, saluting smartly with his free hand.

"What's going on?" Winter said, nodding at the stalled column.

"Wagon train merging," Marsh said. "One of the forage parties. It'll be another half an hour before they clear the road."

Winter glanced at the sun, which was already well past the overhead and sinking fast toward the horizon. The days were getting rapidly shorter as the year slipped away, something that still surprised her after three years in more equatorial Khandar.

"We're not going to get more than another mile today, then," Cyte said, making the same calculation.

Marsh nodded. "Bobby and Captain Verity have gone ahead to secure a campsite."

"Six miles, maybe?" Winter said, looking back the way they had come. "That's pretty mediocre marching."

"Janus isn't pushing us," Cyte said. "Any faster and we'd outrun the wagon train."

Unlike on the Khandarai campaign, where the ships of the Vordanai transport fleet had been able to keep the small Colonial army supplied, Janus' Army of the East had to rely on slow-grinding supply convoys taking the coast road from depots at Essyle. Fortunately, the battle—known as the Battle of Diarach after the tiny village where Janus had made his headquarters—seemed to have taken all the wind out of the sails of the League army.

Given a thrashing when they'd expected to deliver one, the divided components of di Pfalen's force had retreated in two different directions. Di Pfalen's own army, with mostly Hamveltai troops, had fallen back to the north toward the great bastion of Antova, while a smaller force of mostly Deslandai troops had moved off to the east toward their home city. Janus had left a small force to watch di Pfalen, and marched the majority of his troops, nearly forty thousand strong, down the road to Desland. So far, however, he'd been content to match the pace of the slow-moving Deslandai army, rather than outrunning his supplies in an effort to cut the enemy off.

"Desland hasn't got a modern fortification," Marsh said. "If we get our guns up, we'll pound their walls to splinters in a few hours."

Winter nodded. "They'll have to turn and fight before we get there. How many miles left?"

"Forty-five, after today," Cyte said. Unsurprisingly, she'd turned out to be an expert with maps. "Maybe a week's march at this pace."

"So we'll have a fight sometime before then." Winter shook her head. "Marsh, go and tell Captain Verity to make sure there's a space for drilling in the camp. We'll have time this evening while we wait for the wagons, and I think we'd better polish up."

"Yes, sir!" Marsh saluted again, turned his horse with a light touch on the reins, and trotted up the length of the column.

By the time the wagons had moved on, the men and women of Winter's regiment had fallen out all over the road and the surrounding fields, and had to be rounded up by their sergeants. Winter was obscurely pleased to see that the Royals were no better in this respect than the Girls' Own, although she had to admit they got themselves together a bit faster. The column got moving again as the sun reached the horizon, and it was well into twilight by the time they arrived at the campsite, marked out by pegs in a broad expanse of empty fields. Winter's tent stood all alone in the center, with a flag planted beside it. Before long, the designated space was a mass of confusion as the long column straggled in and more tents started going up.

Bobby was waiting with a pair of younger girls. Winter dismounted, wincing at the soreness in her muscles, and handed over Edgar's reins. The girls saluted—they were noticeably better at it than many of their older compatriots—and led the gelding away.

"Sir!" Bobby said. She offered a Winter a folded scrap of paper. "From the general. Marching orders for tomorrow."

Winter broke the seal with her thumb and glanced over the short document. "We're to stay in camp until noon, and follow on after the Sixth and their artillery. Another six miles."

Compared to the trek across Khandar, moving the Army of the East was a terrifyingly complicated endeavor. With more than ten times as many men, moving in a single column would have left the army hopelessly slow and strung out. Instead, Janus had organized a complicated progress by multiple parallel roads, with a cavalry screen protecting the whole unwieldy mass from enemy ambush. In lesser hands, it easily could have collapsed in a mess of snarls and confusion, but so far delays like that afternoon's had been rare. Winter sensed the hand of Fitz Warus— now commanding the Colonials—in the meticulous allocation of march routes and detailed orders.

"Better to wait here than on the road, I suppose," Bobby said. She looked tired, Winter thought, with a pang of guilt. Ever since her promotion, she'd pushed a great deal of work onto Bobby's young shoulders. "Shall I pass the word to let the rankers sleep in?"

"No. I want *you* to take a rest, but the regiment should be up and breakfasted as usual. We've got some drilling to do."

Bobby raised her eyebrows. "The girls aren't much used to drilling, sir."

"It's about time they had a taste of the real military life." Winter flashed Bobby a grin she didn't feel. "Just like we did, eh?"

"Yessir!"

Bobby saluted again, and Winter waved a hand. "Go find your tent."

Marsh would be waiting for her, Winter knew. She hadn't heard any rumors about the two of them yet, but it was only a matter of time.

Not, Winter thought, *that I have any right to register a complaint.* No sooner had she ducked into her own tent than Jane was kissing her, arms wrapped around her shoulders to pull her close. Winter was stiff with surprise for a moment, then softened in her lover's arms, worming her fingers into the sweaty red tangle of Jane's hair, which now nearly reached her shoulders.

"You really ought to salute first," Winter said when they finally pulled apart.

"Sorry." Jane snapped a crisp salute. "Sir! Permission to stick my tongue down your throat, *sir!*"

Winter put a hand over her face to hide a grin. "You want to shout a little louder? I'm not sure the whole camp heard you."

"I'm pretty sure the whole camp already knows Captain Verity and Colonel Ihernglass are fucking." Jane lowered her voice. "It's the details of how we go about it that might surprise some of them."

Jane's hands descended from Winter's shoulders to her hips by way of the small of her back. The feel of her fingers left Winter flushed and breathing fast, but she managed to disengage from Jane's grasp and take a step back.

"Not now," she said.

"Spoilsport."

Winter rolled her eyes. "You're incorrigible."

"I'm sure if I took the time to look up what that meant, I'd be very insulted."

They stared at each other for a second, straight-faced, then broke down in silent laughter. It was at moments like this that Winter felt her love for Jane most keenly. This was the old Jane, the Jane who'd lived with her at Mrs. Wilmore's and taken the worst the old harridans running the place had to offer with a cocky grin.

Sometimes, though, the surface cracked, and something ugly showed through. Winter remembered the quay back in Vordan City where she'd only just talked Jane out of cold-blooded murder. There was a rage in her, simmering just out of sight, and Winter sometimes wondered if this semblance of the girl she'd known long ago was all an act for her benefit.

Jane, watching Winter's expression, let her smile fade. "What's wrong?"

"Nothing." Winter sighed. "I need to see Captain Sevran."

"Uh-oh. Should I be jealous?"

Winter rolled her eyes. "I doubt he's read my new edition of the handbook yet."

"Are you going to get him to make that idiot Novus stop sending you complaints?"

"I doubt he can," Winter said. "But I think we need to do some joint drill. My guess is there'll be fighting in less than a week, and the Girls' Own and the Royals are going to have to learn to work together at some point."

Jane made a disgusted face. "The girls will do what I tell them to. Just make sure the Royals will do the same, and be ready to kick Captain Sevran's ass if he tries to pull what de Ferre did. We'll be fine."

"A little practice won't hurt."

"If you say so." Jane shrugged. "Personally, I'd rather have the extra sleep, but you give the orders around here."

"I'm going to go track down Sevran. Pick your best company and let them know they'll be on the spot tomorrow."

"Yes, sir!" Jane accompanied her salute with a lascivious smile. "Hurry back."

Captain Sevran's men had erected his tent in the middle of the space marked off for the Royals, and teams of them were hard at work putting the rest of the camp together.

Their rows were a bit neater than the Girls' Own, and their cook fires were a lot more organized, each "pot" of men gathered around its own cook fire. Outside the captain's tent, a sentry saluted crisply and knocked on the tent pole.

"Sir? It's the colonel."

Winter's lip quirked. In Khandar, "the colonel" had always been Janus. Hearing the phrase used in reference to herself always made her want to look over her shoulder.

The tent flap opened, and Sevran straightened, the silver stripes on his shoulders gleaming. His salute was as neat as his sentry's.

"Sir!" he said.

"There're a few matters I thought we might discuss," Winter said. "Do you have a few minutes?"

"Of course, sir." Sevran held the tent flap open. "After you."

Sevran's tent was much like her own, with a few well-worn pieces of nonstandard equipment—a trunk, a portable writing desk—marking it as the residence of a long-serving officer. Sevran himself was in his late thirties, his clean-shaven cheeks pockmarked like a crumbling wall from some long-ago illness. He had a long nose and a well-trimmed brown mustache that had yet to show a hint of gray, and he wore his well-tailored uniform with the unconscious comfort of someone who'd spent nearly his whole life in it. Winter fought down a wave of self-consciousness—meeting these old soldiers always made her feel like a fraud, no matter how many promotions Janus had showered on her.

"Welcome, sir," Sevran said. "What can I do for you?"

"I'm sorry we haven't had time to really get acquainted," Winter said. "Things have been a bit busy."

"Of course, sir."

"How are your men settling in to the new organization?"

His expression flickered, just for a moment. Winter recognized the signs of someone preparing to tell a superior what he wanted to hear.

"As well as could be expected, sir," Sevran said. Winter,

who'd bullshitted her share of officers, smiled inwardly at the neat ambiguity of the phrase.

"I've received a number of . . . requests from your staff lieutenant. He doesn't seem pleased."

"Novus?" Sevran asked. Winter nodded, and the captain sighed. "I'll speak with him. It's nothing against you personally, sir. Some of my officers aren't happy about being placed alongside the volunteers."

"Not just volunteers, but *girls*," Winter said. "I know that must bother some of them."

"I've made it clear to them that the First Battalion is to be treated like any other body of men—of soldiers," Sevran said.

Winter guessed that someone higher up—probably Janus himself—had expressed the importance of this point to the captain. She felt a sudden pang of sympathy for him; the situation he'd been thrust into would have been an awkward one for any officer. He had the clear-eyed look of someone determined to do his best under difficult circumstances.

I think I like him, Winter thought. At the very least, he was not Colonel de Ferre.

"What do the men think about the situation?" Winter said. "The rankers, not the lieutenants."

Sevran hesitated. "Speaking in confidence, sir?"

"Of course."

"There's a fair bit of grumbling, of course. A lot of them don't think the First Battalion will fight. I've told them that you were in a pretty serious scrap at Diarach, but I'm not sure they really believe it." He paused again. "A lot of them also think that you're favoring the First, sir. Because you've . . . served with them longer."

And because I'm sleeping with the captain. No doubt that had made the rounds already. "I've tried to be even-handed."

"Some details *do* seem to fall inordinately on my men," Sevran said, then hastily added, "Not that it isn't your right to assign duties as you like, of course. But it isn't helping morale."

"I'm not sure what you mean."

"Latrine duty, for example." Sevran spoke with the air of someone inching across a crumbling bridge. Winter wondered if he thought she was testing him. "My men have been assigned to digging the latrine ditches for the last three camps. Cleaning the horse lines, too."

"Lieutenant Cytomandiclea draws up those orders," Winter said, frowning. "I'll speak with her. That does seem unfair."

"Thank you, sir," Sevran said. "That will help a great deal."

"I'd also like to try some joint drill between the battalions tomorrow morning," Winter said. "I have some tactical ideas that will need some practice. Can you pick your best company and bring them out to meet me?"

"Of course, sir. I think that's an excellent idea."

"Good. Then I'll see you in the morning, Captain."

Winter accepted his salute with a nod and ducked out of the tent. *That wasn't so hard*. Sevran looked as though he was willing to work with her, and he could help her keep the lieutenants in line. As long as the rankers didn't cause trouble, a few blue-blooded officers weren't much of a concern. *This might actually work*.

This, Winter thought, *is never going to work*.

Weak sunlight shone down through a layer of clouds on the square of packed, furrowed earth designated as a drill field.

"All right," she said. "Let's try again."

"Close *up*!" Folsom bellowed. Winter had borrowed the leather-lunged lieutenant for his volume. "Skirmish line, *forward*! Main line, *loading drill*!"

One company of the Royals was drawn up in a three-deep line, about forty yards from end to end. At Folsom's command, echoed by Lieutenant sur Gothin and his two sergeants, the men began going through the manual of arms, lowering their muskets from their shoulder to the ground, opening an imaginary cartridge, and sliding the ramrod in and out of the barrel. When they'd brought their weapons back to the ready position, sur Gothin shouted, "Fire!" and a hundred empty locks clicked closed. Then they began the pantomime again.

In the meantime, a company from the Girls' Own, led by Abby Giforte, was going through a very different drill. They'd spread out in pairs, each ten yards or more from the next, raggedly spaced and a hundred yards up from where the Royals had formed their tight formation. There they pretended to fire by turns, one woman loading—much easier outside the shoulder-to-shoulder press of the line—while the other aimed, pulled the trigger, then switched off.

So far, so good. The loose skirmish line that Janus had improvised at the Battle of Midvale had confounded the regulars by depriving them of a solid target, and in the weeks since Winter and the other commanders had expanded the idea into a workable set of tactics. The problem was that while their loose formation protected them from massed infantry volleys and artillery, the skirmishers could never stand up to a determined bayonet charge, and without any way to form square they were vulnerable to being ridden down by enemy cavalry.

That was, in theory, where the Royals came in. Winter's hope was that the two halves of her regiment might complement each other; the Girls' Own could disperse to fight in its own style, and fall back behind the solid wall of the regulars' line when danger pressed too close. It was this second part, the falling back, that had proven to be the problem.

"Go ahead," Winter said to Folsom.

"Skirmish line, *fall back!*" he bellowed. "Main line, prepare to pass skirmishers!"

The women of Abby's company stopped what they were doing and ran back toward where the Royals were waiting. The Royals were supposed to open their formation slightly by turning sideways so the skirmishers could filter through it, then close up again. Twice already it hadn't worked that way—somehow an extended arm or leg always found its way into a running woman's path, sending a whole section of the line sprawling to the ground and throwing the whole formation into confusion. Some of the women were getting frustrated, too, and had taken to running full tilt, slamming bodily into whatever was in their way.

This time, Winter could see, was not going to be any different. A few of the fleetest-footed girls made it through before the main press arrived, but then a grinning, redheaded ranker in the center of the Royals' line stuck a foot out in the path of a sprinting woman and sent her sprawling to the turf. Her companion, outraged, slammed into him shoulder first, carrying both of them into the man behind him. From that point it was half collision, half brawl.

And we really ought to be doing it with fixed bayonets, if we expect to stand off cavalry. Winter shook her head. In the center of the line, things had devolved into actual fisticuffs, with a heavyset woman in a loose blue jacket giving a gangly young ranker a pounding. Sergeants on both sides waded in to break it up while other rankers shouted encouragement.

"You little shit!" the woman shouted. "You want to grab my tit so badly, maybe try buying me dinner first!"

"Who'd want to?" the Royal spit back, wiping blood from under his nose. "The thing looks like a paper sack full of lard."

"Be kind to the boy, Vena," another woman said. "He hasn't seen one since his mam tossed him out."

"And you haven't had a prick in so long you whittled yourself one!"

"I ought to. It'd stand up better than yours!"

"That's *enough*!" Folsom roared. "Companies separate and form ranks, *now*!"

The sergeants set to pulling men and women apart and pushing them into some semblance of formation. Winter waited until they were approximately in line and had quieted down before she spoke.

"Lieutenants sur Gothin and Giforte, with me, please. The rest of you are dismissed."

The two lieutenants followed Winter to the edge of the drill field, where Captain Sevran and Jane had been watching the carnage. The rest of the rankers dispersed, heading to their respective camps in opposite directions.

"That could have gone better," Jane said. A curl at the corner of her lip told Winter she'd been laughing.

Sevran shot Jane a look, then shook his head. "I agree that the men need more practice, sir. It's a difficult maneuver."

"It's not difficult," Abby said, taking a position at Jane's side. "Your *men* are deliberately fouling it up."

Sur Gothin, a thin, prematurely balding man, removed his cap and scratched the top of his head. He looked at Sevran, then at Winter.

"They might be, at that," he said eventually. "I'm sorry, sir. I'll try to put the fear of God into them, but they're a bit angry about all this."

"*They're* angry?" Jane snapped. "How do you think we feel?"

"J—" Winter checked herself. "Captain Verity, please. We need to make this work. Captain Sevran, please spread the word that I'm not happy about this, and that we'll be making some changes." She sighed. "No specific punishments yet. We'll work out something more . . . general."

"Yes, sir." Relief was obvious in Sevran's face. It would have been well within Winter's authority to demand that examples be made, but she guessed it would be counterproductive. "I'll make that clear, sir."

"Thank you. That's all for now."

Sur Gothin and Sevran saluted and left in the direction of their camp.

"Should I be calling you Colonel Ihernglass, *sir*?" Jane said, smiling.

"In front of them, yes."

The smile faded. "You don't have to put on a show for them. You remember what the general told you. If they don't respect you, we can always shoot a few of them."

"That wouldn't help." Winter looked sidelong at Jane. "When you were running the Leatherbacks, did you shoot anybody who talked back?"

"I had to crack heads from time to time." Jane frowned. "But we were all on the same side, more or less. This is different."

"It shouldn't be. The other side is over *there*"—Winter waved in the general direction of east—"the Leaguers, not the Royals."

Jane shook her head. "It's a nice sentiment, but I still don't trust them farther than I can spit."

And that, Winter thought as Jane walked away, *is exactly the problem.*

"Lieutenant?" Winter said. "Are you there?"

Cyte folded the tent flap open and blinked in the sun. It was nearly noon. "Sir! What can I do for you?"

"I have some ideas I want to run by you."

Cyte waved her inside. The ex-student had a tent to herself, next to the one Bobby and Marsh shared. A folding desk featured centrally, occupied by an unrolled leather map painted in fine detail. A magnifying lens and a pair of dividers sat atop it. Winter looked at them curiously.

"What are you looking for?" she said.

"Oh." Cyte flushed slightly. "Just . . . an exercise, sir. I plan my own route of march for the army and try to guess where the enemy might be. Then, when the general's orders come down, I figure out where I went wrong."

"Or where the general went wrong."

Cyte laughed. "That seems unlikely, sir."

Winter smiled. Something about Cyte reminded her of herself, when she'd first come to Khandar. Cyte didn't have the fear of discovery driving her, of course, but she had the same quiet dedication to mastering all aspects of her new profession that had driven Winter to memorize the drill books. That enthusiasm had been beaten out of Winter by a succession of vicious, lazy sergeants and the general lassitude of life in the garrison; she hoped that she would do better by Cyte.

"We've been having some . . . problems with the drills we came up with." Winter sketched a summary of what had happened that morning, and Cyte frowned.

"There's bad feeling between the Royals and the Girls' Own, then?" she said.

"You might put it that way, yes," Winter said dryly.

Cyte had a gift for maps and history but could sometimes be oblivious of what the people around her were thinking. "By the way, have you been handing the Royals all the scut-work on purpose?"

"Scut-work, sir?"

"Latrine ditches, horse lines, that sort of thing."

"Oh," Cyte said. "I thought you asked for them to get all the nasty stuff. Captain Verity came by to tell me while I was drawing up the rotas. Did I get it wrong?"

Jane. Winter ground her teeth. It wasn't that she couldn't *appreciate* Jane wanting to shift the worst chores away from her girls and onto the Royals, but . . . *She's not helping.*

No sense in taking it out on Cyte, though. "Don't worry about it. But in the future, try to divide things up evenly. It'll be good for morale."

"Of course, sir."

"Now, when you lay out today's camp, I'd like to do it a little differently." Winter grabbed a pencil and a piece of scrap paper and started sketching.

The day's march, commenced just after noon, was over by sundown. Following behind the wagons at a leisurely pace, they'd covered another six miles. Cavalry scouts reported there were still no signs the enemy planned to make a stand any time soon.

Winter had sent Cyte and Bobby ahead to lay out the camp, keeping Jane by her side. It was a cowardly move, just as it was cowardly not to broach the subject of Jane using Winter's name to fudge the duty rosters. But either was going to provoke an argument, Winter sensed, and she only wanted to have it once.

She glanced at her lover as they rode together, through the failing light, into the campsite. Given the choice, Jane liked to walk alongside her men, but she'd been happy enough to ride beside Winter for the day's journey. She was better on horseback than Winter would have guessed— another legacy of Mrs. Wilmore's institution—but still not as comfortable as Winter herself, or soldiers like Marsh, who seemed born to the saddle.

"Getting cooler," Jane observed, holding up one hand to test the breeze. "We'll need coats before long. I . . ." She hesitated, peering at the colored markers and the tents going up between them. "Something's gotten screwed up here."

Winter sighed. *Sometimes you just have to tear the scab off.* "It's not screwed up. I told Cyte to change the layout."

"What? Why?" Jane looked around. "You've got us all mixed up with the Royals!"

"Alternating lines by company, in a checkerboard pattern," Winter said. That left each line of Royals' tents directly facing a line of Girls' Own.

Previously, the two battalions had camped separately, with the drill field between them like the neutral territory between two feuding powers. In addition to the sentries who guarded the entire camp from ambush by the enemy, Jane always posted lookouts from the Girls' Own to watch the Royals for mischief.

"You can't be serious," Jane said. "Do you have any idea what's going to happen?"

Winter shrugged. "Maybe they'll compare cooking?"

"Don't play dumb."

Jane turned her horse into Winter's path, forcing her to stop, and fixed her with a glare.

Winter sighed. "We can't have the Girls' Own treating everyone else in the army as the enemy, Jane."

"It's not like I *want* to. But—you know the Royals, the way they behave! De Ferre was ready to leave us to die. They *are* the enemy, whether we like it or not."

"That was de Ferre." Winter thought of the piles of complaints. "I'm sure some of the nobles hate the Girls' Own, but the rankers don't. They come from the streets and the farms, the same as your girls do."

"If they're on our side, they should have come to help us," Jane said. "Whatever de Ferre told them."

Winter shook her head. Jane had still not really gotten the hang of the military mentality. "They had *orders*. You can't blame them."

"Orders." Jane spit the word. "I think you were a soldier too long."

Winter took a deep breath and rallied to try again. "Look. You had men helping the Leatherbacks. We didn't capture Bloody Cecil or take the Vendre with just your girls."

"I'm not saying they can't *help*," Jane said. "But there are good reasons I didn't let them into the building." Her eyes were flashing with anger. "You have *no idea* what can happen—"

"I do," Winter said quietly. "I saw what happened when we overran a camp full of Khandarai civilians. I know what happens when soldiers get . . . out of hand. But that's not going to happen here, understand? Because *we're on the same side*." *And*, she added privately, *because I'm not going to let it*. No soldiers under *her* command were going to engage in that kind of pillage and destruction, of allies or enemies. "Everyone will be safe. We've still got the Girls' Own in companies, a hundred altogether. They can take care of themselves."

"It's too dangerous," Jane said. "I won't do it."

And there it was, the line Winter had been dreading. She took another long breath and blew it out.

"I'm not *asking* you to do it," she said slowly. "I'm giving orders."

Jane stared at her for a long, silent moment, her green eyes hooded.

"And what are you going to do if I refuse?" she said after a moment. "Shoot me?"

In theory, Winter knew, she could. Balking at a direct order, in the field, could be declared summary treason. But that was out of the question, and they both knew it. Fortunately, Winter had thought this through ahead of time.

"Of course not," she said. "I love you, Jane. You know that. But . . ." She swallowed. "If you can't take orders you don't like, you can't be in command. It's as simple as that."

"So you'll bust me down to ranker?" Jane sneered. "Fine. Go ahead—"

"I'll send you home."

"You wouldn't," Jane said. "Half the battalion would come with me."

"I doubt it," Winter said. "As I said before, they're not

here for you, *or* for me. They're here because they think this is the right thing to do."

Jane stared, her face rigid. A muscle twitched in her cheek.

"Please don't make me do that," Winter said, throat clenching. "I need you for the Girls' Own. *I* need you. But *everyone* in this regiment is my responsibility now, and I need to do what will keep as many of them alive as possible."

Another, longer silence. Then, finally, Jane saluted, without changing her expression.

"Yes, *sir*," she said through gritted teeth. "I had better go and find where your new orders have placed my tent, *sir*."

She pulled her horse around, sawing viciously on the reins, and kicked him into motion. Winter stifled an urge to call after her, and closed her eyes until her heart slowed down. Then, suddenly weary, she turned in search of her own tent.

CHAPTER FOUR

MARCUS

The blindfold was heavy black linen, scratchy and awkward. Marcus resisted the urge to tug it into a more comfortable position, for fear one of the guards in the carriage would take it as an attempt to peek. Janus' Mierantai had been ordered to preserve absolute secrecy, and they took their orders very seriously.

Marcus had dispatched his report shortly after the queen departed, along with an urgent request for instructions. This involved leaving a folded message in a certain cubbyhole at a certain wine shop, one of several clandestine drop-offs that he'd been forced to memorize. He'd spent the rest of the evening and all of the following day trying to puzzle out what answer might possibly come back. It was a fruitless endeavor, as Marcus would be the first to admit. Unlike Janus, he had no head for politics. He'd watched the increasingly heavy-handed rule of the Directory and the Patriot Guard with a vague distaste, but it didn't seem relevant to his own mission, so he hadn't paid any particular attention.

Truthfully, Marcus wasn't entirely sure what he was supposed to be *doing* in Vordan City. It had all sounded very logical when Janus explained it before leaving for the front, but Janus' explanations had a habit of evaporating in the morning light like demon gold, leaving nothing behind but vague memories of something very convincing. He was intended to be Janus' representative in the city, but so far that involved little more than sending back reports on the state of affairs.

Janus had a habit, though, of putting the people he trusted into positions where he thought they might prove useful, even if he wasn't exactly sure how. When the courier had arrived—dressed in plainclothes, but in possession of the prearranged password—Marcus had a strong suspicion it was his turn, like an actor waiting in the wings receiving a cue. Being treated like a game piece would have been more grating if he hadn't long ago accepted that this was simply how Janus bet Vhalnich treated everyone.

He'd climbed into a battered carriage with FOR HIRE signs on the sides and found it occupied by two more young men, with the keen look and mountain accents of Janus' Mierantai Volunteers. They'd given him the blindfold, and he'd tied it with a resigned sigh. There was a point, he thought, where security passed into paranoia, but he wasn't confident in his ability to identify the boundary.

They drove for perhaps a half hour, changing direction frequently, the carriage's poor suspension bumping and rattling over the cobblestones. When it finally came to a halt, one of the guards opened the door and took Marcus' hand, leading him across a gravel drive. A gate squealed open.

"You can take the blindfold off now, sir," the guard said. "My apologies. Welcome to Willowbrook."

Marcus pulled the cloth away from his eyes and blinked in the sun. He stood on the grounds of a small estate, shielded from the road by a tall hedge and a thick wood-and-iron gate. A number of men in plain leathers stood around the grounds, ostensibly tending the plants. They were rather more observant than the typical gardener, however, and Marcus suspected that if he'd tried talking to them he'd hear the gravelly Mierantai accent again. He also suspected their long rifles were not far away.

The courier knocked at the door, and a liveried servant opened it. Once Marcus stepped inside, the guards became more obvious; they still didn't wear their red uniforms, but they did carry the long rifles of the First Mierantai Volunteers, and wore swords at their belts. The pair nearest the door saluted smartly.

Willowbrook was a simple dwelling, as such things went, with the hall, dining room, receiving rooms, and servants' quarters on the first floor and bedrooms on the second. Its only architectural oddity was a four-story tower topped by a broad solar, built for someone who wanted to soak up the sun unimpeded by trees or other buildings. From that perch, Marcus imagined one could not only keep an eye on the streets for a good distance in any direction, but see all the way to the edge of the city and the forested hills to the north.

Captain Alek Giforte waited at the end of the hall. Like the guards, he was out of uniform, though Janus had appointed him an army captain when the Armsmen were dissolved. Marcus had had to coax Giforte into accepting, ashamed as the former vice captain had been over his former accommodation with Orlanko. Marcus was still surprised Janus had trusted the ex-traitor so quickly, but he had to admit the gesture had brought out the best in Giforte. He snapped a brisk salute.

"Sir!" Giforte said. "Welcome to Willowbrook."

"Thanks," Marcus said. "I can see you've settled in."

"Yes, sir." Like Twin Turrets, the house was showing the wear and tear of being used as a barracks. Furniture was shoved out of the way, floors were muddy, and stacks of soiled linens were everywhere. Giforte gestured to the stairs. "If you'll come upstairs?"

"Has something gone wrong?" His messages from Janus originated here, he knew, but usually they were brought to Twin Turrets, disguised as ordinary post.

"No, sir. But our instructions were that the message not leave the room."

That *did* seemed paranoid, even for Janus, but Marcus was curious to see the station in any case. He followed Giforte up the stairs to the second floor, then into a winding tower staircase that curved up another forty feet to a broad room at the very top. Here, the comfortable furniture and decorative touches had all been trundled out of the way, to make room for desks, chairs, and stacks of file folders. Enormous open windows—so big that glassing them in would have cost a small fortune—looked in every direction, all blocked to cracks by wooden shutters.

Five or six young men were hard at work, scribbling in books or doing calculations with small metal counters. They all had the pasty look of fellows who didn't get out in the sun enough, and from the state of their hair and clothes, they didn't even manage to get downstairs for a wash very often. Trays of half-eaten food were piled by the stairwell.

"This is the day shift," Giforte explained. "Mostly coding and decoding. At night we've got a few lads with good eyes and quick pens to keep watch. White?"

One of the men looked up, his spectacles slightly askew. "Sir?"

"This is Colonel d'Ivoire," Giforte said. "Colonel, this is Lieutenant White, He's in charge of this end of the flik-flik line."

"Flik-flik?" Marcus said.

"That's just what the boys call it," White said, getting to his feet. He was in his early twenties, with blue eyes and hair the color and general appearance of a haystack. Noticing Marcus' attention, he ran one hand through it, which produced no notable improvement. "Sir. I mean, that's what they call it, *sir*."

"Why?"

White walked to one of the windows, where something a bit like a box lantern was mounted on a tripod. A lever projected from one side of the box. White pressed down on it, and something inside the box slid open with a sound like *flik*. When it let go, it closed. He did it again. *Flik. Flik, flik.*

"This is the . . . device?" Marcus said. "I thought it would be bigger."

"It's not actually terribly complex," White said. "Not much more than a standard oil lamp with a mirror backing to concentrate the light. They use something similar in the theater, I understand. The shutter is finely balanced, so we can keep up a good speed, but that's just a little bit of machinery. The real genius of the system is in the coding."

"All this?" Marcus said, indicating the books.

"Yes, sir. The idea's not a new one, of course. Signal fires have been used since ancient times. But Janus' system lets us transmit a lot of information very quickly, as long as both sides are working from the same scheme."

Marcus hid a smile. Everyone, down to the lowest private, seemed to have caught the habit of saying "Janus" or "the general," never anything as formal as "General Vhalnich" or "Count Mieran." "How fast is it?" he asked.

"We can send a hundred and twenty symbols in five minutes," White said proudly. "Assuming good weather, the message travels down the line at nearly a hundred miles per hour."

Marcus tried to picture it. Through a crack in the shutters, he could see the hills north of Vordan, miles away. Somewhere on that hilltop was another team of men, with another device like this one. When night fell, they would wait for the distant flashes of an incoming message, then work like mad to flash it along to the next hilltop. More men there would send it to the next, and the next, and so on until it reached the Army of the East more than four hundred miles away. A message could get there and back in a single night, where a fast rider might take days.

It was a fragile connection. Hazy nights could interrupt it, or rain, or even enemy action. The messages it passed along were necessarily brief and often full of ambiguity. Still, it was a tremendous advantage, which was why Janus had been so careful about setting it up. The concept, Marcus knew, had come from the Desoltai of Khandar, whose messages Janus had decoded to lure the desert nomads into a deadly ambush. The general believed in making use of good ideas, regardless of the source.

"Very good, Lieutenant White," Marcus said, sensing that the man wanted praise. White inflated visibly. "Very good indeed. Now, I'm told you have something for me?"

"Oh! Yes, sir. Here." He handed Marcus a scrap of

paper. "This is the expanded version. We use a great deal of abbreviation and substitution, obviously, even within the coding, to keep the messages short."

Marcus nodded. The message, in a neat, well-trained hand, said:

Marcus—
 Yours of last night received. Threat to R. of great concern, agree that M. is a likely suspect. Approve of her plan. Assist R. to obtain evidence, render all possible aid. Trust her judgment. Keep me informed.
 Possible additional threat reported by Downstairs. Have given instructions for you to be briefed. Stay on guard.
 Matters here satisfactory. Aim to capture Antova by end of season, secure our position, return to capital. Await developments.
       —Janus

Well, Marcus thought, *that's one question answered.* He had no idea how Janus expected him to "obtain evidence"— for all that he'd been briefly head of the Armsmen, Marcus had no training in criminal investigation. *Maybe Raesinia has some ideas.* If the general was uncomfortable with the Queen of Vordan running around playing private investigator, he hadn't put it in his message.

More alarming, to Marcus' military mind, was the last line. *He plans to take* Antova? Antova was the great fortress of the Velt Valley, constructed where a tributary of the Velt reached within fifty miles of the primary passes leading over the mountains from Vordan. No army could debouch from the passes and leave the fortress and its garrison active in their rear. The great seven-sided star of its outer trace was familiar to every graduate of the War College; it was the master work of the great Hamveltai engineer Dreiroede, and its plans were included in military textbooks as the epitome of modern fortifications. Such was its reputation that it had never been besieged, let alone captured.

And this is what Janus casually says he'll take by the end of the season? Marcus shook his head. A proper assault, with approaching parallels, breaching batteries, and all the rest, would take months, stretching through the winter with the army strung out at the end of a slow and vulnerable line of supply. *He can't be serious, can he?*

But there was never any arguing with Janus, least of all from the other end of a flik-flik line. Marcus sighed and went to put the message in his pocket, only to be halted by Lieutenant White clearing his throat.

"Sorry, sir," White said. "The coding instructions were clear. The message isn't to leave this room, and we're to destroy all copies once you've seen it."

"Ah. Of course." Marcus handed the paper back to White, who put it with a small stack of others and took it to a small metal bin, already half-full of ashes. A splash of lamp oil and a match later, and the messages were blazing merrily.

"Thank you, sir," White said. "It's good to finally meet you. If you're interested in the details of our operation here, I can put together a basic overview—"

"That's all right," Marcus said hurriedly. White seemed the type who would go into excruciating detail at the drop of a hat. "Thank you for answering my questions." He turned to Giforte. "The message said something about Downstairs?"

"Ah," Giforte said, looking uncomfortable. "That's what we call . . . well, Downstairs. I'll show you. Follow me."

"Where did White and the others come from?" Marcus said as they descended the tower stairs.

"Volunteers, mostly," Giforte said. "I only know their end of it, but apparently the general had some men sorting through the new recruits for candidates. We never have enough boys who can write and figure. He took some from the old navy, too, signalmen and the like."

Marcus nodded. The combination of the revolution and the declaration of war had sent a patriotic thrill through the nation, and while the aristocracy might be unhappy with the new order, the common folk had signed up in huge numbers to help defend Vordan against its foes. Unfortunately, Vordan needed more than bodies—without muskets, training, and leadership, the new soldiers were only extra mouths. *Thank God for Murnskai tardiness.* The League cities, with their standing armies, were quick to mobilize, but Imperial Murnsk was famous for moving with the agility of a glacier. It would be next year before Vordan had to face the full might of the vast hordes at the emperor's command.

"I've heard," Giforte said, "that he also had people looking for recruits for Downstairs. Though what qualifications they needed I have no idea."

He led Marcus back to the first floor and into the kitchen, where a low-ceilinged doorway led farther down. Two guards stood beside it, rifles at the ready, and saluted at the two officers' approach. The stairway beyond had been cut into the bedrock, lit by candles resting in wall nooks crusted over with wax. It went down at least fifteen feet before straightening out into a short tunnel.

"This was originally a wine cellar," Giforte said. "Whoever lived here must have had quite a collection."

The tunnel ended in a wooden door, caked with dirt and grime. Giforte knocked twice.

"Yes?" The voice from within was a young woman's, oddly slurred.

"It's Captain Giforte," Giforte said. "I've brought Colonel d'Ivoire."

Something opened with a *snick*, and the door swung inward. The woman beyond was barely out of her teens, wearing a dark robe that pooled around her ankles and hung loose at her wrists. It had a hood, but this was pulled back, and her face in the candlelight was alarming. It was round and pleasant, even beautiful, but the right half hung drooping and slack, like the skin of a corpse. Her right eye was milky and sightless, and even her hair on the right side was coming in stark white at the roots, displacing her natural brown.

"Captain," she said, with a slight bow. "Colonel. Welcome. I am Auriana Daatifica." When she spoke, the right half of her mouth didn't move, giving all her words a slight lisp.

Marcus nodded nervously, trying not to stare. "I was told you had a message for me."

"We've been expecting you." Auriana stepped out of the doorway and gestured. "Come in. Captain, I must ask that you remain behind."

"Of course," Giforte said, looking relieved. "I'll see you upstairs, sir."

Marcus stepped through the doorway, and Auriana shut and bolted the door behind him. They were in a small chamber with bare rock walls, lit by more candles. Auriana led Marcus through another arched stone doorway, walking with a slow, gliding gait that could not quite conceal a limp.

"You were in Khandar with the mistress, weren't you?" Auriana said.

"I was with the Colonials there, yes," Marcus said carefully.

"She has told us about you. You fought to bring us our sacred texts."

"I'm not sure I understand."

"Here," Auriana said.

They were walking down a long gallery, with more archways on both sides. Auriana indicated one of the left, and Marcus peered inside. There was a closet-sized space beyond, empty except for a pair of candles and a massive steel tablet propped against the far wall.

Marcus' breath caught in his throat. The last time he'd seen one of those tablets, they were hidden in a nightmare temple under a mountain in the Great Desol, two thousand miles away and a lifetime ago. The light playing over the deeply incised runes on their surfaces brought back memories of smoke and fire, of corpses with glowing green eyes lurching through the darkness to rend and tear, of magic that screeched like knives on glass and blasted solid stone to fragments. Of looking down the sights of musket at Jen, beautiful and terrible, wreathed in sorcerous power, and pulling the trigger.

Not that it was worth a damn. Musket balls had been

no more effective than mosquito bites. They'd survived thanks to Ihernglass, who'd somehow acquired a power from these very tablets. They were the treasure Janus had gone to Khandar to find, his *other* secret weapon. *The Thousand Names.*

He'd known they were somewhere in the city, but he'd done his best to put them out of his mind. Demons and sorcery, he'd decided, were above his pay grade, no matter how high that pay grade ended up rising. *Leave that sort of thing to Janus.*

But Janus was in the League, and the Names were here in Vordan.

"I was there," Marcus said. "But I'd rather not talk about it."

"As you will," Auriana said. "Come with me. The mistress is waiting."

At the far end of the gallery was another archway, blocked off with a curtain. Auriana pushed through, and Marcus followed her into a somewhat larger room. Here someone had made an effort to make the raw stone chamber more comfortable—lamps shed a bright, warm light, and overlapping carpets underfoot cut the chill. A half dozen sleeping pallets clustered against one wall, and a pair of portable writing desks of the sort Marcus had used in his army tent sat against the other. Small cushions were scattered everywhere, mounding up in the corners. In the center of the room a young woman sat, eyes closed, hands folded in front of her, breathing slowly and deliberately.

"Mistress," Auriana said diffidently. "Colonel d'Ivoire is here."

The young woman opened her eyes. She was dressed in a robe like Auriana's, gray instead of black, and had the dark hair and gray skin of a Khandarai. Marcus recognized her, vaguely, from a hurried introduction before they'd all taken ship. He gave an awkward nod and dredged up his rusty Khandarai.

"It's Feor, right?"

She got smoothly to her feet, speaking in good, if accented Vordanai. "It is. It's good to see you, Colonel d'Ivoire." Feor gestured to Auriana. "I will speak to the colonel alone, Auri."

"Yes, Mistress." Auriana sat where Feor had been, with some difficulty from her stiff leg. Feor took Marcus' arm and led him back through the curtain.

"Your Vordanai has gotten a lot better," Marcus said. She'd been able to manage only a few halting words the last time they spoke.

"Out of necessity," Feor said. "I have had a great deal of practice."

"Who are those two?" Marcus indicated the curtain. "If I'm allowed to be in on the secret."

"Janus told me I could tell you whatever you asked," Feor said. "Though I am not to bother you unnecessarily. Auri and Justin are my students. There are three others as well, though they are not here at the moment."

"Ah." Marcus shifted awkwardly. "You're teaching them . . . magic?"

Feor gave a wan smile. "I am teaching them what I can. Mother knew a hundred times what I know, but she is not here, and our need is great. We must unlock the power of the Thousand Names if we are to defeat the *abh-naathem*."

Marcus could parse that, after a fashion. *Naathem* was the Khandarai name for someone who could use magic, a sorcerer; it literally meant "one who has read." *Abh* was false, deviant, deformed, disgusting.

"People like Jen, you mean. The woman we fought in the temple." An agent of the Priests of the Black. She'd called herself one of the Penitent Damned.

Feor nodded. "They know that we have the Names. They will try to destroy us. I believe that the gods have set us against them, as a trial of strength."

"So you're training them to be wizards?" The idea seemed ridiculous, something out of a fairy story.

"I am training them to read a *naath* from the Names. They must learn the characters, but more important, they must prepare their spirits. Reading a *naath* is a trial that few escape unscathed."

"Is that what happened to Auriana? She seems . . ."

"Yes. She was fortunate. Others have . . . not been so lucky."

There was something deep and haunted in Feor's eyes. Marcus coughed, nervously, feeling as though he were standing at the edge of a vast abyss.

"I got a message," he said after a moment. "There was something you needed to tell me."

Feor nodded again. "Every *naathem* can feel others of our kind, if they are close enough, depending on the strength of the *naath* on both sides. There are a few small powers in the city, but in the past few days I have felt something . . . larger. An *abh-naathem* of great strength. Janus wanted you to be warned."

"One of these Penitent Damned?"

"I have no way of knowing, but Janus thought it likely. That a wild *naathem* could be so strong is vanishingly unlikely."

"Wonderful," Marcus muttered. He had met two of the Penitent Damned, the demon-bearing agents of the Priests of the Black. The first, Jen Alhundt, he had fallen in love with, right up until she'd tried to kill him in the underground Desoltai temple. The second, Adam Ionkovo, had tried to get him to betray Janus, dangling the truth about what had happened to Marcus' family as bait. After Orlanko's fall, the Penitent had slipped out of a locked and guarded prison cell without leaving a trace. "Can you tell me *where* this *abh-naathem* is?"

"Not unless he comes very close to here."

"So what am I supposed to do?"

"Be careful," Feor said. "And keep your eyes open. If you catch a hint of anything amiss, tell me at once." She hesitated. "I lack the power to confront an *abh-naathem* directly, but it's possible I will have information that can help."

Marcus nodded slowly. *That's not exactly reassuring.* "All right. Thanks for the warning. Anything else?"

"No." Feor hesitated. "May I ask you something?"

"Certainly."

"Do you have any word of Lieutenant Ihernglass and Corporal Forester?"

It had been Ihernglass and Forester, Marcus remembered, who rescued Feor during the Khandarai campaign. Ihernglass had taken the quick passage back to Vordan with Janus and Marcus himself while Feor and Forester had stayed with the rest of the regiment on the slower transport.

"I know they're both in the east with Janus. Ihernglass raised a company of *women* to help defend the city, if you can believe that." Marcus still wasn't sure he could, or why Janus had allowed it. "I think Forester was helping him. They all marched out with the Army of the East."

"They were well?"

"They were the last time I saw them, after the Battle of Midvale. There's been fighting since then, and we haven't gotten much word."

Feor nodded gravely. "Thank you."

"Of course. If you get any more information, about this *abh-naathem* or"—Marcus wanted to say "any other weird nonsense," but thought it might not be politic—"ask Giforte to send word."

"I shall. I wish you the best of luck, Colonel."

"Thanks." Between the queen and this mysterious sorcerer, Marcus was beginning to think he'd need it.

The actual trick of faking the queen's exit from the city was accomplished with a minimum of fuss. The first step was the queen's announcement that, in the interest of safeguarding the Orboan line, she had reluctantly agreed to leave the city for an unnamed, more secure location. She gave quite a nice speech for the occasion, Marcus had to admit, but the occasion was somewhat spoiled by the fact that it was only lightly attended; the commons had apparently decided it was dangerous to get too close to the queen. Those who did attend, forced to by custom or social position, came with conspicuous bodyguards. Combined with the heavy presence of Patriot Guards, Grenadier Guards, and red-coated Mierantai, the armed men probably outnumbered the civilians.

Marcus had reluctantly agreed that the performance was necessary to reassure the public that the queen had not, in fact, been killed in the blast, contrary to rumors already racing through the city. Having proven that she was still in one piece, at least to those who'd bothered to show up, Raesinia was whisked down from the platform and into a waiting coach, guarded by a phalanx of Grenadier Guards on horseback.

It headed north, toward the road that led past Ohnlei and into the country. Near the edge of the city, however, they stopped to collect the queen's luggage and supplies for the journey. A servant girl, dressed in a hooded robe, climbed into the darkened vehicle with a few personal effects. Raesinia, suitably reattired, climbed out. The double would be told the switch was for security reasons, to guard against an ambush on the road.

Marcus waited beside Raesinia, watching the convoy of coach, wagons, and guards rumble away. He had to keep reminding himself that it was the *queen* standing beside him. In plainclothes, she looked like any other pretty young girl, her slight figure making her look younger than her twenty years.

"Colonel?" she said as the convoy turned a corner and passed out of sight.

"Yes, Your Majesty?"

Raesinia winced. "For starters, you're going to have to stop calling me that, or this ruse isn't going to last very long."

"Oh." Marcus tapped the hilt of his saber uncomfortably. "Then . . . my lady?"

"Raesinia," said Raesinia. "I have a name. Raes, even, if you prefer. Remember, I work for you now."

Officially, Raesinia was now a courier in Marcus' service, giving her a plausible excuse to be staying at Twin Turrets should anyone inquire. Only Lieutenant Uhlan and his Mierantai guards knew the truth.

"All right." Marcus gritted his teeth. "Raes."

"Is something wrong?"

There were at least a hundred things wrong that Marcus could think of, starting with the fact that Marcus had been ordered to try and protect the Queen of Vordan while she wandered around incognito playing at being a private investigator. He forced a smile. "I'm just worried that you won't find the accommodations at Twin Turrets up to your usual standard."

Raesinia waved a hand irritably. "Never mind about that. Are you ready to get started? I have a few ideas, but of course I welcome anything you can come up with."

Marcus closed his eyes for a moment and blew out a long breath. *All right.* This was the assignment, the mission Janus had handed him. Marcus might not approve—the thought of being personally responsible for the safety of the queen while she wandered around the city might leave him a bit weak at the knees—but that was neither here nor there. *Trusting Janus' judgment has gotten me this far. It's too late to stop now.*

"Of course, your—Raes," he said. "I'm at your disposal." He pursed his lips thoughtfully. "And, come to think of it, I may have a notion of where to begin."

CHAPTER FIVE

MARCUS

"Hello, Colonel!"

"Preacher!" Marcus waved aside his old friend's salute and shook his hand enthusiastically. "Thanks for lending a hand."

"It's nothing," the Preacher said. He was a balding, wiry man with blotchy skin pockmarked by old powder burns. "God and the general have endowed me with this troop of half-wits, and I'm glad to be able to put 'em to some use."

The half-wits in question, standing in a neat line behind the Preacher, bore this abuse without comment. Some of them had regulation army uniforms, but more wore only blue jackets over civilian clothes, like most of the volunteers. They had the soft look of a good upbringing in their faces, and they wore serious expressions. To Marcus' surprise, one of them was a young woman, in a neatly tailored uniform with her hair tied up in a severe bun.

The skies had cleared, and the autumn sun warmed the flagstones of Farus' Triumph. Patriot Guards were everywhere, patrolling by the half dozen or standing watch over the hulking metal shape of the Spike. Patriot-Doctor Sarton's invention had been getting quite a bit of employment of late. Nearly every day, the broadsheets boasted of more traitors discovered and spy rings unraveled. The bleachers had been expanded since the day of the attack on the queen; apparently, the novel executions were a popular entertainment.

The Preacher's troop had already torn apart the wooden platform that had covered the site of the royal box, exposing the shallow bomb crater in the center of a ring of cracked flagstones. At a gesture from their leader, the students offered Marcus a passable salute and returned to what they'd been doing, which seemed to involve going over the ground with measuring tapes and taking a lot of notes.

"I was surprised to hear you were still in the city," the Preacher said. "I'd have thought Janus would want you at his right hand when the lead starts flying."

"I'm a bit surprised to be here, to be honest," Marcus said. "But he says he needs someone he can trust in the city to keep an eye on things."

"They need looking after, that's a fact," the Preacher said, shooting a sour look at the nearest squad of Patriot Guards. "I've never seen such a gang of useless arse-polishers."

"That's starting to become an unhealthy sentiment to express out loud," Marcus said. The latest round of victims of the Spike had included several men whose crime was "discouraging confidence and enthusiasm for the government and the war."

The Preacher spit on the cobbles. "If they don't like me, they're welcome to file a complaint. I answer only to God and General Vhalnich."

"I'm surprised," Marcus said, eager to change the subject, "that you're not out in the field yourself."

It was hard to tell behind his ferocious beard, but it looked as though the Preacher was blushing. "Ah, well. I'm getting old for that sort of thing, you know? Keeping up with the boys in Khandar just about wore the legs off me." He shook his head. "Besides, for all that they're Sworn Church lackeys, the Leaguers still believe in Karis and His salvation. It never sat right with me, fellow Karisai killing each other over who kneels to who. That's how I ended up in Khandar in the first place, you know. So I could point my guns at proper heathens."

"So you're still training down at the University?"

"To the extent that such a thing is possible with this bunch of fumble-thumbed lack-brains. With the Lord's help, I may be able to pound a thing or two about laying guns into their skulls before sending 'em off to war." He turned to the scurrying students and raised his voice. "Johannes! You got an answer for me yet?"

A gangly youth barely out of his teens shot to his feet. "Yes, Captain!"

"Let me see it."

Johannes approached, glancing nervously at Marcus, and handed his notebook to the Preacher. The artillery captain's eyes flicked over the columns of figures.

"You lost a ten in there someplace," he said, "but I don't reckon it matters. This is how much powder you think you'd need to make a blast this big, is it?"

"Yes, sir," Johannes said, standing at such strict attention he was vibrating. "Judging by the radius at which the blast cracked the flagstones, and the distance—"

"Yes, yes. Now, how big a pile would that much powder make?"

Johannes' eyes crossed as he calculated. "If you just dumped it? It'd be roughly a cone. We can reverse the volume formula—"

"You're not getting it. Lord knows I'm not surprised. Colonel, how big was the royal box?"

"Maybe ten by ten," Marcus said.

"And how much space under it?"

"Not much. Less than a foot."

The Preacher looked at Johannes. "Could you fit that much black powder in there?"

The boy blinked. "Er . . . no, sir. Not even close. But I'm sure my calculations weren't *that* far off—"

"What it means," the Preacher said, "is that we're not dealing with ordinary black powder. Which you ought to have known from the start, because without a complicated fuse you can't get a whole pile of powder to go off at once. It'd get sprayed around, you see?" At Johannes' expression, he sighed. "You don't see. God help us all."

"So what happened?" Marcus said. He was starting to feel sorry for Johannes. "*Something* exploded."

"You ever hear of flash powder?" the Preacher said, turning away from his hapless student. "Stage magicians use little bits of it sometimes. It's basically your standard powder but ground up much finer so it burns faster and hotter. Not much good for guns or muskets, 'cause you'll bust the barrel wide-open. It works for blasting, though, if you can afford to waste it."

"I'm not sure I follow," Marcus said.

"Flash powder's expensive. It's dangerous to make—the finer you grind powder, the better the chance that something'll accidentally touch off the lot, you know? And like I said, it's not good for much. You can usually get the job done with black powder just fine." The Preacher looked back at the crater. "Unless you need to stick a big bomb in a small space."

"So that's what they used here?"

"Has to be. Quite a bit of it, too." The Preacher shook his head. "I wouldn't have wanted to be anywhere near it. It's God's grace that Her Majesty wasn't there."

"I can agree with that," Marcus muttered. "Okay. Flash powder. Do you have any idea where that might come from?"

"Somewhere close by is the best I can tell you. It doesn't travel well. Even a little damp will ruin it."

"That's something." In truth, it was much better than Marcus had expected. He'd hoped the Preacher could tell him something about the bomb, but he hadn't expected much. All Marcus knew about powder was that it came in little paper cartridges. "Maybe we can track down the source."

The Preacher nodded. "Good luck. My boys and I are at your disposal if you need anything."

Marcus looked at the scurrying students. They *were* boys—and one girl—young, unseasoned, and enthusiastic.

After a few more weeks of the Preacher's instruction, they'd be handed off to Janus, who would throw them into the fire. After that . . .

"Luck to you, too," he said quietly as he turned away.

Marcus walked back to Twin Turrets, by way of the Saint Dromin Street Bridge. Vordan City was changing around him, and one of the most visible signs of the times was the near disappearance of carriages from the streets. The army had an insatiable demand for horses, both to mount the outmatched Vordanai cavalry and to serve as beasts of burden alongside oxen and mules. The Ministry of War had scoured the streets for animals, and those that remained commanded ten times the price they had previously.

There were still two in the stables at Twin Turrets, along with a small coach, but any vehicle was an object of curiosity now, and Marcus preferred to avoid the attention. Those carriages he did see were pulled by laboring teams of unfit animals, and carried men wearing the blue-and-black-striped sashes of the Patriot Guard. These rattled back and forth between the Cathedral, where the Deputies-General sat, and the Hotel Ancerre where the Directory had its headquarters.

Other effects of the war were more subtle. The price of a four-pound loaf, the staple of the working poor, had dropped after the revolution, but it had never reached the one eagle that Danton had promised, and since the start of the war it had begun a steady upward march. Armed guards once again stood outside bakeries, protecting the proprietors from hungry customers. Prices of other goods fluctuated wildly, but always with ruinous effect: coffee had virtually disappeared from the shops, while warehouses bulged with stacks of cheeses and bolts of cloth unsalable at any price.

It all went back to the blockade; Marcus was no expert, but he knew that much. Trade overland to the north and east, with Murnsk and the League, was obviously impossible. At the declaration of war, the mighty Borelgai fleet had weighed anchor and put Vordanai ports from Nordart to Essyle under their interdict. Any Vordanai trader who wanted to take his goods to a foreign market risked being blown out of the water by a ship-of-the-line, and the only cargoes coming in did so in black-sailed ships, by the dead of night. Fortunes were being made, rumor said, by cruel men who risked capture or death for the chance to sell their wares for a hundred times what they'd cost.

North of the Triumph, at the base of the bridge, a pamphleteer had set up shop. His table was covered in stacks of flimsy paper, each weighed down with a stone against the wind. The pamphlets had changed, too. Instead of the familiar caricatures that had served as bylines—the Hanged Man, the Drunkard—each sheet bore spots of colored ink in its top-left corner for easy identification. Two black dots meant the author was aligned with the Conservatives, who dominated the Directory, while a bewildering array of colors indicated allegiance to the hundred different factions that made up the Radicals. Other combinations meant other splinter groups Marcus had never heard of, some of which might have merged or disappeared by the time their manifestos came back from the printers.

Cartoons were popular, as usual. Marcus stopped to examine one marked with blue and green dots. Directory President Maurisk, caricatured as a near skeleton, was strapping a fat man in a headsman's black hood to the table of the Spike. "I'm sorry," he was saying, "but you're now surplus to requirements." He was surrounded by hundreds of double-circle grave markers, piles of them reaching into the sky like jagged mountain peaks. The caption read HAVING SPIKED THE REST OF VORDAN, THE PRESIDENT ELIMINATES THE EXECUTIONER.

Farther down, where the rainbow of color turned to solid black-on-black, another cartoon showed a heroically proportioned Maurisk with a sword in either hand, facing down slavering caricatures of a Borel, a Hamveltai, and the Emperor of Murnsk, along with another figure Marcus didn't recognize. Behind him was a girl, her dress half torn off—nothing like a woodcut nipple to boost sales—labeled

VORDAN. The caption read YOU'LL HAVE NO MORE OF HER, YOU BLAGGARDS! The girl was weeping in her hands, but Marcus thought she was intended to look a little bit like Raesinia.

The pamphleteer, a fat man with wispy eyebrows and a bald, spotted pate, caught Marcus' frown and raised his hands defensively.

"I just sells 'em, sir," he said. "I ain't responsible for the contents."

"Who's this?" Marcus said, tapping the fourth figure. It was a big man with a hatchet nose, almost birdlike in appearance.

The pamphleteer looked around conspiratorially, then shrugged. "Supposed to be Durenne, the Minister of War. Not much of a likeness, if you ask me."

"No," Marcus said. He frowned. "What's he done to get the Conservatives so mad?"

"He's the closest thing the Radicals have to a leader, and he's on the Directory. Some people says he's a spy for the Borels, or the Sworn Church, or somebody." The man shrugged again. "Like I said, I just sell 'em. You want that one?"

Marcus gave the pamphleteer a couple of pennies, but left the cartoon under its stone paperweight. There had been plenty of politics when he was at the War College, of course, but after his exile to Khandar his life had been blessedly free of it. The Colonials never attracted anyone with any ambition, and there had been a brutal simplicity to their relationship with the Khandarai, at least until the rise of the Redeemers.

Now, though, politics in Vordan City had risen to a new and deadly level, and Janus had plunged him into the middle of it, right where he felt least prepared to be. Marcus sighed and turned his steps over the bridge. *The Preacher's right. I ought to be out in the field.* Here he felt trapped, useless. *Surely Janus must have someone better for this than me?*

Maybe, he thought morosely, *he just wants to keep me out of the way.*

*　*　*

Marcus' black mood had not lifted by the time he returned to Twin Turrets. He acknowledged the salutes of the Mierantai guards with a grunt and stalked into the grand dining room, where Janus' imported servants laid simple but vast meals for the garrison. It was a bit late for lunch, but there was always something left over.

Ordinarily, the hall would be empty by this hour—the Mierantai servants were very punctual—but today Marcus found one end of the big table occupied by the Queen of Vordan, dressed boyishly in a linen vest and trousers, wolfing down a plate of eggs and sausage while leafing through a stack of broadsheets and pamphlets.

"Marcus!" she said, swallowing hastily. "I've been looking for you."

Marcus swore silently. "I'm sorry, Your—Raes." She scolded him every time he used her title. "I should have left word where I was going."

Raesinia waved a hand dismissively. She held up a pamphlet, which to Marcus' horror bore the same cartoon he'd seen earlier, with Maurisk defending a weeping Vordan.

"Is this supposed to be me, do you think?" she said.

Marcus kept his face wooden. "I really couldn't say."

"I think it is. The hair's about right." She frowned. "Not much of a likeness, really. I haven't got that much . . . chest."

The woodcutter, Marcus had to admit, had used a bit of artistic license where Raesinia's feminine endowments were concerned. He shook his head, trying to banish the disrespectful thoughts, and said, "Where did you get those?"

"Oh, I sent one of the guards to pick them up," Raesinia said. "I hope that's all right. I didn't think I should go wandering off by myself. Sothe usually brings me the lot every morning, but obviously she's not here."

"There's really no need for you to concern yourself with filth," Marcus said. "I—"

Raesinia laughed aloud, until she caught his expression. Then she frowned. "You're serious?" She waved at the pile. "How else am I supposed to know what's going on?"

"I wouldn't trust *those* things to give me an accurate picture of events in the city," Marcus said stiffly.

"They tell me what people are *saying* about events in the city," Raesinia said. "That's better." She shook her head when his face remained grave. "Come and sit down, would you? And get something to eat if you're hungry."

Feeling as if he were on a parade ground, with every senior officer in the College watching him, Marcus went to the serving table at the other end of the room. Metal army plates and trays looked out of place against the elegant wooden furniture, which needed silver and dainty pastries instead of piles of fried eggs, strips of roast beef, and a stack of rough bread. Marcus took a modest portion and turned back to Raesinia. To his horror, she'd pulled out the seat beside her and was gesturing for him to take it.

"Your—" He swallowed. "I couldn't. I mean, I was going to take this to my room. I thought—"

"You are really going to have to get over this," Raesinia said. "Would it help if I ordered you to treat me like a scullery maid?"

Marcus blinked.

"I don't think I will," Raesinia muttered. "Your head might explode. But if I'm supposed to be incognito, you're going to have to unbend a little bit."

"Yes, Your—" Marcus took a deep breath. "Yes, Raes. I'll try."

"Sorry," she said as he sat down. "I know this is hard for you. I spent the better part of a year disguised as a commoner. I've gotten used to it."

Marcus had spent only a little time around Raesinia before the bombing, but her manner had definitely changed. Going through her official functions as queen, she'd seemed—dignified, possibly, or even a bit morose. Now she had the bubbling cheerfulness of someone who'd sloughed off a great weight. Combined with her change of costume, it made it difficult to see her as anything but a pretty young girl, intelligent eyes alive with humor as she flipped through the day's crop of scandals and diatribes.

She is the Queen of Vordan, *for God's sake. It is not*

appropriate to be contemplating her bosom or lack thereof.
Marcus addressed himself to his plate. The food was actually quite good, though the combination of spices was unfamiliar. Presumably it was in the Mierantai style, whatever that was. The mountain folk had been unfailingly polite and obedient, but something about their manner discouraged casual questions.

"So," Raesinia said, flipping over another broadsheet and squinting to read the fine print on the back, "we need to discuss where to begin our investigation into the bombing."

Marcus paused, fork halfway to his mouth. He'd been hoping the queen hadn't been serious in her desire to take an active role. "Yes." He took a bit of sausage and chewed slowly, buying time. "Actually, I believe I may have a place to start. I asked Captain Vahkerson from the new artillery school to have a look at the site and see if there was anything he could tell me."

"A friend of yours?"

Marcus nodded. "He was our artillery commander in Khandar. He knows his business."

"And did he find anything useful?"

"I think so." Marcus related the Preacher's description of flash powder and why he thought it must have been employed in the bombing. "He says that transporting it long distances is difficult," he concluded, "and I would think that's doubly true now, with army agents requisitioning every bit of powder they can get their hands on. So if we can figure out where there might have been a store of flash powder, that could give us a lead."

"That's a definite possibility." Raesinia tapped her finger on the table. "How many mills near the city can make the stuff, do you think?"

"I have no idea," Marcus admitted. He congratulated himself for suppressing his desire to add a title. "But there must be a way to find out. I was going to go looking after lunch."

"Do you have an idea of where to start?"

Marcus had had the vague thought that he should ask

the army quartermasters, but since the sources of the Vordanai army's powder might come under the heading of state secrets, he wasn't sure he'd get an answer without a direct appeal to Janus. He shrugged. "Not specifically."

"I think I might," Raesinia said thoughtfully. "There's somebody you ought to meet."

Marcus had spent so much time riding in carriages since his return to the city that he hadn't quite appreciated how *big* the place felt to a pedestrian. By the time they'd recrossed the Saint Dromin Street Bridge to the Island, then walked the length of the Grand Span to the South Bank, he found himself short of breath. *Too much time on horseback, not enough time marching with the troops.* The worst of it was that none of his companions seemed affected; he might have expected that from the two Mierantai guards, but Raesinia kept up easily, clomping along in big, practical, unladylike boots.

On reaching the South Bank, they'd taken a left turn and walked along the river through Newtown toward Oldtown. Looking up at the decaying tenements and around at the teeming streets, Marcus was glad he'd insisted on bringing the guards. The two Mierantai had left their red uniforms and rifles behind in favor of plainclothes, but they carried long walking sticks and, like Marcus, wore swords on their belts.

Newtown was even more crowded than it had been before the revolution. After the declaration of war, people had flocked to the city, mostly from along the League border or from coastal towns threatened by Borelgai raids. Many of the men had been absorbed into the new army, issued blue jackets and antique muskets and sent to the front, but thousands of women, children, and men too old or infirm to fight remained. Those with money fought over increasingly rare rooms at inns and boardinghouses, or rented the estates of nobles who'd fled to their country estates. Those without camped in the streets of Newtown.

Their small party drew a considerable amount of attention, mostly from people desperate to sell whatever they had to make a few coins. Marcus was offered household furnishings, pots and pans, a dented silver cup, and any number of bottles of wine. Having arrived with whatever they could throw into their farm carts, the refugees were now trying to trade those meager belongings for food. They were also trying to trade themselves, at depressingly low prices; the influx of new prostitutes had evidently lowered both prices and standards, and every few yards Marcus got shockingly direct offers from ragged young women. Some of them were clearly novices at the trade, farm girls tarted up in ratty lace and too much makeup. He saw one girl who couldn't have been more than fifteen staring fixedly at the cobblestones while her father, one arm around her shoulders, solicited offers from the crowd. Marcus forced himself to look away.

Raesinia was getting a fair number of offers herself, usually shouted from a safe distance out of respect for the armed Mierantai. She seemed able to ignore them, but Marcus flinched with every lewd remark.

"I could have done this myself," he said into her ear. "I'm sorry."

"No, you couldn't," Raesinia said. "And I've seen worse, so there's no need to apologize. You should have seen the crowd that stormed the Vendre."

"I did," Marcus muttered. Though, admittedly, the view had not been great from his prison cell.

"We'll be fine. Here's the Cut."

The border between Newtown and Oldtown, where the money had run out for Farus V's grand plan to rebuild the capital along rational lines, was as vivid as a scar in the fabric of the city. On one side, the buildings stood ten stories high, and the streets were a neat grid; across the broad avenue of the Cut, half-timbered buildings leaned drunkenly against one another along winding avenues that followed the tracks of medieval cow paths.

Here the poverty was of a different sort. People might be crowded ten to a room, but no one was sleeping in the streets. When Marcus had been Captain of Armsmen, Giforte had explained that Oldtown was firmly in the grip of a network of gangs nearly as ancient as the monarchy, who ruled their territory with iron fists and sharp knives. Those who wouldn't abide their rules ended up shoved into Newtown, or the even worse shantytowns to the south, where the city faded into the swamps. Those who made trouble were found floating down the river in the morning.

Prostitution, too, was kept behind closed doors. The Cut was thick with brothels, but there were no girls on display. Every other doorway seemed to boast a pair of toughs, escorting a steady stream of customers inside. Marcus could feel many eyes on him, with more purpose than the casual curiosity of the Newtown residents. Watchmen on the roofs and in the alleys marked their progress. He recalled that Armsmen hadn't patrolled here in squads of less than a dozen, and found himself wishing he'd brought *more* guards.

"You don't see any Patriot Guard here," Raesinia said. "Not in Newtown, either."

"What would they do in Newtown?"

"Keep the peace?"

"I think people are taking that into their own hands," Marcus said grimly. "And there's never been much peace *here* to begin with."

Raesinia looked around and frowned. At her direction, they turned off the River Road and into the labyrinth that was Oldtown's inner lanes. Fortunately, their destination was visible from some distance away, towering among the ancient, shingle-roofed buildings like a great stone ship. It was an old Sworn Church, complete with a bronze double circle atop its spire, though the windows—which had presumably once borne the mosaics of colored glass so beloved of the Elysians—were now boarded over.

The front doors, ancient, scarred things that looked as though they'd been through a siege, were firmly closed. Iron letters, weeping long stains of rust, proclaimed this to be the Third Church of the Savior Karis' Mercy. Raesinia pulled back the big knocker, which squealed in protest, and slammed it against the door as though she were trying to break it down.

"Mrs. Felda is a bit deaf," she said to Marcus when he winced at the sound.

"Who's Mrs. Felda?" Marcus' ground-in reticence in the presence of his monarch was warring with his desire to understand what the hell was going on.

"The priest's wife. She runs this place."

"And she knows something about gunpowder?"

Raesinia laughed. "Not that I know of. But I have to admit I've never asked."

"Then why—"

The door opened with a drawn-out squeal of desperate hinges, but only wide enough to reveal a frowning face. It was a young man, with a laughably wispy attempt at a mustache on his upper lip, but he was at least half a head taller than Marcus and much broader across the shoulders.

"What?" he said. Then, as he took in his visitors, his big face flickered quickly through expressions. Delight at the sight of Raesinia, replaced immediately by guarded caution at seeing Marcus and the two armed Mierantai. "Raes? Who's this?"

"A friend," Raesinia said. "We're here to see Cora."

"I suppose that's all right, then," the young man said, with the air of someone working out a complicated intellectual puzzle. "Come in." He opened the door a bit farther, then turned over his shoulder and bellowed, *"Mrs. Felda! Raes is here!"*

"I thought," Marcus said as they slipped inside, "we were keeping a low profile."

Raesinia shrugged, but Marcus thought she was fighting a grin.

Like most of Vordan's old Sworn Churches, this one had been remodeled considerably. In this case, most of the interior walls had been torn down and the grand altar and rows of pews replaced with a more modest worship space at the far end, beside a grand hearth and a huge table. The rest of the room was full of mismatched bedrolls, with hanging curtains creating smaller semiprivate spaces.

People were everywhere, sleeping on every available inch of floor space, standing around the table eating, or simply slumped against the walls. A flock of old women tended several huge pots suspended above the fire, from which they dispensed bowls of brown stuff that reminded Marcus of the "army soup" of his Khandarai days.

Raesinia was staring around, wide-eyed. Marcus wasn't sure what she'd been expecting, but this clearly wasn't it. Before he could ask, a large, heavyset woman bustled over to them, holding up her long black skirt to keep it from dragging on the filthy stone floor.

"Hello, Raes!" she said, her voice loud enough to cut through the babble of many voices.

"Hello, Mrs. Felda," Raesinia said.

"I heard you were dead," Mrs. Felda said.

"I'm not."

"Very good!" With that subject disposed of, Mrs. Felda looked up at Marcus. "Who's this?"

"His name's Marcus," Raesinia said. "He's a friend of mine."

"Fair enough," Mrs. Felda said. "And these two lads?"

"Protection," Marcus said, feeling as though he ought to hold up his end of the conversation a bit. "The streets aren't safe."

"The good Lord knows it," Mrs. Felda said. "Cora's over at the back. Look for the stacks of books. Help yourself to a bowl if you're hungry."

She moved off without waiting for an answer, attracted by someone shouting her name on the other side of the room.

"She runs some kind of charity?" Marcus said.

"More or less." Raesinia scanned the room, her mouth set in a frown. "Come on."

"Stay here," Marcus told the two guards, and hurried to keep up with Raesinia. They had to step carefully, since every flat surface was occupied, and Marcus had to stop himself from apologizing for nearly treading on people.

Eventually, they made it to the vicinity of the big table, and he saw that in the corner beyond it there was what he could only think of as a small fortress made of books. Two haphazard stacks made the walls, with a narrow gap between them. A lantern glowed inside, and by its light Marcus could see a pale teenager bent over a stack of papers.

"Cora?" Raesinia said when they were close enough that the noise from the hall wouldn't drown her out. "It's me."

The girl, Cora, looked up. Her round, freckled face showed signs of many nights without enough sleep, with dark crescents under her eyes that made her look as though she'd been in a boxing match. When she saw Raesinia, though, she lit up, and shot to her feet as if she'd been mounted on a spring.

"Raes!" She ran forward, kicking several books out of her way, and wrapped Raesinia in a hug. Raesinia seemed to take this act of *lesse majeste* in stride, and ran her fingers affectionately through the girl's short, spiky hair.

"Cora," Raesinia said. "This is Marcus."

Cora looked up and blinked. "You're Captain d'Ivoire."

Marcus frowned. "Have we met?"

"Not exactly. I was in the Vendre," Cora said matter-of-factly. "The night of the siege. The guards were beating a woman because she didn't want to . . . service them. You came and stopped them, then sent the Concordat men away and put your own in their place."

"Oh." Sometimes that awful night blurred together in Marcus' memory into the roar of the crowd and pools of blood on the stone steps of the ancient fortress. "I'm sorry we had to keep you there."

"It's not your fault. It was Orlanko who had us arrested. And you probably saved a lot of us from having a . . . a bad night." Cora dipped her head. "Thank you."

Marcus returned the nod, feeling himself blush a little.

"Cora," Raesinia broke in, keeping her voice low. "What is going on here?"

Cora suddenly looked guilty. "Just the usual. Mrs. Felda—"

"Don't give me that. You've got a hall full of Borels and Murnskai!"

Marcus, surprised, looked around the room again. Borelgai men were usually easy to spot by their full black beards and side whiskers, but there were only a few men in the room. On the street, Marcus might have identified Borelgai women by the fur-collared cloaks they wore, but here everyone was dressed in castoffs and rags. Even so, he did see a lot of pale, blond northerners, and the babble of voices, now that he was paying attention, had a distinctly polyglot air. There were a fair number of Vordanai, many of them maimed or otherwise unhealthy, but most of the room was full of women and children. They huddled together in small, nervous groups, mothers keeping their sons and daughters close.

"They didn't have anywhere else to go," Cora said.

"Where did they come from?" Marcus said. "I wouldn't have thought there were many Borels left in the city." What the mobs had begun, the Patriot Guard had finished. Even Vordanai with Borelgai ancestry had to fend off suspicion.

"That's the problem," Cora said. "After the revolution, all the Borel merchants and traders who could got out of town. The Murnskai did the same once the war started. But they left in a hurry, and they didn't all bother to make arrangements for the staff they'd brought with them."

"But how did *you* get involved?" Raesinia said.

Cora blushed. "A lot of them were on my payroll. You'd be amazed what you can do in the market with a little belowstairs gossip. A few of them came to me for help, and then . . . word spread, I guess." She stared up at Raesinia, cheeks burning but eyes defiant. "Mrs. Felda said it was all right. She told me I ought to help them."

"Cora . . ." Raesinia hugged the girl again, then pulled away and looked her firmly in the eye. "I know you want to help people, but this is dangerous. If the Patriot Guard find out, you know what they'll say. A whole nest of Borelgai and Murnskai?"

"That's why I couldn't turn them away!" Cora lowered her voice. "You haven't *listened* to them, Raes. It's not just the Guard. If you're Borel and you're caught on the streets, anyone who wants can just drag you away, and nobody will lift a finger to stop them now that the Armsmen are gone."

Hell. Marcus frowned. "It's really that bad?"

Cora nodded.

"You still can't keep them all *here*," Raesinia said. "Someone is going to notice. You and Mrs. Felda could get *spiked* for harboring enemies of the state."

"I had some ideas," Cora said. "We might be able to get them out of the city—"

"And then what?"

"I haven't gotten that far," Cora said. "What do you want me to do? Tell them to clear out?"

"I . . ." Raesinia looked around the room, then shook her head. "No, of course not. You were right. But I don't know what we're going to do now."

Marcus cleared his throat. "I might be able to offer some assistance."

The two young women looked up at him in surprise, as if they'd forgotten he was there.

"Supply trains leave for the Army of the East every couple of days," he said. "I may be able to arrange to start sending people with them."

Cora frowned. "Would the soldiers stay quiet about it?"

"They will if Janus orders them to. I'll speak to him about it. It may take a while to move everybody, though."

"I think we've got time," Cora said. "Everyone knows Mrs. Felda keeps a charity here, so nobody asks questions when we have food brought in. And the Patriot Guard hardly ever come into Oldtown anyway."

Raesinia nodded. "It could work. Thank you, Marcus. And I'm sorry I blew up at you, Cora."

"It's all right." Cora sighed and ran her hands through her hair, further mussing it. "I've been a bit frantic myself. You have no idea what the war is doing to the markets."

The markets? Marcus shot Raesinia an inquisitive look.

"Cora is a genius at anything involving money or commerce," Raesinia explained.

"I wouldn't say that," Cora said, blushing furiously. "I just keep my eyes open."

Looking down at the frazzled teenager, Marcus had a hard time believing it. "So she's the one you wanted to talk to?"

"Right," Raesinia said. "I'd nearly forgotten about that. Cora, we need your help with something. How many major powder mills are there within easy overland shipment range of Vordan City?"

"Five," Cora said immediately. "The di Bartolo in the south, the Neffoy east of the Thieves Island, the—"

"How many of them can manufacture flash powder?" Raesinia said.

Cora blinked. "Flash powder?"

"It's a sort of very fine gunpowder," Marcus explained. "It takes special equipment to make."

"There must not be much trade in it," Cora said. "I don't recall off the top of my head. Hold on."

She turned and dove into one of the piles of books, delicately shifting volumes in a way that kept the whole structure barely standing while she excavated the one she wanted. All of the books were thick leather-bound tomes, marked only with numerical codes that meant nothing to Marcus, though Cora apparently knew them intimately. She had one particular book open in a matter of moments, and flipped rapidly back and forth through the pages.

"Ah," she said. "Got it. Flash powder. Local sales only, no long-range trade. That's a bit odd."

"It doesn't travel well, I'm told," Marcus said.

Cora nodded absently, her finger tracing a line in the book. "Last year . . . it looks like there are a couple of bespoke places producing it a pound or so at a time . . ."

"It would have to be more than that," Raesinia said.

"Dozens of pounds at the least," Marcus agreed. "Maybe hundreds."

"Then it has to be the Halverson Mill. They're on the north bank, up the river a way. As far as I can tell from this, they're the only ones who make it in bulk."

"Does it say how much they've made recently? Or who buys it?"

Cora shook her head. "These are compilations of last year's stock books. There's nothing that detailed."

"It's still something," Marcus said. "We can find the owner and ask him."

"I'm not sure that would be a wise idea," Raesinia said. "If he's involved, then he'll just deny everything, and then they'll know we're looking for them."

"Ah," Marcus said.

For a moment he'd been thinking as though he were still Captain of Armsmen, or at least the second in command of the First Colonials, with a regiment of musketeers at his back. Here and now, he had no official authority to investigate whatsoever, and all he had to back him was a single squad of riflemen. If Maurisk really was involved in the bombing, then he had thousands of Patriot Guard he could call on against anyone he could plausibly accuse of being a traitor. *If Raesinia is serious about this, we're going to need more men.* He resolved to write to the Preacher when he got back to Twin Turrets and see if he could scrounge up a few more reliable bodies.

"This is about the bomb at Farus' Triumph, isn't it?" Cora said, breaking in on his thoughts like a bucket of cold water. "The day they unveiled the Spike. They said you were nearly killed."

"Wait," Marcus said. "She *knows* you're the queen?"

Raesinia nodded. "My old . . . identity is supposed to have died at the Vendre. There's only a couple of people who know the truth. Cora, Sothe . . ." She hesitated. "And Maurisk."

"Excuse us a moment." Marcus grabbed Raesinia's shoulder and pulled her away from Cora, his voice a hiss. "You did *not* tell me about Maurisk."

"It didn't seem relevant," Raesinia said, with a note in her voice that said she'd known exactly what she was doing.

"Not *relevant*? That the top suspect in your attempted

assassination knows you have a tendency to wander around incognito and will recognize your former identity? You might as well paint a target on yourself!"

"Only if he knows I'm here!"

Marcus scowled. "That won't take long, if you keep visiting old friends."

"Cora's the only old friend I have left," Raesinia said, a bit of pain in her voice. She took hold of Marcus' hand and pushed it aside irritably. "Anyway, are you supposed to be manhandling your monarch?"

Marcus looked down at his hand as though it had caught fire, and swallowed hard. "Sorry."

Raesinia waved his apology away. "I hardly think Mrs. Felda or the people here will tell the Patriot Guard we've been by. And we need Cora's help."

"If there's anything else I ought to know," Marcus grated, "please bring it to my attention."

"I'll keep that in mind." Raesinia walked back to Cora. "Sorry. Yes, it's about the bombing. I wasn't nearly killed, though. I wasn't even there. But some other people *were*."

"You're trying to figure out who did it?" Cora said.

Raesinia nodded.

"What we'd really like to know," Marcus said, "is who bought the flash powder from Halverson, and what happened to it after that."

"If they're in on the plot, they're not likely to have kept records," Raesinia said.

"They'll have to write *something* down," Cora said. "Powder production is tightly monitored by the army. You couldn't just take hundreds of pounds away from a mill without fudging the books *somewhere*. The mill's capacity is a constant. The raw materials are recorded. From there it'd just be a matter of math to figure it out."

Raesinia and Marcus looked at each other.

A genius, eh? "If we could get you those records," he said slowly, "you could tell us where the powder went?"

"Probably," Cora said.

"Then we might be able to track down where they assembled the bomb," Marcus said. "That would be a start."

"Where would the records be kept?" Raesinia said.

"At the Exchange Central Office. There's a military post there to handle war supplies."

A grin spread across Raesinia's face. Marcus looked from her to Cora, and stifled a groan.

CHAPTER SIX

WINTER

The game known as "handball" had ancient origins, though nobody was quite certain *how* ancient. It went back at least as far as the reign of Farus the Conqueror, who was supposed to have won the allegiance of one recalcitrant noble by his prodigious feats on the field. According to Cyte, there was some evidence it was much older, being descended from the ceremonial contests of the Mithradacii Children of the Sun thousands of years before the birth of Karis.

Whatever its origins, handball had been played throughout the history of Vordan, in many forms and under many names. It had been called "grand melee," "pushers," and, confusingly, "football"—not because it involved the feet, but to differentiate it from other popular ball games played on horseback. It always involved two teams, a hard leather ball about the size of a man's head, and two scoring areas some distance apart, but details like the number of players, the permissible ways of advancing the ball, the dimensions of the playing field, and the rules governing the use of weapons had gone through every imaginable permutation over the years.

Winter had learned a version of the game growing up,

not under any explicit set of rules but following a vague consensus of the participants. At Mrs. Wilmore's, ball games were restricted to children under the age of eleven, at which point girls were expected to limit themselves to more ladylike pursuits such as gardening, shoveling animal dung, and preparation for childbearing. Watching the opposing squads square off gave her an unexpected feeling of nostalgia; it had been a long time since she looked back on Mrs. Wilmore's with any good feeling, but a few buried memories of glorious rough-and-tumble merriment in golden summer afternoons wormed their way to the surface, like bubbles escaping from muck.

According to the fairly simple rules of this variant, teams could be of any number of people, provided they were roughly equal. The ball could be thrown, carried, or indeed used as a bludgeon as the players saw fit. Pressing the ball to the ground within the opposing team's scoring area was worth one point. Shoving, grappling, or tackling opposing players was of course permitted, although punching, kicking, biting, or jumping on them was frowned upon.

Each team was made up of a section of Royals and a section from the Girls' Own, for about forty players to a side, evenly split between men and women. Winter had chosen the sections that would play by lot, picking scraps of paper from a cauldron. On the first day, there had been quite a bit of grumbling from both sides. This was the third day, and the chosen sections had erupted in cheers when their numbers were called.

A light rain was falling, just enough to mist the air and turn the dark earth of the fields into thick black mud. The stuff clung like molasses to every inch of clothing and skin, turning men and women alike into earthy golems as they ran, slipped, struggled, and floundered in the mess. One team wore blue bands wrapped around their foreheads, but they were becoming hard to see in the morass, making it hard to distinguish "blues" from "skins" as well as Royals from volunteers.

Tactics were definitely evolving, though. The first game

had been nothing more or less than a giant brawl in the center of the field, won one-to-nothing by the skins when a girl had managed to squirm out of the press with the ball while everyone else was still occupied trying to shove one another into the dirt. Most of the rest of the regiment had turned up to watch out of curiosity, and by the time Winter had called a halt and sent the next set of teams on, she could already hear strategies being plotted on the sidelines.

Today, the blues were from Abby's company in the Girls' Own and Bracht's in the Royals, and both had clearly put some thought into their game plan. Their opponents were doing their best, but they lacked a coherent strategy.

A cheer erupted from the men and women gathered close around the field as a squad of blues, led by a huge woman Winter recognized from the old Leatherbacks, burst through a group of defenders. The largest of the Royals grappled and shoved to keep the gap open while more blues sprinted through, mostly women from Abby's company. One of them, a long-legged recruit whose blond hair was now an unrecognizable tangle of mud, carried the ball under her arm and dodged the incoming defenders as deftly as the difficult terrain allowed.

"She'll never make it," Cyte said, eyeing the play with a professional eye as the girl sidestepped a lunge from an older woman. "Can't keep that up forever."

Winter did her best to remain stone-faced—as the responsible official, she had to appear impartial—but she fought back a smile. Abby had a gift for tactics, and her influence was clearly at work here.

The blond recruit finally ran out of room, slipping in the mud in front of a bull-necked Royal who charged her with his arms spread wide. He grabbed her around the waist, hoisting her bodily off the ground and slamming her with a squelch into the muddy turf, but when he looked around for the ball it was no longer there. The recruit had tossed it straight up, and another woman had snatched it out of the air. Before the skins could react, the blue player skipped lightly into the scoring zone and pushed the ball deep into the mud.

Shouts erupted from the crowd as Winter blew the hunting horn Cyte had cadged from some quartermaster.

She raised her voice, though only those closest by could hear her over the din. "Game over! Three to one to the blues!"

All through the regiment, Royals and volunteers screamed themselves hoarse or shouted curses, depending on which side they were on. Winter had actively encouraged gambling on these matches, to keep the spectators interested. There wasn't much use for money out in the field, and the amount wagered had grown quickly. A small fortune had probably just changed hands, and the blues would be heroes to those who had taken their side. *And the reverse, of course.*

"Time to break camp," Cyte said.

Winter nodded and waved for attention. When the roar had quieted somewhat, she shouted, "Players, go get yourselves cleaned off! Everybody else, break camp and be ready to march in one hour!" That would give the wagon train time to get well ahead of them. "Well played, everyone!"

Another roar of approval. The mud-covered handballers trooped off in the direction of the stream, and a dozen sergeants began shouting at once to get everyone else in order. The crowd gradually dispersed in the direction of the newly integrated camp, slowly sorting itself out into its component companies and sections.

"It seems to be working," Cyte said once the volume level had fallen low enough for ordinary speech.

"For the moment," Winter said. She caught sight of Captain Sevran, on the other side of the playing field. He gave her a rueful smile and shook his head, then saluted smartly and turned to follow his men. "We'll see what happens when we go back to drill."

"Still. They aren't getting into brawls anymore." Cyte cocked her head, reflecting for a moment. "Off the field, anyway."

Another day's march, another seven miles—hardly a stroll, by the standards of Khandarai campaign. The Deslandai army was pulling back toward the town of Gaafen, where a bridge spanned the river Kos. The Kos was tributary to the mighty Velt, running nearly east-west to where the Velt flowed roughly north-south past Desland on its east bank. North of the junction, there were several good fords the Army of the East could use to get across and invest the city, but south of it the big river widened into an uncrossable gulf nearly as wide as the Tsel in Khandar. Gaafen was therefore a good place for the Deslandai army to make a stand; if things went sour, they could always retreat north of the Kos and blow up the bridge, leaving Janus' army a long detour to find an alternative crossing.

Winter could tell that much by reading a map, so she had to assume that Janus had thought it through. As best she could tell, they had a hard road ahead. An assault on an army with its flanks securely anchored on the river would be a straightforward, bloody affair, with little opportunity for Janus' now-famous strategic talent to express itself. Even if they won—which seemed likely, since the Army of the East was half again the size of the Deslandai force—the enemy's secure line of retreat meant that all they were likely to get for it was a town full of corpses.

Janus must have a plan. The Army of the East had thus far followed passively in the enemy's wake, content to keep a safe distance between the opposing forces. *He's not the sort of commander who would bash his head against a wall if he had any other choice. He knows what he's doing.* Faith in Janus had gotten her this far. *There's nothing to do but follow it through.*

Bobby was waiting beside Winter's tent, which stood alone in the midst of the campground. The encampment would grow around it as each company filed in off the road. Winter dismounted and handed Edgar's reins to a waiting soldier—one of the Royals, this time. Cyte was rotating the camp chores more equitably.

"Sir!" Bobby said.

"Come on in." Winter ducked into her tent, blinking as her eyes adjusted to the dimness. Bobby followed. "What have you got for me?"

"Reports." Bobby flourished a stack of papers.

"Anything major?"

"Just the usual. Sick lists are holding steady, a couple of minor infractions."

"Drop them off with Cyte, then." It had become apparent that Cyte had been born to be a staff lieutenant. Her appetite for paperwork and attention to detail was boundless, and she had a deft touch with the military bureaucracy that Winter herself had never been able to develop. *It must come from spending time at the University.* "What's the butcher's bill for this morning?"

Bobby shuffled the papers. "Three broken fingers, two sprained ankles, four pulled teeth. Nothing serious."

"That's good." The handball games kept the regimental cutters busy with minor injuries, but so far nothing more than that. *Thankfully. I don't need my soldiers crippling each other before we even get to a battle.* "Anything else?"

"Um . . . possibly, sir. But it's a little bit . . . personal."

"Trouble with Marsh?" The idea of anyone coming to *her* for relationship advice made Winter want to laugh and cry, both at once. "I'm not sure—"

"Not that kind of personal, sir. The other kind."

"Oh." Winter looked around the tent, then moved to stand by the entrance, leaning against the pole, so she could keep an eye out for eavesdroppers. "What is it?"

Bobby took a deep breath. "I'd better show you."

She shrugged out of her uniform jacket and started undoing the buttons of her shirt. *It's a good thing she gave up her disguise. She wouldn't have been able to keep it up much longer anyway.* Bobby had grown at least an inch taller in the six months or so since they met, and her figure had filled out considerably. Winter did her best to keep her examination clinical.

Bobby's skin had paled a bit since she left the fierce Khandarai sun, but there were still visible tan lines around her neck and at her wrists. Under her shirt, though, she bore other, stranger marks. A small circular patch low on her stomach was from where she'd caught a musket ball at the Battle of Turalin, and a long ragged line that started at her collarbone and ran between her breasts showed where she'd been slashed open by a Desoltai saber, saving Winter's life in the process. These wounds had not scarred or scabbed over; instead the skin had regrown, perfect and smooth, but with the color of polished marble. It was a shiny gray, and flecked with sparking fragments that glittered as Bobby moved.

"They're getting bigger, aren't they?" Winter said.

Bobby nodded, and pointed to the circular patch on her stomach. "I measured this one when we left Khandar, and it was three inches across. It's four and a half now. And this one"—she traced a finger down the long sword wound—"is getting wider."

"But you don't *feel* any different?"

"Not exactly." Bobby poked the gray patch. "It still feels like skin."

Feor had started the transformation, back in Khandar, when Bobby lay dying in Winter's tent. She'd used her *naath* to turn Bobby into what she called a Heavenly Guardian. Winter was still hazy on the theological details—Feor's *naath* apparently gave her the ability to bestow power on *others*, but not use it herself. However it worked, Feor had made it clear that the transformation was permanent as long as Bobby lived, though she'd never been able to say what ultimate effects it might have. The head priestess of the cult Winter had rescued Feor from, the one they'd called "Mother," had kept those details to herself.

Winter's own *naath*, the demon that devoured other demons, usually drew her attention at the presence of any other magic, like a sleepy predator raising its head at the scent of prey. Princess Raesinia—now Queen Raesinia, Winter supposed—had one, as had the doomed orator Danton Aurenne. But she didn't feel anything from being near Bobby, possibly because it was Feor who actually bore the *naath. Or demon. Or whatever you want to call it.* Winter shook her head. She did her best not to think about the supernatural side of her adventure in Khandar, except when it intruded on her nightmares.

"So it hasn't changed much?" Winter said. "It just grows, slowly."

"I'm a little worried about what will happen when it gets to my face," Bobby said. "I won't be able to hide it."

"What about Marsh? I mean . . . he must know."

Bobby looked embarrassed, and Winter was able to follow the flush as it rose up her body and ended at her face. She gritted her teeth and kept her eyes firmly on the girl's face.

"He knows . . . a little bit," Bobby said. "I told him I was wounded, and that a Khandarai priestess saved me with her herb-lore, which left me like this. So far he hasn't pushed me about it."

Winter had to laugh. Men who would swear to being rational and forward-thinking, and therefore dismissive of the supernatural, would also accept almost any claim as to the effectiveness of hidden wisdom or secret knowledge as long as it came from a sufficiently foreign source. She herself had fielded quite a few questions from otherwise modern young women in the Girls' Own who wanted to know if it was true that the Khandarai had discovered a fruit that granted eternal youth, or drank cobra venom to ward off the pox.

"Okay," she said. "At that rate, it should be a while before it's difficult to hide. When we get back to the city, we'll talk to Feor and see if she's been able to figure anything out." After surmounting her crisis of faith, Feor had volunteered to help Janus decode the Thousand Names. They'd left her in Vordan City, partly for security reasons and partly because the massive steel plates on which the archive was engraved were difficult to transport in secrecy. "I know it must be a little odd, but—"

"There's something else." Bobby cast about and found an old tin cup, dinged and battered from years of hard use. She held it in the palm of her right hand, let out a deep breath, and closed her eyes. Then, without any visible sign of effort, she closed her fist, and the cup gave a metallic shriek as it was crushed within.

"Oh." Winter stared. "Wow."

"Yeah." Bobby opened her hand and passed the remains of the cup to Winter. The outlines of Bobby's fingers were dimpled neatly into the metal, and it had bulged at the sides, as though she'd squeezed a handful of butter. "I have to concentrate to make it work, and I can't always do it. But when I can, I feel like I could lift a horse."

"Let's . . . not try that just yet," Winter said. Bobby was clearly relieved to share her secret with someone, and was bouncing excitedly on the balls of her feet, which Winter found a bit distracting. "Put your shirt back on, first of all. I don't want to have to tackle the next person who tries to walk in here."

"Right. Sorry."

Bobby dressed, and Winter turned and stared out through the tiny gap between the hanging tent flaps. Troops of Royals and Girls' Own soldiers were going past, carrying rolled-up tents, boxes of crackers, and other supplies. The steady *tap-tap-tap* of wooden mallets forcing pegs into the earth sounded like a rain of stones on a cobbled street.

"Okay," Winter said, turning back. "I'm going to need to think about this." She turned the crushed cup over in her hands and shook her head. "In the meantime, don't do anything rash."

Bobby nodded. "I'll be careful."

"If Feor can't help us, maybe Janus can," Winter said. "After dumping this whole regiment on my shoulders, he owes me. Between them we should be able to come up with *some* idea of what's happening, and whether we need to stop it."

"Right." Bobby finished buttoning her shirt and took an experimental breath. "Sorry. I didn't mean to spring that on you out of the blue, but—"

"It's fine. I needed to know." Winter set the remains of the cup down on her writing desk. "In the meantime, there are more mundane problems to deal with. Can you run over to Jane's tent and tell her I need to see her?"

Bobby frowned. "I can try. But you know—"

"Just try."

The girl shrugged into her jacket and saluted. "Yes, sir! Just a moment."

She ducked out through the flap and hurried away. Winter, feeling a good bit wearier than she had felt only moments before, sat down on the cushion behind her desk and stretched her back, trying to make it pop.

Since their confrontation over Winter's reorganization of the camp, Jane had been, for lack of a better word, sulking. The thought of it made Winter's jaw clench in frustration. *She knows she's wrong. She just can't bear to admit it.* She walked with her troops during the day, and stayed in her tent the rest of the time. If Winter managed to ambush her, she stood at stiff attention and responded in monosyllables. *God. Was she this frustrating back at the Prison?* Winter shook her head. *I was a different person then, and so was she.*

It couldn't go on forever, though. The Girls' Own needed a captain, and if Jane kept refusing to do the job, eventually Winter would have to replace her. The thought made her feel ill. *It won't come to that. She'll get over it before it actually comes to fighting.* Temper or no, Winter couldn't believe that Jane would let her girls go into battle anything less than well organized.

There was a knock at the tent pole, and Winter straightened up, heart rising for a moment. "Come in."

The flap rustled, and Winter was disappointed, though not really surprised, to see Abby Giforte, Jane's second in command. She wore the rough trousers and linen shirt that had become the makeshift uniform of the volunteers, along with a jacket hastily dyed Vordanai blue. Her curly brown hair was tied back in a frizzy knot, and her pale, freckled cheeks were red and cracking from a day in the sun.

"Sir!" Abby said, saluting. Winter waved for her to sit.

"Where's Jane?"

"She asked me to say that she's busy," Abby said, "and that I should speak to you in her place." She had the decency to blush.

Winter sighed. "She's going to have to come out sooner or later."

"She will," Abby said. "She's just . . . you know how she is. What her temper can be like."

"I remember," Winter said. "I just wish I knew what she was so angry about. It can't just be the mixed camp. That hasn't worked out so badly."

Abby opened her mouth, as though to speak, but then thought better of it.

Winter cocked her head. "What is it?"

"I . . ." Abby frowned. "I'm not sure it's appropriate for me to talk about this."

Winter studied her face, and felt a faint pang of jealousy. Abby had been with Jane through most of her Leatherback days, helping her forge a gang of scared young girls into a force that could protect itself and fight the tax farmers Orlanko had unleashed on the Docks. Somewhere during that time, Abby and Jane had become lovers. Jane had broken the relationship off when Winter returned, except for a single drunken mistake, and Winter didn't think Abby would be willing to pick it up again. Still, for all that Winter and Jane had been together as children, in a real way Abby knew this new, adult Jane better than Winter did.

"You can talk about whatever you like," Winter said carefully. "I won't hold it against you."

"It's not that; it's that I don't know. Not really. I just . . ." Abby sighed. "I think Jane is feeling . . . lost. Envious, maybe."

"Envious?" Winter snorted. "Of who, me?"

Abby nodded.

"Why, because Janus promoted me?" Winter shook her head. "If she wants the colonel's job, tell her she can have it. It's just a load of worry and—"

"It's not that. You *fit* here. In the army. It looks . . . natural on you." Abby touched the shoulders of her jacket, where a crude stripe had been sewn to mark her rank. "The rest of us sometimes feel like we're playing pretend, but not you."

"You don't play pretend with live powder," Winter said.

"How can you feel like it isn't real when people are getting hurt?"

"It's not the fighting," Abby said. "We're used to that, or at least the old Leatherbacks are. We fought the gangs, the tax farmers, whoever needed fighting. People got hurt. We know what that's like. It's all *this* that feels like playing dress-up." She waved a hand vaguely. "The tents, the uniforms, the saluting. Taking orders. Sometimes I expect somebody to come along and tell us to stop being silly."

"Nobody is going to do anything like that. Not if I have anything to say about it," Winter said. "I'd put the Girls' Own against any other battalion in the army, royal or volunteer."

"I know," Abby said, raising her hands soothingly. "I'm just . . . trying to explain. I think Jane feels out of place, and then she looks at you and you make it seem so effortless. You just *know* what to do, how to behave."

Winter wanted to laugh. *Effortless?* She spent her days on a knife edge of exhaustion, worn ragged by the worry that something new would go wrong. *How do I tell her that I'm making it up as I go along?*

"I think, also, she's a little jealous," Abby said. "She sees you pulling away from her, into this world of flags and drums and cannon, and she doesn't think she can follow."

"You think she's jealous of the *army*?" Winter said.

Abby nodded. Winter searched her face for a hint of malice, and found none. It would be understandable for Abby to be angry with her. *I would be, in her place.* But all Winter could see in her expression was a deep concern when she spoke of Jane.

Is that what love is supposed to look like? Wanting the best for another person, regardless of what it means for yourself? Winter closed her eyes and shook her head. *Now is not the time, damn it.*

"Okay. Thank you," Winter said. "But enough about Jane. She'll come around eventually. What about the rest of the Girls' Own? How are they taking it?"

"Better than I might have expected," Abby said, looking relieved at the change of topic. "They wouldn't say so if you asked them, but I think a lot of the rankers are happy to have some proper soldiers around, to show them how things are done. Especially the new girls, the ones who joined up after Midvale."

Approximately half of the Girls' Own was made up of women from Jane's old building, or their friends and family from the Docks. The other half had been recruited afterward, from a steady trickle of female volunteers who'd heard the new government's call for soldiers and followed the Leatherbacks' example.

"It's the old Leatherbacks who do most of the complaining," Abby went on. "The ones who've been with Jane from the beginning. They don't like working with the Royals."

"Anyone in particular?" Winter asked.

Abby shifted uncomfortably, but after a moment she said, "Becca and Winn. Becca thinks all men are rapists and murderers, and that we'd be better off without them. Winn just worships the ground Jane walks on."

"All right. I'll see what I can do to bring them around." Winter sighed. "The fact is that we've got to work with the Royals, unless Janus changes his mind. We'd better get used it."

"I know," Abby said. "Like I said, the Leatherbacks aren't used to taking orders and not asking questions."

"Any discipline problems on your side?"

"Not as such." Abby paused again. "There's a little bit of . . . fraternization."

"That's more or less the idea—"

"I mean fucking," Abby interrupted. "It happens when you get a lot of men and women together. Not that it doesn't happen when it's only men, but—"

"I get the point," Winter said hastily. "But the rankers sleep four to a tent. How do they—"

"They find ways," Abby said. "Do you really want details?"

"I suppose not. But I don't want anyone sneaking out beyond the sentries. We're in enemy territory, even if they haven't been so unfriendly thus far."

"I'll pass the word."

Now it was Winter's turn to hesitate. "When the Leatherbacks were in Vordan, there seemed to be a fair amount of . . . that sort of thing. I assume the girls take appropriate measures to avert . . . potential consequences?"

Abby nodded. "We educate them quite thoroughly on that subject."

"Make sure it gets passed along to all the new recruits, too. And please tell the officers to keep an eye out for anyone who looks like they might be getting pushed into something they're not happy about. I want to hear about anything like that, understand?"

"Yes, sir," Abby said. "We're used to looking out for one another."

"I know." Winter glanced at the tent flap, gauging the time by the lengthening shadows. "All right. I'd better get to dinner."

"Of course, sir." Abby stood up.

"Tell Jane . . ." Winter stopped, and stared at Abby for a moment, then shook her head. "Tell her I'm waiting for her."

"I will, sir," Abby said, lifting the tent flap. "But I think she knows."

When Winter had first been made a sergeant, in what now seemed like another lifetime altogether, she'd spent her first few days in her tent, hiding from the men newly placed under her command. It had been Bobby who eventually coaxed her out, encouraging her to have dinner with the men and get to know them. It had worked on Winter then, so she had decided to try it again, on a larger scale.

As in Khandar, enterprising locals had taken to following the army around in carts, hoping to sell their wares to the foreign soldiers. The sentries were ruthless about keeping them off the roads during the day, but in the evenings they could be found at the edges of the camp, laundering fresh clothes and hawking food, wine, and other luxuries. Cyte had managed to pry a little bit of hard coin out of the quartermasters—a bit of Winter's back pay, actually, that she didn't ever expect to be able to spend—and Winter had used it to bring in a better class of dinner than the rations the soldiers normally received. Every night, she brought in two companies, one from the Royals and one from the Girls' Own, in strict rotations, and they ate together around a roaring fire in the center of camp.

Tonight dinner was a whole roast chicken for every two men or women, purchased live from a local farmer for what was probably ten times the going rate, plus baskets of late berries sold by a pair of ambitious ten-year-olds. Winter's guests were Lieutenant sur Gothin and his company from the Royals, and a company of new recruits from the Girls' Own led by Lieutenant Virginia Malloy. Captain Sevran was also in attendance, with Lieutenant Novus from his staff.

Winter had expected trouble from sur Gothin's people, given their performance in that first abortive drill, but so far she'd been pleasantly surprised. The soldiers were apparently willing to overlook their prejudices, at least when food was involved. They milled around in eager groups, waiting for the chickens to finish roasting, mixing with the women from the Girls' Own. Unlike the Leatherbacks, who shared a common origin either at Mrs. Wilmore's or from the Docks, the newer recruits were a mixed bag, drawn from almost every walk of life. Some of them had distinctly upper-class accents and bearings, like Cyte, while others spoke with the broad dialect of Newtown or the twang of the country. Sur Gothin himself gamely made the rounds, introducing himself to the women and joking about the day's handball matches.

The other officers sat in a circle around a fire. Lieutenant Malloy was a small, dark-haired young woman with the soft accent of the Transpale and the fair skin of someone not used to working outdoors. She'd lost a bit of that during the march, but no one would be mistaking her for a sunbaked Leatherback any time soon. Her attitude, shared with Cyte and many of the other recruits, was a quiet determination to do her best and overcome any obstacles the world might throw in her way. Winter supposed that was the kind of woman who was attracted to the idea of joining up with the only female battalion in the army. She'd won her position by the good opinion of her peers—the Girls' Own had held elections, early on, to fill out its slate of lieutenants and sergeants.

Lieutenant Novus, on the other hand, was an entirely different sort of officer. His uniform, though dusty and sweat-stained from days on the road, was still obviously well tailored and embroidered with more gold thread than the regulations strictly called for, and the sword that hung at his belt had a chased silver scabbard and gold filigree around the hilt. The stripe on his shoulder was plain white, not silver, a distinction Winter had learned to appreciate: only an officer who was a graduate of the War College, like Marcus d'Ivoire, was entitled to wear the silver. Novus had purchased his commission, or more likely inherited it as part of the family fortune.

The similarity to her first lieutenant, d'Vries, was striking, as though there were a printing press somewhere in Vordan City that stamped out these handsome, preening sons of privilege. Winter was doing her best to keep an open mind, although given how d'Vries had ended up, this was not easy. But Novus had stayed with the army, when many noble or wealthy officers had fled, which had to say *something* about his character. He was currently not helping his cause, however, by maintaining a stiff formality and refusing to participate in the conversation.

Winter tried again, as Bobby removed a trio of chickens from the fire and set to work carving. Their fire was in the middle of the feast, and she was very aware that her conversation would be the object of everyone's attention, if not now, then later on when the soldiers whispered about it in their tents.

They'd already exhausted the subjects of the weather, the march, and the pleasant smell of the chicken. Every time Winter tried to get a topic going, it ran into Lieutenant Novus like a tennis ball hitting the net, as he turned his grim stare on each of them in turn. Now, as Bobby served the chickens and even the lieutenant was briefly distracted by the prospect of food, she took a deep breath and tried again.

"Lieutenant Malloy," she said. "I don't believe I've heard the story of how you joined us. If you're willing to share it, of course."

"Not much t' tell, sir," Malloy said, not meeting Winter's eye. She had an awed expression, as though she were dining with a live saint, which made Winter distinctly uncomfortable. "I'm from Appes, on the Fal. Family's in wool. Papa sent me an' two of my older brothers to Vordan City, t' finish up a contract with a new buyer. When the king died, we heard the roads weren't safe, so we stayed put until it all blew over. My brothers were more worried about what this would do t' prices than about watching out for me, so I was out on the th' streets when the Vendre fell. I watched th' Colonials march out to fight Orlanko, and I saw you leading the Girls' Own in the parade afterward."

Her eyes got a strange shine, a glow that seemed entirely independent of the firelight. She wasn't looking at Winter, but past her, into the night sky. Novus, who'd been delicately nibbling his chicken, stopped to fix Malloy with a glare, but she didn't notice.

"I went back t' my brothers an' told 'em I was joining the army," she went on. "They called me crazy and laughed at me. Then they said Papa would disown me, and Benji told me to stop being silly an' tried to grab me, so I popped him one on the nose. Got blood all over his new shirt. Then they shouted at me, said I'd end up as a whore an' it'd be no business of theirs if I did, an' I said it was no business of theirs anyway. An' probably some other things I shouldn't have. Then I grabbed my stuff and left."

Winter was trying to think of what to say to that when Novus saved her the trouble, tossing his plate with its barely touched chicken into the fire. He got to his feet, a thunderous scowl on his face, and turned his back on the company without a word. As he stalked away, Winter got up to follow, gesturing at Bobby to keep the conversation alive. Bobby stuttered a bit, foiled by the sudden silence, but Captain Sevran came to the rescue with a question about the morning's handball match, and everyone piled back into the talk with relief.

Winter found Novus standing by a vacant tent on the edge of camp, staring out toward the line of lights that were the torchbearing sentries. On either side, tents stretched away, neat lines fading into the darkness. The camp was alive with conversation, the crackle of fires, and the soft sounds of horses and oxen settling down for the night. Winter hesitated, not sure what to say, and was considering leaving the man alone when he rounded on her.

"How do you do it?" he said.

"Excuse me?" Winter said, a bit startled.

"Sit there and listen to that . . . that *absurdity*."

"I'm not sure I understand," Winter said. "You have some problem with Lieutenant Malloy's story?"

"I find the sight of Lieutenant Malloy offensive, sir," Novus spit. "It's fucking unnatural and makes me want to vomit. It's like someone put a wedding dress on a sow, or gloves on a horse. It's absurd. Except you're sending her into battle, so it's like taking that horse and trying to make him box, or marrying the sow, taking her home, and fucking her. This so-called 'battalion' is a sick joke."

Now that he was going, the floodgates were well and truly open. Winter's hackles rose, but she tried to keep the anger from her face.

"You heard her story," Novus said. "Every one of your 'Girls' Own' has a story like that. Some father or brother or uncle that they've turned on, in defiance of the laws of God and man, to run off and play at soldiers. And I have to stand here and watch as *my* battalion, which I chose to stand with when the war came, is perverted by this . . . this *ridiculous* farce. If I had my way, I'd tell the lot of them they could go home, if their families will still take them, or stay here and be whores. At least then they'd be good for something." He sneered. "They seem well on their way to that already."

He ran out of breath, and stood there for a moment, panting.

"Is that all?" Winter said, keeping her voice mild with an effort.

"You're the one I don't understand, sir," Novus said. "These *volunteers* don't know anything about war. But you're a man, and you were a *real* soldier, in Khandar. How can you lead these girls out there knowing what'll happen to them? They'll be overrun the first time they meet the enemy, and those of them that don't eat cold steel will spend the rest of the war sucking Hamveltai cock at knifepoint." He eyed her dubiously. "Are you just too afraid of the general to speak up, is that it? If you had any balls at all, you'd resign rather than lead this freak show."

Winter wanted to laugh and cry all at once. She swallowed hard. "Very well. Your point is taken, Lieutenant. And what do you suggest I do with you now?"

"I'll tell you exactly what you're going to do," Novus said. "Nothing. Because you know as well as I do that I'm right, and every man in the Royals agrees with me. Captain Sevran's a coward, but if you lay a finger on me, the whole damned battalion will be on my side. We'll see what your *girls* are worth then."

For just a moment, Winter was back in Khandar, with Sergeant Davis looming over her with his great scarred fists raised. Her breath caught, but when she blinked, the image was gone. Novus was no Davis, had none of the sergeant's strength or brutality. Looking at him now, she could see he was *scared*, talking big because he knew he'd backed himself into a corner.

"Thank you for being frank with me, Lieutenant," Winter said. "I'll consider what you've said. You're dismissed."

Fear turned to triumph in Novus' eyes. "Oh yes. *Consider* it." He shook his head. "You *are* a fucking coward, aren't you? I can see that now. I should have known it all along. Go ahead, then. Lead us to disaster. Once your girls get slaughtered, we'll be there to pick up the pieces."

He turned on his heel and stalked away. Winter sucked in a long breath and blew it out again.

Well, then. She looked after the lieutenant and shook her head. *Now what?*

"You'll have to get rid of him," Cyte said as they watched the formations assemble. "I probably would have fired him on the spot. Or slugged him."

"It's more complicated than that," Winter said. "Being an asshole isn't against regulations."

"Using that kind of language to a superior officer is," Cyte said. "Besides, I think Janus has already set the precedent when he kicked out de Ferre and his friends."

"I'm not Janus," Winter said. She caught sight of Lieutenant Novus, on the other side of the drill field. He looked from Winter to the men and women getting into formation and back again, then shook his head and stalked away.

"Janus would back you if Novus tried to go through channels. And if he tried anything else, you'd be within your rights to have him arrested."

"Maybe." Winter was only half listening, scanning the crowd that had turned up to watch the morning's drill. "I need to talk to Sevran and see what he thinks."

"Don't wait too long," Cyte said. "If Novus gets it into his head that he can run roughshod over you, there's going to be trouble."

"Yeah."

Winter went stiff as she found what she was looking for. A flash of glorious red hair, in the middle of a knot of Girls' Own spectators. She tried to catch Jane's eye and failed. *But at least she's out of her tent.*

"Okay," she said to Folsom, who stood ready to repeat her commands. "Let's get started."

"Close *up!*" Folsom's voice rang through the misty morning air like a clarion call. "Skirmish line, *forward!* Main line, *loading drill!*"

It was Lieutenant Vidolet's company on the field. He wasn't part of the noble clique around Novus, and Winter didn't think he'd deliberately sabotage the drill. His men certainly looked as though they'd been practicing, going through the manual of arms with smooth precision. He shouted, "Fire!" and a chorus of clicks answered him.

Abby's company of the Girls' Own had improved as well. Their loading was faster, and they seemed more comfortable in their two-woman teams, trading off firing as fast as they could ram home imaginary musket balls. They also seemed to be more enthusiastic about the exercise. Playful shouts went up with each shot.

"Got one!"

"Take that, you damned Elysian!"

"Bagged myself a general!"

"No, you didn't, you only knocked off his hat!"

But the next part is the real test. Winter nodded to Folsom, who took a deep breath.

"Skirmish line, *fall back*! Main line, prepare to pass skirmishers!"

Abby's company turned at once and sprinted back toward Vidolet's, where the men halted in their loading and firing and presented their muskets in a stiff line, as though they were brandishing bayonets. The Girls' Own soldiers surged toward them, a confused mass of running, laughing women, and Winter braced herself for the collision.

It never came. The Royals turned neatly in place, opening holes in the line just wide enough to run through, and Abby's company passed through as cleanly and quickly as a pebble dropped into a cup of water. The women came out the other side of the line, whooping and hollering; Abby herself, who was waiting there, immediately began getting them to form a line of their own. In less than a minute, they were all through, and the Royals closed ranks again to present an unbroken line of muskets to the "enemy."

"Fire!" Vidolet shouted, to another round of clicks.

The soldiers began their loading drill again, and Winter let out a breath she didn't know she'd been holding.

"It works," Cyte said.

"Get them to try it again," Winter said. "Then switch companies. I want every soldier to have a chance to practice before we break camp today. If that all goes well, tomorrow we'll see if they can do it with bayonets fixed." *Assuming we get another day to practice.* They were only fifteen miles from Gaafen, where the enemy was reported to be digging in.

"Yes, sir!" Cyte said.

"And once we make camp tonight, go and get decent food for everybody. Spend whatever we've got left."

Cyte nodded. "Yes, sir. What about Novus?"

There had been a moment, as Novus had unleashed his tirade, that Winter felt absurdly grateful she hadn't abandoned her male disguise, as Bobby had. It wasn't a feeling she was proud of. But Novus' reaction was the one she'd always expected would follow discovery—if not the outright rape and murder that had been on Sergeant Davis' mind—and though when he'd found out Janus had not lived up to her fears, she suspected that Janus was, as usual, exceptional. If the old-fashioned royal officers or traditionalists like Colonel d'Ivoire found out, she suspected a verbal explosion like Novus' would be the least of her worries.

It's all well and good for Bobby. As an officer in the Girls' Own, she only has to answer to Winter. I have to work with the rest of the army . . .

"We'll get rid of him," Winter said, shaking her head to clear her brief reverie. "But he's Royal Army, so we need to do this properly, or he'll tie us in knots with regulations. I'll have to write to Janus. We'll see if he grins at me when I've got a letter from the commanding general backing me up."

"I look forward to seeing his reaction, sir."

Winter awoke to the sound of a whispered argument outside her tent.

The news that they were getting a decent meal in place of army rations had lent the camp a carnival atmosphere. While Winter hadn't issued any alcohol, there were plenty of locals willing to remedy that deficiency. Trying to keep it out of the camp altogether would have been futile, so Winter passed the word for the sergeants to circulate and make sure nobody got more than tipsy. There was another march tomorrow, after all, and possibly a battle after that.

Even so, several competing choruses had kept up a running contest late into the night, alternating between patriotic anthems and the endless, bawdy camp songs that any group of soldiers seemed to generate spontaneously. Winter was fairly sure there was a bit of Abby's "fraternization" going on as well, and that thought was almost enough to drive her from her tent in search of Jane. Instead she stayed put, going over regimental paperwork until her eyes drooped, then lying awake on her pallet, aware of every footstep nearby. If Jane was going to come back, after all, this would be a perfect time, and Winter kept expecting to hear the soft rustle of the tent flap and the murmur of her lover's voice in her ear. Eventually she fell asleep, and dreamed of Jane's lips on hers and Jane's fingers sliding over her skin.

She'd left instructions for the camp to be awoken a half hour later than normal, in deference to the fact that a few men and women would probably have sore heads. Blinking, she saw that it was still well before the appointed hour. The light trickling in through the canvas was the bright, angled sunshine of just past dawn, and the camp still seemed quiet.

"I'm awake," Winter said. The two voices broke off. "Bobby, is that you? Who's there?"

"It's Captain Verity," Bobby said. "She . . . would like to see you."

Winter sat up abruptly. "Send her in!"

"Sir—"

Jane pushed through the tent flap. Her hair was a tousled mess, and she wasn't wearing her uniform jacket, as though she'd just rolled out of bed. Winter's greeting died on her lips when she saw Jane's face, which was a mask of fury.

"This is your fault," Jane said. "I fucking *warned* you, didn't I? You think we keep watches around the camp for *fun*?"

"Jane?" Winter said. "What's going on?'

"What's going on is what *always* goes on. You had to trust Captain fucking Sevran, because he's so delightfully charming, and he promised his men would be on their best behavior." Jane snorted. "Like a gang of fucking soldiers is any better than a bunch of apes."

"Jane—"

"One of your precious fucking Royals decided he didn't have to ask permission to lay hands on one of my girls. What the *fuck* did you expect?"

Winter sucked in a breath. "Balls of the Beast. Is—"

"I *think* he'll live," Jane said. "But things have gotten a bit out of hand. Bit of a *fracas*, you might say."

Winter could hear more voices from outside, Cyte's and Folsom's. And, behind them, a rising chorus of shouts, yelps, and thuds, mixed with the *crunch* of breaking tent poles and the ripping sound of tearing canvas.

Oh, Brass Balls of the fucking Beast . . .

CHAPTER SEVEN

MARCUS

The war, as best Marcus could see, was going very badly indeed.

It was difficult to get an accurate picture, of course, from Vordan City. In part this was because news took a long time to arrive from the frontiers, and longer from some frontiers than from others. A dispatch from Vayenne might take a week to be sailed up the Vor, while messages from the Murnskai frontier, seven hundred miles of awful roads, washed-out bridges, and treacherous passes away, might take a month to come if they got through at all.

The other problem was that the news that arrived was often wildly inaccurate, or at least inaccurately reported and promulgated. The agents of the broadsheets and pamphleteers were everywhere, nosing up to every deputy and ministry for the latest tidbits. Every part of the new government leaked information like a sieve, but often only when it suited that particular individual's purposes, or when that information could be carefully doctored to appear in a favorable light. Thus, one broadsheet might announce a famous battle won at the same time another blared about a military disaster, and various towns, fortresses, and river crossings changed hands with bewildering speed, depending on who was doing the writing.

As time passed, however, the stories became more solid, and actual eyewitnesses to distant events began to trickle in, so some bits of truth could be discerned. Marcus' instructions told him to pass along anything he thought credible to Janus, via the flik-flik line, and so he'd sat down with his maps and some of the more reliable reports to cull the wheat from the chaff. Once he began paying attention, however, the picture that emerged was worrying.

The worst disaster had come in the north, on the Borelgai coast. There had been persistent rumors since just after the declaration of war that the Borelgai navy had laid siege to Nordart, Vordan's primary northern port, and the Army of the Transpale under General de Brolge was variously reported to be relieving the garrison, maneuvering for a field battle, or retreating in disorder after a defeat by Borelgai forces. Now, however, all the reports agreed that things were far worse than that. After a brief standoff with the Borels, de Brolge had in fact gone over to the enemy, bag and baggage, declaring his support for Orlanko—rumored to be in exile in Borel—and his contempt for the Deputies-General. Most of the royal regiments in the Army of the Transpale had followed him, and the volunteers had scattered in a panic, leaving no significant army between the Borelgai and Alver on the Pale. Ecco Island, once the primary base of the now-defunct Vordanai fleet, had been captured, and Enzport, at the mouth of the Pale, was widely expected to be next.

Meanwhile, General Hallvez of the Army of the North, on the Murnskai border, had decided to steal a march on his opponents. The legions of Imperial Murnsk were vast, but also notoriously slow to muster and deploy, and Hallvez had thought that delivering an early blow was just the thing to rock the enemy back on his heels. What had happened next was not clear, but Hallvez had apparently marched his twenty-odd battalions into a trap, where they had been decisively beaten by a Murnskai force less than half their number. Hallvez, raving about sorcery, had retreated into Vordan with the remnants of his army, and sent message after hysterical message to the Ministry of War demanding reinforcements.

Everyone was demanding reinforcements, in fact. The commander of every post within sight of saltwater, from Enzport to Essyle, was convinced that his little garrison was going to be the next target of the Borelgai fleet, and they all wanted more guns and more men. The generals and colonels had taken to writing editorials for the broadsheets, in an effort to stir the public about their particular menace and demand action through the Deputies-General. The Deputies, in turn, issued complicated and often contradictory instructions to Durenne at the Ministry of War, and were contradicted in turn by the decisions of the Directory for the National Defense. The fact that there were virtually no guns left to be had, and not many men, didn't seem to bother the commanders fighting over scraps.

The only good news came from the east, where news of Janus' victory at Diarach was now becoming generally known. It was widely acknowledged to have been unsatisfactory, however. Di Pfalen had been permitted to escape, withdrawing with most of his army toward Antova, the central nail on which the League hung its defense of the valley of the Velt. As long as the fortress remained untaken, no real progress could be made, but Janus had not even moved in that direction, instead pursuing a secondary enemy east toward Desland. Moreover, the Hamveltai had organized a second army, under their aged but famous Marshal Jindenau, which was expected to proceed to Antova for winter quarters and launch a direct invasion of Vordan in the spring once the passes were clear.

Radical papers were shouting that the Directory was to blame, dominated as it was by Maurisk and the Conservatives, and that change was needed if victory was to be achieved. The Conservative press, for their part, had taken the defection of de Brogle very badly, and now saw treason and betrayal in every setback. Maurisk had ordered General Hallvez to report to the capital, along with a number of colonels suspected of less than enthusiastic prosecution of their duties, and dispatched representatives of the Patriot Guard to ensure that they complied. And every day, like the clockwork beast it was, the Spike did its bloody work, cutting the hearts out of the men and women the Guard dragged off the street. Yesterday an old woman had been spiked for wearing a fur coat of a vaguely Borelgai cut in public, thus expressing sympathy with the enemy; her protests that she had five grandsons serving with the armies had been in vain.

Condensing all this down to the few sentences the flik-flik line was capable of transmitting was not an easy task. Marcus sent boxes of paper reports by courier, but by the time they arrived they would be doubly out of date. The most important thing, Janus had emphasized, was the conditions in and around the capital itself, and Marcus was doing his best to express the panic he saw rising in the screaming headlines.

Political situation here v. bad, he wrote. *Streets afraid and ready to turn on anyone suspect. Mass Patriot Guard presence keeping basic order for now, but maybe not for long. M. getting harsher by the day.* He paused for thought, and rewet his pen. *Military officers esp. under suspicion after defections. Watch for traps.*

He laid the pen aside and left the note to dry, just as there was a knock at his study door. Marcus had learned by now how to distinguish Raesinia's excited rapping from the polite taps of the Mierantai servants, and this was the latter.

"Come in."

"Sir," said Lieutenant Uhlan, commander of the half dozen Mierantai riflemen Janus had left behind. "There's a couple of soldiers at the door. They claim they were sent here by a Captain Vahkerson at your request."

Marcus stared blankly for a moment, then remembered the note he'd sent to the Preacher asking for extra men to hold down the fort. *Reliable as always.* "Yes, of course. Send them in and have someone see to their things if they have any."

"Sir." Uhlan saluted and slipped out. Marcus listened to his boots clomp down the hallway, and went back to scanning the panicky headlines. Before long there was another knock, softer and more hesitant.

"Come in," Marcus said again.

Two soldiers, in the homespun and approximately blue jackets of the volunteers, came in and stood stiffly at attention in front of his desk. They saluted, and the young man on the left said, "Sir! Rankers Feiss and Dracht, reporting as ordered."

Ranker Feiss was a boy of seventeen or so, tall and lanky, with sandy hair and a face that was just emerging from childlike plumpness, badly savaged by acne. He stood at attention with such concentration that his back was as taut as a bowstring, his eyes firmly fixed somewhere above Marcus' left shoulder.

Ranker Dracht, in contrast, met his gaze levelly. Marcus guessed she was the same age as Feiss, but she was a head shorter, with unkempt brown hair tied back in a short queue.

"Ah," Marcus said, somewhat taken aback. "Welcome. Feiss and . . . Dracht, was it?"

"Ranker Andria Dracht, sir," the girl said. "But you can call me Andy. Everyone does."

Feiss nudged her with his elbow, which she ignored.

"How much did the Preacher—that is, how much did Captain Vahkerson tell you?"

"That you were in need of assistance on a matter of the utmost secrecy, sir," Feiss said, a note of excitement creeping into his voice. "And that he was sending us because he was certain of our discretion."

"Where were you before this?"

"In the hospital, sir. Soldiers who are rated fit for duty again are sent to Captain Vahkerson for reassignment."

"You're recovered now, I take it?" Marcus said.

"Sir, yes, sir!" the boy barked. "Broken leg, sir, but it's all healed now. I ran laps around the University."

Marcus' lip quirked in a slight smile. "How did you come by the wound?"

"I volunteered before Midvale, sir. Had a horse fall on me during training."

"Bad luck."

"My fault, sir. I was racing her and misjudged a jump."

"I see." Marcus transferred his attention to Andy. "And you?"

"Volunteered with Mad Jane's company, sir," the girl said.

"Do you know how to load a musket?" Marcus said, his smile widening a little.

"Load, fire, and fix a bayonet, sir," Andy said. The lamp on his desk gleamed in her spectacles. "And what to do with it afterward. I fought at Midvale. Would have joined Captain Ihernglass' Girls' Own if I hadn't been in the hospital."

Marcus' smile faded slowly. "What happened?"

Andy held out her right hand, which was missing the two smallest fingers, and bore a ribbon of shiny scar tissue. "This went bad on me. Nearly lost the hand, the cutters tell me."

Marcus felt his jaw tighten. He'd opposed letting Jane's Leatherbacks into the battle, but Janus had overruled him. It was all very well to say that they needed every musket, but there was something deeply unnatural about a girl practically young enough for dolls bearing the scars of battle. It went against something deep in Marcus' nature; women were to be shielded from danger, not deliberately exposed to it. In his opinion, the time for girls to pick up weapons was just after the last boy had been buried.

The Preacher thinks I can trust her, though. He shook his head. *Lord knows I could use more hands, but . . .*

There was another knock at the door, this one the frantic banging that announced Raesinia.

"Well," Marcus said, "you'll both be assisting me here. I want your word that you'll say nothing of our business to anyone outside this house, not even fellow soldiers."

"Yes, sir!" Feiss said. Andy nodded and saluted again.

"All right. Uhlan will show you where you're sleeping."

He waved them away, and they went, hampered somewhat in Feiss' case by his reluctance to relax his parade-ground posture.

"Who are those two?" Raesinia said once they'd gone.

"Reinforcements, apparently," he muttered, then

blinked. The person in the doorway wasn't someone he recognized. It took a moment for his brain to kick in.

"How do I look?" Raesinia said, spreading her arms.

"Not like the Queen of Vordan, that's for sure," Marcus muttered.

"That's sort of the point. *They* certainly didn't recognize me."

Marcus had to admit the change of costume had been effective. It wasn't a disguise, exactly, but she'd drawn up her hair and tucked it under a stiff-brimmed red cap, which gave her face a slimmer, boyish cast. Her jacket was bright red, too, with a high collar and polished bronze buttons in a double row down the front, and her trousers were dark gray with a red stripe on the outside seam. Black leather shoes with brass buckles completed the ensemble.

She looked, Marcus thought, like the better class of circus performer, or possibly the impresario of a brass band. He stared at her dubiously. "Do the Exchange Central couriers really dress like that?"

"It's traditional," Raesinia said. "This is one of their official uniforms."

"Do I want to know how you came across it?"

"We . . . acquired them, for a job back before the revolution. They're useful. The couriers can go everywhere without being noticed. Cora's been storing them down at the church."

"All right." Marcus frowned. "I still don't like this. You ought to stay here, where it's safe."

"Except *I'm* the one who knows where we're going."

"You could draw me a map . . ." It sounded weak, even to Marcus. "What if we get caught?"

"We won't get caught."

"And if we do?"

Raesinia shrugged. "You're a colonel in the army, for God's sake. What are they going to do? Just tell them you got lost."

Marcus glanced down at the papers on his desk. "Being a colonel may not be all the protection it used to be."

"Have you got a better idea? Every day we wait is

another day Maurisk has to muddy the waters. If this doesn't pan out, we don't have many options."

The truth was, of course, that Marcus didn't have a better idea. *But that doesn't mean I have to like it.*

RAESINIA

The realization that she was having fun hit Raesinia about the time they crossed over the Saint Uriah Street Bridge to Exchange Island, and it was nearly enough to stop her in her tracks.

It had been a long time since she genuinely enjoyed herself. Not since before the fall of the Vendre, for certain; before Ben and Faro had died, and Maurisk had turned against her. The nights of drinking and plotting in the back room of the Blue Mask felt like stories from another, rosier age, before the dark curtain of reality and responsibility had descended.

In some ways, this made sense. Since the revolution, the country had lurched from one crisis to another, each contributing its own unique flavor to the never-ending whirl of politics in the Deputies-General. Raesinia had watched with a feeling of helpless despair, simultaneously responsible for whatever happened and powerless to affect it. It would have led to many sleepless nights, if sleeping was something she'd still needed to do.

But things hadn't gotten any *better*, and here she was, feeling light as a feather. For the first time since the Vendre, she was on her own again, walking the streets without royal raiment or escort. And she had a goal she could actually reach with her own hands. If she lost sight of that, she only had to close her eyes to see little Emil dragging his mother's body across the cobbles. Whoever had done that had to pay. *And if Maurisk was behind it . . .*

There was guilt at the back of her mind, of course. Guilt for putting Sothe in danger, for dragging Marcus into her affairs. Guilt for feeling happier than she had in weeks while people were suffering. But Raesinia had been living with guilt for a long time, and she'd learned to push it aside, to get the job done, to take her pleasures where she could.

"Something wrong?" Marcus said. He looked uncomfortable in his full dress uniform, with silver embroidery at his collar and a golden eagle on his shoulders. He'd insisted on wearing his old, battered sword, which was out of place among the polished buttons and neat, shiny leather straps.

"Nothing," Raesinia said. "Just thinking that this place has changed."

Which was true enough. The Exchange, an irregular expanse of open, muddy courtyard, occupied almost the entirety of the small Exchange Island, with only a single row of large buildings surrounding it. It was the beating heart of Vordanai commerce, a cyclone of paper and coin, spitting out a storm of letters and messengers to every city in the land. The briefest nod or handshake in the Exchange might mean the launching of a fleet a thousand miles away or the felling of a mighty forest, the destruction of a generations-old family concern or the formation of a new merchant empire.

The permanent structures around the edges of the courtyard represented the princes of commerce, the great banks, the merchant houses, and the mightiest of shipping concerns and traders. More mundane traders had to make do with wooden planks laid across a couple of barrels, set up in clusters around the courtyard according to some arcane scheme that took into account their line of business, seniority, and general respectability. Cora had tried to explain it to her once, but Raesinia's eyes had begun to glaze over after only a few moments.

Even Raesinia, however, could see that things were different now. Many of the great buildings were shuttered and dark; the foreign banks and merchants had abandoned their outposts, either with the revolution or at the advent of the war. Some had been vandalized, especially the Borelgai banks, where the mob had battered the marble and painted vicious slogans across the facades. Others had attracted squatters, traders setting up their temporary desks on the steps or in the lobbies, looking like pygmies invading the homes of giants among the massive pillared porticos.

The Vordanai traders were still there, but there was a frantic, desperate edge to the activity in the courtyard. Couriers, dressed in the traditional red and gray like Raesinia, rushed to and fro in torrents, and men ran from one table to the next, waving their arms and shouting. Patriot Guards were everywhere, bearing halberds and black-and-blue sashes, and they had their hands full keeping the peace. Fights broke out with alarming regularity, well-dressed, portly men swinging at one another like schoolboys until the Guards arrived to pull them apart.

Exchange Central was an old, squat building on the eastern edge of the square. It had begun as a tavern, Cora had once told Raesinia, where traders liked to gather, and then become a kind of headquarters where the business of the Exchange in general was discussed. At some point, the old tavern building had burned down and been replaced with this unlovely but functional three-story brick block, which looked more like a warehouse than anything else. Exchange Central was so old and so embedded in tradition, Cora had said, that it didn't need the elaborate marble facades of the banks to convince people that it was trustworthy. Everyone simply took it for granted.

Someone had at least considered the possibility that it might be a choice target for enemy saboteurs, though, because there was a squad of Patriot Guards standing outside. There was also a group of regular troops, with muskets and army-blue uniforms, since the army's quartermaster services kept their city headquarters here. These men all saluted as she and Marcus approached and they spotted the eagles on his shoulders. The Patriot Guards did not, but they didn't bar the way, either. Raesinia stayed a step or two behind Marcus, trying hard to look like a dutiful servant.

Inside was a vast lobby, low-ceilinged and claustrophobic, with at least two dozen doors leading deeper into the building. Couriers, in uniforms that matched Raesinia's, came and went constantly with envelopes and parcels. More guards, both army and Patriots, waited by the walls, and behind a circular central desk four harassed-looking young men frantically shuffled files and barked terse instructions at a waiting queue of couriers and servants.

Marcus headed for the desk, following Raesinia's instructions. She was surprised to see his manner change, as though he'd slipped on a mask. Around her, he had to fight his tendency to be deferential, so it was a bit startling to see him put on the stern, impatient face of an army officer. Raesinia supposed that commanding troops required a kind of acting all its own, projecting an unwaveringly confident persona to keep morale up. *Marcus may be better at this sort of thing than he gives himself credit for.*

"Yes?" the secretary behind the desk said, then looked up and added, "Sir?"

"Commercial records," Marcus said.

"What about them?"

"I need to examine them." His tone was clipped and dismissive.

"Sir," the secretary said, with a strained smile, "while we strive to be helpful, our commercial records fill quite a large part of this building. I can't have them all brought to you. Is there something particular you're interested in?"

"I'll know it when I see it," Marcus said.

"I'll be assisting the colonel," Raesinia said. The secretary raised an eyebrow at the sight of her, but no more than that—female couriers weren't common, but they were hardly unheard of. "Just point us in the direction of this year's local shipping records and we'll be out of your hair."

The secretary sighed and indicated a door. "Make sure he doesn't disturb anything," he said to Raesinia. "It's your job's worth if you leave a mess in there."

"Of course." Raesinia looked up at Marcus. "Come along, sir."

The guard standing beside the door unlocked it with a key from his belt, and closed it again once they'd passed. They found themselves in a wooden-floored corridor leading to a rear staircase, with no one else in sight.

"That's it?" Marcus said. "I can't believe that worked."

"Uniforms." Raesinia plucked at one of her buttons. "It's something I learned from Sothe. Get the uniform right and you're most of the way there. A little bit of bluster usually does the rest. Come on."

The staircase led straight to the third floor, which was, as the secretary had implied, mostly full of records. Bookshelf after bookshelf of heavy tomes with cheap linen covers stretched to the walls, but Raesinia led Marcus past them without a glance.

"These are all old," she said. "The Exchange has them copied out and bound after a couple of years. What we want is further on." She was only repeating things Cora had told her, of course, but it was hard to resist the opportunity to look like an expert. Marcus seemed suitably impressed, and Raesinia grinned to herself.

There was apparently not a great deal of demand for commercial records, since the floor seemed almost abandoned. At the back of the large room of bookshelves, there was a set of corridors leading back into a maze of smaller rooms, each behind a cryptically labeled door. Raesinia, experimentally, tried one with a tacked paper scrap that read GNS0708 and found it full of mountains of ledgers, bound up with twine and adorned with more cryptic messages. The next two doors she tried were solidly locked, and the one after that led to an empty room.

Cora had told her approximately what to look for, but the girl had never been in here herself, and she'd obviously not been versed in the Exchange's arcane filing system. Raesinia looked around at the rows of identical doors, frustrated.

"What now?" Marcus said, stepping forward to look both ways down a cross-corridor.

"I'm thinking."

"Think quickly."

Raesinia opened her mouth, but didn't get the chance to speak, because Marcus grabbed her by one arm and pulled her hastily around the corner. She let out an undignified squeak as he pressed her against the wall and huddled beside her.

"*What* are you doing?" she hissed.

"Someone's coming."

"Would you *stop* acting like we're trying to spring somebody from the Vendre? We're supposed to act like we belong here." Raesinia slipped free of his grasp and peeked around the corner. An old man in a leather apron was walking slowly down the corridor, humming tunelessly to himself. She pulled back before he noticed her. "Stay here."

Marcus looked aggrieved but didn't protest. Raesinia stepped away from the wall, backed up a little, and walked casually out into the junction with a distracted air, peering at the labels on the doors. When she saw the old man, she smiled, and he grinned back at her.

"Sorry," she said, endeavoring to look sheepish. "I'm supposed to be looking for local shipping records, but I think I'm lost."

"It does take a while to get used to the filing system," the old man said agreeably. "Any particular product?"

"Gunpowder." It was a risk to admit what they were looking for, lest it tip off their prey, but the conspiracy against her couldn't include *every* random caretaker who happened by. "Stuff from the past few months."

"You want PEX08," he said. "It's just around the corner that way. You've got the key?"

Raesinia nodded. "Thanks! Let me just collect my burden here." She went back around the corner and grabbed Marcus by the arm.

"Look stuck-up," she hissed at him, then led him back past the old man. To his credit, Marcus managed a very credible look of disdain as they went by. Raesinia raised her eyebrows theatrically, and the old man winked at her as he went past.

When he was out of earshot, Marcus looked down at her quizzically. "Stuck-up?"

"Best way to get on someone's good side is to make it 'me and you against the idiots.' My guess is that the Exchange staff isn't too pleased at having to live side by side with the army."

"I'm glad I could serve as a convenient idiot," Marcus said. "Now where are we going?"

"Right here." Raesinia stopped in front of a door labeled PEX08. She tried the latch and as she'd expected, found it locked.

"Let me guess," Marcus said, a faint smile on his face. "Sothe taught you to pick locks as well?"

"Nope." Raesinia undid the buttons at her collar, opening her coat enough that she could reach down to the small of her back. From there, she removed the thin, flat metal bar that had been rubbing against her spine all morning. It was about two feet long, and tapered into a wedge at one end.

"What she taught me," she went on, fastening her collar again, "is that only polite burglars pick locks." She slipped the thin end of the wedge between the door and jamb, just in front of where it latched, wiggling it back and forth with wooden splintering sounds until it was solidly stuck in place. Raesinia let go of it and stepped back, leaving the metal bar sticking out at a forty-five-degree angle to the door. "Pull on that, please. As hard as you can."

Marcus paused, looking over his shoulder, but the old caretaker's footsteps were no longer audible. He took hold of the bar with both hands and set his feet. When he pulled, leverage worked its magic, and the wood holding the latch in place on the other side of the door gave way with a *crunch*. The door swung inward.

Raesinia collected her pry-bar and threaded it carefully back past her collar into its hiding spot. Marcus examined the doorjamb, frowning.

"Someone may notice that," he said.

"We'll be long gone by then. It doesn't look like these rooms have gotten much use lately." Dust lay heavy on the stacks of ledgers in the room, piled haphazardly in twine-wrapped piles. "You take that side, I'll take this."

"What am I looking for?"

"Anything that says Halverson."

He nodded, and they began their search. The dust was thick enough that Raesinia had to run her finger along the spines of some of ledgers to see the names penciled there. There were more ledgers than she'd initially anticipated, but they were tied up and grouped together, so she made relatively quick progress. She was nearing the back of the room when a sound from outside made her stand up straight.

"Think I've got it," Marcus said. "There's a whole stack that says Halverson, anyway—"

"Shh." Raesinia raised a hand. The distant footsteps were getting closer. "Someone's coming."

"Should I try looking stuck-up again?"

"That would have worked better before I broke the door open."

"Maybe you should learn to be a polite burglar."

Raesinia couldn't help grinning at that. Marcus could be witty, when he forgot he was talking to the queen. It felt a little like working beside Sothe, with her dry, dark humor.

The footsteps came closer still. Raesina crept up to the doorway and risked a peek. Just turning the corner was a young man in a three-cornered hat and a blue-on-black sash, looking from door to door as though he was searching for something.

"Patriot Guard," she whispered. "I think he's come to find us."

Marcus pressed himself against the open door on the other side of the doorway. "Any ideas?"

"When he comes in here, I'll get his attention, and you jump him."

"Any *good* ideas?" Marcus said, but the footsteps were close now. He waved frantically to Raesinia, not daring to speak.

Raesinia cast around. Against the wall on her side was an invitingly large wooden box, which was probably intended as a wastepaper basket. She grabbed it and turned it upside down, then looked speculatively at Marcus. The guard had been roughly his height. *I'll have to jump a bit.*

Marcus apparently guessed her intention, because he made more frantic hand signals, waving *no, no, no*. Raesinia bounced once or twice on the balls of her feet, getting ready.

The guard rounded the corner, glancing at the splintered jamb and then looking for the door. That left him facing away from Raesinia, which was precisely what she needed. She leapt at him, box in her hands, and slammed it down over the top of his head. The guard let out a startled squawk and stumbled forward, and Marcus grabbed him by the arm and spun him face-first into the wall, knocking the breath out of him with a *whoosh*.

Raesinia was right behind him in an instant, pressing her index finger into the small of his back. "Make a noise, and you'll get it in the kidneys," she said in her best thug's voice. She didn't actually have a knife, but she didn't think he could tell the difference through his jacket. "Stay quiet and you'll get out of this. Get his sword belt."

The guard whimpered but stayed silent. Marcus extracted his belt, set the sword on the floor, and used it to tie the man's hands behind his back. Raesinia undid his sash, stood on tiptoes to pull the box off his head, and then looped the roll of blue-on-black fabric over his mouth. She tied it tight at the back of his neck, then stepped back to admire her handiwork.

Marcus looked at her and raised his eyebrows. Raesinia went to the stack of ledgers he'd been investigating and picked them up with a grunt. Once she was out of the room, Marcus pulled the broken door shut.

"I can carry those," he said.

"I'm supposed to be your courier. It's my job to carry things." She had to tilt her head back to put her chin on top of the stack and see where she was going.

"So we're just going to walk out of here?"

"Exactly. Nice and slow. Nothing wrong, nothing to see here."

"But be ready to run?" Marcus said.

"Of course."

MARCUS

Marcus never would have believed it, but that was exactly how it went, nice and slow and completely uneventful. He and Raesinia strolled out of Exchange Central with the records, past a dozen Patriot Guards and as many army soldiers, and no one said a thing. Whatever had sent the guard to investigate, it apparently hadn't called for anything like a general alarm.

Once they were out in the bustle of the Exchange crowd, Marcus felt a lot safer. He directed Raesinia to a nearby alley, where a few twists and turns put them among the back entrances to the Exchange's buildings, right on the waterfront. They took shelter in the lee of a stairway, and Raesinia set down the stack of ledgers. She was fitter than she looked—she wasn't even breathing hard.

"That," he said, "was not a good idea."

"It worked, didn't it?"

"Just because it worked doesn't make it a good idea. If he'd shouted for help first thing, we'd have been in serious trouble."

"Not much to be done about that, unless you wanted to try and cut his throat before he got the chance. I figured you'd rather not."

"You figured correctly," Marcus said. He might not care for the Patriot Guards, but killing one in cold blood for doing his job properly wouldn't have sat well on his conscience. "I hope you've realized that once someone finds him, word is going to get out eventually that records are missing."

"I know," Raesinia said, untying the twine of the stack of ledgers. "That'll get back to the conspirators. Sooner, rather than later, if it is Maurisk that we're dealing with." She flipped open the top book and turned a few pages, then shook her head. "We've got to get these to Cora. It would take me weeks to make anything out of it, and we haven't got that kind of time now."

Marcus looked down at her, in her boyish red courier's uniform—now stained with dust—and jaunty little cap. He shook his head.

"What?" she said.

"I was just thinking that it would be hard for you to be less like I expected."

Raesinia rolled her eyes. "I'm sorry to be such a disappointment."

"It's not a disappointment," Marcus said, surprised to find that he meant it. "Just a bit of a surprise."

"See if you can find us a boat," Raesinia said, tying the ledgers up again. "That'll be the easiest way back to Twin Turrets, and then we can change into something inconspicuous to visit Cora. I doubt she gets many Exchange Central couriers."

"As Your Majesty commands," Marcus said, bowing low.

"Don't make me hit you with something."

CHAPTER EIGHT

WINTER

In the course of a single afternoon, the camaraderie Winter had worked so hard to build between the Royals and the Girls' Own had evaporated. Getting the brawl broken up had left them barely in time to join the day's march, and their assigned route took them off the road and up a wooded ridge, so they'd arrived later than usual. Without orders, the Girls' Own had camped separately again, with armed sentries standing guard. Many of them bore the marks of the morning's fighting—bruises and black eyes, bandaged cuts and the occasional splinted finger. The same marks were visible among the Royals, and there was a great deal of grumbling coming from that quarter.

Finding the man who'd started it all had not been difficult, since he'd been lying insensible in the dirt when Winter arrived to restore the peace. His identity, in retrospect, was not a surprise.

"Lieutenant Novus," Winter said, standing just inside the tent they'd pressed into service as a prison. Novus was tied to a camp chair, sporting a huge bruise that covered half his face, and his carefully coiffed hair now looked more like a rat's nest. In spite of all that, he summoned up a smirk to greet her.

I should have seen this coming. Novus had made it

perfectly clear he had no respect for either the Girls' Own or Winter's authority, and she'd let him believe he'd gotten away with his ranting without repercussions. *He was bound to try something stupid.*

"Colonel," he said. "I assume you're here to clear up this misunderstanding?"

"Something like that," Winter said.

"Ranker Valon struck me in the face, in full view of witnesses," Novus said. "I trust she'll be disciplined appropriately."

Winter stared. Novus had a mad gleam in his eyes, and she couldn't tell if he expected a serious answer to that or not.

"Ranker Valon," Winter said, "told me that you grabbed her chest and then attempted to push her to the ground. Do you deny that?"

Novus shrugged, as best he was able in his restraints. "She made the offer obvious."

"She didn't mention anything about an offer."

The lieutenant raised an eyebrow. "If a woman walked past you half-naked, making sure you got a good look, what would *you* think, Colonel?"

"That she was coming back from her bath?" Emily Valon, the blond woman who'd done so well in the handball match, had told her that Novus had been waiting by the path leading up to the stream the soldiers had been using for that purpose. Novus claimed he'd just happened to be passing, but no one believed that.

He gave her a pitying look. "Well. Some of us have been around the block a few times."

"I thought the sight of someone like her made you sick."

Another half shrug. "Everyone knows Captain Verity's 'soldiers' are servicing half the battalion by now. Why should I abstain?"

Winter took a deep breath. She wanted to scream at him, take a rock and beat a lesson into his tiny skull. *Jane must be rubbing off on me.* It wouldn't be appropriate behavior from a superior officer; fortunately, she had other options.

"Lieutenant Benjamin Novus," she said, "you are hereby relieved of your command. You'll be returned to Vordan City with the next supply train and held there to await the judgment of the army commander."

"You're not serious." He jerked, as though he wanted to jump to his feet, and tugged against his ropes. "She *struck* me!"

"Ranker Valon was defending herself against assault, in the best traditions of the army."

"You incompetent fool," Novus spit. "You have no idea who my family is, do you? If you planned on having a career after escaping from this freak show, forget about it. You'll be lucky if they don't ship you back to Khandar!"

"You're right that I have no idea where you come from," Winter said. "Nor do I care. More important, I doubt Janus cares, either. He sent a dozen colonels packing, so one lieutenant is not going to trouble him." She leaned a little closer. "More to the point, Lieutenant, *you* are lucky I'm willing to be so lenient. I'd be within my rights to shoot you."

That might be stretching the point a bit, but not too far. There was nothing in the Regulations about attempted rape, but "unprovoked assault on another soldier resulting in serious harm" could be a capital offense in the field, at the commanding officer's discretion. Valon's well-thrown punch had most likely saved Novus' life, not that the lieutenant was ever likely to thank her for it.

Novus gaped. "You can't do this. You can't! We'll be fighting tomorrow. The men *need* me."

"I think the men will manage." Though Winter did feel guilty about depriving Captain Sevran of a staff lieutenant on the eve of battle. "Now, if you'll excuse me, I need to go and clean up the mess you've made."

Novus was correct about one thing—there would be fighting tomorrow. The Deslandai army showed no signs of pulling back from its position around Gaafen, a semi-circular line anchored on the outlying edge of the town and some surrounding farmhouses, with each end snug against the river. The brilliant stroke Winter had hoped Janus would come up with to avoid a frontal battle had yet to make an appearance. Orders had come down before dusk that the Third Regiment of the Line was to seize a ridge about a mile forward of their current camp in the morning, then wait for further instructions.

Winter badly wanted to see Jane, but it was Sevran who was waiting for her when she returned to her tent. She waved away his salute, wearily, and gestured him inside.

"I wanted to apologize, sir," he said. "Novus is one of mine, and I ought to have kept him under better control."

"I should have done something about him myself." Winter sat heavily on her sleeping pallet and started unlacing her boots. "Any of your other young nobles likely to try something similar?"

"I doubt it." The ghost of a smile crossed Sevran's face. "I think the lesson was pretty clear. Captain Verity's soldiers defend one another." He shrugged. "You may find this hard to believe, but a lot of the rankers are just as angry with Novus as the Girls' Own."

"That didn't stop them from getting into a punch-up this morning."

"They didn't know what had happened. When you see people from your unit in a brawl, you don't ask questions, you just jump in and help out. Afterward . . ." He shook his head. "But Captain Verity's people are back to treating us like the enemy."

"I'm not sure I can blame them." Winter sighed. "I'll speak to Captain Verity. But we haven't got time to smooth things over."

"You've gotten our orders?"

She nodded. "We move three hours past dawn. Make sure all the officers get the word. I want everyone up as soon as there's light, in time to get a hot breakfast and get formed up."

"Understood, sir." Sevran turned to leave, then hesitated. "Again, for what it's worth, I'm sorry."

The day of battle dawned bright and clear, with a chilly autumn wind playing over the field and shredding the wisps of cloud overhead. Winter, back astride Edgar, blinked back the gummy feeling in her eyes and watched her regiment advance across the browning stubble of harvested fields.

So far, everything was going according to the book. Each battalion was marching in a two-company column—with two companies side by side in the lead, followed by two more, and so on—and there was enough space between them that they could both deploy into line. The Royals, it had to be said, kept their formation a bit better than the Girls' Own, who were less used to maneuvering in the open, but on such easy ground even relative novices could keep their lines straight. Folsom and Graff led the two companies at the front, and even from where she sat, well ahead of the line, she could hear the steady beat of drums and Folsom's barked orders. At the head of each battalion, color parties carried blue Vordanai flags that snapped in the steady breeze.

Farther out, the rest of the Army of the East was emerging from the wooded ridge. That height, a long rill running roughly east-west, was perpendicular to the line of the advance. The land sloped down to a streambed, running too low this late in the season to be an obstacle, and then up again to a shallower ridge. From that modest elevation, where Winter was currently positioned, she could see that the fields ran downhill all the way to the Kos, visible as a ribbon of silver in the middle distance.

The ridge was too far from the river for the Deslandai to contest it with more than a few scouts, who took off at a run when they saw the blue-uniformed line advancing. Winter guessed it was more than a mile from the edge of the town, which was a neat cluster of shingled and whitewashed buildings, like a larger version of the little villages they'd been passing by. Tiny figures scurried everywhere, wearing flame-colored yellow-orange jackets darker than the bright yellow of their Hamveltai allies. At this distance, they looked like a swarm of colorful insects.

Her regiment was on the far right, at the eastern end of the Vordanai line. To her right, there was only a battery of artillery, moving laboriously uphill as the horses strained at their limbers, and a few squadrons of cavalry keeping pace at a walk. On her left, another regiment, this one in three battalion columns, was working its way up the ridge. Beyond that was another, and another, with still more following in reserve and cannon interspersed at intervals. *Forty thousand men make for an impressive array.* On the march in separate columns, it was easy to forget how big the Army of the East actually was, six or seven times larger than the whole Colonial force Janus had led in Khandar.

Winter shaded her eyes, searching the line for a familiar flag. The Colonials had become something like Janus' personal guard and his most reliable troops, following him into battle and doing the jobs he could trust to no one else. Ordinarily, they would be in place at the very center of the line, but either they weren't there or some trick of the ground was hiding them. *Maybe he's holding them out of sight as a reserve.* She shook her head and turned back to more immediate problems.

She and Edgar, with Bobby and Cyte mounted and waiting nearby, now occupied roughly the position Janus had ordered her regiment to take. The ground was mostly harvested fields, with only the occasional rocky outcrop or hedgerow to disturb the smooth order of the advancing lines. A few hundred yards ahead, where a tiny stream emerged from the earth and trickled down toward the river, there was a small cluster of buildings—a sprawling one-story farmhouse and a couple of barns, surrounded by a white waist-high fence. A few chickens were visible in the yard, but nothing else moved; the farmers had either fled or hidden in a cellar.

For a moment, waiting for her troops to mount the slope, Winter felt a strange peace. Men and women were about to die in large numbers—she herself could die, with no more warning than the scream of a cannonball—but it somehow seemed unreal, inappropriate for this picturesque valley with its perfect little town and gently winding river. She felt as if the morning had reached this moment and gotten stuck, as though they'd all been frozen into a painting.

"Sir?" Bobby said.

"Hmm?" Winter blinked and looked around. The columns had reached the top of the hill, and the peace was broken by the close-up roll of the drums and the shouts of the sergeants. While the front two companies of each battalion waited in place, the rest of the column split down the middle, each company marching sideways enough to clear the one in front of it and then forward until it was level with the rest. That was the theory, anyway. The Royals did a passable job, but the companies of the Girls' Own tended to misjudge the distances and end up overlapping or too far apart. Lieutenants gestured imperiously while sergeants swore and screamed and shoved women to where they were supposed to be standing. In a few minutes, the regiment made a nice neat line, blue-on-blue uniforms on the Royals to her left and blue-jackets-on-whatever-they-could-find among the Girls' Own to her right.

"Not too bad," Winter said. "Bobby, go and tell Captain Sevran I want a word. Cyte, would you fetch Jane?"

"Sir!" The two lieutenants saluted and rode off in opposite directions.

Jane arrived almost immediately, apparently having been headed to see Winter to begin with. Winter felt silly, looking down at her from horseback, so she swung herself off Edgar and acknowledged Jane's salute with a nod.

She found Jane's cool green stare oddly disconcerting. They hadn't been able to exchange more than a few words since the incident with Novus; Winter had thought she'd detected a little thawing in Jane the night before, but now she had no idea where they stood. *Where we stand is as colonel and captain, on the battlefield. We can figure the rest out later.*

"We're in position, sir," Jane said, as though Winter couldn't see that for herself. "What happens now?"

"Now we wait," Winter said.

"Just wait?"

"We're where Janus wanted us. Unless the enemy does something, we stay put." Winter glanced over her shoulder toward the center of the line, where larger columns of Vordanai blue were gathering. "My guess is the first attack will be over that way, but with Janus, who knows? We just have to be ready."

"Yes, sir." Jane saluted again. "Is that all?"

Winter hesitated. She had the feeling Jane was looking for something from her, some gesture, but this was not the time or place, with half the army looking on. She gave a curt nod, though her stomach felt as if she'd swallowed a hot coal. Jane turned around and stalked back toward the Girls' Own.

Captain Sevran arrived a few moments later. He wore a fresh uniform, which looked as though it had come straight from the tailor, and carried a bronze spyglass tucked into his belt. His salute was rigidly correct.

"Sir!"

"Captain," Winter said. "Well deployed."

"Thank you, sir." Down in the valley, flame-colored dots were milling about in front of the town as the Deslandai made their preparations. Sevran watched them, his eyes distant.

"Is something wrong, Captain?"

"No, sir." Sevran hesitated. "Just . . . twitchy. This is my first honest-to-goodness battle."

Winter felt a surge of sympathy. She remembered what it had been like in Khandar, having memorized the Regulations and the manual of arms, but never having faced a real enemy. Sevran, a graduate of the War College, had spent his whole life training for exactly this moment, and now it had finally come. *"Twitchy" doesn't begin to describe it.*

"Well, things seem quiet enough for now," Winter said in what she hoped was a reassuring tone.

"Yes, sir." He pointed at the farmhouse. "Should we consider occupying that? It would make for a nice strongpoint."

"Not yet," Winter said. "We may not even be headed in that direction. Wait for the enemy to make a move. We'll see them coming in plenty of time—"

"Sir," Cyte broke in. "Something's wrong."

Winter and Sevran turned to follow her pointing finger. The artillery battery on their right had crossed the crest of the hill, but showed no signs of stopping. Winter squinted, trying to guess what they were up to.

"Hell," Sevran said. "Someone's got their position wrong. If they go too far, they're going to get bitten off."

Winter nodded. There were several squadrons of cavalry visible down behind the Deslandai line, and a battery of guns with no infantry support would be easy prey for horsemen.

"Bobby!" she shouted. When she appeared, Winter pointed to the wayward battery. "Ride over to that battery and tell the commander he's headed straight for the enemy. He needs to come back up to the crest of the ridge."

"Yessir!" Bobby saluted and dashed to find her horse. Sevran had his spyglass out, studying the Deslandai at the edge of the town.

"They're doing *something*," he commented. "There's more confusion than I'd expect if they were going to just dig in and wait. They'd have had everything prepared by now."

Winter watched Bobby mount up, then turned back to the town. As she did, there was a flash from a barricaded street and a billow of smoke, followed by a shower of dirt as the cannonball plowed into the hillside a hundred yards short of the advancing Vordanai line and well to her left. Then, belatedly, the distant *boom* of the shot echoed through the valley.

A battery of big twelve-pounders just at the crest of the ridge answered, flashes rippling across the ranked guns like fire racing up a fuse. With the advantage of height, they outranged their Deslandai counterparts, and the solid shot arced over the head of the advancing troops to plow into the streets of Gaafen. One hit the roof of a house and crashed through without slowing, blasting neat shingles in every direction. Another skipped merrily off the cobble-stones, raising sparks with every bounce as it bowled down the street and eventually smashed into the side of a house.

"We could sit here all day and blast them out," Sevran said. More Deslandai artillery was opening fire, but it was still falling short. "Janus has them ranged in nicely."

Winter shook her head. "The guns are too inaccurate at that range. It's easy enough to hit the *town*, but it's not the town that shoots back. Prying men out from behind barricades is much harder. This is just a little brisk warm-up."

Sevran shot her a glance that she had trouble reading at first. It was respect, she realized after a moment. For all that he'd been to War College to learn his trade, Winter was the one who'd already smelled the powder. She'd marched in a firing line as muskets and canister tore great gaps in it, and led a company in a screaming bayonet charge that swept the enemy from the field. *Someday I'll stop dreaming about it, too.*

"Sir!" Bobby, returning at a full gallop. Winter had to look farther down the slope to find the artillery battery, which hadn't slowed its advance. "Sir! They wouldn't listen!"

"Saints and martyrs," Winter swore. "Can't they see what they're riding into?"

"No, sir." Bobby reined up in a shower of dirt and pebbles. "There's a fold in the ground. It's hard to see from here. The captain in charge thinks the ridge he was supposed to stop on is still ahead of him."

"Did you get his name?" Sevran said.

"Captain Altoff, sir!"

Sevran rolled his eyes.

"You know him?" Winter said.

"A bit. He's a stiff-necked old dinosaur. Too proud by half. I'm not surprised he wouldn't listen to a volunteer lieutenant."

"Let me see that." Winter held out her hand for the spyglass, and Sevran handed it over. She swept it down until she found the Deslandai line, the yellow orange uniforms jumping into sharp relief. They were definitely forming up for something, battalions arranging themselves in columns, with cavalry lining up behind them. As of yet, they hadn't seen Altoff's battery, but once it came into view the horsemen would be on it before it had time to withdraw.

Winter swore again. "Balls of the Beast. I'm going over there. If he won't listen to a lieutenant, he'll damned well listen to a colonel. Cyte, with me. Bobby, tell Jane what's happening. Sevran, you've got command here until I get back. Where's my damned horse?"

*   *   *

"Sir," Captain Altoff said, "I protest. I was ordered to plant my battery on the ridge!"

Sweat was pouring down his face and soaking into his collar as he mopped at it ineffectually with a handkerchief. Altoff was a portly man who gave the impression he was gradually being blown up from within, like a paper balloon. This was particularly visible because his uniform had evidently been tailored in his younger and slimmer days. Now the buttons were straining with his girth, and the collar dug so tight into his neck that the veins stood out like a relief map.

"Yes," Winter said, pointing over her shoulder. "*That* ridge, there, where my regiment can support you."

"I won't have the range to hit anything from there!"

"If there's any shooting to be done, they'll come to us."

Altoff frowned. "I'll not have it said I kept my men out of a fight."

"If anyone blames you, I'll take responsibility. Will you please just get this battery turned around before we're knee-deep in enemy cavalry?"

The captain looked unhappy, but he jerked a nod at a nearby lieutenant, who started shouting at the drivers. Each gun was attached by its trail to its caisson, a cart that held spare ammunition and supplies, so that its muzzle pointed backward and down. Teams of four horses pulled the carts, with some of the gunners riding while others walked alongside. Getting them turned around was a laborious process that involved leading the teams by hand, and Winter watched and fretted while the men worked, expecting to see orange jackets coming over the fold at any moment. She breathed a sigh of relief when they were straightened out and headed in the right direction.

The crackle of musketry caught her attention. The cannoneers of both sides had continued their long-range argument, a distant rumble and thump that quickly became almost subliminal. This was different, sharp *cracks* coming from nearby. Winter turned to look, but the dip in the ground obscured most of the field from view. She could see smoke rising, though. Above that, the ranks of the Girls' Own were visible, but the space beside them on the ridge was empty.

"Cyte," she said, "where the hell are the Royals?"

Cyte turned her horse with her knees and shaded her eyes with her hands. "Don't know, sir."

Shit, shit, shit. Goddamn this idiot. "Altoff!"

"Sir?" The fat captain was climbing up onto a caisson.

"I'm going back to my men. Get your battery to the top of the ridge and wait for orders."

"Yes, sir," Altoff said, obviously put out. Winter couldn't spare him any more of her time. She snapped Edgar's reins, and he trotted back up the hill, Cyte trailing behind her.

Once they'd gained enough height to get a view of the town again, Winter paused. The musketry was coming from the little farm, and she could see the pink-white flare of muzzle flashes amid growing drifts of smoke. Blue-clad figures knelt behind the fence and rushed in groups across the courtyard, making for the farmhouse. More flashes from the windows told her that the place was occupied.

"That has to be Sevran," she said. "So why are the Girls' Own just standing there?"

Cyte shook her head. "No idea, sir."

Winter blew out a long breath. "All right. You go find Sevran, get a report, and get back here. I'll go get Jane and get him some support."

"Yes, sir!"

If Cyte was nervous about being ordered to go where the lead was flying, she didn't show it. She turned her horse about and headed for the farm. *She's changed,* Winter thought, watching her go. She was used to thinking of the ex-student as someone who added things up and did paperwork, for all that they'd fought side by side at the Vendre. *I think I've been selling her short.*

She shook her head and continued up the ridge. Jane was waiting in front of the Girls' Own, with Bobby standing anxiously beside her. The lieutenants of the battalion were gathered in a loose group nearby, Folsom standing out among the women like a tree trunk in a clump of ferns.

Winter was swinging out of the saddle before Edgar had a chance to stop, and he shifted uneasily underneath her and nearly dumped her on her face. She hit the ground in a crouch, and Bobby was at her side immediately.

"Are you all right, sir?" she said.

"I'm fine. What the hell is going on?"

"Ah—" Bobby looked back at Jane.

"Captain Sevran took it into his head to take the fight to the enemy," Jane said. She had a smug expression, like a cat that had gotten away with some mischief. "He took the Royals down to occupy the farm."

"I saw," Winter snapped. "So what are *you* doing here? Did he tell you to stay behind?"

"No, sir," Jane said. "But your instructions were to stay put. I didn't think Captain Sevran had a good reason to—"

Oh, saints and martyrs. "I left him in *command*," Winter grated. "If he ordered you forward, you should have damned well gone forward!"

"I don't take orders from him," Jane said, frowning. This was clearly not how she'd expected this conversation to go.

"You do if I fucking well tell you to," Winter said, her anger boiling over.

"Winter—"

"Don't!"

"Colonel Ihernglass," Jane said. "Do you think we could speak privately?"

"No, I don't," Winter said. "I think we will get this battalion down there this goddamned minute."

"I don't see what your hurry is," Jane said. "It's just a bunch of Royals. Remember what they did to *us*, last time? And Novus—"

Winter crossed the distance between them in two steps and grabbed Jane's collar, pulling her close. Her voice was low and fierce, for Jane's ears alone.

"You know I love you," she said. "And I know you're angry at me, and you're angry about what Novus did. I understand all that. But if you *ever* deliberately leave soldiers under my command in danger without a good reason,

I swear by Karis and all the saints I will ship you back to Vordan. I am *responsible* for every one of those men down there, just as much as I am for every woman up here."

"You think they'd come and help *us*?" Jane hissed back.

"Yes," Winter said. "Now come on." She raised her voice. "Follow me! At the double!"

"At the double!" Folsom bellowed, and the other officers took up the cry. The drums thrilled, and the women in the ranks shouted their approval. The line lurched into motion, erratic in places but still moving as a body in the direction of the farm.

Winter left Edgar behind—*no sense in making myself more of a target than I have to*—and scrambled to keep ahead of the advancing formation. A few moments later, Cyte reappeared, sliding off her own mount and hurrying to keep up.

"Sir, Captain Sevran says he saw an enemy formation trying to occupy the farm in advance of an attack. He decided the best way to stop them was to get there before they did."

Winter grimaced, but truthfully it wasn't a bad call. If the Deslandai really were going to launch an assault on this quarter of the field, it would be better to be behind the farm's walls and fences. *And if they get guns placed in there, we'd have a hell of a time staying on the ridge.*

"I take it things didn't go as planned," she said.

"No, sir. He got to the fence line and one of the barns, but the enemy has got the main house. He's tried two charges, but they can't get across the courtyard." Cyte gestured downslope. "And there's more of them coming, sir."

Winter looked and saw that she was right. The columns she'd seen forming earlier were advancing, at a measured pace. *At least four battalions, plus cavalry and guns. If we're dug in here, we've got a chance of turning them back.* She looked over the layout of the farm, rapidly considering. "Cyte, go back to Altoff. He knows you're with me now. Tell him he'd better listen or I'll have his hide. I need his guns down here, as quick as he can."

"Yes, sir!"

"Jane!"

"Sir?" Jane's tone was acid, and it sent needles through Winter's heart, but she ignored the feeling.

"Pick your best rider. Have her take Edgar and go back up along the ridge. Find Janus and tell him we're going to need help over here, sooner rather than later."

"Right." A little of Jane's anger seemed to dissolve. "Jennie! Up here!"

Winter turned back to the farm as Jane dealt with that. The area enclosed by the fence was roughly square, with a barn at the two right-hand corners and the farmhouse in the far left. The yard between, where the chickens had been, was now sown with a new crop of blue-uniformed bodies. Musketry rattled from behind the scanty cover of the fence, and muzzle flashes blazed from every window of the house and around the edges of the farther barn.

When Jane turned back to her, she was ready. "Take four companies and find Sevran. Tell him to wait ten minutes, then try the yard again. I'm going to take the other four and swing around the left, and we'll hit them from both sides at once."

Jane looked dubiously at the corpse-strewn yard. "I—"

"Don't fucking argue," Winter said. "You say 'Yes, sir' and then you damned well do it."

There was a dangerous light in Jane's green eyes. "Yes, *sir*," she said.

As she turned away, Winter felt her throat go thick. *Is this how I lose her? Screaming at her on some battlefield?* She swallowed hard and looked away.

Off to the left, the Vordanai center was in action against the town itself, musketry and cannon-fire intermingled to a dull roar. Winter barely spared them a glance, and gave the Deslandai troops approaching from the direction of the town scarcely more thought. They would be a problem in a half hour; what mattered now was getting through the next few minutes.

Bobby was at her side, and she'd taken Abby and Graff as well. They were a hundred and fifty yards from the farm, standing in the stubble of a shorn cornfield, while the other half of the Girls' Own marched on toward where Sevran's men were fighting.

"On my signal," Winter said, "we're going to run like hell. Don't worry about formation, and *don't* stop to fire. See the apple tree, where the fence runs close to the house?" She pointed. "That's where we're headed. Get to the fence, as close to that tree as you can, and get some cover. *Then* you can fire." She turned to Abby. "Get together twenty or so of your best, and keep them together. Fix bayonets. Once we've got someone keeping their heads down, we'll go over the fence and in the side door."

Abby saluted. Winter let her have a few minutes to choose her soldiers, then pointed again. "Remember, to the apple tree. Ready?"

There were shouts of assent from the Girls' Own. Three hundred young women in blue coats clutched loaded muskets. Winter eyed the farmhouse, where muzzle flashes still stabbed out toward Sevran's Royals. "Go!"

She ran, pounding across the soft dirt and crunchy, dead stubble. That many blue-coated figures couldn't help drawing the attention of the men in the house, and soon enough muskets were flashing in their direction, filling the air with the *zip* of flying lead. Winter heard the soft thump of balls hitting the earth, and the sharp *thock* as they found flesh and bone. Beside her, a woman's head snapped back, and she crumpled to the ground like a broken toy. Someone was screaming, the high-pitched wail of a girl for her mother. Winter's pulse roared in her ears.

It had looked as if it were only a little way to the fence, but the distance seemed to stretch on forever, telescoping with every step she took. Every window in the wall of the farmhouse blazed with hellish pink fire.

The fence appeared with such shocking suddenness that Winter nearly pitched herself over it. Instead she put her shoulder against it with a *thump*, feeling it vibrate as dozens of women joined her. The fence was only slats and boards, not much as far as cover went, but worlds better than nothing at all. Across it, the only thing between her and the house was the apple tree, a tall, spindly thing with wide-spreading branches and leaves already yellowing at the edges.

From either side of her came the blast of close-up musketry, and smoke billowed all around. Only twenty yards separated the two sides, and at that distance the fire was murderous. There weren't enough windows for more than a dozen of the enemy to fire, against several hundred of the Girls' Own, but they had the advantage of better cover and a safe place to load.

Beside Winter, a stout older woman—one of the Docks people, she vaguely remembered—crawled the last few feet to the fence, musket in her hands. She pushed herself up onto one knee, shouldered the weapon, and aimed, but a Deslandai musket *cracked* and the woman spun away, clutching a bloody, shattered hand. Winter snatched up her musket and put it to her own shoulder, sighting on a yellow-orange shape. The weapon delivered its well-remembered kick to her shoulder, and she had the satisfaction of seeing the Deslandai drop out of sight with a scream.

More Girls' Own soldiers were reaching the fence, putting out a steady fire that made the Deslandai reluctant to risk standing at the windows. Glancing over her shoulder, Winter could see bodies sprawled along the path they'd taken, but only a few. Their position was not one that could be maintained for long, though, not with Deslandai reinforcements on the way.

Now, Jane. Smoke was boiling along the fence, filling the space under the apple tree. *Now, now, now.*

Hoarse shouting rose from the other side of the farmhouse, and Winter caught both men's and women's voices raised in battle cries. The sound of firing from that direction suddenly intensified.

"Hold fire unless you've got a clear shot!" Winter shouted to her own men. "Abby, your squad, with me! Over the fence!"

Abby gestured, and two dozen women, bayonets already fixed to their muskets, surged to their feet and clambered over the waist-high barrier. Balls zipped around them, *thok-*

*thok-thok*ing in the dry earth. A tall, gangly young woman took one high in the chest and flopped forward over the fence, hanging across it like a sheet set out for drying as her blood gushed across the whitewash. The women who'd remained behind fired at every sight of yellow-orange, and the wood around the windows of the house was rapidly being torn to splinters by misses and ricochets.

Having cleared the fence, Winter led Abby's squad at a dead run across the open ground under the tree, smoke parting around them like a wake. There was a side door in the center of the farmhouse wall, and she aimed for that, throwing herself flat against the plaster wall. Abby was right behind her, along with another redheaded girl Winter didn't know who wore sergeant's pips. The others spread out along the wall, out of sight of the windows.

Winter was thinking quickly. The windows were high and narrow—no getting in that way without being an easy target. That left the door, but they'd be waiting inside.

"First six, into the doorway, but only on my signal," she said. Balls clattered and *cracked* all around her, and Jane's attack in the main yard was well under way. *Hopefully, the Deslandai are spread thin.* "Next six, wait half a minute, then follow. I don't want us jammed up in there. Remember, wait till I say!"

Winter got nods or grunts of assent. She edged beside the door and lifted her borrowed musket, butt first. Back still to the wall, she swung it inward as hard as she could, slamming the wooden butt against the door right above the latch. The farm door, never designed to stand that kind of abuse, gave way with a crash, and Winter snatched her arm out of the way. Just in time—at least three men inside fired, balls whining past the tips of her fingers.

"Go!" Winter shouted. "Before they can reload!" *And hope none of them held their shots.*

One had. One of Abby's soldiers leapt into the doorway, and another musket *cracked* from inside, catching her in the belly and sending a spurt of blood and gore out the small of her back. She crumpled with a moan, and the woman next to her leaned into the doorway and fired.

Someone inside screamed. Abby went next, stepping over the writhing woman. Her sergeant stayed beside her, and Winter followed.

She had time only for brief impressions. There was a single hallway, leading to a T-junction with a larger hall that went from the back to front of the house. Doorways led in both directions, to what had been a kitchen and a dining room, and Abby's soldiers burst through them. More shots and more screams followed, along with the clash of steel on steel.

Two Deslandai came around the corner from the back of the house, bayonetted muskets in hand. Smoke still trickled from the barrels, and they gaped at the sight of the Vordanai women. One of them clawed at his belt, where Winter saw he had a pistol. At this range, he could hardly miss, so she didn't give him a chance to fire—she charged, tossing her own spent musket aside and clawing the sword from her belt. The Deslandai boy raised his bayonet to spit her, but at the last moment Winter twisted adroitly aside and let the momentum of her run carry her blade into his ribs. He folded up, gurgling, and she jerked the weapon free.

The other Deslandai backpedaled rapidly into the corridor. Winter waved at the hall behind her, where more of Abby's squad were coming in. "After them! With me!"

She turned the corner without waiting to see if they followed. A musket *cracked*, and wood exploded from the ceiling over her head. Another Deslandai, a young man with a downy beard and wide, terrified eyes, stared at her through the cloud of powder smoke from his missed shot. Winter crossed the distance between them in three strides, batted his bayonet away, and sank her sword in his throat.

Abby, coming up rapidly behind her, shouted a warning. Winter looked to her right as the young man crumpled, and found another door leading into a room full of yellow-orange uniforms. There were three of them, two more carrying muskets and an officer, gold epaulets gleaming, in the act of drawing his sword.

Abby's musket *cracked*, deafening in the tight space, and

one of the soldiers spun away. She charged at the other, and he parried crosswise with his own weapon. Her momentum drove them against the wall of the room, grappling and struggling for the locked muskets. It gave the officer a golden opportunity to plunge his sword into Abby's guts from behind, so Winter stepped forward with a slash that forced him to back off, raising his guard. He dropped into a fighting stance, weight low, eyes confident.

Winter had never been much of a duelist. It wasn't a skill that came up in the thick of battle, where opportunities to match skills against a comparably armed opponent were uncommon. Now, doing exactly that, she ventured another thrust at the Deslandai officer and watched him effortlessly flick her blade away and riposte with a strike that she avoided only by dancing clumsily backward. It came to her that she was going to die, right here, in the next few *seconds*. She could see by the officer's eyes that he knew it, too.

The red-haired sergeant rounded the doorway, bayonetted musket in hand, paused a moment, then went after the enemy officer. He swept her thrust away, then turned and parried a cut from Winter, shouting what had to be Hamveltai obscenities. Winter gestured at the sergeant to move right, spreading out to get through the officer's guard, and the woman nodded.

Whoever their enemy was, he was an experienced fighter. Rather than wait to be surrounded, he rushed at Winter, sword cutting downward in a desperate two-handed blow. When the sergeant thrust her bayonet at his back, he sidestepped, pulling his blade back from Winter's parry and leaving her stumbling and overbalanced. Before she could step back, he lashed out with the hilt, a vicious short jab that drove the heavy metal pommel into her temple.

Black stars flashed behind Winter's eyes, and she stumbled away, legs suddenly wobbling underneath her. The officer spun to engage the sergeant, who tried to slash at him with her bayonet and cut nothing but air. He extended his front leg in a textbook lunge and spitted her through the belly. The sergeant dropped her musket and closed her hands around the blade where it had gone in, making mewling, gasping sounds. The Deslandai pulled the weapon free, and she sank to the floor, curled around a spreading bloodstain.

The officer whipped his sword around, sending a line of hot red blood across the floor, and turned back to Winter. He stepped forward, and Winter realized her own sword was lying on the floor, fallen from nerveless fingers. Blackness nibbled the corners of her visions, and her head pulsed with agony with every heartbeat. She wondered if he'd cracked her skull.

The man regarded her curiously, then looked back to the sergeant and shook his head.

"You Vordanai," he said, speaking with a heavy accent. "I never kill a woman before."

He sighed, and raised his sword. Before it could fall, there was movement in the doorway, and the man's head turned. Winter got a glimpse of a blue uniform, and then Bobby stepped into the room.

"Winter!" she shouted, looking around. The Deslandai officer stepped into his swing, a heavy sideways cut at head level. Bobby looked up, far too late to bring her musket up to parry, and brought her left hand up into the path of the blade.

Her fingers closed around the steel. Winter, watching as though in a dream, saw blood well where the edge bit into Bobby's palm, but she effortlessly brought the stroke to a halt. Before the startled officer could react, Bobby jerked the sword forward, tearing it from his grip. A twist of her fingers folded the thick metal in half as though it were made of paper.

The Deslandai could only stare, muttering something Winter didn't understand. Bobby dropped her musket and swung her fist square into the man's face, and there was a *crunch* like someone smashing a sack of raw eggs. The officer was slammed against the wall, his head spraying blood across the wood where it struck, his face a red ruin. He sank down, slowly, and did not move again.

Winter blinked. Everything was moving slowly now, so slowly. She watched Bobby pick up her sword and run to where Abby was struggling with the other soldier, cutting the Deslandai down from behind. Then she blinked, and when her eyes opened, Bobby's face filled her vision. Her voice clanged in Winter's ears, as though they were underwater.

". . . all right? Sir? Are you all right?"

"I'm . . ." Winter wanted to say that she was fine, but the effort of speaking was apparently the last straw. The darkness that had been marshaling its forces in the corners of her eyes surged up again, with a pain like her skull being split open. Falling into unconsciousness was a welcome relief.

Chapter Nine

MARCUS

Marcus spent the rest of the day after his trip to Exchange Central looking over his shoulder, and went to sleep in the full expectation of being awoken by the news that Twin Turrets was under siege. All through the next day, Lieutenant Uhlan and his Mierantai maintained a high alert, and Marcus insisted Raesinia remain inside, no matter how eager she was to deliver their stolen book to Cora.

He passed the time by putting his new recruits through their paces. Ranker Feiss, whose first name turned out to be Hayver, went through the manual of arms with a stiff-armed precision that spoke of time spent on the drill field but little else. Andy—Marcus still had a hard time thinking of her as "Ranker Dracht"—was much smoother, working the musket and ramrod with a fluidity that spoke of real experience, and the missing fingers on her right hand seemed to make little difference. There was nowhere on the grounds safe to fire live balls, but she claimed to be a decent shot, and watching her work, he was prepared to believe it. Even Uhlan, as taciturn as all Mierantai seemed to be, gave a grunt of approval.

The following day, when no official retribution for their theft materialized, Marcus relaxed sufficiently to be convinced that a trip to Mrs. Felda's to deliver the books to Cora wasn't too great a risk. Raesinia, straining at the leash to depart, stomped up and down the front hall while Marcus spoke to Uhlan and arranged an escort. Before he was finished, the front door opened, and the young Mierantai ranker who had the watch appeared.

"Sir?" he said. "Got a note for you. Army boy delivered it."

"Give it here," Marcus said. Janus was unlikely to use a regular army courier—messages from Willowbrook came via Mierantai messenger or more circuitous routes—but stranger things had happened.

When Marcus broke the army-blue seal on the single page and unfolded it, however, he found not Janus' neat handwriting but the blockier script produced by the Preacher.

> Colonel d'Ivoire—
>   Need to speak with you, most urgent matter. Come at once.
>
> > By the Grace of God,
> > Captain S. Vahkerson

"Damn," Marcus said. Raesinia stepped up beside him and read the note, frowning.

"That's awfully mysterious of him," she said. "This is your friend from the artillery, isn't it?"

Marcus supposed that one did not upbraid the Queen of Vordan for being nosy. "Yes. We call him the Preacher, though not to his face. But it's not like him to be so circumspect." The Preacher had more sense than, say, Give-Em-Hell, but a man who spent his life around cannon was unlikely to make subtlety his watchword.

"Are you sure it's from him?"

"It's definitely his handwriting," Marcus said, feeling another burst of paranoia. He examined the seal, which bore the imprint of the Royal Artillery, and didn't show visible tampering. "I can't imagine anyone forcing him to write it."

"Maybe he was worried who else might read it."

"Maybe. As far as I know, all he's doing is training new artillery officers."

Raesinia hummed thoughtfully. "Are you going to go?"

"I should." He looked down at her and sighed. "Lieutenant Uhlan, would you please escort Raesinia to Oldtown? I'll take Hayver and Andy to the University."

"Of course, sir," the Mierantai officer said.

"And be careful." It was just barely possible this was some plot to separate the two of them, though that was stretching suspicion a bit far. "Make sure you aren't followed."

Uhlan gave him an "I'm not an idiot" look, but forbore to comment. Marcus watched him and three more Mierantai riflemen follow Raesinia outside, then went in search of the two rankers.

"I didn't know you were friends with Captain Vahkerson, sir," Hayver said as the carriage rattled along Second Avenue toward the Dregs.

Andy gave him a withering look. "They were captains together in the Khandarai campaign under Janus."

"And for years beforehand, under Colonel Warus," Marcus said, only half paying attention to the conversation. He peered out the carriage window, searching the street behind them for some sign of a tail. It was futile, not just because Marcus' knowledge of espionage was minimal, but given that their carriage was one of the only horse-drawn vehicles still on the road, a blind man could follow their trail.

Most of the traffic was pedestrian, but not all. The citizens of Vordan's South Bank, ever resourceful, had begun hitching themselves to light carts and offering rides to the affluent Northsiders. Marcus watched several of these strange vehicles go past, and shook his head. Human adaptability never failed to surprise him; enough time could make even the strangest situation routine. *Just look at us in Khandar, before the Redeemers turned everything upside down and the Steel Ghost started raising hell.*

He shook his head and looked back at Hayver. "How do you know the Preacher, anyway? Were you in artillery training?"

The boy shook his head. "After the battle, some of the wounded were transferred to the University hospital. Captain Vahkerson would come around to read to us from the *Wisdoms*."

Andy rolled her eyes. Marcus, who had sat through a few of the Preacher's readings, was inclined to agree, but he did his best not to show it.

"What do you think he wants, sir?" Hayver said.

"I have no idea," Marcus said.

"I bet," Andy said, "it has something to do with that."

She pointed out the other window, and Marcus leaned over and looked ahead as the carriage slowed. They had crossed the Dregs and come onto the grounds of the University itself, where the curving cobbled road led across the fields, past the various outbuildings, and up to the walled compound that was the ancient core of the institution. There it passed through the pompously titled Gateway of Wisdom, a tall arch of stone that was another of Farus V's affectations. The great iron gates were ornamental, bracketed to the wall and never closed to demonstrate that the pathway to wisdom would never be barred—though the faculty *had* been forced to barricade the gateway at times.

If the gate was ornamental, the wall was decidedly not. It was old stone, twelve feet high and topped with rusty iron spikes. It dated from a time when the citizens of Vordan would periodically take it into their heads to burn the scholars of the University for sorcery, though nowadays it was more useful for keeping unruly students away from the taverns of the Dregs.

Today, though, the wall was again serving its original function. A mob had gathered outside the Gate of Wisdom, mostly Southside laborers by their clothes but a few better-dressed young Northside men mixed in. They all seemed to be shouting at once, producing an incomprehensible babble, from which the occasional disjointed phrase emerged.

"—spies! They're all spies—"

"Turn them over!"

"Spike! To the Spike!"

A line of Patriot Guards with halberds kept the crowd out of the University. There were only a dozen of them, spread thin across the broad gateway, and Marcus could see only fear and force of authority was keeping the mob back. A concerted rush would batter the guards to the ground, halberds or no.

"Hell," Marcus said, rapping on the front panel to alert the driver. "Stop here."

"Sir?" The driver, one of the Mierantai servants from Twin Turrets, had the same harsh accent as Uhlan and the others.

"We'd better not try to push through that." Marcus opened the door. "We'll go on foot from here and make our own way back. Take the carriage back to the house."

"Yes, sir."

Marcus couldn't tell if the driver was relieved to hear this or no. Hayver definitely blanched, though.

"Right," Marcus said as the carriage wheeled around. "Stay close, you two." He looked at Andy as he said it, and she gave him a grim smile.

"I grew up in the Docks, sir. I know my way around a mob."

Hayver stepped in close to Marcus' right side as he led the way to the gate. "What do you think they're so angry about, sir?"

"Damned if I know. I expect we'll find out."

That was their last coherent bit of conversation before they plunged into the shouting, gesticulating mass of humanity. No one attempted to bar their way, but people were packed so tight Marcus had to elbow and shove to make any progress. While Marcus hadn't grown up in the Docks, he *had* spent years in Ashe-Katarion, a city that considered orderly queues a dangerous foreign invention, so he was no stranger to the art of strong-arming his way through a press. Hayver trailed in his wake while Andy made solid progress of her own on the other side.

As they got closer to the front, the shouting got a little more coherent. The crowd, kept a few paces back from the line of guards by the lowered halberds, shouted insults and curses.

"You should be fucking ashamed! Protecting Sworn scum!"

"Out of the way!"

"They can't hide in there forever!"

Marcus shoved a particularly obnoxious ranter out of the way and secured a place in the front rank. He paused to make sure his escort was still with him—Hayver had one hand on the back of his coat, while Andy was rubbing her elbow with a satisfied expression—then stepped forward, sliding between two protruding halberds. The guards, seeing his uniform and the eagles on his shoulders, looked at one another uncertainly.

"I need to get through," Marcus shouted, over the roar of the crowd.

"I've got orders to keep the public out!" one the guards shouted back.

"I'm not the public," Marcus snapped. "I'm Colonel Marcus d'Ivoire, personal liaison to General Janus bet Vhalnich."

The guard exchanged a glance with his nearest companion, and then stepped aside, lowering his halberd. Marcus moved through the gap, towing Hayver and Andy, and sidestepped to allow the guard to get back into line. The crowd roared its disapproval.

"Down with army traitors!"

"To the Spike with all the officers!"

"Shame! Shame!"

Marcus would have liked to question the Patriot Guards about what was happening, but they were fully occupied. Beyond the Gateway of Wisdom, the University was a maze of ancient stone buildings and courtyards, built out and added to haphazardly over the centuries. Marcus had only the vaguest idea of the layout, and he stood looking at the mess with a sinking heart. On his previous visits, he'd always asked a passing student for directions, but the near riot at the gate was apparently keeping everyone inside. The lanes and courtyards he could see were deserted.

"I know the way, sir," Hayver said, guessing the problem. "You do?"

"Yes, sir. I spent a fair bit of time wandering around on crutches while I waited for my leg to mend. Captain Vahkerson's offices are over in the Old Bully."

"Lead the way, then."

Hayver headed off down a lane at a confident walk. Evidently, being asked to lead made him feel buoyant, because as they went he pointed out various ancient landmarks and structures along the way and explained their origins and nicknames. Marcus soon learned more than he ever wanted to know about the Vermillion Hall, Bungo's Ass, the Three Virgins, and other minutiae of University life.

"Where did you learn all this stuff?" Andy said as they passed a cracked, faceless statue that, for some reason lost in the mists of time, was called the Pole-Vaulter.

"While I was in the hospital," Hayver said, looking suddenly apologetic. "I had a lot of time on my hands."

"I spent most of my time in bed with a fever," Andy said. "But still!"

"I just talked to people." He shrugged shyly. "I like finding things out."

"Remind me to introduce you to Fitz someday," Marcus said. "I think you'd get along."

"Here we are, sir." Hayver gestured to another long, low building, covered in wilted, browning ivy. "The Old Bully. I think the captain is on the second floor."

The doors—heavy oak studded with iron, looking as old as the University itself—were solidly closed. Marcus rapped as loud as he could, then rubbed his knuckle.

"Yes?" said a nervous voice from inside. "Who is it?"

"Colonel Marcus d'Ivoire," Marcus said. "I'm here to see Captain Vahkerson. He asked for me."

A whispered conversation took place behind the door, and then there was the squeal of a rusty bolt being drawn. The door swung inward, revealing dusty, gloomy darkness. Two young men in the traditional black robes of University students stood behind it, squinting in the daylight.

"He's upstairs," one of the students said. "Come in, quick. I have to bolt the door."

That took quite a bit of effort, the young man grunting as he forced the rusty bolt closed. He looked at his palms afterward and frowned.

"Cut myself," he said, wiping away a little trickle of blood.

"Bad essence in rusty metal," the other said. "Better clean it out. Argvine pollen and honey—"

"Don't be stupid. De Calabris says argvine pollen makes things worse—"

"De Calabris wouldn't know a bone saw from a tooth pick. All his really good work was done after Effartes joined his salon, and he was clearly cribbing."

"Oh, if you're so fond of Effartes, why don't you suck his fucking cock?"

"Better him than de Calabris. He died of quicksilver sores—"

"Excuse me," Marcus said. "Medical students, right?"

"That's right," the first student said, rubbing at his lacerated palm. He appeared to notice Hayver and Andy for the first time, and his cheeks flushed. "Oh. Sorry for the language, miss."

"Please," Andy said. "I could swear in five languages by the time I was ten."

"Which five?" Hayver said.

"Would you *please*," Marcus interrupted, "tell me where Captain Vahkerson is?" He'd raised his voice a little, but he was still surprised to find all four of them staring at him. He cleared his throat.

"Also," he went on, "I'd like to know what the . . ." He paused, glancing at Andy, and then deliberately went on: ". . . what the *hell* is going on outside. If you wouldn't mind."

The University's vaunted gas lamps were shut off, and all the windows had heavy curtains drawn across them. They made their way down the corridor by the light that leaked past the heavy cloth. Paintings hung on the walls, darkened and anonymous, and here and there sculptured busts or ornamental tables made for dangerous obstacles.

"It all started," said the first student, whose name was Norman, "with one of those awful broadsheets."

"*The New Patriot*, it calls itself," said the other, who was called Geoff.

"Somebody got their hands on the University records—"

"Probably bribed the bursar, the man could have given Rackhil Grieg lessons—"

"—and found out that there were a bunch of foreigners still here."

"Most of the students left when all this started," Geoff explained. "And a lot of the rest volunteered for the army. That's why they put Captain Vahkerson's gunnery school here, and moved the casualties who need long-term care into our hospital. There was plenty of space. It's mostly just us medical types left."

"Along with a few foreigners who couldn't go home or didn't want to. They're not *spies*." Norman gave a disgusted snort. "But this *New Patriot* person started giving the mob ideas, and before long they're convinced we've got a whole nest of conspirators in here."

"What's that got to do with Captain Vahkerson?" Marcus said.

"Well, the thing is, there's nobody really in charge around here anymore," Norman said. "The master and his people took off during the revolution, and now the bursar's locked himself in his cellar and won't see anybody. Captain Vahkerson's the only one willing to give orders, so people are listening to him."

"He does have a talent for being obeyed," Marcus muttered.

"He's using Professor Indica's office, since it's got a good view of the gate," Geoff said. "Here. Captain? I've brought Colonel d'Ivoire."

The door, one of many identical doors on the second-floor corridor, was so dark with multiple coats of resin that it looked as though it might be made of iron. It opened, and to Marcus' surprise a young woman stood behind it. It was the girl he'd seen at Farus' Triumph with the Preacher, her dress still severe, her tight hairstyle showing some signs of coming apart at the edges.

"Colonel!" the Preacher said. "It's all right, Viera. The colonel's here to help." The Preacher strode over. The office was a large one, with a full table and chairs in addition to a massive desk and liquor cabinet. In the back wall, a large multipaned window was covered by a curtain, and three more students were clustered around it, peering through a narrow gap.

"Captain," Marcus said. "I came as quickly as I could. It looks like you're having some problems."

"Not really my problems, in truth, but I can't just leave 'em be. Did Norman and Geoff fill you in?"

"Somewhat. How many foreigners have you got here?"

"Just Viera and the three lads over there. She's one of mine, and the other foreigners are all medical types." The Preacher's bearded face clouded over. "I'll not hand any of 'em over to be spiked, you understand? It'd be plain murder."

A woman cannoneer? Marcus looked at Viera, who stared back at him icily.

"I don't suppose you happened to bring about a company of grenadiers with you?" the Preacher said.

"Just the two you sent me. I didn't know we'd be standing a siege."

He wished, momentarily, that he'd brought Uhlan and his men—if it *did* come to a fight, the veteran Mierantai riflemen would have been a reassuring weight on his side. *Then again, if it comes to shooting down unarmed civilians in the street . . .* He shied away from the thought.

"I thought as much," the Preacher said. "How many do you figure at the main gate?"

"Maybe five hundred," Marcus said.

"There's more now," one of the boys called from the window. "At least a thousand. They're going crazy!"

"Listen." The Preacher stepped closer and spoke quietly. "We've got to get these lads out of here. It's only a matter

of time before someone decides to push through those
Patriot Guard. I need your help."

"You've got it, but I'm not sure what you want me to do."

"If we can get them off the campus . . ." The Preacher
eyed Marcus sidelong. "I hear tell that you're sneaking
Hamvelts and Borels out of the city."

Cora's refugees. Marcus thought he'd been careful.
Cargo ships left every day for the front, with army crews,
and he'd impressed on them the need for silence about
their extra cargo. The name of Janus bet Vhalnich was
one to conjure with, as he'd found at the Gateway of Wisdom, and mentioning that this was all part of the general's
plan was usually enough to secure enthusiastic coopera-
tion. It made Marcus feel guilty, but only a little. *Janus
would certainly approve, if he knew.*

They'd been sneaking the refugees out slowly, one family every few days. *But if the Preacher knows about it . . .*

"Don't worry too much," the Preacher said. "Nobody's
been telling tales. But sometimes I inspect those ships,
when we're sending cannon and powder, and I saw something I shouldn't have. A few of the boys admitted it when
I asked them, on the condition that I keep it quiet."

"They shouldn't have even done that," Marcus grumbled. But he couldn't bring himself to be too angry—the
Preacher could be very persuasive.

"You're doing God's work, keeping those women and
children from the Spike. You must be keeping them somewhere beforehand, so I thought if we could sneak this lot
over the walls, then you could get them away to wherever
the hideout is."

Balls of the Beast. This is not what I signed up for. Marcus sighed. "We could probably manage it. But are you
really sure this is necessary? It seems like—"

"They're breaking in!" one of the young men at the window shouted. He had a broad Borelgai accent.

"What?" The Preacher whirled and sidestepped the
desk, pushing the students aside. "What happened to the
Patriots?"

"They just . . . left," said one of the other students. "I

was watching. Someone came to talk to them, and they just marched away!"

Marcus was only a step behind the Preacher, tugging the curtain farther aside. The window had a view of one of the main avenues through the maze of courtyards, ending in the Gateway of Wisdom. The halberds of the Patriot Guard were indeed nowhere to be seen, and the crowd grown considerably since they'd passed through—had flooded past the walls out of sheer momentum. They milled in the first courtyard, uncertain what to do with their sudden victory, but before long a new wave of arrivals seemed to infuse the mob with a sense of purpose. Large groups fanned out in every direction, waving sticks, cudgels, and other impromptu weapons.

"Saints and *fucking* martyrs," Marcus swore.

"Why would the guards leave?" said one of the students, this one Hamveltai. "Oh God." He lapsed into his native language, muttering to himself. Another young man, who looked enough like him that Marcus guessed they were brothers, put an arm around his shoulders and spoke to him quietly in the same tongue.

"The Directory wishes to throw us to the mob," Viera said. It was the first time she'd spoken, and her voice was as clipped and precise as her appearance. Her accent was hard for Marcus to place, with the Hamveltai tendency to turn *W*'s into *V*'s but without the broad vowels.

"Why would they do that? We swore to their inspector we were loyal to nothing but knowledge!"

"I do not think they care what we swore," Viera said. She turned away from the window. "Colonel d'Ivoire. Do you have somewhere we can hide?"

"I might," Marcus said, eyes still tracking the mob. "The problem is going to be getting off the grounds. There's plenty of them still left at the gate."

"There's the Porter's Gate on the north side," the Preacher said. "But that's locked up tight. I had hoped we could rig some kind of rope ladder to go over the walls—"

"We don't have the time," Viera said.

"What about the Students' Gate?" Hayver said.

Marcus turned, startled. He'd forgotten the two rankers were there. Andy still stood by the door, looking nervous, but Hayver had stepped forward.

"There isn't a Students' Gate," said the Preacher.

"I have never heard of one," Viera said.

Hayver shrank a bit, cheeks burning. Marcus caught his eye and nodded encouragingly, and that seemed to hearten him.

"It's not really a gate," he said. "It's a bit of a secret, really. Passed down among the older students. There's a spot on the south wall where there are holes in the brickwork, under the ivy. You can climb over, and then some of the iron spikes come off."

"How do you know this?" Viera demanded.

"I . . . talked to people. While I was here. One of the men in the hospital with me was a student who'd gotten hurt at Midvale. He told me all about what it was like when he was here . . ." Hayver swallowed. "Before he died."

"Can you find this place?"

Hayver nodded. "Once I could get out of bed, I went to look for it. I know how to get there."

"Then what are we waiting around for?" Viera said.

"Wait," said the younger of the two Hamveltai. "Just wait a minute. If we go out there, if we run into them . . ."

"Maybe we should stay here. The Patriot Guards will be back eventually," the other said. "If we barricade the doors, perhaps we'll be safe."

"I wouldn't count on the Patriot Guard for anything," the Borelgai said.

"I'm forced to agree," Marcus said.

"Then maybe we could talk to them?" the younger brother said. "Someone must be willing to listen to reason—"

"Try it if you like," Viera snapped. "I for one am not willing to take a chance on gang rape and vicious execution. Colonel?"

Marcus eyed Viera curiously. If she was afraid, it didn't show in her face. Her eyes were still ice-cold. He gave a quick nod.

"She's right," he said. "We'll make a try for this Students' Gate, if Hayver's sure he can find it. If you want to stay, stay."

The Borelgai crossed immediately to Marcus' side of the room, beside Viera. The two Hamveltai fell into a heated discussion in their own language, and the Preacher edged closer to Marcus and spoke quietly.

"I'm going to stay behind," he said. "There's a whole hospital full of boys who can't be moved."

"They're not foreigners," Marcus said. "They should be safe, shouldn't they?"

"Maybe. But there's no telling what a mob will do when its blood is up." He shook his head. "Besides, there's the powder magazine to think of. If they take it into their heads to start torching the place . . ."

"God Almighty." Marcus hesitated. "Are you sure you'll be all right?"

"If the Lord wills it." The Preacher smiled. "I expect He will, though. That lot are all cowards at heart."

"All right." Marcus extended a hand, and the Preacher gripped it. "Send a runner when things die down so I know you're all right."

"I will. And if you could contrive to get a message to me, just to say that things worked out?"

Marcus nodded. "I'll find a circumspect route."

"Right." The Preacher looked at the window and grinned. "I feel like I'm back in Ashe-Katarion. Where's Janus when you need him, eh?"

In the end, the two Hamveltai—brothers named Karl and Fredrick—came along. The Borelgai student, Volaht, stuck close to Marcus' side. Hayver led the way, with Viera close beside him, while Andy had volunteered to bring up the rear.

"I'll take us out the back door," Hayver said. "There's a courtyard that connects to the Longer Hall, and from there we can stay indoors most of the rest of the way."

"What if they find us?" said Karl, the younger of the pair.

"Then keep your mouths shut and I'll try to reason with them," Marcus said.

"What if that doesn't work?"

"Then we run," Viera said.

They walked through the gloomy shadows of the Old Bully, Hayver turning corners and hurrying down stone-flagged passages without apparent hesitation. Marcus caught glimpses of comfortably furnished rooms, chairs drawn into circles or set around tables. Other doors opened onto tiled chambers like giant washrooms, with stained stone slabs. Surgeries, he guessed, or dissection rooms. *Or both.*

At the far end of the seemingly endless hallway was another big double door, closed and bolted. A little sound leaked in from the outside, and Marcus could hear shouts and the occasional tinkle of breaking glass. Now and then there was a *crunch* as something toppled, followed by a cheer.

"What are they doing?" said Volaht. "I thought it was us they're after. Why are they wrecking the place?"

"When a mob gets loose, it destroys whatever it finds to hand," Viera said.

"Oh God," Karl said, shrinking against the wall. "They'll kill us. We won't even get to the Spike. They'll tear us to pieces." He murmured prayers in Hamveltai, fast and nearly inaudible.

Marcus edged up to the curtain and twitched it back a half inch. There was a courtyard outside, longer than it was wide. Hedges ran around the outside, and a gravel path wound through a browning lawn. A small marble statue of a frolicking nymph had already been pushed off its plinth.

"Hayver," Marcus said. "Which way are we going?"

Hayver put his eye to the window while Marcus steadied the curtain.

"All the way across. Looks like the door's open."

Marcus looked again. At the other end of the courtyard, another pair of doors stood ajar.

"That's got to be a hundred yards," Marcus muttered.

"We'll never make it," Karl wailed.

"Will you shut up?" Andy spit.

She'd acquired a broomstick from somewhere along the way, a big one with a long, sturdy handle. She propped carefully against the wall and stomped on it, just above the head. The wood broke with an almighty *snap*, spraying splinters.

"I thought I said to be quiet!" Marcus said.

"Sorry, sir." Andy hefted the orphaned handle, now reduced to a serviceable club with a jagged, splintery point. "Thought it might be best to have something to hand."

Karl moaned again. Andy rolled her eyes.

"Leave him alone," Fredrick said. "He's too sensitive for this."

"All *right*," Marcus said. "I'll go first. Everyone stay close. Walk fast but *don't* run until I say. From a distance we're just another group of rioters, right?"

There was a chorus of assent. Viera walked to a small marble bust and lifted it, testing the weight.

"Your girl is right," she said when Marcus gave her a questioning look. "Best to be prepared."

Marcus shrugged. "Hayver, can you get that bolt?"

Hayver threw his weight against the rusty metal, and it moved with a squeal of complaint. The door opened, letting in daylight that cut through the shadows of the dusty hall like a knife, illuminating a swirl of dust motes. Marcus blinked a few times to let his eyes adjust, then started forward, trying to walk with confidence. He spared only a brief look over his shoulder to make sure the others were following.

The hundred yards to the other side of the courtyard stretched out beneath his feet, until he was certain he could feel the distance increasing with every step. Unbidden, his hand drifted to the hilt of his sword. He hadn't expected a fight, so he was the only one who'd brought a real weapon, but he didn't want to use it on what were, after all, civilians. *Let's hope it doesn't come to that. Nearly there.*

They'd crossed three-quarters of the distance when a party of shouting, laughing men entered the courtyard through one of the side paths. There were at least a dozen of them, and they pulled up short in shocked silence, taking in Marcus' army uniform and the students' robes.

"It's them!" one of the rioters shouted.

Now would be my chance to reason with them, Marcus thought, *and chide them for making unwarranted assumptions. Try to bluff our way out.* He took in the look on the man's face, the fury rising in his eyes.

"Run!" he shouted.

They ran. Andy and Hayver, in their uniforms, easily outdistanced the four scholars, who were slowed by their clumsy robes. Marcus stayed in the rear, ready to grab anyone who stumbled. He looked over his shoulder and found the rioters closer than he'd thought, practically on their heels. Spinning, he clawed his saber from its scabbard and raised it to block the way, bringing the first pursuer up short.

"Get him!" another shouted, pushing forward and swinging a wooden post like a club.

It would have been easy to skewer him, but Marcus wasn't ready for that, not yet. Instead he sidestepped the clumsy blow and rammed the saber's guard into the man's face, feeling bone crunch in his jaw. He dropped like a broken puppet, clutching his face and writhing in pain, and Marcus took advantage of the respite to backpedal. They were nearly to the door, Hayver standing beside it, white-faced.

"Marcus! They're inside!"

"Good!" Marcus turned his back on the rioters and edged past the ranker. "Close the door!"

"No, I mean—"

"Colonel!" Andy said. "A little help?"

Hayver dragged the door shut, plunging them back into gloom. Before the light vanished, however, Marcus saw another half dozen men, advancing down the corridor toward them.

They must have been inside already. No wonder the door had been open. Marcus swore and jogged forward, sword at the ready. Andy had her broken broom in a passable attempt at a guard position, and Viera stood behind her, clutching the marble bust. Karl and Fredrick were pressed against the wall while Volaht hovered uncertainly nearby.

"Out of the way!" Marcus bellowed in his best parade-ground voice. "These people are under the protection of the Royal Army of Vordan!"

"It's the Army of the Republic now," one of the men blocking the corridor spit back. He had what looked like the leg of a chair in one hand.

"Yeah, you work for us!" another said.

"Put the sword down!"

"Get out of the way," Marcus repeated. "I don't want to hurt any of you."

"Oh yeah, soldier boy?" said one of the men, from the safety of the rear of the back. "Gonna stab us?"

Marcus took a step forward. The man in the lead had the expression of someone comparing his chair leg to Marcus' polished steel and coming up short. He gave ground, pressing into the huddle behind him. Encouraged, Marcus took another step forward, flicking the point of his weapon forward until it was practically under the man's nose.

That was a mistake, he saw almost immediately. With his arm at full extension, he wasn't in a position to attack, and one of the smaller men lurking behind the leader sprang forward before he could recover. He got both hands on Marcus' wrist and pulled him sideways, slamming his hand into the stone wall of the corridor. Marcus' fingers exploded with pain, and his saber slipped away, clattering noisily on the floor.

"Get 'em!" the leader shouted.

The rioters rushed forward. Marcus, still clutching his hand, managed to stick his leg out to trip the nearest, sending him sprawling to the flagstones. Then the man who'd grabbed his hand was on top of him, wrapping his arms around Marcus' shoulders and trying to bear him to the floor. It was the move of someone who'd been in more drunken wrestling matches than honest-to-God street fights, and Marcus let him come close before driving a knee up hard into his groin. All the strength went out of his assailant, and he folded up like a damp cloth.

Andy, standing in the center of the corridor, met the rioters' rush head-on. The leader came after her with his chair leg, a clumsy overhand swing, and she moved neatly out of the way and cracked him on the back of the head with the end of the broom handle as he went past. The next man hesitated, pulling up short, but misjudged the distance—he ended up stopping at the perfect range for her to swing the broom into his face with all the leverage of three feet of solid wood. The *crunch* of his nose breaking was audible, and he tumbled bonelessly backward.

The last two rioters were big men, and they moved as though they'd fought together before. They spread out, one going left and one going right, and when Andy wound up to hit one of them, the other moved like a snake, grabbing her arm with both hands and locking her elbow behind her back. She gasped in pain and let the broom handle fall.

Marcus' right hand still hurt, badly enough that he was certain he'd broken something. He stepped up behind Andy's attacker, ready with a kick to the back of the knee that would have sent him sprawling, but something snagged his foot. He looked down to find the man he'd tripped grabbing his ankle, hanging on like a drowning man clutching a log. Marcus spun and kicked him in the side of the head, once and then again when he didn't let go.

One of the big men punched Andy, a hard blow across the face and then a jab to the chest that connected with a flat *thud*. He followed it up with a knee to the stomach, and she doubled over with a choking wheeze. The man holding her arm let go, turned around to face the others, and found the marble bust of a long-forgotten scholar coming down fast into his forehead. The blow dropped him with a sound like two billiard balls meeting.

The last rioter raised his fists, confronting Viera, who was still holding the bust and breathing hard. After a moment, Hayver joined her, holding his own fists up in a way that made it clear he didn't have the faintest idea what to do with them. Volaht stepped forward as well, face white as a sheet.

"That's *enough*," Marcus growled. He'd retrieved his sword, holding it awkwardly in his left hand, and he leveled it at the big rioter's throat, taking care to keep well out of range of a sudden grab. "Sit down and put your hands on the floor."

The man raised his hands in surrender, sliding down the wall to a sitting position. Marcus looked over the other rioters, but none of them seemed about to get up and renew the contest. Andy, curled in the fetal position, was alternately coughing and swearing imaginatively.

"Volaht, Viera, help Andy up. Hayver, is that door bolted?"

"Yes, sir," Hayver said, glaring at the sitting man.

"Then keep going. You know the way." He beckoned to Karl and Fredrick, who were huddled together against the wall. "Come on, you two. It's over."

As the brothers picked their way through the fallen, groaning men, and Andy was hauled to her feet, the sitting man's expression became a snarl. "Fucking foreign trash," he muttered. "Need a Vordanai girl to fight for you."

"May I hit him, Colonel?" Viera said.

"Please do," Marcus said. "We can't have him following us."

"Wait—" the man managed, before the marble bust came down again.

"Are you all right?" Marcus said as they hurried through the corridors of the Longer Hall as fast as Andy could manage.

"'M fine," she said. A bruise was already swelling over one cheekbone, and she spoke as if her mouth were full of cotton. "Had worse kickings than this."

"And delivered worse, I'd guess."

She gave a lopsided grin. "You have no idea."

"Through here!" Hayver said, standing beside another double door. "Looks clear."

There was another courtyard beyond, this one shaded by evergreens and heavy with the scent of pine. It was hard up against the outer wall, and more of the ubiquitous ivy grew across the brickwork. Marcus glanced nervously at the archways leading in either direction, but no rioters were in evidence. Sounds of breaking glass and shouts from elsewhere on campus indicated that the destruction continued.

"Here." Hayver rushed to the wall and fumbled with the ivy. "Some of the bricks are missing, I'll show you."

"I'll go over first," Marcus said. "Hayver, you bring up the rear. Andy, are you going to be all right?"

"I'll manage," Andy said. "Will you?"

Marcus tried flexing the fingers of his right hand. They hurt abominably, but they moved. He winced. "I think so."

"Two of the spikes at the top just come off if you pull on them," Hayver said.

Marcus looked up at the wall, which suddenly seemed quite formidable, and its spiky crown. "Right," he said.

Truthfully, the climb wouldn't have been at all difficult to someone who had full use of both hands. As Hayver had promised, there were handholds in the brickwork, and at the top Marcus was able to lift two of the iron spikes out of their sockets and set them aside. More bricks were missing on the other side, and he picked his way down, using his right hand as little as possible. By the time he dropped to the turf, Viera was already coming over, taking a moment to smooth her long skirts at the top before descending.

They followed, one by one. Marcus helped Andy to the ground after catching her wince as she bent to turn around at the top. Hayver, coming last, conscientiously replaced the two spikes before making his way down.

"Now what?" Fredrick said. He had one arm around his brother, who hadn't spoken since the fight in the hall-way. "Where are you taking us?"

"Oldtown," Marcus said. "But you'll need to ditch the robes first, or we'll be followed."

"They'll be watching the road to the west," Viera said.

"I know. We'll go south to the Old Ford. It'll be a bit wet, but we'll get across."

"We're going to *wade* the river?" Fredrick said. "Don't be ridiculous."

"If you'd care to head in any other direction, be my guest." Marcus gestured south. "Come along, if you're coming."

They all followed, of course. The University grounds outside the walls were grassy hillsides dotted with a few small trees, descending gradually until they met the river. The Vor was placid here, only a foot or two deep and broad enough that it might have been a lake. Long before the network of bridges to and from the Island had been built, the Old Ford had planted the seed of Vordan City, the medieval village whose bones still lay underneath Oldtown.

It didn't come to actually wading the river. A number of enterprising bargemen sold their services to those who had cargoes to bring across and couldn't afford a cart, poling their shallow-bottomed craft just barely above the gravel of the riverbed. Marcus herded his charges onto the first such boat he could find, gave the owner ten times his usual fare, and told him to head for Oldtown and not ask any questions. This was apparently not an unusual request, and the gap-toothed Southsider remained silent for the entire journey and pushed off again once they'd disembarked without a complaint.

From there, Marcus waited with the students and Hayver while Andy went off to secure more suitable clothing. She returned a quarter of an hour later with sacklike brown tunics and britches for the men and a shapeless green dress for Viera. The students, grumbling, changed clothes in the shadow of an anchored riverboat. Marcus got a long linen cloak, which would at least hide his uniform from casual observers.

The walk to Mrs. Felda's wasn't long, but Marcus felt every step of it, forcing himself to stop staring at everyone who passed with suspicious eyes. Andy, in the rear, kept a wary eye out for any tails, and when they finally stood in front of the old church she reported that no one had taken a more than usual interest.

Hell. Marcus gritted his teeth. *I'm not cut out for this. Give me a nice battlefield and an enemy that wears uniforms.*

He knocked at the church doors, expecting Mrs. Felda or her son, and when they squealed open was surprised to find himself facing Cora. By her little squeak of surprise, she was evidently taken off guard as well.

"Colonel!" she said. "We weren't expecting you for hours."

"Expecting me?" Marcus shook his head. "How could you be expecting me?"

"I sent a boy to Twin Turrets," Cora said. "Just a few minutes ago. He can't have even got there yet."

"What's happened?"

"We found something. Me and—" She eyed the figures clustered behind Marcus. "—our mutual friend."

Marcus shook his head. "I haven't been back there all day."

"Then—"

"Let's get this lot off the street," he said. "Then maybe we can straighten this out."

Mrs. Felda took immediate charge of the four students, shuffling them off in the direction of a wash and a hot meal. She cooed over the bruise on Andy's face as well, but the girl waved off all offers of sympathy. She and Hayver stayed with Marcus, who followed Cora to the fortress of ledgers at the rear of the repurposed building. Raesinia was there, carefully tracing something in one of the books with her forefinger. She looked up as Marcus approached, and gave him a broad grin.

"We've got something!" Her smile faded as she took in his expression. "What's wrong? What did the Preacher want?"

"Help," Marcus said. "A mob stormed the University because they'd heard some foreign students had stayed behind."

"Balls of the Beast," Raesinia swore. "Was there a lot of damage?"

"When we left, they were still wrecking the place."

Marcus sighed and pulled over an ancient chair. He tested it with his weight, gingerly, and when it didn't collapse at once he sat down. "I got the foreign students here, but the Preacher stayed behind to take care of the people in the hospital. I'm not sure what happened."

"Oh hell." Raesinia came closer and put her hand on his arm. "I'm sure he'll be okay. Not even the maddest mob would hurt an army officer in wartime."

"They did their damnedest with me," Marcus said, flexing his right hand. Pain flared in his bruised fingers.

Now that the immediate danger had passed, the emotions he'd been suppressing came to the fore. Worry about the Preacher, disgust at the stupid, shortsighted anger of the rioters, and something more: a hint of despair.

This was, after all, Vordan City, a place he'd always considered to be the center of the civilized world. Watching his city tear at itself like a crazed animal affected Marcus more than he cared to admit. During the revolution, there had been Orlanko and his black-coats to blame, but now there was no one but the Vordanai themselves.

Or maybe not.

"I think Maurisk wanted this," Marcus said. "Or someone in the government, anyway. There were Patriot Guards protecting the University, but they marched off somewhere just before everything started."

"That sounds like Maurisk," Raesinia said. "He's running out of the food for the Spike. But listen!" Raesinia grabbed Cora, who'd been hovering nearby, and pulled her over. "Tell him what you told me."

"What?" Cora said. "Oh. Yes. I went through the records you got me, from the Halverson Mill. Something is very wrong there. A lot of capacity is missing, and a lot of raw materials. They've tried to cover it up, but not very effectively."

Marcus massaged his temples. He'd almost forgotten why Raesinia had come here. "So, what does that mean?"

"It means that there's a lot of gunpowder unaccounted for. A *lot*."

"But it gets better," Raesinia said, unable to restrain herself. "Cora figured out where it's going!"

"Probably," Cora said, blushing a little. "I'm not certain. But there's a warehouse in the Docks that Halverson owns, and if you cross-reference all their wagon traffic, there's more trips coming out of it than going in. So either they're manufacturing horses and wagons in there, or somebody neglected to write down what they've been sending over. Officially, the place is standing empty."

"So all we've got to do," Raesinia concluded, "is go over there and take a look!"

"Go and take a look," Marcus said. He blew out a long breath. "If there *is* something bad going on, it'll be dangerous."

Raesinia's face fell. "I don't—"

"This is real progress," he said. "Enough that we need to talk to someone who actually has some authority." He paused thoughtfully. "I think I need to have a word with an old friend."

PART TWO

INTERLUDE

IGNAHTA SEMPRIA

As best Wren could see, the city wasn't burning.

They'd been hearing rumors all day, from folk jamming the road to the north, laden with all the possessions they could carry. Poor laborers carried packs strapped down with food, tools, and small children, with their families flocking behind them. Wealthier refugees rode or drove carriages, though Wren had seen more than one man in expensive clothes staggering on foot after he'd driven his horses too hard.

He had a barrel of water, which he refilled periodically from a stream a few minutes' walk from the road, and offered a wooden cupful to anyone who asked. In return, they gave him information, of a sort. The Vordanai had won at Gaafen. No one was quite sure *how*, but the Deslandai didn't seem curious; their city did not have a glorious military tradition, and this defeat was one more in a longstanding pattern.

Instead the rumors focused on what the Vordanai, newly fired by the spirit of their bloody revolution, would do to the city. That they would pillage anything they could get their hands on and rape any women they could catch was taken as a given, and the stories only grew more grotesque from there. Whole blocks had been fired, one woman assured him, the doors of the houses barricaded so the occupants cooked inside. Sworn Priests were being sacrificed to dark powers on their own altars. Several well-dressed refugees swore that the nobility of the city was already being rounded up, and the Vordanai general had brought one of their horrible "Spikes" with them to begin spreading his new, vicious creed. A mother, clutching her young daughters, told him that the Vordanai had a legion of unnatural woman soldiers with unhealthy desires, and that they were gathering all the virginal girls of Desland to induct them into their ranks in a perverted, orgiastic ritual.

Wren just smiled, nodded, and agreed that it was all terrible, while compiling the mad tales to try and extract some nuggets of truth. His demon, pressed into his ears, let him overhear conversations among those passing even when they thought themselves alone, and he added these to the mix as well. As evening fell, the flow of fleeing Deslandai slowed to a trickle, which was in itself a significant data point. He lit a fire beside his water barrel, offered drinks to the few stragglers, and waited.

To Wren's ears, the sound of horseshoes on the packed dirt of the road was audible long before the horses came into view. He could even pick out his companions' animals, having ridden so long beside them, and so he was not surprised when Twist's big gelding hove into view, followed by the Liar's more modest mount. What did surprise him was the third man, sitting beside Twist, his hands tied in front of him. Wren could hear his heart beating in a panic and the breath that rasped in his throat.

"You were supposed to be back by sundown," Wren said as the two Penitent Damned brought their mounts to a halt. The Liar slipped carefully from the saddle, favoring one leg in a long-suffering fashion Wren suspected was affected.

"We were delayed," the Liar said, stretching his back, "by an unexpected opportunity."

"Him?" Wren said, indicating the stranger as Twist lifted him, one-handed, to the ground.

"Yes," the Liar said. "We should get off the road."

Wren dumped the rest of the water and carried the

barrel, and Twist led his horse with one hand while carrying the stranger over his shoulder. The Liar brought up the rear, leading his own mount and muttering about his aches. Wren let his demon flow into his eyes, until the growing darkness was as bright as noon and he could see every snag and deadfall. When they reached their little camp by the stream, where the rest of the horses were tethered, Twist set the stranger down on a rock.

He was an old man, much older than the Liar, with silver hair and a pained, wrinkled face. He wore neatly tailored black, as the better class of servant might, and he stared at his captors with a defiant expression.

"Who is he?" Wren said, examining the man with his enhanced vision. He could count the hairs in the man's nose, and the signs of his fear were obvious, though he was doing a good job of concealing it from ordinary notice.

"I am assured," the Liar said, "that he is the personal servant of no less than General Janus bet Vhalnich himself. A man who has accompanied him everywhere, including on the Khandarai campaign."

Wren regarded the old man dubiously. "Khandar? Him?"

The Liar looked down at his inch-long fingernails. They were lacquered white, but the tip of each was stained the brown of dried blood. "So I am told. While my informants cannot lie, they may of course be mistaken."

"Even if it's true," Wren said, "does he know anything useful?"

"There's an easy way to find out," the Liar said.

The old man had watched the conversation, head turning between the two of them in an oddly birdlike motion. Wren hadn't thought he understood—the two Penitent Damned had been speaking in Murnskai, which few understood this far south—but to his surprise the prisoner spoke in the same language, heavily accented but understandable.

"You may as well kill me and get it over with," he said stiffly. "I'll tell you nothing, you know."

The Liar raised an eyebrow. "Do you deny you work for General Vhalnich?"

"I have had the privilege of serving him for many years." The old man raised his chin. "Whatever it is you think you can do to me, I guarantee it won't be enough."

"Under ordinary circumstances, I don't doubt it," the Liar said. "After all, you're not in the best of health. There's a limit to how long we could usefully torture you. However." He spread his hands, nails gleaming in the light of the small campfire. "Twist, hold him still."

Twist grunted and put one hand on each of the old man's shoulders. The prisoner struggled uselessly against the huge man's colossal strength, and then froze as the Liar came close. The pointed tips of his thumbnails came to rest on the old man's forehead, and he cupped his wrinkled face in his fingers, tenderly as a lover.

"Now," the Liar said, repeating the assurance that had earned him his name, "this won't hurt a bit."

His fingers began to glow, blue and white, outlining the bones of his joints and knuckles. The light ran down to his fingertips, then out along his nails, caging the old man's head in a radiant web. Then, slowly but inexorably, the nails sank smoothly into the prisoner's face, cutting through flesh, skin, and bone without pausing. Blood welled around them, dribbling down the old man's cheeks like tears. The prisoner opened his mouth and tried to scream, but his voice never emerged; instead a faintly glowing blue mist gushed out of his throat and swirled around his head in a thick cloud.

"What is your name?" the Liar said.

"Augustin," the man said, slowly and precisely. "Jean Rigas Augustin."

"Good. And do you know who we are?"

"Agents of the Elysian Church. Penitent Damned."

"*Very* good." The Liar glanced at Wren, then back to his prisoner. Augustin's eyes were locked forward, wide-open. "Now. Were you with General Janus bet Vhalnich in Khandar?"

"I was."

"And were you privy to his private conversations?"

"Yes. My lord trusts me implicitly."

"Well, then," the Liar said, "tell us what happened there. In particular, tell me everything you know about the Thousand Names."

Wren leaned forward as the old man began to speak, and listened with all the power of his demon.

"That was more informative than I expected," said the Liar, wiping blood from his nails with a damp cloth.

"Vhalnich has the Names," Wren said. "He knows what they are. He was *looking* for them."

"As our lord the pontifex suspected. It's possible the entire Khandarai expedition was a ruse for that purpose."

"We still don't know if he bears a demon himself," Wren said.

"At least one of his subordinates does," the Liar said. "This Ihernglass. He must be the power I can feel in the city."

Wren nodded. His own magical senses, ironically, were far less developed, but as they'd come closer to Desland he felt the vague pressure of a powerful demon at the back of his mind.

Twist shoveled another huge load of dirt over his shoulder. His hole was already waist-deep, his massive strength making short work of even the dry, rocky ground of the woods. The body of the old man waited beside him, the cloth that covered him mercifully sparing them the sight of his final, twisted rictus. Even Wren, who had seen the Liar work many times, felt a little uncomfortable when he watched the man's demon slowly burn someone alive from the inside out.

Before the magic killed him, they'd gotten a lot of information, but Augustin hadn't known everything.

"We don't know the nature of the demon Ihernglass bears," Wren said.

"I can feel its strength," the Liar said. "I have only felt such power a few times before. A Demon Lord, for certain, and not the weakest among them."

"It still need not be a threat," Wren said.

Even the most powerful demons didn't always grant their bearers dangerous abilities. There was a man in

Elysium, for example, whose demon allowed him to copy entire books in a matter of hours. While the Church made good use of such abilities, of course, Wren was glad his own demon gave him the strength to work in the field, combating the enemies of God directly.

"We know Vhalnich left the Thousand Names in Vordan," he went on. "Finding them should not be difficult. If Ihernglass is here, so much the better. He will not be able to interfere."

"So we assume. The powers of hell continue to surprise us." The Liar shook his head. "We cannot leave a Demon Lord to roam unchecked, not so near at hand."

Twist climbed out of the hole and pushed the old man's body into it, where it landed with an undignified *thump*. The Penitent lifted his oversized shovel again and started filling the grave back in.

"We will have to kill Ihernglass," the Liar said. "It should be simple. He was injured in the battle, I'm told."

"Attack him without knowing the nature of his demon?" Wren said.

The Liar shrugged. "A risk, of course. I will attempt to gather more information, but I suspect only Vhalnich himself knows, and he is still too well protected."

Twist grunted. From the rare words he'd spoken so far, Wren had gathered he favored simply attacking Vhalnich to end the danger quickly. Twist always preferred the direct approach to any problem.

"So we kill Ihernglass," Wren said. "Then retrieve the Thousand Names?"

The Liar nodded.

"Well enough." Wren got to his feet. "We'll have to send word to Elysium."

"There is a conduit in Desland. Well hidden. The Vordanai will not have found him," the Liar said. "Are you finished, Twist?"

Twist grunted again, tamping down the earth with the back of his shovel. This far from the city, out in the woods, the old man's body would never be found. Wren closed his eyes and sent up a silent prayer; even heretics were human, after all. He did not bother with a matching prayer for himself or his companions. They had all chosen damnation the moment they spoke the name of a demon, and weighed against that monstrous sin, any other crime against God was paltry by comparison. All that remained was to make certain their lives in this world served His interests sufficiently to counterbalance the loss of their souls.

A Demon Lord. Wren was human enough to feel a bit of curiosity, even anticipation, at the prospect. No matter how powerful Ihernglass' demon was, it was unlikely to threaten three trained Penitents, but the thought made Wren's pulse quicken a bit nonetheless. *I hope he can at least put up a fight.*

THE DIRECTORY OF NATIONAL DEFENSE

Johann Maurisk, President of the Directory of National Defense, stared at the crystal decanter on his desk. It was one-third full of a thick golden liquid, Hamveltai *flaghaelen* brandy, whose price had risen from merely expensive to unobtainable now that the war had begun. When he'd started his day, that decanter was full, as it was every morning in accordance with his strict instructions. He'd had one glass, a couple of fingers, no more, and yet here it was, nearly empty.

Someone was stealing it. Someone on the Hotel Ancerre's staff, most likely. The manager bowed and scraped obsequiously, but Maurisk had always found his protestations of loyalty suspect. Clearly, he was harboring a nest of traitors, right here in the headquarters of the Directory. The thought made Maurisk's head swim. *Traitors everywhere.*

He reached for the decanter and splashed a little more brandy into his glass, then settled back in his chair with a grin. *Well, we know how to deal with traitors.* Sarton's

Spike was operating with metronomic efficiency. One or two more traitors wouldn't tax it.

"Sir?" Kellerman said, standing by the door. "They're ready."

"Send them in," Maurisk said. "Let's get this over with."

Kellerman opened the door. Maurisk's office was on the top floor of the hotel, in a suite that had once been reserved for visiting ministers or heads of state. It had an impressively large and polished desk, bookshelves lined with matching sets of all the great works, and deep leather armchairs just a bit shorter than the massive wingback throne in which Maurisk himself sat. Perhaps a *bit* too opulent for Maurisk's tastes, truth be told, but impressions were important.

Outside, in the well-appointed waiting room, three men stood between a pair of Patriot Guards with sashes and halberds. Two of them Maurisk had expected: General Martin Hallvez, author of the disaster on the northern front, and Robert Zacaros, commander of the Patriot Guard. The contrast between them was strong: the former was a spare man with thin features and a white goatee, wearing an unmarked army uniform, while the latter was thick-bodied and sported a bushy brown beard shot with white streaks, and wore not only the blue-on-black sash of the Patriot Guard but a gold starburst pin he'd designed himself to denote his rank. Zacaros' hair was thinning on top, and he grew the sides long and slicked them over to cover his scalp. More gold gleamed at his collar and dripped from his cuffs.

It was the third visitor who made Maurisk's lip curl. Giles Durenne, a pair of tiny spectacles perched on his famous beak of a nose, dressed in shabby blacks that made him look like an unkempt crow. Even his eyes were dark and colorless, and his black hair was pulled back in a short queue.

His appointment to the Ministry of War had seemed like a safe sinecure for a leading Radical in the first days after the revolution, since the new government had intended to dismantle most of the army until it could be rebuilt on more

Republican grounds. The declaration of war had changed everything, of course. While Durenne had never disputed the Directory's ultimate authority, as a matter of course the Ministry of War—still mostly staffed by officers appointed in the old king's time—did much of the business of the military and thus held considerable power there, especially among the old regiments. Maurisk was thus obliged to take him seriously. *At least for the moment.*

"Gentlemen," Maurisk said. "Come in. Your guards may remain outside, Commander. I don't believe we'll need them."

Zacaros nodded—he never saluted, considering it beneath his dignity—and waved the two halberdiers away. Hallvez stepped in front of the desk and stood with military stiffness, his face schooled into impassivity. Zacaros slumped into a chair beside him, sighing. Kellerman closed the door.

"General," Maurisk said.

"Sir." Hallvez gave a definite ironic twist to the word.

"I've read your report." Maurisk tapped a stack of paper on his desk. "It seems to contain some . . . irregularities."

"Such as?"

"You claim you were ordered over the Murnskai border in a preemptive attack, over your own protests. But my colleagues at the Ministry of War seem certain no such order was issued." He nodded at Durenne, who remained stone-faced.

"That's because the order didn't come from the Ministry," Hallvez said. "It came from this office, by Patriot Guard courier, as a *suggestion*. When I objected, I was told to obey or face removal from my post for treason."

"And so you marched your army, unprepared, into Murnskai territory, taking no precautions—"

"My *precautions* were not the issue," Hallvez said, showing a hint of emotion for the first time. "Two-thirds of my troops were volunteers, with no training or drill. The *fallorii*, the Murnskai border guards, are light cavalry famous for their deviousness. They started cutting us to pieces within days."

"Because you were unable to bring them to battle, and let your men fight piecemeal."

"How would you suggest bringing them to battle, *sir*? A swarm of riders with three horses each, who know every inch of their damned country?"

"Enough," Maurisk said. "It's clear that *this*"—he waved dismissively at the report—"is a tissue of lies intended to cast blame on this Directory for your failings and undermine the war effort. Which, I may remind you, is treason. Do you have anything to say for yourself?"

Hallvez' lip twitched. "Only that I ought to have resigned on the spot rather than obey your *suggestions*. Thousands of Vordanai boys that you asked to protect their country are dead or prisoners in Murnsk because of my cowardice. I will live with that until the end of my days."

"Fortunately," Maurisk drawled, "that will not be very long. Commander, please take this traitor away. Make sure the broadsheets print the time of his appointment with Dr. Sarton so the public can observe the fate of those who betray our homeland."

Zacaros dipped his head, heaved himself to his feet, and took hold of Hallvez' arm. The general shook himself free and walked out of the office, with the Patriot commander following. Maurisk waited until they were gone, then tossed back his brandy and poured himself another.

"I heard in the papers Hallvez had gone mad," Durenne said from where he was leaning against the bookshelves.

"Mad, traitorous, or both," Maurisk said. "What does it matter?"

"Are you sending *suggestions* to all our generals?"

"Too many of our officers have dubious loyalties," Maurisk said. "They need to be reminded of their duty."

"I wonder what you sent to de Brogle. Instructions to feed his men on rats and patriotic rhetoric, perhaps?"

Maurisk slammed one hand on the desk. "De Brogle will pay for his crimes. As will *anyone* who works against Vordan." He eyed Durenne. "What do you want?"

"I just wanted to hear what Hallvez had to say for myself," Durenne said. "Being Minister of War, you know."

"I remind you that Directory business is confidential," Maurisk said. "I don't want this treasonous nonsense to spread."

"As would happen if, for example, Hallvez had a trial in the Deputies?"

Maurisk's hand clenched into a fist. In theory, the Ministry of War, like all the ministries, was now subject to the authority of the Deputies-General, which had in turn delegated power to the Directory. So far, though, the ability of the Directory to enforce its will on the Minister of War had not been seriously tested, as Durenne, in spite of his Radical politics, had been willing to play along. If Durenne brought things to a head, he would almost certainly lose in the end, but he probably *could* force a public vote on the matter. If that happened, no oath of secrecy would keep Hallvez' story out of the papers.

Durenne laughed. "You shouldn't scowl so much, Johann. It makes you look constipated. I'm only tweaking your tail, of course. How could I object to the punishment of such an obvious traitor?"

"I don't appreciate being toyed with," Maurisk said. "Is there a point to this?"

"Only that if the Directory is going to be in the business of issuing orders directly to the military, I think we might as well pack up the Ministry of War and be done." Durenne leaned forward. "I have worked with you because the good of the state requires it. But if you continue to go behind my back, I will have no choice but to bring matters to a public vote. Don't push me, Johann."

"I'm sure it was just an oversight," Maurisk said stiffly. "We'll consult you in the future, of course."

"Of course."

Durenne opened the door to leave, and Maurisk spotted Kellerman hovering outside. He beckoned the young man in and poured a little more brandy into the glass.

"We have someone watching him, don't we?" Maurisk said when he heard the outer door close behind Durenne.

"Yes, sir," Kellerman said. He was a treasure Maurisk had picked out from the initial flood of volunteers: prim, efficient, and a rabid idealist, someone who wouldn't shrink from any task that furthered the cause. *We could have used him in the old days.*

"Good. I want to know who he talks to, who he spends time with. What messages he sends. Use more men if you need to, and don't worry about being spotted. A little reminder will do him good."

"Of course, sir." Kellerman bowed and withdrew, closing the door behind him.

"What an obedient little viper." A pleasant voice, with the hint of a Murnskai accent.

Maurisk shoved his chair back from his desk, scrabbling for the knife strapped to its underside. His fingers found the hilt, but he couldn't get the damned thing out of its sheath, and before he figured out what he was doing wrong his slightly brandy-fogged mind had finally caught up with events. There was a man standing in front of the desk, a man who hadn't been there moments earlier. He was young and handsome, with brown hair and a well-trimmed goatee, dressed in close-fitting black. The corner of his mouth turned up in a slight smile, and in one hand he carried a bottle labeled with the image of a charging bull.

"I brought you a gift."

"You," Maurisk said, heart hammering in his chest.

"Hamveltai *flaghaelan*," said Adam Ionkovo, placing the bottle on the desk. He sat in the chair Zacaros had vacated, as casually as if he had not just walked into the most heavily guarded room in Vordan without even opening the door. "It's your favorite, if I remember correctly. I imagine it's hard to come by these days."

"I . . . yes." There was dust on the bottle. A ninety-one, Maurisk noted absently. A good year, and rare even in the best cellars. A full bottle was worth several thousand eagles. He blinked. "What are you doing here?"

"I thought I would check up on things," Ionkovo said, folding his hands in his lap. "Given how circumstances have . . . evolved. Your attempt to eliminate the queen did not go as planned, I take it."

Maurisk's hand twitched. His office was as secure as it

was possible for a room to be, but speaking those words aloud still made him cringe. He fought down the urge ruthlessly, sat up a little straighter, and pulled himself back to the desk.

"She left the box too early," he said. "Regrettably. But I have her under control."

"So I hear."

"I can deliver her whenever you like. If our agreement still holds."

"It does," Ionkovo said. "Bring me Raesinia, Vhalnich, and the Thousand Names, and Vordan will have peace."

"It would be easier to secure Vhalnich and the queen if we were to bring the war to an end," Maurisk said. "As it is, the people—"

"The Pontifex of the Black is not in the habit of delivering payment without results. The agreement stands."

Maurisk regarded his guest coldly, his fear finally coming under control. Ionkovo was the very embodiment of everything he hated about the Sworn Church: the ancient, hidden hand of Elysium, reaching out like a puppeteer to make the world dance to its tune. Once, he would never have consented to speak with such a creature.

But Raesinia's betrayal had opened his eyes. After the fall of the Vendre, he'd genuinely hoped that the world might change; the will of the people was sweeping away the old chains, and—properly guided—it could lead to a new era of enlightenment. Then he'd seen Raesinia, the young woman he'd trusted as one of his closest companions, now dressed in the garb of a queen.

He'd realized then that nothing had changed. The old chains still held. They'd all meant nothing to her, less than nothing; the will of the people had been a useful tool to bend to her own ends. It had opened his eyes to what was needed. A true revolution required a *purge*, as Farus IV had understood over a hundred years before. It needed a man willing to do what was necessary, without restraint.

Ionkovo had come to him soon after the war had begun, and laid out his price. Maurisk hadn't hesitated. He needed peace to continue his work. Raesinia, Vhalnich, and some dusty Khandarai artifact were a small price to pay.

"As you say," Maurisk finally said, "the queen is in hand."

"What about Vhalnich? He keeps winning battles."

"Vhalnich will need to be . . . reined in, but I don't anticipate any difficulty. Once our position is secure, he will either deliver himself to us or reveal himself as an outright traitor, and any support he has will melt away. Once we have him, it shouldn't be difficult to force him to reveal where he's hidden your Thousand Names."

"That's good," Ionkovo said. "That's very good. I wanted to be certain you were still committed." He leaned forward. "Because if Vhalnich's little successes make you think you can stand against us, you had better think again. The Borelgai fleet dominates your coasts, and the Emperor of Murnsk is coming with all his power. Hamvelt is a sideshow. If you don't give us what we want, we will crush this city under our heel." He grinned, showing teeth. "Not that you, personally, would be around to see it."

"I told you, everything is in hand." Maurisk was appalled to find himself sweating. "You have nothing to worry about."

"I'll tell that to the pontifex," Ionkovo said. "He'll be pleased to hear it. When will your position be 'secure'?"

"Another few weeks, at most. Preparations are well under way—"

"Very well." Ionkovo stood up and bowed. "A pleasure speaking with you, as always."

The Penitent Damned circled around the desk, coming to Maurisk's side. Maurisk started to turn in his chair, but Ionkovo laid a hand on his shoulder, and he froze in place. Ionkovo passed out of sight, behind him, and there was a whisper like silk brushing silk.

It was several long seconds before Maurisk risked turning around. There was no rear door in his office, not even a window. No way out, but Ionkovo was gone nevertheless.

Maurisk pulled his chair back up to his desk and took a moment to compose his features and let his hammering heartbeat slow. Then, once he was certain he was in control, he said, "Kellerman?"

The door opened. "Yes, sir?"

"That colonel, the one who was in here breathing fire. Do you recall his name?"

"De Ferre, sir."

"Is he still in the city?"

"I don't know, sir. But I will find out directly."

"Do so. And tell him I would like to speak with him." Maurisk had dismissed the old nobleman as a hopeless reactionary, and only listencd to his complaints with half an ear. But he remembered the venom the man had aimed at Vhalnich. "Tell him I may have an assignment for him after all."

CHAPTER TEN

WINTER

Winter opened her eyes with some difficulty. It felt as though someone had glued them closed with spirit gum. She sat up, or started to; the slight movement set off a pain in her head like a cannon going off.

"Rest easy." Her mind felt fuzzy, and it took a moment to recognize the voice. *Janus.* "What did I tell you about leading from the front? Here."

Winter blinked, and her surroundings became a bit less blurry. There was a canteen in front of her, and she took hold of it greedily, sucking down cold, clear water until it was empty. Then, cautiously, she tried sitting up again. Her heartbeat thudded in her head, each pulse producing a stab of pain, but this time she managed to get upright.

It took her a moment to realize what was so disorienting about her surroundings—she was not in a tent. Instead she found herself in a bed in a well-appointed bedroom, with heavy curtains drawn across the windows. A table and chair were pulled up by the bedside, and Janus sat with his hands folded, regarding her with broad gray eyes. She handed back the canteen, and he gave her a full one, which she swallowed from a bit more slowly.

"The cutters have been all over you," Janus said. "From the Girls' Own, naturally. Your Lieutenant Forester was quite the watchdog. They tell me that if you were going to develop a fatal swelling of the brain, you would have done it by now, so you'll probably recover."

Winter reached up to touch the side of her head. There was a lump there, although *lump* was probably not an adequate description of a swelling bruise bigger than her palm. Touching it brought on another shooting pain, and she closed her eyes and took deep breaths until it steadied.

"You're lucky it didn't break your skull," Janus said. "Do you remember what happened?"

"I got into a sword fight," Winter said. Her tongue felt thick. "With someone who actually knew what to do in a sword fight."

"In that case, it's fair to say you got off lightly."

"Bobby. Lieutenant Forester. She's all right?"

"She is."

"What about . . ."—*Jane*—"the rest of the regiment?"

"Losses were light, I'm told. Your charge carried the farm, and Captain Altoff brought his battery forward to break up the Deslandai attack."

"Did we win the battle?"

"Oh yes." Janus seemed vaguely amused that she'd asked. "We're in Desland. The city has capitulated."

"Oh." Winter blinked and took another swallow of water. "Congratulations."

Janus smiled, just a moment. "Thank you. It's a step in the right direction, but only a step."

"How long has it been?"

"A couple of days," Janus said. "I hoped you'd wake up today. I wanted to speak to you before I left."

"Left?" Winter felt as though her mind was still not working properly. "Where are you going?"

"North. Most of the army is already on the road. I'm leaving the Third"—Winter's regiment—"here in Desland for the moment. You'll keep order in the city and organize our supplies. I intend to make Desland our base for the rest of the campaign."

"I don't . . ." Winter blinked and rubbed at her eyes. "I don't know how to organize a supply base."

"The clerks from the Ministry will handle the details. You'll be in overall command." He leaned forward. "Now, it's possible that I'll have need of the Third before long. You must be ready to march at an hour's notice, and march hard. We're entering a critical period."

"Command." Winter tried hard to concentrate. "Command of *what*?"

"The garrison. The city, in effect. Don't let the locals get the better of you. If you have to, remind them who has the upper hand here."

"You're leaving me in charge of the *city*?"

"Don't worry too much. I imagine it mostly takes care of itself." Janus got to his feet. "Now I must be going. Get some rest. I'll have them send your officers in later."

"Sir—"

"One other thing." A look of unaccustomed uncertainty crossed Janus' features. "Augustin's gone missing. I would appreciate it if you kept an eye out." He sighed. "He's not the sort to wander off, and I'm worried."

"I'll . . . see what I can do, sir."

"Thank you. Now, I'll be in touch by courier. I have every confidence in you."

"Thank you, sir."

"Incidentally, your part of the battle was excellently fought. Well done." He gave another brief grin. "Try to do it without getting bashed over the head next time."

He bustled out, calling orders before he'd closed the door behind him. Winter took another long drink of water.

In command . . . of the city?

It was too much for her to wrap her battered mind around at the moment. She laid her bruised head gingerly back on the pillow and let her eyes close.

When she next awoke, the pain had receded a little, and Bobby and Cyte were waiting by her bedside. Winter pushed herself back in the bed until she was propped up against the headboard and groaned.

"I had a really terrible dream," she said. "Janus had marched off and left me in charge of Desland."

Bobby and Cyte looked at each other, worried.

Winter groaned again. "All right. I didn't get hit *that* hard. He's really gone?"

Bobby nodded. "This morning."

"And how does he expect me to run a city? I don't even speak Hamveltai."

"Most of the Deslandai upper class is bilingual," Cyte said. "Historically, the region has been heavily influenced by both Hamvelt and Vordan. It was actually a Vordanai protectorate until—"

Winter winced and held up a hand. "Later. Okay. So how bad was it for us?"

"Captain Verity reports twenty-two dead, thirty-six wounded," Bobby said, consulting a folded page from her pocket. "Captain Sevran reports fifty-four dead, sixty-two wounded. I'll have a more detailed report on the injuries soon."

Losses were light, he said. Winter remembered the red-headed sergeant—*I didn't even know her name*—whimpering and clawing at the wound in her chest. *Twenty-two dead. Twenty-two who followed me from Vordan because I told them it was the right thing to do. Twenty-two daughters who won't be back.* She didn't even want to think about the wounded, the cutters' tents with the piles of arms and legs outside. *"Light."*

"What about . . ." The question made her feel absurdly guilty, but she had to say it. "Jane?"

"She's fine," Bobby said, an unhappy look on her face.

Winter's heart twisted. "What's wrong?"

"I think she's still angry at you."

"Oh." Winter let out a deep breath. "I'll talk with her. Later." Guilt prickled. "Is Marsh all right?"

"Yes, sir."

"Who's been in command while I've been . . . out?"

"Sevran and Abby having been working together, sir. There's a lot to be done, but they seem to be on top of things."

"Still. I need to be up and about." Winter began to move, but pain lanced through her head again, and she moaned involuntarily. Bobby rushed to press her back into the bed, and Cyte held up her hands.

"It's nothing you need to concern yourself with, sir," Cyte said. "We can handle it. Just supply requisitions, transport arrangements, that sort of thing. The Deslandai have been very cooperative."

"You've got quarters for everybody? Somewhere to care for the injured?"

"Yes, sir," Bobby said. "We're taking care of it, don't worry. Just rest for now."

Winter nodded carefully. Her eyes went to Cyte, and she cleared her throat. "Do you think you could give me a moment alone with Bobby?"

"Of course, sir." Cyte got to her feet and saluted. "I'll be outside."

She left, closing the door behind her.

"What about you?" Winter said in a low voice. "Are you all right?"

Bobby held up her right hand, and Winter noticed for the first time she was wearing a dark glove on it. She tugged at it with her other hand until her palm was exposed. A streak of sparkling gray ran across the living flesh.

"God," Winter said. "I'm sorry."

"It's nothing," Bobby said, pulling her glove back into place. "Better than losing the hand."

"You saved my life."

Bobby's face colored. "I just . . . I saw you fighting, and I wanted to help. I'm sorry I didn't get there sooner."

"Did Abby see anything?" She'd been in the corner, grappling with a Deslandai soldier. "She's not hurt, is she?"

"Just a little bruised, sir. And I talked to her, but she didn't mention anything unusual."

Winter smiled weakly. "You'll have to be careful about snapping swords in half if you want to keep your secret."

"Sorry, sir."

Her evident sincerity made Winter laugh out loud,

however much it hurt. "Thank you, by the way. For saving my life. It seems to have become a habit."

Bobby grinned. "I do my best, sir."

By the next morning, Winter felt well enough to walk, albeit with exaggerated caution. She discovered she had been sleeping in the upper room of an abandoned house near the gate, which Janus had appropriated as his head-quarters. It was nearly empty now, with the army departed, and Bobby and Cyte arrived to escort her to the new regimental quarters up in the citadel.

Desland was closer to being two cities than one. Like Vordan City, it was divided by a mighty river, but here there was no convenient island to serve as a footing for bridges, so the Velt flowed on placid and unimpeded. Innumerable barges, skiffs, and other watercraft crossed and recrossed the flat expanse many times a day, from the cargo warehouses and docks of the low-lying west bank to the residences of the upper class on the cliffs of the east.

Only the east bank had a wall, and it was of medieval construction, a crumbling stone barrier long ago leap-frogged by the expanding city and useless in any case against modern artillery. It also had a citadel, originally intended as a final holdout for the cities defenders in case of a siege. Equipped with barracks and training fields, it made a convenient base, except that it was naturally located at the highest point inside the walls, looking off a cliff over the river. Winter, legs shaky and head throbbing, tried not to think about how much farther they still had to go.

This part of Desland was not too dissimilar from a well-off district of Vordan City, though the Hamveltai influence was apparent in the steeply sloped roofs with carved wooden buttresses at the corners. Carriages rattled back and forth, and pedestrian traffic was light but steady. There had been an exodus in the first few days as those who were convinced the Vordanai would exact vengeance fled the city, but now the locals who remained had apparently decided their conquerors were not going to put the place to the torch after all.

The three blue uniforms—one of them worn by what was clearly a woman, and one with a colonel's eagles—drew quite a bit of attention, and they walked in the center of a bubble of stares. Passersby detoured to give them a respectful distance.

Winter forced herself not to stare back, and instead tried to focus on what Bobby was saying, which was a slightly overexcited explanation of how Janus had won the Battle of Gaafen. Cyte, on her other side, listened with the indulgent air of someone who had heard it all before.

"—Give-Em-Hell and the Colonials crossed the river upstream, fifty miles short of Gaafen. They had to detour to find a good road, which is why we moved so slowly on the approach. Every day *we* marched six miles and *they* made fifteen. Give-Em-Hell started raiding the Deslandai supply lines so they'd think that was all that was going on, and the cavalry kept the scouts from figuring out the infantry was there. They were all in position the day before we reached the Gaafen line."

"Wait," Winter said. "That means the Colonials went over the river *before* we knew the Deslandai were going to fight at Gaafen?"

Bobby nodded vigorously. "Janus knew. It's like he could read their minds. The morning we attacked, Fitz Warus led a company from the Colonials down to the Gaafen Bridge and captured it before the Deslandai engineers could set off the charges they'd rigged to destroy it, and then the rest of the Colonials came over and attacked the town from behind. After we threw back their first attack on the right, Janus brought the center forward, and they just started to panic. The whole Deslandai army fell to pieces in an hour."

Winter smiled ruefully. *And I thought we might be reduced to battering a fortified position head-on. I ought to have more faith in Janus.* Such faith had been justified many times over by now, even if the general was not in the habit of explaining his plans to his subordinates.

"And the city just surrendered?" Winter said. "We were still on the wrong side of the Velt. They could have tried to keep us from crossing."

"Apparently there was a bit of a coup," Cyte said. "Or at least a shift in government. Desland's ruled by a merchant's council, but Hamveltai interests had always held a lot of sway. Nobody seems willing to say exactly what happened, but those members of the council seem to have left town rather suddenly, and what was left didn't have a lot of interest in continuing the fight."

"Better to make money off us than try to fight," Winter said. "Ashe-Katarion was the same way, until the Redeemers turned on us."

"I don't think that's very likely here, sir," Cyte said. "Most of the Deslandai are Sworn Church, but there's always been a substantial Free Church minority, and they're on relatively good terms. I don't think there's many who are eager to die for Elysium."

"That's something we have in common, then. So there hasn't been much trouble?"

Cyte shook her head. "No, sir. Nothing significant."

"A few incidents of . . . overexcited carousing," Bobby said. "But Sevran and Abby have been keeping things under control."

"Abby? What about Jane?"

Bobby looked embarrassed. "You'll have to talk to her about that, sir."

What the hell am I supposed to say to Jane, anyway? She'd blown up at her on the battlefield, in the heat of the moment, but ultimately she'd meant every word. *I don't care what she thinks of the Royals. You can't leave fellow soldiers to fight on their own if you've got a choice.* Just thinking about it made Winter feel angry, but that only made things worse. *I can't lose her. Not again.*

The citadel was surrounded by a stone curtain wall, three stories high, enclosing a drill field and a stone keep along with various wooden buildings. The huge doors, solid oak planks banded with iron, stood open. By the rust on the hinges, Winter guessed they hadn't been closed in decades. She was gratified to see sentries on the wall walk, though, Girls' Own and Royals both.

Passing under the wall—the ceiling was full of holes,

where medieval defenders in the gatehouse could have poured boiling oil on attackers who'd breached the first set of gates—they emerged into the courtyard. About half of it was taken up with tents; Winter guessed the citadel only had room for a few hundred. In the other half, several companies were drilling while a group of men in regulation uniforms inspected a cartload of crated goods. Soldiers were everywhere, maintaining gear, cleaning linens, or just sitting in the weak autumn sun.

As soon as Winter entered, silence spread throughout the yard, spreading like a ripple from a stone dropped into a pool. The shouts of the drilling sergeants quieted, and every head turned to stare. The closest soldiers to Winter, two Girls' Own rankers and a royal corporal working on coiling ropes, bounced to their feet and saluted. Soon that was spreading, too, every man and woman in the yard straightening up and putting a hand over their heart. Winter heard Bobby and Cyte follow suit.

Winter was certain her cheeks were flaming red. She waved a hand awkwardly.

"Thank you, everyone." She patted the bandage that ran around her head. "I'm all right, as you can see. Thank you." Winter paused. "The general asked me to tell you, 'Well done.'"

No one moved, but she saw smiles spreading.

"That's all," Winter said. "Thanks."

The crowd of soldiers relaxed, and a low buzz of conversation began again. The three directly in front of Winter stood aside to let her pass.

"You don't have to keep thanking them," Bobby said. "You're the colonel here."

"Sorry," Winter muttered. "I couldn't think what else to say. Is Sevran in the keep?"

Cyte said, "I'll take you up. Bobby, you need to go find Marsh, don't you?"

Bobby blushed but nodded and hurried away. Winter stared after her a moment, then shook her head.

"You don't approve?" Cyte said.

"It's hardly my place not to."

Cyte shrugged. "You seem to worry a good deal about her."

"Bobby . . ." Winter sighed. "It's just that I knew Bobby in Khandar, and . . . she feels very young sometimes."

"War has a way of burning that out of people," Cyte said, then laughed. "Look at me. Half a year ago I'd never swung a sword in anger, and now I can act cynical with the best of them."

Winter smiled. "Don't let Graff hear you say that. He considers cynicism his personal prerogative."

"Sir!" Sevran said, rising. "It's good to see you on your feet."

"Right now I'm eager to get *off* my feet," Winter said, collapsing into a chair and waving away the captain's salute. "This is quite a hill they've stuck us on top of. Could I trouble you for some water?"

"Of course!" Sevran gestured at one of the young rankers waiting by the door, and the boy dashed off.

Winter waited, but the captain remained standing. Eventually she felt compelled to break the silence. "Is something wrong?"

"Sorry, sir. It's just . . ." He straightened back to attention. "I wanted to say that I realize I acted against orders, during the battle. I advanced my battalion from the position I was assigned. Captain Verity was correct not to—"

"No," Winter said. "She was not. I didn't just leave you orders, I left you in *command*. That means making decisions. You saw a threat, and you acted to forestall it. It was the correct decision. Whether or not Captain Verity agreed with you, you were within your rights to order her to support you."

Sevran deflated slightly. "Thank you, sir. I recognize that it's put you in a difficult position."

"My personal life is my own problem," Winter said with more confidence than she felt. "It's not your responsibility, Captain."

The ranker returned with a glass carafe, still cold from the well. He poured a cup, which Winter took gratefully. The keep reminded her a little of the barracks of the

Heavenly Guard in Ashe-Katarion. It was richly furnished, with solid furniture, wall hangings, and rugs, but there was no concealing the fact that it had originally been intended as a fortress. The ceilings were low, the walls stone, and the windows were narrow slits that let in hardly any sun. Captain Sevran had taken an old common room on the second floor for a planning room, laying a map of the city out on the big polished table and surrounding it with scraps of notepaper carrying various details. A desk bore stacks of paper, both flimsy army foolscap and thicker pages that must have come from civilians in the city.

"I've made a start on getting the supply lines organized," he said, following Winter's gaze. "Janus left us several wagonloads full of people from the quartermaster's office, and they're working on securing what we need. Our biggest problem is upriver transport. Goods move north from here mostly by barge, and a lot of the bargemen are Hamveltai. So far they haven't been very cooperative."

"If that's our biggest problem," Winter said, "we're having an easy time of it. We haven't had any riots, protests, that sort of thing?"

"No, sir. Not so far. The Vordanai community here has been very accommodating, and the Hamveltai are keeping their heads down. We're eating better than we have in weeks."

"That's something to look forward to. How are your men holding up since the battle?"

He pursed his lips. "I'd say they're doing well, sir. The . . . uh . . . story of your altercation with Captain Verity spread pretty quickly, and it seems to have done a lot for their respect for you." He smiled. "I haven't had a single formal complaint, not even from the noble-born lieutenants. Although Lieutenant Novus' dismissal may have something to do with that."

"People heard what I said to Jane?" Winter winced. She'd hoped to keep that between them. "The Girls' Own can't be happy about it."

"You'd have to ask Captain Verity or Lieutenant Giforte about that, sir, but my impression is that a lot of them think you were right. There may be . . . pockets of grumbling, though."

I'll bet. Jane's old cronies—Becca, Winn, and the others from the Leatherbacks—wouldn't be so quick to forgive Winter for humiliating their leader. *Thank God Abby seems to have a good head on her shoulders.*

"With your permission, sir, I'd like to begin daily drill again tomorrow. I'd like to use an old racecourse down in the city. I think it would do everyone good to get most of the regiment practicing at once, and it can't hurt to be seen exercising a little discipline. A lot of people are still frightened."

And if the locals are *thinking of turning on us, a little show of force might be a good idea.* "Do it," Winter said. "Use everyone you can spare from other duties. I'll tell Abby."

"Thank you, sir." Sevran cocked his head, listening. "I believe I hear Lieutenant Giforte now."

A moment later, Abby swept in from the corridor, with several other Girls' Own officers trailing behind her. She looked unhappy until she saw Winter, and then her expression became one of relief.

"Sir! Are you feeling better?"

"Enough to walk short distances, anyway," Winter said. "I think we need to talk."

Abby nodded emphatically. "Virginia, Nel, go over my plan with the captain and get his notes. Colonel, I think we can use the room next door."

With some reluctance, Winter levered herself up from her chair and followed Abby out into the corridor. The freckled young woman was showing some serious signs of sunburn on the back of her neck, and she'd tied her frizzy brown hair up into a bun that bobbed as she walked. She opened the door to the next room over, which was a dusty pantry that looked as though it hadn't been used in months. A handful of empty crates lay on the floor, and Abby grabbed one and brushed it off before presenting it to Winter.

"Who was using this place before we moved in?" Winter said as Abby cleaned off another crate for her own use.

"An outfit called the Falcon Guard. Strictly ceremonial, sons of privilege riding around in fancy costumes, that sort of thing. After the real army surrendered, they've been too embarrassed to show themselves, and the merchant's council said we could help ourselves. They're eager to be seen being helpful."

"Let's hope nothing changes their attitude." Winter had no illusions that the Deslandai had suddenly seen the virtues of the revolutionary cause. Their loyalty would last up until the moment Janus' army was no longer a threat. "Sevran said things have been going well."

"More or less." Abby sighed. "I've had to keep the Girls' Own from going out nights. There's a lot of strange rumors going around about us."

"I can imagine. Do what you need to keep them safe."

"I will, sir. But they're not happy about it. The Royals get passes to go out on the town."

Winter nodded. "Let me think about it."

There was a moment of silence, which stretched out into an awkward pause. Winter finally said, "I wanted to thank you for what you did in the battle. Your squad carried the farm."

Abby shrugged. "I was only following your orders, sir."

"It still took a lot of courage. I'm glad you're all right."

"Thank you, sir." Abby sighed. "But it's not the battle you want to talk about, and you know it. It's Jane."

Winter winced. "I'm that transparent?"

"More or less."

"So, where is she?"

"Last I heard," Abby said, "she was in a tavern called the Loose Cannon, about a mile from here. But they may have tossed her out by now."

"Is she alone?"

Abby shook her head. "Most of the older Leatherbacks are with her. Becca, Winn, and the rest. Forty or fifty in all. They take over a tavern and drink it dry, then move on to the next."

"How long has this been going on?"

"Since the battle, I think. Things got a little confused when we entered the city."

"Saints and martyrs. What the hell is she up to?"

"Celebrating, she calls it. I think she's still hiding."

"From who?" Winter said.

"You? Me? Sevran? The rest of the Girls' Own?" Abby looked uncomfortable. "The Leatherbacks are still mostly behind her, but the newer recruits weren't happy when she told us we couldn't go and help the Royals. They'd just as soon be rid of her."

Winter looked at Abby thoughtfully. She still lacked a formal uniform, but her rumpled blue jacket seemed to fit her like a second skin, and the battered leather bandolier that went over her shoulder looked like a natural fit. She'd become a soldier, somewhere over the past few months, in much the same way that Khandar had molded Winter herself into one.

"You've been running the Girls' Own in the meantime?" Winter said.

"More or less. I don't have any actual authority, but the others listen to me."

"I'm changing that, as of now. You're acting captain."

"What about Jane?"

"Jane is obviously not terribly interested in the job," Winter said, unable to keep a certain bitterness out of her voice. "I'll deal with her, but it may take some time. It's my fault for letting this thing between us get so bad. In the meantime, the battalion needs a commander."

"Understood, sir. Just . . ." She hesitated.

"What?" Winter said.

"Don't be too hard on her. Please."

"I'll do my best," Winter said.

The soldier's life had never agreed with Jane, not in the way it obviously suited Abby. She wasn't used to drills, discipline, taking orders. *She was never good at taking orders.* Even the mistresses at the Prison had given up trying to get Jane to do anything she didn't want to do, until they'd finally thrown her in a closet and married her off to a brute. *The army is never going to be her home, not the way it is for me or Bobby.*

Winter shook her head and got to her feet. "All right. Have I got a room in this place?"

"Of course, sir. You've got the commander's suite on the top floor. I'll show you the way."

The commander's suite turned out to be almost ridiculously luxurious, like the bedroom of a particularly avaricious king. It was so crowded with gold and silver bowls, candelabra, plate, and other precious odds and ends that there was scarcely room to do more than make her way to and from the big bed, and the sitting room was a mass of elegant paintings, vases, and polished hardwood. Winter decided that first thing tomorrow she was going to have the clutter packed away into a cellar. As it was, she felt that if she turned around too quickly she'd bump a spindly little table and shatter some priceless heirloom.

Rankers brought her food, which was served on polished silver plates with a crystal goblet of wine and was indeed considerably better than what they'd been eating on the march. Abby had told her the storerooms were filling up with "gifts" for the colonel from local notables eager to court her favor. The wine must have been one of them, because it was worlds different from the awful stuff available from the merchants who followed the army. This was cool, clear nectar from the Old Coast, golden as the sun, with such a smooth flavor that Winter didn't realize how much she'd drunk until her head was swimming.

Cyte returned, with a batch of reports—the next of kin for the dead and details of the injuries of the wounded, who was expected to recover and who to die, the state of the regiment's weapons and ammunition, guard rotas and infractions to be dealt with. Winter looked it all over, a little unsteadily, and told Cyte to take care of whatever she could on her own. She relayed her order putting Abby in charge of the Girls' Own, too, which the ex-student seemed to thoroughly approve of. Then, perhaps sensing her commander's weariness and slight inebriation, Cyte withdrew, leaving Winter to shrug out of as much of her uniform as she could easily remove and crawl into bed.

The sun wasn't yet touching the horizon, but the long walk through the city earlier and the pounding pain in her head made her want to curl up and hide under the thick wool blankets and silk sheets of the big four-poster. But actual sleep eluded her. When she closed her eyes, she found herself back in the battle, not watching the Girls' Own rankers shot down around her or in her desperate final struggle with the Deslandai officer, but delivering her warning to Jane through clenched teeth. Again and again, she saw Jane's eyes widen in shock, as though Winter had just run her through the belly with a rapier, then narrow in—what? Rage? Frustration? Chagrin? She could picture the expression exactly, but not read it.

I should never have brought her here. Jane had done the impossible—escaped from the Prison and her husband, built a life for herself in Vordan City, and helped hundreds of others along the way. Winter had come into that life like a hurricane and knocked it to pieces. *I should have made her stay behind. Made them all stay behind. Janus would have listened to me. He could have made them do it.*

But if Jane wasn't fitting into the army, others—Abby, Cyte—had taken to it like a duck to water. *Should I have sent them home, too?* She'd told Jane that the women of the Girls' Own knew what they'd signed up for, and that was true, too. *Why do I get to make the choice for any of them?*

And no matter what, the thought of sending Jane away—of being separated from her again—made Winter feel as if someone were tearing her ribs out of her chest. *But why does my pain trump hers? If being with me means ruining her life, how is that worth it? If I really loved her, I should have been willing to stay by her side in Vordan, and to hell with Janus and the army.*

Of course, that had never been a realistic option. The passenger in the pit of Winter's mind rarely made itself felt, but she could feel it if she turned her attention inward. *Infernivore.* A devouring beast, slumbering until it felt the approach of prey. Army or not, since the moment she took on the demon—*or the* naath, *or whatever it is*—she'd marked herself. According to Janus, it would stay with her for the rest of her life.

"Fuck." Winter pressed her face into the thick down pillow, muffling her voice. "Fuck, fuck, *fuck*. Balls of the fucking Beast. What the hell do I do now?"

Then, a bit unsteadily, she rolled out of bed and went in search of the rest of the bottle of wine.

The next day dawned clear and—to Winter's eyes— uncomfortably bright. She shaded her forehead with one hand and gulped water from her canteen. Her head still throbbed, although this morning it was perhaps for different reasons.

The racetrack—it was called the Campus—was at least a square mile of open land in the midst of one of the wealthier parts of Desland. The houses that looked on to it were some of the biggest and most expensive in the city, equaled only by the mansions lining the river cliffs. Horses, their breeding, racing, and trading, had always been the center of the Deslandai economy, and all of the city's oldest and most noble families had equine interests. The Campus was the site of the Golden Laurel, arguably the most prestigious set of horse races in the world, and afterward played host to the most exclusive and expensive of the city's many horse markets.

Racing and trading horses was a summer affair, however, and this late in the year the Campus was just a square of browning grass and dirt, scattered with scraps of wood and bits of canvas left over from the great fairs. It was easily large enough to accommodate the entire Third Regiment, along with the crowds of curious Deslandai who had come to see the show.

The spectators kept a respectful distance from the troops, and here and there a blue Vordanai flag waved in a show of goodwill. In the center of the rough ring of onlookers, the Girls' Own and the Royals went through a set of evolutions that Abby and Sevran had worked out between them the night before. The two battalions deployed from columns into line and ployed back again, companies marching and countermarching to the beat of the assembled regimental drums. They formed two squares, bayonets gleaming dangerously, and at a drumbeat of command melted back into column and marched proudly around the square.

Some of the maneuvers, to Winter's eye, were a bit ragged, especially on the part of the Girls' Own. Tight formation drill had never been a priority in a battalion where most of the soldiers had barely handled a musket before. But they'd made a lot of progress, and it was evidently enough to impress the Deslandai, who shouted and applauded with each barked command. There were a fair number of whistles and catcalls mixed in, of course. The women in the front of the formation responded to lewd suggestions from the crowd with equally foul hand gestures, provoking roars of laughter.

Winter sat astride Edgar, with Cyte mounted beside her, and tried to enjoy the show. Every time she saw Abby, walking at the head of the Girls' Own and shouting orders to the drummers, it made her think about Jane. She and the older Leatherbacks hadn't returned last night, and according to reports had moved from the Loose Cannon to the Golden Goose for another round of revels.

"The Girls' Own ought to have proper uniforms," Cyte said, drawing Winter up from her thoughts.

"I put in a request to the Ministry," Winter said, "but there are a lot of volunteer battalions. Somehow I think providing a bunch of women's uniforms is not at the top of their list."

"Plenty of tailors here in Desland," Cyte said. "We ought to be able to get them made locally."

"I don't think I can afford it." Winter sighed. They'd spent nearly all her back wages—all the money she had in the world, she thought ruefully—on providing better food and drink for the troops on the march.

Cyte shot her a crafty look. "You wouldn't have to pay. The quartermasters have authorization to draw on the credit of the Crown."

"Since when does the Vordanai Crown have any credit in Desland?"

"Since Janus marched in and pointed twelve-pounders at their fancy banks," Cyte said bluntly. "They've been very good about extending loans."

"That sounds more like robbery."

Cyte shrugged. "It's war. Read a little history, and you'll find this is polite by any standard. We're already taking all kinds of supplies, especially horses. A few hundred yards of cloth will hardly make a dent."

"All right," Winter said, watching the Girls' Own maneuver. Their jackets, each a different shade of blue, flapped against whatever homespun or linen each recruit had brought with her. "Do it. If they're going to risk their lives for Crown and Deputies, they deserve to look like soldiers."

"Yes, sir." Cyte grinned.

"And see what you can do about boots." Too many of the women had come with footwear adequate only for city streets, which was falling to pieces after weeks of marching hard country roads. "As long as we're looting, we might as well make ourselves comfortable."

"Now, there's the right spirit for a conquering commander," Cyte said. "We'll make a proper tyrant of you yet. I'll see what I can do in terms of slave girls for your bedroom."

It was a joke, and Winter did her best to smile, but she must not have done a very good job of it. Cyte blanched.

"Sorry," she said. "I . . . sorry."

"It's all right," Winter said, ignoring the ache in her chest that matched the throb in her head. "Come on. We should get back to the citadel before the crowd breaks up."

A couple of companies of soldiers had been left on guard duty, and the sentries Winter saw on her return looked very unhappy at being unable to join the demonstration. She passed the word that they'd be the next to receive passes to head into the city, which cheered the Royals up considerably. Abby hadn't wanted the Girls' Own to go out, which rankled a bit, but was probably sensible; Cyte's notion of using the Crown's credit to secure supplies had given her an idea, though. She spent the next couple of hours in the big room

Sevran used as an office, writing orders and consulting with a few local representatives.

"Sir?"

Winter looked up to find a ranker from the Girls' Own at the door. The young woman—she couldn't have been more than seventeen—was obviously intimidated at the prospect of talking to her colonel, and she drew herself up into what she probably thought was a properly stiff military bearing. Winter suppressed a smile.

"Yes, Ranker?" she said.

"Captain Giforte requests permission to bring a matter to your attention."

Winter frowned. "Of course. Tell her to come in."

"She requests you join her in the yard, sir."

"All right." Winter set down her pen and stretched, kinks popping in her back. Her headache, at least, had subsided a bit. "What's going on?"

"Best she tells you, sir."

Abby was waiting in the yard, in front of the entrance to the keep. Behind her, the troops had returned to their tents and were cooking lunch, though quite a few seemed to have drifted over to see what was going on.

Behind Abby stood three young women. The one on the left was enormous, a head taller than Winter and broad-shouldered, with short hair and a guarded expression. To her right was a younger woman, slim and sallow-looking, dressed in battered leather and fraying homespun.

The third woman made a point of not looking at her two companions, or indeed anyone else in the yard. She had the pale skin of someone who'd spent her life sheltering from the sun, and long golden curls that cascaded down to the small of her back. Her dress, elegant pink and gold with matching jewelry at her throat and wrists, was already stained at the hem from the mud of the yard. Her eyes snapped to Winter as soon as she emerged, bright blue and disconcertingly piercing.

"Abby," Winter said as the acting captain saluted briskly, "what's going on?"

"These three came up to me after the demonstration, sir," Abby said. "They want to join up."

"Join up?" Winter looked at the three women incredulously. "Why?"

"You'd have to ask them, sir."

Winter turned to the large woman. "What's your name?"

The woman's eyes flicked to the smaller girl beside her, who stepped forward. "She's Joanna, sir. Or Jo. I'm Barley." Her Vordanai was good, with only the faintest trace of an accent.

"Jo and Barley."

"Yes, sir. Jo doesn't talk."

Jo gave a passable imitation of a military salute, fist thumping against her chest.

"And what are you doing here?" Winter said.

"What the captain said, sir. We want to join the Girls' Own."

"You're Deslandai. We're still at war."

"Pardon, sir, but we're Vordanai. At least, I am, more than half, and Jo's grandma didn't speak a word of Hamveltai. Down where we live, people cheered when they heard the army got whipped."

Winter paused. Desland did have a substantial minority of Vordanai, mostly in its poorer sections. "We're not going to be staying in Desland. Sooner or later, we'll join up with the rest of the army, and I have no idea if we'll ever be back."

"Fine with me, sir," Barley said. "There's nothing here for us but working the docks and getting spit on by Hamveltai nobs. If you can keep us fed, we'll follow you wherever you want to go."

Winter wanted to say no, to tell them that however bad things were on the docks, it was better than facing musket balls and cold steel and the prospect of a shallow grave on some battlefield. But there were soldiers all around, from the Royals and the Girls' Own both, and in the face of their scrutiny she couldn't make herself say it.

Who am I, she remembered from the night before, *to decide for any of them?*

"Jo," Winter said. "You agree with everything Barley is saying?"

The big woman nodded emphatically and put a hand on her smaller companion's shoulder.

"Captain Giforte," Winter said. "Have you got a company that could use these two?"

"I think I can find one, sir," Abby said, with the hint of a smile in her voice.

"All right, then." Winter turned to the third woman, who again met her gaze without flinching. "And who are you?"

"Anne-Marie Gertrude di Wallach," she said. Unlike Bailey, she had a heavy Hamveltai accent, rolling her R's and turning her W's into V's.

"You're not Vordanai."

"No."

"So what are you doing here?"

Anne-Marie frowned in concentration. She spoke with the air of someone working through a puzzle; the Vordanai language was clearly something she'd only encountered in a schoolroom. "I want . . . to fight. Fight with you."

"Why?"

"Because you fight for everyone." She dug in a hidden pocket of her dress and produced a small, battered book. It was Voulenne's *Rights of Man*, the founding tract of the University rebels back in Vordan. "I read . . . papers. Things that come from Vordan. People rule themselves. No more kings. I want to fight for that."

Winter looked her over. Anne-Marie's hands were soft and uncalloused, her arms skinny and unfamiliar with work.

"You want to fight for that?" Winter indicated *The Rights of Man*. "You're ready to die for it?"

"Yes," Anne-Marie said, standing up a little straighter.

"You're ready to kill for it?"

"Yes." Though this time, she hesitated a little.

"Walk for miles in the mud? Carry a heavy pack? Eat squirrel or whatever else you can catch?"

Anne-Marie's cheeks were reddening, but she remained standing. "Yes."

Winter let out a long breath and turned to Abby, speaking quietly. "What do you think?"

"I think she's very determined," Abby said. "I also think she won't last five minutes."

"We can't turn her away and let the others in," Winter said.

"Leave it to me," Abby said. "Tell her she can stay, and I'll make sure she gets a taste of what things are really like. She'll run home soon enough."

Winter nodded. Turning back to meet Anne-Marie's eyes again, though, she was uncertain. There was a determination there that struck a chord; it reminded her of another girl who'd run away from everything she'd ever known with the mad idea of joining the army.

Of course, nobody at Mrs. Wilmore's ever had soft hands like hers. Still, Winter thought she deserved a chance. *It's the best I can offer, anyway.*

"Captain Giforte will find you a place," she said. "You'll need new clothes, though. And you'll probably have to cut your hair."

Anne-Marie's hand went involuntarily to clutch her golden curls. With an effort, she straightened up again. "Yes. Sir. I . . . understand."

Barley, who had been staring skeptically at Anne-Marie, looked up at Winter. "We're not the only ones, sir. There's lots of girls from the Docks who'd join if they knew you were taking recruits."

"I also have friends." Anne-Marie patted her book. "They believe this."

Great. There would be no way to keep *this* news from spreading across the city like wildfire. *Just great. What the hell have I gotten myself into now?*

CHAPTER ELEVEN

MARCUS

It had been a long time since Marcus spent much time in Farus' Triumph. Superficially, things hadn't changed much. The cafés around the edges of the vast square were still open, spilling cast-iron tables out onto the flagstones to take advantage of the weak autumn sun. The great equestrian statue of Farus V looked out as majestically as ever, surrounded by his worshipful coterie of water-spouting nymphs and swans. To the south, the Grand Span leapt from piling to piling, and a steady stream of pedestrian traffic came and went from the South Bank.

After some time sitting in a café by the side of that stream, though, Marcus could see the differences. The Island had once been the most cosmopolitan part of the city, where Vordanai rubbed shoulders with fur-clad Borelgai merchants, Murnskai traders, or businessmen from the League cities. Even Khandarai, thousands of miles from home, had not been unheard of. Now the foreigners were gone, and in their wake some of the Triumph's businesses had shuttered. Gareth's, the Vordanai branch of the great Hamveltai jewelry empire, had boards nailed across its windows, and the Hotel Vichk, for decades the most expensive and exclusive address in the city, had closed its doors.

At the north end of the square, the Hotel Ancerre was

lit up like a candelabrum, but its patrons weren't the wealthy merchants and nobility who'd once rented its apartments. As the headquarters of the Directory and the Patriot Guard, it was ringed by halberdiers, and carriages hastily painted with blue and black stripes came and went constantly from its stables.

The crowds were different, too. Marcus remembered children running through the square, laughing at the fountains and buying sweets from the vendors. Not only were there no families now, but he scarcely saw any young men—and no wonder, when anyone who looked as though he might be capable of carrying a musket risked being harried by accusations of cowardice whenever he went out in public.

He leaned back in his chair, trying to work some of the stiffness out of his back, and looked forlornly at the mug in front of him. He'd discovered the hard way that what was being sold as coffee smelled and tasted as though it had been brewed from tree bark, and after a cautious sip he'd left it well enough alone. Marcus would happily have done terrible things for one small cup of coffee the way they served it in Khandar, black as the Beast and strong enough to melt copper.

Andy returned, pulling out the chair opposite him with a nasty screech of iron on stone and sitting down. She slapped a broadsheet in front of him, and he put his hand over it before it was caught by the afternoon breeze.

"This was the best they had," she said, frowning. "Doesn't sound like what *I* saw happen, though."

Marcus looked down at the paper. It was headlined FOREIGN ELEMENTS CAUSE CHAOS AT THE UNIVERSITY. The text recounted how a band of right-thinking citizens had assisted the Patriot Guard in suppressing a disturbance at the University and contributed to the arrest of several foreign spies. It said the grounds had been slightly damaged and "some injuries were suffered," although it neglected to mention by whom.

"Nothing about the Preacher."

"It doesn't say that any army officers were arrested," Andy said encouragingly. "You'd think they'd mention that."

"Unless they're keeping it quiet," he said. "Did you see the Patriot Guard arresting anybody?"

"No," she admitted. "But we left in a hurry."

Marcus sighed. The more he thought about what had happened at the University, the less he liked it. It was *possible* that the Patriot Guard had retreated in the face of the mob from cowardice, or bureaucratic error, or even because their commander thought he was in danger of being overwhelmed. But the timing—just after Marcus himself had arrived—was a fairly startling coincidence. He hadn't made much of a secret of his visit, and he had a nasty feeling that he'd been the cause of what had happened. *Maurisk must know by now that we were poking around in Exchange Central. If he's not confident enough to have me arrested outright, getting me involved in a riot would be just the thing.*

That felt like paranoia. For that matter, what he was doing now felt like paranoia, treating a meeting between two old school friends like a cloak-and-dagger rendezvous from a penny opera. But he was starting to think a bit of paranoia was justified.

Enough. His thoughts had been chasing around and around in circles, faster and faster. He felt like a dog that had worn itself out in pursuit of its own tail.

He looked up at Andy, who was drinking the not-coffee with every sign of enjoyment. One side of her face was a single massive bruise, fading now to a slightly alarming shade of yellow and green.

"How do you feel?" he said.

"I'll live," she said. "The coffee's not *that* bad."

Marcus grinned and tapped the side of his face.

"Oh." Andy shrugged. "It hurts a bit. But like I said, I've had worse."

"Really?"

"Oh yes. When I was nine I was in a fight and ended up with a broken arm and three cracked ribs."

"I'd hate to see what happened to the other fellow."

"There were three of them, and yes, it wasn't pretty." She drained the cup and set it down. "Why do you ask?"

"Just curious. You certainly know your way around a

broken broom handle. I was just thinking I'd never had a soldier under my command . . . quite like you."

Andy barked a laugh. "I suppose that makes sense."

"How did you get involved in all this?"

She cocked her head. "You mean, why am I not at home sewing and making babies like a proper young lady?"

"I . . ." Marcus felt himself reddening under his beard. "I wouldn't put it quite like that."

"It's all right. I guess it goes back to Mad Jane. You know her?"

"We've met briefly," Marcus said. There had been a few hurried introductions before Midvale, and the occasional briefing afterward, before the Army of the East had departed for the front. He recalled flashing green eyes and a fierce expression. "She helped Captain Ihernglass put together his . . . female contingent."

"Ihernglass, right. He . . . I mean . . ."

Andy hesitated. Marcus wasn't certain why, until he recalled that Ihernglass had been in disguise as a woman while he was with the Leatherbacks. He felt a pang of sympathy. *It can't be easy finding out someone has been fooling you all along.*

Andy cleared her throat. "Anyway. I grew up in the Docks, more or less on my own. When I was ten the Armsmen got me for stealing. Nobody to pay fees or speak on my behalf, but the magistrate said he liked the look of me, so he sent me to Mrs. Wilmore's. You know anything about Mrs. Wilmore's?"

Marcus shook his head, feeling out of his depth. He'd had a few youthful misadventures that had ended with a run-in with the Armsmen, but they'd never resulted in anything more serious than a clip round the ear followed by a stern talking-to from his father.

"The Royal Benevolent Home for Wayward Youth." Andy pronounced the words with distaste. "We always called it Mrs. Wilmore's Prison for Young Ladies. Girls got sent there if they got caught stealing or whoring, or sometimes if their parents went to prison. We were supposed to be raised into proper and productive members of society, until someone came along to marry us."

Marcus wanted to say that this didn't sound so bad, but a look at Andy's expression told him this would be unwise. He nodded instead.

"Mrs. Wilmore," Andy said, "would *arrange* a marriage for the girls who were old enough and properly educated. Farmers from the deep country, mostly, or the mining villages. A man needs a wife to run a farm, she was always telling us, and bear his children and raise them to be good little workers. A farmer could come to the Prison and buy himself a sweet young wife, like a new plow. The girls didn't get a choice in the matter."

"That can't be right." Marcus' forehead creased. "The government would never allow such a thing."

Andy smiled grimly. "Of course it would. Can't have too many little vagabonds and prostitutes running around, and can't ship the girls to Khandar." She sighed. "Truth be told, most of the girls went to their marriages willingly enough. Sharing a man's bed isn't so bad if you get food and a roof out of the bargain. Only another kind of whoring, if you look at it that way.

"Not Jane, though. She was too much for even Mrs. Wilmore to deal with. Fought the mistresses, fought the proctors, refused to sit still and be educated. They striped her black and blue with the switch, locked her up, tried whatever they could think of, but they couldn't break her.

"So Mrs. Wilmore found this farmer named Ganhide. He was a big brute of a man, ugly as a pig, and he agreed to take Jane as his fourth wife. Nobody asked too hard what happened to the first three. They were just glad to be rid of her. She tried to tear his eyes out when they brought her to him, but he just laughed.

"And then . . ." Andy paused and leaned forward slightly, eyes sparkling. "I was at the Prison when Jane came *back*. Nobody had ever come back before. She walked right in, bold as brass, and told the girls they weren't going to be married off to anybody anymore."

"Nobody tried to stop her?" Marcus said.

Andy paused, then gave an awkward shrug. "They tried, but most of the girls were with her by then, and they weren't going to stand for it. We followed her out of the Prison and all the way to the city."

"And that's how the Leatherbacks got started?" Marcus said.

"More or less." Andy's face clouded. "Things were . . . bad, for a while. Jane was always trying her best to keep everyone going, and some of the older girls started helping her. We moved into the Docks, and we fought the thieves and the pimps and the tax farmers and anyone else who got in the way. And *that*," she said, taking a deep breath, "is why I know my way around a brawl."

Saints and martyrs. Marcus wondered if Ihernglass knew all this. It was widely agreed that he and Jane were lovers. *If nothing else, it explains where he found so many women ready to pick up muskets. With an upbringing like that, it's no wonder they're abnormal.*

"Well," Marcus said, "that's quite a story. I always wondered why they called her Mad Jane."

"You'd be a little mad, too, if you went through what she did," Andy said. "Sometimes you have to be crazy to fight back."

"Mmm," Marcus said noncommittally. He wasn't certain it was a good idea to encourage hero worship of a murderer, but Andy was clearly not open to discussion in that direction. Glancing around for a distraction, he was relieved to see a bearded man in a blue uniform hurrying across the square in their direction. "Ah. I think we may finally be in luck."

"I'll make myself scarce, then," Andy said. "But give a yell if you need me."

"Hello, Robbie," Marcus said, rising, as his old friend approached the table. He laughed as the other man made to salute, waved it away, and they shook hands instead. Robert was still careful not to sit down first, Marcus noticed, in deference to a superior officer.

Robert Englise had always been one for doing things properly. He had been Marcus' best friend at the War College when they enrolled together at the tender age of sixteen, and they'd spent much of the first two-year term in each other's company. Even then, Robert's fierce devotion to the army had been evident, though back then Marcus had aspired to live up to his example.

The fire at the d'Ivoire estate, which had killed Marcus' parents and his four-year-old sister, Ellie, had driven them apart for a time. Marcus now knew this had been deliberate murder, perpetrated by the minions of the Last Duke, but at the time he'd believed it to be a tragic, stupid accident, and it had sent him spiraling into depression. He'd turned his back on Robert and his other friends, and it had only been the insistent intervention of Adrecht Roston that had kept him from leaving the College.

Afterward, while they'd all remained friends, Marcus had drifted out of Robert's straight-and-narrow orbit and toward Adrecht's more indulgent lifestyle. The War of the Princes had interrupted their term in the field; while Marcus had been closest to the action, serving in the supply train and joining the general chaos after the disaster at Vansfeldt, Robert had been placed on the staff of a prestigious regiment, on track for an important command. In their second stint at the College, they'd been more distant, but they hadn't lost touch entirely until Marcus volunteered to accompany Adrecht to exile in Khandar.

"Robbie," Robert said reflectively, settling into his chair. "I don't think anybody's called me that since graduation."

"Sorry," Marcus said.

"It's fine." Robert smiled, a hint of the old twinkle in his blue eyes. He'd grown from a slim youth into a solid man, with a thick beard shot through with white and with just a hint of paunch. "'Captain Englise' would feel wrong, coming from you."

"Just so long as you don't call me sir," Marcus said. "It was bad enough getting that from Adrecht all those years."

"I'll try to restrain myself." Robert grinned. "We always

said you'd go a long way. After you left for Khandar, the boys and I used to say we didn't think you'd take us literally." Robert eyed the colonel's eagles on Marcus' shoulders. "Now it looks like we were right after all."

Marcus searched his old friend's face for a hint of jealousy. In the old Royal Army, captain was the highest rank a War College graduate could hope to achieve, lacking a noble pedigree. Colonelcies were reserved for the scions of ancient bloodlines. The colonel of a regiment, they'd used to joke, was there to look good at the head of the parade, while the captains ran things for him. No doubt it had been true in many outfits—the system had always been an awkward compromise between the noble tradition of martial leadership and the need of a modern army for officers with specialized training.

Now Marcus had been promoted beyond what he could have dared to hope for, in the old days, thanks to Janus bet Vhalnich, and much of the Royal Army tradition had been swept away. The new volunteer battalions *elected* their officers, putting men who'd never even set foot in the College in the higher ranks. *Not to mention Ihernglass and his battalion of* women*!* Amid this change, Robert had made his career in the bastion of tradition, the Ministry of War itself. As the colonels had departed for the front lines, he'd quietly risen, until he'd become the senior military subordinate of Giles Durenne, the new Minister of War himself.

Not jealous, Marcus decided, *or else very good at hiding it.* That was good. He hadn't been sure what to expect when he asked Robert to meet.

"Is that coffee you're drinking?" Robert said, raising his hand to signal the waiter.

"I'm honestly not sure," Marcus said, pushing it away and making a face.

"Wine, then."

It seemed a bit early in the day, but Marcus let him order two glasses. When they arrived, Robert raised his in a toast.

"To Adrecht," he said. "He deserved better."

"To Adrecht," Marcus murmured. His old friend had

indeed deserved better. Janus' campaign had broken him, costing him an arm and finally driving him to mutiny and betrayal. His bleached bones lay somewhere in the shifting sands of the Great Desol. He sipped the wine and set the glass down, feeling awkward.

"So, what can I do for you?" Robert said. "I'm assuming this isn't just a sudden desire to catch up with old school friends."

"I . . ." Marcus hesitated, and Robert laughed out loud.

"Oh, just come out with it," he said. "You go cross-eyed when you're trying to be subtle. You want a favor."

"Something like that." Marcus shook his head. "I'm sorry to have to come to you."

"Don't worry about it," Robert said. "I'm used to it. Since I took over at the Ministry, you wouldn't believe how many old classmates have suddenly remembered we used to be pals when they come asking for supplies." He smiled as he said this, but it still stung a little.

"It's not that kind of favor." Marcus hesitated, but there was nothing to do but come out with it. "You know I've been working for General Vhalnich."

"So I'd heard. They say you're his right hand."

"That might be a stretch." *If I was his right hand, I'd expect him to tell me more about what was going on.* "But he trusts me, and I've been representing his interests in the city. After the attempt on the queen's life, Her Majesty asked General Vhalnich to investigate. I've been leading that effort."

"Interesting. I understood that the Directory and the Patriot Guard had determined the bomb was planted by Borelgai spies."

"The queen had reason to believe that elements in the Patriot Guard were involved. She thought it best to have an independent inquiry."

"I see." Robert's lip quirked. "You've found something, or you wouldn't be here."

"I have." Marcus swallowed and barreled past the point of no return. "I believe that the President of the Directory was responsible for the bombing."

Robert blinked, but showed no other sign of surprise. He stared at Marcus for a long, silent moment, then took a swallow from his glass. "You don't set your sights low, do you?"

"Believe me, I'd rather not be involved at all," Marcus said. "But I can't ignore the truth."

"You have evidence?"

"Just . . . hints, so far," Marcus said. "But we've identified a location used by the plotters as a base. There may be records there, documents, correspondence, that sort of thing."

"I begin to see the picture," Robert said. "You can't exactly ask the Patriot Guard to stage a raid."

"No. And I don't have the authority to do it on my own." Raesinia was all afire to investigate on their own, but Marcus had convinced her to let him try going through channels. *I have to try.* "With the Armsmen dissolved, the Ministry is the only organization with the standing to look into it."

"If the Directory is involved, how do you know you can trust the Ministry?"

Marcus grimaced. "Minister Durenne is Directory President Maurisk's chief political opposition. He's not likely to be involved in his conspiracy. And besides . . ." He shook his head. "I don't trust the Ministry, but I trust *you*, Robert. I know that if there's a plot, you'd never be part of it."

"I'm honored," Robert said dryly. "I might have changed since we were at the College together, you know."

"We've all changed," Marcus said. "But not that much."

Robert drained his glass and set it on the table. He traced one finger around the edge, pensively, and there was a long, quiet moment.

"It puts me in a hell of a spot, you know," he said finally.

"I understand," Marcus said. "I wouldn't do it if I felt like I had any choice."

"I know." Robert put on a faint smile. "People change but, as you say, not that much. The Marcus d'Ivoire I knew wouldn't put a friend on the spot, unless he was certain his duty demanded it."

For a moment, Marcus saw Adrecht's face, scared and pleading. He said nothing.

"And please believe me," Robert said, "when I say you *are* still my friend. I wish we'd come back together under better circumstances."

"So do I."

"So take it from one friend to another when I tell you that the best thing you can do is to drop this, right now, and never mention it to a living soul."

Another pause stretched awkwardly.

"The minister . . . ," Marcus began.

"The minister does not have as much power as many believe," Robert said. "He leads the Radical party, yes, but they are far from united, and in any case the Conservatives are currently ascendant. Suppose I take this to him. Suppose, for the moment, that he believes you completely. What then? You're asking him to risk everything—his *life*—on one gambit, one chance to bring Maurisk down. If he can't convince the Deputies-General the allegations are true, Maurisk would have him on the Spike before dawn as a traitor, and who knows how many others with him."

"You don't think he'd risk it?" Marcus said.

"I'm certain he wouldn't. Durenne dislikes Maurisk, and I'm sure he'd be happy to see the Directory fall, but above all he's concerned with maintaining his position. Balancing the demands of the Radicals and the orders from the Directory is hard enough without bringing on a crisis. If I brought this to him, he'd ask me where I heard it, and when I told him he'd tell Maurisk, to keep the peace. Then *you* would be the one who'd find the Patriots at your door some morning."

Marcus shook his head. "If we had *proof* Maurisk was trying to kill the queen—"

"He'd say it was fabricated," Robert said. "The Conservatives would believe him, the Radicals wouldn't, and they'd shout at each other twice as loud as before." He shrugged. "If you brought proof to the deputies yourself, some of them might listen. But Durenne would bury it first, and I can't say I'm certain he'd be wrong. Have you considered what it would do to the country to have this crisis *now*? Things are bad enough at the front."

"Then what should I do?"

"Your duty, of course. Serving your country, its queen, and its people." Robert gave a wry grin. "It's never quite as clear as they make it seem in class, is it?"

When Robert had departed, leaving a few coins to pay for the wine, Andy returned and sat down in the chair he'd vacated.

"What happened?" Andy said. "You don't look happy."

"He wouldn't listen." Marcus pressed one hand into the other, listening to the knuckles pop.

"He didn't believe you?"

"I don't know if he believed me or not. But it doesn't matter. The Ministry won't help us."

"But—" Andy shook her head, confused. "But then what do we do now?"

Our duty. "What Raesinia wanted to do all along. Go down to that warehouse and find out for ourselves." Marcus gritted his teeth. "*Every* member of the Deputies can't be as cowardly as Durenne. Once we splash this across the broadsheets, they'll have to do something about it whether they want to or not."

RAESINIA

Of late, Raesinia had been spending more time at Mrs. Felda's church than Twin Turrets. She told Marcus this was because she needed to consult with Cora, but in truth she was more a hindrance than a help to the girl's continuing efforts to pin down the web of false orders and missing documentation that outlined the missing gunpowder. Tracking to the warehouse had been simple enough, but finding out where it went from there was proving more difficult. Cora was still hoping to find a pattern in the records that would lead them to a suspect, but Raesinia wasn't optimistic.

We have to go and see what they're hiding. Marcus was determined to do things by the book, which meant trying to convince the army to launch an investigation. Raesinia wasn't optimistic about that, either. *Durenne would be a fool to provoke a confrontation, unless he wants to end up on the Spike. Backing Maurisk into a corner is too dangerous.* But Marcus had refused to be persuaded. *His naïveté can be sweet, when it's not so annoying.*

While the colonel had waited for his audience with his friend in the Ministry, therefore, Raesinia had stewed. She came to Mrs. Felda's because there was always something for her to do, while at Twin Turrets there was only the watchful silence of the Mierantai guards and a trunk full of books she'd already read. Today Lieutenant Uhlan and Hayver were her escorts, both in plainclothes and armed with cudgels.

Mrs. Felda put them to work, as she did anyone who appeared to be the least bit idle. Raesinia wasn't sure if she knew they were soldiers, but it wouldn't have mattered; she was fairly certain that Mrs. Felda would still have conscripted her to fold laundry or stir pots even if she knew Raesinia was Queen of Vordan. Currently, Lieutenant Uhlan was carrying heavy sacks of provisions from the back door into the basement, while Hayver sewed up worn-out clothing. The boy had proven to be a dab hand with a needle.

Raesinia was cutting vegetables for the endless cauldrons of soup that were the cornerstone of meals at Mrs. Felda's. The diet of bread and broth was dull, but there were few complaints from the refugees. Every day, new stories trickled in about fresh atrocities visited on foreigners or other undesirables in the name of national security. Every night, Mrs. Felda led a prayer for the safety of those Marcus had already passed along to the Army of the East's supply train, in which Free and Sworn residents both joined.

Beside Raesinia at the chopping table was the tall, severe young woman who'd returned with Marcus from the University. She attacked a pile of potatoes as though they had done her a personal injury, hacking them into irregular chunks with a long knife. Raesinia discreetly moved her own work a pace farther down the table, to avoid being pelted with flying bits of spud.

"*Verdoht!*" the woman said. It sounded like a curse. The knife jangled as it bounced on the floor, and the woman held one hand in the other, blood welling between her fingers.

"Are you all right?" Raesinia said, taking care to enunciate clearly. She didn't recognize the language the woman was swearing in, but it had a far eastern tone. Most of the refugees spoke at least a little Vordanai, but their skill varied widely.

"No, I am not," the woman said in a clipped, precise accent. "I am losing a knife fight to a *folgaht* potato. I doubt my honor will ever recover."

Raesinia found herself smiling. "I can't do much for your honor. How about your hand?"

"My hand is not bleeding *too* badly." The woman wiped her palm on her trousers, heedless of the bloodstains, and peered at the long cut along her index finger. "I will survive, I suspect."

"We ought to bind it up," Raesinia said. "I doubt Mrs. Felda would appreciate blood as an extra ingredient in her soup."

The woman smiled. "It might give it some more flavor."

Mrs. Felda kept strips of clean linen handy for bandages, an essential precaution with so many children about. Raesinia grabbed one, dunked it in the boiling water of the cauldron, and gestured for the woman to hold out her hand. She gritted her teeth and hissed as Raesinia pulled the bandage on, but made no other complaint as she wrapped the wound and tied the cloth tight.

"There," Raesinia said. "Can you still bend your finger?"

The woman tested it, winced, and nodded.

"What happened to the knife?"

"Over there, I think." The woman pointed, and they fished around under the table until they found it, steel still spotted with blood. Raesinia tested the edge with her finger and found it dull.

"No wonder. This needs seeing to. Do you know how?"

"No," the woman said. "This is my first time for kitchen work."

"Come on. There's a stone in the pantry."

"Thank you. Ah . . ."

"It's Raesinia. Raes, if you like."

The woman nodded, following in Raesinia's wake. "I'm Viera."

The pantry was a small room off the main hall, its theological function long forgotten. It had no windows, and rows of shelves held any food that wouldn't bear long storage. There was also a basin and a whetstone, as Raesinia remembered. She pulled them out and demonstrated the long, easy strokes that would sharpen the blade, then let Vicra try for herself.

"You came here from the University, right?" Raesinia said as the scrape of metal on stone formed a steady rhythm.

"Yes," Viera said. "Colonel Marcus kindly came to fetch us when the crowd wanted us on the Spike."

"Had you been there long?"

"Not long. I came after your revolution."

"What were you studying?"

Viera gave a brief grin. "Guns. Under Captain Vahkerson."

"That's . . . unusual, isn't it? For a woman."

"Before this I was studying with an alchemist in Hamvelt. He felt it was beneath him to have a girl as an apprentice, but my father paid him a great deal. Unfortunately, I succeeded in burning down the greater part of his laboratory, so my status was in some dispute at the time of the revolution. When I heard what had happened, I decided to come here."

Raesinia nodded sympathetically. "I suppose you found out it wasn't all it was cracked up to be. Freedom and equality for all and so on."

"Philosophy and nonsense," Viera said, her tone implying the two were synonymous. "I came because I heard your women were permitted to fight. At Midvale, and now in the Army of the East."

"Fight?" Raesinia blinked. "But why come and fight if you didn't care about the revolution?"

"Because I love to see things explode," Viera said matter-of-factly. She gave the blade a final pass and held it up to admire her handiwork. "My father says it is a sickness with me, this love, but after the fourth tutor quit he began sending me to alchemists in the hope that I could at least learn to do it *safely*. I was glad to be able to study with Captain Vahkerson."

"Oh," Raesinia said. "What will you do when you get to go home?"

"Begin again, I suppose." Viera shrugged. "But home is in Vheed, which is a very long way from here, especially in wartime. So meanwhile I make do. Is there news of Captain Vahkerson, do you know?"

Raesinia shook her head. "Nothing that I've heard."

"A pity." Viera regarded her curiously. "And you? You work with Colonel Marcus?"

"Y . . . yes." It took Raesinia a moment to remember her cover story. *I'm getting sloppy.* "I'm a courier, mostly. There's not enough soldiers left to do everything, so he hired a few civilians."

"Do you know him well?"

"A little bit, I suppose."

"He has a wife?"

Raesinia shook her head. "He spent most of his career in Khandar."

"Hmm. You think he would be averse to finding one?"

"I'm sure I have no idea," Raesinia said, cheeks reddening a little. "Why, are you planning to marry him?"

"I'd thought about it. He saved my life, after all, and that is supposed to make me go all starry-eyed." She shrugged. "He is a kind man with a fine figure, and I think Father would accept a colonel for a son-in-law. It would keep the proposals away, at least. What do you think?"

"I think," Raesinia said, "that we have more potatoes to chop."

"There must be a more efficient way," Viera said as they wandered back to the table. "If the potatoes were strapped to the outside of some sort of explosive chamber, and the powder input carefully regulated—"

"Raes!" Cora was waiting by the mound of spuds, waving frantically. "There you are. The colonel's been looking for you!"

"Duty calls," Raesinia said to Viera. "Try to make sure the potatoes end up *chopped* instead of blown to smithereens."

Viera snorted. "Powder residue would ruin the flavor anyway. I need to think of a better design."

"Do you know what happened?" Raesinia asked Cora.

The girl shook her head. "It can't be good, though. He looks like he's in a temper."

Raesinia sighed. He shouldn't have bothered. It couldn't be helped, though. Sometimes you needed to hit the wall headfirst before you know it was there.

Marcus, Andy, Hayver, and Lieutenant Uhlan were gathered in the quiet corner where Cora piled her books, Marcus and Uhlan in quiet conversation while the two rankers looked on uncomfortably. Marcus looked up as Raesinia approached, and she paused for a moment.

A kind man with a fine figure. I suppose he is.

"Raes?" he said. "Is something wrong?"

"No." She shook her head and stepped into the little circle. "So, what's the plan?"

CHAPTER TWELVE

WINTER

"We're eager to work with the Vordanai, of course," the tradesman lied. "And the terms your general offered us were more than fair."

"More than fair," his fat companion agreed. "I won't hear a word said against General Janus." He pronounced the name wrong, jah-noos instead of ya-nuhs.

"It's the quartermasters," the tradesman continued. "They've been promising us payment for days, and now they say they've delivered it. But what am I supposed to do with this?"

Winter looked at the paper the man held out to her. It said, on embossed parchment with many elaborate curlicues, that it was a bill to be drawn against the treasury of the Vordanai Crown and Deputies-General, to the amount of six thousand five hundred crowns, payable no more than six months after the conclusion of "the present hostilities."

"I got one, too," said the fat merchant. "I delivered six wagonloads of hardtack and four hundred head of horses, and they gave me a paper with a stamp on it."

"I'm sure the Vordanai treasury will honor those bills in full, once the war is over," Winter said, though she was actually certain of no such thing. Finance, beyond the kind that clinked in your pocket, had always been vague and mysterious to her.

"What am I supposed to do until then?" the tradesman said. "Cut this into pieces and feed it to my family?"

Winter sat back in her chair and looked desperately at Cyte for help. The ex-student stepped in smoothly.

"I suggest," Cyte said, "you take it to a bank. I'm sure they would be happy to convert it into coin for a reasonable percentage."

"I tried that," said the fat one, "and they told me to shove it where the sun don't shine." He eyed Cyte and added, "Begging your pardon, ma'am."

"Lieutenant," Winter said, "would you make a point of visiting Gold Row tomorrow morning and impressing on the local financiers the absolute sincerity of Her Majesty's government? I'm sure once you explain the position, they'll be happy to assist these gentlemen." Winter looked from one man to another. "Will that do?"

The tradesman scratched his cheek and nodded. The merchant looked unhappy, but he turned to follow his companion out, which was all Winter really wanted. Once the office door closed behind them, Cyte gave her a mischievous grin.

"You're getting the hang of this. I take it I'm to tell these bankers what will happen to them if they *don't* play along?"

"Be as polite as you can," Winter said.

Cyte nodded. "You should know, though, that this can't go on indefinitely. It's just pillage by degrees."

"Without the rape and murder," Winter said.

"That is an improvement," Cyte admitted. "But we're already not getting enough food in the city. The merchants won't bring it in once they figure out that we're only paying in paper promises. The nobles are already moving everything they can carry to the country, and the bankers will follow suit before long."

"Our squads at the gate are going to have to start searching any cart or wagon that leaves," Winter said. "I don't want an ounce of gold or a pound of food to leave the city if we can stop it. Anybody who tries forfeits their property."

"That may not go over well."

"As long as the quartermasters keep 'requisitioning' everything in sight, we don't have a choice." The Ministry of War seemed to view Desland as a storeroom to be sacked, regardless of the fact that its inhabitants had surrendered peacefully and largely sympathized with the invaders.

"I know." Cyte sighed. "Hopefully Janus will send for us before too much longer."

"Funny how marching off to a battlefield to get shot at can seem like an improvement—"

They were interrupted by shouting from outside the door. Winter could hear Bobby, telling someone to calm down, but she was mostly drowned under a rising voice with a heavy Hamveltai accent.

"—I will not, sir! I have been waiting an hour and a quarter and I will not wait a moment longer. Now you open that door at once or—"

"Bobby!" Winter shouted. "Who is it?"

Silence fell. A moment later, Bobby said, "It's the Baron di Wallach, sir. And his wife. He says it's important."

"Important!" someone, presumably the baron, sputtered. "I should say—"

"Let him in," Winter says. "I've been . . . expecting him."

The door opened, and a tall, thin man in late middle age stormed in. He was impeccably dressed in what must have been Hamveltai fashion—high, flop-brimmed boots, gray tights, a long belted doublet, and a light wool coat, with a big wide-brimmed hat tied up on both sides and topped by a long white plume. Behind him came a plump woman swathed in so many layers of velvet and lace that the outline of her body was difficult to discern. She wore heavy makeup around her eyes, but it had run down her cheeks in streaks, as though she'd been crying.

"My lord." Winter got to her feet and bowed. Di Wallach looked at her as a man might regard a roach that had crawled out onto the table during a fancy dinner party.

"You are Colonel Ihernglass?" he said. His Vordanai was good, in spite of his accent.

"I am."

"Then your ruffians have *kidnapped* my daughter, and I demand her release *at once*. And I swear to you, if they've laid a finger on her—"

The Baroness di Wallach burst into tears at the mere suggestion of this, pressing her hands to her face and heaving huge, racking sobs. Winter resisted an urge to pat her on the shoulder and offer her a handkerchief, which she suspected would have gone over poorly. Instead she sat down behind her desk, which seemed to incite new heights of rage in the already apoplectic baron.

"This would be Anne-Marie Gertrude di Wallach, I take it?" she said.

"Of course it would," the baron said. "Have you got many other daughters of nobility locked in your dungeons?"

"I don't have anybody locked in my dungeons, but there are at least three daughters of nobility in the regiment at the moment. They all came here of their own free will and asked to enlist."

"That's the most ridiculous thing I've ever heard," di Wallach said. "It's bad enough that your army lets its prostitutes dress like soldiers, but *recruiting* from the ranks of the quality is beyond the pale. You can get your rent girls from the brothels across the river like everyone else. I don't believe for a moment that my Anne-Marie—"

"Shall we ask her?" Winter said. She turned to Cyte. "Send someone for Ranker di Wallach, would you?"

Cyte nodded and slipped out of the room, leaving Winter alone with Anne-Marie's parents. The baron looked uncomfortable.

"My daughter is only nineteen," he said, "and is subject to irrational feminine fancies from time to time. Whatever she may think she wants, I have every right to stop her. I am her father and she cannot leave my house without my permission."

"I would suggest that she has done exactly that."

"Which is why you are obligated to return her."

Winter permitted herself a slight smile. It was nice, for once, to be holding all the cards. "I'm afraid that I don't see it that way."

"The law is on my side, and you know it."

"Actually, my lord, since your city has surrendered to the Vordanai army, and I happen to be the ranking member of that army here, I think you'll find the law is whatever I say it is." She saw the door open again, over the baron's shoulder. Anne-Marie and Cyte were standing in the doorway, and Winter raised her voice. "Let me make myself absolutely clear. I will not keep any Hamveltai citizen here against his or her will. However, if I have accepted someone into the ranks of this regiment, they will not be dismissed from it unless *I* deem it necessary. Is that understood?"

"What do you want?" the baron said. "Is it money? How much is my little girl worth to you? A thousand eagles?"

"It's not about money, my lord. The Vordanai army needs good soldiers more than it needs coin." Not *quite* true, Winter had to admit, but it was a nice sentiment.

"She's just a little girl," said the Baroness di Wallach, breaking out of her sobs. Makeup ran in rivers down her face, and her nose was sticky with snot. "She's scarcely been off our estate in her life! You can't expect her to march around in the *dirt* and sleep in a camp with a bunch of *men*. God only knows what's happened to her already!"

"Have you considered that getting off your estate may have been one of her goals?"

"But she could get hurt! People *die* in battles."

There was a pause.

"A great many people get hurt in battles," Winter said. "Some of my friends have died. If things had gone differently, I might have been killed myself. Every one of them had family who would have preferred someone else pay the price."

"But she's my little girl," the baroness said. "You can't . . ."

Looking at the woman's watery eyes, Winter almost softened. Fortunately, her husband cut in.

"It's one thing when a bunch of peasants get themselves killed," he said. "It's quite another thing for a daughter of a noble family to put herself in danger."

Winter set her jaw. "My lord, I have served both alongside and against the sons of noble families, and let me assure you that they die just like anybody else. The same goes for their daughters." She raised her eyes. "Lieutenant, did you find the ranker?"

Cyte was now alone in the doorway. "Yes, sir. She indicated she didn't wish to speak to the visitors."

"She'll speak to me, by God, or else—"

Winter cut the baron off. "Then we have nothing further to discuss. Please escort our guests out."

Di Wallach whirled to face Cyte. "You have some cheek, telling me I can't speak to my own daughter. I will not leave this room until . . ."

He trailed off. In the antechamber, six big rankers from the Royals were standing at attention, muskets on their shoulders. Cyte stood in front of them, her expression neutral.

"Baron? Baroness? If you'll come with me?"

Baron di Wallach hesitated, caught between his pride and his desire not to suffer the insult of being physically dragged from the room. Finally, he straightened up, smoothed his coat, and marched out as haughtily as he could manage. His wife followed him, sniffling, only after throwing Winter a last pleading glance. Their "escort" fell in around them and filed out the door.

Cyte was grinning again. "Also nicely done, sir."

"Would you tell Ranker di Wallach I would like to speak to her, please?"

Cyte nodded and returned a moment later with Anne-Marie, who must have been waiting just out of sight. A few days had wrought quite a lot of change in the girl. Her hair had been inexpertly cut short, all those waves of blond curls traded for a flyaway mess, and her dress and court shoes had been swapped for good leather boots and the blue trousers and jacket of the Vordanai army. The uniforms Winter had requisitioned for the Girls' Own had arrived only the day before, and as she'd predicted they'd done wonders for morale.

Anne-Marie's pale skin was red from the sun, and her hands were cracked and blistered. Abby and her sergeants had been working her hard, along with all the other new recruits, but somewhat to Winter's surprise the girl had borne everything they'd thrown at her. Her friends, more daughters of the elite of Deslandai society, had done like-wise, as had the several dozen recruits of more humble origins. As Winter had predicted, word had gotten around.

"Sir!" Anne-Marie said, with an excellent salute.

"You didn't want to speak to your parents?"

"No, sir," she said. Her Vordanai was still a bit broken. "You already say . . . everything I want to say."

"Glad to hear it."

"Hard to see Mother," the girl said. "I thought she never like me. See her crying . . ." She shook her head.

Winter fought the urge to tell Anne-Marie to run after her mother, hug her, and go home. *Not my choice to make.* Even if all that was waiting for the girl was a musket ball on some muddy battlefield, it was her choice whether or not to go there.

"You're doing all right, then?" Winter said, a bit lamely.

"The work hurts," Anne-Marie said. "But I stick to it. Learning better Vordanai, and how to make jokes."

"That's good." Winter had no doubt the Girls' Own would have Anne-Marie swearing and telling filthy stories like a native in no time. "That's all, then."

"Thank you, sir." Anne-Marie saluted and went out, and Cyte returned.

"Would you have credited it?" Winter said, nodding at the retreating girl.

"Not a bit," Cyte said. "But I'd bet you she makes cor-poral before the end of the year."

"No bet," Winter said. "I'm inclined to think it'll be sooner." She noticed Cyte was holding a crisp white paper, folded and sealed. "What've you got there?"

"Ask, and you shall receive," Cyte said. "Orders from

the general. There was a courier waiting when I went to retrieve Anne-Marie."

Winter reached out eagerly, and Cyte handed the packet over. The seal was army blue and stamped with the official Ministry device, and Winter broke it open with her thumb. Inside was square onionskin paper, folded many times over and bearing the sweeping lines of a map in what Winter thought was Janus' own delicate hand. The letter itself read:

> Colonel Ihernglass,
>
> The time has come for you to rejoin us, some-what sooner than expected. I need you to do everything in your power to bring your regiment to the location marked on the enclosed map, on the morning of the day there noted. You will be met there by friendly units with further instructions.
>
> I know this will be difficult, but you have yet to disappoint me. If you succeed, the entire Army of the East—all of Vordan—will owe you and yours a great debt.
>
> Lose no time that can be avoided. I rely on you.
>
> —J

Winter blinked, and showed the note to Cyte, who had already unfolded the map. The lieutenant gave a low whistle.

"That's . . . *Difficult* isn't going to be the half of it." She stiffened her fingers into a pair of dividers and walked them across the map. "That's close to a hundred miles. If he wants us there in the morning, and assuming we leave tomorrow, we'll be four days on the march. And it looks like there's a good road only half the way. After that we're in the backcountry."

Twenty-five miles a day. That was faster than the Colonials had marched at their hardest in Khandar. A killing pace, even for veteran soldiers. Winter drew in a deep breath, and exhaled slowly.

"I could catch the courier," Cyte said, as though reading her commander's thoughts. "Tell him we're not going to make it."

"Do you think we can do it?"

Cyte tilted her head, considering. "Some of us can. The wagons would never keep up, so we'll have to leave them behind. That means carrying provisions on our backs, which makes it harder." She shook her head. "We'll get there, but I don't know how many soldiers we'll have left when we do. Anybody who gets hurt or drops out is going to get left behind. And we'll probably be awfully hungry when we arrive."

"We leave the road *here*." Winter stabbed a finger at the map. "That's not far from the river. We've been floating supplies upriver all this time, so some of them must still be in transit."

"That's a thought," Cyte said. "Send riders ahead to flag down some of the barges and off-load enough to make a supply dump for us. It'll help."

"Do it," Winter said. "Right away. Then start working out a marching schedule."

"Yes, sir." Cyte paused. "What about the celebration tonight?"

"Oh, damn."

She'd almost forgotten. The Girls' Own had become nearly mutinous over the fact that they weren't allowed out into the city for recreation like the Royals, and so Winter had arranged to bring the city to them, so to speak. Wagons full of food and drink were waiting to be brought into the citadel at the start of the festivities, and all sorts of hopeful vendors were lining up to hawk their wares. The Royals, grumbling, had been ordered to abstain and help keep order.

"It'll have to go ahead," she said after a moment's thought. "There'd be a riot if we tried to stop it now. But pass the news that we're marching in the morning, and tell the Royals to pull out anyone who looks like they'll be too drunk to walk tomorrow. We'll wrap up early, too."

"I'm on it," Cyte said. "I'll have our supplies waiting at the gate in the morning. That just leaves—"

Winter sighed. "Jane. I know."

"We could leave them behind." Cyte smiled, to show it was a joke, and Winter forced a faint smile in return.

"Abby would never forgive me." *I would never forgive myself.* "I'll go and talk to her now. Maybe they haven't had time to get drunk yet."

I shouldn't have left this so long. But there had been a million things demanding her attention—angry merchants, new recruits, supplies and schedules and duty rosters—and she'd been so *sure* that Jane would eventually come to her senses of her own accord. Now that she thought about it more clearly, it was obvious that wasn't ever going to happen. *She'd never just slink home with her tail between her legs.* Her continuing debauch was as much a challenge to Winter as anything else. *And I just left her to get on with it.*

The current haunt of the Leatherbacks was a tavern called the Linked Rings, whose sign was a pair of barrel hoops welded together and optimistically slathered with gold paint, now mostly flaked away. It wasn't in the worst part of town—the true slums of Desland were across the river to the west—but it was about as bad as one could get while remaining on the eastern bank. Shabby row houses stretched down winding streets, and a fair number of angry or avaricious looks followed Winter as she brought Edgar to a halt in front of the tavern, dismounted, and handed his reins to the dirty young man who emerged from the neighboring alley.

She pressed a coin into his hand. "Keep him saddled. I won't be long."

The tavern was a two-story building, with a common room and a kitchen on the ground floor and private rooms upstairs for those who wanted to do their drinking in more select company. It was clear that any non-Leatherback clientele had abandoned the place, and the proprietor was also nowhere to be found. Clay mugs, wooden cups, and plates of half-eaten food still littered the big, solid tables of the common room, and the women of Jane's Leatherbacks were strewn about like detritus from a shipwreck. It was well past noon, but many of them were still asleep, snoring on the benches or curled up on the floor with their clothing in various states of disarray.

Some were up and moving, though, picking through the remains for tidbits. A couple of women were behind the bar, helping themselves to beer from the big kegs there. Near the door, Winter recognized Becca, one of Jane's lieutenants, in the process of carving an elaborate design into one of the tabletops with the point of a long knife. The woman looked up at her as the door swung closed, and Winter coughed.

"Where's Jane?" she said.

Becca got to her feet, knife in one hand, and glared. Winter wondered for a moment if it had been wise to decline Bobby's offer of an escort. She hadn't seriously thought that Jane's people would hurt her, but having a half dozen armed soldiers at her back would have been reassuring.

"Why?" Becca said eventually. A couple of other Leatherbacks were looking in their direction. Some of them had the same belligerent expression Becca did, but others looked more guilty than angry.

Winter raised her hands. "I want to talk to her, that's all."

There was another long, dangerous moment. Finally, Becca shrugged and gestured toward the stairs with her knife. "Up there."

"Thank you," Winter said. She slipped across the room, through the slowly rousing Leatherbacks, and made her way to the second floor.

Most of the private rooms there had their doors closed, and Winter dreaded the prospect of having to knock on each to find Jane. The rooms she could see were occupied by more Leatherbacks, in various stages of inebriation or consciousness. She found Winn, a tall, skinny woman who was another of Jane's lieutenants, naked and sleeping on a tabletop, curled around a similarly unclothed Deslandai boy with dark hair and a peach-fuzz beard. Another young man, wearing only a shirt, snored in the corner. Winter pulled the door closed, gently, and shook her head.

"Aha!" A door at the end of the hall opened, and there was Jane, leaning against the doorframe. An unmarked bottle of something green dangled from her fingers. The sight of her familiar, cocky smile made Winter's heart jump. "I thought I heard someone. Finally decided to pay us a visit?"

"I need to talk to you." Winter looked around at the other rooms, where Jane's voice had started a few Leatherbacks stirring. "Alone."

"Well, then. Come into my parlor." Jane stepped back and swept her arm out. Her room had a circular table and two semicircular benches, with a window that overlooked the alley outside. "I'm sure I can find a bottle for you."

"I don't need a bottle," Winter muttered, pushing past Jane. "And neither do you."

Jane nudged the door shut with her hip. "No?" She looked down at the green stuff and frowned. "I suppose not. I'm not even sure what the fuck this is, to be honest."

There were several other bottles on the table, and more on the floor, most of them empty. Winter carefully stepped through them to the window and glanced outside, then turned around and took a deep breath. "Jane—"

The kiss caught her by surprise. Jane was on top of her, arms thrown around her shoulders, lips rough against her. Winter retreated a step, and Jane leaned forward, pressing her against the wall beside the window. Her mouth tasted of alcohol, and faintly of vomit, and her lips were cracked and dry. Winter hesitated, long enough for Jane to press her body close, her breasts tight against Winter's uniform and one knee tangling between Winter's legs.

"Stop." Winter grabbed her by the shoulders and shoved her away. "Jane, stop!"

"What?" Jane cocked her head. "Don't tell me it's not what you want. I know it's been hard for *me*, with temptation all around." She grinned wickedly. "Did you see Winn, with her pretty boys? And one of the serving girls definitely gave me a wink. I've been frigging myself to sleep every night, wondering if you're doing the same thing up there in your castle—"

"Jane—"

"Oh, don't pretend you haven't."

Winter's cheeks were beet red. "Would you listen to me for a minute?"

"Oh, I see." Jane sat down heavily on the bench and let her head loll back. "It's not my Winter who's come to see me, it's Colonel Ihernglass."

"It's *me*," Winter said. "Jane, what are you doing?"

"Having a good time. Have you forgotten how?"

"It's been days."

"I know. The tavernkeepers here are a bunch of fucking puppies. I just glare at them and they hand over their keys and their virgin daughters." She caught Winter's expression and rolled her eyes. "Figuratively speaking. But they wouldn't last five minutes back in the Docks."

"And what about the regiment?"

"What about it? We fought the fucking battle, didn't we? We deserve a bit of a rest."

Winter stared, not sure what to say. Jane looked back, green eyes slightly bloodshot, then looked away uncomfortably.

"Besides," she said. "I figured you'd come and get me when you wanted me."

"I'm sorry I was so hard on you during the battle. I was—"

"You were angry," Jane said. "And you were probably right. Sevran knows about"—she waved a hand vaguely—"troops and lines and ranges, things like that. What do I know?"

"You've been a good captain for the Girls' Own—"

"No, I haven't." Jane crossed her arms. "Let's not lie about it. I make a shitty officer, and we both fucking know it."

"Being an officer isn't just about training. It's about your relationship with the soldiers. The girls worship you."

"The ones downstairs do," Jane said. "They've been with me a long time. The rest of them have found a new idol to bow to, I think."

"Abby was right," Winter said before she could stop herself. "You're jealous."

"You and Abby talk about me?" Jane smirked, but Winter could see the hurt in her eyes.

"She came to me, Jane. She's worried about you. We both are."

"She's a sweet girl. Tell her I can take care of myself."

Winter gritted her teeth for a moment. "We don't have time for this. I have orders from Janus. The regiment is leaving the city in the morning, and I need you to get your people here back to the citadel."

"Ah," Jane said. "I was wondering why *now* was the time to rein me in."

"This is not the time for . . . whatever this is. You and me. Please. Come back."

"Or what? You'll leave me behind?" Jane cocked her head, examining Winter's face. "You would, wouldn't you? If the general says march, you march, whatever I have to say about."

Winter stiffened. "I have a duty—"

"To who? The queen? The Deputies?"

"To the men and women in my regiment."

"Of course." Jane exhaled slowly. "Abby *was* right. I am jealous. You were upset when you found out she and I were together, weren't you? It's awful discovering your lover has fallen in love with someone else."

"I haven't fallen in love with anyone."

"You have." Jane reached out a hand and flicked the silver eagle on Winter's shoulder. "You've fallen in love with Janus bet fucking Vhalnich."

"That's not fair."

"Probably not." Jane let her hand fall and turned away. "Now get out of here. I'm half-drunk and my head hurts and I haven't had a proper fuck in days, and it doesn't look like any of those things are likely to change in the near future. Go back to your tidy fucking toy soldiers."

"We still need you. I still need you."

"Just go." Jane sat down heavily on one of the benches, groping among the detritus for a bottle.

Winter slipped out of the Linked Rings, through the waking Leatherbacks, and reclaimed her horse. Her chest felt hollow, an empty space behind her breastbone surrounded by a seething mass of mingled anger and grief and guilt.

The emotional storm even seemed to reach the Infernivore, which perked up at the back of her mind and thrashed about in the murky parts of her subconscious.

I should go back to the citadel, get two companies, and drag the lot of them back to dry out overnight. Winter took a deep breath, bouncing against the gentle rhythm of Edgar's walk. *I should go back to Jane and beg her to forgive me.* Her head was pounding, as though she were the one who'd been drinking all day. *I should go back up there and kiss her, tear off her clothes, and kiss every inch of her, over and over—*

"Sir? Can I take your horse?"

Winter blinked. A Girls' Own ranker, a thin-faced woman with dark curls, stood with her musket at the citadel gate. Inside, Winter could hear shouts and laughter, and the courtyard was ablaze with light.

Oh yes. The party. Probably the news that they'd be marching in the morning had pushed the regiment into celebrating all the harder. *Good for them. It's the last chance they'll have for a while.*

She got down without a word and handed Edgar's reins to the ranker. No one noticed her as she passed through the courtyard, or at least no one spoke up. One didn't accost a colonel, Winter supposed. She was reminded of the night she'd spent outside the Vendre, drifting through the crowd, the mad carnival atmosphere contrasting with her own gloom. That had been just before she caught Jane and Abby together.

That was unlikely today, at least. She caught a glimpse of Abby in the thick of it, surrounded by recruits and old Leatherbacks alike, leading one of the endless, bawdy soldier's camp songs with a tankard as her conductor's wand. Winter smiled, briefly, and turned away before anyone noticed her.

The keep was deserted, except for a pair of Royals on guard inside the door. They saluted as Winter passed, as did the pair on watch outside her office. One of these two was a Royal, an unhappy-looking man who kept looking longingly toward the party outside, but the other was a woman. Winter waved aside her salute and stopped in front of the door.

"I thought the Girls' Own was off duty for the night," she said.

"Punishment detail, sir." The sentry, a short, muscular woman, vibrated with the stiffness of her rigid posture. "For smuggling drink into the camp."

"Ah. I hope you've learned your lesson."

"Yes, sir!" The ranker cracked a smile. "Don't get caught next time."

Winter smiled in return and went inside. Her office, well lit during the day, was huge and shadowy in the darkness. Only a few candles burned on the big central table, and Winter was surprised to see Cyte and Bobby there, poring over maps and scribbling notes and figures.

"Welcome back, sir!" Bobby said, popping to her feet. "Did you talk to Jane?"

"I talked to her."

"And will she be returning to camp?" Cyte said without looking up.

"Maybe. I hope so." *Probably not.* Winter sat down at her own desk, slumping into her chair. "We'll see. If she's not back by the time the party's over, I'll send some men to bring her in."

Bobby winced. "Let's hope it doesn't come to that."

"What are you two working on, anyway?" Winter said to change the subject.

Cyte seemed to understand, and gathered a stack of paper to bring to Winter's desk. "Arrangements for tomorrow. I've already sent couriers to intercept the upriver barges. I'm working on arranging our wagon train."

"I thought we were leaving the wagons behind."

"They can follow as best they can, sir. I'll detach a couple of dozen soldiers to look after them. If they take the same route we do, it should be safe enough." She paused. "They'll also be on the lookout for anyone we have to leave behind on the march. That could save lives."

Winter nodded, flipping through the pages. "It's a good thought." *I wonder if I should just have Jane and her*

people assigned to the wagons? It would look like a punishment detail, and Winter wasn't sure that was a bad
thing, given the way the Leatherbacks had been behaving.
But it's not going to make her like me any better.

Cyte came over to the desk to explain the details, and
Winter let herself be immersed in the columns of figures
and map notations. There was no need for her to attend to
any of it, truthfully, but she was grateful for the work, and
Cyte sensed her need for distraction. Bobby brought her a
tankard of watered wine, which Winter drank without much
enjoyment.

Sometime later, as Winter was idly flipping through
reports while her two lieutenants copied out orders, there
was a knock at the door.

"I'll get it," Winter said, springing to her feet before
either of the other two could move. "Get that finished up
while there's still time to go outside and relax a little."

"All I'm planning to do is go to bed," Cyte muttered,
but Winter saw that Bobby perked up and moved her pen
with a little more vigor. Winter crossed to the door and
opened it, feeling as she did another pulse of pressure in
her head. *Maybe I ought to go to bed myself.*

"Colonel Ihernglass?" The visitor was an older man in
a Vordanai uniform, standing relaxed between the two
sentries. She didn't recognize him. *Someone from the
quartermasters' people?*

"Yes?" she said. "Can I help you?"

She couldn't have said what it was that saved her life.
There was something *wrong* with the picture—the man's
shoulder straps made him a corporal, but he hadn't offered
a salute, and he was far too old. The way he stood was
unmilitary, and his coat was tight, as though it had been
tailored for someone smaller.

Infernivore roared and thrashed at the back of her
mind, half warning, half frantic hunger.

Winter threw herself backward, and the old man's hand
slashed through the air inches in front of her face. His
fingernails were as long as talons, painted with a strange
white lacquer.

"Winter!" Bobby shouted, coming to her feet as Winter stumbled backward against the table.

Cyte was only a fraction slower, waving to the two guards. "Stop that man!"

The old man spun, faster than he had any right to, and the first guard through the doorway got raked across the face by those white talons. They passed through flesh and bone without slowing, leaving horrendous open tears in their wake. The guard dropped his musket and screamed, falling to his knees and clutching his hands to his ruined face.

The Girls' Own guard, a step behind, had her musket up before the old man could get to her. Winter saw her pull the trigger, and the old man threw himself sideways before the shot went off, staggeringly loud in the tight quarters. The ball *zinged* off the stone wall and the ceiling, raising sparks, before it embedded itself in Winter's desk with a *thok*. The guard didn't give the old man a chance to recover himself, charging through the cloud of powder smoke with her bayonet fixed, forcing her assailant to scramble backward to avoid being spitted.

Winter was pulling herself to her feet, looking for her sword. It was where she'd left it, in its sheath on her sword belt hanging from her desk, on the other side of the big table. Cyte had her own sword belt closer to hand, however, and she tore her rapier from its scabbard. Before she could move to help the guard with the old man, the injured man just outside the door straightened up and gave a gasp, then slumped limply forward. Past him came another figure, dressed in drab gray and black. His face was obscured by a mask, a thousand tiny chips of obsidian shifting and glittering as he moved.

The sight of such a mask was burned into Winter's memory. She'd last seen it in the Sworn Cathedral, the night Orlanko had attempted to capture the Deputies-General. The night Danton had been assassinated by a man who'd disappeared as quickly and impossibly as he'd arrived. *The Penitent Damned.* Infernivore was flinging itself against her mind like a starving predator against the bars of its cage.

"Colonel Ihernglass?" he'd asked. A realization crashed down around her like chill water. *They're here for* me.

The black-clad figure had a knife in each hand. Cyte extended her sword, trying to keep him at bay, but the Penitent sidestepped and closed with her; when she flicked the blade toward his throat, he leaned back slightly, letting it pass him by less than an inch. His left-hand knife swung up, almost in passing, and slashed a deep cut across her arm. Cyte's eyes went wide, and she stumbled backward but hung on to her sword.

Winter edged left around the table, toward where Bobby was standing. Her lieutenant, as though reading her thoughts, tossed Winter her own sword and darted back toward the desk to get Winter's. Winter tore the short, unfamiliar blade from its scabbard and swung it overhand at the Penitent. He dodged the cut as easily as he'd avoided Cyte's blade, but it forced him to give ground, giving Cyte the chance to regain her balance at Winter's side.

On the other side of the room, the old man backed away from the bayonet-wielding guard, leading her toward the room's other door, which opened onto a narrow stairway from behind Winter's desk. At first Winter thought the old man wanted to escape, but he backed past the door without pausing. A moment later, the thin wood exploded as though it had been hit with a cannonball, fragments scattering across the room.

Standing amid the wreckage was another man, a giant, easily seven feet tall and broad to match. Winter was forcibly reminded of the *fin-katar*, the sacred eunuch she'd had to kill when she rescued Feor in Khandar. He had been huge, but running to fat, while this man seemed to be a slab of solid muscle. The giant wore the same blacks as the knife man, and the same glittering black mask.

Winter had to admire the courage of the Girls' Own soldier, if not her good sense. She turned on her heel and lunged with the simple bayonet thrust that they'd practiced so often in the yard. The giant half turned, letting the blade sink into the meat of his side until the barrel of the musket pressed against him. Then he swatted the weapon aside and grabbed the guard by the shoulder. She had time for a scream as a huge hand closed around her face and twisted her head one hundred eighty degrees without apparent effort, bones snapping with an ugly crunch. The giant tossed the limp, twitching corpse aside and looked down at Winter, ignoring the blood matting his clothes.

"Balls of the fucking Beast," Cyte swore. "What in all the hell—"

The knife-wielding Penitent came at Winter again, and she struggled to avoid him. He wasn't fast, at least not any faster than any trained fighter, but he seemed aware of what she was doing almost before she did it, gliding smoothly around her clumsy attempts at parries and ripostes. Winter was only able to keep him off by exploiting her longer reach and giving ground, and even so she quickly accumulated a half dozen shallow, painful cuts on her fore-arm where his knives had scored. Her sleeve was dark and sodden with blood, and Infernivore screamed at the back of her mind.

It wants his demon. Infernivore could devour it, but she had to lay a hand on him to unleash the thing, and the Penitent in front of her seemed as insubstantial as mist. She hurled herself desperately to one side to avoid getting backed into a corner, taking a cut on the leg as she passed, and had a moment to spare for the rest of the room.

The old man had backed Cyte into a corner. He kept his distance, wary of the reach of her rapier, but shock and pain were catching up to her, and she was visibly flagging. On the other side of the room, the giant slammed Winter's desk out of the way with one hand, coming toward her with strides she swore made the floor shake. Bobby, who had been wrest-ling to free Winter's sword from its scabbard, found herself directly in the monster's path. The giant aimed a casual backhand cuff at her head, and Bobby's hand came up and grabbed his wrist. Both of them seemed surprised when she halted the blow in its tracks, leaving the huge man stumbling and off-balance. He brought his other hand around in a wild roundhouse punch, and Bobby caught his fist in her palm. Winter distinctly heard the *crunch* of breaking bone, but

Bobby's arm didn't even waver. She leaned forward, matching the giant strength for strength, and the huge man gave a roar of anger and disbelief.

Then Winter had no attention to spare for anything but her own fight. She was backing into a wall, increasingly desperate sword strokes cutting nothing but air. *If I can only lay a hand on him* . . . She drove him back for a moment with a wild horizontal cut, then lunged. He slipped aside, as she'd expected, drawing the knife across the back of her hand. Her fingers spasmed and the sword fell from her grip, but she was already turning, grabbing for the Penitent's arm. Almost, *almost*, her fingers brushed against his sleeve, but he danced sideways and behind her, one arm raised for a strike that would bury his dagger in her kidneys.

The sound of a musket going off, only a few paces in front of her, was shatteringly loud, and the muzzle flash was almost blinding. Winter saw blood explode from the giant, high on his right shoulder, and he took a staggered step backward. She was already twisting away from her own opponent, skin tingling in the expectation of a blow that hadn't fallen. But he was backing away, hands pressed to his eyes, face contorted in agony. His knives lay discarded on the floor.

Jane stood in the doorway, breathing hard, the dead Royal's musket in her hands. Winter barely had time to register her presence. She threw herself forward, wrapping a hand around the Penitent's wrist, and sent her will down into the pit of her soul where the Infernivore dwelt. *Now. Now!*

The demon surged forth in answer, rushing through her hand and into the young man. Winter could feel his demon, a wispy, insubstantial thing, and feel its panic as Infernivore began to devour its substance. Energy crackled and sparked between them. Back in the physical world, she heard the Penitent scream.

Pain lanced through her, and her attention returned to her physical body with a lurch. The old man had two of his nails embedded in her arm, and he was bringing his other taloned hand toward her face. Winter released her grip on the Penitent, feeling the demons tear apart, the

Infernivore's hunger and frustrations hitting her like a punch to the gut. She collapsed to the floor, but instead of following her down the old man lurched backward, dragging his still-stricken companion. A moment later Jane came into view, the bayonet on her musket gleaming, standing in front of Winter like a growling attack dog.

The old man barked a word in a language Winter didn't understand. He ran for the back door, dragging the young Penitent behind him. As they passed, the giant—as unhindered by the musket ball in his shoulder as he had been by the bayonet—tore free of Bobby's grip and followed them, backing out through the door and around the corner. Bobby fell to her knees, breathing hard.

Winter struggled to her feet, clutching the deep cuts the old man's nails had left in her arm. Jane, musket still raised, looked around the room and then back to her.

"What the *fuck*?" she said. "Holy Karis buggered with a bloody pike, what the *fuck* was that?"

Two soldiers were dead, Cyte was badly hurt, and Winter's own pain was rapidly closing around her. But she couldn't deny—even if it made her an awful person—a tiny bit of pleasure at the look of utter stupefaction on Jane's face.

CHAPTER THIRTEEN

MARCUS

Standing in front of the polished dining room table of Twin Turrets, looking down at the hastily sketched map and deciding how best to deploy his forces, Marcus felt a powerful sense of coming home. It brought to mind memories of Khandar, which appeared increasingly attractive in retrospect; the situation had been desperate, but at least the sides had been clear and the enemies obvious. *Until the very end.*

He shied away from that thought, memories of his brief time with Jen Alhundt still too painful to touch, and returned his mind to the current problem. Desperate as Khandar had been, he didn't think he'd ever led *this* small a contingent. His army consisted of six Mierantai riflemen, two half-trained rankers, one completely unblooded and the other female, plus himself and a teenage financier. *Oh, and the Queen of Vordan.*

On the other hand, it was unlikely that the enemy expected them. This was good, because if Marcus had his way the whole thing would go off without a shot being fired. The Patriot Guard might work for Maurisk, but they were still Vordanai, and for the most parts they *were* patriots. *We can't shoot them just for being in the way, not unless there's no other choice.*

"This is what we know," he said, tracing the outline of the big building on the map. "Cora's people have been keeping watch for the past few days, so we have a pretty good idea of what to expect."

The girl blushed at the mention of her name and kept her eyes on the table. Cora's contacts, spread throughout the Oldtown and the rest of the South Bank, had been invaluable. Boys who normally earned a few coppers keeping tabs on food shipments coming up the Green Road or boat traffic on the river had instead turned their eyes to the innocuous warehouse off the River Road, so nondescript that it was only labeled with the number 192.

Raesinia stood beside Cora, one hand on her shoulder. Lieutenant Uhlan was there as well, along with Hayver and Andy. *With only eight soldiers, the line between officers and men gets a little fuzzy,* Marcus reflected.

"It doesn't look like there's any guards within the building itself," Marcus went on. "There's only one door, though, and there's four men on it day or night. They're all in plainclothes, but we're pretty sure they're Patriot Guards. Around here"— he tapped a spot on the map just in front of the warehouse's front door, where a pier jutted out into the river—"they have a riverboat they tie up at night. Four more men there, two sleeping and two on watch."

"There'd be less opposition during the day, then," Uhlan said.

"We're hoping we don't have to fight them at all," Marcus said. "You want to explain what you found, Cora?"

The expression on her face made it clear that she would rather not, but Raesinia squeezed her arm, and she spoke in a small voice.

"Th-there's a back door. Or there was. Someone got rid of it, the last time they fixed that place up. But Gregory went up to have a look, and it's not bricked in, just boarded up and plastered. A man with a crowbar should be able to make short work of it."

Uhlan raised his eyebrows, and Marcus held up a hand to forestall his objection. "Yes, that'll be loud enough that the guards will hear. So we're going to need a distraction.

That's the part I'm still working on." He tapped the pier again. "We'll hire a boat to drop us by the door. After that, I'm thinking that someone needs to get onto the Guards' boat from the river side and set a fire. Once that's got them occupied, we should be able to get the door open and get in without anybody getting wise. Once we have what we need, we can get back out by boat."

The Mierantai officer considered for a moment, then nodded. "Seems simple enough. When are we going in?"

"Tomorrow night. Before that, we'll need a few things. Cloaks for everyone, and some hurricane lamps. That warehouse may be stuffed with flash powder, and I don't want to take any chances."

"I can get whatever you need," Andy said. She sounded eager to be a part of things. "I'll make a trip down this evening."

"Good. Lieutenant, anything else you think of that we might require, let Ranker Dracht know."

"Yes, sir." Uhlan saluted. "I'll speak to my men."

He bustled off, and Marcus stepped away from the table to let the others know they were dismissed. Andy followed Uhlan, with Hayver trailing in her wake. Raesinia tried to catch Marcus' eye, but he pretended not to notice, slipping out of the dining room and up to his office while she spoke with Cora in low, urgent tones. It might have been a cowardly move, but Marcus was expecting harsh words from his monarch, and she often didn't give enough thought to the possibility of being overheard.

In any event, it only won him a few minutes' respite. He'd managed to uncork his ink bottle and sharpen his quill by the time there was a knock at the door.

"It's me," Raesinia said. "I need to talk to you."

"Come in," Marcus said, making a show of setting his pen aside as she entered. "But I still need to write to our illustrious general."

News of the great victory at Gaafen and the fall of Desland had come via flik-flik within hours, but only trickled into the rest of the city by more conventional means over the past few days. The mood was subdued. While the surrender of a League city was by no means a small triumph, the Hamveltai army at Antova made it a temporary one. It was widely agreed that Janus would have to confront the fortress next, or risk being cut off from Vordan in the event of a sudden enemy thrust. The general opinion of his prospects seemed low, though Janus' messages to Marcus were nothing if not confident.

Raesinia frowned. "It hardly matters, does it? It's not like he can send us any help."

"I like to keep him up-to-date." Marcus sighed. "Maybe it's just for my benefit, but it eases my mind. But all right, shut the door."

Raesinia did, then stood opposite the desk, looking thoughtful.

"I have an idea," she said finally. "For the distraction."

"Oh?"

"I talked a little with Viera, one of the students you rescued."

"The Vheedai girl?" Marcus nodded. "What about her?"

"She was studying with your friend the Preacher."

Marcus nodded again, a bit slower. She'd mentioned that, but it hadn't really registered.

"And before that, she worked with an alchemist in Hamvelt," Raesinia went on. "I think we should bring her in and put her to work on making our distraction a good one."

"That does sound better than just lobbing a torch over the rail," Marcus said. "But do you think we can trust her?"

"I think so. She seems to . . . have a lot of respect for you." Raesinia looked slightly embarrassed, for some reason, and shook her head. "She certainly has no reason to help Maurisk or the Guard. And she was working with the Preacher before I was even attacked, so she can't be a plant—"

"All right." Marcus held up his hands. "Will you talk to her?"

"I can." Raesinia fixed Marcus with a hard stare. "I also talked to Cora. She said you asked her to come along."

Marcus took a deep breath and blew it out. "I did."

"You know that's crazy. She's not cut out for this."

"It won't be dangerous if the plan works," Marcus said, knowing as he spoke how weak that was. *Since when has a plan ever gone perfectly?* "We need someone who knows what to look for. We'll probably only have a few minutes once we get in."

"You can't bring her," Raesinia said flatly. "She's my friend, and I love her, but she needs a book or a banknote in her hand, not a pistol."

"No one said I was giving her a pistol. Besides, you were the one who got her involved in the first place."

"She's been *involved* the whole time. She was with us from the beginning, before the revolution. You saw what she did for the refugees before we even got there. It's not that she isn't *brave*, but she's not a soldier. You can't take her into danger like this!"

"I don't have a choice," Marcus said. "We're short-handed as it is. If I thought I could get away with it, I'd leave Andy and Cora here with you, but—"

"You . . ." Raesinia paused, and cocked her head. "You'd leave *Andy* and take *Hayver*? Hayver would trip over his own foot even if he only had one leg!"

Marcus had to admit that, if push came to shove, Andy would probably be more useful to have at his back in a fight than the awkward boy. *But still.* Seeing Andy with her face bruised and bloodied, and knowing she'd gotten that way defending *him* made Marcus feel deeply wrong. Inadequate, as though he'd failed in some primal duty he could barely articulate. It was not a position he wanted to put himself in again.

"It doesn't matter," Raesinia said brusquely, "because the solution is obvious. I'll come with you, and Cora will stay at Mrs. Felda's. I can find the evidence we need as easily as she can."

"No," Marcus said. "Out of the question."

"I—"

"You are the *Queen of Vordan.* You are not going to come with us to skulk into some warehouse that could easily be a trap!"

"But you're willing to bring a girl like Cora along?"

"Don't think I like it, but yes. Raesinia—Your Majesty—you are *more valuable* than she is, whether you like it or not."

"That—"

"If Cora were to die," Marcus ground out, over whatever Raesinia had been about to say, "it would be a tragedy. She's a wonderful person, and I understand that she's your friend. But if anything happens to *you*, the entire kingdom will suffer. Millions of people, just as wonderful as Cora. You are the last of the Orboans. Without you, at worst we'd have civil war. At best we'd have someone like Maurisk claiming the throne."

"Or someone like Janus?" Raesinia snapped.

"Janus swore an oath," Marcus said. "As did I. We are bound to protect and defend the kingdom and the queen. I can't do that if I deliberately take you into danger."

"So you'll leave me here," she said. "Unguarded."

"We'll lock the building down. I should be gone only a few hours."

Raesinia's face was calm, but he could see rage in the depths of her eyes. "And if I order you to let me come?"

"Then you can find someone else to lead this raid."

"I could have you thrown in prison." She put on a vicious smile. "Or sent to the Spike."

"That would be Your Majesty's prerogative."

There was another drawn-out silence. Then, without a word, Raesinia turned away, wrenched the door open, and disappeared, slamming it so hard it bounced off the doorframe and rebounded. Marcus winced.

He got to sleep surprisingly easily that night, settling into the soft bed in his second-floor room more comfortably than he had done in weeks. His dreams were full of fire, and when a knock at the door dragged him out of slumber, he found himself reflexively looking around for signs of a blaze.

"What?" he managed, blinking and shaking his head. "Is something wrong?"

"Open the door," Raesinia said.

"Raesinia? What's happened?"

"Nothing's happened. Just do it."

Marcus rolled out of bed and pulled on his undershirt before crossing the room and pulling the door open. He'd extinguished all the candles before going to bed, but left the curtains open, and a square of moonlight fell on the carpet and edged the shadows with a silvery glow.

Raesinia pushed into the room before he could say anything, slamming the door behind her. Marcus hastily backed away a step as she turned to shoot the bolt, then fixed him with a stare.

"Your Majesty . . . ," he said. "I . . . uh . . ."

He noticed—it was impossible *not* to notice—that Raesinia was wearing a sheer silk nightgown that did little or nothing to hide the shape of the figure beneath it. A woman's figure, Marcus had to admit. The queen's diminutive height made it easy to forget that she'd passed her twentieth year. When he wrenched his eyes away from *that*, he took in the knife in her right hand. It was a long, thick blade, probably filched from the butcher's block in the kitchen.

"You shouldn't be here," Marcus said. "Dressed like that." He took another step backward, doing his best to keep an eye on Raesinia without actually looking at her. "And . . . perhaps you should put down the knife?"

"Colonel Marcus d'Ivoire," Raesinia said, with a note of command in her voice. "Sit down on the bed and be quiet."

"I—"

"Am I your queen or not?"

"You are," Marcus said. "Your Majesty."

He sat, and she stepped forward, into the square of moonlight. It made her skin look as pale as parchment, and her eyes glowed.

"I am going to show you something," she said. "It's something I have never shown to anyone, at least not of my own free will. I'm doing this because I trust you, and because I don't want us to have any more . . . misunderstandings."

Marcus swallowed hard. "I don't understand."

"If you ever breathe a word of this to anyone, the consequences would be . . . dire. For me." She cocked her head. "Janus already knows, of course. I know you don't understand. Just nod."

Marcus nodded.

"Fuck." Raesinia took a deep breath. "God, sometimes I wish I could still get drunk. All right. You helped Janus capture the Thousand Names in Khandar, correct?"

"Yes." A chill ran along Marcus' spine. "How do you—"

"So you know magic is real," Raesinia interrupted. "You know that a person can carry a demon inside her."

Marcus saw Jen's face, two images superimposed: eyes closed, resting in his camp bed, calm and beautiful, and with her features twisted into a snarl as she hurled rock-shattering magic in the Desoltai temple.

"I know," he said softly.

"That makes this easier. Watch closely, and *don't move*."

Raesinia raised her left hand, and brought the knife up, blade flashing silver in the moonlight. Marcus half rose from the bed, intending to tackle her and wrench the weapon away, but the force of her gaze pinned him to the spot. He stared as she held out her left palm and, deliberately, carved a gash across it. The knife was well honed, and her flesh parted easily under it, like a well-cooked roast. Blood welled, coating the blade and dripping to the floor in a steady patter.

"Your Majesty," Marcus said, his throat tight. "Raesinia. *Please*."

"Just watch."

She stared at her hand, as though she felt no pain at all. The patter of blood slowed, and finally stopped, leaving her palm coated with gore. She frowned and wiped it against the front of her nightdress, leaving crimson streaks on the pale fabric. Then she held the hand out for Marcus' inspection. The skin was unbroken, perfect and smooth, as though the wound had never been.

Marcus looked from the queen's hand to her face. There was still resolve there, but also fear, the tension of someone expecting a blow.

"How did this happen?" Marcus said.

"Orlanko." Raesinia let her hand fall to her side. "There was a time when I was very sick. The Last Duke sent word to Elysium, to—"

"—the Priests of the Black."

Raesinia nodded. "I don't remember much. One of them came to see me, before I . . . expired. He brought me back, with this *thing*. Ever since then . . ." She shrugged. "I can't be hurt, not for long. I can't die. I've been shot, stabbed, fallen from more tall buildings than I can count, had my brains blown out and my limbs broken. None of it sticks."

"Balls of the fucking Beast," Marcus said, forgetting himself enough to swear in the presence of his monarch.

"More or less. Orlanko wanted a regency when Father died. He planned to marry me to some Borelgai prince; then I would conveniently 'die' and be spirited away to Elysium to spend the rest of eternity in a cell. He and his cronies would have ruled Vordan, and made us all kneel to the Sworn Church." She sighed. "You and I tossed that plan out the window, obviously. So now the Church wants to take Vordan by force. After all, it has a demon for a queen."

"Who else knows?"

"Janus. Sothe. Cora. Orlanko, obviously. My father did, though I only found that out too late."

"The king knew?"

"He was the one who asked Janus to try to find a solution." She looked down for a moment, face shadowed. "He was trying to protect me, and I had no idea."

It was easy to forget, with all the talk of the death of the king, that to Raesinia he'd been a father instead of a sovereign. Marcus hesitated, uncomfortably, then said, "Why tell me?"

Raesinia closed her eyes. "I once had a dear friend who thought I was in danger. He did something foolish, and now he's dead. He wasn't the only one. Everyone is always so . . . so *ready* to sacrifice themselves for me, and they have no idea it's all *pointless*." She opened her eyes again, unshed tears glittering in the silver light. "I'm finished with that, you understand?"

"I . . . think so."

"I understand if you think I'm . . . a monster, a demon, any of that. But please understand that I only want the best for Vordan. That's *all*. I didn't ask for any of this."

"I know." Marcus shook his head. "I would never—"

"It's all right. I *am* a monster. Someday I'll leave this kingdom and never come back." Her face tightened. "But not before Vordan is safe."

"Raesinia . . ." Marcus trailed off, not sure what he'd intended to say. There was a long pause.

"So. Now you know." Raesinia wiped the blade of the knife on her nightshirt, smearing it further. "Cora stays behind. I come along. Agreed?"

"Agreed," Marcus said.

"Good." Raesinia turned. "Get some sleep. Tomorrow will be a long day."

"Raesinia!" Marcus called as she reached for the door. She looked over her shoulder. "What?"

"Here." He walked across the room, avoiding the spatter of blood, and handed her a folded robe. "The guards might be making the rounds. You don't want to cause . . . comment."

"Ah." Raesinia looked down at herself. "Good point."

RAESINIA

On the whole, she thought, watching Marcus plan the raid the next day, *that went as well as could be expected.*

The silk nightgown had probably been a little over-the-top, but it was an impractical piece that she'd always hated, and it was good to finally have an excuse to feed it to the fire while indulging her occasional taste for melodrama. And, she had to admit, it had been fun to watch Marcus' eyes pop.

Viera's offhand comment had made her wonder a little about Marcus. He didn't seem to have pursued female company since his arrival in Khandar, but nothing she'd heard made her think that he had left a particular companion somewhere, or that he preferred men for that matter. He had an odd prudishness that made it hard to imagine him, for example, visiting a whorehouse, but at the same time a soldierly earthiness that made it difficult to believe that he *never* indulged. *Perhaps he does, but feels guilty about it afterward. That* sounded like Marcus.

Now Viera was hard at work in what had been Twin Turrets' sitting room, mixing and grinding while there was still daylight to work with. She'd responded enthusiastically to Raesinia's tentative approach, and hadn't even asked to hear the plan before beginning her work. *I guess she really does just enjoy blowing things up.* Andy, for her part, had acquired a riverboat and other necessary gear with impressive efficiency. Whatever Marcus might think, Raesinia was glad to have the girl on her side. *Hell, I would have liked to have one or two like her before the revolution.*

Marcus, going over details of the escape plan with Uhlan and Hayver at the map table, caught sight of Raesinia and straightened up. He gestured for the others to continue what they were about and came in her direction, expression dark. Raesinia gritted her teeth. *Don't tell me he's changed his mind* now.

"I've been thinking about what we discussed last night," he said quietly. "I've got a question."

She nodded, and they ducked through a doorway into a spare room piled high with furniture from the rest of the house. There was barely room to stand among the overturned chairs and overloaded tables, and she felt reasonably secure they wouldn't be overheard.

"What is it?"

"You said Cora knows?"

Raesinia pursed her lips. "She knows . . . something. She saw me get shot at the Vendre, but she hasn't asked for any details on how I survived." There had been several times when Raesinia nearly spilled the whole story, but she worried that Cora might find the truth a burden. *She'll need to know, someday, but not yet.*

"What about the others from your old group?" Marcus said. "What about Maurisk?"

"That's . . . difficult." Raesinia blew out a breath. "I

met with Maurisk after the revolution, and I told him I used a double that day. Whether he believed that, I honestly don't know. If he *was* behind the bombing, then presumably he bought my story, or he'd know that wouldn't have killed me."

"Unless . . ." Marcus scratched his beard. "Something feels wrong. We know there's a Penitent Damned in the city—"

"We do?" Raesinia said. "How?"

"Janus left behind some . . . sources of information," Marcus said. "But the Priests of the Black would know about your . . . abilities, so they wouldn't try to blow you up, either."

"And someone planted the bomb under the noses of the Patriot Guards," Raesinia said. "Which leads right back to Maurisk, or someone close to him."

"Right." Marcus rolled his eyes. "Saints and martyrs, give me enemies who wear proper uniforms. Then I know who to shoot at."

"Have you thought about what happens if we find proof Maurisk was involved?"

Marcus nodded. "The Deputies-General will be in session tomorrow. We'll dress you back up as the queen, march onto the floor, and present the evidence. Durenne won't be able to sit on *that*. You can demand that the Deputies revoke the emergency powers of the Directory and put someone else in command of the Patriot Guard."

"If Maurisk still thinks I'm in the country, that ought to catch him off guard," Raesinia said. She sighed. "I'm worried about Sothe."

"I'd be a little more inclined to worry for anyone who tried to cause trouble for her."

The ghost of a smile crossed Raesinia's lips. "That, too."

They spent an hour at Mrs. Felda's, getting into costume and waiting for the last light of the sun to leave the sky, and then set out for the Oldtown docks. The boat Andy's contact had promised was just where it was supposed to be, a flat-bottomed river tub that could be propelled by either poles or oars. Eight men and two young women clambered on board, and Marcus, sitting in the stern, shoved them away from the bank.

The six Mierantai wore plainclothes and long coats, not too out of place in midautumn. They'd kept their long-barreled rifles concealed on the quick walk through the streets, but now they held them openly, trusting the darkness to conceal them from other river traffic. This was at a minimum in any case; before the war, boats had plied the river by lantern light, but as trade had dwindled, reasons to risk a nighttime trip had become rarer. There were even rumors that bands of outlaws were operating off Thieves Island once again, preying on incautious travelers.

Andy and Hayver each had a musket and a pistol, as well as a sword from Twin Turrets' small armory. Neither looked terribly comfortable. Hayver handled his weapons gingerly, checking and rechecking some memorized list of preparations, while Andy looked as though she'd prefer something long and heavy to swing in the place of powder and blades. Marcus also carried a pistol and his saber, the battered weapon looking more in keeping with his plainclothes outfit than it ever had on his dress uniform. Raesinia herself had a pair of pistols, though she freely admitted it was more for the look of the thing than because she expected to present an enemy with a serious threat.

It was an easy trip downstream, drifting with the current, Marcus keeping them near the bank with periodic shoves of his pole. Raesinia would have been hard-pressed to pick out warehouse 192 from the ranks of brick-sided structures with darkened windows that lined the river, but Andy pointed it out as they approached. A lonely lantern hung near the front door, and two more illuminated the little two-decked riverboat tied up to a short stone pier.

They all watched as their target drifted past. Once they were well beyond the pier, Marcus started poling them closer, until their little boat scraped against the muddy bank. One of the Mierantai got out, taking a coil of rope with them, and held the craft in place while everyone else disembarked. Marcus handed the pole to Lieutenant Uhlan, who remained behind with two of his men and the "distraction."

Viera had produced three wine bottles full of a viscous black stuff, which she'd promised would take fire instantly, even on a damp surface, and not only burn hot enough to ignite wood but give off copious black smoke. Once everyone was clear—Hayver managed to nearly tumble on the slippery mud, soaking his pants to the knees—Uhlan pushed the boat back into the river, and his men unshipped the oars. They made their way slowly upstream, against the current, toward the lights of the Patriot Guard boat.

The rest of them stood in an alley between warehouse 192 and one of its neighbors, illuminated by nothing stronger than moonlight. Marcus had a bull's-eye lantern, which he opened a crack, enough to send a spot of brilliance onto the wall of the building. It was plaster over a brick wall, gray with age and rotting where rain had gotten through the whitewash.

"The door is closer to the river side," Marcus said in a whisper. "About fifty paces along."

Andy nodded and drew a long fighting knife from her belt. She walked to the corner of the building and started pacing, counting under her breath. When she got to forty, she began sinking the knife into the plaster, listening to the tip scrape on the bricks underneath. At fifty-two, the knife hit wood with a *thunk*.

"That's it," Marcus said, waving the Mierantai forward. "See how much of the plaster you can get off, but stay quiet."

Raesinia stood with Hayver, watching the end of the alley for any movement amid the shadows, while the soldiers attacked the wall with their knives. Great chunks of plaster peeled away, and white dust covered everyone's clothes and cascaded across the ground. In a minute or so they were able to reveal the rough shape of a doorway, lined top to bottom with wooden boards, as well as a bit of the brickwork around the edges.

Two of the men produced crowbars and stood ready. Marcus held up his hand and stared upward, listening.

The signal, when it came, was unmistakable. A soft

whoosh echoed across the water, followed a moment later by a much louder *crunch*. Flames leapt into the sky, visible over the roof of the warehouse and reflected on the surface of the river. A moment later, the stars began to flicker and dim, outlining a rising column of black smoke. Men's voices raised in alarm rang through the alleys.

"Go!" Marcus said. "Get it open!"

The two Mierantai attacked the door with vigor, wrenching the boards away with a series of *cracks* and *crunches* that would have been as audible as musket shots if not for the roar of the burning riverboat. Once they had the old door clear, Marcus grabbed one of the bars and, glancing at Raesinia, worked it under the doorframe right beside the latch.

"Polite thieves?" she said.

"Right." He grinned and threw his weight against the bar. The latch gave way with a splintery *crunch*, and the door swung open.

They slipped inside and into darkness. Marcus kept his lantern shuttered until they'd closed the door behind them, then opened it enough to allow two of the soldiers to light glass-enclosed hurricane lamps. As the flames caught, shadows danced and wavered throughout the warehouse, and tiny points of fire gleamed on polished metal. Raesinia's breath caught in her throat.

"That," Andy said, "is a lot of cannon."

They were lined up, hub to hub, rank after rank of them, at least three dozen in various sizes. Beside them stood stacks of chests that Raesinia assumed contained the ammunition. An equal number of caissons, small carts that would be dragged behind the cannon into battle, stood in neat rows. Beyond that was a shadowy mountain of small kegs; Raesinia made a quick estimate of her size and did some rapid calculations in her head.

"That's got to be most of what's missing from the powder mill's output," she said. "I don't think I realized how much that actually was. It looks like enough powder for an—"

"For an army," Marcus said grimly. He gestured past the gunpowder, where Raesinia could see more stacked crates the size and shape of coffins. "Those are muskets. There's got to be enough here for ten regiments."

"I thought Maurisk was making bombs," Andy said. "What's he going to do with all this?"

"It has to be for the Patriot Guard," Marcus said. "Halberds are all well and good for standing in front of buildings, but with this . . ."

"He must have friends in the armament factories as well as the powder mills." Raesinia raised her lantern. "Come on, spread out."

"What are we looking for?" Hayver said.

"Paperwork." Raesinia looked at the neat rows of weapons. "Nobody puts something like this together without paperwork."

They found a clerk's desk near the center of the warehouse, overflowing with stray paper. Raesinia hurried over, and Marcus and Andy stood beside her while Hayver and the three Mierantai kept looking, picking their way carefully closer to the front door of the warehouse.

"Well?" Marcus said as Raesinia rummaged through the sheets. "We could just take it all."

"I don't know if there's anything useful here," Raesinia said. "A lot of this is in code."

She set aside a stack of gibberish pages, then caught a scrap of readable text out of the corner of her eye and pounced. They were messages, written on flimsy foolscap with the message ENCODE AND DESTROY printed at the top.

"Keeping your plaintext around after encoding?" Raesinia murmured, flipping through. "Naughty, naughty. Sothe would show you a thing or two."

Most of the messages, whose dates went back at least two weeks, were concerned with the movement of hidden shipments through the city, and all were unsigned. She put these aside, with mounting frustration. *There has to be something here to tie Maurisk to all this.* He'd been a canny conspirator when they worked together, but not always a cautious one. *He has to slip up somewhere.*

There. A long document, with the heading DIRECTORY

FOR THE NATIONAL DEFENSE. A list of names—her eyes flicked down it, and then back to the top.

"In the interests of state security and given the present emergency, the following persons are to be arrested with all dispatch . . ."

"The present emergency . . . ," Raesinia whispered under her breath, scanning the list. The first name on it was Giles Durenne. "Marcus, I've got it."

"Got what?" said Marcus, who'd been poring through another stack of papers.

"Here." She thrust the list under his nose.

He read for a moment, frowning. "Half these people are deputies. And Durenne?"

"It's a coup," Raesinia said. "That's almost the entire Radical caucus, and a lot of their allies."

"Nice to see that I rate a mention," Marcus muttered.

Raesinia looked back to the paper. The name "Colonel Marcus d'Ivoire" was in the midst of a mixed bag of officers of all ranks.

"This is dated two days ago," Marcus said.

"He's getting ready." Raesinia looked around the warehouse. "It can't be much longer—"

There was a groan of metal, and the front door of the warehouse opened a fraction, letting in the lurid glow from the ship burning outside. Marcus slammed the bull's-eye lantern closed and dropped to his knees, and Raesinia followed suit. Andy flattened herself behind the nearest caisson. Closer to the door, Raesinia saw the other lantern vanish as Hayver snuffed it and took cover.

"Damn," Marcus whispered. "I thought we'd have longer."

Something stabbed into Raesinia's skull, a sudden pain behind her eyes that throbbed with every heartbeat. She blinked, breathing hard, and it faded slightly, leaving a coppery taste in her mouth.

Raesinia swallowed hard. "What now?"

"Hope they go away."

"If they don't?"

He shrugged. "Then we'll see if they're willing to risk firing near this much powder."

The door opened wider. The fire on the ship was still crackling, but over the top of it Raesinia heard another sound, a high-pitched *ting* that repeated every few seconds. She held her breath for a moment, then peeked around the edge of the desk as strange shadows twisted through the vast space.

Four men in Patriot Guard sashes were struggling to haul the main door open on its sliding track. Two more, muskets in hand, stood peering into the darkness, but it was the figure beside them that drew Raesinia's attention. It was a woman, old and gray-haired, walking with the aid of a long, knob-handled stick. The point of the stick must have been sheathed in metal, because it made a *ting* and threw a tiny spark every time it struck the flagstones.

She had one hand outstretched, and hovering above it was something like a miniature sun. It was a ball of flame, about the size of a man's head, colors shifting and twisting under a perfectly smooth surface as though a roaring blaze was contained in a glass bowl. When the woman moved her hand, the flame followed, as though it were tethered to her finger by a string.

Raesinia had become very adept at leaping to certain kinds of conclusions. Nothing of this world could let someone hold a ball of fire in her hands, and that left only a few possibilities.

"It's one of *them*," she hissed. "The Penitents. We have to get out of here *now*."

Marcus risked a glance of his own. "Balls of the *fucking* Beast," he said. "You're not serious."

Raesinia waved to Andy, gesturing toward the back door. The girl nodded and slunk off, keeping to the shadows between the caissons. Marcus ducked back behind the desk, and Raesinia gave his shoulder a tug. She led him on hands and knees, threading their way among the piled implements of war.

"You are here," the old woman said. Her voice was

raspy and nearly unintelligible under a thick Murnskai accent. "I feel you. Do not hide."

She raised her hand, and a portion of the ball of flame split off and rose toward the ceiling. It brightened as it did so, from the light of a bonfire to the light of the sun itself, throwing the whole warehouse into sudden, stark illumination. The shadows vanished.

"There!" one of the Patriot Guard shouted. Musket barrels swung around.

At the same time, the long shapes of Mierantai rifles came up over the boxes of muskets. The blasts were nearly simultaneous, muzzle flashes washed out in the brilliant light. Balls *pinged* and *thoked* among the stacked boxes, and one of the Guards fell backward with a cry and a spray of blood.

"So much for staying quiet," Raesinia said.

"Back!" Marcus shouted, rising to a crouch and drawing his pistol. "Everybody back!"

Hayver and the Mierantai fell back from among the muskets, the riflemen running bent over to present smaller targets while Hayver stood up in full view of the Patriot Guards. The four who'd been wrestling with the door now raised their own muskets, but a shot from Andy sent them scattering for cover before they could fire. The old woman glanced at them scornfully.

"Shoot *her*!" Raesinia hissed. She drew one of her own pistols, aimed, and fired as soon as it looked as though the guards were lining up another shot. It was too far for someone of her low skill to hope to score a hit, however, and besides sending the enemy ducking for cover again, there was no obvious effect. She tossed the empty weapon away and drew the other. "Marcus! Get them to shoot the woman."

A musket *cracked*, and one of the Mierantai stumbled and crashed into a stack of boxes. His two companions dove for cover, and Andy popped up and fired again, raising sparks where the ball glanced off a stone outside. Raesinia caught sight of Hayver, taking cover behind a box and frantically ramming a new round into his musket. The old woman continued her unhurried advance, staff *tinking*

on the floor, while behind her the Patriot Guard fired from
the sides of the doorway and ducked out of sight. One of
them took too long in aiming, and a Mierantai rifle
cracked, sending him sprawling to the floor.

Hayver rose from cover, musket swinging about, aiming
square at the old woman from less than twenty yards. She
had time to turn her head before his weapon bloomed with
fire and smoke. Something fast and bright happened, just
in front of her, the sphere of flame swooping with trip-
hammer speed to place itself between them. Something
spattered across the old woman's clothes, spraying droplets
that smoked wherever they landed.

She melted the ball—

"Hayver!" Marcus shouted. "Back!"

Hayver backpedaled, dropping his musket and scrabbling for his pistol. He backed into a stack of musket crates
and stumbled, sending the topmost crashing to the floor.
Weapons packed neatly in straw spilled across the floor.

The old woman raised her hand, her face gleeful. The
fiery orb subdivided again, and a smaller mote zipped across
the space between them to impact on Hayver's chest. It
spread across him in an instant, as though he'd been dipped
in lamp oil, outlining him in a nimbus of fire that brightened
until it was white-hot. The pistol in his hand exploded as the
charge cooked off, spraying blood across the floor, but Hayver was already screaming. His flyaway hair seemed to glow
as each strand burst into brief, brilliant flame.

"Hayver!" Andy put her musket to her shoulder, sighting on the woman, and pulled the trigger. Sparks flashed
in the pan, but she must have been hasty loading, because
the shot didn't fire. Another shot, from one of the Mierantai, did. The ball of flame skipped across to interpose
itself, again spattering her with molten lead, which she
ignored as though it were drops of rain. Another bolt of
fire slashed out, and the rifleman began to burn.

"Run!" Marcus shouted.

Raesinia watched Hayver collapse, no more than a
darker shape inside his personal ball of hellfire. The
woman glanced at him and extended her hand, and the

flames around him shot back toward her, rejoining the orb hovering before her. What was left behind was a steaming, blackened ruin barely recognizable as human.

Marcus was halfway to the door already, with Andy close behind him. The third Mierantai had thrown himself behind the barrels of gunpowder, loading his rifle, his face the grim mask of someone staring death in the face. The old woman regathered her flame from his burning companion, calling them back to her hand like a medieval falconer and his hunting bird.

We're not going to make it. Raesinia threaded her way back through the piles, ignoring the Patriot Guard musket balls that still snapped and whined around her. The Mierantai got to his feet and fired, producing no more than another spatter of lead, and more fire snapped out. As he burned, the charges in his belt pouch exploded, nearly tearing him in half. The old woman gave a harsh, cackling laugh.

Marcus and Andy had reached the last row of cannon, but there was an open space between them and the back door. *If they run, she'll burn them.* They'd apparently reached this conclusion, and Marcus had hold of Andy's arm, holding her in the protective shadow of the guns. Raesinia found herself among the chests and caissons, huddling as the woman, the Penitent Damned, stalked closer.

Raesinia's eyes fell on the closest chest. It wasn't locked, just latched. She pried it open an inch with one finger, and found it full of linen bags. Her knowledge of artillery was limited, but she guessed that these were premeasured portions of powder, used for speed in the heat of battle. Each one was about the size of her hand. *They can't be very heavy . . .*

Carefully, she extracted one of the pouches and let the chest close. She hefted it, testing the weight, and then gauged the old woman's unhurried progress. *A few more steps. Marcus, just stay put a little longer . . .*

"Andy, go!" she heard Marcus shout. The girl ran, and he stood up, pistol in hand. The old woman smiled.

Goddamn all chivalrous bastards!

Raesinia sprang to her feet as the report of his pistol

echoed through the warehouse. She took a step forward, winding up, and hurled the sack of powder toward the old woman with all the strength she could muster.

It wasn't a very accurate throw—she probably wouldn't have done much more than bounce the sack near her feet. But, as she'd hoped, the flaming orb snapped across to intercept it with all the speed of instinct. The powder charge went off with a roar, blowing the flaming sphere apart as though it were made of burning oil. Fragments of flame went everywhere, scattering across the warehouse like from a flint. In the center of it, wreathed in flame, the old woman had gone to one knee.

"Go!" Raesinia shouted, running for the door at top speed. Andy was already out, and Marcus needed no urging. He dropped his pistol and ran.

It's all going to go up. The warehouse was full of powder—packed securely, to be sure, but no one had anticipated the kegs being splashed with liquid fire. *God Almighty. It'll take out half the Docks.* She wondered, idly, what it would feel like—if she would be literally blown to bits, or just badly burned. *If I get blown to bits, which part of me does the binding stick to? The heart?*

Every step toward the door seemed to stretch. When she finally reached it, she couldn't help looking over her shoulder. The old woman was back on her feet, face dark with concentration. All around her, bits and pieces of flame were rising into the air, falling inward toward her hand like an explosion in reverse.

Well, thanks for that.

Uhlan had the boat against the dock, though there was no sign of the two men who'd been with him. Andy was the first over the side, and Marcus wasn't far behind, shoving frantically against the bank. He held out his hand as the boat wobbled out into the current, and Raesinia grabbed it, clasping him wrist to wrist. He swung her into the boat, tumbling over himself, so they ended up side by side in the bottom, along with a half inch of scummy water.

"Away from the bank!" Marcus gasped. "Now!"

Uhlan had the idea already, shoving the little craft

deeper into the current. Raesinia hauled herself to the rail, watching the shore and waiting for a figure escorted by a ball of fire to emerge. But none did, and within a few minutes the gloom of night swallowed warehouse 192.

Lieutenant Uhlan pushed the boat so far into the middle of the river that his pole lost touch with the bottom, and they were obliged to row. He and Marcus took the oars, driving the boat across the dark water and toward the dim lights of the Island.

"A Penitent," Raesinia said to Marcus, no longer caring whether Uhlan and Andy overheard. "That was one of them. The Penitent Damned."

"It seems like it," Marcus said, panting with the effort of rowing.

"Maurisk must be working with the Priests of the Black."

Marcus gave an assenting grunt.

"That hypocritical, double-crossing *fucker*," Raesinia hissed. "After everything he said . . ." She trailed off, still feeling dazed. "What the hell do we do now?"

"Get back to Twin Turrets," Marcus said. "Warn Janus."

PART THREE

THE DIRECTORY FOR
THE NATIONAL DEFENSE

Maurisk took up the bottle of *flaghaelen* with a shaking hand and tipped it over his glass. After a moment, a single amber drop ran down the side of the bottle, hung suspended on the rim for a moment, then splashed into the bottom of the glass. Maurisk stared at the bare smear of liquid, gritted his teeth, and shoved glass and bottle aside.

There was a soft knock at the door.

"What?" Maurisk snapped.

"Zacaros is here, sir," said Kellerman, from outside.

"Finally. Bring him in."

The commander of the Patriot Guard had evidently taken the time to put on his elaborate, immaculate uniform, or else he'd still been wearing it in the small hours of the morning. Maurisk wouldn't have put a bet either way. But while his gold lace was carefully arranged, his hair was askew, inexpertly tugged across his balding pate, and sweat coated his jowly face.

"President," he said, with a nod. Zacaros refused to offer salutes to civilians, which Maurisk thought was rich from a man who'd been a banker only months before. "I got here as soon as I was brought up-to-date on the situation."

"Really?" Maurisk said. "Then perhaps you can enlighten me as to the *situation*."

Maurisk had received a private briefing—practically a scolding—at the hands of Ionkovo. *And may demons hurry up and devour that smug priest.* But it wouldn't do to let anyone know that, least of all Zacaros. The commander of the Patriot Guard was a stupid man, but an ambitious one.

"Warehouse 192 was attacked by an unknown force," Zacaros said. "Our riverboat was burned, and the assailants forced their way into the building through a hidden door and did some small damage to the contents. A skirmish apparently followed, and . . ." Zacaros paused. "The results are not clear. A number of bodies were found badly burned, as though they'd been doused in oil. All six of our men who were present were killed."

That would be the work of Ionkovo's associate. The Penitent Damned called her *Cinder.* It was a pity about the men guarding the warehouse; he'd chosen them specifically for their loyalty. But Ionkovo had warned that anyone who saw his agents at work would be eliminated, and Maurisk had to approve. As the old saying went, "Three men can keep a secret only once two of them are at the bottom of the river."

"And have we *identified* these 'assailants'?"

"No. There was nothing remarkable on the unburned bodies. I believe they were hired thugs from Oldtown, and my men are making inquiries."

If there was anything less likely to produce results than asking pointed questions in Oldtown, Maurisk didn't know it. *Unless it's relying on idiots to make decisions.* Zacaros' only usefulness was in the loyalty he inspired in his men and his willingness to obey orders.

"More important," Maurisk said, "do we know what they took?"

"It's not clear," Zacaros said. "Nothing of military importance."

"I'm not worried they stole a *cannon*. Was there anything there that could compromise us?"

"Possibly. Copies of some messages, perhaps—"

"Messages are to be destroyed once encoded!"

"The clerks may have been . . . lax. But it seems likely the attackers were surprised before they had time to investigate."

"Likely." Maurisk drummed his fingers on the desk. There was only one decision he could possibly make, one throw of the dice that might produce success, but still he hesitated. *Damn, damn, damn. I need more time.*

"I—" Zacaros began.

"Shut up. We're moving up the timetable."

The Patriot Guard commander blinked. "When?"

"Now. Tonight."

"That's not possible," Zacaros said. "We need time to prepare—"

"You've had weeks. If you're not ready now, you never will be. All the orders are already printed. You only need to hand them out. If the enemy—whoever they are—knows about the warehouse, they'll know everything soon enough. This is the only chance we have to still achieve surprise."

"But—"

"Don't forget it's your head in the noose, too." Maurisk smiled nastily. "Or possibly the Spike. That bastard Durenne has always been fond of poetic irony."

Zacaros swallowed, swiping his hand over his scalp and further disrupting his hair. After a moment, Maurisk saw his eyes harden in decision, and he straightened to his feet, coming to the best approximation of military attention his overweight frame could manage.

"As you say. I'll make the arrangements at once."

"I want regular reports."

"Of course." Zaracos nodded again. "If you'll excuse me?"

He went to the door without waiting for an answer. Once he was gone, Kellerman looked in.

"Sir? Can I—"

"A drink." Maurisk waved the empty bottle.

"I believe that was the last bottle of the *flaghaelen*, sir."

"I don't care what *kind.* Just get me a goddamned drink!"

"Yes, sir."

Maurisk leaned back in his chair and settled in to wait.

Three hours. Three hours to go from despair to euphoria.

It had little to do with the indifferent white wine Kellerman had scrounged up. Maurisk had stared into his glass, imagining his orders fanning out across the darkened city, thinking of everything that could go wrong. Zacaros could betray him, or simply bungle the job. The Patriot Guard might balk, in spite of all their careful preparation. The Radicals might be more prepared than they seemed. The Beast of Judgment might appear in Farus' Triumph to proclaim the End of Days. *Waiting*.

And now . . .

Giles Durenne's famous nose had been broken rather badly, and was now turning a ripe red color and swelling to twice its original side. Maurisk watched the Radical leader as two Patriot Guards forced him to his knees in front of the desk, and decided he liked the way it looked. *He's practically a clown already.*

He'd wondered, over the past few weeks, what Durenne would say when it all finally played out. Even made little bets with himself, in fact. Now he waited, savoring the moment, as the Minister of War coughed and spit blood on the floor.

"Have you," Durenne said, voice made stuffy by his broken nose, "have you gone *mad*?"

Dreadfully unoriginal. That was Durenne, though. Unimaginative to the last.

"No," Maurisk said. "Merely had my eyes opened."

"This is absurd. Release me at once."

"So you can continue your treasons with your Radical friends? I think not."

"I am an elected deputy and Minister of War! I demand—"

"You are in a position to demand nothing." Maurisk felt suddenly tired. It was nearly five in the morning, and the nervous tension that had kept him going all night seemed to go out of him in a rush, leaving him barely able to keep his head up. "You will have a trial, eventually. We both know what will happen when the truth comes out."

He fixed Durenne with a very slight smile, which said, *I win. You lose. That's all there is to it.*

"If there's a traitor here, it's you," Durenne snarled. "But you won't get away with it. The army won't sit still for this."

"We'll see." Maurisk sat back and waved at the guards. "Take him away."

Kellerman appeared again, a paper in his hand, as the frantic Radical was dragged off.

"Matters are proceeding on schedule, I trust?" Maurisk said.

"Yes, sir," his assistant said, consulting the page. "Two-thirds of the arrests have already been carried out. No real resistance thus far."

"I want every one of those men under guard before dawn."

"They will be, sir."

"Has d'Ivoire been taken?"

"Not yet, sir."

"You gave the commander my instructions?"

"Yes, sir. D'Ivoire is to be taken alive, no matter the cost."

Maurisk grunted. With the queen in hand, and arrangements already made to draw Vhalnich's fangs, that left the Thousand Names. What Ionkovo wanted with a Khandarai relic, he had no idea, but d'Ivoire was their best chance of finding the blasted thing. *The last thing I need is for him to be killed in the cross fire.*

Speaking of Vhalnich.

"Send a messenger to *General* de Ferre. Tell him the new Minister of War directs him to begin his mission at once."

CHAPTER FOURTEEN

WINTER

"Magic," Jane said.

"I know it sounds crazy," Winter said. "I wouldn't have believed it if I hadn't been there."

It was the first day out from Desland, and the Third Regiment was marching along in fine style on a pleasant autumn morning. Winter, Jane, Bobby, and Cyte rode together near the head of the column, far enough from anyone else that their conversation wouldn't be overheard. Beside them, the Girls' Own tramped in loose ranks, chatting and joking. There was a nasty edge to them, Winter thought. They were angry.

They had a right to be. In addition to the two guards who'd died trying to defend her office, they'd found two other soldiers dead: a young man from the Royals with wounds to his face, who'd been stripped of his uniform, and a woman on watch at one of the gates, who'd been snapped in half like a toothpick by the giant on his way out.

Winter hadn't told everyone that the attack had been made by the Penitent Damned, of course, but there was no hiding the fact that there had been an attempt on her life. Rumor had filled the gap left by the absence of facts, and it was now widely accepted that the assassins had been sent by the Kommerzint, the Hamveltai intelligence service. Winter was happy enough to let that stand, since it was close enough to the truth to be believed.

After the attack, when soldiers had rushed into the blood-spattered room and then out again to put the whole citadel on alert, Winter had only been able to steal a few moments with Jane. She'd promised a full explanation, but they'd passed a sleepless night simultaneously directing the search for the vanished attackers and rechecking the preparations for the next day's march. At Cyte's insistence, Winter had taken a few hours to fall into an exhausted sleep, but she'd been up with the late dawn to get the troops on the road.

Now, with the march well under way, she reviewed the story she had to tell and winced. *Damn. I wouldn't believe me, either.*

"Me, either," Bobby said. "I didn't believe it, I mean. Not at first. Not until after Feor healed me."

"Who's Feor?" Cyte said. Winter had expected more of a reaction from her, but she was only listening carefully, brow furrowed, as though she expected to be quizzed on the material later.

"I'd better start from the beginning," Winter said. "Which is Janus' arrival in Khandar."

It took longer than she'd expected to lay out the bare facts. The Khandarai campaign, her own unwilling promotion, the Battle of the Road, and her chance discovery of Feor in the aftermath. Bobby's nearly fatal wounding and her miraculous recovery. The fire that had consumed Ashe-Katarion, and their confrontation with Onvidaer and Mother. And, finally, the night that still lived in Winter's nightmare, trapped in an underground temple full of walking corpses with glowing green eyes. How, with Feor's guidance, she'd read the *naath*, or the name, or *whatever* it was that had invoked the Infernivore, and how she'd used it to defeat Jen Alhundt.

"She worked for *them*. The Priests of the Black," Winter said.

"There aren't any Priests of the Black," Jane said.

"There used to be," Cyte said, "but they were disbanded

nearly a hundred years ago. And the Priests of the Black were devoted to destroying the supernatural in all its forms. How could someone like that be one of them?"

"Janus only explained a little," Winter said. "He said the Priests still operate, but they do it in secret, because nobody believes in magic these days. They have these . . . agents, who call themselves the Penitent Damned. They believe that anyone who uses a demon is condemned to hell, but they do it anyway, because it helps to advance the cause."

"That," Jane said, "is fucked up. This is why I never paid attention in church."

"Those three yesterday were Penitent Damned?" Cyte said.

Winter nodded. "I think so. I can sense them, when they get close enough. The Infernivore gets . . . restless."

"You can feel what the demon is thinking?" Jane said.

"Not exactly." Winter sighed. "It's hard to explain. It feels like it's this *thing*, living inside my mind. Like it's part of me, but it's *not* me, if that makes any sense. I don't think it's very smart, but I can tell when it gets hungry."

"Yuck," Jane said. "No offense. That sounds awful."

"Apparently, I'm lucky to be alive," Winter said. "Janus told me most people who try to bind to a demon die in the attempt. I suppose I didn't have much of a choice at the time."

"So that's why he brought you with him from Khandar?" Jane said. "Because you had this thing he wanted to use?"

"That's one of the reasons," Winter said, a little embarrassed. "It's always hard to tell with Janus."

"What about you?" Cyte said to Bobby. "Can you feel your demon?"

Bobby shook her head. "Feor tried to explain it to me. She's got the demon, but she can't use its power herself. She granted the power to me, but I don't get the demon. If I died, she could give it to someone else."

"And it makes you . . . what? Invulnerable?" Jane said.

"It keeps me alive," Bobby said, with a wince. "But it still hurts."

There was a moment of silence. Winter could hear

singing from somewhere up the column, the tramp of many feet, and the jingling of her horse's harness. Absent were the creaking sounds of wagons and the occasional lowing of oxen. The slow-moving vehicles had been left to make their own best speed behind the column, bearing most of the regiment's baggage and reserve supplies.

"So, what does he want, in the end?" Jane said.

"Who?" Winter said.

"Janus." She held up a hand and ticked off points on her fingers. "The Church, or the Priests of the Black, anyway, want to get rid of magic because the *Wisdoms* tell them it's evil. So if this Thousand Names is like a giant spell book—"

"It's a set of steel tablets eight feet high," Winter interrupted. "Not a book."

"Whatever. The point is, it lets you do magic, so they want to destroy it, or hide it until Elysium. I follow that much. But what does Janus want it for? You said he went to Khandar to get it."

Winter frowned. "It's not as if he shares his plans with me. But if I had to guess, he wanted it to help him get rid of Duke Orlanko. He told me that he always knew the Concordat were working with the Priests of the Black."

"Did he really need to go all the way to Khandar for that?" Jane said. "We threw Orlanko out, and I didn't notice him blasting anyone with lightning bolts at the time."

"I have no idea," Winter said. "Maybe there's more to it than that. Does it matter?"

"I . . ." Jane shook her head. "I'm not sure. This is a lot to take in."

Winter let out a deep breath. She felt curiously *free*, now that she'd told the story from beginning to end. *No more secrets.* "I'm sorry I didn't tell you before."

"It's all right," Jane said. "I can't imagine I'd have believed you."

"Those three last night," Cyte said. "You think they were there to kill you?"

"That's the only thing that makes sense to me. We're only one regiment. It's flattering to think that I might be a good enough officer that they'd want me assassinated, but even if that were true they wouldn't send Penitent Damned to do it. It has to be because of Infernivore."

"Do you think they'll come back?" Cyte said.

"We'll be keeping better watches now that we're in enemy country," Jane said. "They won't be able to sneak up on us again."

That was more confidence than Winter felt, but she nodded anyway. "They're not invincible. Frightening, but not unbeatable."

"And I'm going to stay close," Bobby said. "Just in case."

As the day wore on, the march began to drag. They'd begun at first light, with only a short break around noon for lunch, and by the time the sun touched the horizon they still hadn't reached the place the scouts had designated as a campsite, twenty-five miles from where they'd started. It was well into dusk before the head of the column got there, and mounted officers roamed the road by torchlight rounding up stragglers for hours afterward.

Winter stood on the edge of the grassy hillock that was their campsite and watched the horsemen come and go, lights moving in the dark like windblown sparks. Captain Sevran, standing beside her, twisted his lip in concern.

"Something wrong?" Winter said.

"Just imagining what would happen if we got hit by a cavalry raid," Sevran said. "They couldn't ask for a better target."

"It's a risk we're going to have to run. If we take the time to be cautious, we'll never make it." Winter shook her head. "As it is, we'll have to start well before dawn tomorrow. We can't keep fumbling around in the dark like this. Get them on the road as soon as you can see your hand in front of your face."

"Yes, sir," Sevran said, saluting. "After today, we've got a lot of sore feet and sprained ankles. Some of them are going to have to be left behind."

Winter winced, but there was nothing for it. Marching wore down men just as surely as it broke down wagons and animals, and abandoned casualties were one of the prices of fast movement. "Make sure they have enough food and water to last until the wagon teams catch up." The lamed soldiers wouldn't arrive in time for the battle, assuming Janus' timetable was accurate, but at least they wouldn't be on their own in enemy country. "And get me a report of how many men we're talking about."

"Yes, sir." The captain saluted again. "If you'll excuse me, I'm going to get a little sleep myself."

Winter waved him away. She herself was sore—she hadn't been riding long enough that twelve hours in the saddle was something she could shrug off—and the day had been a long one. But there was one more thing to attend to, and once again she'd been putting it off. She turned her back on the stragglers and went looking for Jane.

The camp bore little resemblance to the organized tent villages of earlier marches. The tents had been left behind, along with all the other equipment that the wagons normally carried, leaving the soldiers with only bedrolls and blankets to make themselves comfortable. Small fires blazed everywhere, and the men and women of the Third Regiment sat around them, leaning on their bedrolls or already stretching out on the uneven ground. The banter was good-natured—legs were sore and feet blistered, but for the moment morale seemed to be high.

She found Jane in a rocky copse, near the edge of the hill, where Edgar and some other horses had been tethered. Their saddlebags had been neatly piled nearby, and Jane was rooting through hers. As Winter approached, she straightened up, triumphantly holding her prize.

"Socks," she said. "There's a hole in mine and it's rubbing me something awful. I knew I bought an extra pair after we got to Desland."

Winter did her best to put on a grin, but it must have looked as sickly as it felt, because Jane's expression darkened.

"We need—"

"To talk." Jane sighed. "Come on."

Winter followed her into the trees, out of sight of the

rest of the camp. Jane found a small boulder and sat down, gingerly, and started unlacing her boots. Winter stood opposite her, arms folded. She realized she had no idea how to begin.

"What were you doing at the citadel?" she said after a moment. It wasn't the right question, but it was the only one she could think of. "You said you weren't coming back."

"I'm not sure I remember anymore," Jane said, pulling off one of her boots and setting it on the ground. "I think I came looking for a fight."

"You found one."

Jane chuckled. "Not the kind I wanted. I just thought . . . I don't know. I was going to grab you and shake you until you understood."

"Understood what?"

"I'm not sure I knew. I was pretty drunk." Jane sighed. "It doesn't matter."

"You saved me. Probably Cyte and Bobby, too."

"I didn't mean to."

"Still." Winter took a deep breath and hugged herself a little tighter. "Thank you."

Jane tugged off her sock and held her foot in the air, wiggling her toes. "Ahhh. Much better."

"Jane—"

"What do you want me to say?" Jane looked up. "I was acting like an ass. I'm sorry. I'm sorry you nearly had to get killed before I realized it."

"It's all right," Winter said.

"No, it's not," Jane said. "When you came back to me in Vordan, and told me your story, I don't think I understood it. I thought you were . . . hiding, pretending, when you talked about being in the army. But this is your life."

"It is," Winter said. She wasn't sure she'd understood that herself until Jane had said it out loud. "I didn't mean for it to be. But . . ."

Jane cocked her head, emerald eyes reflecting sparks from the campfires out in the darkness. Winter uncrossed her arms.

"Do you mind if I sit down?"

Wordlessly, Jane shuffled over on her rock, and Winter took a seat next to her. They sat side by side for a moment, in silence.

"I spent two years living in fear," Winter said. "After I ran away from Mrs. Wilmore's, I was so sure someone would come after me. I ran all the way to Khandar, and then I was afraid of what would happen if someone found me out. I had this sergeant, Davis, who was . . . a monster." Winter touched her cheek. Davis' bruises had long since faded, but something in the bone remembered. "If he'd ever discovered who I really was, I don't know . . ."

Jane put a hand on her arm, and Winter let out a long breath.

"It all changed when Janus arrived. They made me a sergeant, and then our lieutenant got himself killed, and the men in the company *needed* me. No one had ever needed my help before. Except for you, and that time I ran away."

Jane squeezed Winter's arm. "You know you can't blame yourself for that."

"Thanks." Winter swallowed. "Once people start to rely on you, you can never really get free."

"I know all about that." Jane leaned back, kicking her feet, one bare and one booted. "I didn't mean to start the Leatherbacks, obviously. When I went back to Mrs. Wilmore's, I was looking for *you*. But I ended up with a couple of hundred girls expecting me to tell them what to do, and I couldn't just leave them. And one thing just kept leading to another . . ." She shrugged. "The hell of it is, now they don't need me anymore. They've got you. And I don't know how to feel about it."

"*I* need you," Winter said.

"Not in what you might call a professional capacity," Jane drawled, and Winter laughed. "So, what are you going to do with me, Colonel Ihernglass?"

"I think Abby should stay in command of the Girls' Own," Winter said.

Jane nodded. "She's better at the organizational bullshit than I could ever be. Even back in Vordan it was her and Min who kept everybody fed and made sure the laundry got done."

They were silent for a moment. Min had died at the Vendre, shot by a Concordat sniper.

"I'll put you on my staff," Winter said. "I can't imagine Janus will object."

"Just don't expect me to write out marching orders and file reports."

"Cyte can handle that. I'll keep you around for when some idiot officer needs to be beaten into submission."

Jane laughed, and slipped her arm around Winter. Winter sagged against her, with a happy sigh, and rested her head on Jane's shoulder.

"What happened to Sergeant Davis?" Jane said. "Will I get the chance to beat the hell out of him?"

"No." Winter closed her eyes. "I killed him myself."

"Oh." Jane thought about that for a moment. "Good."

After a moment of silence, Winter felt Jane's finger under her chin, tilting her head back. Jane leaned over her, red hair falling around them like a crimson waterfall, blocking out the world as their lips met. The kiss lasted for a long time.

"We haven't got a tent," Jane said, pulling away just far enough to speak. Her breath was hot on Winter's face.

"I don't think anyone can see us in here."

"They might hear us."

"I can stay quiet."

"Oh?" Jane murmured, pulling Winter closer. "Is that a challenge?"

Late that night, the rain began.

It was a light drizzle, not a downpour, but it was continuous and unrelenting. By the time the soldiers awoke, an hour before dawn, uniforms and blankets were already soggy. The road, which was little more than a ribbon of dirt running parallel to the river, slowly but surely transformed into a ribbon of mud. It was churned a little more by every pair of boots that passed over it, until the unlucky companies at the end of the column were slogging through glop as deep as a man's thigh. Whole groups abandoned the road altogether and wandered through the brush beside it, losing their way or flailing through grass and bushes.

In spite of the early start Winter had ordered, it was obvious by midday that they were not going to reach their campsite until long after dark. Winter let Edgar pick his way through the mud, snorting in irritation, while she listened to Sevran's reports.

"We're down about thirty, all told," he said. "Better than I expected. They should be all right until the wagons catch up."

"That may take a while, if the rain doesn't stop," Winter said.

Sevran nodded. "I'm more worried about tonight. We're already getting a lot of stragglers."

"At least we should be in the dry when we get there." The supplies she'd ordered unloaded from the barges included enough tents to keep the regiment out of the rain, if they were willing to squeeze tight. More important, there would be enough food there to fill the soldiers' knapsacks, which they'd deliberately kept light to make the marching easier. "Start sending officers to round up the laggards while we still have some light to see by."

"Good idea." Sevran saluted, water dripping from the brim of his cap, and rode off.

Winter went in search of Abby, riding past rank after rank of struggling Girls' Own soldiers. She saw Anne Marie, a flash of golden hair amid the drab, wet blue uniforms. The Deslandai girl stumbled and went to her knees, but two of her neighbors caught her by the elbows and swung her back up. Winter smiled to herself and rolled on.

Abby, mounted, was at the very head of the column, where the mud was only an inch deep. Edgar liked this much better than slogging through muck in the rear, and tossed his head excitedly as Winter urged him into a trot.

"Not exactly ideal conditions," Abby said as Winter came alongside.

"How are you holding up?"

"All right, I think." Abby looked over her shoulder at

the women of her command. "I won't know for sure until we round everybody up and count noses."

Winter nodded, and hesitated for a moment. "I talked with Jane. She agrees that you should keep the Girls' Own."

Abby blinked and straightened up, setting off a waterfall from some recess of her cap. "She . . . she's not coming back?"

"She'll be on my staff, so she's not going anywhere. But you'll be captain of the battalion. You've done an excellent job so far."

"I . . ." Abby swallowed, then saluted, heedless of the rain. "Yes, sir. Thank you."

"If any of the old Leatherbacks give you problems, let me know."

"Yes, sir. I'll need another lieutenant to take my place with the Third Company."

Winter nodded. "Go ahead and promote someone. I'll leave the choice to you. Anything else?"

"I'll let you know when I think of it." Abby shook her head, spilling more water. "Looking forward to drying out tonight."

"You and me both." Damp had never been a problem in Khandar, and Winter hadn't spent much time in her uniform in the rain. The tight undershirt she used to hide her breasts was chafing badly enough that she thought she'd have blisters. *Thank God I insisted on getting everyone fresh boots before we left.*

The march went on, and on, and on, through the afternoon and into the evening, after the sun hid its face beyond a veil of clouds. Torches, spitting and flaring in the rain, marked the length of the column, giving the men and women trudging through the dark something to guide themselves on. It was easy to put a foot astray in the dark, to turn an ankle on a rock or get stuck in a deep mud puddle, and the mounted officers spent more time orchestrating rescues than collecting stragglers.

Winter pushed forward to the head of the column, hoping to find the campsite, only to meet a pair of scouts returning. She could tell from their faces that the news was not good.

"I'm sorry, sir," the young man said for the twentieth time.

"It's all right," Winter said. "It sounds like there's nothing you could have done."

"No, sir." He swallowed. "We rode upriver with the barges, as ordered." She'd sent four men with each convoy, to guard against bandits or pilferage by the bargemen themselves, but she hadn't expected this. "Once we met with the courier, we told the bargemen we were going to stop and wait. They weren't happy about that, sir. They had other cargoes, they said. But we got them to pull in to bank."

"And then they attacked you?" Jane said.

The ranker nodded, looking around the circle of officers. Abby, Sevran, Bobby, and Cyte were there, in addition to Winter and Jane, standing on a muddy bit of grass overlooking the river Velt. A ring of torches defined the camp, which was conspicuously lacking the tents that Winter had expected to find there.

"It wasn't . . . I mean, we didn't *fight* much. There were twenty of them and four of us, and they grabbed Clarke while he was taking a piss. And it was raining, so we'd put our powder in our packs. They didn't hurt us any, just put us over the side and pushed off. Though one of them did shout some lewd things at Ranker Verra."

"Any idea where they were going?"

The young man shook his head. "Somewhere upriver. But we lost sight of them pretty quickly in the rain. I'm really sorry, sir."

"Thank you, Ranker. You're dismissed."

He saluted and squelched away. Winter waited until he was out of earshot, then turned to the others. "All right. How bad is this?"

"Pretty bad," Abby said.

Sevran nodded. "We're low on food. Most of the rankers took a little extra, so there's enough left for maybe a half ration tomorrow, but that's all."

"If that much," Abby said. "I'm hearing from the sergeants that we've got a lot of 'lost' bedrolls and packs today. Everyone was sure there'd be plenty to eat when we got here."

"And there are *still* some wandering in," Sevran said. It was nearly midnight. "If we want to keep to the same schedule tomorrow, some of the rankers are going to be on barely an hour of sleep."

"How about ammunition?" Winter said.

"Forty rounds each, as usual, but no reserve supplies," Sevran said.

"And cartridge boxes may be getting lost, too. Or wet."

"Hell," Jane said. "We're fucked, aren't we?"

The gloomy sentiment passed around the circle, and no one offered an objection. Winter took a deep breath. "So what do we do?"

She looked at Sevran, who shrugged. "If it were just me, I'd go back the way we came until I met up with the wagons. Plenty of supplies there."

"At the wagon's pace, it might take us two weeks to get to Janus."

Sevran nodded. "That's the problem."

Winter glanced at Abby, who stood up a bit straighter. "We should keep going," she said. "Nobody's going to starve in a couple of days, and we can gather up all the horses and use them for foraging parties. That ought to get us through."

"Assuming there'll be supplies waiting when we get to wherever we're going," Jane said. "Otherwise it could be a lot longer than two days if we have to wait for the wagon train to catch up."

"Cyte?" Winter said.

"I'm not sure how much of a regiment we'll have left when we get there if we push on," Cyte said. "The way people are straggling, we might end up leaving half the soldiers behind. Is that really going to be any good to Janus?"

Winter nodded and looked to Bobby, who shrugged. "I'm with Abby. If she thinks we can make it, we can make it."

"And you're with Sevran, Jane?"

Jane frowned. "Hell. It's not that we couldn't do it. But people are already hurting themselves, and it's only going to get worse."

"That makes three to two," Cyte said.

"It's not a vote," Sevran said. "We provide our advice to the commander, and he makes the decision. If the colonel says we're pressing on, I'll press on."

"Thank you," Winter said. "I need a minute to think about this. Go and see how we're doing on rounding up our stragglers."

The five of them saluted, picking their way through the mud and out into the chaos of the camp. Winter stayed where she was, looking out at the nearly invisible river. Faint lights on the other side marked a hillside village, shimmering through a curtain of rain.

Jane's right that people are going to get hurt. There had been a few broken bones already, and that was only among the men and women who'd made it into camp. *Who knows how many are still out there? Or how many have decided to wander off?* There was no way the sergeants could police for desertion with straggling as bad as it was. *If we press on, with no tents and no food . . .*

When she closed her eyes, she could see the note Janus had sent, his neat handwriting aglow in her inner vision.

. . . do everything in your power . . .

. . . you have yet to disappoint me.

Failing Janus was unthinkable, somehow. *He's always come through for us, in the end.* Now that he was relying on her, could she do less than everything in her power to help? But . . .

Janus hadn't come through, not for everyone. Not for Adrecht Roston, whose bleached bones were lost somewhere in the Great Desol. Not for all the men they'd lost on the trek to the Desoltai temple, in pursuit of the Thousand Names. Not for Min, or Chris, or all the rest of the young women who'd died thus far following Winter and Jane. *There are going to be more names on that list, whatever I do now. Can I really ask them to keep going, with no food, no shelter, and maybe a battle at the end of it all?*

Drums rolled an hour before dawn the next morning, tearing the soldiers of the Third Regiment from their all-too-brief

slumber. The rain had slackened but not stopped, so the rankers rolled their blankets and assembled their sodden kit under
a gray, drooling sky.

The officers, meanwhile, assembled in a semicircle in
front of a flat boulder, where Winter could stand and be
heard. Sevran and Abby were on either side of her. True
to his word, Sevran hadn't flinched when Winter told him
of her decision, only nodded and calmly issued orders for
the continued march.

The lieutenants and sergeants, thirty or so in all, milled
about in a loose crowd. She could see Folsom, standing
stolidly in the center with Graff hunched to one side and
Marsh, Bobby's lover, on the other. The noble lieutenants
of the Royals, Maret and sur Gothin and the rest of Lieutenant Novus' erstwhile friends, kept to themselves in a
sullen group, as did Becca, Winn, and the rest of Jane's older
Leatherbacks. In between were the rest—long-serving, hard-
bitten sergeants from the Royals mixed women from the
Girls' Own who had largely been promoted by Winter
herself or elected by their own companies. Their expressions were downcast, the recruits affecting the cynicism
of the veterans, but underneath it Winter could feel an
almost childlike need for reassurance. She coughed, and
swallowed hard.

"You've probably heard by now," she said, voice thin
and reedy in her own ears, "that a bunch of bargemen
turned traitor and made off with the supplies we were
counting on. We've got fifty miles to go before tomorrow
night, and that's going to mean some empty stomachs.
There's no way around it."

There was a chorus of low groans and whispered
comments.

"We'll be lucky to get half that far," a woman said. The
Girls' Own hadn't had the grin-and-bear-it attitude toward
orders ground into them like the regulars. "The mud is
sucking the boots off my rankers' feet."

"We'll keep going as long as we have to," Winter said.

"Why?" the woman shot back. "What good is one more
regiment going to do, out of a whole battle?"

"I have no idea," Winter said. "But Janus told me it was important, and that's good enough for me."

More grumbling, this time from the two isolated groups of the nobles and the Leatherbacks. In between, though, Winter saw mostly nods, led by Folsom and Graff. For the recruits, Janus' name was a thing to conjure with, the genius who'd led them to nothing but victory. Even the Royals were starting to come around.

"We'll do what we can about food," Winter went on. "As of now, I need every horse we've got for foraging teams. That includes mine."

"You can't be serious!" Lieutenant de Vend burst out. He was one of Novus' cronies. "You expect us to slog through the mud?"

"I'm happy to slog through the mud all day if it means we'll have something to eat at the end of it," Marsh shot back. De Vend scowled, but said nothing.

"That's all," Winter said, ignoring them both. "Let's get moving."

There was a shuffle as the assembled officers made a ragged salute, and then they dispersed. As the crowd cleared, Winter saw Jane coming over through the muddy grass of the campsite.

"Something wrong?" Winter said.

Jane looked grim. "You'd better come see."

Hanna Courvier was the cutter for the Girls' Own, the closest thing the battalion had to a doctor. She'd taken on several of the young girls, those too small to carry muskets, as her assistants, and they'd designated a stretch of soggy hillside as a field hospital. Blankets, sewn together at the edges and staked up with bayoneted muskets wedged in the mud, provided a modicum of shelter from the drizzle.

Hanna was a solid-looking, tanned woman with long, frizzy hair pulled back into a tightly controlled bun. Winter didn't know very much about her, other than that she'd come with Jane from the Docks. She realized, belatedly, that it must have been Hanna who treated her after the battle of Gaafen. *I never even thanked her.*

The cutter was not in the mood for pleasantries now. She glared at Winter as though holding her personally responsible for the weather, the mud, and everything else that had gone wrong.

"Miss Courvier," Winter said, ducking her head politely. "How bad is it?"

"Pretty fucking bad," Hanna said. She had the same Docks accent—and accompanying foul mouth—that Jane had picked up. "I've been making do with less than nothing. Most of my kit is back with the wagons." She waved at the area under the blankets. "There's already more than I can handle. Marching this hard, in the rain and the mud . . ."

There were at least a score of soldiers lying there, packed shoulder to shoulder, asleep or staring up at Winter, Jane, and Hanna. They were surprisingly quiet, though one man at the edge moaned in a soft, low voice and a woman gave periodic hacking coughs.

"How many of them can walk?" Winter said.

Hanna snorted. "I already sent all them that can walk back to their units. These are the ones that're going to have to be left behind." She lowered her voice. "Or those who aren't going to make it, regardless. I've got two legs with infected punctures that need to come off, but nothing to do it with. A few others . . ." She shook her head.

Winter looked over the injured soldiers, feeling sick to her stomach. She paused and turned to Jane. "Is that Molly?"

Jane nodded. "She and Becks joined up before we left Vordan."

Molly had cut her ringletted hair back to a boyish fuzz, and marching had melted the plumpness from her face. Winter remembered her and Becks at the Sworn Cathedral, helping to rescue Danton when Orlanko tried to arrest the Deputies-General. *I didn't know she'd come along.* She didn't look injured, but her cheeks were flushed and her breathing shallow.

"What's wrong with her?" Winter said.

"Shaking fever," Hanna said. "Exhaustion and damp bring it on. Too many bad vapors."

"Will she be all right?"

"If we had her in the dry in front of a roaring fire, with something besides hardtack to eat, she might be. Out here?" Hanna spit on the grass. "Might as well start digging a grave. She's not the only one."

More names on the list. Winter closed her eyes for a moment and fought down a sour taste at the back of her throat. She turned to Jane, who was doing her best to remain expressionless. Winter knew her too well for that, though. There was accusation in those green eyes, and she found herself looking away.

"Find some volunteers to stay with them," Winter said. "It shouldn't be difficult. Four rankers. Leave as much food as you can spare, and tell them to keep a fire going. The wagon teams have cutters. They'll do what they can when they get here."

"That could be days," Jane said very quietly.

"I know." Winter gritted her teeth. "We haven't got a choice."

That became her mantra, repeated at every step along the road on a day that seemed as if it would never end. *We haven't got a choice.* She couldn't bring herself to fail Janus, not if there was any other option, and that meant *this.* Winter started at the head of the column, but it wasn't long before she drifted rearward, the bigger and stronger soldiers passing her by as the weaker and smaller filtered toward the back. Mud sucked at her feet with every step, clinging to her boots in great grimy chunks, making her feel as though she wore iron weights around her ankles.

The rain stopped, began again in a sudden, violent torrent, then died away to a drizzle once more. The sun was invisible behind the clouds, the world illuminated by a sourceless gray light that left everything flat and without shadows. In her idle moments, Winter wondered if she'd died and gone to her own personal hell. *But I'm not alone. Are there hells for entire regiments?* Those moments were few and far between, though, and most of the time she had eyes only for the ground directly in front of her. Each tiny puddle might be an inch deep, or an ankle-breaking hole;

each stretch of mud could slide underneath her or sink her to the knee.

She chewed a hardtack cracker as she went, without enthusiasm. The men and women around her slogged on, not singing, not even speaking, with no energy to spare for anything except the next breath and the next step. Sometimes they tripped and fell, or flopped to the ground and lay gasping in the mud. More often, when they couldn't bear any more, they simply vanished, slipping to the side of the road and away into the underbrush.

It grew darker so gradually that Winter didn't notice the sun had set until she held up a hand and realized she could only see the outline of her fingers against the sky. Full dark came not long afterward, and torches blazed along the column, making it feel even more like some sort of demonic procession. The entrance to the campsite was marked by a blazing bonfire, which ought to have been ominous, but after so long in the cold and wet, Winter wanted nothing more than to lie down amid the flames and let them roast her dry.

The scouts were waiting there, and they had food. Chickens were cooking over smaller fires, fat dripping and sizzling, and the delicious aroma of roasting pork served as a beacon. Just the smell revived Winter somewhat, and she sat down beside one of the fires, among the other soldiers.

"—didn't want to sell," one of the scouts was saying, a hard-faced woman with a Docks accent. "Said our money wasn't worth anything, and he wouldn't sell to the enemy anyway. So I told him, 'You see these muskets? They mean we're taking your goddamned chickens. Your only option is whether you get anything in return.' He decided he wanted the money after all."

"Fucking Hamvelts," someone else said. "If this is what their country is like, no wonder they're such ugly bastards."

"I don't know," someone else said. "Place we stopped, there was a daughter who gave me quite a looking-over, and I can't say I would've minded a turn."

"When that dark-haired lad smiled at Neyve, I thought

she was going to fall off her horse," the scout said. "I had to watch to make sure she didn't sneak away and ride back to have a roll."

"Forget the pretty boys," another woman said. "What about the wine cellar?"

Winter's eyes closed, unstoppably, as though they had weights attached. The smell of food made her stomach rumble, but the lure of sleep was stronger, and the voices faded away.

"Isn't that the colonel?" someone said in the distance.

"Let him rest," someone else said. "He's had a long day. He's not used to walking with the rest of us . . ."

The drums the next morning woke her into a world of pain, cramps and bruises and aching muscles. The sky was lightening back into gray, trees and soldiers stark black silhouettes against it. Winter forced herself up, feet squelching inside the still-soaked boots she hadn't had the chance to remove, and stumbled toward the nearest collection of officers.

"Good morning, sir," Bobby said.

She seemed unaffected by the brutal march—more gifts from Feor's *naath*, if Winter had to guess. She directed a mental glare at the Infernivore. *Why can't you give me the strength of a giant or let me fly or something like that?* The demon made no answer, not that she'd really expected one.

"Morning," Winter mumbled.

"We're less than twenty-five miles from where Janus wanted us," Cyte said. She looked as haggard as Winter felt, eyes feverishly bright above dark circles like bruises against her pale skin. She held up the map and pointed to something Winter couldn't manage to focus on. "I think the officers should ride with the scouts today. We need to start laying plans for tomorrow."

"Ride." The idea of being on a horse, of not having to lift her own legs out of the mud, sounded like heaven, but Winter couldn't bring herself to accept it as possible. "Don't we need the horses for foraging?"

"Rich pickings yesterday," Bobby said. "We got more than we needed."

"And straggling has gotten worse," Cyte said darkly. "Which means fewer mouths to feed."

And, no doubt, more men and women left behind, collapsed on the road or abandoned in their blankets with the shaking fever. *We haven't got a choice.*

The mention of food made her suddenly, ravenously hungry, as though her stomach had been waiting for the perfect moment to pounce. Bobby directed her to the remains of a campfire, where half a roast chicken sat cold and greasy on a tin plate. Winter tore it to pieces with her bare hands, pulling the thin bones apart to suck the dark meat from them and licking the grease from her fingers afterward. When she stood up, she felt a bit more human, and brushed hopelessly at her muddy, sweat-stained uniform.

The scouts rode out, a handful of men and women on horses that looked almost as hard-used as the soldiers. Winter, Abby, and Sevran rode with them, with Jane, Bobby, and Cyte following, while the rest of the officers coaxed the mass of exhausted rankers into one last effort. Edgar was muddy and tired-looking, and Winter rode him as slowly as she could afford to while Sevran filled her in on the latest dismal reports.

"My sergeants tell me men were still wandering in this morning, saying they'd walked all night. There are probably more who took a nap in a hedge somewhere and got left behind."

"They won't get lost," Winter said. "A blind kitten could follow our trail through the mud."

Sevran nodded. "But roll call was down about two hundred. If today is the same, we'll be lucky to have four hundred men fit to fight tomorrow morning."

"The Girls' Own are holding up a little better," Abby said, with only a hint of competitive pride. "But I can't hope for more than five or six hundred."

That made nearly half the regiment left behind on the road to Desland, straggling, wounded, or dead. Winter wondered if any of the new Deslandai recruits had made it. *I doubt this was what they had in mind when they signed up.* She couldn't bring herself to blame them if they'd turned back; no doubt more of the Vordanai would have done the same, if they weren't so far from home.

"We'll have to hope that's enough," Winter said.

"And that whatever Janus has planned for tomorrow doesn't involve much marching," Jane muttered.

"Janus knew what he was telling us to do when he sent his orders," Cyte said. "A good general knows exactly what he can ask of his soldiers."

Jane only grunted.

The day wore on. Winter found herself dozing on Edgar's back, only to shake awake again as the horse navigated around a hole or a mud puddle. She'd long ago given up trying to give him much direction, as he was clearly better at picking his way through the drenched ground than she was. From time to time a scout rode back from the vanguard to report that they hadn't encountered anything worth noting, friendly or enemy. At lunch, they ate hardtack and cold chicken from their saddlebags in the saddle.

The rain had stopped, and after noon the sun finally broke through the clouds, a blindingly brilliant light after the dim morning but one that seemed to have lost all power to warm. The autumn wind cut through wet clothes like the sharpest of knives, and without the effort of walking to keep herself warm, Winter found herself shivering. She wrapped herself in a blanket from her bag that had stayed mostly dry, and hunched close to Edgar's solid warmth.

As the sun was setting, she was woken from her half-conscious reverie by calls from the scouts.

"Riders! Cavalry ahead!"

Awake at once, Winter blinked away the fog in her head and reined Edgar to a halt, the other officers clustering around her. Her hand went to her sword, for all the good it would do. If the cavalry were Hamveltai, they would face little opposition from the exhausted Third Regiment.

But no. When the approaching horsemen became visible, they wore blue jackets and trousers, along with the gleaming steel cuirasses that were the pride of Vordan's elite heavy cavalry. Each man carried a carbine, a shortened musket that could be used from horseback, along with his cavalry saber. In the lead was a diminutive figure standing tall in his stirrups, wearing a tall, plumed hat. He waved excitedly.

"Oh Lord," Winter said.

"You know him?" Jane said.

"He was our cavalry commander in Khandar. Captain Henry Stokes," she said. "We called him Give-Em-Hell."

"Why?" Cyte said.

"You'll see."

CHAPTER FIFTEEN

MARCUS

In spite of the fact that his only physical pain was the aching of his arms from rowing, Marcus felt bruised.

Again. Once again, he'd led men into a nightmare, a confrontation with forces they couldn't hope to match. He remembered the sick lurch of his stomach as the dead had risen in the Desoltai temple, the feeling that everything he knew about the world was coming apart. The screams of the soldiers the walking corpses had torn to pieces. *What good are ordinary people against creatures like* that?

For a moment, he damned Janus, the Thousand Names, and everything that had happened since the day Colonel Vhalnich stepped off the boat onto the rocky shore of Khandar. *Maybe it would be better if the Redeemers had slaughtered us all.*

Except, of course, it wasn't Janus' fault. The Priests of the Black were real, working under the surface, still manipulating events a hundred years after they'd supposedly been abolished. Raesinia was proof enough of that. *Janus only opened my eyes. But he never asked if I'd rather have kept them closed.*

"Marcus?" Raesinia said.

"Hmm?" Marcus blinked. They were sitting in the

dining room of Twin Turrets, with the map still laid out on the table. It had gone four in the morning, and exhaustion was settling over him like a cloak. "I'm sorry, what did you say?"

"How long will it take your message to reach Janus?"

"If we're lucky, by tomorrow night." Marcus silently cursed the elaborate security measures that kept him ignorant of the location of Willowbrook. He understood the necessity, but he wanted to sit by the flik-flik line until new instructions came through, not wait for a signal and a courier handoff that might be flubbed. "And if he's prompt, we could have a response by the day after tomorrow."

"That's too long." Raesinia bit her lip. "I think we should go to the Deputies in the morning."

"With just the arrest list?" That was all they'd gotten out of the night's disaster, and that only because Raesinia had had the presence of mind to stuff it in her pocket. "It's hardly proof."

"The warehouse is still there. The Deputies could send investigators. Maurisk can't move all that equipment overnight."

"Are you certain? Maybe he has someone who can make cannon get up and dance."

Raesinia shook her head, smiling slightly. "That would be something to see, at least."

"I'll think about it." Marcus squeezed his eyes shut for a moment. "Sleep on it."

This time Raesinia's smile was more genuine. "Get some rest."

She, Marcus noted, didn't seem tired at all. He wondered if she slept, and if her condition prevented it how she occupied herself all night. The thought of his own bed, so sinfully large and soft compared to the camp beds he'd spent his campaigns on, was extremely attractive. *Just a little more to take care of first.*

Marcus got up, stumbling a bit over his chair, and excused himself to go in search of Uhlan. He found the Mierantai lieutenant by the back stairs, talking in a low voice to one of the serving women. Her eyes were full of tears, an uncharacteristic display of emotion for the stoic mountain people. One of the men had meant something to her. *Sweetheart? Brother?* Whatever it was, he hadn't come back.

"Sir." Uhlan patted the woman on the shoulder and she hurried away, ducking her head perfunctorily in Marcus' direction. Marcus cleared his throat, uncomfortably.

"Is she . . . going to be all right?"

"Yes, sir," Uhlan said.

Marcus couldn't bring himself to ask for details. He shook his head. "I'm sorry about your men."

"Thank you, sir," Uhlan said. "We volunteered for this. It was a risky assignment."

I didn't know their names. The Mierantai had been happy keeping themselves to themselves, and Marcus had always left it that way. *I ought to have at least known their names.*

"If there's anything I can do, for the families, or anything . . . ," he managed.

"It will be taken care of," Uhlan said. "But thank you."

What is Mieran County like, if it breeds people like this? Marcus shook his head. "All right."

"Our security here is poor, sir, now that it's only Ranker Dracht and myself," Uhlan said. "In my opinion, we ought to relocate to somewhere more defensible and request reinforcements."

"I've sent to Willowbrook." There was at least a company of Mierantai there, Marcus knew. "In the meantime, all we can do is be ready. Make sure everyone knows we may have to leave in a hurry."

"Yes, sir."

"Have you seen Andy?"

"I believe she's in the kitchen, sir."

Andy was indeed in the kitchen, sitting at the plain wooden table the servants used for their meals. She had a bottle of something sticky and red, which was already half-empty. When she looked up at Marcus, her eyes were fever-bright.

"Hello, Colonel," she said, slurring only a little. "You want a drop?"

"No, thank you." Marcus pulled out a chair beside her and sat. "Are you all right?"

"No injuries to report, sir," she said, saluting with the bottle. A few drops splashed onto the tabletop.

"Andy . . ."

"Sorry." She took a pull, then put the bottle down. "I'm just a little drunk."

"I can see that," Marcus said gently.

"I just . . ." She swallowed. "Hayver was screaming. He looked like a roast someone had left in the fire too long, and he was still screaming."

"I know."

"I've never seen anyone burn to death before." She took a deep breath. "Stabbed, bashed over the head, shot. I helped with the wounded after Midvale. I thought nothing could be worse than that. There was this girl, she kept calling for help, but when we lifted her up her guts just fell out. Like she was giving birth to a pile of snakes. And she's still crying . . ." Andy closed her eyes. "I thought nothing could be worse than that."

Marcus fought a powerful urge to fold her in his arms. *She's still half a child.* But she was a ranker, a soldier, and colonels didn't embrace their rankers. *But . . . hell.* His lip twisted, thoughts a tired muddle.

"When you told me to run," Andy said, "and stood up to shoot . . . you thought you were going to burn, didn't you? That woman was . . . throwing bombs, or something . . ."

Marcus recognized the look in her eyes. He'd felt it himself, the sense of trying to reconcile what you knew was impossible.

"I thought I had a good shot." Marcus sighed. "Not that it did much good."

"Still. Thank you."

Andy blew out a breath, straightened her shoulders, and took another pull. "When you've been in a fight and you're hurting, what you need is a bottle and a warm body to hold close. That's what Mad Jane used to say, when we were fighting the tax farmers." She looked at the bottle. "You want a drop, Colonel? You look like you could use it."

For a moment, Marcus strongly considered it. *Lord knows I've crawled into a bottle from time to time.* But he was the responsible officer here, for better or for worse. He shook his head, wearily, and pushed his chair back from the table. "What I need is sleep. Good night, Ranker Dracht."

"Good night, sir."

Halfway to the door, Marcus paused. "I'm . . . sorry about Hayver."

"Thank you, sir." Andy waved the bottle at him.

Marcus stumbled twice on the stairs, and it took him far too long to figure out how to work the doorknob on his bedroom door. By the time he made it to the bed, it was just a matter of falling over in the right direction.

When he opened his eyes again, it was still just before dawn, with the dull glow of Vordan City coming in through the window and a few bright stars twinkling in the sky. He'd managed to get his boots off, but he still wore his jacket, and the buttons had pressed painfully against his sternum. He groaned again, rolled over, and shrugged out of the sweat-stained blue coat.

"We meet again, Captain d'Ivoire."

Marcus spun, heart suddenly thudding in his chest. His room at Twin Turrets was small, just a bed to sleep in and few personal effects. Sitting on the trunk that contained these was a figure dressed all in black, fingers steepled in front of a neat goatee. He wore a smile—closer to a smirk—that Marcus last remembered seeing on the other side of a set of iron bars.

"Ionkovo," Marcus said.

His sword was four steps away, hanging from a peg on the back of the door. A nearby candlestick might do as a club, in a pinch. *How the hell did he get in here?* Presumably the same way he'd gotten *out* of a locked cell, murdering an Armsman in the process.

"My apologies," Ionkovo said. "I see that it's *Colonel* d'Ivoire now. And you won't need your sword, I assure you. I haven't come to do you any harm."

"Then what the hell are you here for?" Marcus felt his anger rising. "*You* told me you had answers. You knew Orlanko had my family killed, didn't you?"

"I set you on the path to find the answer," Ionkovo said. "Isn't that worth something?"

"You—" Marcus' hands tightened to fists.

Ionkovo shrugged and raised his palms. "All right, I admit it. I had hoped the search would . . . distract you, at a critical time. Obviously, that did not go as we had planned it."

It had nearly worked. Marcus had left Danton's arrest to Vice Captain Giforte, and when Orlanko had interfered, a mob laid siege to the Vendre. Marcus had only barely made it there in time to take command, not that it had done much good. Only the timely intervention of Winter Ihernglass had kept *that* debacle from ending in a bloodbath.

"If you're not going to try to kill me," Marcus said, "then give me one good reason I shouldn't call the guards and have you thrown in the cellar. I know Janus would very much like to talk to you."

"The feeling is mutual," Ionkovo said, "although we perhaps imagine different circumstances for the conversation. But your guards will have their hands full in a moment. I have come, Colonel, to once again offer you my help."

"What the hell are you talking about?"

"Directory President Maurisk has finally decided to deal with his opponents once and for all. Tonight the long knives come out, and there's a blade intended for you. Answer my question, and I will delay them sufficiently for you to retreat and fight another day."

"Don't be absurd." Marcus' heart beat faster. *He had the arrest list ready. Could he have moved so quickly?* "The Deputies wouldn't stand for it. Neither would Janus."

"Maurisk believes he has General Vhalnich in hand. Whether he does or not . . ." Ionkovo gave an exaggerated shrug. "It will be all the same to you, however."

"I don't believe you."

"Then you will die. Tonight." Seeing Marcus' eyes flick to the sword again, Ionkovo laughed. "Oh, I won't need to dirty my hands."

"I—"

There was a knock at the door, loud and frantic. Ionkovo frowned. "Time's running out, Colonel. You have to decide."

"You haven't asked me your question," Marcus said, buying time.

"I think you know what it is." Ionkovo leaned forward and spoke in a hiss. *"Where are the Thousand Names?"*

That's what I was afraid of. "I don't know what you're talking about."

"Of course not." Ionkovo rolled his eyes. "I must say—"

The door broke open with a shattering crash, bits of the lock spraying across the room. Uhlan stood in the doorway, Raesinia at his side. Ionkovo looked them over, lazily. When he reached Raesinia, his face froze.

"Here." A slow smile spread across his expression. "You had her *here.* Oh, well done, d'Ivoire. Very well done."

"Colonel, down!" Uhlan raised a pistol.

Marcus sprang sideways, landing on the bed and clearing the line of fire. Uhlan pulled the trigger, but Ionkovo was faster still. He leaned backward from his seat on the trunk, letting himself fall into a reverse roll that ought to have ended with him sprawled awkwardly against the wall. Instead he hit the stark shadow cast by light from the corridor and fell *into* it, the dark surface rippling like water. A moment later the pistol roared, and the ball punched a splintery hole in the woodwork.

Uhlan lowered his smoking pistol, staring at where Ionkovo had disappeared. Raesinia pushed past him and ran to Marcus' side.

"Are you hurt?" she said.

Marcus groaned and sat up. "Fine, thank all the saints. But I think we're in trouble."

"I'm sorry to have broken down your door, sir," Uhlan said, emerging from his paralysis. "She insisted."

Marcus looked questioningly at Raesinia, who looked away.

"I had a . . . feeling," she muttered. "A sort of pain. I felt it when we saw that woman yesterday, and when it came back, I thought she might be here."

"Every naathem *can feel others of our kind,"* Feor had said. Marcus hadn't considered that it might apply to Raesinia as well, but she'd obviously sensed Ionkovo's presence. He glanced at Uhlan—at some point they were going to have to bring him up to speed, now that he'd seen this much. *No time.*

"Tell me if you ever feel it again," Marcus said quietly.

Raesinia nodded. "It's still there, but getting weaker. Who *was* that?"

"One of them. The Penitent Damned. His name is Ionkovo."

"You *know* him?"

"I took him prisoner during the revolution," Marcus said. "Or he let me take him. I had no idea what he was. I think he wanted to find out how much I knew. When he was finished he just walked out of a locked cell."

"I heard him talking, and I thought you might be in trouble."

"He told me Maurisk is coming for us. For me, rather. I don't think he knows you're here."

"When?"

"Now. Tonight." Marcus got to his feet, head spinning a bit. "We have to get out of here."

"He just told you this? Why?"

"He wants"—Marcus looked at Uhlan again, who was studiously pretending to ignore them, and grimaced—"the things Janus brought back from Khandar. He thought I could tell him where they were. I think the backup plan is to lock me in a cell until I let something slip."

"Oh hell," Raesinia said. "That means it's all happening tonight. The coup. I have to get word to Sothe."

Marcus nodded. "First we need to get out of here. Uhlan!"

"Sir!" The lieutenant saluted.

"We have to leave—now."

"I made sure the carriage was ready, sir. I'll send word to harness the horses."

Marcus frowned. Fleeing in a carriage would have been a lot less conspicuous before the war had mostly banished horses from the streets of the city. Then another thought occurred to him.

"What about the staff?" There were three Mierantai women who cooked and cleaned at the Twin Turrets, along with two stable boys and the carriage driver. "We can't leave them."

"You think they'd be hurt?" Uhlan sounded genuinely shocked.

"Maurisk will want to know whatever they know," Marcus said. "That means grabbing everyone in the area for questioning."

"I'll go and wake them," Raesinia said as she hurried off.

A hasty muster in the living room produced three middle-aged Mierantai women, looking stolid and unflappable even in their heavy cotton nightdresses. Uhlan ran to the stables to get the cart ready.

"We're leaving," Marcus said. "And I think you ought to come with us. I won't force you, but if you're coming it has to be *now*. Get dressed and leave everything else behind."

The oldest of the three women looked at the other two, then nodded wordlessly. They bustled back to their rooms as Uhlan came back in.

"The carriage will be ready in five minutes, sir," he said. "But Aldio is missing."

"Hell. If he's snuck out, I hope he has the sense not to come back."

Raesinia's voice came from the top of the stairs. "Marcus! I can't find Andy! Her room's empty!"

Marcus blinked, then got it. "Squeeze them into the carriage. Whoever doesn't fit will ride outside. If you've got time, load some pistols."

"Marcus!" Raesinia's voice again, more urgent now,

from the landing window. "I see torches coming up the street!"

Marcus ran toward the rear of the house, checking the hall closet, the spare room, and the kitchen. They turned out to be in the pantry; he hauled the thick door open to find a tangled blanket on the floor and the Mierantai boy frantically tugging his trousers back on. Andy, mostly naked, sat against the back wall.

"Sir—" the boy began, accent even thicker than Uhlan's.

Marcus snatched his shirt off the floor, thrust it into his arms, and shoved him out the door. "The stables. Go!"

Andy got up as the boy rushed off. Marcus kept his eyes resolutely on her face, but nevertheless she flushed under his gaze. "Are you sober enough to shoot?"

"Probably." Andy blinked. "What's happening?"

"Patriot Guards coming to get us. We're leaving. Get something on and get to the stables."

"Oh." She paused a moment. "Oh, *fuck*."

"Go!"

She ran. Marcus followed her as far as the landing, where Raesinia had her face pressed to the window. Marcus could see a row of lights halfway down the street and getting closer fast.

"There's at least twenty of them, all with muskets," Raesinia said. She had her hands cupped against her eyes to shut out the lights. "Maurisk isn't fooling around."

"Get to the stable."

"Are we going to have room for everyone?"

"We will if some of us sit on top."

Raesinia grinned. "I always wanted to try that."

Andy appeared at the top of the stairs, trousers and boots on, still pulling a shirt down. Raesinia raised an eyebrow.

"I seem to be walking straight," Andy said to Marcus.

"Good." Marcus led the two women downstairs and through the short covered passage to the stables.

The carriage, four-wheeled and fully enclosed, sat facing the closed front door, in front of the empty stalls. One door was open, and Marcus could see the three Mierantai women and the two stable boys inside, while the driver sat in front on the box, nervously holding the reins. Uhlan was ramming a charge into a pistol, with another three lined up in front of him on an overturned feeding trough.

"Raesinia, you take the top." She was the lightest, and Marcus wasn't at all confident about the carriage's ability to bear weight on its roof. "Andy and I will take the doors. Uhlan, stay on the box."

"Yes, sir." Uhlan handed a pistol to Marcus. Raesinia hopped up on the box and scrambled up to the roof.

"Not much to hang on to," she said. "If we take a turn too hard I'm going to fall off."

"Here." Marcus grabbed a knife from Uhlan's belt and tossed it up. Raesinia unsheathed it and stabbed into the thin wood as hard as she could, embedding the blade in the carriage's roof. She gave it a tug, and nodded.

Marcus examined the door. There was a metal rung to help shorter passengers step inside, and that combined with the leather strap that served as a door handle would make for a precarious perch. He climbed on, holding the strap in his left hand and the pistol in his right.

Uhlan handed a pistol to Andy and passed another up to Raesinia. He went to the stable door and tugged it open. The gravel drive was illuminated only by a trickle of light from the house windows.

"Where are we going, sir?" he said as he climbed up on the box and readied his own weapon.

"Oldtown," Marcus said. Mrs. Felda's was the obvious place for a bolt-hole. "But not straight to the church, not unless we want to bring the Guard on behind us."

"Just get us to Oldtown," Andy said. "I'll tell you where to go from there. It's an easy place to get lost in if you're trying."

"All right." Marcus looked back at the driveway. The end of it was starting to brighten, and long shadows flickered across it. "Get moving!"

The driver needed no urging. He snapped the reins, and the already-nervous horses jerked forward.

"Are we shooting at the Patriot Guard?" Andy said. "Last time you wanted us to try not to."

"I think we are officially done with such niceties," Marcus said. "But try not to waste—"

"D'Ivoire!" someone yelled from the end of the drive, now rapidly approaching. "Is that—stop at once!"

"Keep going," Marcus said.

"D'Ivoire!" A figure, outlined by the torches, stepped in front of them. "I have a summons to—stop, stop!"

"Faster!" Marcus shouted.

The horses hadn't had time to get up much speed, but the carriage was heavy enough that the prospect of being run over was not attractive. The Patriot Guard dove aside, dropping his musket. Behind him were several men with torches in one hand and muskets in the other, a combination that proved less than immediately effective.

"Left!" Marcus shouted. The driver hauled on the reins, and the axle screeched as the carriage rose for a moment on two wheels and slewed around behind the team. Ahead of them, he could see more Patriot Guards. The group had apparently spread out to encircle the Twin Turrets. "Go through them!"

The men up ahead had a few moments to react to the carriage bearing down on them. Several dove aside at once, but three braver men tossed their torches away and shouldered their muskets. Marcus took aim as best he could and pulled the trigger, hoping to scare them aside at the very least. The flash left him blinking, and the pistol's report came simultaneously with the deeper sound of the muskets. His ears rang, and he swung wildly from the leather strap for a moment.

He got a brief view of the musketeers, their weapons expended, rolling out of the way as the carriage clattered past. Then they were through, accelerating down the street into the darkness. More musketry thundered from behind them as the startled men at the end of the driveway recovered their wits, but though Marcus could hear the *zip* of the balls, none of the shots came close.

"Everyone okay?" Marcus said. "Turn right at Saint Uriah—*right*—"

The intersection passed in a blur. The team, at a full gallop now, strained at the traces, pulling the carriage at an impressive speed. Every rut and bump in the road was magnified, and Marcus' next attempt to speak nearly cost him his tongue as his teeth came together hard.

"I'm hit," Uhlan said in a strained tone. "And I believe Delcot is dead."

Marcus tossed his useless pistol aside and swung himself to grab the edge of the box, until he could look over Uhlan's shoulder. The Mierantai lieutenant had one hand pressed to his thigh, where a dark stain was rapidly spreading. Beside him, the driver had slumped back and let the reins fall. A musket ball had made a ruin of his throat, coating the front of his shirt in gore.

"Shit," Marcus said. He tightened his grip and tried to gauge his chances if he let go of the door handle and swung up onto the box. *If I time it just right, I am* definitely *going to fall off and get crushed.* "Raes! Can you get to the reins?"

"I can try!" Raesinia's head appeared at the edge of the roof and she appraised the situation. "Oh damn."

"Hurry, please."

Second Avenue was a relatively straight run between Saint Uriah Street and the Dregs. They'd covered nearly half that distance already, though, and when they reached the Dregs, which ran along the front of the University, they would be presented with a sharp turn in either direction and nothing straight ahead but buildings. The horses might see the danger, but without the brakes the carriage would simply run them over.

"Damn, damn, *damn*," Raesinia repeated, like a mantra, as she pulled herself forward to the edge of the roof. Most of the street was dark, but even the war could not completely quash the nightlife of the Dregs, and the line of lamps that marked the end of the street was getting closer fast. "Sorry about this."

She put a hand on the dead driver's shoulder and gave him a shove. His limp body slid sideways, then tumbled from the box, and the carriage gave an almighty lurch as the wheels went over him. Marcus nearly lost his footing and clung to the strap for dear life. He heard a heavy *thump* as Raesinia slammed against the roof.

"Raes?"

"Still here!" She spit blood onto the box. "Somehow. One moment . . ."

Marcus could hear Andy laughing, high and a little mad. Raesinia pulled herself forward and down onto the box, flopping gracelessly into a heap beside the wounded Uhlan. She scrambled to right herself and got hold of the reins.

"Now what?" she said.

"Stop us!" Marcus shouted back.

"How?"

"I—" Marcus was astonished to find that he had no idea. Horses and vehicles had never been his strong suit.

"Brake," Uhlan gasped. "Between us. Then pull the reins."

Raesinia yanked up on a metal lever, and the carriage's axle started screaming like a banshee. She hauled back on the reins, shouting unintelligibly at the horses. The sudden loss of speed left them weaving drunkenly across the street, and for a horrible moment Marcus thought they were going to tip. Then, with a final lurch, the carriage came to a halt just short of the Dregs, where curious pedestrians gathered to stare. A burned-metal smell was everywhere, and when Marcus looked back he could see trails of smoke rising from the back wheels.

Marcus let go of the strap, dropped into the street, and fell over when his legs refused to support him. He heard footsteps, and a moment later Andy appeared, holding out her hand to help him up.

"*That* was quite a ride," she said. "Are you all right?"

He nodded, brushing himself off, and went to Uhlan. The lieutenant gave him a tight smile, teeth gritted.

"Not too bad, sir. Gone straight through, I think."

"Mrs. Felda will know someone who can help," Marcus said. "We'll get a bandage on it for now."

"Better hurry," Andy said. "They'll be after us."

A scream, from farther up the street, told Marcus that someone had discovered the body of the driver.

"Here." Marcus took Uhlan's arm, and he and Andy helped the wounded Mierantai down. "Do you think your women can tie a bandage?"

"Of course."

With a certain amount of squeezing, they managed to get the lieutenant in among the servants, who showed no sign of fainting at the sight of blood. Marcus climbed up on the box beside Raesinia, and Andy resumed her place at the door. Gingerly, Marcus released the brake and took the reins himself. Fortunately, the horses were well trained, and didn't seem to require much handling.

"We'll take the Old Ford," Marcus said as they trotted down the Dregs at a more sane speed, leaving gaping men and women in their wake. "Then we're going to have to ditch the carriage. Andy, you said you had something in mind?"

"Yes," Andy said. "I know a few people."

"What then?" Raesinia said.

Marcus looked down at her. She'd been holding her hands over her face, and now she let them fall to show that there was quite a bit of blood on her cheek and temple. Only small cuts remained, though, and as Marcus watched, they closed up and vanished as though they'd never been. Raesinia wiped the blood on her sleeve and waggled her eyebrows conspiratorially.

"Then . . ." Marcus shook his head. "I'll think of something."

RAESINIA

"You're the queen," Andy said.

"Yes," Raesinia said.

"The Queen of *Vordan*."

"Yes."

"*The* Queen of Vordan."

"Last I checked, there was only one."

"But . . ."

Raesinia sighed. "Let me guess. I'm not what you expected?"

She set off down the street at a determined walk, leaving Andy staring after her. The ranker shook her head and jogged to catch up, and they walked in silence for a moment. Even here, only a block from Farus' Triumph, pedestrian traffic was scarce. An older man hurried past, eyes down.

"Sorry," Andy said. "I just . . . I mean, that's a hell of a thing to drop on someone."

"I thought it would be better to get it out of the way." She and Marcus had decided last night that Andy deserved to be brought into their confidence, at least partly. Raesinia wasn't about to tell her about her own condition. "I'm surprised that you believe me."

"I . . ." Andy frowned. "I guess people wouldn't, would they?"

"I haven't really been in a position to tell many people, but I would imagine not."

"It just seems like the sort of thing that might happen these days," Andy said. "I mean, why not?"

"Solid reasoning."

"Well, excuse me for being gullible." Andy cocked her head. "You're not joking, though. Are you?"

"No." Raesinia closed her eyes for a moment. She was angry, and a little frightened, but it was unfair to take it out on Andy. "If we go over to the palace, I could show you some portraits."

"Does Marcus know?"

Raesinia nodded. "That's why I was staying at Twin Turrets."

"That explains a lot."

"It does? Like what?"

"I was starting to think he was in love with you."

Raesinia missed a step, stumbling slightly over a loose flagstone.

"But in a creepy, worshipping sort of way, you know?" Andy went on, without pausing. "The way he treats you so carefully. But this makes more sense."

"I suppose it does." First Viera, now Andy. *Why is everyone suddenly obsessed with Marcus' love life?*

"What about Uhlan?" Andy said.

"I *think* he knows, but he's never mentioned anything." The Mierantai lieutenant was still abed, but according to Mrs. Felda wasn't in serious danger. They'd had to haul him to the church on two lengths of board after ditching the carriage in an empty yard. "Cora knows, too. But no one else. Obviously, I'm going to need you to keep quiet about it."

"Obviously. Your Majesty." Andy grinned at Raesinia's warning glance. "Sorry. But you really lived up in the palace?"

"All my life."

"That must have been a nice life," Andy said, with a wistful sigh. "Good food, people waiting on you hand and foot, nothing to do but . . . what *do* princesses do all day?"

"Not a lot, it turns out. I spent a lot of time reading, or studying with my father when he wasn't ill."

"Your father . . ." Andy paused. "Oh. I'm sorry."

"It's all right."

"It's so strange to think of the king as . . . well, as a man. With a family. As opposed to just a beard with a crown that gets stamped on coins."

"I wish more people could have known him like that," Raesinia said, a lump forming in her throat. "I don't know if he was a good king. I suppose not, given how things have turned out. But he was always a good father. After my brother died . . . it took a lot out of him."

There was another awkward pause. Andy pointed to a café, its colorful banner showing a crane in flight against a setting sun. The cloth snapped in the stiff, chilly breeze.

"Is that the place?" she said.

"Looks like it," Raesinia said.

"I don't understand why Janus wouldn't tell Marcus where this Willowbrook place is. Or tell *you*, for that matter. If he can't trust *you*, then what's the point?"

"Operational security," Raesinia said, parroting Sothe. "People should know only what they need to. Less chance of someone giving something away by accident, or under torture."

"Under *torture*?" Andy shook her head. "Janus must be a cheery guy."

"He takes things seriously."

They reached the front door of the café. It was nearly empty; a trio of old men huddled against a long wooden counter were the only customers. Raesinia looked over the abandoned tables, all bare and gleaming with chairs neatly pushed in.

Except for one, near the front, where a broadsheet had been left behind. It was folded between its corners, to make a triangle. Not the way you'd normally fold something like that, or crumple it in your pocket.

"It's there," Raesinia said.

"You're sure?"

"Act calm." Raesinia gestured at the tired-looking woman behind the counter, and pointed to the table. The woman gave a resigned wave, as though to say, *Under the circumstances, just sit wherever you like.* Raesinia and Andy pulled back two chairs and sat, and Raesinia unfolded the paper.

"Now what?" Andy said.

"Now we wait."

Raesinia's time with Sothe had made her at least minimally conversant in this kind of operation, which everyone at Mrs. Felda's seemed to take to mean that she was some kind of expert. In fact, her time in the conspiracy had included very little cloak-and-dagger stuff, until the very end. *Mostly it was drinking and talking to people.* With Uhlan badly hurt, and the Patriot Guard actively on the lookout for Marcus, it was left to Raesinia and Andy to check for replies for Marcus' message to Willowbrook.

Andy has a point about the secrecy. She understood why Janus would want to keep the location of the Thousand Names a tightly guarded secret, but she could hardly see how telling *her* was going to cause any problems. *And it would have been helpful in an emergency.*

"Should I order something?" Andy said.

"We'd better," Raesinia said. "Otherwise this will look pretty odd."

She waved to the woman behind the counter, who reluctantly came over to serve them. Raesinia bought a loaf of fresh bread and butter for a shockingly high price, and a bottle of wine for a startlingly low one. While they waited, she looked over the broadsheet, which turned out to be *The Patriot*, a solidly Conservative paper and one of the most popular at the moment in the mad whirl that was Vordan's press.

MORE ARRESTS MADE was the leading article. "Following the shocking revelation of the treason of the Minister of War, Giles Durenne, the Patriot Guards continued their laudable efforts to purge the rottenness from our government. Several more associates of the former deputy were brought into custody, and information he and his cronies provided led to the capture of a number of enemy spies. We trust that the removal of these discordant elements will bring unity to our people, and thus gain for Vordanai arms the laurels of victory that have thus far been lacking . . ."

It went on in that vein, with eloquent praise for the "genius" of the "benevolent President of the Directory" and the salutary effects of his program of public executions. Not mentioned were the arrests among the Radical deputies, except in passing as additional spies and traitors. Or, for that matter, was there any word from the Army of the East, or acknowledgment of its past victories.

That has to mean something. If she went to the corner pamphlet seller, Raesinia knew, she would find *The Patriot* and its like to be the only things on offer. If the Conservatives had dominated the press before, now they had simply extinguished all other voices. Several Radical printers and writers had been arrested in the general roundup, and now languished in the impromptu cells beside the Hotel

Ancerre. *I'm surprised Maurisk hasn't gotten around to reopening the Vendre.*

The fact that these government-approved publications said nothing at all about Janus' army, even though—according to Marcus—the news from that corner was good, could only mean that Maurisk was not interested in the general further enhancing his reputation. *With Durenne disposed of, Janus is the only remaining threat. We have to get in communication with him.* Hence the frantic efforts to contact Willowbrook.

"Can I ask you something?" Andy said.

Raesinia folded the paper—in the more usual way, this time—and looked up. "What about?"

"If you're the queen"—Andy kept her voice low—"what are you *doing* here?"

"It's kind of a long story," Raesinia said.

"I can imagine," Andy said. "But I think we've got time."

The proprietor arrived, bearing a wooden tray of steaming bread, a bottle, and two glasses. When she retreated after a few moments of slicing, uncorking, and pouring, Raesinia looked thoughtfully at Andy.

What the hell? Why not tell her?

So she did. Not everything, obviously—not her death and Orlanko's demon. But the story of how she'd founded the conspiracy against her own rule, in order to fight back against the increasing influence of the Last Duke, and how it had ended in blood and revolution. Andy listened, absorbing everything in silence.

"That's . . . wow," she finally said when Raesinia sat back.

"When I tell it like that, it all seems a little mad," Raesinia said.

"What happened to the rest of the conspiracy?"

"Cora was one. Maurisk was another." Raesinia was surprised to find that she still felt a sense of betrayal there. "The others . . . died. One of them was working for Orlanko. Another . . . he was in love with me, and got himself killed trying to keep me safe."

"Ah." Andy shook her head. "I think Hayver had . . . feelings for me. He kept trying to work himself up to talking about it. I thought it was cute, stupid tongue-tied boy, but I didn't want to encourage him." She looked down at the table. Raesinia heard screams in her head, and knew Andy was hearing the same.

Silently, Raesinia picked up the bottle and poured Andy a full glass, followed by a token amount for herself. Alcohol was more or less wasted on her, since the binding didn't allow even a pleasant fuzziness.

"I still don't understand," Andy said, coming out of her reverie.

"Don't understand what?"

"Why you did it. I mean, Orlanko was going to take over. So what? You'd still get to be queen, even if you didn't actually do anything."

"He would have married me off to some Borelgai prince and ruled Vordan himself. We got a taste of what that would have been like. Concordat agents at every window, bodies in the river every morning, and anyone who objects gets hauled off to the Vendre or worse. And he was selling the country to the Borels and the Sworn Church, piece by piece. I couldn't just stand by and let it happen."

"I can think of worse fates," Andy said. "Swanning about the palace eating off silver plates while other people do the work of running everything. Having to roll with some nasty foreigner from time to time doesn't seem like too high a price, and as for the rest of it . . . what makes it your responsibility?"

"I . . ." Raesinia paused. "It has to be my responsibility. That's what kings and queens are *for*, to take care of their people."

"Just because you were born to the wrong family, the fate of the whole kingdom is your problem?"

"More or less," Raesinia said. "That's just the way it is."

"Color me glad I wasn't born royal, then."

Raesinia shrugged. She couldn't explain, not completely— her ageless state meant that Orlanko would have had to eliminate her sooner or later, presumably by announcing her "death" and shipping her off to the dungeons of Elysium.

But the truth was that she'd never really considered giving in. Raesinia frowned, trying to sort her feelings into something that would make sense. The luxury of palace life had never mattered to her, but that was because she'd grown up with it as the default. *How can I explain what that was like?*

She gave up. There was another, truer answer in any event.

"I hate him," she said. "Orlanko. For what he did to me, for the way he treated my father. I couldn't just lie back, not if it meant letting him win."

"Ah." Andy smiled and raised her glass in salute. "Fair enough. If you'd been a Leatherback, I think we'd have made you into a proper scrapper in no time."

"I'm sure." Raesinia raised her own glass and took a sip. "Maybe I went looking for revolution in the wrong place."

Andy laughed, then froze and set her own glass down. A young man in the worn linens of a common laborer approached their table, heedless of the look he drew from the proprietor.

"Hello, ladies," he said. "Where might you be headed?"

"Somewhere there's willows," Raesinia said.

He nodded, as if this answer made sense. "Not going my way, then." As he turned away, his hand passed over the table, and a folded scrap of paper fell from his sleeve. "Best of luck!"

Raesinia put her hand over the note and waited until the courier had gone. She pretended to stare at the broadsheet, engrossed in its hyperpatriotic idiocy, while she unfolded the message. Andy leaned across to get a better look.

The note was written on thin foolscap, in a neat hand, and read:

Your message received and transmitted. Still secure here but not sure for how long. Backup plans under way. Will bring you over here as soon as I can, but

may take some time to arrange secure transport.
Contact again using usual arrangement. Giforte.

"Well," Andy said, "that's something."

"At least Maurisk hasn't found them," Raesinia said. "Come on. We'd better show Marcus, before he goes mad with waiting."

Chapter Sixteen

WINTER

"**—A**nd then we'll ride out and give 'em hell!"

Winter exchanged a look with Jane, and tried not to smile.

She and the other officers had followed the cavalry commander back to the designated campsite, which was in a broad meadow beside a belt of woodland. A few fences indicated this land was used to pasture animals, but whatever farmer did so had long since fled, and the soldiers had mostly torn the split-rail barriers down to feed their fires. Give-Em-Hell had about five hundred cavalry camped there, a regiment that, like Winter's command, was a mix of old Royal Army horsemen and post-revolution recruits.

They'd already kindled fires, and as the men and women of the Third stumbled in, the cavalry brought them food and water. As on the previous days, the regiment had stretched into an extended column on the march, so its soldiers didn't arrive in a body but in an extended trickle. At Winter's request, Give-Em-Hell had sent more of his men back down the road with torches, to help gather up stragglers and show the way in the dark.

In the meantime, he'd been explaining the plan in his typical idiom, which involved a great deal of slashing at imaginary foes with an imaginary saber. It was short on tactical niceties, however, and Winter cleared her throat.

"Colonel?" Give-Em-Hell had gotten his own promotion, presumably around the same time Winter had. "Did Janus leave you any written orders?"

"Yes, he did, as a matter of fact." The cavalryman dug around under his breastplate and came out with a much-folded sheet of paper, which he passed to Winter. "He's got everything laid out, as usual."

Winter unfolded the note and read. While she did, Give-Em-Hell turned to Abby and looked her slowly up and down.

"You're a woman," he said, with a faint note of surprise.

"So I've been told," Abby said dryly.

Winter paused, holding her breath and waiting for the explosion. The old cavalry commander had not exactly been famous for his open-mindedness.

"So it's true that there's a women's battalion?" Give-Em-Hell said. He sounded more curious than angry.

"Yes," Abby said.

"And they'll fight?"

"They certainly have so far."

"Hell." The cavalryman broke into a gap-toothed smile. "I always said infantry was such an easy job that girls could do it."

Winter rolled her eyes. *Not perfect, but I'll take what I can get.* Any reaction was better than Lieutenant Novus'. She turned her attention back to the note, which included a hastily sketched map that she compared to the terrain she could see with the last of the fading light.

"All right," she said, looking up. "I think I understand. Thank you for your help, Colonel. I understand we've got an artillery battery?"

"Captain Archer," Give-Em-Hell said, nodding. "He's camped over there a ways."

"Janus says here that I'm to be in overall command of the force," Winter said. "That's not going to be a problem, is it?"

Give-Em-Hell pushed his hat back and scratched at his

thinning hair. "Not unless you're planning on keeping me out of the action."

"You'll get plenty of action, don't worry. But it needs to be on my order."

"I understand," he said. "Just wave your hat, and we'll give 'em hell."

"Excellent." Winter glanced at her officers and nodded toward the woods. "Follow me."

It was fortunate that the moon was high and three-quarters full, because Winter forbade any of the torch-carrying cavalry pickets from accompanying her and the small group of officers into the forest. It wasn't a true wild wood, but a well-tended belt of trees occupying the rocky ground at the top of the ridge, separating one shallow valley from the next. Still, picking their way through it went slowly, and it was a half hour before they were at the other side and looking down on what would, tomorrow, be a battlefield.

Campfires sparkled in long, parallel lines, marking the positions of the opposing armies. On Winter's left, an irregular series of hills was topped by a few farmhouses and barns, and studded here and there with the regular shapes of orchards. Small fires burned all through their yards and down their slopes, avoiding the low-lying gaps between them. On her right, across two or three miles of valley flatland, another army was camped in a tighter mass behind the protection of a wandering stream.

Now and then, nervous pickets down between the two forces fired at one another, or at fleeting shadows. Each musket shot was a sharp pinprick of fire, followed seconds later by the distant clap of the report.

"That's Janus," Winter said, pointing to the left, then sweeping her arm across the valley. "And that's di Pfalen."

"Unless he's building fake campfires, that's a hell of a lot of Hamveltai," Cyte said.

Winter nodded. "At least as many as Janus has, probably more."

"So what does he want us to do?"

"Only to win the battle for him." Winter blew out a

breath and tried to picture things unfolding as Janus had explained in his note. The battalions marching with fluttering flags, the guns coughing smoke and flames. "We're on the left end of the Hamveltai line, and they don't know we're here. He's going to bait them into attacking his center, and while the battle's going on we're supposed to descend on their flank and send Give-Em-Hell into their rear."

They looked out at the field in silence for a while.

"Sounds like a fine plan," Sevran said cautiously. "Except that it requires di Pfalen to be so idiotic as to not take any precautions."

"Like sending someone up here to occupy these woods," Abby said. "I certainly would."

"Janus thinks he'll send at least a regiment of yellow-jackets," Winter said. "However, he's 'confident that a sudden attack, launched from under cover, will put them to flight.'"

This time it was Jane who broke the silence. "I don't know if we'll be up to delivering an attack, sudden or otherwise. The soldiers we've got left are going to be exhausted. I don't want to run my girls down, but nobody is ready for a fucking bayonet charge after walking a hundred miles in four days in the rain."

Sevran nodded agreement. "We won't have the strength."

"We have to try," Abby said. "What else did we come all this way for?"

"We have to try *something*," Winter said. "Janus wants us on their flank, but I don't think he cares how we get there. I have an idea, but I want you all to tell me what you think . . ."

It was nearly midnight before Winter returned to the camp, to find that the slow trickle of haggard infantrymen and their cavalry escorts had nearly come to a stop. A patrol of four horsemen trotted up to the camp, with three women riding behind them. Winter recognized Anne-Marie's blond curls first, and then identified the other two as Joanna and Barley.

"Are those three all right?" she shouted to the lead cuirassier.

"Just tired, I think," he called back. "When we found them the big one and the little one were carrying the blonde between them."

At least some of the recruits made it, then. Winter found herself smiling.

"You've got some tough ladies in this regiment, sir," one of the other cavalrymen said. "Hell if I'd have been able to walk through the shit we've seen on the road."

"Wait until you see them in action tomorrow," Winter said. "You'd better get some sleep if you want to keep up."

"Don't worry, sir," the leader said. "We'll give 'em hell."

They continued on their way, and Winter continued on hers, finding a tree stump among where the Third Regiment soldiers had spread themselves over the still-wet ground. She sat down against it and closed her eyes, expecting sleep to come as instantly as it had the night before, but found herself disappointed. The battle she'd conjured, gesturing out at the field in front of her officers, continued to dance behind her eyes.

She heard footsteps, and then a warm, soft body settled itself beside her. Winter opened her eyes and found Jane's head on her shoulder, sodden red hair in a tangled mess against her sleeve.

"Sorry," Jane said. "I didn't mean to wake you."

"I wasn't asleep." Winter blew out a breath. "Are you all right?"

"Tired." Jane hesitated. "You're sure this is going to work?"

"No. There's a million things that could go wrong." Winter let her head rest on the rough bark of the tree stump. "But it's the best I could come up with."

There was a long pause.

"Remember what Janus told you, about being more careful?" Jane said.

Winter nodded.

"He may only want to keep his special demon safe. But I'm going to say it, too, and I really fucking mean it, all right? No more leading charges." Jane's hand found Winter's wrist and gripped it tight. "We need you too much."

Winter shifted her hand to interlace her fingers with Jane's and squeezed tight. This time, when she closed her eyes, sleep came quickly.

The day of battle brought a blue sky, cloudless from edge to edge, with a cold, distant sun and a chill wind that made the branches rattle in the woods and brought down drifts of crunchy brown leaves. Winter stood where she had the day before, borrowing Cyte's spyglass to examine di Pfalen's dispositions.

It certainly made an impressive array. Battalion after battalion of infantry in splendid yellow and black formed in front of the distant village of Jirdos, yellow banners rigid and snapping in the wind, displaying the roaring bull of Hamvelt. Cannon, still limbered and ready to deploy, formed neat lines in the gaps between the infantry columns. Behind the first line stood a second, and behind that came the cavalry, hundreds of horsemen sitting calmly in formation, each man's boot only inches from his neighbor's.

"That's the Guardians," Cyte said when Winter passed her back the spyglass. "They're supposed to be the elite. Every wealthy family in Hamvelt sends their spare sons to serve with them."

Jane snorted. "Rich men make bad soldiers. They've got too much to lose."

On the heights opposite, Janus' army made for a less intimidating picture. Guns were parked hub to hub on each hilltop, flanked by infantry, but even at this distance the volunteer battalions looked shabby with their particolored clothes and improvised banners. Another mass of troops, mostly regulars in their solid blue uniforms, was forming in front of the line of hills, with more cannon alongside them. There was hardly any cavalry to be seen.

"I would have thought Janus would keep all the guns on the heights," Sevran said, frowning down at the maneuvering soldiers.

"He knows what he's doing," Abby said.

Winter turned away at the sound of horses crashing through the brush. A moment later, the animals emerged, snorting and irritable, the cannon that they were pulling bouncing on its wide wheels. A young captain who Winter vaguely recognized spotted the eagles on her shoulders and hurried over.

"Sir!" He saluted. "We're coming into position now."

"Good." Winter cocked her head. "It's Archer, isn't it?"

"Yes, sir."

"You were in Khandar?"

"Yessir. Under the Preacher."

"And you came to rescue us at Diarach."

He blushed slightly and nodded. "Janus thought we might work well together, given our history."

"I'm glad to have you. You know what you're supposed to do?"

Archer nodded again. "I'm worried that we won't be able to pull out in time. These woods aren't too bad, but we got stuck a couple of times on the way up."

"Jane!"

Jane turned, and Winter gestured to Archer.

"Gather up a company or so from the Girls' Own and help the captain clear a path for his guns. We don't want them getting hung up here when we have to pull out."

Jane nodded and hurried off, back through the woods to the field where the Third Regiment was shaking itself out and trying to make ready for battle. Winter looked down at the Hamveltai, who so far showed no signs of movement.

"Sevran, you'd better get back to your people," she said. "I'll send a runner when things start to happen here."

"Yes, sir!" Sevran saluted. "Good luck."

The battle began on the Hamveltai right, the extreme opposite end of the line from where Winter and the Third were waiting. From their wooded ride, they could see the banners of the yellowjackets as they advanced, but the troops themselves were concealed by a fold in the ground. Guns on both sides opened fire, filling the valley with low, distant booms. Before long, a cloud of powder smoke boiled up over that end of the line, lit from within by the flashes of musketry and cannon-fire.

"Janus is moving in the center," Cyte said not long after.

It was true. The blue-uniformed infantry moved forward in neatly aligned columns, crossing the valley floor at a leisurely pace with several batteries of guns alongside them. As they came into range of the Hamveltai cannon, puffs of smoke blossomed along the yellowjacket line, and Winter could see the dirt fountain where the balls struck the earth. From this vantage, it was easy to see how the round shot bounced, skipping over the ground like a stone skimmed into a lake in a series of shortening arcs. Where those arcs intersected with the Vordanai columns, they left a scattering of broken men in their wake, patches of blue against the brown of the fields.

About seven hundred yards out from the Hamveltai line, the advance stopped, and the troops deployed from columns into long lines as the guns unlimbered. That was still much too far for musket-fire, but the cannon were soon banging away, their coughing booms mingling with those of their Hamveltai counterparts. The long, thin formations were less vulnerable to the bouncing cannonballs, but each hit still sent men pinwheeling away or staggering out of line. The tiny shapes of wounded soldiers walked or crawled toward the rear, like a tide of ants picking their way through a lawn.

The exchange of fire went on for at least a half hour. Then the Vordanai began an unceremonious retreat, lines deploying back into columns and turning to march the way they had come. Cannon relimbered and rumbled off, leaving the occasional broken gun behind. A neat line of corpses marked the spot where they had stood.

"What was the point of that?" Bobby said, frowning.

"I think," Winter said slowly, "that Janus wanted to convince di Pfalen that was the best he's got."

"If that's true, it may have worked," Abby said. "They're on the move."

The center and left of the Hamveltai line, so far idle except for the cannoneers, lurched into ponderous motion.

Thick columns of yellow-uniformed men splashed through the small stream that had guarded their front and pushed across the valley toward the heights. Their cannon raced ahead, teams of horses laboring to pull them past the infantry and then turning around to set up for firing. As they came closer, the hills seemed to explode with fire and smoke, a rippling volley of guns like distant thunder. Now it was the yellow line's turn to dribble corpses and wounded to the rear as it advanced, battalions closing up whenever a ball cut through them like waves crashing around a rock.

"Yellowjackets coming our way," Cyte said, peering through her glass. "Three columns."

It was a few moments before the rest of them could see. The left-most regiment of Hamveltai had peeled off from the general forward advance and was headed toward the wooded ridge. As Winter had predicted, di Pfalen was not totally blind to the danger presented to his flank; as his main line advanced past the woods, he'd sent troops to guard against an attack from that direction.

"Bobby, go find Archer," Winter said. "Tell him to hold his fire as long as they keep coming. It's when they get too comfortable that we'll need to sting them. Then find Abby and help her get the Girls' Own ready."

Bobby saluted and ran off. Winter stayed where she was, watching the approaching yellowjackets. Three columns probably meant three battalions, or something like three thousand men, opposing the bare thousand or so that remained in the Third Regiment after the hellish march. Janus' original plan, that they charge from cover and catch the Hamveltai by surprise, might have worked if they'd been at full strength, but with the odds that far against them, it would have been a disaster. *So even Janus isn't omniscient.* Winter wasn't sure if that was comforting or terrifying.

The first question, whether the Hamveltai colonel intended to occupy the woods or merely to screen them, was soon answered. He halted his men in column at the bottom of the slope, facing up toward Winter but not yet deployed into a combat formation. *He still doesn't know we're here.* More than likely, the yellowjacket commander expected to be called into action somewhere in the front line now engaging Janus' army, once the danger of a flank attack failed to materialize. *Time to show him otherwise.*

The cannon opened fire, right on cue. The closest gun was a dozen yards away, and the blast was enough to rattle Winter's teeth in her skull. More fire came from all along the edge of the woods, where Archer had positioned his guns to take advantage of the cover and the high ground. The cannonballs followed long, arcing trajectories down toward the Hamveltai troops below, and even the first volley plowed into the tight-packed yellow ranks, knocking men down like toys. Winter gave an appreciative whistle. *Archer knows his business.*

For a few moments, confusion reigned down below. Winter could see men on horseback galloping back and forth, presumably the Hamveltai colonel and his officers. Orders went out, even as the shots continued to fall, and after no more than a few minutes the columns began to advance up the hill. With no guns of his own, the Hamveltai commander could either retire out of range or advance and silence the troublesome battery. As Winter had hoped, he'd chosen the latter course.

What he was *not* doing, she saw, was deploying into line as he came on. That was less encouraging. Tactics manuals said that all attacks should be delivered in line, but the long, cumbersome formation was difficult at best in rough ground like the woods. She'd hoped the Hamveltai would stick to their doctrine and get bogged down, on ground that would favor the Girls' Own and their skirmish tactics. Clearly, though, the enemy intended to simply bash ahead by sheer numbers, not bothering with the niceties of a firefight.

On the other hand, the tighter confines of the columns gave Archer's guns a better target, and as the range shrank the cannonade began to inflict serious damage. Yellow-clad bodies littered the slope, and a well-aimed shot could plunge through an entire column, snatching a dozen men out of the ranks and laying them in pieces on the hillside. Hamveltai discipline held, however, and they kept to their formations in spite of the pounding they were taking.

Bobby returned, with Abby and Jane at her side. Behind them came the women of the Girls' Own, those who'd kept up on the march and were still fit enough to fight. They spread out along the edge of the woods, not attempting any kind of formation but taking whatever cover they could find among the trees and rocks. Folsom led his company to the area where Winter and the other officers were standing, offering a cursory salute before turning to his rankers and assigning positions. The soldiers looked grim, and their new blue uniforms were travel-stained, but Winter was glad to see determination in their faces. *After coming this far, they won't break easily.*

But anyone could break in the face of overwhelming numbers. Winter turned to Abby and Jane.

"Remember the plan," she said. "Stand as long as you can, but give ground when they push too hard. No heroics." *Not yet, anyway.*

Abby nodded. "We'll bleed them."

"That's all we need." Winter turned to Bobby. "Find Archer and tell him to give them one round of canister at a hundred yards, then pull back. I don't want him around when it comes to musket range."

Bobby saluted and rushed off again.

"Speaking of musket range," Jane said, looking at the approaching Hamveltai. "You should be moving back, don't you think?"

Winter chewed her lip. She was right, of course. Once the fighting started, here in the woods, there was nothing she would be able to do, no meaningful control she'd be able to exert over the battle. All she could do was put herself in danger, and risk disorganizing the whole regiment if she was injured or killed. *But I can't just* leave *them.*

Jane seemed to read all that in her expression. She gave a crooked smile and put a hand on Winter's shoulder.

"Go back," she said. "We can handle things here."

"Sevran might need you to hold his hand," Abby said.

"All right, all right," Winter said. "But I mean it when I say no heroics, all right?" She caught Jane's eye. *Be safe. Please.*

"Understood, sir."

They both saluted, though in Jane's case it felt as though the gesture was a little mocking. Winter turned and hurried back through the forest, where the Girls' Own were still filing into position, picking out positions, and loading their muskets. Broad paths had been chopped from the underbrush, leading from Archer's guns back through the woods. It would still be rough going, and Winter hoped the cannoneers would be smart enough to save themselves and leave their pieces behind if they got stuck.

Too late to give orders on that subject now, though. She emerged, blinking, into the meadow on the other side of the woods, and found the Royals drawn up in a solid line of blue in front of her. With so many lost or straggling on the road, they made a very thin line, sometimes only one man deep, but it was still an impressive sight. Sevran, mounted, rode along the front of the formation inspecting their alignment. When he saw her, he waved to another officer, and a sergeant rode out with Edgar trailing behind him.

"Everything ready here?" Winter said.

"Ready, sir," Sevran said. "They're going to get a hell of a surprise if they make it this far."

"Let's hope it's enough." Surprise and terrain were what they had to work with, against superior numbers and training. "What about Captain Stokes?"

Sevran nodded to the end of the line of Royals, where the horsemen were assembling in a tight-packed mass. "Champing at the bit, as it were."

"He's sure he can get through the trees?"

"He rode through this morning and said it shouldn't be a problem."

Winter wasn't sure she trusted Give-Em-Hell's assessment of what was and was not a problem, but she had no alternative. She followed Sevran around the end of the line, to where the lieutenants, dismounted, stood behind their companies. Sergeants waited between them, and in the center a color party carried the Vordanai flag, surrounded by drummers poised to relay signals.

Turning back to the woods, Winter could see almost

nothing, just the swaying branches of the closest trees. She closed her eyes and listened instead. In the distance, the racket of Janus' fight was swelling, but it was drowned out by the closer booms of Archer's guns. They'd have switched to canister by now, each shot spraying musket balls into the enemy ranks like an enormous shotgun. The lead ranks of Hamveltai would be cut down, but they'd come on, stepping over their dead like automata. Four hundred yards, three hundred, two hundred, one hundred . . .

The cannon fell silent. In their place, she heard the tearing rattle of musketry, a scatter of shots at first that quickly rose to a continuous roar. It was punctuated by clattering thunderclaps, the sound of a disciplined volley being delivered by trained troops. That would be the Hamveltai columns, finally able to fire on their tormentors. Then, barely audible over the shooting, Winter heard the skirl of drums and the shouts of men as they charged.

The woods began to boil with powder smoke, wisps of blue-gray tugged out of the trees by the steady wind. Muskets popped and clattered, and now they were mixed with screams and curses in more than one language. Women were dying in there, Winter knew, torn by musket balls or pierced with bayonets. Men in yellow were dying, too. *And I can't even see what's happening.* Her hands had gone tight, fingernails digging painfully into her palms.

Archer's guns burst from the edge of the woods, first one and then the others, dragged by wild-eyed horses clearly glad to be away from the fighting. The mounted sergeant who'd brought Winter her horse waved them on, around one side of the Royals' formation. Winter held her breath for a moment—if the Girls' Own had given way completely, and the enemy was hard on the gunners' heels, there would be a dangerous moment while the Royals' fire was blocked by their own men. No yellowjackets appeared, however, and the firing went on in the woods. Muzzle flashes were visible now, coming steadily closer as the Girls' Own fell back in the face of the more numerous Hamveltai.

Finally, women in blue uniforms started to emerge

from the edge of the woods, stopping to fire one final last shot at fleeting forms in yellow, then running for the safety of the Royals' line. Answering flashes came from among the trees, and one tall woman doubled over and crashed to the turf. The others kept running, and were joined by other companies, up and down the line. Winter saw Abby in the center, her sleeve damp with blood, waving her sword back toward the Royals.

"Open the line to pass skirmishers," Winter said to Sevran.

The captain repeated the command, and the drums thrilled. The men of the Royals turned in place, opening gaps as the Girls' Own reached them to let the desperate, bloodied women through. They were all in the meadow now, and yellowjackets were starting to appear in pursuit. The fleeing women mostly obscured their view of the Royals, or else they saw the gaps in the Royals' line and thought they were about to flee as well. Either way, they kept coming, pouring into the meadow, all formation lost in the vicious running battle in the woods.

The last of the Girls' Own passed through the line, only thirty yards or so separating them from the closest yellowjackets.

"Close up," Winter said, and at another drummed command the blue line straightened out, gaps shutting like slammed doors. The sight of them brought the Hamveltai up short, and here and there a musket popped. The yellowjackets hung in a strange limbo for a moment, too broken up to maneuver, not ready to charge that steady line but with their retreat blocked by their companions still coming out of the woods.

Winter drew her sword and slashed the air. "Fire!"

Even reduced to four hundred muskets, a battalion volley at close range was deafening. The balls cut through the mass of Hamveltai, dropping men by the score. The yellowjacket officers were shouting, but they'd lost control of their men. Some were attempting to load and fire back, others were edging backward, while still others simply milled in confusion, unable to see. They were still shuffling thirty seconds later, when another volley slammed out, tearing great holes in the yellow ranks.

By the third volley, they were joined by Archer, who'd gotten his guns turned around and loaded with double canister for close-range work. The combination of point-blank artillery fire and rapid musketry from the Royals convinced any yellowjackets who still had doubts that discretion was the better part of valor, and they poured back into the woods. Some ran; others took cover to load their weapons. Winter slashed the air again.

"Hold fire! Fix bayonets!"

The Royals, after loading another round, drew their bayonets and attached them to the lugs behind the barrels of their weapons. Archer's guns fired one more time, flailing the brush with musket balls with explosions of splinters and falling branches.

"Charge!"

Four hundred men shouted and stormed forward, weapons lowered. Here and there, shots dropped a blue-uniformed soldier, but the yellowjackets didn't stick around to be on the receiving end of the Vordanai bayonets. They ran, all cohesion lost, and the Royals plunged into the woods after them. Winter rode in their wake, walking Edgar down one of the trails they'd cut for the guns, until she could see out the other side. The Royals had stopped at the forest's edge, as ordered, but the Hamveltai were still running, three solid columns of yellow converted into a mass of fleeing men no more capable of offering resistance than if they were unarmed. Winter turned her horse about and rode back to the meadow, where Give-Em-Hell was practically bouncing in his stirrups.

"It's all yours," she said. "Those Guardians are still in reserve, though, so you're in for a fight."

Give-Em-Hell didn't bother to shout an order, only unsheathed his saber and pointed. He rode into the woods, and his men pounded after him, rank after rank of cavalry in gleaming cuirasses. Winter watched them disappear under the trees until the last had passed out of sight.

The Girls' Own had gathered just behind where the

Royals had been. Winter was pleased to see that none of them had kept on running, always a worry in any retreat. She sought out Abby, and to her relief found Jane by her side, winding a strip of bandage around her arm.

"Are you all right?" Winter said.

Abby grinned. "I wasn't looking where I was going and ran into a tree."

"Typical." Jane tied off the bandage, tight enough that Abby squeaked.

"How was it?"

"Hot," Abby admitted. "But we did all right."

"They certainly lost a hell of a lot more than we did," Jane said.

"They had more to lose," Winter said. "Take another few minutes to rest, then get back into the woods. They may try this again, and in the meantime we should pull all the wounded back here."

As if to compensate for not being where the fighting was hottest, Winter found herself helping with this latter task, scouring the underbrush and following the cries of the injured. There were, as Jane had said, many more dead and injured in yellow uniforms than blue, but there were plenty of both. Every rock and ditch had been a defensive position to be fought over, and she found dead yellowjackets drifted three or four deep at the base of a boulder. A young woman had climbed a tree to get a better shot, and gotten her leg stuck there when she was hit, so her corpse hung upside down with her arms dangling and loose hair drifting in the wind. A Hamveltai boy with his intestines coiled in a gory pile in his lap calmly asked in heavily accented Vordanai if Winter could please kill him. She drew her saber and cut his throat.

When Bobby found her, they had run out of wounded, and had turned to the task of extracting the corpses. Winter was holding the legs of an older woman while one of the Royals took her shoulders. One of her hands had flopped loose and trailed limply in the dirt.

"Sir!" Bobby said.

"What?" Winter stopped. "Are they coming back?"

"No, sir! It's Give-Em-Hell!"

Winter waved over a nearby soldier to take up her burden and hurried back with Bobby to the edge of the woods.
Yellowjacket corpses covered the slope of the hill, whole
mangled rows of them lying where they'd been cut down
by canister from Archer's guns. Scattered bodies in blue
lined the edge of the woods, where they'd been caught by
answering volleys. The men and women tasked with retrieving them had stopped to watch the drama going on below.

Winter shaded her eyes with her hand, trying to make
out what was happening. A large body of horsemen was
in motion—that was Give-Em-Hell, the uniforms were
blue, and the Vordanai flag snapped at their head. It was
more of a disorganized mass than a formation, but it hung
together, which was more than could be said for the Hamveltai cavalry. Yellow-clad riders galloped in every direction, escaping their blue pursuers, while riderless horses
ran about and added to the confusion. A sprawling mass
of dead and wounded men and animals marked the point
where the two sides had first come together; evidently, the
Hamveltai Guardians had not been as elite as they'd been
made out to be.

As Winter watched, the Vordanai cavalry overran a
line of guns that had been firing at the Vordanai on the
hilltops. The cannoneers struggled to turn their pieces
around and face the oncoming threat, but before they
could get into firing position the cavalry was on top of
them, sabers rising and falling. Panicked artillerymen fled,
not just from that battery but from the guns on either side
as well, and the horsemen rode on without a shot being
fired at them. Ahead was the Hamveltai infantry, deployed
into line for the final advance on the heights. Their officers
saw the cavalry coming, and drums beat a frantic tattoo
while the lines writhed and attempted to shape themselves
into squares.

They didn't make it. Artillery fire from Janus' army was
still coming hard and fast, sowing confusion and death in
the Hamveltai ranks. When their men turned around, they
could see the wreckage of the once-proud Guardians

scattered across the field, and their own artillerymen running for their lives. The first battalion in the horsemen's path had half completed its evolution into a bayonet-fringed square, and a ragged volley of musketry emptied a few saddles, but Give-Em-Hell's men rode around the firm part of the formation and cut into it from the sides. Without the solidity of a line of bayonets, the foot soldiers were no match for the armored horsemen, and they knew it. A few moments of bloody saber-work, and the battalion was in full flight, scattered beyond any hope of recall. The two nearest Hamveltai units, still struggling to form their own squares, broke into panicked flight along with it as the men ignored the shouts of their officers and took to their heels.

Just like that, five hundred horsemen had put to flight five or six times their number. But the Hamveltai infantry were thick on the ground, and a canny commander might still have saved the situation. Before anyone could try, however, a wave of blue appeared at the crest of the hill, Vordanai infantry filing out into line and marching down to join their mounted countrymen. The artillery paused to let them pass, then thundered over their heads at the Hamveltai battalions that had managed to form square, wreaking havoc on such tight-packed targets.

It was too much. First one battalion began to crumble, then another, and then the entire Hamveltai flank fell to pieces before Winter's astonished eyes. Ten thousand men, as finely trained and equipped as any army in the world, were converted in a moment into a fleeing, helpless mob. They overran their own guns and the few officers who tried to stop them, sitting helplessly on their horses amid the human flood. They didn't try for long, as the Vordanai infantry broke into a charge, firing wildly into the mass of panicked enemy. Hundreds of yellowjackets, unable to get clear, were throwing down their weapons and waving frantically in surrender.

For a long moment, there was dead silence on the wooded ridge, among the piled dead.

"Sir?" Bobby said, stunned. "What just happened?"

"We won the battle," Winter said.

There was still firing at the far end of the line, men fighting and dying for a cause they didn't yet know was lost. Heavy columns of Vordanai infantry were marching down from the hills in that direction, in case they needed convincing.

Two women standing beside Winter let out a hesitant cheer, which was quickly joined by a half dozen more. Moments later the whole forest was ringing with triumphant shouts, and bayonetted muskets waved in the air. Winter snatched off her cap and joined in, though in truth she was still too numb to feel much elation. In any case, once the celebration was done, there was still the grisly work of clearing out the corpses to attend to.

THE DIRECTORY FOR
THE NATIONAL DEFENSE

The triumphs of the past few days had done much to insulate Maurisk against shock, or else he was still feeling the effects of the treasures he'd looted from the liquor cabinets of Durenne and his allies. Either way, when he turned back to his desk to find Ionkovo standing in the corner of the room, he gave little more than a startled grunt. *Maybe I'm just getting used to him.*

"It appears," the Penitent Damned said, with his customary lack of preamble, "that congratulations are in order."

"I'm not sure I'd go as far as congratulations," Maurisk said. "But things do seem to be in hand, for the moment."

"In hand," Ionkovo said. He stepped away from the wall and circled the desk. Almost unconsciously, Maurisk retreated, sidestepping to put the desk between them. "Yes, I think that might be a good description. *Your* affairs are in hand."

"I'm not sure—"

"Your enemies languish in dungeons, the Deputies-General are firmly cowed, and that toad who commands your guard will jump whenever you dangle a pretty bauble in front of him." Ionkovo leaned forward and put his hands on the desk. "*My* affairs, however, would seem to have been . . . neglected."

"Plans are in motion, I assure you."

"Like your plan to seize d'Ivoire? Your men were *late*." Ionkovo straightened up. "I cannot abide lack of punctuality."

"D'Ivoire can't hide forever," Maurisk said. "And we still have the queen—"

"You do not, in fact, have the queen," Ionkovo grated. "Indeed, I begin to doubt if you ever did."

Maurisk found the courage for a bit of indignation. "If you doubt my word—"

Ionkovo cut him off again. "I don't doubt your word, only your competence. Let me remind you that all of your political triumphs will be worth *nothing* if I don't get what I want. The legions of Murnsk and the Borelgai fleet will grind this country to dust, and you will be remembered as the man who presided over the final destruction of Vordan."

Sweat trickled down Maurisk's neck and into his collar. "I assure you, I am making every effort. I will investigate the matter of the queen. And in the meantime—"

"Forget the queen for now," Ionkovo said. "One of my associates will see if there is anything useful to be learned from that farce. But more important, you have captured one of Vhalnich's men, have you not?"

How could he possibly know that? Maurisk swallowed and nodded. "Yes. He denies it, but we're certain he's working for Vhalnich. He must have left a cadre in the city to protect the Thousand Names."

"Of course he did. And what has he told you?"

"Ah . . . nothing, so far. But I have men who are skilled in loosening tongues. He'll talk before much longer."

"I have extremely limited patience. Your men are restricted to . . . conventional methods, while my associates are not. One of them is waiting outside. You will accompany him to this prisoner, and he will practice his craft. I will join you there. Understood?"

"Now?"

Ionkovo smiled. "Now."

It was only a short walk to the old Butchers' Union building, a blocky brick structure on one of the streets that led away from Farus' Triumph. Maurisk spent the time glancing at his companion, who seemed a remarkably ordinary sort of man, balding and a bit paunchy, walking with a slight limp. The only oddities were his fingernails, which were as long and white as an eagle's talons.

The Patriot Guards outside the Butchers' Union saluted and opened the doors, and Maurisk led the stranger through the darkened space. The sun had set, and no light came in through the many narrow windows. This had once been the killing floor, before the pressures of commerce had moved sanguinary operations to less savory districts south of the river. After that, the vast open space had been sluiced down, refurnished, and rented to firms in need of temporary accommodation. With the drop-off in trade caused by the war, it had rapidly emptied out, and been taken over by the Directory for its own ends. During the day, it served as a muster hall and meeting ground for the Patriot Guard, and the cellars that had once secured sides of beef and curing hams had proven ideal for sensitive prisoners.

Another pair of guards waited at the stairs, and yet another outside the room itself. Maurisk kept looking over his shoulder, expecting to see Ionkovo skulking in the shadows, but the Penitent Damned made no appearance. One of the guards unlocked the door with a key from his belt, and Maurisk led the bald man into a dry, windowless space, illuminated by a single candle in a wall bracket.

In one corner, tied to a chair at his wrists and ankles, was the prisoner. He was a lean young man, with several days' growth of beard and a wound under one ear that was crusty with dried blood. His clothing was rank and filthy.

"Shut the door," the bald man said. He had a Murnskai accent, much thicker than Ionkovo's.

Maurisk glanced nervously from the prisoner to the guards, then put his shoulder against the door. It swung shut with a hollow *boom*, locking itself with a final-sounding *click*.

"This is our man, then?" said Ionkovo, stepping out of the shadows.

Maurisk gritted his teeth to keep from shouting. *Sorcery.* He swallowed, regaining his composure, and nodded.

"What makes you think he's one of Vhalnich's?"

"He made regular visits to a particular set of cafés, always waiting in the same places, and every so often he'd leave what looked like a sign. Folded papers, twisted napkins, that kind of thing. A local woman tipped us off because she thought he was a spy."

"So he's a spy. But is he Vhalnich's?"

"He's Mierantai. If you can persuade him to speak, you'll hear it in his accent. The men of Mieran County are notorious for their close-minded loyalty, so I can't imagine him working for anyone else."

The prisoner raised his head, regarding his captors through a ragged fringe of hair. His eyes went from Maurisk to Ionkovo as they spoke, but his face remained impassive.

"Well," Ionkovo said, "we'll know soon enough. My associate here is known, in our circles, as the Liar, and this is his area of expertise. If you would?"

"Gladly," the bald man said. He stepped in front of the prisoner, regarding the man blandly. "Now, this won't hurt a bit."

"Watch," Ionkovo said. "You may find this instructive."

Maurisk watched. He watched as the Liar's nails began to glow a bright blue, and watched as the bald man sank these burning claws into the prisoner's face as though it were made of butter. Maurisk felt his gorge rising, but he felt Ionkovo's eyes on him, and dared not look away. It was obvious that there was a purpose to this exercise beyond simply gathering information. *He wants me to know that it could as easily be me in that chair.*

As his blood ran down his face and dripped onto his shirt, the Mierantai spoke in a slow, careful voice, answering every question the Liar put to him. It was, Maurisk thought, when his instinctive horror of the supernatural subsided a little, considerably more efficient than the beating and flaying his own people relied on to achieve the same end. When the Liar was satisfied there was nothing more to be wrung from the wretch, he withdrew his hand. The young man gave a few final twitches and died.

"Well," Ionkovo said, "it appears you were correct."

"I'll get a force together."

"Do so," the Penitent said. "One of my people will accompany them."

"Cinder?" Maurisk said apprehensively. The old woman's ability was anything but subtle, and keeping her involvement a secret always involved a regrettably large number of extra casualties.

"No," Ionkovo said, with a slight smile. "Not this time. Liar, would you please inform Twist that his services are required?"

"Of course," the bald man said, ducking his head. The politician in Maurisk noted that there was a simmering resentment in the Liar's gaze when he looked at Ionkovo. *So there are rivalries among even the Penitent Damned?* He filed the thought away for later perusal and kept his face blank.

"This time," Ionkovo said, stepping back into the darkness, "there are to be no mistakes."

Chapter Seventeen

WINTER

The river Piav was a large tributary of the Velt, running down from the Keth Mountains until it met up with the greater flow somewhere north of Desland. Rivers like it ran from east to west across the Velt Valley at regular intervals, carrying rain and snowmelt from the mountains down through the hills to nourish the lowlands and ultimately flow out to the sea. The Piav happened to flow within fifty miles of the Orlan Pass, the largest of the gaps in the mountain range and the only one capable of accommodating a large army. It was here, therefore, around the small town of Antova, that the Free Cities League had built its great fortress.

Dreiroede of Hamvelt, probably the greatest siege engineer who had ever lived, had laid it out at the very height of his powers and influence. The town itself was pressed against the riverbank, and what had once been a fishing village was now dwarfed by the system of fortifications that surrounded it. Seen from a distant overlook, as Winter was seeing it now, it resembled a massive exercise in geometry, sketched onto the land by some idle deity. On the west side of the river, around the town, six points of a great star were traced by a ditch and a massive earthen rampart, pockmarked with embrasures for defending artillery. A seventh point, like a massive spike, stretched on the other side of the river, with additional protection provided by a swampy moat created with water diverted from the Piav. Between the points of the star were the outworks, ravelins and lunettes, from which the defenders could create a vicious cross fire and slaughter the crews of any cannon trying to breach the walls.

It was Dreiroede himself, who had been as expert in attacking fortresses as he had been at building them, who had insisted that there was no such thing as an impenetrable fortification. Given sufficient numbers, artillery, and willpower, any fortress could be reduced; bastions could be toppled, outworks seized, and eventually a breaching battery established close enough to the wall to blast a hole in it and permit an infantry assault. The fortress builder's art was therefore all down to buying time—angled walls of earth would deflect cannonballs rather than shatter beneath them, overlapping rings of defense would each cost time and lives to penetrate, and defending cannon could sweep the attackers back from the defenses until they were finally silenced. The strength of a fortress was measured in *time*, how many months the defenders could be expected to hold out without relief.

Antova, his greatest work, was a year-strong fortress. Any attacker was supposed to have to batter the walls for at least that long before gaining entry, while deflecting the efforts of the garrison and surviving a cold and hungry winter. In the meantime, relief forces would be approaching, and the attacking army risked being caught between them and the fortress like iron between a hammer and the anvil.

Janus was evidently not concerned. From where she stood, on a height in the mountain foothills, Winter could see blue-uniformed troops hard at work digging trenches. The Army of the East now numbered some thirty-five thousand. Di Pfalen's routed army had nowhere near the numbers Dreiroede's calculations required—even the strongest fortress required soldiers to man the walls—but even so the massive construction with its killing fields and siege guns seemed a daunting prospect. And to the north, approaching with the slow inexorability of a glacier, came Hamvelt's greatest living soldier, Field Marshal Jindenau, with another thirty thousand soldiers.

Janus spread a map of the Velt Valley on the grass and weighed it down with stones, explaining all of this in a slow, patient tone while he pointed out the geography with a stick. The colonels peered at the map and furrowed their foreheads, eager to impress with the depth of their understanding.

Winter felt uncomfortable in their company. Some of them were Royals—Janus' purge of the old, noble colonels meant that these were mostly younger men, War College graduates like Captain d'Ivoire, new to their posts and hungry for glory. The rest were volunteers, men who had either been elected to high rank by their troops or gained promotion on the spot in battle, who wore homemade uniforms and looked skeptical at the talk of ravelins and breaching batteries.

But none of them murmured an objection, or even a question. Janus, thin-faced, gray eyes blazing, held them rapt. Looking at the faces around her, Winter found herself able to understand Jane's qualms about Janus. After Diarach, Gaafen, and the latest Battle of Jirdos, their trust in the general was complete. They would storm the gates of hell against a legion of demons on his order, in full confidence that he would produce victory out of a hat like a street-corner conjuror.

"That about sums up the situation," Janus said, sitting back on his heels. The others, thirteen of them including Winter, sat or knelt in the damp grass around the map. "It will take another day to fully invest the fortress, but I don't expect any interference from the garrison before our preparations are complete. It will take them some time to assemble an effective resistance."

"We should storm the walls tonight," one of the volunteer officers said. "They'll never expect it, and as you say, they're still disorganized. Why give them a chance to catch their breath?"

"An attractive thought, but it would be far too costly," Janus said. "Di Pfalen's army is shattered, but the walls are strong, and they have heavy siege guns we can't match. We might be able to find a weak spot, but we'd lose half the army."

The rest of the officers hurriedly murmured agreement, throwing nasty looks at the man who'd spoken out, who hung his head. It reminded Winter of the prefects back at Mrs. Wilmore's, competing to see who could most effectively kiss up to the mistresses. Janus looked around the circle, and when his gray eyes met hers his mouth twisted in a tiny, knowing smile, as though the two of them were sharing a joke.

"No," he went on. "We'll invest the fortress, and dig trenches to keep the garrison from making trouble. We should be able to contain the Hamveltai and leave a substantial force free to maneuver."

More mutters of agreement, loudest of all from the man who'd spoken out the first time. Winter cleared her throat.

"Maneuver where, sir?" she said. "Given the size of the fortress and the garrison, even dug in we'd need a sizable force here to keep them in check. That would make us substantially smaller than the field marshal's army, and he'll have the advantage that we'll be tied to the siege. If he gets too close to the fortress, he could combine with the garrison and crush us."

"Di Pfalen outnumbered us," one of the royal colonels said, with a touch of condescension in his voice. "And we've whipped him twice now. This Jindenau will fare no better."

Janus has whipped him, Winter thought. *My soldiers and I have whipped him, marched through hell and mud to turn up on the enemy flank and beat three battalions to give the cavalry a shot at his rear. Where were you? Up on the hills, watching the artillery do the work?*

It was unfair, she realized. Men had fought all along

the line, though casualties had admittedly been light among the troops nearest the Girls' Own, where the Hamveltai line had given way. On the other side, where di Pfalen had led his initial attack, only desperate fighting had kept him from pushing the defenders off their hilltops, and those troops had retreated in good order when the rest of the line collapsed. It was largely thanks to the rearguard action of these disciplined Hamveltai regulars that di Pfalen had an army left at all.

But it hurt Winter to watch the way the men all around the circle nodded, with solemn pomposity. Another Royal, a big man with heavy sideburns and a neat mustache, said, "Don't worry. The general will find a way."

None of them were in Khandar, Winter realized. Fitz Warus, now commanding the Colonials, was conspicuous by his absence; she guessed he was down organizing the construction of the trenches. Give-Em-Hell was off with his heavy cavalry, who'd taken serious losses in their hell-for-leather ride. The Preacher and Colonel d'Ivoire were back in Vordan.

None of these men had seen Janus when his back was truly to a wall, as Winter had, the night of Adrecht's mutiny and then again in the Desoltai temple. They thought that there would always be another scheme, another gambit, that his calm facade came from deep-down certainty that he would come out on top. Winter knew different. She'd seen Janus run out of tricks, trapped under a statue and facing certain death at the hands of the Penitent Damned Jen Alhundt. His calm had never wavered. *When the day comes that he throws the dice once too often, you won't see it on his face.*

"Thank you, Colonel, for your confidence," Janus said. "For the moment, shovel-work is what is required. Colonel Warus is working to distribute the necessary orders. I need you to impress upon your men that this is just as important to our final victory as courage on the battlefield."

"Yes, sir!" the big colonel said, followed by the others in ragged chorus. They saluted, and Winter joined in.

"Very good," Janus said. "See to your men. Colonel Ihernglass, if you would remain a moment?"

"Sir?" Winter said, frowning.

Janus smiled at her again, but said nothing while the others walked away, down the slope of the hill to where their aides waited with the horses. His eyes never left hers, and she wondered if her dark thoughts had been visible in her expression. Janus sometimes seemed as though he could read minds, although she was reasonably sure this was only his remarkable insight and not an actual supernatural ability. Infernivore never so much as twitched in his presence.

When they were alone, he said, "I must say, Colonel, you look worn out."

Winter looked down at herself. She'd changed from her mud-spattered uniform into a fresh one, but there hadn't yet been time to do much else. Her hair was getting shaggy, and her face had to show the effects of several nights of poor sleep and days of exertion and fear.

"I am worn out, sir," she said.

"And how fares the Third?"

"Worn out as well. We lost half our strength on the march. They're still trickling in, and we're hoping to recover the rest when our wagon train finally catches up." She thought of Molly, sweating and pale. "Most of them, anyway."

"I must apologize for the exertion I asked of you. In spite of what Colonel Gordace would have you believe, I am not infallible, and Baron di Pfalen is a canny soldier, if somewhat lacking in imagination. He behaved more aggressively than I had expected, and my timetable had to adapt accordingly."

"Yes, sir."

"Your men and women did a fine job under extremely difficult circumstances. Please convey to them my thanks, and tell them the entire army is in their debt."

"Thank you, sir. I will."

"As for you, Ihernglass, I see that I was not wrong in

considering you an extremely promising officer, regardless of your other qualities." He cocked his head. "May I ask you a question?"

"Of course, sir."

"Why do you continue your . . . charade? Your current position would seem to be a good one for revealing the truth."

"A few people know, sir. Bobby, Jane, some of the Leatherbacks. For the rest . . . it just seems easier to keep things as they are." Winter thought of Novus and his tirade. "It would be one thing if I had just joined up, but it's been so long. People might be upset that they'd been fooled. And . . ."

Janus raised an eyebrow. Winter hesitated.

"It's all right for the Girls' Own," she said. "They joined up because Vordan needs them, and when the war's over they'll go home. I . . . I haven't got anywhere to go." She tugged the collar of her uniform. "This is who I am now, for better or worse. This is my home. After the war, maybe it will be all right for a woman to keep this on, but . . . maybe not."

Winter found her throat getting thick. She'd never put it that way before, never even thought it so bluntly. *This is my home.*

"I leave it to your discretion, of course," Janus murmured, after a moment of silence. "What of Captain Verity?"

Winter took a deep breath and blew it out. "I've put Abby Giforte in command of the Girls' Own, sir, and kept Jane on my staff. I'd appreciate your official endorsement of Abby's promotion, incidentally, on the off chance that we ever get the chance to claim any of our pay."

"Certainly. Captain Giforte—the younger Captain Giforte, I suppose I should say—seemed a most capable young woman. But it was Captain Verity I was asking about. Have you encountered difficulties with her?"

Winter hesitated, but something about Janus' penetrating gaze made her think that trying to conceal anything from him was a lost cause. "A few, sir. But we're working them out."

"If it would make things easier for you, I could order her back to Vordan. I'd make it clear it wasn't at your request."

Winter's breath caught. The thought of sending Jane away made her want to curl up and die on the spot, but her immediate protest froze in her throat. *If it means no more days like yesterday . . . no more standing by and waiting to see if she stumbles out of the cloud of smoke, or if I'm going to find her sprawled and cold on some battlefield . . .*

"No, sir," she said after a long moment. "That won't be necessary."

"As you like," Janus said. "Now, I received your report concerning the attack in Desland. You're certain the three assassins were Penitent Damned?"

Winter blinked at the sudden change in subject. "Uh . . . no, sir, not completely certain. But they wore the obsidian masks, and all three seemed to have . . . abilities that were more than ordinary. One bore a demon for certain—I nearly devoured it with the Infernivore. I understood that only the Penitent Damned carried demons."

"The truth is more complex, but only slightly. You haven't seen them since?"

"No, sir." Winter frowned. "If they wanted to kill me, on the march would have been an ideal time. Our security fell by the wayside after the rains started."

"I can imagine," Janus said, "So either they were no longer interested, or some other target had become a priority." He grimaced. "I can only think of one that would qualify. If they knew you carried a demon, they must also know that we have the Thousand Names. I fear poor Augustin must have fallen into their clutches."

Winter had almost forgotten about the aged manservant. "We never found a trace of him."

"You wouldn't have, if he was abducted by Penitent Damned." Janus sighed. "He had served my family his whole life. This was a poor way to repay him. I hope he didn't suffer unduly."

There was a moment of silence.

"Well," Janus said, "I'm glad you escaped, and I thank

you for the information. I will do what I can. We still have work here—"

"General Vhalnich?" a voice called, from farther down the slope. It took Winter a moment to recognize Fitz Warus. The young man had acquired an air of authority that matched his advancement in rank.

"Yes, Colonel?"

"A party's just arrived from the capital. It's—you'd better come and see, sir."

The last time Winter saw de Ferre, he'd been slinking off with his tail between his legs, summarily sacked by Janus after his performance at the battle of Diarach. If he'd had a tail, it would have been bristling now. He rode a tall white stallion, and a dozen officers and as many guards, all mounted, rode in his train. The eagles marking his colonel's rank were gone from his shoulders, replaced by silver stars amid a tangle of gold braid.

A ranker stood nearby, waiting to take de Ferre's horse, but he'd apparently refused to dismount until he saw Janus approaching. Now that he'd sighted the general, he swung grandly out of the saddle, gilded spurs jingling on the stony ground. His escort followed suit. They'd halted on the open ground south of the camp, where the uneven lines of tents petered out. While much of Janus' army was off digging fortifications or standing guard against the possibility of a Hamveltai sortie, a good number of off-duty rankers had drifted over to see what was going on.

"Colonel de Ferre," Janus said, no hint of surprise on his face. Winter stood respectfully behind him, flanked by Fitz. "What brings you back to the Army of the East?"

"General Vhalnich," de Ferre said. He strove to keep his expression neutral, but didn't have Janus' control. There was the hint of a smile at the corners of his mouth, and his tone was that of a man savoring every word. "Orders, of course. But I must correct you. It is *General* de Ferre now."

"So I see," Janus said, looking over the officers and men de Ferre had brought.

"In accordance with the orders of the Secretary of War"—de Ferre raised his voice—"as of this moment, I am assuming command of the Army of the East."

A mutter ran through the crowd of watching soldiers. Winter suppressed a start and tried to emulate Janus' carefully bland expression.

"May I examine these orders?" Janus said. "For form's sake."

"Of course you may." De Ferre stepped forward, pulling a sealed paper from his breast pocket, and handed it to Janus with the air of a fencer delivering a killing stroke. Janus examined the seal for a moment, then broke it with his thumb and read.

"I see," he said. "By the order of Secretary of War Johann Maurisk."

"That's right."

"And I am further ordered to place myself under your authority," Janus said quietly.

"You are." De Ferre was openly grinning now, decorum forgotten.

There was a long pause. Janus folded the document, carefully, and handed it back.

"General," he said finally. "I wonder if we might speak . . . more privately."

De Ferre's eyes narrowed. "Surely you don't intend to question the Minister's orders?"

"Of course not. But there are matters of . . . operational detail that you should be made aware of."

"Very well. Colonel Pahn will accompany me, if you don't mind?"

"Not at all. Colonel Ihernglass, Colonel Warus, would you also join us?" Janus stepped aside and picked out an officer among the watching men. "Captain, would you make sure the rest of the general's escort and their mounts are cared for?"

The man saluted, and Janus led the way through the tents to his own. It was, Winter noticed when they went inside, even more spartan than she remembered, presumably because of the lack of the missing Augustin's touch.

A folding table, a camp bed, and an open trunk packed full of books were the whole of the furnishings. De Ferre's lip turned up in a sneer; clearly he was used to more comfortable surroundings.

"I think," Janus said when they were all inside, "that you—"

"*Sir,*" de Ferre growled.

Janus paused.

"The Minister has placed me in command of all soldiers of the Army of the East, including you. You will therefore address me as *sir.*"

Winter sucked in a breath, and waited for the explosion.

"As you wish, sir," Janus said mildly.

"*Very* good." De Ferre waved a hand magisterially. "Continue."

"Matters have progressed a bit further than the Minister was aware when he gave you your orders. We have fought and won a great battle here—"

"And you think that will reverse his decision?" de Ferre snarled. "Not this time, Vhalnich. Your luck has finally run out."

"I think nothing of the kind, sir," Janus said. "But it means our strategic situation is changed. The army is currently laying siege to the fortress of Antova."

"I'm not *blind*, thank you."

"While Marshal Jindenau's army approaches from the north," Janus went on, "I am curious, sir, if you have any thoughts on what our next move should be."

De Ferre frowned. "Obviously, we storm the fortress at once, before the enemy can unite his forces. Basic strategic principles."

"It is my opinion that any attempt to storm Antova will very likely be repulsed with heavy loss. Sir."

"Oh, I *see*. That's your opinion, is it?"

"Yes, sir. I'd like you to consider—"

De Ferre drew himself up and sucked in the considerable stomach that his tailored uniform could not quite conceal. "Let me tell you what I think, Vhalnich. I think you've

bought in to your own legend. The military genius, the hero
of the hour. *Of course* you know better. Us ordinary mortals
can only watch and learn, eh?" He waved a finger under
Janus' nose. "The fact is that there's nothing special about
you. You've been lucky on the battlefield, that's all. That
may be enough to make the rankers worship you, but it will
not work on me, do you understand?"

"Of course, sir. But I might offer some suggestions—"

"So you can take credit for my victory?" De Ferre
snorted. "I think not. I have been commanding troops
since you were in britches, and I like to think I know my
way around a siege. All I require from you is that you obey
my orders and provide such information as I request. Is
that clear?"

"Yes, sir," Janus said. His huge gray eyes were impassive.

"Now. You will instruct your colonels to prepare
detailed reports on their strength and dispositions. Send
along any plans you've already drawn up for the assault
so my staff engineers may assess their merit."

"As you wish, sir." Janus saluted, as crisply as any War
College sentry. "If you'll excuse me, then? I have a great
deal of work to do."

"Indeed." De Ferre turned around with a jangle of
spurs. Colonel Pahn, a small, rat-faced man with an
unhealthy-looking mustache, gave Winter and Fitz a sneer
and followed. Janus stood silent and unmoving until their
footsteps had faded away.

"I wonder," he said thoughtfully, "if that was as satisfying as he thought it would be. He clearly spent the whole
ride over practicing."

"Sir . . . ," Winter said hesitantly.

"Colonel Warus," Janus said, still not turning around.
"In the small case by your feet, there's a crystal bottle.
Would you be so good as to hand it to me?"

Fitz bent, plucked up the bottle, an elegantly carved
thing that looked out of place in the sparse tent. It was
half-full of something that looked like liquid gold. Janus
accepted it, opened the stopper, and took a deep breath.

"They make this in the mountains at home," he said. "A sort of apple liquor. It's an acquired taste." He drained the bottle in a few gulps and made a face. "I don't know why one would bother, to be honest. But Augustin always insisted we have some along, for medicinal purposes."

Then, fast as a snake, he spun and hurled the bottle at the trunk on the other side of the tent. It struck the leather-bound side and shattered with a satisfying crunch, spraying fragments of glittering glass into the air.

For the first time Winter could remember, there was fury in Janus' face. His eyes *burned*. His lips curled back from clenched teeth, an animal's snarl.

"It's too *soon*," he said. "Too *fucking* soon. Blind, blind, how could I have been so blind! That clever god-damned bastard."

"De Ferre, sir?" Winter said.

Janus barked a laugh. "De Ferre couldn't plot his way out of a sack of puppies. I mean our eminent President of the Directory for the National Defense, who is now also in his person the Minister of War."

"Do you have any idea what happened, sir?" Fitz said. "News from Vordan takes days to get here, but—"

"That's the point. That's exactly the point." Janus took a deep breath. "I received word, by private means, that there had been major changes back home. Maurisk has seized power for himself."

"What?" Winter said. "But—"

"It was bound to happen," Janus said dismissively. "He's not the sort of man to be easily satisfied. I had a number of scenarios ready. But I thought I would have more *time*. If de Ferre set out the moment of the coup, he'd still be riding through the pass, a hundred miles away."

"Which means he set out beforehand," Fitz said.

"Exactly. Maurisk gave him postdated orders and sent him out *before* he made his move. Probably to wait some-where nearby for a prearranged signal. An obvious move, in retrospect." Janus turned to Winter, with a fleeting smile. "If we extricate ourselves from this situation, please remind me of this the next time someone claims I am infallible."

"So Maurisk stole a march on you," Winter said. "But that would only be a few days, wouldn't it?"

"A few days can make all the difference. In a few days' time, the army would have been on the march. Even de Ferre would have hesitated to interfere. Now, though. If he sits here assaulting the walls, everything I've done this season will be for nothing!"

"We could work with the colonels to plan the assault," Fitz said. "Make suggestions to de Ferre through them."

"It won't work. If we're fortunate, we might take the fortress, but we'd never hold it against Jindenau's army." Janus' expression darkened again. "And Antova is the key to the valley. Without it, we'll have no option but to retreat when winter sets in."

"Not to mention," Winter said quietly, "how many soldiers we'll lose."

"Yes," he said. "Though I doubt that enters de Ferre's calculations."

There was another moment of silence.

"Antova must fall," Janus said, half to himself. "It *must* fall, soon. A fortress can fall by storm, by siege, by betrayal, or by surrender. We can't storm it with a good chance of success, and they've got more than enough supplies to hold out until Jindenau gets here and forces a field battle we won't be able to win."

"You had a plan," Fitz pointed out.

"The beginnings of one," Janus admitted. "But de Ferre will never agree. And it's moot in any case if he gets half the men killed in the first assault."

"Finding a traitor inside the fortress would take more time than we have," Fitz said.

"And why should they surrender?" Janus said. "They know their army is on the way."

Winter chewed her lip for a moment, then said, "There's a new Vordanai general. A cruel, heartless bastard. He's brought twenty fresh regiments to storm the fortress, and he promises to kill everyone inside the walls, soldiers or not. No quarter, unless they surrender at once."

Fitz and Janus looked at her, then at each other.

"It might help," Fitz said. "If they believed it."

"But why should they?" Janus said.

"I have . . . an idea. Let me talk to my people. And we'll need some help from the other colonels."

"I'm sure they'd be willing, if the alternative is storming the walls," Fitz said. "Sir?"

"Do it," Janus said. "Whatever you need. De Ferre will be watching me, so I won't be able to be much help." He glanced at the remains of the bottle. "I apologize for my . . . nerves."

"Understandable," Winter said. "Frankly, I'm surprised you managed not to punch him in the face."

An hour later, with the sun sinking toward the horizon, Winter sat in her own tent with Abby. The story of de Ferre's arrival had made the rounds of the camp by now, in various distorted versions, and she'd been full of questions. Winter explained what had happened in Janus' tent, and laid out her idea. Abby gave a low whistle.

"That's . . . bold," she said.

"It's all I could think of. Fitz is making the rounds of the other colonels to get them to do their part, but I wanted to get your opinion before I talk to Anne-Marie."

Abby shook her head. "I don't like it. Do you have any idea what they'd do to a girl like her if they found out who she really is?"

"Yes," Winter said, "I do. But if de Ferre has us try to storm the walls . . ." She frowned. "You don't think she'd do it?"

"She'll do it. She'd jump at the chance." Abby's brow furrowed. "I'm just not sure we should ask her to."

"If she knows the risks . . ."

Winter paused. *It doesn't work like that. Rankers don't get to assess the risks and decide if something's worth doing. We point, and they go. Working out whether it's worth it is our job.* It wasn't so long ago that she'd been marching in the ranks herself, but it was easy to forget how it felt.

"I think," she began again, "that this is the best chance we have of preventing a massacre."

"You may be right." Abby grimaced. "What happens if it works? What then?"

"Let's worry about that once we get there. Can you find Anne-Marie for me?"

"Yes, sir." Abby stood, saluted, and left. Winter stared after her, trying to fight a sick feeling in her stomach.

Anne-Marie, when she arrived, was as excited as Abby had predicted. She seemed to have suffered nothing in the march or the subsequent battle that a few nights' rest hadn't been able to cure. Her uniform bore signs of recent, careful patching, and her blond hair, cut short when she'd joined, was just getting long enough to curl at the ends. She saluted and stood at attention, practically vibrating with the effort.

"Sit down," Winter said. "How much did Abby tell you?"

"Only that you specifically requested me for a special mission, sir." Anne-Marie's Vordanai was much improved, though her Hamveltai accent remained strong. She sat cross-legged, and daintily picked a stray bit of mud off her boot.

"Something like that. I need you to do a bit of playacting."

Anne-Marie blinked. "Sir?"

"We need to give the Hamveltai in there"—Winter gestured in the general direction of the fortress—"the impression that we're about to come in and slaughter them all. Unfortunately, Janus has been making a point of being correct toward Hamveltai prisoners, so he doesn't have the right kind of reputation to be convincing. I thought one of their own—an escaped refugee, perhaps—might go a long way toward spreading the news of our new commander."

"You want me to go into the fortress?" Anne-Marie said. "And . . . convince them?"

"Yes, in a nutshell." Winter shook her head, suddenly

embarrassed. "It's a hell of a thing to ask, I know. But you're Deslandai, you know the language, and you're . . ." She waved a hand vaguely.

"Sir?" Anne-Marie said again.

"A pretty girl," Winter managed to get out. "Men are always a bit more gullible when there's a pretty girl involved."

"Oh." Anne-Marie went quiet for a moment, cheeks slightly flushed.

"If you don't think you can do it, we'll think of something else," Winter said, forcing herself to ignore the fact that she had no idea what "something else" would be. "But it has to be tonight."

"Of course, sir. I'd be glad to." Anne-Marie smiled brightly. "I was just trying to think of where I'd left my dresses."

It turned out that Anne-Marie's trunks, containing everything she'd brought with her when she ran away from home, had been thrown on the regimental wagon train by the quartermasters, which meant they'd arrived along with the rest of the baggage. It took Winter, Abby, and a whole squad of rankers nearly an hour to locate them, until finally they found the battered, expensive-looking luggage under some empty ammunition cases.

"I don't know why I thought I'd need any of this," Anne-Marie said, opening the case right on the back of the wagon and sorting through a mess of frilly, lacy things. "I just tossed in whatever I could lay my hands on."

She selected a green velvet dress of a conservative cut, and jammed the rest carelessly back in the case. Winter watched in bemused surprise as Anne-Marie wadded up the flimsy garment, took it to the nearest wagon rut, and dunked it liberally in mud. She held the filth-encrusted thing up and inspected it with a critical eye.

"Let me get it on," she said, "and I'll see what I can do with a pair of scissors and a few good tugs."

While she worked, Winter had a hurried conference with Fitz. A half dozen regiments were ready to execute their part in the charade, which would consist of unscheduled "exercises" lasting all night. They'd march, up and down, tramping and shouting and generally making a racket the defenders would have to be deaf to miss. With judicious use of a few empty carts and caissons thrown in, it would sound very much like the arrival of considerable reinforcements.

"Your job is going to be to stall de Ferre if he starts asking questions. You can give him the runaround, take him from one camp to the next, and—"

"Colonel Ihernglass," Fitz said, smiling, "I mean no offense, but I've been handling inconvenient superiors for quite some time. I know what I'm doing."

Winter nodded. "Right. Well. Good luck."

She and Abby had arranged passage for Anne-Marie through the section of the lines held by the Royals. They met there soon after full dark, and Winter studied the Deslandai girl's disguise in the light of the sentry's lantern. It looked, she had to admit, convincing. In addition to getting filth on the dress itself, Anne-Marie had coated her hair and skin liberally in the stuff.

She'd made some changes to the dress as well—one shoulder was ripped, so she had to clutch it at her collar and looked constantly at risk of baring her breast, and tears in the long skirt gave glimpses of dirty but shapely legs. The general effect was something out of a melodrama, the beautiful, bedraggled girl just waiting for someone to sweep her up and place himself between her and danger.

Looking at her, Winter felt obscurely out of her depth, as though she were catching a glimpse into some alien world. It was clear that, while she might need work on the manual of arms, in the areas her training had prepared her for—which obviously included securing male attention—Anne-Marie had long since mastered the essential skills.

"Good," Winter managed. "You're clear on what you have to tell them?"

Anne-Marie nodded. "We have a new general with plenty of new troops. Marshal Jindenau's army is defeated and retreating, and there's to be no quarter unless they surrender. And I have my heartbreaking adventure and escape ready."

"Remember, try and talk to di Pfalen personally if you can," Winter said. "Janus has whipped him twice already. He'll be ready to believe that we can do it again."

"Yes, sir." Anne-Marie's eyes twinkled. "You can count on me."

"Okay." Winter looked at Sevran, who was waiting nearby. "Your people are ready?"

He nodded, taking his eyes away from Anne-Marie with some difficulty. "They know not to fire."

"Right." Winter felt there should be something more to say, but she couldn't think of any grand sentiments. "Good luck."

Anne-Marie grinned. Janus' ring of fortifications was barely begun, so there were no trenches here yet, just a line of sentries out of cannon range of the nearest bastion. Once Anne-Marie took a few steps beyond them, she was lost to the lantern light, appearing only as a slender shadow flitting across the invisible barrier between the opposing armies.

Winter held her breath until the girl was out of sight completely, and then a little longer. For all that she worried about Anne-Marie being discovered as an imposter, this was the most obviously dangerous moment. If some trigger-happy sentry on the other side saw someone moving and decided to fire . . .

But no muzzle flashes lit the night. Winter let out her breath, feeling something clench tight in her chest.

"Well," she said to Abby and Sevran, "now we wait until morning."

To Winter's surprise, Jane was waiting for her when she returned to her own tent. Wordlessly Winter took her arm, and they slipped through the tent flap together. As soon as they were inside, Winter pulled Jane close and kissed her thoroughly, fingers tangling in her slick red hair.

"What's wrong?" Winter said when she pulled away.

"It's . . ." Jane grimaced. "I heard about what happened. De Ferre's really in command?"

"Apparently."

"Have you . . . I mean . . ." Jane, uncharacteristically, seemed hesitant. "Have you figured out what you're going to do?"

"About de Ferre? I have no idea." *One crisis at a time.* "I don't know that there's anything I *can* do."

For some reason, Jane's tense expression relaxed at this. "Good."

Before Winter could ask for an explanation, Jane was kissing her again. Winter relaxed into her arms and tried not to think about what might happen in the morning.

Chapter Eighteen

RAESINIA

The silence in the wagon was oppressive.

There was no real reason to be quiet. It was true that they were hiding, but between the rattle of the wheels and the creaking and shifting of the cargo, the chance of being overheard was too small to worry about. Nevertheless, Raesinia found herself reluctant to speak, and her companions apparently shared the feeling. They sat side by side in the warm darkness under the tarp, and she listened to the soft whistle of Marcus' breath. His shoulder was pressed against hers, and she could feel his arm tense as he clenched his fists in his lap.

She understood, in principle, the need for secrecy. Janus had given strict orders that Willowbrook's precise location was not to be revealed to anyone who didn't need to know, and furthermore too many furtive visitors would raise questions. About the only vehicles still regularly seen on the streets of the city were the wagons that delivered provisions to the estates of the wealthy, though more and more of these were pulled by mules these days instead of horses. The Micrantai courier had explained that the easiest way to get them in without alerting anyone was to put them on the regular supply run.

So, if all went well, no one was even paying the cart

much attention. Raesinia found herself tensing anyway, every time a wheel bumped over a stone or they halted for a few moments to let someone pass. By the time the tarp was pulled back, letting in the late-morning sun, she'd been starting to wonder if the journey would *ever* end.

A middle-aged man in a captain's blue uniform stood at the back of the cart, holding a salute.

"Good to see you again, sir," he said.

Marcus got to his feet, tentatively, and hopped down from the cart before holding out a hand to help Raesinia. Beside him, Andy stretched, shoulders popping audibly. Raesinia climbed down and looked around, curiously. Outwardly, Willowbrook looked like any other small estate that a minor noble or successful merchant might maintain, though the single high tower was architecturally a bit of an oddity. Men in plainclothes worked at the garden or simply stood around in pairs, watching.

"I'm sorry it took so long to arrange," the captain said. "As you can imagine, we have to be more careful than ever."

"I haven't got much experience being a wanted man," Marcus said, then turned to Raesinia and Andy. "Let me do the introductions. This is Captain Alex Giforte, formerly Vice Captain of Armsmen and in command here. Alex, this is Ranker Andria Dracht—"

"Andy, if you please," Andy said, saluting.

"—and this," Marcus went on, "is Her Majesty Raesinia Orboan."

"You may as well call me Raes," Raesinia said. "I've gotten used to it."

Marcus had explained that all his communications with Janus went through Giforte's people, who were therefore privy to her identity already, but it still felt odd to reveal herself so openly. Giforte saluted again, but he wore a bemused expression that Raesinia was beginning to recognize. *He's thinking, Wait,* this *is the Queen of Vordan?* She put on a rueful smile.

"Welcome to Willowbrook," Giforte said. "Colonel, we've just had a message from Janus that you'll want to see. Please, come with me."

He led them up the path from the end of the drive to the house, as some of the other men closed in around the wagon and started unloading the genuine supplies that had come with them. The door opened at their approach, and though the man behind it wore servant's clothes, he carried himself with a soldier's bearing.

As Raesinia crossed the threshold, something lurched unpleasantly in her skull, and she felt a sharp pain for a moment behind one eye. She stopped, shaking her head, and the others pulled up short as well.

"Raes?" Marcus said.

"I feel . . ." She lowered her voice. "Marcus, it's like at Twin Turrets. There's someone—"

"Ah," Giforte said. "She warned me this might happen. Feor?"

A young woman came forward, dressed in a plain black robe. She had dark hair, and skin the pale gray color of ashes. Raesinia found herself staring; while she'd read descriptions, she'd never met a Khandarai in the flesh before.

"Your Majesty," the woman said. She was younger than Raesinia herself, maybe not even twenty. "My name is Feor."

"You're . . ." The pain in her head had subsided, but there was still a faint feeling of *presence*, and it grew stronger when she looked at Feor.

"Yes." Feor looked at Giforte and Marcus. "I think Her Majesty and I should speak in private."

Feor took Raesinia down a long flight of stairs and into a long underground corridor, lit by hanging lanterns. They passed a heavy-looking door, which a young man in a gray robe bolted behind them, then bowed and withdrew.

"You're not a Penitent Damned," Raesinia said. "Obviously."

"No."

"But you're . . . you have a demon."

"My people would say I am a *naathem*." Feor smiled slightly. "As are you."

Raesinia blinked. "How—"

"*Naathem* can sense one another's presence. As you sensed mine."

The old woman at the warehouse, and that priest, Ionkovo. Raesinia hadn't fully considered the question, but it made sense that if she could somehow *feel* other demons, then they could feel her, too. *That might make it more difficult to hide than I thought.*

"Janus asked me to speak to you," Feor said. "In fact, his plan was eventually to move me into the palace, to be a . . . tutor to you. Obviously, that scheme has been overtaken by events."

"You work for Janus?"

"I suppose I do, though I prefer to think that we are allies." Feor chuckled. "In truth, it is Winter Ihernglass to whom I owe a debt. He saved my life when by rights we ought to have been enemies."

Raesinia had met Winter only briefly, at a few official functions before the departure of the Army of the East. "He's the one commanding Janus' battalion of women, isn't he?"

"Yes, I believe he is." For some reason Feor's smile grew wider. "In any event, Janus and I share an enemy, and that is what is most important."

"The Church," Raesinia guessed. "The Priests of the Black."

"Yes."

"Why? What did they have to do with you in Khandar?"

Feor hesitated a moment. "My own history is . . . complex. I was born to a secret sect of our religion, whose purpose was to safeguard knowledge of the *naath*. I learned very little of our history, but I believe the group I knew was a remnant, the remains of a once-mighty organization that had withered away over the years. We were taught that the *abh-naathem*—you call them the Penitent Damned—would stop at nothing to destroy us, because they craved the power of the Thousand Names. When the Redeemers overturned Khandar, they got their chance."

Raesinia nodded. "Janus told me their agents tried to kill him and take the Names."

"The rest of my sect was killed trying to protect the Names. It was Winter who showed me that it was not my duty to die with them. The gods have another purpose in mind. I believe they allowed the Names to fall to Janus because he will use them to finally break the power of the *abh-naathem* once and for all. My task is to help him as best I can."

"I see." That kind of sincerity, whether it was religious faith or political idealism, made Raesinia vaguely uncomfortable, as though there was something fundamental that she wasn't getting. "Are they here? The Thousand Names. They, it, whatever you want to say."

"Yes." Feor beckoned Raesinia forward. "I will show you."

The other end of the short corridor was blocked by a curtain, which Feor pulled aside. Beyond was a long gallery, with archways on either side leading to small alcoves that might once have been filled with storage shelves. Feor gestured to the first of these, and Raesinia approached to take a closer look.

She'd expected some kind of *book*, leather-bound and ancient. Crumbling scrolls, or maybe even clay tablets. Instead there was a steel plate taller than a man and wide enough that she would have difficulty getting her hands on either side of it. Its burnished surface shone gently in the lantern light. From top to bottom, it was deeply incised with line after line of an elaborate script Raesinia didn't recognize.

She raised a hand, then hesitated. "Will something terrible happen if I touch it?"

"No," Feor said. "It is only steel."

Raesinia ran her fingers over the surface, feeling the shapes of the unfamiliar letters, edges still unrounded in spite of their age. *Whoever made this thing built it to last.*

"The *naath* only have power inside a human soul," Feor said. "The letters are only sounds, until they are spoken aloud."

"It's just a list? Of names, or spells, or whatever they are?"

"There is a good deal more than that. Commentary,

warnings, ritual, and practice. They were created over many decades, or perhaps centuries, I believe."

"Are there really a thousand?" Raesinia looked at the giant plate. "That seems like a lot to fit in, even on something this size."

"There are seven more." Feor waved a hand at the other archways.

"Oh." Raesinia felt suddenly small. "And you're working on . . . what? Translating them?"

"In part. There are hints at pieces of our history that I believe nobody living remembers. And descriptions of what purposes the *naath* serve, although they are often vague or metaphorical."

"Okay." Raeisnia turned to face her. "So if I read one of these out loud—assuming I learned how to read this language—then that's it? Poof, I'm a *naathem*?"

"In your case, no. One soul cannot hold two *naath*. A *naath* read aloud by a *naathem* does nothing."

"Right. But someone else?"

"Perhaps." Feor shook her head. "The *naath* binds to the soul, and the soul must be strong enough to bear it. Some *naath* are weak, and nearly anyone may bind them. For the strongest, only one in a thousand might be able to speak the *naath* without dying in the attempt. And each *naath* can only be spoken once, until the bearer dies."

Raesinia closed her eyes. She remembered lying in bed, every breath a labored agony, while a bearded priest had knelt beside her. He'd asked her to read something, and there had been pain. She'd never been sure whether the episode had been part of her fevered delusions. *They gave me something like this to read.* She stared, inwardly, at the binding. *And it made me into . . . this.*

"Can you . . . stop being a *naathem*? Is there a way to get rid of one?"

"Janus said you might ask that." Feor sighed. "In short, I do not know, assuming you want to survive the process. I hope the answer may be here, somewhere."

"Somewhere." Raesinia looked up and down the massive plate. "It's going to take a while, isn't it?"

"Years, perhaps," Feor said. "But I would persevere, even if Janus had not asked. It has become clear to me that Mother—the leader of our sect—concealed a great deal from us. This is the closest to the truth that I can get."

"Do you know where these came from? How old they are?"

"Not precisely. The language is not Khandarai, though there are hints of an influence on modern Khandarai. Nor is it directly connected with any of the modern languages of your people, though again there are a few odd similarities. As best I can tell from events that are mentioned, the plates were carved sometime in the second or third century before the life of your prophet Karis."

That made the Names at least fourteen hundred years old. Raesinia didn't know much ancient history, behind what had made it into *The Wisdoms* and Church doctrine. The time between the Fall of the Tyrants and the Judgment was a vague era of chaos and destruction, where the lands were ruled by sorcerer-kings and demons of all sorts. All that wickedness had prompted God to send the Beast of Judgment to exterminate mankind, and only the intercession of Karis the Savior had convinced Him to stay His hand. Afterward, the Church had launched the beginning of its endless campaign against sorcery and sin, to prove to the Almighty that His continued mercy was warranted.

That was the version old Father Nuvell had taught her, anyway. There was nothing in there about the Priests of the Black employing sorcerous assassins, so she was pretty certain there were probably some other missing pieces.

"I'm interested to hear what you find," Raesinia said. "Even apart from . . . my condition. If I ever get to be a proper queen, you'll have any support I can offer. You won't have to live in a basement, to start with."

"Thank you, Your Majesty," Feor said. "But as long as the Black Priests exist, the Names will never be safe in the open. I am afraid hiding in basements may be my lot in life."

"Then at least we can get you a nicer basement," Raesinia said.

She grinned, and Feor smiled back. Before Raesinia could think of another question, there was a sharp pain at the back of her head, as though something had popped underneath her skull. She saw Feor stagger slightly.

"Is that . . . ," Raesinia said.

"Another *naathem*," Feor said. "Very close by."

"A friend of yours?"

She shook her head, face white. "They have found us."

MARCUS

Marcus—

Yours received. Timing unfortunate. M.'s representatives already arrived here, situation unstable. Will send word of further developments.

R must be kept safe, Willowbrook secure, all else secondary. Suggest remaining at Willowbrook until safe route out of the city can be secured, then hide in the country. R may object, but no more good options now that M. has revealed his hand. Suspect PD on their way to Vordan, do not risk operating with them at large.

If things resolve in our favor here, I will be able to assist you. If not, you will be on your own. In the latter case, I have sent instructions home; in the event of my death, take R to Mieranhal. The people there will keep you both safe.

Hope to see you again soon. If not, it has been an honor.

—J

"This is *all*?" Marcus said.

"We've gone over it several times," said Lieutenant White, who ran the flik-flik station. Around them, the solar was a mess, as men packed books and papers into trunks. "Orders for us came through a little later. We're moving the station out of the city down to the first waypoint, in the forest behind the University. Most of our gear is already there."

"But this . . ." Marcus gestured at the page. "What the hell does he mean 'in the event of my death'? What's going *on* out there?"

"Sir, I don't *know*," White said.

Giforte put a hand on Marcus' shoulder. "Let the lad keep packing."

"Sorry." Marcus shook his head. "It's just . . . not what I was expecting."

"This has caught us all by surprise."

"So you're pulling out? What about the Names?"

"Downstairs is staying here. The idea is that if nobody knows about this place, moving the flik-flik station will remove the most obvious way they might find out. We'll leave a guard as well, of course."

"It still seems like it would be safer to move everything out of the city."

"The problem is transportation. All those tablets weigh tons—getting them out without drawing attention would be difficult."

Marcus thought for a moment. "Maybe we can put something together with the army supply services." It was working for the refugees—or *had* been working. They'd put the whole thing on hold when Maurisk had launched his coup. "I'll see—"

"Marcus!" The shout came from below, accompanied by a Mierantai voice.

"You can't go up there!"

"Marcus!" Raesinia called again. "We're in deep shit!"

"Is that the queen?" Giforte said, frowning.

"You get used to it," Marcus said, already headed for the stairs. He pounded down several circular flights to find Raesinia restrained by two sheepish but firm Mierantai guards. Feor hovered anxiously on the other side of the door to the rest of the house.

"What's going on?" Marcus said.

"Someone's coming." Raesinia tapped her head. "Like that night."

"An *abh-naathem*," Feor said, her gray skin very pale. "Not far away."

"Oh, Balls of the fucking Beast," Marcus swore.

"What?" said Giforte, descending at a slightly less precipitous rate.

"They've found us," Marcus said. "Maybe they followed me here after all."

Giforte looked at the two Mierantai. "Go find Goffa and Ithan. Tell them to get everyone inside and prepared to defend the house. Now!"

"Sir!" The two men sprang away from Raesinia, saluted, and ran off. Giforte cupped his hands and shouted up to the top of the tower.

"*White!* We're moving you out *now!* Grab your gear and move. We'll burn the rest!"

The clatter coming down from the solar increased in tempo. Feor, having stepped out of the path of the hurrying guards, pressed forward again.

"We must defend the Names," she said. "If they fall into the hands of the *abh-naathem*—"

"We'll do our best," Giforte said. "It depends how many men they've brought. If they don't know what we've got here, it may take them a while to organize a real force, and we'll have time to ship everything out. Otherwise . . ."

"We cannot leave the archive behind!"

"Unless you've got a way to carry a ton of steel on your back, we may not have a choice. Like I said, we'll do what we can." Giforte paused. "Do you have any idea what this . . . *abh-naathem* can do?"

Feor shook her head, looking nearly in tears. "I do not."

"Can you or your students do anything?"

"No." Feor's voice was small. "My own power . . . no. Auriana, perhaps, but it would be very dangerous to her—"

"More or less dangerous than being shot?" Giforte shook his head, and his voice softened. "Sorry. Please, do whatever you can."

"Marcus." Raesinia beckoned him over and spoke quietly. "If it's Patriot Guard out there, and not just Penitent

Damned, I could try talking to them. They might not be willing to shoot the queen."

"Assuming they believe you're the queen," Marcus said, indicating Raesinia's not terribly queenly attire. "In any case, I'm sure they'd be willing to haul you back to the Hotel Ancerre. Try it if we've got nothing else left, but . . ."

"What if it's that woman from the warehouse out there?"

Marcus looked at the hurrying Mierantai, all carrying their deadly long rifles. "Then we're going to find out how many shots she can stop at once."

Marcus' position, amid the chaos of running, shouting men, was a somewhat ambiguous one. Technically, he was the senior officer on the scene, and therefore in command of this whole mess. But he was smart enough to know that Giforte and his subordinates had obviously spent time preparing for this circumstance, while he himself knew nothing about their plans or even the layout of the house. Any order he gave was only going to increase the confusion and slow things down. Instead of interfering, he took charge of Raesinia, shepherding her to a second-story window with a good view of the front lawn. Feor had disappeared back into her basement.

The chaotic state of the Mierantai garrison was at least partly an illusion. For secrecy, none of the riflemen were wearing their neat red uniforms, instead being dressed up for a variety of civilian roles: gardener, servant, laborer, and so on, with quite a few who were apparently on the night shift and wore little more than long linen nightshirts. This did nothing to impede their efficiency, however, as they stationed themselves at the windows, pushed furniture in front of the doors, and distributed boxes of ammunition. The general effect was that of a country estate threatened by bandits, where servants and bedraggled guests had taken up arms to defend it with slightly alarming efficiency.

Giforte stood down in the main hall, invisible from where Marcus had stationed himself but clearly audible as he shouted orders. He'd lost none of the assertiveness that had kept him as the effective leader of the Armsmen for so many years.

"Movement along the back fence!" one of the Mierantai shouted. "Hard to see how many. Muskets for certain."

"More on the left!"

"Moving on the right!"

"Patriot Guard coming up the drive!" another man shouted. Marcus looked out the window, with Raesinia beside him, and saw that it was true. A big four-wheeled carriage had parked at the bottom of the drive, and at least a dozen men were waiting behind it while a party of four made their way up toward the house. All wore the sashes of Patriot Guards, and one had shoulder decorations suggesting he was an officer.

From the outside, Marcus imagined, the house must look quiet. The riflemen had drawn most of the curtains to slits, and the cart they'd arrived on stood with its traces empty just in front of the side door. The Patriot Guard officer held up a hand to his men, then came up to the front door alone and slammed on the knocker.

"Open the door!" he said in a voice that betrayed only a little bit of fear. "In the name of the Directory for the National Defense!"

"What does the Directory want here?" a muffled voice answered. It was Giforte, Marcus thought.

"We've received information suggesting there may be contraband on the premises. We'll need to search the house. Cooperate, and no one will be harmed."

"That's not going to be possible. My master instructed me to allow no one inside."

The Guard officer frowned. "I don't give a damn what your master said. Open this door or we'll have you on the Spike!"

"I suggest you leave the premises at once. And tell your men to withdraw."

The officer spun on his heel and stalked back to his three men. "Break the door down!"

The trio, obviously unaware of how many weapons were trained on them, moved up to the front door. They all carried heavy axes, which Marcus recognized from his brief time in the Armsmen as weapons designed for exactly this situation. A few well-aimed blows would open most stubborn portals, but in this case he doubted they'd get the chance to even wind up. It was hard to watch anyone, even the enemy—*how did they become* the enemy?—walk into certain death. *Go back, you stupid bastards . . .*

The Patriot Guards raised their axes, the officer watching from a few yards back.

"That's it," Giforte shouted. "Fire!"

The *crunch* of breaking glass came from all over the house, as one Mierantai in the pair at each window slammed his rifle butt against the windowpane. His companion leveled his rifle through the gap in the curtains, took aim for a moment, then fired. A staccato series of *crack*s echoed weirdly through Willowbrook's rooms.

The three men at the door, who'd lowered their axes at the sound of breaking glass, collapsed instantly. Behind them, the officer's head snapped back, spraying blood and brains, and he took a single involuntary step before collapsing nervelessly to the gravel. More balls raised splinters from the wagon, and at least one found one of the horses, who started to rear and thrash desperately in its harness. Shouts from the sides and rear of the house indicated the volley was having an effect there, too.

"Fire! Fire!" someone outside screamed as the rifle shots died away. The Patriot Guards obeyed, sliding their muskets out from behind the wagons and blazing away at the house. Balls pattered and *thocked* into the facade, like hail falling into stiff mud. As they loaded, the second man in each pair of Mierantai leaned out and fired, and Marcus saw several men fall drunkenly away from the wagon and sprawl in the street. Smoke boiled from most of the windows of the house and around the hedgerows that surrounded it.

It was a patently unequal contest, Marcus could see at once. It was hard to see how many Patriot Guards there were, but he doubted it was as many as a hundred, spread around the house on four sides. Giforte had nearly that many Mierantai, and they held a much stronger position.

Further, the grounds of the house offered little cover—given how long the Mierantai had been here, Marcus doubted this was an accident—so the Patriot Guards were firing from the edges of the property, fifty or seventy-five yards away. At that range, their smoothbore muskets were a distinct disadvantage against the long Mierantai rifles; while the larger weapons were clumsy and awkward to reload, they were much more accurate over any distance, a fact that the Mierantai were proving with deadly efficiency.

"I don't see the old woman," Raesinia said.

"Or Ionkovo." A thought occurred belatedly to Marcus. "Damn, he could be inside the house. He can turn invisible and walk through walls, or something like that. I have to warn Giforte."

Raesinia nodded, and they left the window and hurried together down the main stairs. Feor was just emerging from the basement, with her students in tow: Auriana, white-haired and limping, and the young man she'd called Justin.

"Giforte!" Marcus called. "I thought of something. You remember Ionkovo?"

When Giforte nodded, Marcus explained about his second encounter with the Penitent Damned.

"I'd keep a few men back to watch out for surprises," Marcus concluded.

Giforte nodded. "Good plan." He looked at Feor and Raesinia, then pulled Marcus aside and spoke quietly. "We're going to have to try a breakout."

Marcus grimaced. "You seem to be holding them."

"There's too many for us to pick off from here, though. And you can bet they sent a runner screaming for help. This place isn't a fortress—if they get any kind of gun up here, they'll bring it down around our ears."

Marcus pictured cannonballs tearing through wood-and-plaster walls and nodded. "What about the Names?"

"I don't think we have any choice but to leave them." Giforte shook his head. "You know all this nonsense better than I do, and you know Janus. Are a bunch of Khandarai artifacts that critical?"

"I think so," Marcus said thoughtfully. "But we're not going to be able to get them out with us, and you're right, we can't just stay here. I think we may have to count on coming back for them."

"That sounds more possible," Giforte said, brightening. "We can keep an eye on the place and jump the Patriots if they try to move them."

"Which way are we breaking out?"

"Toward the back. There's a garden path there that leads down to the Dregs. We should be able to get clear pretty quickly."

"I'll stay with Her Majesty," Marcus said. "Your people can handle the flik-flik team."

"Right." Giforte took a deep breath. "I'll give you the word when we're ready."

Raesinia was talking quietly to Feor. A bit belatedly, Marcus realized that all this business of combat and musketry, to which he'd long since become accustomed, represented a new world for her no matter how many clandestine exploits she'd had. He looked over her face, and found no trace of fear there. *Maybe being immortal makes it easier to get used to.*

"We cannot just *leave* them," Feor said. "You don't know what was sacrificed to get the archive here."

"We can't ask Giforte and his men to die to no purpose," Raesinia said. "We have to—"

Marcus was interested to know whether Raesinia had come to the same conclusions he and Giforte had, but she was interrupted by shouts from the front of the house. A sudden increase in the volume of rifle fire was followed by screams, and the splintery, rending crash of shattering wood.

The main hall, where they were standing, looked through an open foyer onto the front doors. Marcus saw them bow inward, wood cracking and sagging in its metal frame as though it had been hit by a battering ram. *Or a cannonball.* For a mad moment he thought the Patriot Guard had already gotten a gun in place, but they'd have heard the report—

Another blow tore the doors apart, fragments of wood

spinning away and metal bands peeling back. They shuddered open, and through the battle smoke a huge figure loomed. Four Mierantai, who'd backed away from the windows and shouldered their rifles, all fired at once; at such close range they could hardly miss, but the figure didn't flinch. Two huge strides covered the distance separating it from the soldiers, and it grabbed the closest rifle, tore it from the owner's hands, and swung it into the next man like a club. The impact snapped the weapon in two and sent the soldier flying across the hall.

It was a huge man, all in black. Smoke clung to the giant, blowing off him like steam. When he turned to regard Marcus and the others, his face was hidden behind a dark mask, covered with glittering fragments of black glass.

"*Abh-naathem,*" Feor said. Her voice was barely a whisper.

"Giforte," Marcus roared. "Break out *now*!"

Giforte shouted orders at the Mierantai. More men appeared on the stairs, and more rifles fired. Marcus could see the balls striking home with little puffs of dust and torn cloth, but they bothered the giant no more than flea bites. He snatched up another soldier in one hand and *squeezed*, the *crunch* of breaking ribs audible even over the firefight, then flung the spasming victim aside. As the rest scrambled out of the way, he focused on Raesinia, and the glass on his face shifted as though he was grinning under the mask. The floor shook as he stepped forward.

"Mistress!" Auriana said, moving to stand between the apparition and Feor. "Run!"

"No!" Feor's voice was thick with despair. Justin, her other student, grabbed her by the arm and dragged her back toward the kitchen, and Marcus and Raesinia followed suit.

Auriana raised her hand, and the giant suddenly paused. He leaned forward and took another step, straining as though walking into a heavy wind. His back foot, digging in for purchase, broke through a floorboard with a *crunch*.

"No . . . ," Feor moaned, looking over her shoulder.

"Can she hold him?" Marcus said.

"She's not strong enough—"

Auriana looked back at them. Her face was a crimson mask, blood pouring from her nose and the corners of her eyes.

"Mistress, *run*." Her voice was a bubbly rasp.

"Marcus!" Giforte shouted. "Come on!"

There was firing in the backyard. Giforte had gathered two dozen Mierantai, and they charged the thin cordon of Patriot Guard hiding in the back hedges. Several were hit by musketry as they ran, but the Guards took to their heels before their opponents reached them. Lieutenant White and several of his flik-flik crew, sacks of equipment on their back, followed at a dead run.

Marcus took hold of Raesinia's arm in one hand and Feor's in the other, and ran, Justin keeping up behind them. A rear guard of Mierantai followed, while the second floor of the house still spit and fumed rifle fire, keeping the Patriot Guards hunkered down. A piercing scream cut through the battle racket, and Marcus knew the monstrous Penitent had broken through Auriana's desperate defense.

Giforte, ahead, was beyond a small gate in the hedge and waving frantically. Marcus and his two charges reached it just as the kitchen door of the house exploded, bits of doorframe flying into the yard as the giant shouldered his way through.

"Just run!" Marcus shouted.

But the rear guard was already turning, rifles lowered and bayonets fixed. A volley crashed out, balls *pocking* the wood around the door and scoring again and again on the monster. His huge head snapped back, and Marcus could see a strip of the black mask hanging loose where a ball had torn it, with a smudge of red underneath.

Marcus ran, following Giforte and the flik-flik team. As the captain had said, the hedge door led onto an alley, twisting between the rear walls and hedges of other estates. Screams from behind them indicated that the Penitent was in pursuit.

"Giforte!" Marcus said. The captain slowed enough for

him to pull alongside, breathing hard. "We'll lead him off, through one of these other yards. You get clear!"

"But—"

"White and the others will never outrun him!" The flik-flik team was visibly flagging under the weight of their equipment. "He wants Raesinia. We'll draw him off and try to lose him. You have to get word to Janus."

Giforte considered only for a moment, then gave a quick nod. "Good luck!"

We're going to need it. Marcus drew up short, and Raesinia skidded to a halt beside him. Feor stopped, too, with Justin trailing behind her like a kite.

"Did you catch that?" Marcus said to Raesinia.

"Most of it." She wasn't even winded. "It's a good plan."

"You two should go with Giforte—" Marcus began, turning to Feor.

At that moment, though, the Penitent burst through the hedge, enormous strides devouring the distance between them. *Too late.* Raesinia gave him a cheery wave and ducked through the nearest open gate, onto the elaborately landscaped grounds of the elderly manor house. Marcus, Feor, and Justin went after her.

"We'll never outrun him," Marcus said. The giant's head was visible over the hedge, coming closer preposterously fast. "If you take Feor and stay hidden while I run the other way—"

"What did I *tell* you?" Raesinia said, turning and planting herself in plain view. "*I'll* draw him off, *you* hide."

"But—"

"I can't fucking die, Marcus."

"They can stuff you in a barrel and ship you off to Elysium," Marcus said. "I can't let that happen."

Raesinia looked up at him, then at Feor, jaw set. "I—"

The hedge gate was ripped from its hinges, and the giant stepped through, turning sideways to fit between the close-set plants. He'd been hit by so many rifle balls that his black clothes were in tatters, and blood dripped from his fingers. Marcus couldn't tell if it was his or his victims'.

I can't leave her. That was what it came down to. *She's the queen, and I'm a soldier. And—*

He drew his saber, setting himself in front of Raesinia.

"He's bleeding," he said. "That means he can be killed."

"Marcus!"

The Penitent Damned nodded, as though acknowledging a challenge, and lumbered into a run. Marcus raised his blade, ready to throw himself to one side. He didn't seriously expect to survive the first few moments of the confrontation, but he wasn't going to make it easy.

Raesinia . . .

Wind, sudden and hot, hissed through the manicured garden. It had a smell that Marcus knew, taking him across thousands of miles in an instant. It was the sandy, dry scent of air that had been baked under the sun of the Great Desol, the smell of the east wind in Ashe-Katarion, blowing sand and grit off the desert through the streets of the city. And there was sand in the air now, impossibly, whipping against Marcus' skin and lodging in his beard. He closed his eyes for a moment against the stinging onslaught and took a step backward.

When he opened his eyes again, the giant had stopped, surrounded by a cloud of flying sand that thickened by the moment. It swirled around the huge man in waves, a dust devil that rose out of nowhere to engulf the Penitent in a whirlwind of blown grit. The giant lashed out, trying to push through the cloud, but his punches met nothing solid. Whenever he tried to take a step, the sand thickened, shoving against him and driving him back.

"I can't hold him for long." The voice spoke in Khandarai, and Marcus thought it was just on the edge of familiarity, like someone he'd known in another life. He turned away from the giant, and froze.

"You're dead," he managed. "You're not even *real*."

The man standing behind him, in the midst of another swirl of spinning sand, wore the traditional loose brown garments of the Desoltai tribes, with dark gloves on his hands and his hair hidden under a black cloth. His face was concealed behind a mask, a simple metal oval with square slits for eyes and mouth but otherwise featureless.

"Malik-dan-Belial," Feor said, with something like awe. *The Steel Ghost.*

Marcus knew him. Or knew the mask, which in the end was all there *was* to know. The Steel Ghost had been a *trick*, an illusion, a bogeyman the desert tribes had created out of a mask and a costume to frighten invaders. In the end, his legendary sorcery had been nothing more than a clever means for flashing messages from one place to another, the "language of light" that Janus had used as the basis for the flik-flik system.

But the sand that rolled around him now was no illusion, nor was the force of the wind holding the massive Penitent in place.

"I have done my best to keep the shadow priest in check," the Steel Ghost said. "But there are too many *abh-naathem* in the city now. You must stop them, d'Ivoire." The blank mask turned to Raesinia. "Keep the queen safe. Retrieve the Thousand Names. I will help where I can, but my power—" The giant threw himself against the whirlwind, and the Steel Ghost flinched. "My power has limits."

"Who *are* you?" Marcus said. "You're not—I don't—"

"We share an enemy, but we are not allies. The *abh-naathem*'s ambition has no limit, and they must be stopped before they undo the work of a thousand years and bring ruin to us all. That is all you need to know."

"Marcus?" Raesinia said. "What is he saying? Marcus!"

"Go now," the Ghost grated. "I will keep this one here as long as I can."

"He says we should run," Marcus said in Vordanai. He took hold of Feor and Raesinia and dragged them after him a few steps, until they got the message. Justin, eyes wide, held Feor's other hand.

"But—" Raesinia began.

"Later!"

Marcus led them around the side of the house. Ahead was the Dregs, crowded even in wartime. But there were

Patriot Guards there, too, moving down the street in small groups. Word of the breakout had clearly gotten around.

"Now what?" Raesinia said.

"Back to Mrs. Felda's," Marcus said, eyes tracking the guards. "If we can."

"What about Giforte?" Feor said.

Marcus looked over his shoulder. They'd drawn off the Penitent Damned, but the city was still full of Patriot Guards. There was no way of knowing whether Giforte and his men had made it to their forest bolt-hole without going after them, and that might bring down even more attention.

"He'll have to manage on his own," Marcus said. "Right now we need a very deep hole to hide in."

Chapter Nineteen

WINTER

It took some doing, but they managed to suggest to General de Ferre that—in accordance with the generally accepted rules of civilized war—it would be only fair to offer the Hamveltai a chance to surrender before beginning the assault. The general grudgingly conceded this, but insisted on issuing orders drawing up the attack formations while the ultimatum was delivered to the fortress and a response awaited.

Winter had been worried that the general would insist on writing the note himself, but it happened that de Ferre spoke no Hamveltai, so the task was delegated to Fitz Warus. It therefore agreed with the story they'd given Anne-Marie to carry the night before, saying that—*against* all the generally accepted rules of civilized war—the fortress had one hour to capitulate, and that if no surrender was received, not only would it face an assault but no quarter would be offered to prisoners or even civilians.

Of Anne-Marie herself, there'd been no sign since the previous evening. Winter had no idea whether she'd been taken in as a guest, as a prisoner, or even had her head mounted on a pike. It gnawed at her as she drew up the Royals and the Girls' Own, in accordance with de Ferre's orders, in two compact columns facing the southeast section of the fortress.

That the assault would be a disaster was obvious even to Winter, who was no student of siege warfare. While not as intimidating as the high walls of a medieval castle, the defenses of Antova were formidable. Instead of solid stone, the "walls" were layers of defenses. First there was a slight rise to deflect incoming cannonballs, then a ditch with an earth rampart behind it, topped by wooden barricades and studded with slits for firing. Beyond *that* was a narrow track, followed by an even deeper ditch and a higher mound of earth, rising to the parapets themselves, which were crenellated in brick and lined with cannon.

To reach the top, Winter's soldiers would have to cross the open field at a run, struggle over the first ditch and up the wall. Having reached the lane, they would once again be in the open, facing the deadly close-range fire on the next line of defenders, and an even taller wall to scale. To make matters worse, the star-shaped design of the whole affair meant that each side of the fort was in easy range of at least one other side, so the attacking force would be taking fire from behind as well as ahead.

De Ferre was confident that di Pfalen's men were demoralized, after their succession of defeats, which Winter didn't doubt was true. But it didn't take much morale to stand behind a rampart shooting down helpless enemies. *Even de Ferre must see that this will be a bloodbath.* If the general could see it, now that he'd had time to inspect Dreiroede's masterpiece, he refused to admit any error. The minutes of the hour's grace he'd given the Hamveltai ticked away, and the moment of the assault approached.

Winter, standing in front of the line, looked at the assembled ranks of the Royals and the Girls' Own. They'd grown somewhat fuller since the battle, bolstered by recovering casualties and stragglers who'd caught up or been brought in by the wagons. The men and women in the front rank were staring at the defenses, and no doubt making the same mental assessment Winter was.

Will they go, if I tell them to? She was almost certain they would. *Why?* It was idiotic—*anyone* could see it was idiotic. Some would go because they were afraid of being disciplined, others because they didn't want to look like cowards in front of their fellow soldiers. *But mostly they'll go because they think I know what I'm doing. They trust that, if I give the order, it must not be certain death after all.*

It was that kind of faith—in her, but most of all in Janus' guiding hand—that had held the Army of the East together. And it was about to be broken beyond repair, thousands of lives thrown away for the pride of a puffed-up nobleman. *Janus is right. This will be the end of the campaign.* It wasn't just the casualties. *If this assault goes forward, even if we take the walls, the army will never fight again. Not for de Ferre.*

"Sir," Cyte said. Forty minutes had passed. "If we don't get word, are we going forward?"

"We have our orders."

"A lot of the volunteer officers talked about refusing."

"They'll go." Winter's voice was bleak. "Nobody wants to be the only one to disobey. They'll go, until the wheels come off the cart, and then it'll be too late."

"Then we should be the first," Cyte said, low and urgent. "This is suicide. It's a thousand yards to the wall, under all those heavy guns. Half the soldiers won't even reach the first ditch!"

"I *know.*" Winter bit her lip, hard enough to draw blood. "But if we're the first, God alone knows what de Ferre will do. He'd be within his rights to have every officer shot." Winter herself, of course, most of all.

"Better a few dozen of us than a thousand rankers," Cyte said, but her voice was tight. "You can't do this."

Winter looked, instinctively, for Jane. But Jane was over with the Girls' Own, beside Abby. It wasn't where she was supposed to be—as a staff officer, she belonged out front at Winter's side—but Winter couldn't bring herself to reprimand her. *And anyway, I know what she'd say. We should march the regiment in the other direction and never look back.*

"Sir!" Bobby was running along the line, waving. For a horrible moment, Winter thought she'd mistaken the time, and that this was the order to attack. She'd left Bobby with Fitz and the Colonials, where de Ferre had his command post, so she could bring any new developments.

"What is it?" Winter said, trying and failing to keep the anxiousness from her voice.

"Truce flag on the walls, sir. The fortress wants to parley."

Winter could *hear* the news spread through the ranks, as those close enough to eavesdrop repeated it to their companions. A kind of collective exhalation of breath spread through them, nearly two thousand men and women relaxing simultaneously. If they were going to die, it wouldn't be *quite* yet.

"Sevran!" she said. "Give Bobby twenty men, and you're in command until we get back. Bobby, come with me. I need to see this."

"Yes, sir!"

Winter attached herself to the truce party by the simple expedient of turning up and offering to provide the general's escort. Fitz, who was coming along as translator, made no objection, and though a sour look crossed de Ferre's face at the sight of Winter, he didn't bother to overrule her. Bobby arrayed the twenty Royals in two lines, on either side of the party of senior officers, and they walked out from the waiting ranks of the Colonials. Antova's main gate was directly ahead, a road passing over the ditches by two removable bridges, leading to a stone gatehouse with massive, iron-banded doors. A white flag waved from the parapets, and a moment later the doors swung ponderously outward, revealing a group of elaborately uniformed Hamveltai officers followed by a dozen yellowjackets in tall shakos.

The two groups met halfway between the Vordanai lines and the fortress walls, within easy cannon-shot of both sides. Winter didn't know how to read the Hamveltai insignia, but judging by the amount of gold braid and decorations pinned to his chest, the white-haired man in the lead was di Pfalen himself. His right arm hung limp in a sling, and his face was tight and puffy from pain and lack of sleep. Carrying himself with obvious effort, he looked over the Vordanai party and spoke in Hamveltai. Winter could more or less decipher this, but de Ferre was obviously in complete ignorance.

"Which one of you is Vhalnich?" di Pfalen said.

Fitz took a step forward, bowed, and asked in Vordanai, "Do any of you speak Vordanai?"

There was a bit of muttering and head-shaking from the Hamveltai officers. Fitz nodded, switched smoothly into Hamveltai, and went on. "Then I will translate for the general. Is that acceptable?"

Di Pfalen grunted approval. "Then this is Vhalnich?"

"He wishes to speak to General Vhalnich," Fitz said to de Ferre.

"Tell him Vhalnich is no longer in command here. I'm the one he has to deal with now," de Ferre said.

"General de Ferre has replaced General Vhalnich in command of the Army of the East," Fitz repeated dutifully.

Another round of muttering. Winter's heart leapt when she heard one of the officers say, "It's true, then!" *Our message must have gotten through.*

"The terms presented in your note," di Pfalen said, "go against every principle of civilized war. I must protest in the very strongest terms."

"He isn't happy we've asked them to surrender," Fitz said to de Ferre.

"He's not meant to be happy. Tell him I want to get this over with one way or the other," de Ferre said.

Fitz turned back to the Hamveltai. "The general says he meant what he wrote. We demand your immediate surrender, or else you face an immediate assault."

Di Pfalen's mustache twitched. "You're bluffing. You'd lose thousands just getting to the walls."

"He thinks you're not serious," Fitz said to de Ferre.

"Not serious, am I?" De Ferre advanced a step and waved a finger under di Pfalen's nose. "Tell him to turn around and step back inside his little castle if he wants to see how serious I am. And if he insults my courage again, I'll slug him, white flag or no white flag."

"The general says," Fitz translated for the wide-eyed di Pfalen, "that casualties mean nothing to him. Ours, or yours. He says he is quite prepared for the battle to start right here." Fitz swallowed, and did a good impression of someone who was terrified. "I suggest you don't test him on this point. He has quite a temper."

Di Pfalen spun and spoke to his officers, voice low and urgent. Winter caught, "Mad! The man must be mad!" and "Can't be bluffing. We heard their men marching in."

"Eh? What's going on?" de Ferre said.

"I think you've disconcerted them," Fitz said. "They're considering your offer."

Finally, looking a bit ashen, di Pfalen turned back to the Vordanai.

"If we surrender," he said, "we require guarantees of safety for all ranks, as well as for the personal property of officers."

"Agreed," Fitz said. "Your men will surrender their arms and all equipment within the fortress intact, and give their parole not to fight against the Vordanai for a period of one year. All who agree will be permitted to depart immediately, with provisions and personal property."

"What?" de Ferre said.

"Done," di Pfalen said, looking pained. "But you should know that as soon as I return home, I intend to publish an account of your tactics. The world will know of your infamy."

"Is he insulting me again?" De Ferre raised a fist. "Tell him to step up, if he's half a man."

"The general accepts your surrender," Fitz extemporized to di Pfalen, "and, if you are unhappy with the terms, extends an invitation to personal combat, armed or unarmed, as you choose."

"Mad!" one of the other Hamveltai officers said. "A bloody mad dog!"

Di Pfalen himself bowed at a shallow, correct angle and turned away. The other Hamveltai fell in behind him, leaving de Ferre looking deeply confused.

"Warus? What happened?"

"They offered their surrender, sir," Fitz said. "The fortress is ours."

"Surrender? Really?" De Ferre looked back at the waiting ranks of Vordanai troops. "Well, I suppose it's for the best, but you wouldn't catch me giving in so easily." He sounded almost disappointed.

"Fitz," Winter said when they were back in the safety of their own lines, "I could kiss you. That was fucking *brilliant*."

"I think di Pfalen was ready to topple," Fitz said. "I don't blame him, with what he's been through. I just gave him a little push."

He smiled modestly. Winter, bouncing on her heels with released tension, fought a strong urge to hug him.

Around them, cheers and shouts were spreading, and the formations were breaking up as the news spread. Men less reticent than Winter tossed their muskets away and hugged one another, or sat down heavily in the brown grass, or professed disappointment and boasted about what they would have accomplished. Across the way, white flags were rising from other places along the fortress walls.

"I'd better get things organized," Fitz said, watching the Colonials celebrate. "There're several thousand men in there who need to give their parole, not to mention all the equipment."

"Go ahead. I'm going to give my people the news."

A surging crowd was forming around them, and Fitz turned away and started shouting orders against a background of cheers and backslapping. Winter fought her way through the press and found Bobby and her escort of Royals waiting, all of them grinning from ear to ear. They jogged back to where they'd left the rest of the regiment, only to find that the news had outrun them. Girls' Own and Royals had mixed into a single joyous cacophony of self-congratulation.

Cyte hurried up to her, pushing through the close-packed soldiers. "It worked?"

"It fucking worked!" Winter shook her head. "I don't believe it. Di Pfalen was a little angry about our 'infamy.'"

"He's going to be even angrier when he finds out we don't have half the men we said we did," Cyte said.

"Fitz is already working on it. By the time they figure out they've been tricked, we'll have all the guns."

"Thank God," Cyte said. She let out a long breath, looking up at Winter, then shook her head. "You should see Jane."

Winter nodded, patted Cyte on the shoulder, and moved off through the crowd. Abby and Jane were together in the middle of a knot of cheering Girls' Own soldiers, but the press melted away as the women caught sight of Winter, shoving each other aside to clear a path for her. Winter trotted past, and they closed up again behind her, cheering.

Jane's face was drawn, and there was something odd in her eyes. She tried to say something, but even leaning close Winter couldn't make it out above the tumult. In lieu of speech, she simply drew Jane close, wrapping her arms around her. Then, with sudden mad elation—*everyone already knows, even if they've got the genders wrong*—she tugged Jane's head around and kissed her, prompting another wave of cheers and whistles from the women in the crowd.

Jane's lips were soft and warm, but Winter could feel a reluctance in her that made her pull back.

Are you all right? she mouthed. Jane blinked, and shook her head.

"Colonel! Hey, Colonel!"

Winter turned to find the tall form of Jo beside her, accompanied by the diminutive Barley. The latter's voice was louder than it had any right to be, as though to make up for her companion's silence.

"Yes?" One did not normally address a superior as "Hey, Colonel!" but at the moment Winter was willing to forgive the lack of etiquette.

"What about Anne-Marie?" Barley shouted. "Is she back yet?"

"Not yet." Winter felt her elation deflate a little bit. *She's okay, I'm sure she's okay.* Even if the Hamveltai discovered her *now*, they'd hardly dare harm her while they were at the mercy of their enemies. "I'll tell Fitz to be on the lookout when he sends men into the fortress."

Barley nodded and Jo fixed Winter with a meaningful look. A moment later, they were swept away by the crowd, and the celebration went on, but Winter felt more than a little subdued. She was thinking beyond Anne-Marie, to what would come next, and was not at all sure she liked what she could see. *This isn't over yet.*

Winter meant to corner Jane and get her in private so she could vent whatever was bothering her, but Fitz arrived before she got the chance. The crowd was breaking up, lieutenants and sergeants herding their soldiers back to the camps to impose some kind of order. From the general mood, Winter guessed a few carefully hoarded bottles were going to be breached tonight, and she wouldn't be surprised if there was quite a bit of "fraternization" between (or within) the two battalions. *There's nothing quite like having mortal danger suddenly called off to put a new edge on living.*

Fitz drew congratulatory shouts from those who recognized him, though only a few did. He waved Winter over, and his expression was worrying.

"Something wrong?" she said.

"Not sure," he said. "The occupation is going all right. Janus and I have everything laid out. But he sent me away and said I should tell you he wants to see you as soon as possible."

That *did* sound ominous. "Where's de Ferre?"

"Last I heard, planting our flag on the battlements and

personally receiving di Pfalen's sword. If he follows the plan I laid out for him, he'll be busy for hours."

"That's something." Winter looked around. Abby and Sevran seemed to have things well in hand, so it was unlikely her presence would be urgently required in the near future. "I'll see what he wants, then."

"Good luck. Tell him to send for me if he needs me."

Winter trotted through the long arc of the camp, bending around the periphery of the looming, defanged fortress. Janus' tent was near the area occupied by the Colonials, but slightly apart from it, as befit the army commander. No one was on watch outside, so Winter rapped at the tent post. The gesture reminded her of the old days in Khandar; colonels didn't do much standing at the door of other people's tents.

"Colonel Ihernglass?" Janus said.

"Yes, sir. You wanted to see me?"

"Come in."

The tent was the same as before, except that someone had erected a tall lacquer folding screen in one corner, behind which Janus was changing. Winter let the tent flap fall and stood, somewhat awkwardly.

"I'm sorry," Janus said. "It's been a busy day."

"Yes, sir."

"I understand I have you to thank for our triumph this afternoon?"

"No, sir. I mean, only a little bit. Colonel Warus did the clever part."

"So I heard. But the idea, I think, was yours. I will happily admit that this time I thought the game was up. I owe you my thanks, and many of the men and women in the army owe you their lives."

Winter flushed a little and shook her head. "Anne-Marie—that is, Ranker di Wallach, sir—volunteered for an extremely dangerous mission. We couldn't have done it without her."

"I've heard that as well. I would nominate her for a decoration, except that we haven't got any at the moment.

The Deputies-General got as far as abolishing the old royal orders, but a set of new Republican commendations appears to have bogged down in committee."

"Have you heard anything about Anne-Marie, sir?"

"Not yet. But it's a bit chaotic in there. We've made it clear that nobody is to be harmed, and they haven't admitted to mistreating any of our prisoners."

Winter nodded, realized Janus couldn't see her, and said, "That's good, sir."

There was a moment's pause, and the leathery sound of a belt being drawn tight.

"Have you read Goekhol, Colonel?"

Winter blinked. "I can't say that I have, sir."

"You should. There was a time when I thought that one could learn everything one needed to know about the military arts from his *On War*. My perspective has expanded a bit since then, but . . ." He sighed. "In any event, in *On War*, Goekhol describes the perfect battle, the perfect victory."

"Is there such a thing, sir?" Winter thought about the aftermath of some of her victories.

"In a manner of speaking." Janus emerged from behind the screen. He was wearing his dress uniform, crisp regulation blue with gold braid and silver stars on his shoulders. A dress sword, so small Winter doubted it was functional, swung at his hip. "Goekhol wrote that just as war is the last resort of statesmen, combat should be the last resort of generals. A great general would only fight when the outcome is a foregone conclusion. And a *perfect* general would outmaneuver his enemy so utterly, leave the position so completely hopeless, that the futility of fighting would be obvious to even the most dim-witted foe. The perfect victory is the battle that is decided before it is even fought, and therefore never needs to be fought at all."

"I see," Winter said. "Certainly to be preferred from the perspective of the soldiers in the ranks."

"History is a strange beast, Colonel. Goekhol is remembered as a warmonger, because he wrote about how to fight wars efficiently and with as little suffering as possible. Vou-lenne wrote *The Rights of Man*, in which he says that men are born with a right to happiness and self-determination, and is remembered as a peacemaker even though his words have caused God knows how much death and destruction." He cocked his head. "Do you wonder what they'll write about you?"

"Nothing, if I'm lucky," Winter said. "Or maybe, 'She died at age ninety-nine, a wealthy and comfortable woman.'"

Janus grinned, just for an instant, gray eyes sparkling. "Well said. We should all be so lucky."

"I think you're more in danger from historians than I am, sir."

"Probably." He stared into the distance, as though he could see through the walls of the tent and the detritus of the camp, all the way to the horizon. "Would it surprise you if I said I don't particularly care?"

"Nothing you say is going to surprise me, at this point."

"If they knew . . . if the historians knew what *I* know, I think they'd be appalled. So much blood, for such a small thing. One raindrop in the river of history." He sighed. "Fortunately, I don't plan to tell them. No doubt they'll spin many entertaining theories, once we're all dead and gone."

He was silent a moment, adjusting the hang of his sword, and Winter felt compelled to speak.

"Sir? Is something wrong?"

"The next battle, Colonel. It is . . . not perfect. I have done my best, but I do not know if I see the way clear, and I find it lies heavy on me."

If it was anyone else, Winter would have said he sounded nervous. But this was Janus bet Vhalnich. "Nervous" didn't apply to him. "What battle, sir? With Jindenau?"

Janus laughed. "Oh no. No, the great field marshal will no doubt scuttle back to Hamvelt with his tail between his legs. The campaign in the east is over, though I doubt anyone yet realizes that but you and me. The next battle will be quite different."

"Then—"

"Vhalnich!" It was de Ferre's voice, loud and imperious.

"He's not supposed to be back yet," Winter said. "I should probably leave you alone, sir—"

"I suspect," Janus said very quietly, "that if you were to step outside you would be very unpleasantly surprised."

"Sir?"

"I recommend you take cover behind the dressing screen," Janus said. "And be very quiet."

"I—"

"*Now*, Colonel."

"Yes, sir." His tone of authority was such that Winter only barely managed to stop herself from coming to attention and saluting. She dodged around him and put herself behind the lacquered screen, using the edge of the camp bed to conceal her feet where a gap at the bottom might make them visible from the tent flap. She could see, just barely, through a crack between the sections.

"Yes, General?" Janus said, once Winter was concealed.

"So you are in there." De Ferre pushed the tent flap aside and straightened up. Two men accompanied him—not officers, Winter was surprised to see, but musket-bearing Patriot Guards. De Ferre looked over Janus' dress uniform with suspicion. "What do you think you're doing?"

Janus shrugged. "I was expecting . . . something like this. Although not quite so promptly."

"Ha! I can tell when I'm being run around the bush." De Ferre ran a finger along his mustache. "Did you put the Warus boy up to that?"

"Of course not, sir."

"Doesn't matter, I suppose." De Ferre drew himself up. "Count Janus bet Vhalnich Mieran, you are hereby summoned to testify before the Directory for the National Defense, to answer charges of high treason."

"Ah," Janus said, showing no sign of surprise. "I'm to be permitted a defense, then?"

De Ferre grinned nastily. "The president always lets

his generals have their say before he sends them to the Spike. You'll be joining Hallvez and the others who got too big for their boots, while I clean up the mess you've left behind."

"I think you'll find the Army of the East in excellent condition."

"Really?" De Ferre snorted. "You've got a battalion of *women*, for God's sake. I'll send *them* home where they belong. And the proper soldiers are mixed up with the hangers-on and vagabonds. Sorting all that out is going to take weeks." The general paused. "You're awfully calm, for a man who's just been told he's going to be spiked. Have you got ice in your veins? Or do you not think I mean it?"

"I'm sure you mean it."

"I hope you're not counting on any of your men to help you. That would be high treason for all concerned." De Ferre leaned forward. "Not to mention, they're all too busy getting drunk, which is why you're leaving tonight. Didn't expect *that*, did you?"

"A masterstroke," Janus murmured. "Sir."

"We'll see how calm you are when you get to the city," de Ferre said, obviously disappointed by the lack of reaction. "By all the saints, I'm sorry I won't be there to see your smug face when they finally strap you to the Spike."

Janus sighed, straightening his shoulders and subjecting de Ferre to the full force of his dispassionate gaze. Even in his moment of triumph, the general couldn't help flinching slightly.

"You're a fool, de Ferre," Janus said. "I would say I expected better of you, but it would be a lie. You've played the part Maurisk assigned you to perfection, and when it's finished I expect he'll sweep you up with the rest of the trash."

De Ferre's cheeks went red. "You—you *dare*! I could have you shot!"

"I don't think you could." Janus grinned at de Ferre. "I have an appointment with the Directory for the National Defense."

"Very funny." De Ferre turned to the guards. "Watch him until it gets dark. We'll move him then."

They saluted, and the general turned on his heel and stalked from the tent. The two Patriot Guards took up station on either side of the flap, staring pointedly at Janus, who sighed and sat down at his folding table.

Behind the screen, Winter had been watching the exchange, full of a paralyzing mixture of rage and fear of discovery. Now that de Ferre was gone, rage was rapidly winning out, and she gauged her chances carefully. *If I knock the screen over, I could clear the bed and be on them before they can fire. Get the musket away from the first one, shoot the other. Then—what?*

"Then what?" was the basic problem. De Ferre was keeping Janus' arrest secret, which meant that he didn't trust the army to swallow it without question. But if Winter started shooting Patriot Guards, and de Ferre ordered the troops to stop her, would they? *Depends on the troops.* She could rely on the Girls' Own, and probably the Royals, if they understood what was going on well enough. The rest of the colonels were loyal to Janus, but how loyal? *More to the point, de Ferre won't tell them what's happening. All he needs is to fire a few volleys into the confusion and express his regrets afterward.*

It's too dangerous. I need help. She took a deep breath and backed away from the screen. *Which means I have to get out of here.*

She turned to the wall of the tent behind her. It was a finer fabric than the standard cheap army-issue canvas, no doubt purchased by the late Augustin with his master's comfort in mind. She drew her belt knife and poked a hole in it at head height, bunching the fabric in one hand and moving slowly so as not to make too much noise.

Behind her, something started to rattle noisily. It took her a moment to place the sound: Janus was washing the dregs out of his teapot. *He is a damned genius, isn't he?* With the racket as cover, she drew the knife down sharply, parting the bunched fabric into a slit wide enough for her to wriggle through. There was a bad moment when her boot got tangled up with one of the tent ropes, and she thought she was going to fall, but she managed to end up on hands and knees and crawl clear.

No one was near enough to notice. Most of the camp, in fact, seemed empty, aside from distant sentries and a few details standing around cauldrons to get an early start on cooking dinner. Winter stood up, dusted herself off, and walked determinedly in the direction of the Girls' Own camp, trying to project the air of someone with something important to attend to.

"Hello, sir," said Bobby. She sat between the neat rows of tents, taking advantage of the waning daylight to scribble in a notebook. This part of the camp wasn't as abandoned as the rest—the women of the Girls' Own seemed to have the afternoon off, and they were taking their ease, talking, playing cards, or getting dinner started. There were no Royals to be seen, however.

"Fitz has most of the men in the fortress," Bobby explained as Winter looked around. "Processing the prisoners, taking inventory, making sure nobody sets a match to the powder magazine, that sort of thing. He said to tell you that he's sorry, but that he thought bringing the Girls' Own in might be too hard on Hamveltai pride, and he doesn't want them doing anything rash."

"That . . . makes sense." Winter kept her voice carefully neutral, aware how many people were in earshot. "I need to speak with as many officers as you can round up. Sevran's inside, I take it?"

"So is Cyte," Bobby said. "She volunteered. Abby and the others are over with Anne-Marie by the pots."

"Tell them—" Winter stopped. "Anne-Marie's back?"

"Oh!" Bobby shut her notebook and grinned. "I forgot you hadn't heard. She turned up just a little while after you left."

"She's all right?"

Bobby nodded. "Not a scratch. It worked perfectly, I gather."

Winter exhaled, feel a tiny sliver of relief. *That's something.* Though in the light of what she'd overheard, it might not mean much. "I'll find them, then. Meet you in my tent in five minutes."

"Yes, sir!" Bobby stood up. "Is something wrong?"

Winter shook her head. "Later."

She headed for the center of the camp, where the big iron cauldrons that boiled the regimental meals were kept. One of them had been overturned, and Anne-Marie was sitting on top of it, looking dainty perched on its black bulk. She still wore the torn green dress from the night before, but she appeared to have had a bath and a chance to work on her hair in the meantime. She was beaming down at the small crowd of women who'd gathered round, with Barley and Jo flanking her like honor guards.

"He was there when the sentries brought me in. The sergeant was very suspicious, but I started crying, and before I knew it the colonel was telling off the sergeant for mistreating a lady. Then he threw his cloak over my shoulders, which I thought was a very nice gesture." The crowd laughed, and someone whistled. "He took me up to his quarters—it's a little town in there, you know, very civilized—and asked me what had happened. Well, I had my story all ready, about a Vordanai officer who'd plucked me up on the street in Desland and treated me *ever* so roughly on the march. I may have been sobbing a little. By the time I was done he was practically a puddle on the floor, and he asked me what this man's name was so he could seek him out and kill him in the battle."

"And you spent the night?" someone called out from the crowd.

"*I* did," Anne-Marie said primly. "He slept on a sofa in the foyer."

Everyone roared with laughter, Anne-Marie included. When she caught sight of Winter, she waved, feet kicking against the side of the cauldron like a little girl's.

"Sir! A Hamveltai colonel has asked me to marry him." She grinned. "Do you think I should accept?"

"That's an attractive offer," Winter said, forcing a smile

of her own. "He might not like having a soldier for a wife, though."

Anne-Marie put a finger to her cheek, making a show of being deep in thought, and then shrugged. "Oh well," she said. "In that case, the hell with him!"

Another explosion of laughter. Winter raised her voice over the tumult. "Captain Verity? Captain Giforte? Could I see you for a few moments, please?"

Abby and Jane struggled to the edge of the crowd. Abby was grinning, but Jane's expression remained troubled. They both saluted.

"Sir!" Abby said. "What's going on?"

"We need to talk. In private." Winter looked around suspiciously. "Now."

"Sir?" Abby looked confused, but Jane's eyes had gone grim.

Winter led them back to her own tent, where Bobby was waiting. They sat around the tiny folding table, the four of them more or less filling the little space to capacity. Winter took a deep breath, not sure how to begin.

"Sir?" Bobby said. "Has something happened?"

"I was speaking with Janus," Winter said slowly. "And then de Ferre showed up. He's had Janus arrested, to be brought to the capital and tried for treason. They're shipping him out tonight."

There was a hiss of indrawn breath. Jane lowered her head, fists tightening.

"He's going to disband the Girls' Own, too," Winter said. "Send us 'back where we belong.'"

"He can't be serious," Abby said. "They want to try *Janus* for treason? He's the only general who's been worth a damn!"

"Even if they try him," Bobby said, "it's not like there's any evidence. He'd be cleared in the end, wouldn't he?"

Winter shook her head. She remembered the Borelgai and Hamveltai "spies" who'd been hanged from the Cathedral, back when the Deputies-General had barely been formed. Somehow she didn't think the invention of a machine to make it more efficient had really improved the process.

Another, longer silence. Abby coughed.

"So," she said. "What are we going to do about it?"

Jane's fist shot out, slamming down on the table and making the ink bottle jump and rattle. Winter started, then turned to her, staring. Jane was breathing hard, and her eyes were wide.

"Winter," she said very quietly, "could we have a few moments alone?"

Winter looked from Bobby to Abby, then nodded.

"Bobby," she said, "go to the fortress and get Sevran and Cyte back here. Abby, see if you can spread the word among the lieutenants that no one is to get drunk tonight."

"Yes, sir!" Bobby shot to her feet and slipped outside. Abby followed more slowly, giving Jane a last look before withdrawing.

When their footsteps had receded, Winter reached across the table for Jane's clenched fist. Jane snatched it away, crossing her arms and looking up at Winter.

"You're going to *do something about it*," Jane said. "Aren't you?"

"I don't . . . I don't know." Winter shook her head. "We can't—"

"Don't lie to me. You will. You just haven't talked yourself into it yet." Jane looked down again. "I knew this would happen. I *knew* it."

"Knew *what* would happen?" Winter took a deep breath. "Jane, I don't understand. What's going on?"

"You don't see what he's done to you."

"Who?"

"Janus. General Janus bet *fucking* Vhalnich. How did you end up hearing all this?"

Winter briefly sketched what had happened, her hiding place behind the screen when de Ferre had stormed in.

"If de Ferre had seen me, he might have had me arrested, too," Winter concluded. "So Janus told me to hide."

"Of course he did. And so you heard just what he wanted you to hear."

"He wasn't expecting de Ferre to come back so soon. He said so himself!"

"Would you listen to yourself? Do you honestly think this was an *accident*?" Jane shook her head. "He set the whole thing up, because he *knows* that you'll go charging off to rescue him. He's got you eating out of his god-damned hand."

"That . . ." Winter paused. "If that's what he wanted, he could have just told me."

"Oh no." Jane put on a rictus grin. "This way is much better. You convince *yourself* that it's necessary. It's how he works."

"You barely know him!"

"I know the story *you* told me. The one where you went back into that temple and risked your life to summon a fucking *demon* to save him."

"I didn't know—"

"The one where he *sent* you to me, because he knew he needed the Leatherbacks on his side. And who comes charging to his defense, right when he needs us?"

"But you—"

"We marched ourselves half to death because you couldn't stand the thought of letting him down. Some of my girls are buried under a few feet of mud, somewhere on the road, because you didn't dare disappoint Janus bet Vhalnich."

Jane paused, gasping for breath. Winter felt her pulse throbbing in her skull.

"How long have you been thinking about this?" she said.

"Since Desland." Jane's voice was suddenly small. "Since you finally told me the truth. He's *using* you, Winter, and he's got you so wrapped up you'd hang for him and smile while you put your own head through the noose."

"That's . . ." Winter shook her head. "It's not like that."

"As soon as de Ferre arrived, I knew. The Directory

can't leave Janus to win any more victories, so now he has to turn on them. But it wouldn't look good, too much like making a grab for power. So he'll get *you* to do it, like he always does."

"It's not like that!" Winter said, more angrily than she would have liked. "I . . . respect Janus. I believe he wants what's best for the country, and for everyone under his command."

"More fool you," Jane said. "Is that what he wanted when he led the Colonials into the desert?"

"He needed the Thousand Names."

"For what?"

"*. . . If the historians knew what I know, I think they'd be appalled. So much blood, for such a small thing. One raindrop in the river of history.*"

Winter shook her head again, throat tight.

Jane gave a hollow laugh. "Now he needs you to save him again. All for the good of Vordan, of course."

"I'd do it for you," Winter said. "Or Bobby, or Cyte, or . . . or *any* of my friends. I wouldn't let de Ferre haul any of them away."

"Those are your *friends*. They would help you in return. Janus will use you until you're of no more value, then throw you away."

"How can you say that? He gave you back to me."

Jane rocked backward, gritting her teeth. "And how do you think I felt about that, when I found out? He brought us together, like he was a fucking playwright and we were the actors, because it was what the script needed. He couldn't have just *told* you where I was? Of course not."

Winter felt tears in her eyes, and blinked them angrily away. "What do you want me to do, then? Stay here with de Ferre?"

"*No.*" Jane sounded suddenly urgent, and she leaned in. "Winter, listen to me. This is our chance to get *out* of this, don't you see? You, me, everyone in the Girls' Own. De Ferre wants to be rid of us. We could be done with this, done with war and marching and dying."

"And do what?"

"Whatever we want! Go back to Vordan, or out into the country. Settle down and fucking raise pigs, if we want to. *Please*. I know he's got his hooks in deep, but *listen* to me." Jane was crying now. "This is the only chance we're going to get. If we don't get them out now, every one of those girls out there is going to end up like Chris or Min or any of the others. Because he's not going to *stop*."

"I can't do it," Winter said.

"That's Janus talking. You can! We can lose ourselves so thoroughly that not even the Black Priests will be able to find us. I know how. We—"

"It's not that." Winter shook her head. "It's not about Janus, not really. Think about it, Jane. Even if de Ferre let us go, what about the rest of the army? How long until he marches them on another suicide mission? Or until the Directory sends someone even worse?"

"*Fuck* the army. Fuck the Directory. Fuck all of them. It is *not your responsibility*, don't you understand? You don't have to care." Jane sucked in a long, shuddering breath. "Just because you weren't brave enough to save me doesn't mean you have to save the whole world to make up for it."

There was a long, pregnant pause.

"I'm sorry," Jane said. She curled in on herself, head cowed. "I shouldn't have said that. I'm sorry. Winter, please—"

There was a knock at the tent pole.

"Sir?" Bobby said from outside. "Sevran and Cyte are here, and Abby's on her way."

"Please," Jane whispered. "Please."

Winter looked at Jane in her blue uniform, red hair in gorgeous disarray, eyes bloodshot and sparkling with tears.

"She sees you pulling away from her," Abby had said. "Into this world of flags and drums and cannon, and she doesn't think she can follow."

"You've fallen in love with Janus bet fucking Vhalnich."

You don't have to care.

But I can't help it, can I?

"I can't," Winter said in a very small voice.

"Sir?" Bobby said again.

Jane stood up, rubbing furiously at her eyes. Winter held out a hand, but she batted it aside as she stalked past, out through the tent flap and past the startled group outside. Winter's hand dropped to the table and lay there like a dead thing.

"Sir?" Bobby said hesitantly. "Winter?"

Winter swallowed, and found her voice.

"I'd be grateful," she managed, "if you'd give me a minute or two. In fact, go and find Colonel Warus as well. Tell him it's an emergency, but don't let anyone else know." She looked down at herself. *Jane was right about one thing, at least. I know what I need to do. I just didn't want to admit it.* "We're going to need him."

The perfect victory, Winter thought, *is the battle you don't have to fight.*

She remembered Janus in Khandar, facing down the mutinous Colonials led by Adrecht Roston, and how the colonel had turned the whole situation to his own advantage with nothing more than a little guile. *And a bit of help from me, I suppose.* She'd thought about calling a similar meeting, but after her conversation with Jane she wasn't at all sure she could pull it off, and in any case the Army of the East was too large to gather that way.

Instead she'd gone to a few commanders she knew she could rely on. Fitz Warus and Give-Em-Hell, of course, had agreed eagerly, but their very eagerness had shaken her. *Is Jane right? Will we just do anything for Janus, and damn the consequences?* She'd expected Sevran to be more difficult, but he'd promised to get the support of the Royals and make sure his lieutenants were on board.

Last, and most critically, she'd gone to Abby. As Winter had feared, Jane had already been there, and Abby looked as shaken as Winter herself felt. Abby's expression was firm, however, and her voice steady.

"Jane's being an idiot," she said. "Which is hardly unprecedented. She's gone to sulk with some of the old Leatherbacks." Abby took a deep breath, steadying herself. "What do you need us to do?"

That, and some hasty planning, had led to this rocky hillside, a few miles outside the camp and well beyond the view of the outlying pickets. This was the road that led up to the pass; with the fall of Antova, the direct route back to Vordan City was open, as opposed to the roundabout trip through Desland and Essyle. A few days' travel through the gap in the Keth Range and a quick downstream river journey would see the Patriot Guards and their prisoner back in the capital.

Give-Em-Hell had volunteered to seize the carriage by force, vaulting from horseback to the driver's seat, but Winter had vetoed the idea. Instead she'd borrow a squadron of light cavalry, hard-riding men who'd mostly seen service in Khandar, equipped with stubby-looking carbines and fast horses. They'd left Give-Em-Hell with Fitz Warus, to execute the other half of the plan, and set off just before sunset through the Colonials' pickets.

There was still a great deal that could go wrong, and Winter chewed her lip as she waited. De Ferre might have been lying, or he could have been tipped off by their preparations. *If they send the carriage by another route, tonight is going to be bloody chaos.* She therefore felt a knot in her chest loosen when the sound of hoofbeats and rattling wheels reached her around the bend in the road.

She had her back to a huge pine tree, felled by the cavalry and dragged across the road to create a barricade. It smelled of needles and sap, and scratchy pine needles brushed against her every time she moved. Winter raised her head enough to see the road, and waited until the lanterns of the carriage came into view. Then she stood up, uniformed but unarmed, and waited.

They'd picked a stretch of road where the carriage would have plenty of time to brake—it wouldn't help anybody if the whole thing toppled over the hillside. The vehicle slewed to a halt in front of the barrier, horses sidestepping nervously as far as their harness would allow. The driver had the reins in one hand and a long-barreled shotgun in the other, and four escorting Patriot Guards rode alongside with muskets. They gathered in front of the pine and leveled their weapons when Winter stepped up to stand on the trunk.

"What's this? Who're you?" one of the escorts, a lieutenant, barked. He was obviously on edge, and his finger was already on the trigger of his long, unwieldy weapon.

"Colonel Winter Ihernglass, of the Third Infantry," Winter said. She held up her hands. "As you can see, the road is blocked."

"Not for long," the lieutenant said. "Ferrer, Gunter, hitch your horses to that mess and drag it out of the way." To Winter, he added, "*You*, get down and don't move."

"Before you do that, I suggest you look up at the hill," Winter said. "Carefully."

"Sir!" One of the Patriot Guards gestured wildly with his musket, making Winter wince.

On the hill, above the road, two dozen men in blue had risen to their knees, short-barreled weapons trained on the guards. Carbines might be less accurate at range, but the distance was barely twenty-five yards. The other side of the road was a steep drop, impassable to horses. The lieutenant's eyes went up to the cavalrymen and then back to Winter.

"You wouldn't dare," he said. "This is treason."

"Probably," Winter said agreeably. "But that's not *your* problem, is it?"

Sweat gleamed on the man's face. "General de Ferre instructed me to break through any resistance."

"You could try that," Winter said, trying to keep her tone calm. "And then some people are going to end up dead. That might include me, but it will *definitely* include you, because the men up there had instructions to leave no survivors once the shooting starts."

"I . . ." The musket wobbled.

"Think of it this way," Winter said. "If it's treason, I'll be punished for it in the end. No need for *you* to die, right here, if that's inevitable anyway. Why don't you and your men drop your weapons?"

There was a long, strained moment before the lieutenant uncocked his musket and tossed it on the ground. His men hastily followed suit.

Winter breathed out. "Lieutenant Corder? You can come down and secure the carriage."

Half of the cavalrymen put their weapons away and descended the slope, while the other half kept watch. Winter let them deal with the Patriot Guards. She went to the carriage door and opened it, to find Janus sitting calmly on a cushioned seat, reading from a thin volume. He marked his place with a ribbon as she entered, shut the book with a snap, and looked up.

"Colonel," he said. "Nicely executed, as always."

"Thank you, sir," she said, wishing he'd chosen another word. "Execution" was not something she wanted to think about at the moment.

"May I ask as to your next step?"

"The cavalry will get the carriage turned around, and we'll head back to the camp. By the time we get there, Fitz and Give-Em-Hell will have disarmed the rest of the Patriot Guards and taken de Ferre into custody."

"And after that?"

Winter shrugged. "After that I was hoping to leave it up to you. Sir."

"I see." Janus paused, looking briefly at the ceiling, and then turned back to Winter. "What about the rest of the army? What will they do?"

"If I'd tried to get them to come after you, I think there might have been a lot of arguments, and maybe some fighting. But if we can get you back and de Ferre under guard before they realize what's going on . . ." Winter shrugged. "They'll follow."

"Like most soldiers, I suspect." He patted the cushion opposite him. "You might as well have a seat, then."

Winter sat. Janus leaned back and closed his eyes, and she remained silent while the cavalrymen led the horses around and went through the tricky operation of turning the carriage on the narrow road. Before long they were heading back the way they had come, toward the river and Antova, with their Patriot Guard prisoners in tow.

"Sir?" Winter said.

"Hmm?" Janus said without opening his eyes.

"Was this the right thing to do?"

"Are you really expecting me to have an answer to that question, Colonel?"

Winter considered. "No. I suppose not."

"Well, then."

"May I ask another?"

"Of course," he said.

"You hid me in your tent on purpose, didn't you?"

Janus opened his huge gray eyes and stared at Winter in the semidarkness. "Yes."

"Why? If this is what you wanted, why didn't you just tell me?"

"He's using you, Winter, and he's got you so wrapped up you'd hang for him and smile while you put your own head through the noose . . ."

"It's . . ." Janus paused. "It is difficult to explain."

Winter said nothing.

"There is a way," he said eventually, "in which you are a better officer than I will ever be. I can lead an army, but I can never be a *part* of it. I am too . . . different." He sighed. "I think I see the way forward, and to me it seems so *obvious*, but somehow others fail to grasp it. It is something I have struggled with all my life.

"I think I know what to do now, and I thought that the army might support me. But if I was wrong, if I failed— as I have often failed—to understand the thoughts of other men, then the Army of the East would tear itself apart. I could not allow that.

"So I left the decision to you. You understand the . . . the *feelings* of the men and women in the ranks, in a way I do not. I presented the opportunity, confident that you would be able to exploit it if you felt it was the correct decision."

"What if I'd decided the other way?" Winter said.

Janus closed his eyes again. "Then they would have taken me to Vordan, and I'd probably have been executed in due course. I sent appropriate instructions to Colonel d'Ivoire against that eventuality."

There was another long silence.

"You said you know what to do," Winter said quietly. "So what happens next?"

Janus grinned, his smile there and gone again like summer lightning.

"What do you think, Colonel?" he said. "We're going home. All of us."

The carriage rattled to a halt beside the sentry line, where in spite of their efforts at secrecy a small crowd had gathered. Janus emerged first, and the sight of him drew cheers. Muskets waved in the air, fixed bayonets glinting dangerously.

They have no idea what the politics are, Winter thought, looking at the excited men. *They don't care about the Directory or the Deputies-General. All they know is that this man has always brought them victory.* With him to lead them, they'd smashed the vaunted armies of the Free Cities League and captured the impenetrable bastion of Antova without firing a shot.

Framed in the carriage doorway, Janus looked back at Winter and gave a slight nod, as if in thanks. Then he hopped down and, flanked by cheering Colonials, rejoined his army. It was only once most of the crowd had moved off that Winter saw Abby waiting, with a set to her jaw that meant that something had gone badly wrong.

She hopped down herself, stomach tight. Abby gave her a tight salute, which Winter waved away.

"I'm sorry, sir," Abby said. "I couldn't stop her."

"What's wrong?" Winter said. "Did de Ferre get warning? Is there fighting?"

"What?" Abby blinked. "Oh no. Nothing like that. The Patriot Guards practically fell over themselves to surrender. I think someone's been telling tall tales about the Girls' Own, because they looked like they expected us to rip their throats out with our teeth. De Ferre swears a lot,

but Graff stuck a sock in his mouth and that shut him up."
She swallowed. "No, it's Jane."

"Oh, saints and martyrs," Winter said. "Where is she?
I'll talk to her."

"She's gone," Abby said. "Along with a dozen of the
Leatherbacks, and as many horses. In the confusion,
nobody thought to stop her."

"Gone?" Winter shook her head, as though trying to
make the statement fit better. "Where would she go?"

"Away from the army," Abby said.

Away from Janus, Winter thought. *Away from me.*

PART FOUR

THE GRAY ROSE

The grounds of Clover-by-Ost stretched from the house itself—a four-story, multiturreted thing—down toward the river, widening as they went to encompass a considerable stretch of bank. There were rolling, gently sloped meadows, cobbled lanes that snaked back and forth to take in the most breathtaking views, and little clumps of carefully tended trees surrounded by artfully deployed "wild" flowers. Most of the plants were brown and dead now, of course, and the picnic umbrellas had been stored for the season, but it was still warm enough to make for a pleasant evening walk when it wasn't raining.

Sothe didn't walk because it was pleasant, obviously, any more than she neglected her duty when it was raining. She had men posted at strategic points all along the vast, sloping estate, covering all the major approaches and a few more imaginative possibilities. They were supposed to stay awake and alert throughout their shift, and Sothe liked to encourage this by visiting them unexpectedly. This had the added bonus of letting her practice her stealth, which had grown dangerously lax in Raesinia's service. She considered it a personal failure whenever one of the guards failed to jump in surprise at her discreet cough.

Soft, she said, working her way along a fold in the ground that covered her from the (hopefully) watchful eyes at the next guard post. *I'm getting soft.*

And old, of course. This was a young woman's game, and Sothe could smell age stalking her like an invisible, infinitely patient predator. She could still sneak up on a stray cat, or hang from her fingertips, but she wasn't as *fast* as she'd been at eighteen. Some of that was natural—no one could stay at their peak forever—but Sothe was convinced that some of it was the result of getting too comfortable.

The girl who'd done Orlanko's dirty work for so many years, who'd flitted from shadow to shadow like a breeze and spent hours waiting for a single unguarded moment, that girl would never have let the queen come so close to disaster. Just thinking about it brought bile to the back of Sothe's throat, the *thump* of the explosion and the rush of realizing how close they'd come. *Soft.*

So she stalked through the grounds of Clover-by-Ost, sneaking up on her own men, trying to approach as an intruder might. A smart, patient, knowledgeable intruder, someone who knew the security inside and out and wasn't afraid of dying if it meant success. Herself, in other words.

She'd chosen Clover-by-Ost, an estate that had been gifted to the crown by the late queen's family, because its remote location and rambling, enormous size meant that the illusion she planned to create was that much more plausible. The staff was as big as the house, and Sothe had taken care to give the various branches contradictory instructions in the matter of cleaning, meals, and laundry. The resulting confusion, with bedding regularly changed twice or not at all, feasts delivered to the wrong room, and garments ruined from overwashing, meant that it was easy to conceal the fact that meals went uneaten and beds unslept in.

Everyone knew the queen was staying at the house. No one had seen her, of course, but everyone had a *friend* who'd caught a glimpse, or knew someone whose cousin had been scrubbing a window when the royal presence had turned the corner, or—

It was a simple game, almost a childish one. Sothe played it out more from habit than anything else. Gossipy staff worried her less than the watchers the Directory deployed, official and unofficial. She thwarted these spies by layering the house around with elaborate security—easily justified, in the name of protecting the queen—and a great deal of straightforward bribery. Maurisk's agents wrote long, carefully annotated reports, unaware that the couriers they trusted to deliver them instead handed them to Sothe to amend. Their simple ciphers would have made the least of the Last Duke's analysts roll his eyes in contempt.

Standards, Sothe reflected, had certainly fallen since the old days. Orlanko had been a vicious, backstabbing, power-mad bastard, but no one could say a word against the efficiency of his organization. Sothe had always respected efficiency.

The guard she was approaching had his station in the shadow of a huge, spreading oak, whose dried leaves, spread underfoot, made the approach tantalizingly challenging. She padded across them, stepping so slowly and carefully she hardly seemed to move at all. The guard was a silhouette against the tree, leaning on the trunk and staring out toward the river. Sothe was so absorbed in keeping her progress silent that it took her a few moments to catch the absolute stillness of the shadowed shape, or the scent of fresh blood on the wind.

She stiffened, then ran the last few steps, leaves scattering and crunching underfoot. The guard, a thin, rangy man, had been pinned by the shirt to the trunk of the tree, his throat slit as neatly as a pig at a butcher shop. Sothe looked him over briefly, then turned up the slope toward the house.

None of the Directory's agents had dared do anything so overt, at least not yet. But there were other powers interested in the welfare of the Vordanai queen who might not be so circumspect. Borel, Murnsk, and Hamvelt certainly had their own agents, and the Hamveltai *Kommerzint* in

particular was—though overestimated, in Sothe's professional opinion—still worthy of respect.

He killed the guard. It was the move of someone who
didn't plan to stay undetected for long. Bodies had a way
of causing alarms, by their presence or their absence. *So
either he's testing the defenses or he's here to break in and
doesn't much care about getting out again.*

She covered the distance to the house at a jog, crunching across the gravel path that separated it from the
grounds and heading for the closest door. The illusion had
to be maintained at all costs, even in an emergency—if the
queen *had* been here, the first thing Sothe would have
done on discovering a dead guard would be to make sure
she was safe. So that was the first order of business, followed by a quiet alert, and an effort to mousetrap whoever
had the temerity—

There were two guards beside the door, day and night.
Both were now dead, sprawled in the gravel. Knife wounds,
fast and precise. One guard had fumbled a pistol out of
his belt, and it lay nearby.

That, Sothe thought, *makes no sense.* There were far
easier ways to gain access to the house itself. Clover-by-Ost
was too large to be very secure, and a little climbing would
have given the intruder a way in without the chanciness
of a fight. *So he's either a lunatic, or . . .*

She stepped over the bodies, pushed open the door,
and headed through the maze of servants' corridors for
the stairs. A few turns on, she encountered the next body,
a teenage maid with a single stab wound on the side of her
head, just forward of the ear. A silver tea service lay where
she'd dropped it, undisturbed.

A lunatic who knows what he's doing. The young woman
hadn't even had a chance to scream. Sothe ghosted past the
corpse, up the servants' stairs to the third floor. Another
pair of bodies, another maid and a groom, lay atop each
other where they'd fallen in a tangle of limbs. The young
man's face showed nothing but blank surprise.

The "queen's" chambers were on the fourth floor. Whoever the intruder was, he'd followed the direct route,

making no attempt at stealth, and had simply silenced everyone who happened across his path. The door to the royal suite was kept locked, and Sothe was unsurprised to find the latch simply kicked out of the doorframe. *Not subtle. But efficient, curiously efficient . . .*

She crept up to the door, glad she'd been out on her rounds—and thus armed and dressed for stealth—rather than dressed up in her Head of Royal Household guise. Not a floorboard squeaked underfoot, and the deep carpet absorbed her cautious steps without a whisper. She pressed herself against the side of the door and listened.

Footsteps. The intruder was one room beyond, across the sitting room and in the queen's bedchamber. The tone of his steps changed as he entered the washroom, boots clicking on marble, then changed back. *Searching.*

That the man had to die was now apparent. Sothe would dearly have loved to capture him and find out where he'd come from, but his evident skill was such that she couldn't risk it. She had a half dozen throwing knives tucked into her well-fitted blacks, along with two longer fighting knives in greased sheaths at the small of her back. She drew one of the smaller blades, a carefully balanced steel needle only a little bigger than her palm. The footsteps were coming closer—the intruder was returning to the bedroom door. She heard the door creak, ever so slightly, as he pulled it open –

Without looking, she wound up and whipped the knife around the edge of the door. She aimed it squarely at where the center of an ordinary man's chest would be—without looking, it was too risky trying for a fancy shot. It wouldn't be fatal, but this was in the nature of opening remarks, rather than final arguments, and slowing him down would be helpful.

There was a curious absence of sound, not the thump of blade in flesh but not the wooden *thok* of a miss. *Maybe he ducked and I hit the bed.* She was already making her next move, pushing herself out and spinning across the doorway to the other side. This was reasonably safe; even if he was waiting for her to appear, she'd be moving too fast for him to throw or shoot, and she'd have a quick glimpse of him and the room beyond.

As she cleared the doorframe, she saw a figure in dark clothes, across the sitting room in the doorway to the bedroom, right where she'd expected him. He wore a linen mask over his face, and it glittered darkly, as though covered in shards of black glass. Of more concern to Sothe was his posture, right arm forward, as though just finishing a throw of his own.

Something punched her hard in the midriff, throwing off her momentum. She grabbed the doorframe and pulled herself sideways, out of view, but at the last moment she could see the intruder's *left* hand was still raised in front of his chest. Steel gleamed between his fingers—what looked very much like her knife, as though he'd picked it out of the air. *Which is impossible.*

She thumped against the wall, awkwardly, and flattened next to an ornamental table. One hand went to her side, where she found the bare-metal hilt of a throwing knife much like her own, the blade buried deep in her flesh.

Pain was just starting to bloom, and she fought it down with all the ruthlessness of two decades' practice. Her heart wanted to pound, and her breathing to deepen. She denied these requests from her body, keeping her mind clear. *The situation is not what was expected. Reassess.*

First step, damage control. She pulled the knife free, took a deep breath, and evaluated the resulting agony dispassionately. *Tolerable.* Judging by the wound depth and location, it wouldn't be seriously hampering, and blood loss would remain within acceptable levels.

Second step, threat assessment. *That throw was impossible.* The flight time of a flung blade was an appreciable fraction of the time it had taken her to spin across the doorway. That meant her opponent had made his move *before* she had, timing the throw so perfectly it had intercepted her in midmovement. Even if she had known someone was going to leap across a doorway, and had been waiting for precisely that moment, she didn't think she could have done that. *Which means that nobody can.*

And my knife— He'd *caught* it. There had always been fanciful stories about men so fast they could catch a blade thrown at their face, but experiments and experience had taught Sothe that no one was *that* fast, except by luck. *He doesn't seem like the lucky type.*

The black mask rang alarm bells, too. Not conclusive, of course—anyone could wear a mask; that was the *point* of a mask—but how many people knew about this particular style?

Tentative conclusion: *sorcery.* The man across the way was one of the Penitent Damned, a supernatural assassin.

Course of action: unclear. It was possible that she would be able to defeat him, in spite of his evident advantages. Sothe had beaten many men over the years (and a handful of women), some of whom thought they'd had her in a bad spot. She'd been wounded, starved, tortured, outmuscled, and outgunned. In the end, she'd always come out on top.

Her hands itched to draw the knives at her back, burst through the doorway, and see if the intruder's skill at throwing knives extended to hand-to-hand combat. But she took a long breath, feeling blood drooling down her skin, and waited.

No. Objectives first. Mission first. Her mission was to make sure the illusion of Raesinia's presence here was maintained. The only chance of success was to kill this man, and even then the secret might get out in the confusion that followed the slaughter. *Secondary objective.* If secrecy could not be maintained, she had to warn Raesinia the ruse had come apart. That would be impossible if the intruder killed *her.*

The right course was apparent. *Retreat.* It hurt her pride, but her pride was not important. *Mission first.*

That decided, how to execute? The stairs, behind her, were in full view of the doorway. There was another set, but that would involve going through the sitting room, and the intruder would probably be able to run her down. *Window, then.* The nearest one of *those* was also in the sitting room, but much closer.

Perhaps a second had passed.

She grabbed the ornamental table by its spindly base, tipping china ornaments to shatter on the floor. Raising it in front of her like a shield, she bulled through the doorway. One knife *thocked* into the surface of the table, and Sothe ducked her head when she saw the man in black winding up for another throw. A moment later, the blade whistled an inch over her head.

She threw the table, a clumsy effort, but enough that he had to step back into the bedroom for a moment. That bought her a moment to roll sideways, coming up with a knife in hand, whipping it at where he would have to be in order to attack. He twisted, letting the blade rip past his cheek by a hair's breadth, and snatched another blade from a sheath at his side.

Sothe bounced up and jumped, headfirst, at the window. It was four-paned, with a wooden crossbeam, but her momentum was enough to drive her through it in a splintering crash. Shards of glass surrounded her for a moment, and she felt cuts open on her cheek and forehead. Then she was falling.

The third-floor roof sloped out several feet beneath the four-floor windows, and Sothe hit it and rolled across the wooden shingles. The edge was just ahead—from there, it was an easy twenty-foot drop into an ornamental shrubbery, and then a quick run to the stables. She popped to her feet, jumped—

The next knife intercepted her in midair. *No, no, no. Nobody is that precise. Not possible.* It was a perfect shot, a kill shot, just under her left breast and in between the ribs to find the heart. Sothe caught the hedge at an awkward angle, tumbled, and sprawled spread-eagled in the dust of the yard.

She felt no pain, though the cuts on her side and face were a spreading agony now. *But I don't feel dead.* Her heart, leash slipped now, pounded hard and strong in her chest.

Cautiously she brought one hand up and found no blade embedded in her ribs. She brushed herself where she'd felt the impact, and nicked her finger on a shard of glass. When she sat up, more pieces cascaded off her.

Part of the window must have lodged in my clothes. Right there, over her heart, right at the spot where—

Lucky. For a moment, it felt as though she didn't dare breathe, or the world would collapse on top of her.

Then she was in control again, up and moving, more glass falling away from her. There were horses in the stables, and arrangements with inns all along the road to Vordan City. This was not a completely unexpected result, though she'd been thinking more in terms of a small army than a lone intruder.

Either way, the game is up. Raesinia has to be warned.

THE DIRECTORY FOR THE NATIONAL DEFENSE

The President of the Directory for the National Defense, who was also in his person the Minister of War, looked across his desk at General de Ferre and saw a dead man looking back at him. De Ferre had always carried a few extra pounds, but his recent ordeal seemed to have left him half-melted, his face loose and jowly and his stomach sagging. His uniform, in contrast, was polished and immaculate.

Maurisk picked up the glass from his desk and tossed back the bit of wine that remained. Vordan might have run out of brandy, but wine it had in plenty, and with the blockade strangling the export trade even the finest vintages were being dumped on the market for whatever they would bring. This had come from a particularly dusty and distinguished-looking bottle, but it might as well have been paint thinner to Maurisk's numbed palate. He drank it anyway.

"He let you go," Maurisk said after he set the glass down.

"Yes, sir," de Ferre said.

"Why?"

"He said . . ." De Ferre paused and took a breath. "He said he wanted to be sure you knew he was coming, sir. Asked me to be certain to tell you everything I'd seen."

"Did he?" Maurisk tapped his finger on the desk. *Pretty thin.* "You are aware, of course, of how it must look from . . . my side of the table? In combination with your complete failure, there is a suggestion of . . . collusion."

"I am aware, sir."

"Do you have anything to say about it?"

"Only to assure you that any such suggestion is false, sir. I am the most loyal man in the army. If there is a man who presents any evidence otherwise, I request permission to meet him blade in hand on the field of honor."

"I see." Maurisk's finger tapped again. De Ferre swallowed. "I will consider the matter. You are dismissed, for now, but make sure to keep yourself . . . available."

De Ferre looked surprised, then terrified and relieved in equal measure. He saluted, heels clicking, and left the office as quickly as decorum would allow. Kellerman opened the door for him, and slipped discreetly inside when the general left.

"Shall I have the papers drawn up for his arrest, sir?"

A corner of Maurisk's lip curled in what might once have been a smile.

"No," he said, with a sigh. "No, I think not. I suspect we will find a use for him. After all, he's the one man in the army I can be absolutely certain won't go over to Vhalnich." He sat back in his chair, staring at the empty glass. "Tell Zacaros to begin work on our little contingency plan. He's to have a free hand."

"Yes, sir."

"And draft orders to the colonel in command at Orlan. Tell him he is on no account to allow the Army of the East to pass. Burn the boats, burn the bridges, burn the town, I don't care. Tell him that if Vhalnich leaves the mountains, I will *personally* see to it that he and every surviving man in his command will wish they'd died on the battle-field."

"Yes, sir. Anything else?"

"No." The sickly half smile returned to Maurisk's face. "Yes. Send someone to fetch me the printers and pamphleteers. We must be certain the public is well informed."

CHAPTER TWENTY

RAESINIA

Janus. A week ago, people had argued over the price of bread, the progress of the war, the stupidity of the Deputies-General, or the difficulty of getting coffee and sugar through the blockade. Now there was only one thing anyone wanted to talk about, though always in whispers or behind closed doors. *Janus.*

He was coming, they said, with thirty thousand battle-hardened veterans of the Army of the East, or with a few hundred half-starved men. The Hamveltai army had been scattered to the four winds, or was chasing him over the passes, or marched *with* him as an ally. He'd recruited an army of *women*, unnatural creatures twisted by sorcery, who shrugged off musket balls and ate the dead. He himself was a demon, an agent of the Sworn Church, a spy for Hamvelt or Borel or Murnsk.

But he was *coming.* Everyone agreed on that.

The news had filtered into the city gradually, amid a profusion of other rumors about what had happened in front of the walls of Antova. All the papers were echoing the Directory-sanctioned truth—that Janus had turned his coat, like de Brogle, and brought his army over to the side of the Free Cities League. He was marching toward Vordan, they acknowledged, but loyal units of the army were assembling to stop him, and it was only a matter of time before he was captured or at least forced to withdraw.

The people Raesinia listened to were not so sure. Janus, it was widely agreed, was the best general in the Vordanai army—or any other army, some said—and the prospects of a scratch force confronting his (Hamveltai-aided, possibly sorcerous or female or both) troops seemed grim. If he reached the city, then . . . what?

Some said they would fight, house to house and street to street if necessary. The Patriot Guard had begun enlistments for Civic Defense militias, rough neighborhood mobs armed with improvised or antiquated weapons. These CDs, immediately dubbed "seedies" by the populace, were charged with keeping the peace throughout most of the city. Northside, Raesinia had heard, things were tense but quiet, with regular militia patrols and the semblance of a normal life. The Island and the Exchange were the domain of the Patriot Guard, who kept a tight hold over all the bridges and landings.

South of the river, though, the seedies had a different character. A responsibility for keeping the peace was, after all, also a license to break it, and the militias had begun enriching themselves at their constituents' expense. Food prices rose as seedies imposed impromptu "taxes," or simply charged protection money to remain in their good graces.

On the South Bank, there were those who said they looked forward to the day Janus marched his troops into Vordan. It was Janus and the queen who'd saved Vordan once before, and now that the Directory had gone as bad as Orlanko, he was coming back to do it again. He would sweep away the politicians and the traitors, end the war, lift the blockade, make the streets safe again. When he arrived, it was whispered, he would send Maurisk to the Spike, announce his marriage to Queen Raesinia, and take the throne.

Raesinia was able to take this last rumor in stride. *It*

might come to that, in the end. If Janus demanded the throne, with an army at his back, she wasn't sure she'd be able to refuse. Worse, she wasn't sure if she *should.* She'd started the revolution to take power away from Orlanko and give it to the people. So many had died—her friends had died—to keep Vordan free of tyranny. And then, as soon as war threatened, the elected representatives of the people had happily handed it all back to someone like Maurisk. *Maybe Vordan would be better off with Janus in charge.* Whatever his faults, no one had ever accused him of being incompetent.

There were public executions every day now in Farus' Triumph, enough to strain even the Spike, and they drew huge, jeering crowds. There was no longer a pretense that the accused were spies for the enemy; now they were simply traitors, heard expressing approval of Janus, criticizing the government, or simply turned in by overzealous or vengeful neighbors.

She, Marcus, and Feor had returned to Mrs. Felda's church after their escape from the Penitent Damned, and spent the next few days with their heads down, expecting another attack. Feor had been practically comatose, exhausted and feverish, and Mrs. Felda had taken on the task of nursing her back to health. Marcus, at Raesinia's prompting, had explained what he knew of the Steel Ghost from his time in Khandar, which didn't help all that much.

When it became clear that black-masked giants were not going to break down the doors of the church, it left them with the question of what to do next. They'd been in the midst of an endless, circular argument with far too many unknowns when the news of Janus' march arrived.

"Marcus isn't going to like this," Andy said.

"Marcus wasn't the queen of this particular country, last time I checked," Raesinia said. She and Andy looked at each other, and Andy was clearly stifling a laugh. "Besides, he's got his hands full. Someone has to think about these people."

Mrs. Felda's church was filling up. Some of the foreigners, mostly Hamveltai, had been sent home with the supply convoys, but lately their places had been taken by Vordanai. People from the Docks or Newtown who'd been forced from their homes by seedie "taxes," or fled ahead of accusations of treason. It was all Mrs. Felda and her volunteers could do to feed them all and find them beds, and sooner or later word would get out to the Patriot Guard or the seedies about the church. Just having a building full of Borelgai women and children would be enough to send Mrs. Felda, her family, and everyone who worked with them to the Spike.

Unless we do something about it. Andy stopped in front of a doorway, and Raesinia looked above it to the swinging sign, which proclaimed the establishment the Dead Dog. A canine skeleton, though wired to the wood, managed to look down at Raesinia with what seemed like an aggrieved expression.

Andy squared her shoulders and pushed open the door. Raesinia followed.

The last time Raesinia had done this sort of thing, it had been in the Dregs, in the hothouse intellectual environment of places like the Blue Mask. There had been wine, gallons of it, but it had always been secondary to the exchange of ideas. People came to argue about the deep questions of law and human nature, in the company of other people who understood the importance of such matters.

The Dead Dog, by contrast, was a place where people came to get drunk. It was dark, lit only by a few candles on each table and a fireplace at one end of the room, and smelled mostly of smoke and wine, with a faint undertone of piss. The tables were big, thick things built like ships, scarred and stained black by years of spills of smoke. The chairs were crates, barrels, or loose collections of planks nailed together by someone who didn't care much about comfort. There was no bar, but a trio of colorfully dressed women came and went constantly through a door to a back room, bringing clay jugs to the patrons.

The patrons were Dockmen, Raesinia surmised. There

was a certain uniformity about them, big, heavy men with broad shoulders and arms like wrapped cords, dressed in rough leather and interested only in their drinks. There was practically no conversation, only the occasional exchange of grunts or the rattle of dice where a few patrons were doing a bit of desultory gambling. Aside from the servers, there were no women in evidence.

"What," Raesinia said under her breath, "are we doing here, again?"

"Looking for people I used to know," Andy said. "Just follow my lead."

Raesinia was aware of eyes following them, from behind mugs and under slouched hats. Andy strode confidently through the tables, ignoring the gazes, and Raesinia stuck close behind her.

"Hey," someone said as they passed by. "That's not Wee Andy, is it?"

Andy didn't respond, but a hand shot out and grabbed her wrist. Raesinia tensed. The man who'd seized her was old and running to fat, with gray hair under his cap. He looked up at her, blearily, eyes struggling to focus.

"It is!" he said. "Fuckin' Wee Andy. You used to grab bread for me from the wagons on the Green Road." He turned to his companions, who'd all lifted their eyes to stare. "Wee Andy had the fastest fingers in the Docks." He lowered his voice to a stage whisper. "And the best tongue, too. She had this thing she'd do where—"

"It's good to see you, too, Harry," Andy said, putting her other hand across his. "But I'm afraid I'm a little busy."

"Aw, don't be like that," Harry said, jerking her a step closer. "It's been, what, seven years? You can't spare the time to have a drink with ol' Harry?" He looked her up and down. "You went and grew some tits, too, didn't you? I bet you'd be good for a proper fuck now, what do you say? For old times' sake. Used to be only two bits, but I bet you could charge—"

"If you don't let go," Andy said pleasantly, "I'm going to break your fingers."

"Eh?" Harry's expression changed slowly, as what she'd said worked its way into his sodden brain. "The fuck? I'm just bein' friendly."

"So am I. I haven't broken anything yet."

"Better listen, Harry," one of the other men said. "I heard she's one of Mad Jane's lot."

Harry turned around. "So fuckin' what? Mad Jane fucked off to the wars, and good fucking riddance. Crazy bitch strutting around tellin' everyone what to do—"

A hand landed on Harry's shoulder. It belonged to a very large man with skin like old leather, and it gripped tight enough that Harry flinched.

"Jane will be back," the big man said. "In the meantime, I won't hear that kind of talk."

Harry's friends were suddenly all extremely interested in their drinks. Harry looked up at the newcomer, then released Andy's wrist, looking a bit sick.

"Sorry, Walnut. Just . . . you know. Wanted to catch up with an old friend."

Walnut gave Harry's shoulder a squeeze before letting go, and Harry's face went white.

"Sorry, Andy," he said.

"It's nothing," Andy said, rubbing her wrist. "I came here looking for you. Can we talk?"

Walnut shared a table in the back of the establishment with two other men, who were introduced as George the Gut and Flopping John; the source of the former's appellation was obvious, and Raesinia was not sure she wanted to know the origin of the latter's. She and Andy sat across from the three, Raesinia crossing her legs underneath her to get a little more height and keep her chin above the level of the table.

"I didn't know you were still in town," Walnut said to Andy. "I thought you marched off to war with all the rest."

"Marched off, got shot, spent a while in the hospital at the University," Andy said. "By the time I was better, they'd all gone."

"All the worse for you," John said. "I bet the food's better in the army. Bakers are back to filling out the bread with sawdust, and there's a good trade in rats again."

"I got nothing against rat," rumbled George the Gut. "I got a recipe."

"I'm staying at Mrs. Felda's," Andy said. "And the stories I hear from people who come in . . ."

Walnut sighed. "It's the fucking seedies. Worse than tax farmers. At least with tax farmers it wasn't our own people shoving the boot in."

"Even the Oldtown gangs are having trouble," Jack said. "Lots of fighting over there."

"What about the Leatherbacks?" Andy said.

"Hardly any Leatherbacks left," Walnut said. "The girls all went with Jane, and half the boys joined the army. Only us who've got families to feed stayed home."

"That's something, isn't it?" Andy said. "Harry seemed to show some respect."

"Harry's a prick," Walnut said.

Raesinia took a long breath and said, "Janus is coming back."

The table went silent. Eventually John, looking down at his fingers, muttered, "You want to be careful with that kind of talk."

"Everyone knows it," Raesinia said. "And if Janus is coming, Jane and the rest will be with him."

"Who knows?" George said. "I heard he works for the Hamvelts now. Can't see Jane working for the bulls."

"Besides," Walnut said, "they're going to stop him at Orlan." He grinned. "Has to be true—I read it in the papers."

"He'll be here," Raesinia repeated. "And he's going to need your help."

"With all respect, miss," John said, "who the *fuck* are you? Just 'cause you share a name with the queen doesn't mean you get to give orders."

Raesinia glanced at Andy.

"The thing is," Andy said, "I'm not the only soldier hiding out at Mrs. Felda's. Marcus d'Ivoire is there."

"The Captain of Armsmen?" George said.

"The one who kept the black-coats from firing at the Vendre," Walnut said. His eyes were wary. "Janus' right hand in Khandar, right?"

"Right," Raesinia said. "And he's here to get ready for Janus' return."

Jack's brow furrowed. "Get ready how?"

"There aren't enough troops at Orlan to stop the Army of the East," Raesinia said, trying to sound more certain than she felt. "That's why the Directory is arming the seedics. They're going to fight, and it's going to be bad. Janus is going to have to cut through to the Island, and that means the Grand Span."

This was an assumption, but not a difficult conclusion to reach. The bridges from the north side of the river were all small and mostly arched, and Raesinia could only imagine the nightmare it would be trying to force a passage over them. The Grand Span, on the other hand, was wide, sturdy, and flat, which made it the obvious choice for an army trying to reach the Island. Unfortunately, this would also be obvious to the defenders, and the approach to the Grand Span went squarely through Newtown and the Docks.

The men at the table might not have been well educated, but they weren't fools. They'd all been through the rioting and the skirmishes around the Vendre during the revolution, and she could see they were all only too aware of what it would mean to have a real army going up against a dug-in defender in the streets around their homes. Everyone was silent for a moment.

"I *thought* the Patriots had been busier than usual," John said. "They've been bringing wagons over the Span and down the Green Road the last couple of days."

"Doing what?" George said.

Jack shrugged.

"Defensive positions," Raesinia said. "Ammunition stores. Cannon."

"Saints and martyrs," Walnut muttered.

"Fucking bastards," John said.

"Marcus wants to do something about it." This wasn't

quite the truth, Raesinia was aware, but Marcus was too focused on keeping *her* safe and not worried enough about the city that was in her charge. *It's what he* would *want, if he were thinking straight.* "But we need help. We need whatever Leatherbacks are left, and anyone else you can gather."

Walnut looked at Andy, who nodded encouragingly, then at his two companions. His brow furrowed.

"If—*if,* mind you—we were of a mind to help, what would you want us to do?"

"Help us keep the seedies from hurting people." Raesinia leaned forward. "Mrs. Felda's is full of people who've run away from the militia and the Patriots. We need safe places for them, food, extra hands. And . . ." She hesitated. "Maybe a bit of poking around. Nothing dangerous. But if we can send Janus information, maps of where the Patriots are and what they're up to, it will make the fighting shorter."

George was frowning. John said, "Listen. You mean well, but you have to understand what you're asking. It's all well and good if Janus wins, but what if he loses? The Patriots will ask who helped him, and people will talk. Every one of us could be on the Spike by the end of the year. I've got a wife and kids to think about."

"What makes you think they'll leave you alone if Janus loses?" Andy said. "We fought the tax farmers, we fought the fucking black-coats, and we took the *Vendre.* If the goddamned Directory thinks they can push us around, they've got another think coming."

"You all know what the Patriot Guard are like," Raesinia said. "A bunch of bullies and cowards. If it comes down to them against Janus bet Vhalnich and Mad Jane, which side are you going to bet on?"

Walnut looked at John, then back at Raesinia. Slowly, he nodded, and his huge hands tightened into fists.

"I am supposed to keep you safe," Marcus said. "*That* is what Janus ordered me to do. And I can't do it if you keep running off every time a thought pops into your head!"

They were in the attic of the church, a windowless,

claustrophobic space stuffed with forgotten boxes of holiday ornaments and stacks of unused prayer books. Linen and bedding that hadn't been disturbed in decades had been hauled out to deal with the influx of refugees, disturbing the dust of decades and leaving the air thick and choking. With the number of people now in Mrs. Felda's care, it was about the only place left they could talk without being overheard.

"It had to be done," Raesinia said. "We *need* the Leatherbacks. And they agreed to help!"

"Ionkovo can *walk through walls*," Marcus said. "And that monster from Willowbrook shrugged off musket balls like they were champagne corks. Either one of them could come back at any time!"

"If they do, what makes you think I'd be safe *here*?"

"I've organized watches," Marcus muttered, but the question clearly cut him to the quick. He could see as well as Raesinia that a few half-starved refugees standing guard with cudgels were not going to do much to stop the Penitent Damned. He and Lieutenant Uhlan were the only proper soldiers in the place, and they had only one musket between them and a couple of pistols.

"But you're right," Marcus went on, rallying. "Our only hope is keeping it absolutely quiet that we're here at all. And going out to talk to people isn't going to help!"

Now it was Raesinia's turn to wince, but she had an answer ready. "Word is going to get out about Mrs. Felda's sooner or later. If the Leatherbacks are operating again, then nobody will immediately associate it with us."

"So you're using them as cover?"

"I'm helping people."

"It's not part of our mission," Marcus said. "Janus ordered me to take care of you, not to defend the city."

"Would you shut up about your orders?" Raesinia said. "*I* don't answer to Janus, and I can't stand by and watch." She shook her head. "Besides, if we can get a good map of the Patriot Guards' defenses, that will help when the Army of the East gets here. It'll save lives."

"If he'd wanted me to make maps, he would have said

so," Marcus said, but that was weak, and they both knew it. They'd had no contact with Giforte or the flik-flik team, and had no idea if the line linking them to Janus' army was still in operation.

Raesinia let out a long breath. "Look, it's done. We'll have them come here from now on. Will you at least talk to them? Cora and I can handle setting up safe houses for the refugees, but if we *are* going to be of any use to Janus, you're the one who knows what kind of information we should be looking for."

"All right, all *right*." Marcus looked up at Raesinia, as though considering her in a new light, and she felt herself blush slightly.

"What?" she said. "Am I failing to live up to your expectations for a queen again?"

"In a way," Marcus said. "I was just thinking that maybe this is what I *ought* to have expected a queen to be like."

Raesinia snorted, but her cheeks reddened further. She turned away to hide them. *I don't need his approval.* "I'm glad you've learned something—"

There was a knock on the trapdoor, and she fell silent. Marcus, sitting beside it, said, "Yes?"

"Raes?" Cora said. "There's someone down here asking to talk to you."

"One of the refugees?" Raesinia said. "Or someone from the Leatherbacks?"

"Neither." Cora lowered her voice. "I think it's your friend Rose."

Rose . . . Raesinia shot to her feet after a moment's thought, cursing herself for not getting it faster. Sothe had used that name when Cora met her, during the fall of the Vendre. *She's here!* She rushed to the trapdoor and pulled it up. Cora was already backing down the ladder, too slowly for Raesinia's taste—she nearly jumped, twenty-five-foot drop be damned. *I've fallen a lot farther.*

But there were people watching, so she followed Cora down, carefully. The church didn't have a true second floor, just a balcony that ran along one wall, where seats had once been positioned for distinguished guests to watch the service. Mrs. Felda had used it for storage before the crisis; now the food stocks had mostly been eaten, and bedding laid out on the creaking wooden floor so that refugees could sleep in shifts. This area had been allocated to later arrivals, which meant they were almost all Vordanai—mothers with young children, for the most part, along with quite a few old men and women who'd been forced from their homes by the seedies and left with nowhere to go. Men of fighting age found looking shiftless were liable to be dragged into service in the Patriot Guard, while unaccompanied young women disappeared to even worse fates.

Raesinia picked her way through the makeshift beds, full of exhausted people sleeping in spite of the early hour, and down the rickety switchback stair that led to the main floor. The church smelled mostly of the huge pots of soup Mrs. Felda and her assistants churned out, but with a strong undertone of unwashed bodies and overflowing privies. Filthy children ran about, chasing one another with sticks.

Sothe looked like any other refugee, wrapped in gray, fraying homespun, the dirt of several nights on the road obvious on her face. A thick bandage wrapped her side, and she walked with a limp, favoring one ankle. Raesinia pushed her way through the crowd and wrapped her arms around her maidservant, carefully avoiding her wounded side.

"Thank God," she said. "I was so worried about you."

Sothe, as always uncomfortable with such displays of emotion, patted Raesinia awkwardly on the shoulder. "I'm glad you're well. My mission was successful, I think, until . . ." She lowered her voice. "We were attacked. One man, but he was . . . exceptional. I believe he may have been a Penitent Damned. By now they certainly know that you were never there, and they may know you never left the city. I'm sorry."

"It's all right," Raesinia whispered. "It was never going to hold up indefinitely." Ionkovo had seen her, in any case, so the word was out. "I'm just glad to have you back. We tried to send you a warning, but . . ."

Marcus, a bit slower down the ladder, pushed his way through the crowd and stopped facing the two of them. Raesinia disentangled herself from Sothe and put on a more dignified face.

"I'm not sure the two of you have been formally introduced," Raesinia said. "Marcus, this is Sothe, my head of household and close personal friend." Sothe shifted uncomfortably at this description, but Raesinia didn't give her a chance to object. "Sothe, this is Colonel Marcus d'Ivoire, also my friend and Janus' personal representative."

Marcus, also looking a bit awkward, let courtesy come to the fore and bowed. "Miss Sothe. Last time I saw you, you were fighting a half dozen Noreldrai Grays with admirable efficiency. I regret I was unable to render more effective assistance."

"I believe the *last* time you saw me, I was lying bleeding on the floor," Sothe said. "But thank you. You have my gratitude for keeping Raesinia safe."

"We need to talk," Raesinia said. "All of us. But—"

"Not here," Sothe said, looking at the teeming refugees. "And not now. I've been three days on the road without sleep, so my contributions would likely be . . . minimal."

"Oh!" Raesinia silently cursed Sothe's stoicism. *She'd probably keep chatting until she dropped from exhaustion.* She pointed across the room. "Use my bed. Or would you rather eat first?"

"Sleep," Sothe said. "Thank you. If you'll excuse me?"

Raesinia nodded, and Sothe slipped into the crowd, moving like a ghost in spite of the tight quarters and her injuries. Marcus looked after her and shook his head, his expression thoughtful.

"'Head of household'?" He looked quizzically at Raesinia. "Someday you're going to have to explain to me where you found her."

"You'll have to ask her yourself," Raesinia said. "It's not my story to tell."

MARCUS

Marcus had not been sleeping well.

He was one of a few in Mrs. Felda's with the privilege of an actual bed, rather than a bit of cloth spread over the stone floor, but he was still obliged to share it with two others in shifts. As another nod to his standing, he'd been assigned the night shift, which let him try to sleep during the approximate hours of darkness, but he still had to vacate promptly in the morning to let some other poor soul collapse.

The combination of the ever-noisy church and the enforced schedule meant that Marcus spent quite a lot of time lying down, hoping that exhaustion would finally triumph over the shouting of night-owl children or the clink and scrape of cutlery and carry him off to sleep. *I never thought being on the run from the law would be so* loud. Or, he had to admit, smell quite so bad. The church was developing an odor to rival an army camp.

It gave him plenty of time to think, which was not particularly welcome. The truth was that he felt lost. Ever since he'd first saluted the young colonel at Fort Valor in Khandar, Marcus had found himself swept along in Janus' wake, acting in his name. That was simple enough in battle—executing orders was what an officer was *for*—and even command of the Armsmen had made sense, of a sort. But it bothered him more than he'd realized at the time that Janus had left him behind to go off and fight his war.

Now he had, in any reasonable regard, failed in his mission. The Thousand Names, which he had been assigned to protect, had been taken by the enemy; Raesinia, who had been added to his responsibilities, would have been taken as well if not for the intervention of a Khandarai phantom. He had nothing left—one Mierantai lieutenant, recovering only slowly from a nasty wound, and one girl ranker with little respect for his authority.

More important, he didn't know what to *do*. On the

battlefield, if you couldn't accomplish your goals when you'd done all you could, you fell back and asked your superior for further orders. Without the flik-flik line, though, he was out of contact with Janus, and the situation had changed radically.

In the event of my death . . . That last set of orders was still chilling. Rumor had Janus still very much alive, but how good was rumor? Marcus felt himself instinctively reaching out for reassurance and not finding it.

And then there was Raesinia, with her insistence that they do *something. She's probably right, damn it. But what if I do the* wrong *thing?* The last time Marcus had been without a commanding officer had been after Colonel Ben Warus' death, just before the Redeemer rebellion. *All I managed to do was run away.*

The time was approaching when he'd have to turn over his bed. He resigned himself to the fact that he wasn't going to get any more sleep and opened his eyes. The omnipresent buzz of life in the church went on all around him, laundry and cooking, cleaning and mucking out. Someone had even started a little group to sing prayers in the pulpit, the first time that sacred space had been put to its intended use in centuries.

Marcus stretched and sniffed himself surreptitiously— he hadn't washed his uniform in three days, but given the general state of the place, it would probably be okay for one more. One small corner of the kitchen was reserved for "baths," which consisted of a bucket of cold water dumped over the head and a tag end of soap. There was privacy only for those who could persuade a friend to hold a sheet in front of them; at this point, most of the refugees had stopped bothering, in spite of Mrs. Felda's scandalized looks.

At least there was still food. Daily passing of a collection plate among the refugees secured some coin, and those who'd arrived with extra possessions were eventually convinced to offer them up for sale. Marcus was surprised that this hadn't caused more than a bit of grumbling, but shared trouble had created a bond of solidarity, even across nationalities, and only a few Vordanai had complained at their treasured goods being sold off to help feed Borelgai women and children. Cora, given Mrs. Felda's blessing to organize things, had deputized a troop of young women, older children, and fit old men to go out and purchase necessaries, in addition to dividing up the various cooking and cleaning duties.

It all *worked*, even though the closest thing to people in charge were a forgetful old woman, her slightly thickheaded son, and a teenage financial genius with a tendency to lose herself in books for hours at a time. Marcus had been prepared at first to get things organized on a proper military footing—he'd put camps together before, after all—but he'd quickly realized his assistance wasn't going to be necessary.

But it only works as long as there's food coming in, and nobody asks too many questions. They were relying on finite resources and goodwill, and both would run out eventually. He doubted the camaraderie of the last few weeks would last when rations started to shrink. *Raesinia's right. We have to do something, or this is going to turn into a nightmare.*

He stood in the queue for a bowl of soup and a bit of bread, dunked the one in the other, and ate without thinking hard about what precisely had gone into either. When he'd finished—handing the bowl off to be quickly washed and given to the next hungry party—he climbed the staircase up to the balcony. Raesinia was already waiting by the ladder leading up to the attic, with Sothe beside her. So, to Marcus' surprise, was Feor, looking paler than usual and with dark circles under her eyes but definitely upright.

"Good morning," Marcus said in Khandarai. "Are you feeling better?"

Feor nodded. "I am, thank you."

"She asked to be involved," Raesinia said quietly. "You don't mind?"

"I think," Marcus said, looking around to make sure no one was listening too closely, "that anyone who knows anything about magic is going to have something to add."

That was what this amounted to, Marcus realized. *The "council of people who know magic is real."* Andy, who had actually seen one of the Penitent Damned, seemed to have convinced herself that it had been some kind of chemical trick, and Marcus wasn't yet sure if he should force her to confront the fact that most of what she knew about the world was a lie. That left himself, Raesinia, Sothe, and Feor.

All women, Marcus realized with a sinking feeling as he climbed the ladder. He wished Janus and Ihernglass were here, to even the odds a little. The others were sitting in the small clear space in the attic, dust dancing in the light of the candles they'd brought up, and Marcus closed the trapdoor and sat between Raesinia and Feor. Sothe, having traded her beggar's garb for more comfortable linens, stared at him for a long moment before looking away.

"All right," Raesinia said. "We have to decide what to do next."

Just by coming here, Marcus realized, he'd made the decision that Raesinia was right. They had to do *something.* In the end, he couldn't stand by and watch the people of the Docks suffer, any more than he'd been able to fire on the crowd at the Vendre. Whatever Janus' orders might or might not have been was no longer the issue.

In a way, he was once again under a commanding officer. That it was a woman a decade younger than him, and a civilian to boot, was taking some getting used to.

"We know Maurisk is digging in," Raesinia said. "He can read a map as well as we can. He'll defend all the approaches, but this is the hardest one to block, so he has to assume this is where Janus will make his main effort."

Marcus nodded. "The bridge itself is wide-open. Even with the guns we saw, the Army of the East will probably have superior artillery, so if Janus gets to the riverfront, he can blast a crossing. Maurisk's best chance is to fight it out along the Green Road. If he fortifies the buildings, assaulting them would be too bloody to risk. Janus would have to wait until his guns reduced each position, then move up, block by block. That could take weeks."

"Not to mention reduce half the Docks to rubble," Raesinia said. "That's point one. Point two is that Maurisk is working with the Priests of the Black, and has a number of Penitent Damned on his side. Do we know how many?"

Marcus ticked them off on his fingers. "Ionkovo. That giant who attacked Willowbrook. The old woman who can throw flames."

"The one who attacked me was . . . strange," Sothe volunteered. "Not fast, exactly, but he could predict my movements."

"That's at least four," Marcus said. "Feor, do you have anything that might help us stop them?"

"With the Names . . ." Feor shook her head, then paused. "I can sense them, if they're close enough. Her Majesty ought to be able to as well."

Raesinia nodded. "It took me a while to recognize it, but yes. I don't know how close they have to be, though."

"Janus has a few tricks," Marcus said, feeling guilty for keeping secrets even from this inner circle. He'd seen Ihernglass' power in action, when he defeated his lover/would-be-murderer Jen Alhundt. But that was Ihernglass' secret to tell, or at least Janus'. "Until he gets here, we're going to have to try to avoid fighting the Penitent Damned if we possibly can." He thought of Hayver, screaming as he was engulfed in flames. "And we'll keep a twenty-four-hour watch, so we'll at least have a little warning if Ionkovo decides to pop out of the closet."

"What about the Steel Ghost?" Raesinia said. "He helped us once."

She looked at Feor, who gave an awkward shrug.

"I cannot answer for him," the Khandarai girl said. "That he has helped without coming forward to join us openly is probably a fair statement of his intentions."

"Agreed," Marcus said. "We can't rely on him."

"That's point two," Raesinia said. "Point three is the refugees. We can't keep them here." She sighed. "I wish we could bring Cora up here."

"Fill her in later," Sothe said.

"We need more space and more food," Raesinia said.

"Without drawing too much attention. We'll need to work through the locals."

Marcus nodded. "They seem willing, and Andy will help."

"Lastly—" Raesinia said.

"The Thousand Names," Feor said.

"Right." Raesinia rubbed her eyes. "Maurisk captured them at Willowbrook nearly a week ago. We have to assume he's moved them by now."

"Probably not out of the city, though," Marcus said. "Too much risk of running into one of Janus' cavalry patrols."

"If I may ask a potentially obvious question," Sothe said, "are these Names that important at this stage?"

"Yes," Feor said. "They *cannot* be allowed to be taken to Elysium."

"Why?"

"The *abh-naathem*, the Penitent Damned, already have a great store of *naath* at their disposal. The Thousand Names represents the only archive outside their control. If we lose them, we lose any chance of opposing them."

"Having seen what the Penitent Damned can do, I'm inclined to believe that," Marcus said.

"If Janus takes the city," Raesinia said, "then we may get the Names back in any case."

Sothe shook her head. "If they're as important to the Priests of the Black as you say they are, they would try to get them out before the city falls."

"I agree," Feor said. "They will abandon Maurisk, if it comes to that. Cities and armies are not their concern."

"So we have to get them back," Marcus said. "Eight solid steel plates, taller than I am, that each take at least four strong men to carry. That's not going to be easy."

"Wait until they're in transit," Sothe said. "Then hijack them."

Marcus had had much the same idea at Willowbrook, but since then he'd thought a little harder about the difficulties. "That relies on knowing *when* they're in transit."

"I can find that out," Sothe said.

There was a moment of silence. The queen nodded, decisively, and looked at Sothe. "How badly are you hurt?"

"Not badly enough to slow me down much," Sothe said.

"You're in charge of intelligence, then. We need to know where the Names are now, when they'll be moved. Knowing where the Penitent Damned are would be a big help, too."

"That's a bit of a tall order," Marcus said.

"I can handle it," Sothe said, looking at him coolly. "I still have contacts."

Marcus looked questioningly at Raesinia, who shrugged. Sothe raised an eyebrow.

"I used to work for Orlanko," she said. "Any other questions?"

Another, more strained silence.

Raesinia cleared her throat. "All right. I'm going to work with Cora to help with the refugees. Cora had some ideas on where we can house people, but it's going to take delicate negotiation. Everybody's closed up tight right now, and we can't afford to fight the seedies in the open. Feor, until we find the Names, you can help us."

"I would be pleased to," Feor said, dipping her head.

"Marcus," Raesinia said, "you're on the military side. Andy should be able to get you some eyes and ears, and you know what to look for. We'll prepare maps and notes, and when Janus' army gets close we can send riders to meet him. Or Giforte might get back in touch, in which case we'll want to be able to pass along as much as possible."

Marcus barely bit back an instinctive *Yes, sir!* He grinned and nodded, fighting the urge to salute.

It's always good to have a proper commander in charge.

CHAPTER TWENTY-ONE

WINTER

The Army of the East debouched from the passes of the Kell Mountains, descending in a long, winding column along a road that switchbacked between the steepest hills before leveling out into lush, gentle country. This was the Duchy of Orlanko, the ancestral lands of the Last Duke, and Winter had half expected the whole place to look sinister. Orlanko had been a mostly absentee landlord, though, spending much of his life in the capital, and his realm was a sleepy, well-ordered place of broad pastures and quaint medieval towns.

As a result of the Last Duke's ancestor's good sense in choosing the cause of Farus IV over his noble opponents, the Duchy of Orlanko had never suffered the horrors of the civil war and the Great Purge that had followed. The victorious king had left his greatest ally's lands alone while he reordered the rest of the kingdom, and as a result traveling through Orlanko was in some ways like walking in Vordan's history. The previous hundred years might as well not have happened; riding at the head of her regiment, Winter passed through villages of half-timbered houses with tiny, mottled glass windows and vast fields given over to pasturage for cows. The animals stood by the fences, staring dumbly and lowing now and then as the army trooped past.

The people were another matter. The folk of Deslandai hinterland had been positively pleased to see the Vordanai army, and had been willing to sell to anyone with coin in their pockets. Here, back in Vordan at last, the locals were much less friendly. Winter wasn't certain if they were loyal to Orlanko, to the Directory, or simply scared by the stories that had been spreading ahead of the army, but every building they came to was locked up tight.

Even outriders ranging far from the column found only a few suspicious peasants willing to sell food or fodder, and more often came upon farmsteads whose inhabitants had fled or hidden in the cellar as though they were facing murderous Murnskai hordes. At Janus' express direction, in such cases the scouts were to take only what they thought the peasants could spare, and to leave fair value in coin behind. There was no shortage of money, at least—the Hamveltai baggage train they'd captured at Antova had been a rich haul, both in military supplies and more conventional loot.

Soon after descending from the mountains, the road to Vordan had shifted to parallel a river called the Haggon, which was a tributary to the Ost. The Ost, in turn, joined with the Vor just short of Vordan City itself, so Janus had ordered a day's pause to shift much of the army's heavy baggage to river transport. Once this was accomplished, they made good time down the River Road, with the heavily guarded supply barges keeping pace beside them. It meant longer marches but light packs, and the men and women of Winter's regiment seemed to regard the tradeoff as on the whole a good one.

Janus had given Winter's troops the vanguard, marching at the front of the army while he rode with the Colonials at the tail of the column. It was Winter, therefore, who was the senior officer on the scene when scouts on lathered horses rode in, reporting heavy columns of infantry in Vordanai blue advancing eastward on the road, led by a party of mounted officers under a flag of truce.

* * *

Winter, Cyte, and Bobby waited, several hundred yards in front of the now-halted Girls' Own, as the two colonels dismounted some distance away and approached on foot. They were accompanied by a single ranker, bearing a white flag, while several more stayed back with their horses.

It was past midday, and a chill wind was blowing. Winter shaded her eyes with a hand and examined the two men. She didn't recognize either, but that wasn't unexpected—outside of the Army of the East, she wasn't very familiar with the officer corps.

The pair of them were a study in contrasts. The one on the left was obviously a Royal, an old-time army officer; he wore an expensive, tailored uniform, spotless except for the dust of the recent ride. The eagles on his shoulders were silver, though, which meant he'd graduated from the War College rather than purchasing his commission.

His companion barely had a uniform at all, just a ranker's blue jacket over a dark shirt and trousers. *His* eagles were stitched outlines of white thread, already fraying at the edges, and he wore a battered slouch hat instead of an officer's cap. He walked with an affected swagger, trying hard to seem nonchalant.

When they were a few yards away, Winter offered the formal nod that was due to an officer of equal rank. Bobby and Cyte saluted, and the ranker with the flag did likewise. The Royal colonel returned the gesture, precise and correct, while the other just stared insolently.

"I'm Colonel Winter Ihernglass," Winter said. "Third Regiment of the Army of the East. This is Lieutenant Forester and Lieutenant Cytomandiclea."

The unofficial-looking colonel raised his eyebrows at Cyte's full name, but his companion remained impassive.

"I'm Colonel Zarout, of the Eighteenth Regiment of the Line," he said. "This is Colonel Braes, of the Tenth Volunteers."

"I've sent a rider to bring General Vhalnich," Winter said. "He's at the rear of the column, but I'm sure he'll be here in a few minutes."

"If you don't mind," said Braes, "I'd like to have a chat before he gets here." He had the drawl of the Transpale in his voice. "These your troops in front of us?"

"This is the Third Regiment, yes."

Braes' eyes went to Cyte for a moment. "Can't help but notice that most of 'em appear to be ladies."

Winter's expression hardened. "The First Battalion is female. As are many of my officers."

"I heard some strange things about Vhalnich, but I didn't credit them," Braes said. "There a lot of girls in this army?"

"As far as I know, only my regiment has a women's battalion," Winter said in the iciest tone she could manage.

"I have to tell you, I'd have a hard time shooting a girl," Braes said.

"I assure you that the reverse is not true," Winter said.

Colonel Zarout coughed. "The . . . gender of Colonel Ihernglass' troops is not the issue here."

Braes gave a rolling shrug. "Just curious."

"Colonel," Zarout said, turning back to Winter, "I would like to inquire as to General Vhalnich's intentions."

"I'm sure he can answer your questions when he arrives," Winter said.

"You must know something," Zarout said. "He is marching on Vordan City. Has he said why?"

Winter hesitated, then said, "General Vhalnich believes that the President of the Directory has unlawfully assumed the post of Minister of War, and other powers besides. He is marching to support the queen and the legitimate government of Deputies-General."

"Way I heard it, he's trying to keep himself off the Spike," Braes said.

"General Vhalnich would never disobey an order he believed was legitimate," Winter said. "And I think I should ask *your* intentions. My scouts tell me that your troops are drawn up in defensive positions across the road."

"I have orders," Zarout said, "from the *new* Minister of War, to engage and defeat the Army of the East."

Braes gave a braying laugh, which earned him a cold look from Zarout.

"What he wants to say," Braes said, "is that Maurisk has tossed us in front of a runaway cart and hopes we might slow it down a little."

"I meant nothing of the kind," Zarout said stiffly. "But I will admit you appear to have the advantage of forces."

Winter suppressed a smile. Even with the garrison they'd left behind to hold Antova, the Army of the East was nearly thirty thousand strong. The two regiments in front of her mustered five or six thousand at best, with minimal artillery and no cavalry. She felt a sudden sympathy with Zarout.

"I agree that your position seems . . . difficult," Winter said. "I'm sure I speak for the general when I say that we would like to avoid bloodshed between fellow Vordanai. Is there anything we can do in that regard?"

Zarout's jaw clenched. "I have been informed by the Ministry that if General Vhalnich is permitted to pass, I and every man in my command will be executed for treason."

"That'd certainly keep Dr. Sarton busy," Braes said.

"General Vhalnich would suggest that such an order would be illegitimate," Winter said.

"All well and good if General Vhalnich's . . . opinion carries the day. But at the same time, those of us who have obeyed Directory orders . . ." Zarout trailed off, considering his words. Braes laughed again, and Zarout turned on him. "What do you find so amusing?"

"The way you know what you want to say, but get so tied up trying to say it," Braes said. He looked Winter in the eye. "Look. Here's our problem. If we fight you, a lot of people are going to get killed who don't have to, and it'll all be the same in the end, 'cause you've got six times our numbers. But if we don't fight, and you *lose*, then we're all going to be getting a little prick right *here*." He thumped his chest.

"I can say from experience," Winter said, "that General Vhalnich does not lose."

"That's what I hear. Trouble is, when the top seat changes hands, the new boss tends to get a bit angry with whoever knuckled under to the old boss. There's a lot of us who've just been following orders, and we're all looking over our shoulders after what happened to Hallvez." He waggled his eyebrows. "You follow our predicament?"

"I do." Winter took a deep breath. "I can't speak for the general, of course, but I have served with him since Khandar, and he is not the vengeful sort." For a moment, she thought the ghost of Adrecht Roston might raise a protest. *That was different.* Mutiny was one thing, but Janus wouldn't execute a man who'd happened to be on the other side, especially if he didn't fight. *I hope.* "I'm sure officers who followed their duty and their conscience would have nothing to fear."

Zarout coughed. "Do you think the general would be willing to offer his personal assurance on that? For the men as well as the officers?"

"I suspect so, yes."

"That would be . . . useful." Zarout looked over his shoulder, back toward his own men. "It occurs to me that, positioned as we are, our left flank is unprotected. Since the Ministry of War has neglected to assign me a cavalry force, a threat in that direction would force us into a tactical withdrawal, probably over the river at the nearby crossing." He nodded in the direction of the river. "If the bridge were subsequently destroyed, it would be many days before we could reach another."

Braes was laughing again, and Winter found herself smiling in spite of her best efforts.

"I think," she said, "that something like that could be arranged."

When Janus did arrive, his conference with the two colonels was brief and to the point. A few minutes later, Give-Em-Hell led a force of laughing, whooping cavalrymen on a ride around the end of Zarout's line. Winter, standing beside Janus on a roadside hill, could see the long lines of blue-uniformed troops already beginning to leave their positions, headed for the bridge over the Ost and safety.

"A pity that they couldn't be persuaded to join us," Janus said. "But one can't have everything."

"I don't blame them for being cautious," Winter said. "These are strange times. Zarout seemed like the sort who wanted to do the best by his men, whatever happens."

"No doubt. Strange times indeed when the best a loyal officer can manage is to step aside and let a mutinous army through."

Winter shifted uncomfortably. "I don't like to think of myself as mutinous, sir."

"What else can you call it?" Janus waved down at the road, where the Army of the East was marching on toward the day's camp. "I'm certainly disobeying orders."

"Maurisk had no right to give those orders," Winter said. The story of the coup in Vordan had become common knowledge in the past few days. She guessed that the soldiers passed it round so eagerly in part because many of them shared the same uncomfortable feeling she had; it made things easier if the government they were disobeying was a treacherous one. "He's shut the queen up in the country and locked up anyone who speaks against him. That's hardly the revolution we signed up for."

"No doubt when the histories are written, that's what they'll say," Janus said. "Assuming we win. If we lose, of course, we'll be a lot of dirty traitors." He flashed his summer-lightning smile at her. "But tell the truth. If Maurisk had been content to leave us alone, would you be marching against him?"

"I . . ." Winter shook her head. All she could think was that if matters had never come to a head, she might have had more time to get through to Jane.

"You don't have to answer that."

"May I ask *you* a question, sir?"

Janus raised an eyebrow. "Certainly."

"You seem like you expected . . . something like this."

"It seemed likely. I couldn't have told you who it would be, but after the revolution *someone* would end up taking charge, and the odds were extremely high that they'd make a hash of it." He frowned. "Maurisk has exceeded my expectations there, I must admit. But yes, it wasn't hard to guess that it would eventually come to this."

"Then why leave Vordan at all?" Winter shook her head. "If you *knew* we were going to be coming back to the city with an army . . ."

"Why not take over after Midvale, you mean? Make myself Raesinia's regent, as Orlanko wanted to?"

Winter colored slightly. "Something like that."

Janus looked contemplative. "If you were going to go about taking over a kingdom, how would you do it?"

"Having an army in the capital seems like a pretty good first step."

Janus shook his head. "Not in the long run. The Borelgai defeated our armies in the War of the Princes, but they weren't stupid enough to try and install a new king. If I'd used the Colonials to take over after the revolution, I would have been as bad as Maurisk. I would have *had* to be, in order to stay in power, and in due time some hero would have come along to defeat me."

"But you can go back now?"

"Oh yes." He spread his hands, gray eyes sparkling. "Now *I'm* the hero, come to overthrow the vicious tyrant. That puts things on a very different footing."

Winter stared for a moment, not sure what to say. Janus lowered his arms.

"Liberators are always more popular than conquerors. And a return to law and order is more welcome once people have gotten a taste for what life is like without it." He cocked his head. "What's the matter, Colonel? You look shocked."

"You . . . really planned all this? That far in advance?"

"I believe I told you once that it's not about planning. It's about putting the pieces in the right places, and reacting to whatever opportunities come up."

"But *why*?" Winter blurted. "Just for the power? To make yourself king?"

"I don't want to be king. I think Raesinia will be a good

queen, if she gets the chance. And I don't want the power, in the end. But . . ."

Janus looked away, at the column marching past. Evening was beginning to fall, and the light had turned soft and buttery, painting the brown grass of the hillside so it looked as if it were cast from gold. The silence stretched on, until Winter thought she'd offended the general. When he spoke, though, it was not the dismissal she expected.

"Someone had to do it," he said.

There was another pause. Winter blinked. "That's it?"

Janus shrugged. "Anyone could see the crisis was coming. The king dying, the princess too young, Orlanko too powerful, and the Black Priests . . . It was going to explode, one way or another. The wrong ruler, at the wrong time, can mean decades of poverty and war. Farus the Third, the Wastrel King, let the nobles steal the kingdom from under his nose. Farus the Fifth, Farus the Great, was so in love with his own face that he bankrupted the state building grand monuments. Only the right person could keep us from disaster."

"And you're the right person?" Winter said.

Janus smiled, and fixed her with his fathomless gaze. His eyes blazed in the soft light.

"Of course," he said.

"You didn't believe him?" Abby said.

They were in Winter's tent, after dinner. The camp was in a pasture by the side of the road, and the outer pickets had to fend off determined attempts by inquisitive cows to breach the perimeter. Whoever was supposed to be minding the animals had apparently fled at the army's approach. *He's lucky Janus is so restrained, or we'd all be eating beefsteak.*

Abby had slipped into the tent, quietly, as she had done every night since the confrontation at Antova. In what might have been an effort to delay the main business of the evening, Winter found herself recounting her conversation with Janus, and her impression that, somehow, he'd been lying to her.

"I don't know," Winter said. "Not telling the whole truth, anyway."

"You don't think he's really doing it for the good of Vordan?"

Winter shook her head. "That may be *part* of it, but there's something else. What he told me sounded . . . too pat. Like it was something he told himself, to try and get himself to believe it."

"We've got no choice now but to trust him," Abby said.

"No." Winter let her awareness sink through the layers of her mind, down to the level where she could feel the slow movement of the Infernivore. "It's been a long time since I had a choice."

There was a long pause.

"Jane was wrong," Abby said. "She was wrong, and she's still wrong. You did the right thing."

Winter sighed. "Thanks." Then, steeling herself, she asked the question she'd asked every night. "Any sign of her?"

The forward scouts, some from the Girls' Own and others from Give-Em-Hell's cavalry, had been given quiet instructions to ask the folk they met about others who might have come this way. Winter wasn't sure what she expected to find—traffic on the River Road was heavy enough that a small group of young women wouldn't have attracted much notice—but she had to *try. I'll find her. She wants me to find her.*

"No," Abby said. She looked at the table, on which was spread a map, and put her finger near the spot where they were camped. "We'll make Orlan tomorrow. That's our best chance to pick up the trail, assuming she came this way at all."

"She came this way," Winter said. "This is the way back to Vordan City. Where else does she have to go?"

Abby nodded. "We'll find her. If not before we get to the city, then after."

After . . . Winter hadn't let herself think too much about *after*. What might happen after everything played out, after Janus confronted Maurisk. It seemed like a distant fantasy world, the other side of an endless river with no bridge in sight. *The end of the war.*

"Cyte needs to talk to you," Abby said, seeing the distant look in Winter's eyes. "She's got orders to go over for tomorrow. And I think there were some disciplinary issues Bobby wanted you to look at."

"Right." Winter pulled herself back to the here and now. Since Jane had left, that seemed to be getting harder and harder. "Tell them I'm ready for them."

"And try to get more sleep," Abby said, getting to her feet. "You look exhausted."

"Take the knife," Jane said, as though instructing a friend in how to carve a roast. "Put the point of it about here"— she raised her head and put the tip of the dagger on her throat, just under her chin—"and press in, upward, as hard as you can."

I did it already. Winter could feel the soft flesh of Sergeant Davis' throat parting under her blade, the stunned, stupid look on his face as his blood gushed over her hands.

"*Fuck* the army," Jane said. "Fuck the Directory. Fuck all of them. It is *not your responsibility*, don't you understand? You don't have to care."

I can't help it. Winter let her hands fall, the knife slipping through her fingers. *I'm sorry, I'm sorry. I can't help it.*

"Just because you weren't brave enough to save me doesn't mean you have to save the whole world to make up for it."

How can you say that? Winter squeezed her eyes shut, tears falling. *I came back for you. You never came looking for me.*

"We're together." Jane leaned close to her. "Now, and always."

Her lips touched Winter's. The kiss was sweet, as sweet as it had ever been, as sweet as the first time. Then Winter felt something rising within her, the demon that lived in the pit of her soul, rushing forth and flooding into Jane. She screamed at it, swore at it, but it went on unbidden.

As it had when she'd used it on Jen Alhundt, the thing *spread*, transforming Jane into more of itself, down to her feet and the tips of her fingers. Then, hunger satisfied at last, the demon dove back inside Winter, leaving nothing behind but the fading image of a crooked smile and green eyes full of pain.

I did this to her. I drove her away.

"I'm sorry," Winter said into the darkness. There was no answer.

CHAPTER TWENTY-TWO

MARCUS

The wagon, pulled by a quartet of straining, panting mules, rattled slowly down one of the innumerable alleys that branched off the Green Road north of the Lower Market. The buildings on either side were two or three stories high, not the towering tenements of Newtown but the more modest, ramshackle brick-and-timber architecture of the Docks. Overhead, clotheslines ran between upper-story windows, with a few lonely sheets flapping in the chilly breeze.

Two Patriot Guards, wearing their blue-and-black sashes, escorted the wagon, one on the box beside the driver and the other perched uncomfortably on the roof. Both had muskets, with bayonets fixed. A half dozen big men walked beside the vehicle, too, with the ragged blue armbands that had been adopted by the Civic Defense militia. Seedies, the Leatherbacks called them, and as far as Marcus could see the name fit. They looked like ordinary street toughs, dressed in leather and homespun, with cudgels and long knives at their belts. *No pistols, though.* That was a blessing. *I don't want to kill any more of them than we have to.*

He waited until they'd passed his position, behind the

rag curtain of a second-story window. Once he was satisfied none of them were paying particular attention, he
leveled Lieutenant Uhlan's long rifle, the barrel poking
through the gap in the curtain. It was heavier than a musket, and the balance was different, but Marcus had spent
an evening practicing and felt he grasped the basics. He
was no marksman, but the target was barely ten yards off.

The kick against his shoulder when he pulled the trigger felt harder than a musket's, and the sound was different, a high-pitched *crack* instead of the smoothbore's *bang*.
Clouds of acrid smoke billowed from the lock and the end
of the barrel, momentarily obscuring his vision as shouting
erupted from the street below. Marcus leaned forward and
saw that the man he'd been aiming for, the Patriot Guard
beside the driver, had slumped from his seat and tumbled
into the road. The man on top of the wagon was aiming
his musket, sighting on the window gushing powder
smoke, and Marcus hurriedly jerked his head back. Two
more reports sounded, almost simultaneously, and there
was a crash of falling plaster from the rear wall of the
abandoned apartment he was holed up in. When he risked
another look, the second Patriot was down, swearing and
clutching his gut.

With both musketeers out of action, a loud whistle
sounded, and attackers appeared at both ends of the alley.
Walnut, eschewing weapons in favor of a pair of huge,
iron-studded gauntlets and bracers, led one crew while
Andy headed the other, waving a long wooden club. Their
"troops" were a mix of Leatherbacks and refugee volunteers: Dockmen and women, some of the older boys and
old men still hearty enough to swing a cudgel.

Not much of an army. Marcus set the rifle aside and
swung out the window. Iron bars hammered into the splintering brick made a kind of ladder, and he climbed down
a few rungs before letting go and dropping the rest of the
way to the street, yanking his sword free of its scabbard.
Just ahead, a white-haired, heavily whiskered man and a
boy who could have been his grandson were dodging the

wild sweeps of a swearing, club-wielding seedie, trying to get in close enough to land a blow. Marcus stepped up behind the militiaman and smashed him over the back of the head with the hilt of his saber, dropping him like a sack of rocks.

The melee was just about over. One of the seedies had climbed up to the top of the wagon, brandishing a long knife, a crazed look on his face. Walnut tried to grab hold of the edge and pull himself up, then hastily stepped back as the militiaman swiped at his face.

"You're all going to the Spike for this!" the man shouted. "We're official, damn you! We work for the Directory!"

"We know," Marcus said, pulling himself up onto the box.

The seedie spun, knife thrusting, but Marcus interposed his saber in a lazy parry that sent the smaller blade spinning across the alley and left the militiaman cradling a gash on his fingers.

"Now," Marcus said. "What's in the wagon, and where's it going?"

The man blinked. He had deep-set, piggy eyes, and a scraggly beard that didn't fully hide his sagging jowls.

"I don't know what's in it," he said.

"Fine," Marcus said. "How about we set it on fire?"

"No!" the seedie screamed. "No fire. Please. It's . . . it's powder."

Marcus found Andy in the group near the rear of the wagon and met her eye. She nodded grimly. *Just like the others.*

"And where is it going?" Marcus said, raising the tip of his sword until it was level with the man's eyes.

All the fight had gone out of the militiaman. "Over to Kara Doulson's place, just up the road. I don't know why. I really don't!"

"I believe you." None of the other Patriots or seedies had known the purpose of their cargoes. *Maurisk is playing this one close to the chest.* "Walnut, can you handle dumping this in the river?"

"No problem," the big man said. "What about this lot?" He indicated the unconscious and captive seedies.

"Take their weapons and turn them loose, unless they need a cutter."

Marcus looked at the wounded Patriot Guard, who had subsided into a sobbing ball. *Gut wound like that, he's a dead man*. He caught Walnut's eye and jerked his head in the dying man's direction, and Walnut nodded, his expression souring.

"These seedies aren't much in a fight," Andy said as Marcus hopped down from the wagon and the other volunteers gathered around them. "Boys and fat old men."

"That makes us just about even," Marcus said, grinning at his little squad. They laughed, including the boys and the old men.

One of the women sniffed. "Hardly *even*," she said, provoking another round of laughter.

Marcus had to admit that without the Docks' women, they'd be dangerously undermanned—*outnumbered*, he corrected ruefully. The Borelgai refugees were no fighters, being mostly domestic servants accustomed to a quiet life, but the Docks seemed to have an extensive supply of stocky, muscular matrons who were used to hard labor beside their husbands and not averse to cracking skulls when necessary. At Raesinia's insistence, he'd taken on any who volunteered, along with men older than his father and boys who'd never needed a razor. So far, their confrontations with the seedies had been extremely one-sided, but that wouldn't last. *Maurisk will send more Patriots, with better weapons*.

It didn't have to last, though. Not long. Janus was coming. *We just have to figure out what the hell Maurisk is planning to do when he gets here*.

"More powder?" Viera said.

"More powder," Marcus confirmed, setting the long rifle down on the table. Viera was working in the church's ever-busy kitchen, chopping vegetables for the endlessly boiled cauldrons.

"Flash powder, or ordinary gunpowder?"

"I wouldn't be able to tell by looking," Marcus said, "but the barrels looked the same as all the others."

"Flash powder, then." Viera's faced twisted in thought, and Marcus found himself watching her hands to make sure she didn't remove a finger. "What is he going to do with that much flash powder?"

This was the third convoy they'd ambushed, with the same result. The Patriots had taken possession of nearly all the larger buildings along the Green Road, but they weren't fortifying them as Marcus had expected. *They ought to be blocking up the entrances, loopholing the walls, that sort of thing.* Instead the actual defenses seemed to have been delegated to the seedies, who were throwing up barricades in the streets with a great deal of enthusiasm but little actual military skill.

And flash powder was flowing, from the mills north of the city through a seemingly endless chain of wagons, all destined for one building or another along the road.

"Presumably he wants to blow something up," Marcus said.

"It doesn't make sense," Viera said.

"I don't know." Marcus shrugged. "Hide barrels of powder in the buildings by the side of the road, wait until the army is marching up it, then set them off."

Viera rolled her eyes in a way that was becoming depressingly familiar. "How much would that actually accomplish? You'd collapse a few buildings, maybe hurt some people with flying bricks, but he hasn't got *that* much powder. As a trap, it's not worth much, not the way he's setting it. If he *really* wanted to do some damage, he could bury it under the road—with as much as we've seen, that would leave quite a crater when it went off."

"Even that wouldn't be enough to *stop* Janus," Marcus said. "He might wreck a company or two, but that's not going to make a difference in the long run."

"Exactly." Viera shook her head. "I don't know what he thinks he's playing at."

"Maybe he just doesn't know what he's doing?"

"He must have *some* engineers." She pursed her lips. "If I were him, I'd think about bringing down the Grand Span. That would keep Janus off the Island for a while."

Marcus paused for a moment, taken aback. The Grand Span was part of Vordan City, and had been since before he was born. It was a monument to the foresight and perseverance of the builders, a triumph of modern science, bridging a distance long thought to be impossible. The idea that Maurisk might *destroy* it to gain a temporary military advantage seemed almost sacrilegious.

"Do you think he'll do that?" he said after a moment.

"From what you've brought me, there's no evidence that he's going to try. It's a big bridge, and all stone. He'd need a lot of powder, and the preparations would be pretty obvious."

"He might be worried people wouldn't stand for it. The seedies might turn on him."

Viera nodded, pushed aside the bits of potato she'd been cutting, and reached for a bunch of slightly wilted-looking carrots. Marcus looked around. The population of the church had thinned out considerably since Raesinia took charge, and Mrs. Felda was taking the opportunity to give it a thorough cleaning. The smell of salts and vinegar was strong in the air, as were the shouts of the apparently tireless old woman as she ran after her charges.

"So what should we do about it?" Marcus said.

"The powder?" Viera paused in her chopping, shrugged, and went back to it. "It depends. It's not going to hinder Janus much, so from that point of view we don't need to do much more than warn them when they get here."

Marcus nodded, feeling a little relieved, but she went on.

"On the other hand, if they *are* mining the buildings, and they know what they're doing, then they're going to bring down an awful lot of masonry. And I doubt they'll give the game away by warning the people who live there. So from that point of view"—she separated the top of the carrot with a particularly sharp *whack* of the knife—"it might be worth our trying to stop them."

"Damn," Marcus said quietly. Janus, if he were in command, might weigh the pros and cons of rescuing the people in the rigged buildings. Raesinia would not. *And Raesinia's in command now.*

"One thing we should definitely do is have a firefighting crew ready," Viera said, starting on another carrot. "It's too cold and wet to get a serious blaze going, but flash powder burns spread a lot of hot sparks around."

Marcus nodded absently, distracted by a commotion at the front door. Raesinia had returned. Cora and Walnut went to greet her—the teenager was half a head taller, and the huge man dwarfed the queen, but it was clear nonetheless who was in charge. Marcus had seen it a dozen times now, but he still marveled. *I always wondered how a girl like her managed to put together a conspiracy that toppled the government.* It no longer seemed so mysterious.

It reminded him of Janus, in an odd way. People around Raesinia were drawn into her orbit, the same way the general exerted a palpable force on nearly everyone he met. The difference, Marcus thought, was that where Janus was well aware of the extent of his personal magnetism and used it to his advantage, Raesinia was almost unconscious of hers. *She doesn't plan like Janus. She just keeps moving forward, one step at a time, and we fall in behind her.*

Marcus wondered, uncomfortably, what would happen if these two heavenly forces directed their gravities in opposite directions, and shook his head to banish the thought. *Janus would never allow that to happen.* He picked up his rifle again and raised his hand in greeting as the queen's party approached.

RAESINIA

"You convinced him?" Andy said incredulously. "You convinced *Smiling Jack* to help us?"

"Well," Raesinia said, "I doubt *I* had much to do with it. Cora did all the real work." She put an arm around Cora's shoulders and squeezed her tight. "I just had to go in and say the magic words."

"What?" Andy said. "What magic words? They say the

last man who asked Smiling Jack for charity was found spiked on the weathercocks of six different buildings!"

"Ah, but we weren't asking for charity. We were making an offer."

Andy looked from Raesinia's smiling face to Cora's blushing one and gave her a pleading look. Cora shrugged awkwardly.

"Smiling Jack is having . . . liquidity problems," she said. "A lot of the Oldtown gangs are suffering under the blockade, and now with the seedies cutting down on night-life. I did some research on where he's been going for coin, and bought an appropriate stake in some of the larger institutions."

"In other words," Raesinia said, still grinning, "Smiling Jack is up to his eyeballs in debt, and thanks to Cora a lot of that debt is now owed to *us*."

"Or to banks that we control," Cora said. "It's safer that way. Less of a chance he'll resort to extralegal measures."

"That is, that he'll decide his problems would be over if we were found floating facedown in the river," Raesinia translated. "Once we got him to understand the situation, you should have seen him grovel."

In truth, Raesinia had found the meeting with the crime lord disappointing. She'd heard endless stories of the famous gangs of Oldtown, criminal dynasties that stretched back into antiquity. Some supposedly occupied premises that dated from before the founding of the Vor-danai monarchy, give or take the odd citywide fire. While crime in Newtown rarely rose above the level of petty theft and vendetta, the loose alliance of gangs, families, and guilds that ruled the city's oldest district had loftier ambi-tions. They ran the brothels and gambling houses of the Cut, and controlled empires of smuggling, corruption, and vice stretching from Essyle to the Jaw.

So she'd always been told, anyway. Smiling Jack had been a middle-aged man with a paunch and thinning hair, bedecked in gaudy jewelry and silks. He'd met her in the back of his tavern, the Lion's Den, where he had what

amounted to a throne room. To other criminals, the osten-
tatious display of wealth in the furnishings was probably
impressive; to Raesinia, who'd grown up in the vast, gilded
halls of the Palace at Ohnlei, it felt like an overcramped storage closet.

Smiling Jack's bluster and crude threats had deflated
quickly enough when Cora explained the situation, and
he'd been almost pathetically eager to deal. The prospect
of a suspension of interest on his loans was enough to
wring the promises they needed out of him, and Raesinia
had taken pains to point out that in the event of her and
Cora disappearing, the arrangement would vanish with
them, leaving Jack once more at the mercy of the banks
of the Exchange. *Even crime lords can't stand up to count-
inghouses, it seems.*

The upshot was that Smiling Jack undertook to open
some unused property of his to the refugees who were still
streaming into Mrs. Felda's, and to keep them safe from
the seedies, at least until Janus' army arrived. Similar
arrangements, on a smaller scale, had already relieved the
pressure a bit, but this would improve conditions considerably.

"And," she said, "according to Cora we'll even make a
profit on the deal."

"Smiling Jack's ventures seem basically sound," Cora
said. "We purchased the debt at a discount, but I'm convinced it's viable in the long term. Of course, it does tie
up those assets for a while."

Andy shook her head and looked at Raesinia. "Where
did you *find* her?"

"Working as a messenger for the Exchange," Raesinia
said. "If I hadn't distracted her with helping me save Vordan, she'd probably own half the world by now."

Cora, already red, blushed further and looked at her feet.

"What about your side?" Raesinia said. "Any progress?"

"We grabbed another seedie wagon," Andy said. "More
gunpowder. Marcus and Viera are trying to figure out what
they're up to."

"Anybody hurt?"

"Not seriously. They had more guards this time, though. We had to shoot a couple of them."

"Have you seen Sothe?"

"Upstairs." Andy gestured at the balcony, which with the decreased crowding had been cleared to allow planning in private without resorting to the attic. "She's waiting for you."

"I'd better go, then." Raesinia patted Cora one more time, waved to Walnut and some of the other Leatherbacks who'd come to greet their returning party, and fought her way to the stairs.

Sothe was waiting in what had become an impromptu conference room. A big dining table, donated by one of the refugee families, bore a hand-drawn map of the Docks on big rolls of butcher paper, annotated and scribbled on to represent what they knew of the seedie and Patriot Guard activities. Most of the handwriting was Marcus', but when Raesinia came up the stairs Sothe was adding a few notations in her precise handwriting.

"I take it your plan worked?" Sothe said, setting her stub of pencil aside.

"It was Cora's plan," Raesinia said. "But it worked brilliantly. This is going to make it a lot easier to feed and house everybody who needs help."

"It's still only a stopgap," Sothe said. "We can't feed the entire population of the Docks."

"It only *needs* to be a stopgap. Janus is coming."

Janus is coming. That had been the refrain of the refugees, the mantra recited on every street corner. *Janus is coming.* Even the official papers could no longer deny it, though they continued to insist that only a few traitorous units accompanied him. Raesinia wondered if Maurisk, in the barricaded offices of the Hotel Ancerre, repeated it to himself. *Janus is coming.*

"What about your side?" Raesinia said, looking down at the map.

"As far as the streets go, I'm just filling in what Marcus has already sketched out. The Patriot Guard are preparing some kind of explosives in the buildings on the Green Road between the Lower Market and the Grand Span, but we don't know why." Sothe paused. "I did get a bit more information about the Thousand Names, but I'm not sure if it does us any good."

"You know where they are?"

"Yes. As you might expect, the Patriot Guard moved them by wagon into the basements of the Hotel Ancerre not long after the raid on Willowbrook. Most of them don't know what they moved, of course, but the total picture is unambiguous." Sothe frowned. "Maurisk's people talk too much."

"You can critique their operational discipline after we win," Raesinia said. "I take it we can't get to the Names?"

"We might be able to get there," Sothe said in a way that made it obvious that by "we" she meant "I." "But then what? Spirit away eight steel plates that weigh tons? We'd effectively have to take and hold the hotel, and we don't have the strength."

"But if Maurisk is just going to sit on the Names, we don't need to worry. We'll get them back when Janus crushes him."

"Unless Janus loses."

"If Janus loses," Raesinia said, "I think the Names will be the least of our problems."

"Unfortunately, it doesn't look like Maurisk is planning to sit tight," Sothe said. "He's keeping it very quiet, but there's a big Murnskai trading boat, the *Rosnik*, currently tied up by the water batteries. She was confiscated when the war broke out, and she's been sitting there quite some time, but now it looks like the Patriot Guards are getting her ready to sail. And from the cargo they've been told to expect, he's going to load either the Names or some very oddly shaped cannon."

"Balls of the Beast," Raesinia swore. A boat *would* be the easiest way to get the unwieldy plates out of the city. Moving the Names in a slow-plodding wagon would be too much of a risk; if Janus got wind of it, his cavalry would easily be able to intercept them. But the Vor was navigable to the north for hundreds of miles, and even fast-riding troopers would have a difficult time catching up. "If they get out of the city, they could get all the way to Murnsk before we catch up with them."

"I suspect that's the idea. I think our best chance is going to be once the plates are on the boat. If we can get a large enough party on board, we could take it over." Sothe hesitated. "The trouble is going to be getting away. It'd be easiest to strike while they're still tied up, but . . ."

Raesinia saw the problem. A boat tied up in front of the water battery—Vordan's primary defense against a downriver naval attack—was by definition at point-blank range from some of the largest guns the armories could produce. The needs of the war had stripped away every movable cannon for the armies, but the water batteries included some monstrous siege pieces never meant to be used in the field. Intended to blast holes in Borelgai warships, they would be perfectly capable of reducing a trading boat to kindling.

Blasted to kindling. Raesinia mulled that over for a moment. It felt, oddly, like the beginning of an idea.

"To make matters worse," Sothe went on, "it looks like they're planning to sail just as Janus arrives. Presumably they want to be sure his attention is fully engaged."

"That's going to keep us busy." Raesinia sighed. "So we've got to figure out what he's up to on the Green Road, and then come up with some way to get this boat that isn't actually suicidal."

"That's about the shape of it."

"Raesinia!" Marcus shouted, from the bottom of the balcony stairs. "Are you up there?"

"Something wrong?" Raesinia said.

Marcus pounded up the stairs in his heavy boots, accompanied by another, lighter set of footsteps. This turned out to be Viera, whom he was dragging along by one hand.

"I think," Marcus said, a bit short of breath, "that I figured it out."

"*I* haven't," Viera said. "What—"

"Just explain to her what you were just telling me," Marcus said. "The last bit."

Viera blinked, looked irritable, and straightened up. "All I *said* was that if Maurisk was putting flash powder bombs together to bring down buildings along the Green Road, it wouldn't make much of a trap for anyone not actually in the building at the time."

"Not that. The next bit."

"The next—" Viera furrowed her brow. "That we'd probably want to have firefighting teams ready?"

"Yes," Marcus said.

"Flash powder starts fires," Viera said, more irritated than ever. "If it was drier, or we used more straw in the city, it could be a serious issue, but as things are it'll be more of a secondary problem. We just might want to have a few bucket brigades on hand."

Raesinia got it, and it must have shown in her face. Viera stared at her.

"What?" she said. "Did I say something wrong?"

"No," Marcus said. "It's fine. Can you give us a minute, though?"

"What's going on? If it's to do with explosives, I can help—"

"I think we'll need your help," Raesinia said. "But not right at the moment."

Viera sniffed, but turned about and went down the stairs. Sothe looked after her for a moment, then back to Raesinia.

"I appear to be missing some important context," she said. "Something about starting fires?"

"The woman from the warehouse," Raesinia said.

Marcus nodded. "You saw what she could do."

"She could throw balls of flame," Raesinia said. "But . . . more than that. She wasn't *creating* the flames, she was *controlling* them. I remember her pulling little bits of fire from the guards' lanterns."

"She must have kept that place from burning down," Marcus said. "I was certain it was going to go up in our faces."

"And if she can put a fire out," Raesinia went on, "it seems logical that she could start one. Or more than one. Help them spread once they're going."

"He's mined six buildings on each side of the road," Marcus said, looking at the map. "That's a stretch a couple of miles long. Do you think her power can reach that far?"

"I don't know," Raesinia. "But *he* obviously does, or the Black Priests who are helping him."

"No wonder the bombs didn't make sense to Viera," Marcus said grimly. "She doesn't know they'll have a demon helping them along."

"So he waits until Janus' army has fought its way to the Grand Span, which probably means thousands of soldiers in the city—"

"At least," Marcus said.

"And then turns it all into a firestorm." Raesinia's mouth was dry. "He's lost his *fucking* mind."

"Pressure does strange things to people in power," Sothe said. "Also, I'm no longer certain if Maurisk is running things himself, or taking suggestions from his Penitent friends. The Black Priests certainly wouldn't hesitate to burn down half of Vordan to get what they want."

"Which is why they picked that night to get away with the Names," Raesinia said.

"What?" Marcus said. "Get away where?"

Sothe briefly ran down the information they had on the Names, the *Rosnik*, and their suspicions about the Black Priests' plans. Marcus frowned, brow furrowed, and scratched his beard.

"Even if we can get aboard, there'll be guards," he said. "That will take time. Then there's the chance one of the Penitent Damned will show up."

"The one I fought could be overcome by a reasonably sized force," Sothe said.

"The giant might be more of a problem," Marcus said. "Or the fire woman, if she's not too busy. But even if we *can* get past them, how do we get the ship out of range of the guns before they start shooting holes in it?"

"We could use the Names as hostages," Sothe said.

"How? They're not exactly easy to break. What are we going to do, threaten to sink them in the river?"

"Maybe we could rig a gunpowder charge—"

Something shifted in Raesinia's mind, and she had it.

"I think," she said, "we're going about this the wrong way . . ."

CHAPTER TWENTY-THREE

MARCUS

Why do I feel, Marcus thought, *like I've been here before?*

Once again, he was in a small boat, on an empty, darkened river, rowing into the unknown. The muffled splash of the oars, regular as a heartbeat, was the only sound. To the right, the Island was a blaze of light, lanterns burning even on the abandoned battlements of the Vendre where it stuck out into the river like the prow of a ship. Ahead and to the left was the stretch of noble estates called the Fairy Castles for their fantastical, impractical architecture, where only the occasional glow of some servants' kitchen was still alight. Those of the nobility who'd remained through the revolution and the outbreak of war had finally departed, along with everyone else who had the means, now that Janus' army was camped on their doorstep.

Tomorrow, or so the word went, the Army of the East would begin its advance into the city. Or Maurisk would surrender, or Janus would surrender, or they would meet between the lines to settle matters in single combat. The official presses had gone ominously silent, and in their absence a million rumors bloomed like fungi. Morning would settle the matter, one way or another.

More important, for the purposes of the motley band of refugees and fugitive soldiers, a strong force of Patriot Guards was posted on the outskirts of the city, blocking the roads south. A few brave volunteers had tried to get through to Janus' army in order to establish communication, but they'd all had the sense to turn back in the face of the well-manned patrols. Maurisk clearly knew that there were groups in the city more likely to lend aid to Janus than to fight him, and he was determined to maintain a tight cordon.

Which means we're on our own. Marcus still didn't know if Giforte had escaped and reestablished the flik-flik station, but it didn't matter now. *We're out of time.* Which was why he was out here on the river with the Queen of Vordan, getting ready to board an enemy vessel with a cutlass in his teeth like a pirate in a bad play.

Why carry it in your teeth? he wondered, idly, as Walnut and George the Gut strained to keep the boat steady in the current. *What's wrong with a sheath?*

"There." Raesinia pointed. "That's got to be it."

Directly ahead of them were the ominous fortifications of the water batteries, vast brick enclosures whose blank, gaping portals suggested the mouths of the cannon lurking within. A few lights were visible there, clustered along the small piers that jutted into the river directly under the guns. In front of them, with only a pair of lanterns burning, was a tall, dark shape. Marcus could just make out two tall, skeletal masts against the deeper black of the hillside beyond.

"And we're sure they've loaded the Names?"

"Sothe is sure," Raesinia said, which as far as she was concerned meant it was the next thing down from the word of God. Raesinia obviously placed a great deal of trust in the taciturn ex-Concordat agent, and Marcus had to admit he had no reason to doubt her. But he couldn't help feeling a little strange around Sothe. The woman was reluctant to look him in the eye, and found excuses not to speak to him if she could help it. *Maybe she just doesn't like me.*

Or she doesn't like my getting so close to Raesinia. The latter, he suspected, was more likely. Sothe was nothing if not fiercely protective of her charge.

Convincing Sothe that her talents would be more valuable elsewhere this evening had been the work of a night's furious argument. In the end, though, she had to concede that if they were going to both keep the Names out of Elysium's grasp and prevent the Penitent Damned from reducing the Docks to ashes, someone needed to locate the fire woman and keep track of her, and that nobody but Sothe was likely to succeed in that task. Sothe had then argued that Raesinia should stay behind, but with a fatalistic tone in her voice that made Marcus suspect she expected the queen to overrule her. As expected, Raesinia had insisted on accompanying him to the *Rosnik.*

Marcus tapped Walnut on the shoulder when they were a hundred yards from the boat. He and George stopped rowing, except for small strokes to keep them in place against the gentle current of the Vor. Marcus took a bull's-eye lantern from its peg, checked the shutter, then opened it briefly to send a single flash upstream.

A single flash answered him. That would be Andy, right in position. Turning in his place in the stern of their little craft, Marcus repeated the operation downstream, and got another answering flash. *Viera.* Marcus would have preferred not to bring the student along—she wasn't going to be any use in a fight, certainly—but she'd insisted she might need to make some final adjustments. *I think she just wants to watch the fireworks.*

"Everyone's set," Marcus said.

Walnut nodded. He let go of his oar for a moment, put two fingers in his mouth, and whistled. The high, eerie sound echoed across the water for a moment before dying away. Then, taking up his oar again, he and George started pulling strongly toward the *Rosnik.*

They seemed to cross the hundred yards between them and the riverboat in an eyeblink. If all was going as planned, Viera's boat would be headed for the boat's bow, while Andy's took the stern. Marcus' boat, squarely amid-ships, bumped up against the hull of the much larger craft, rocking gently. The *Rosnik*'s rail was only a few feet over-head, so fortunately actual grappling hooks were not necessary.

Marcus put his hands against the pitted wood of the boat's side, trying to hold steady. Raesinia, barefoot and in short trousers, took a hold of Marcus' shirt and then swarmed up his back until she was standing on his shoul-ders. From there, she could grab the rail and haul herself aboard. Marcus looked up, waiting for the shout of alarm or even a pistol shot, but none came. A moment later, a rope ladder unrolled and landed in the boat, and Walnut immediately went to work securing their small craft to the bottom.

Most of the equipment and expertise for this part of the plan had come from the big man and his Leatherback friends, who, after all, spent their days on and around ships. Marcus' experience with sea and river travel mostly involved vomiting, so he'd been happy to let them take the lead. Letting Raesinia be the first one over the side had been against his better instincts, but as she'd said to him in private: "If someone's going to get her head blown off coming over the rail, probably best that it be me. I can put mine back together."

Once the ladder was secure, Walnut went up it hand over hand, with an easy grace that belied his size. George the Gut followed, a bit more awkwardly, and Marcus brought up the rear. The *Rosnik* had the low profile of a riverboat, with a single deck and all cabins and cargo stowed below. One lantern burned at the stern, and another pair near the bow, where the boat was tied against the pier. Marcus could see one musket-armed guard by the boat's wheel, and several more by the bow, but as they'd guessed the majority of the Patriots were waiting on the pier itself, protecting against an attack from the landward side. *Mau-risk needs to show a bit more imagination.*

"Something's wrong." Raesinia was shielding her eyes

against the lights, looking toward the bow. "I don't see anyone from Viera's team."

Marcus looked the other way. The lanterns had ruined his night vision, but he could just about make out dark shapes slipping over the rail, only a dozen yards from the wheel and the guard. The Patriot, equally blinded, didn't show any sign he'd noticed.

"Andy's here." Marcus drew the pistol from his belt and checked the powder to make sure it was still dry. "Could they be having trouble getting the ladder up?"

"I'm worried they went too far around—*fuck!*"

A shape became visible on the bow rail, the head and shoulders of a boy of fifteen. His name was Peter, Marcus vaguely recalled, one of the refugees who'd eagerly volunteered for a chance to strike back against the Patriots and the seedies. But their boat had somehow missed its mark, and drifted too close to the pier—he was climbing up within a few yards of the pair of guards there. Even as Marcus watched, one of the Patriots turned and gawked at the boy, then yanked a pistol from his belt.

"Stop right there!" he said, loudly enough to carry all over the *Rosnik*.

The boy ought to have ducked back out of view. Instead he pulled himself upward, one hand fumbling over the rail. Marcus drew a breath to shout and distract the guard, but before he could the Patriot pulled the trigger. His pistol *cracked*, and Peter's head snapped back as though someone had yanked hard on his hair. The boy's hands gripped the rail for a moment, then relaxed, and he toppled backward and out of view. Someone screamed below.

Marcus' shout of warning became one of rage, and he sighted down his own pistol. While he badly wanted to shoot the guard who'd fired, military discipline made him target the other, whose weapon was still loaded. The pistol kicked back hard against his hand, and the Patriot spun and crumpled against the rail with a grunt. The second guard turned, empty pistol still smoking in his hand, and Marcus could hear shouting among the other guards on the pier.

And suddenly we're out of time. "Raes!" he shouted. "Get the gangplank!"

Tossing his spent pistol aside, he drew his sword and charged the bewildered-looking Patriot who'd shot Peter. Behind him, back at the stern, there was another pistol shot, but he couldn't spare the time to look. *Andy can take care of things.*

He reached the guard, who was just tossing his pistol aside and going for his own sword. Marcus didn't give him the chance, dropping into a straight-forward lunge that took the man in the belly and came out between his shoulder blades. Hot blood gushed over Marcus' hand, and the Patriot slid forward and died with a gurgle. Marcus pull the blade free and let him fall, looking up in time to see Raesinia sprint past him.

The *Rosnik* was connected to the pier by a pair of heavy lines, and an articulated gangplank that came up to the level of her deck. This was lashed in place by a lighter rope, and Raesinia drew a knife and began hacking at it, even as the guards on the pier started to come up. Marcus realized immediately that she wouldn't make it—someone else was climbing up the rope ladder where Peter had fallen, but they wouldn't be on deck in time. He spun and stepped up beside Raesinia, swinging his sword blindly with a wild roar.

His sudden appearance out of the darkness was enough to startle the first Patriot Guard on the gangplank into lurching backward, where he lost his footing and toppled sideways with a yell, splashing into the gap between the edge of the pier and the boat. The man behind him had better balance and a pistol in his hand, and Marcus threw himself down just as he pulled the trigger. As soon as the shot sounded, Marcus popped back up, swinging his sword low and catching the Patriot in the shins. The blow and the pain sent him sprawling, too, and he caromed off the end of the stone pier with a nasty *crunch* before hitting the water.

"Shoot them!" someone on the pier was shouting. "Fire!"

"Got it!" Raesinia said.

Marcus ducked and took hold of the end of the gangplank

in his off hand, while Raesina grabbed it with both of hers. They lifted the folding wooden bridge until it was clear of the *Rosnik*'s deck, then let it fall, scraping against the side of the hull as it went. Once it was clear, Marcus grabbed Raesinia and dragged her down again, as three or four muskets boomed from the pier. Balls *zipped* overhead, and at least one *thocked* into the hull.

"You all right?" Marcus said, one arm over Raesinia's shoulders.

"Always," she said. "Remember?"

"Marcus?" Andy shouted. "I think there's more of them downstairs!"

"Balls of the fucking *Beast*," Marcus said, rolling back to his feet and running hunched over across the ship. The deck of the *Rosnik* was several feet higher than the pier, which meant the musketeers there didn't have a good shot at anyone who didn't expose themselves along the rail, but that didn't seem to stop them from trying. By the volume of fire, there had to be at least a dozen of them.

At the bow, Viera was aboard, along with two more women volunteers, Maple and Zimona. The pair were sisters who'd been targeted by the seedies after they cracked the skull of a man who'd come to demand protection money, and they'd been eager to help. Maple, the elder, was moving to Raesinia's side, but her sister was on her knees and looking a little gray, spattered with blood Marcus assumed was Peter's. Viera, knife-slim next to the pair of formidable Docks women, followed Marcus toward the midships stairway.

Andy was already waiting there, the Patriot who'd been on guard unconscious and bleeding freely. She held his musket in one hand. With her were Gavin, a balding, muscular Borelgai who had once been some sort of gardener, and another former Leatherback named Brask. Nell, another one of Jane's young women who'd left the troop to stay behind with her sweetheart, was just coming up the rope ladder. A set of stairs went from the level of the main deck down to a thin wooden door, which already had one splintery hole in it.

"I tried to open it, and he took a shot through the door," Andy said. "Missed me, but not by much."

"Is there another way down?" Marcus said.

"There's a cargo hatch," Brask said. He had the thick, heavy build of the men who loaded and unloaded ships for a living. "But you need a crane t' get it open."

"Marcus!" Raesinia said. "They're climbing up!"

Marcus swore again. "Andy, get the guards' muskets and pistols. Fire off a few shots to make them keep their heads down, but don't stick yours *up* if you can help it. Get the bow crew to help you, but send Viera back here."

"On it," Andy said, hurrying toward Raesinia.

"Everybody clear of the door," Marcus said. Nell made it onto the deck and came to join Gavin and Brask, a pistol clutched in one hand. "I'll try and get him to shoot. Gavin, you think you can break that door down?"

The big gardener gave it an appraising glance, then grunted. Marcus left him at the top of the stairs and circled around to where he'd dropped his pistol. Retrieving his weapon, he lay flat on the deck, just above the door—one deck below, the Patriot Guard with the itchy trigger finger was right underneath him. From that position, Marcus could reach down and touch the top part of the door. Holding his pistol by the barrel—still warm from the earlier shot—he swung it as far down as he could, hard, against the door.

This had the desired effect. The pistol's butt slammed hard against the wood, and the guard inside fired, punching another hole in the door but hitting nothing more than the staircase. Gavin, waiting for the shot, ran full tilt down the stairs and put his shoulder to the door. It broke with a crash, and there was another pistol shot. Marcus heard a gasp and a grunt, and Brask, following close behind Gavin, passed underneath Marcus with a long knife in his hand. Marcus pushed himself to his feet and circled around, hopping down onto the stairway.

The Patriot Guard was dead, two smoking pistols beside him and Brask's knife in his throat. Gavin was slumped against one wall, moaning and clutching his side, with blood slick under his fingers.

Didn't think he'd have a second one, Marcus thought, with the numb feeling that always came over him in the midst of a battle. It was the detachment of a commander, watching men fall all around you, and knowing that you couldn't care about it, not yet. *Get the job done first.*

"Get Gavin back on deck," he told Brask. "Nell, make sure that's the last of them."

"Yes, sir!" she said, voice squeaky with fear but determined. Only in the moment after he'd done it did Marcus realize what he'd just done, ordered a girl not yet twenty to go in search of armed men in the midst of a firefight. *Get the job done.* Marcus stood aside to let her pass, then went back up the stairs to find Viera coming his way, lugging her oiled-leather sack.

"Wait until we know it's clear down there," Marcus said. "Then do what you need to do, as fast as you can."

"You can count on that." There was a feverish light in Viera's eyes. "We won't want to hang around here any longer than we have to."

Musket-fire was still coming from the front of the boat, so Marcus ran in that direction, hunching over again to avoid poking his head up. He saw Raesinia and Andy, lying side by side, aiming through the gaps in the rail while exposing themselves as little as possible. Once they fired, they slithered back to accept a fresh musket from George the Gut, who was reloading as fast as he could. Maple was down, lying slumped against the rail, and Zimona was pulling at the back of her sister's dress in tears. Walnut, beside her, hacked at the arm-thick lines tying the boat to the pier.

"Leave those," Marcus told him. "We'll never get the anchor up anyway. Get her out of here!"

Walnut nodded and pulled Maple's deadweight away from the rail and out of sight of the musketeers below, Zimona trailing in his wake. Marcus watched the big woman's limp, dangling arm and thought, *Get the job done first.* He lay down and pulled himself up beside Raesinia to look at the pier.

As he'd guessed, there were close to a dozen Patriot Guards down there, taking cover among the stacks of barrels and coils of rope that littered the pier. One lay in plain view, obviously dead, while another crawled determinedly away from the boat, trailing a slick of blood from his leg. The rest were loading and firing as fast as they could, a thick haze of powder smoke already hanging over the pier like a dirty cloud lit from within by muzzle flashes.

"A couple tried to climb up the ropes, but Andy bashed one over the head," Raesinia reported. "The other jumped into the water."

"I think they're trying to keep us busy while they figure out what to do," Andy said.

"Fine with me," Marcus said. He flinched at the sound of a pistol shot, muffled by the wooden deck. *Nell must have found something.* "You two keep this up. I'll go help Viera."

He had only a moment to reflect on the absurdity of using the queen like a common ranker. Shuffling back from the rail on his elbows, he looked over his shoulder at Walnut, who had dragged Maple to safety. The big man caught Marcus' eye and shook his head; Zimona was bent over her sister's corpse, sobbing. *Damn.* Marcus pointed at George, indicating that Walnut should help load—he would make too big a target at the rail. Walnut nodded, patted Zimona on the shoulder, and loped across the deck as Marcus ran back toward the stern.

Nell was emerging from the stairway, a smoking pistol in one hand. "There was one left," she said, beaming at Marcus. "But I got him."

"Good work. Is Viera already down there?"

"With Brask," Nell said.

"Help Andy and Raes," Marcus ordered, and went down the stairs himself.

Gavin lay to one side, a crude bandage wrapped around his waist already clotted with blood. His breathing was ragged. Beyond, a short passage in one direction opened into the cargo hold, while the other way led to two cabins, both with their doors already broken open. The corpse of a Patriot Guard was sprawled behind one of them, a bloody hole where one eye should have been.

Marcus turned into the hold. Viera was at one end of it, adjusting something, while Brask stood looking down at a massive wooden crate. Marcus joined him, and found one of the huge steel tablets nestled within, packed in straw like wine bottles ready for shipment.

"This is what we came for, isn't it?" Brask said.

Marcus hesitated, then nodded. They hadn't told the volunteers the whole story, of course, only that the mission was important to stopping Maurisk. Brask frowned, then made the sign of the double circle across his chest.

"Good," he said. "Glad we're destroying this heathen stuff. Gives me the creeps just to look at it."

Good enough. "Viera, how long?"

"A couple of minutes," Viera said, not looking up.

"Brask, get Gavin up on deck," Marcus said. The wounded Leatherback probably wouldn't make it, but they owed it to him to at least try to get him to a cutter. "I'll get the boats ready."

"Got it," Brask growled.

Up above, the fire from the pier had slowed down. Marcus suspected the Patriot Guards were low on ammunition, and in any case their own smoke cloud was so thick now they were essentially firing at random. Andy fired back periodically, just to reassure them someone was still there, but Raesinia and Nell had moved back from the rail.

"Nearly there," Marcus said. He ran a quick mental count in his head. "We'll leave one of the boats. George, get the one we came in. Walnut, you take the one at the stern. It'll be a little crowded, but we'll get clear."

"I don't think Zim will leave Maple," Walnut said.

"Carry her," Marcus said. "We haven't got time. Then help Brask with Gavin. He's hit pretty badly."

"Right."

Walnut strode across the deck and grabbed the shrieking Zimona around the waist, pulling her off the prone body of her sister. He carried her to the stern, without apparent effort. George, hampered somewhat by his namesake gut, was lowering himself back down the rope ladder to the other boat.

We're going to pull it off, Marcus thought. It had been bloodier than he'd wanted—he'd hoped to avoid a fight altogether—but the Patriots were out of options. *They can't rush us, and they don't have the angle to pick us off. They could blow us out of the water with the guns, but that would defeat the whole—*

Something moved, on the deck. Marcus blinked and looked down—the shadow of the foremast, cast by the bow lantern, slanted right beside where Nell was excitedly recounting the story of her encounter with the Patriot to Raesinia. A long, sharped-edged shadow, and right at the edge of it . . . *a hand?*

Marcus' perspective swam. A black-gloved hand, gripping the lit part of the deck. Then, in one swift movement, a lithe, dark form pulled itself out of the shadow of the mast like a swimmer hoisting himself out of the water. Marcus caught the glitter of obsidian and started to scream a warning.

Too late. The newcomer grabbed Nell's arm and used it to pull himself to his feet, sending her staggering in front of him. As part of the same, elegant motion, his other hand drew a long knife across her throat, leaving a spray of arterial blood in its wake. Raesinia was just starting to turn when the man spun, slamming a balled fist into her midsection. As she doubled over, he grabbed her hair, jerking her head back, and brought his knife up to her throat.

"Hello, Colonel." Ionkovo's voice. His face was obscured behind the faceted obsidian mask of the Penitent Damned.

Damn, damn, damn. Andy, still lying at the rail, rolled over and froze. There was smoke trickling from the barrel of her musket, which meant that she'd already fired. George was over the side already, Brask and Walnut helping Gavin at the stern. Nell, eyes very wide, took a couple of tottering steps and then keeled over like a collapsing drunk, a crimson pool of gore forming from the weakening pulses from her neck. Her heels drummed a tattoo on the deck, then stilled.

"Not a bad plan," Ionkovo said. "But I don't see how you expected to get away with it. A suicide mission, perhaps?"

Raesinia was gasping for breath, knife pressed against the soft skin of her throat. But her hands were moving, one clutching the other. She drew one finger down the other palm, over and over, but it took him a moment to realize what she meant.

That night, at Twin Turrets. She'd drawn the knife across her palm, to demonstrate her power. *"I can't die."* Raesinia's eyes found Marcus', and her gaze was fierce. *Don't do anything stupid.*

Marcus met Ionkovo's gaze, eyes sunken behind the gleaming mask. There was a steady malevolence there, but also a touch of morbid humor. *He knows. But he doesn't know that I know.*

Without moving his head, Marcus glanced at the stern. Brask and Walnut had already taken Gavin over the side, and he could see Viera at the rope ladder. She took one look at the frozen tableau on the deck and started climbing down to the boat. *Smart girl.*

"Lie down on the deck, Colonel," Ionkovo said. He looked down at Andy. "You, too, unless you're eager to see your friend get a red smile."

"If you hurt her," Andy said, "I'm going to paint the deck with your brains."

Marcus was trying to count heartbeats, but his pulse juddered so wildly he couldn't be certain. *But it can't be long now.*

"Colonel?" Ionkovo cocked his head. "What are you waiting for?"

In the hold, a tiny piece of clockwork went *click* and made a spark.

The blast sounded like a cannon going off, and the *Rosnik* lurched as though a giant had kicked it. Ionkovo staggered, but his grip didn't falter. He flipped the knife in his hand and drove it up, through the soft underside of Raesinia's jaw and upward into her skull. Her legs gave way, and she collapsed to the deck as Ionkovo let her hair slip through his fingers.

Andy screamed and charged the Penitent Damned, only to be intercepted midway there by Marcus, running in the opposite direction. He grabbed Andy by the waist and lifted her bodily off the deck, heading for the bow rail. Ionkovo was saying something, but it was drowned out by a much larger blast, this one from the stern. Bits of flaming wood pinwheeled through the sky, and the rear mast began to topple with a groan like an enormous rusty hinge. The shock slammed Marcus and Andy against the bow rail, which snapped under their combined weight. Marcus kept a firm grip on Andy as they went over the side, splashing into the water a few feet below.

Marcus did his best to keep Andy's head above water as she thrashed and swore, but she got a mouthful in spite of his best efforts. This quieted her a bit, and by the time she'd coughed it up she was composed enough to tread water on her own. *Rosnik* was sinking fast, with a hole across her keel by the bow and the whole of her stern blown out below the waterline. Before long, only her foremast was visible above the surface of the water.

The water was bitterly cold, and Marcus could feel himself losing feeling in his fingers already. He kicked, his boots slowing him, and turned in a circle. Without *Rosnik*'s lanterns, the water was dark, but Patriot Guards were still milling about on the pier, and their lights gave him a brief glimpse of one of their boats, not too far away. He grabbed Andy's arm and pointed, and she gave a convulsive nod and started to swim.

George the Gut, leaning so far over he came close to swamping the little craft, helped first Andy and then Marcus into the rowboat along with a generous quantity of river water. Zimona was curled in the stern, sobbing, and

with all of them soaked, it took Marcus a moment to realize Andy was crying, too.

"What the hell happened?" George said. "I was getting
ready to cut loose when I heard the shouting. Where's
Raesinia and Nell?"

"He fucking killed them," Andy said. "That's what happened! That *fucker*—"

"Nell's dead," Marcus said. "But Raesinia will be fine.
We have to go back and find her."

"Fine?" Andy turned on Marcus. "Have you lost your
fucking *mind*? How can you—"

Marcus slipped between her and George and bent over,
putting his mouth by her ear.

"I will explain everything later, I *promise*," he whispered.
"Right now you're just going to have to trust me. Raesinia
is *alive*, and you cannot tell anyone what you just saw."

Andy's hand gripped his shoulder tight, and her voice
was a hoarse rasp. "You're serious? You think she's alive?"

"I swear by all the saints and martyrs," Marcus said.

Andy pulled back and looked at him, in the shadowy,
flickering light. Whatever she saw in his eyes, it was evidently convincing, because she gave a quick, jerky nod
and sat down beside one of the oars.

"Raesinia is alive," Marcus said, turning back to George.
"But we have to get to her before they do. Help me—"

The night lit up, as though lightning had struck, and a
moment later they were blasted by an enormous roar
louder than any thunder Marcus had ever heard. A hundred yards beyond the little boat, a column of water rose
from the surface of the river, collapsing into a spray of
foam.

Zimona screamed and curled up even tighter. Andy,
hands over her ears, mouthed, *What the fuck?* at Marcus.

"The siege guns!" Marcus shouted, voice barely audible
in his ringing ears. "The water battery is firing at us!"

"Then let's get out of here!" George said, grabbing an oar.

"We have to go back!" Marcus said. "Raesinia—"

He had a sudden image of her, hands on her hips, staring

at him crossly. *What did I tell you, Marcus?* She brought up one hand and drew a line down her palm. *Don't do anything stupid.*

"Those guns are a bear to aim," he said. "I don't think they'll be able to hit us."

"They don't need to hit us," George said, giving the oar a pull and sliding across to yank on the other. "Did you see the size of that spout? They'd have us over if they hit within fifty yards!"

"And there's still musketeers on the pier," Andy said, sitting down at the other oar. "He's right, Marcus."

Damn. Marcus took a deep breath. *All right. They can do whatever they want to her, and it won't matter. She told you it won't matter. As long as they don't get her out of the city, and Janus wins, we'll get her back. Sothe can track her down and make sure they don't try to sneak her off to Elysium.*

Sothe. Marcus groaned aloud. *She's going to have my head on a platter . . .*

RAESINIA

Raesinia awoke.

Ever since she'd died, this wasn't something that happened very often. The binding wouldn't let her sleep, and it took serious injury to her head before she lost consciousness. The last time it had happened, it was because Faro had put a pistol ball through her skull, and she'd awoken upside down in the river, impaled on a rock.

This time, she was reasonably certain her unconsciousness had to do with the knife the Penitent Damned had shoved into her brain, and she wasn't sure if the circumstances of her awakening were better or worse. On the positive side, she was out of the river, laid out on a rocky strip at the base of the water battery fortifications. This was surely better than being upside down and impaled.

On the negative side, the handsome young man dressed

in black sitting beside her was almost certainly the same Penitent Damned who'd stabbed her, minus his obsidian facemask. He was watching her with intense interest, and she would have shifted away from him uncomfortably if she hadn't been more or less dead.

The binding was hard at work, though. Having rebuilt her brain and restarted her consciousness, it moved on to resealing her skull and knitting up the rents in her throat left by the Penitent's knife. Once those were closed, it wrapped around her heart and squeezed tight. Her pulse slammed against her chest and through her skull, so hard she thought she would burst, and stuttered a bit before getting back to its regular rhythm. Raesinia coughed, sending up a small spray of water, and drew a ragged breath. Her body tingled all over as the binding got round to fixing all the little bits and pieces that had gone haywire when her heart and lungs gave up the ghost.

"Remarkable," the Penitent Damned said. "Five minutes ago, I would have sworn to the pontifex you were dead."

Raesinia coughed again, then managed to rasp, "You get used to it."

"I imagine," he said. "I have read about the Eternal Warrior, of course, but I have never been privileged to see it work. Does the time it takes to repair you depend on the degree of the injury?"

"Usually," Raesinia said, then remembered that she didn't owe this man any answers. He smiled at her silence, and looked out at the river, where the *Rosnik* had been.

"I must admit," he said, "it was a bold plan. Not a *good* plan, but I can't fault your courage. Although I suppose in your case that doesn't really apply, does it?"

"The plan seems to have worked fine," Raesinia said. "Aside from me getting left behind."

"Really?" The Penitent looked puzzled. "I'd assumed you intended to extract the Thousand Names *before* sinking the boat, though I admit I don't understand how."

"They all thought the same way," Raesinia said. "But I realized we didn't need to *steal* the Names back, just keep you from getting away with them. A few weeks on the bottom of the river won't hurt them any, and once Janus crushes Maurisk he can fish them out again."

Getting to see the look on his face, Raesinia thought, was almost worth getting stabbed in the head.

Chapter Twenty-four

WINTER

Just after dawn, they ran into the first hint of resistance. Three Patriot Guards, hiding behind an abandoned wagon, jumped out from cover, fired an ineffective shot or two, then ran for it.

"Well," Winter said, watching from Edgar's back, "that answers that question."

They'd camped the night before at the edge of the noisome swamp called the Bottoms, only a few miles from the edge of Vordan City proper. If there had been a hill, a man standing atop it could have seen the lights of the Island, but there were no hills in the Bottoms, only bits of ground that were nominally above water. The Green Road, which they'd been following north, ran along a raised causeway here to keep it out of the mud.

The army was still well outside the formal boundaries of the city, but the first shacks had already started to appear. The Bottoms had always been a place for castoffs, those too destitute, crippled, or mad to survive even in the slums of Newtown. They drifted here, eking a meager existence from the marsh and living in tumbledown huts made of scrap and sod. By and large, they hadn't turned out to welcome the Army of the East. Winter suspected these were people used to hiding at the first sight of armed men, whatever banner they were flying.

Janus had sent riders, the evening before, bearing his terms to the Directory. The Army of the East would remain outside the city if the Directory officially dissolved itself and returned power to the Deputies-General and the queen, to whom Janus would submit himself for judgment. No answer had been forthcoming, so as soon as there was enough light to see, Winter had taken the Girls' Own forward along the causeway. That the Patriot Guard were shooting at them, however ineffectually, more or less decided the issue.

She let out a long breath, staring up the road in the gray light. Jane was up ahead, somewhere, in the midst of a city of frightened people caught in the midst of the clash of armies. It had been more than a century since the capital had suffered invasion.

"Send a messenger to Janus," she said to Cyte, who waited patiently at her side. "Tell him the Patriots seem to be planning to resist, and I'm going to push ahead until I run into something solid."

"Sir." Cyte saluted. Something about the occasion seemed to encourage formality.

The Third Regiment was lined up behind her, the Girls' Own in the lead and Royals in the rear. Winter studied the faces she could see, and found no hesitation there. The women in the front ranks looked eager. For a good portion of them, this was their home, and they were here to retake it.

"Abby?" Winter said.

"Sir!" Abby stepped forward from the front ranks of the Girls' Own.

"Go ahead and move up the causeway. Loose order, and stop as soon as you find anything serious."

"Yes, sir."

Abby turned and began shouting orders. The lead companies of the Girls' Own fell out from their neat ranks into a rough skirmish formation and started up the road at a jog. Winter turned Edgar about and rode past them until she was level with the Royals, where Sevran saluted crisply.

"Once they've cleared the road ahead, move up, but stay in column." There wasn't room for a wider formation, not until they'd cleared the marshes. "You're the reserve, so keep back and be ready to pass skirmishers if they counterattack."

Sevran saluted again, and turned to his tasks. The sun had cleared the eastern horizon, and the low mist of the marshes was beginning to burn off. Winter could see the blue-coated women of the Girls' Own, up ahead, still moving briskly. *No firing yet.*

The approach to Vordan City presented a series of challenges, and the central question was where the Patriot Guard planned to make their stand. The Green Road passed through the Bottoms along a causeway, an earth-and-stone roadbed built several feet higher than the surrounding marshes to protect it from the occasional inundations of the Vor. It was wide enough for two wagons to pass each other, which was barely room for a single-company front. A barricade here, especially with artillery to defend, would be a nightmare to storm from the road, and Winter had been expecting to see one emerge from the mists as the sun rose.

Janus had planned for this, of course. Fitz Warus' Colonials were advancing up the Old Road, to the east, straight toward the Cut that divided Newtown from Oldtown. It didn't offer the advantages of a direct approach to the Island, and risked getting bogged down in the maze of Newtown tenements, but if Winter's Third Regiment got stuck, Fitz would be able to come to her assistance and outflank the defenders. Farther west, Give-Em-Hell's cavalry were taking the long way around, circling the marshes to come up the River Road.

They can't be strong everywhere. Sooner or later, given the numbers, Janus' army would take the city. As he'd emphasized to his commanders, though, *sooner* was a good deal better than later. The longer the battle went on, the more damage they'd cause to the city. And if the Patriots were able to drag things out into a serious siege, it was possible that other army units might arrive, more loyal to the Directory than Zarout and Braes had been.

With Cyte and Bobby at her side, Winter rode forward near the tail of the Girls' Own's extended formation, close enough to see what was going on without getting into musket shot of any enemies. Behind her, the Royals advanced in step to the sound of their drummers.

For a half hour, they advanced like this, women occasionally running up to report that the causeway remained clear to their front. Winter kept a cautious pace, but the complete absence of resistance meant that they made good time nonetheless.

"This doesn't make sense," Cyte said, riding beside Winter. "The causeway is a strong position. They ought to be making the most of it."

"Maybe they're worried about getting cut off." Winter shrugged. "Or maybe they're just stupid."

Cyte grinned. "Farus the Fourth said his favorite prayer was 'God grant me stupid enemies.'"

"I can see the city," Bobby said, pointing.

It was true. The rising sun had burned away the mist, and the buildings of the South Bank were slowly coming into view. The brutally regular tenement towers of Newtown loomed over the smaller buildings around them off to the right, a monument to Gerhardt Alcor's failed vision of a perfectly rational city. Directly ahead, the smaller, older shops and warehouses of the Docks were a confused jumble of slate roofs and protruding chimneys, with smaller, meaner dwellings clustering at the edge of the marshes like barnacles clinging to the hull of a ship.

Far beyond, picked out by the gleam of sunlight on gold, Winter could see the twin spires of the Sworn Cathedral topped by their double circles. Off to one side, the black spike of the Vendre was like a wedge cut out of the sky.

"Coming up on the Lower Market," Winter said.

She'd gotten a passing familiarity with this part of the city during the time she lived with Jane's Leatherbacks, and a few hours with the maps had refreshed her memory. The Market was at the intersection of the Green Road and Wall Street, a broad open dirt square where farmers from the south sold their goods to city merchants. The causeway ended at the southern end of the irregular open space, opening out onto the streets of the city. Winter rode off the elevated highway with a sense of relief. *One obstacle down, and nobody's died yet.*

"Sir!" A young woman ran up and saluted. "Barricade ahead!"

Well, luck can't last forever.

The barricade sheltered the top half of the Lower Market, north of Wall Street, where it would be difficult to outflank from either direction. It was mostly made of wagons and carriage, turned on their sides and buttressed with crates and barrels. Musket barrels poked through gaps and loopholes, like the spikes on a strange-looking porcupine. The Girls' Own had halted out of range, and Winter noted approvingly that Abby had already stationed companies to watch the roads to the east and west. *They might try to jump us while we're engaged here.*

"Any firing?" Winter asked Graff, dismounting and hanging Edgar's reins to a ranker.

"No, sir." Graff, squat and bearded as ever, looked more at home at the head of his company of women than the last time Winter had checked in on him. "Looks like they're sitting tight."

"Might be worth trying to talk, then," Winter said. "Run up a white flag and send someone over. Tell them if they get out of our way, nobody has to get hurt."

"Yessir!" Graff turned away. "Sergeant! Get a truce flag ready."

While he made the preparation, Winter looked back to Bobby, who was still mounted.

"Captain Archer's battery is somewhere behind us," she said. "Would you ride back and tell him that if he could hurry along a couple of guns, it would be helpful? Tell Sevran to let him pass." She looked across at the bristling barricade. "Let's not storm that thing if we can help it."

Bobby nodded and reined about. Cyte, also dismounting,

returned to Winter's side as three women set out from the front line toward the irregular mound of vehicles and furnishings, carrying a white flag.

"You think they'll give way?" Cyte said quietly.

"No," Winter said. "But it doesn't hurt to ask."

The trio of unarmed women walked to within thirty yards of the barricade, and the sergeant cupped her hands to her mouth and shouted while one of the rankers waved the white flag in case the enemy had somehow missed it. There was a moment of silence, then an answering shout from behind the row of wagons. It was too far away for Winter to hear the words, but she caught the tone and let out a sigh. *Probably too much to hope for—*

A musket *cracked*, and then another. Dirt fountained by the sergeant's feet. She backed up a step, still shouting, and another half dozen shots erupted from the barricade. The ranker carrying the flag sat down heavily, as though a chair had been pulled out from under her, then slumped to one side. The sergeant screamed and collapsed, clutching her knee. The second ranker turned to run, but made it only a few steps before she was struck from behind by two balls at once. A spray of blood and torn flesh erupted from her chest, and she fell heavily, face-first, and lay still.

"Bastards!" Graff yelled, raising his sword. Similar cries were going up all down the line of Girls' Own, and a few women started forward. Winter took a deep breath and shouted as loud as she was able.

"Steady! Hold the line!"

A few officers repeated the command. Graff looked up at her, eyes wild with rage. For a moment she thought she was going to have to slap him, or worse, but he mastered himself and added his voice to the chorus.

"Steady! Steady! Hold!"

The sergeant was still alive, crawling away from the barricade with a slick of blood trailing from her wounded knee. Dirt erupted by her head as a Patriot on the barricade took a shot at her, and even across the distance Winter could hear laughter. A moment later, another shot ricocheted off a stone near her foot.

"They're *taking turns*." Graff turned to Winter, his expression pleading. "We have to help her!"

"They want us to charge." Winter's throat was thick. "There's a rank of soldiers waiting behind that thing ready to fire. They *want* us to try storming it."

"But that's Sergeant Bells!" Graff said. "She—"

"It doesn't matter who it is. We can't get to her, not without leaving another dozen corpses out there." She raised her voice again. "Hold the *fucking* line!"

Bells had managed to crawl ten yards or so before one of the men on the barricade managed to hit her, raising a spurt of blood instead of a column of dust. Winter let out her breath, only to suck it in again as the sergeant kept moving, pulling herself forward with a dying animal's tenacity.

I am going to kill you all, Winter thought, teeth clenching so hard she felt they might shatter as more laughter came from the barricade. *Every last fucking one.*

Finally, mercifully, the sergeant shuddered and lay still. The enemy took another couple of shots at her, until the amusement palled. Winter tried to pick out the faces of the men who'd been laughing, but it was too far. She forced herself to swallow, feeling the muscles of her jaw ache where they'd been locked tight.

"Cyte!" she barked.

"Sir?"

"Tell Abby to send a company into those buildings and find me a spot where I can see over that thing."

Cyte saluted and hurried off.

Let's see what kind of trap they're so eager we rush into.

A few minutes later, on the roof of what had been an animal feed shop, Winter stood with Cyte, Lieutenant Marsh, and a few women of his company. They'd found the building abandoned, and Winter had been escorted up the back stairs, through kicked-open doors and the messy hallways of a residence quickly abandoned. The proprietor and his family had lived above the shop, but had presumably sought safer quarters when the barricade went up.

From this vantage point, three stories up, Winter could see the whole curving arc of barricade. It was lightly held, with only a few hundred men in total spread along its length. Enough that they'd take casualties storming it, but not enough to stop a determined charge.

But, a few hundred yards back, a much larger body of men waited. There were a thousand or more of them, bunched in small groups at the north end of the square. Unlike the men at the barricade, they didn't wear the sashes of the Patriot Guard; all Winter could see that resembled a uniform were blue armbands.

"Some kind of militia?" Cyte guessed, looking down at the milling mass.

"Seems like a safe assumption," Winter said. "They're certainly not holding any kind of formation."

"Not many muskets," Marsh said, peering intently. "A few pikes."

"Nasty," Cyte said. "Put just enough real troops on the barricade, taunt us into charging, then counterattack with that lot when we're halfway over. If they time it right they could do a lot of damage."

Winter frowned. It *was* a devious way to use poor-quality troops, especially if you didn't particularly care how many of them came back. *I wonder if they realize that?*

"Bobby's back," Marsh said, looking over at the Girls' Own. "And I think Archer is with her."

"Good," Winter said. "Hold this position, and I'll have Archer send one of his officers up as a spotter."

Marsh saluted, and Winter turned about and pounded down the stairs. Her heart felt as if it were full of ice, and the rage that Graff and all the others expressed so openly burned at the back of her mind like a banked flame. She wondered if Janus ever felt like this—he was always so outwardly calm, but he had to feel *something*.

Archer greeted her with a salute, which she waved away. Two of his guns were pulling into positions, their teams dragging them in tight half circles to get the barrels pointed the right way and detaching them from their caissons.

Cannoneers pushed the guns forward, clear of the ammunition-carrying wagons, and stood ready beside the pieces.

"Can you knock that thing to pieces?" Winter said, nodding at the barricade.

Archer looked at it and raised a contemptuous eyebrow. "With a popgun. Shall I get started?"

"Please. Where's the rest of your battery?"

"Coming. It sounded like you were in a hurry, so we doubled the teams on these two."

"Thank you," Winter said. "You've got howitzers, don't you?"

"A pair of nine-pounders. We won't need them to blast through wagons, though."

"There's a battalion or so waiting in cover." Winter pointed to the building she'd just come from. "Put somebody up there to direct your fire. You should have a good view. Try not to damage the buildings more than you have to."

"Artillery isn't always a precise science," Archer said. "But I'll do my best."

The first shot through the barricade was carefully aimed, and the results were suitably spectacular. A big four-horse wagon that formed the base for a rickety tower of crates and barrels took the six-pound ball near the top of its frame and practically exploded with the impact, bringing the whole stack crashing down along with a pair of unfortunate Patriots. The next shot hit a barrel that must have been full of flour, because it blew apart in a puff of white. As the cannoneers found their rhythm, balls slammed out with the regularity of clockwork, blasting bits and pieces of wood into the air and drawing the occasional scream from the defenders.

Here and there, a blast of musketry marked where some Patriot could no longer stand the tension. Winter's troops were all well out of range, and she'd forbade any return fire. The Girls' Own settled for shouts and jeers, and raucous cheering whenever some section of the makeshift barrier collapsed in a particularly impressive fashion.

Before too long, Sevran sent word that the Royals were ready and waiting at the end of the causeway, and the rest of Captain Archer's battery began to appear. First came two more six-pounders, which Winter dispatched to the ends of the line to spread out the destruction. Then four big twelve-pounders rolled up, which Archer deployed level with the front line of Girls' Own. From that distance, two hundred yards or so, they could fire canister, spraying the barricade with buckets of hard-hitting musket balls. The sound of impacts on the wood of the barricade was like a burst of rainfall, just after the thunder of the main blast faded away, and the soldiers cheered at the clouds of dust and flying splinters these raised.

Finally the two howitzers, looking like nothing so much as fat-bellied kettles on wheels, pulled into position. Unlike the other cannon, they were designed to fire black powder bombs in high, arcing trajectories, reaching out over the barricade and into the square beyond, where the militia were sheltering. One of Archer's officers, from the rooftop vantage, waved semaphore flags down at his companions on the ground, and the two guns were soon belching fire. The spotter watched the fall of the shot and flagged corrections, and the gunners adjusted their aim.

"Right on target," Archer said, watching the flags waggle.

Winter imagined the bombs bursting among the tight-packed militia, spraying them with ruptured metal. She bared her teeth in a vicious grin.

"Abby!" she said. "Get ready."

"For what?" Bobby said.

"They can't just sit there and take it forever," Winter said. "Sooner or later they'll either break and run or come after us. My bet is on the latter." Being under fire without an effective way to fight back was every soldier's worst nightmare, and when it had happened to her, Winter remembered, she wanted nothing more than to get to grips with her tormentors.

As though they'd been listening to her conversation, the men behind the crumbling barricade chose that moment to surge forward. Musket-armed Patriots came first, dashing across the shot-pocked earth of the square to shoulder their weapons and fire. Judging distances in the heat of battle was notoriously difficult, and for the most part this wild fire accomplished little. The Girls' Own, spread across the square in loose ranks, let loose with a ragged volley, delivered at the very edge of their weapons' range, and a few Patriots fell. One of Archer's cannon belched and delivered a load of canister with considerably more effect, cutting a swath through the disorganized enemy.

"Hold," Winter said, seeing the Girls' Own start to edge forward again, eager to close the range. "There's more coming." Abby repeated the command, echoed by officers up and down the line.

Soon the militia started to appear, pushing through gaps in the devastated barricade and the clouds of drifting smoke from the ongoing firefight. They paused behind the loose line of Patriots, gathering in tight knots. Then, at some signal from their leaders, they charged with hoarse shouts, pikes and clubs waving.

"Ready to fall back if they get too close," Winter said to Abby. "We've got the Royals formed up behind us."

The tactic was the same one she'd employed at Jirdos, but she could already see it wasn't going to be necessary here. Having to negotiate the barricade had broken up the mass of militia into a steady dribble of small groups, each of which fought without coordinating with the others. Each would break into a run, attracting more and more fire from the Girls' Own as they came closer, and dribbling dead and wounded like bloody footprints in their wake. Before they got close enough to use their makeshift weapons, the cohesion of the group would break under the shattering fire of the skirmish line, and the survivors would run back to the shelter of the barricade.

After three or four such sorties broke in bloody ruin without getting in fifty yards of her line, Winter nearly found herself feeling sorry for them. Each new group emerged from the smoke without knowing what had happened to the others, and each was shot down in turn. Wounded men and those whose courage had broken were trying to force their way back through the barricade now, clogging up the gaps and creating a mass of shoving, struggling men, those pushing their way forward trapped by those trying to get back. Archer, unprompted, directed his fire at these clots of humanity, bowling solid shot through the press and flailing the edges with canister. Soon bodies were heaped so thick at the choke points that even those militia who wanted to press forward found themselves trapped behind drifts of corpses.

The Patriot Guards, more disciplined, kept loading and firing, though one by one they were deciding the fleeing militia had the right idea and throwing down their weapons. Muzzle flashes from inside the bank of powder smoke that hung over the barricade were increasingly erratic, and it was as much from sympathy as anything else that Winter decided the time had come to finish it.

"Abby!" She had to shout to be heard over the thunder of the guns. "Fix bayonets and charge! Take prisoner anyone who throws down their weapon."

"Sir!"

Winter sent Bobby to make sure Archer ceased fire before the Girls' Own surged forward. Their loose line lacked the shock impact of a formed body of troops, but by this point it was hardly necessary. At the first sign of their opponent's approach, Patriots and militia alike began throwing away their weapons, either redoubling their efforts to flee or raising their hands in surrender.

Ten minutes later, it was all over. The Girls' Own had climbed the barricade, avoiding the corpse-choked gaps to clamber up and over the wagons. The ground on the other side was a charnel house, dirt churned to bloody mud by the work of Archer's howitzers, which had wreaked havoc on the waiting militia. Those enemy who weren't dead, wounded, or fleeing in panic were being corralled to the rear by the Royals, who'd marched in to help with mopping up.

*   *   *

"Sir," Winter said. "Third Regiment reports twelve dead and twenty-three injured." That included Sergeant Bells and her rankers. The rest of the casualties had come from the erratic fire of the Patriot Guard; none of the militia had come close to the line.

"Do you have an estimate of the enemy's losses?" Janus said.

He sat comfortably on his horse, surveying the carnage. Winter's troops had opened a hole in the barricade by harnessing teams of horses to drag the broken wagons aside, and cleared a path through the drift of bodies. Otherwise the enemy lay where they had fallen, cut to pieces by musketry and cannon-fire. The regimental cutters, having dealt with the paltry friendly casualties, moved briskly over the field looking for wounded with a good chance to survive.

"Hard to say, sir," Winter said. "Probably five or six hundred all told? We have a few hundred prisoners, too. But I doubt the militia that got away will be coming back to bother us."

"Agreed," Janus said. "You weren't at the Battle of the Road in Khandar, I recall."

"No, sir," Winter said. "If you remember I was . . . otherwise engaged."

The general nodded. "I commented to Captain d'Ivoire at the time that the first engagement for green troops is crucial. It sets the tone for everything that follows." He smiled, briefly. "I believe you have administered a salutary lesson."

"The Patriots will fight, sir, even if the militia doesn't."

"They have more to lose," Janus agreed. "But even desperate men have a breaking point. We simply need to find it."

"Yes, sir."

"Now. Your regiment is fit for further action?"

"Yes, sir. The Girls' Own is resting now, but if I let the Royals lead we can press on."

"Excellent." Janus glanced at the sun, which was approaching the midpoint of its low sweep through the autumn sky. "We must use what daylight remains to us.

Colonel Warus is facing lighter opposition, but the tight terrain is slowing his progress. Colonel Stokes is just beginning his attack. For the moment, your advance appears to promise the quickest results." He pointed, past the barricade toward the north end of the square. "Keep moving. Your objective is the near end of Grand Span. I will direct forces from the reserve to follow you, including several heavy batteries; once you have the foot of the bridge in hand, we'll need artillery to suppress any guns the Patriots may have covering the Span before we can advance. I'll instruct the commanders to follow your orders as to dispositions."

"Sir!" Winter saluted. Janus had just put her in command of perhaps a quarter of the Army of the East. "Thank you, sir."

"Be careful, Colonel," Janus said. "The enemy have had weeks to prepare this ground. But make haste as best you can. If we are still engaged when darkness falls, the results could be . . . messy."

Winter pictured scared, confused men firing at one another in the gloom, and nodded emphatically. She straightened up and offered a formal salute. "We'll get there, sir!"

Chapter Twenty-five

MARCUS

"I should have known better," Sothe said, flipping open a black-lacquered chest and unwrapping a bundle tied with black silken cord. "I should have known this would happen."

"I'm sorry," Marcus said again. "I tried—"

"I don't blame you," Sothe said. "I am well acquainted with the princess'—that is, the *queen*'s—habit of running foolish risks. She should never have been there in the first place."

"I shouldn't have taken her."

"I sincerely doubt she gave you a choice."

Sothe picked up a long, thin blade, tested the edge with a finger, then slipped it into a sheath. She was wearing close-fitting blacks, leather and rough silk, evidently made specifically for her purposes. They included a slightly preposterous number of sheaths, pockets, and loops for a variety of weapons, which Sothe produced one by one from the black chest and slotted into place. Marcus was surprised she could still stand under the weight of them all.

"You're the one who planned this," Marcus said. "You can't back out of it now."

"Plans change," Sothe said. "Rescuing Raesinia is more important."

"More important than keeping the Docks from burning down and thousands of soldiers from burning alive?"

"Yes," Sothe said. "If she's taken to Elysium—"

"You know what *she* would want you to do."

Sothe slammed her final dagger into place and stood up. Her expression was nearly as calm as always, but not quite, and Marcus got the faintest hint of strong emotion in her voice.

"What *she* wants is not the issue," Sothe said. "Protecting Raesinia from herself has always been among my primary duties."

"When you rescue her, what are you going to say?"

Sothe met his gaze, hesitated for a moment, then looked away. Marcus frowned and shook his head.

"Look," he said. "It's obvious you're not . . . comfortable with me. I'm not going to ask why. Just don't let the fact that it's *me* asking make you do something you're going to regret."

"I have done quite a few things I regret," Sothe said very quietly. She closed her eyes and was silent for a long moment. "But I suspect you are right. It will take time to organize transport for Raesinia with the city in chaos. She would want me to help you."

"If we pull this off, Janus will have a clear shot at the Island, and we'll be able to link up with him. That ought to make getting Raesinia back a lot easier."

Sothe nodded. "I will do my best. I must tell you, though, that I am not confident of the outcome if I must face another Penitent. My last encounter with one of their kind was . . . difficult."

"You think she'll see you coming?" Marcus said.

"When it comes to these Penitent Damned, there is a great deal we don't understand. You said the last time you faced this woman, she was able to deflect pistol balls?"

"More like melt them, but yes."

"That would be impossible if it required her conscious intervention. Perhaps the demon acts for her. Perhaps she can see the shots before they happen. The man I fought could read my intentions before I acted."

"It's a possibility," Marcus admitted. "But we have to try. That's why we have backup plans."

"Make sure they are ready." Sothe picked up Lieutenant Uhlan's rifle and began inspecting it minutely. "I will be waiting."

Marcus left her on the balcony of Mrs. Felda's church and descended to the main floor. The place felt cavernous and empty after so many nights of crowded floors and crowds. The refugees had mostly departed for the new hideouts in Oldtown, out of the direct path of the fighting and protected, hopefully, by Smiling Jack's cutthroats. Marcus had sent Mrs. Felda and her family with them, along with Cora. The girl had been oddly undisturbed by the news of Raesinia's capture, accepting Marcus' assurance that her friend would be all right with blithe optimism. *It's almost as if she knows the truth. I wonder if she's worked it out?*

Left behind were those who'd agreed to fight. Andy, Walnut, George the Gut, and a motley group of perhaps a hundred gathered from the Docks and the refugees. As usual, men of fighting age were notable by their absence—there were girls who'd helped out the old Leatherbacks, solid older men with gnarled, tanned skin the color of hardwood, boys on the cusp of manhood and Docks women in multicolored skirts. All they had in common was their willingness to defend their homes and an almost total lack of preparation for the rigors of combat.

Marcus had done the best he could with them, but he was well aware it wouldn't be enough when the fighting got serious. About half of them had firearms, a mix of old muskets and pistols dug out of attics and basements and some hunting and fowling pieces. The rest carried clubs, knives, and spears, with the occasional sword liberated from some old soldier's box of memorabilia. Twenty of the volunteers, those who'd proven to have the best arms in trials in the alleys behind the church, also carried burlap sacks over their shoulders. Each bag held three tin balls, each of which was stuffed with a measure of the flash powder they'd liberated from the Patriot Guard convoys.

Hand grenades, Marcus had learned at the War College, had gone out of military fashion about a hundred years ago. The theory sounded good, but in practice they'd proven to be more of a danger to their wielders than the enemy. Fuses were unreliable at the best of times, and under battlefield conditions the bombs often failed to go off at all or, more problematic, detonated too soon. In addition, when the grenadiers came under fire, the odds of some poor bastard getting shot after lighting his grenade but before throwing it were fairly high, and the consequential chain reaction could be catastrophic. After decades of experimentation, the Royal Army had followed the example of most other militaries and converted its grenadiers—who had always been required to be taller and stronger than the average soldier—into elite shock troops rather than bomb-throwers.

These hand grenades were crude things indeed, but they had the advantage that they had no fuses or other mechanisms. Viera had assured Marcus that they would explode of their own accord if they were tossed into a fire, and that was all he expected of them. They weren't intended for use against the Patriot Guard, but were very particular weapons for facing a very particular foe.

It had been impossible to keep the fact of Raesinia's capture from the Leatherbacks and refugees, but her absence hadn't produced the blow to morale Marcus might have expected. The men and women who'd chosen to fight were still determined to do so, and they talked in low voices among themselves as he passed through them. Some of the younger boys and girls were boasting a bit, displays of bravado that were painfully familiar to Marcus from every unit of soldiers he'd ever accompanied to its first battle. Many of the older people had seen war, or at least fighting, before, and they were mostly quiet.

He found Andy with her handpicked team, all young, strong men and women. Several of the Borelgai refugees were among them, women who hadn't been prepared to pick up arms but had been determined to do *something*. They'd tied their long skirts up above their knees to make running easier, exposing fish-belly-pale legs. Andy herself wore her Vordanai uniform, though she'd lent her musket to one of the other fighters.

"You've got the signal down?" Marcus said.

She nodded. "I've got it."

"Stay back until you're sure you heard it." He looked over her team, who had recognized him and assembled behind their leader in something approximating ranks. "You'll be awfully vulnerable out there."

"We'll be careful." Andy's eyes went to the balcony. "Did you talk to Sothe?"

"I think I got through to her," Marcus said. "She'll help."

"That's something." Andy blew out a long breath. "I'm all for rescuing Raesinia as soon as possible, but if she's alive, then a few hours probably aren't going to make any difference. And if—"

"She's alive," Marcus said. "And we'll get her."

Andy nodded, though she still seemed skeptical. Marcus hadn't had time to explain the truth to her, but she seemed willing to act on faith for the moment. The same went for her part in the plan, and for that matter everyone else's; no one but Marcus and Sothe knew what they were really up against. Marcus had tried to warn them, without coming out and saying the opposition was demonic. *I doubt that would help morale. Or that they would take me seriously.*

Hopefully, none of it would be necessary. Sothe came down the staircase, long rifle slung across her back, and gave Marcus a wave. He took a deep breath and summoned his parade-ground voice.

"All right!" he said, the acoustics of the church bouncing his words off the walls. "Let's go put out a fire."

Sothe's information indicated that the Patriot Guard were assembling at the foot of the Grand Span, in the crossroads where the Green Road met the River Road. Buildings lined the north side of the road, their fronts to the street and their backs to the edge of the river, whose bank was steep and rocky. They were mostly two- or three-story structures, upscale shops and cafés—by Docks' standards—where the best of the Southsiders could mingle with Islanders who wanted to do a bit of slumming or search for bargains.

South of the River Road, the Docks proper began, shipping company offices and vast warehouses for every kind of good. The streets were reasonably regular, unlike the confused warrens of Oldtown, but they jinked and twisted to make their way between the uneven buildings. Marcus' small group had used this to good advantage, staying well clear of the fighting at the south end of Newtown and approaching the crossroads from the southeast, under cover of a four-story brick building that bore the sign of the Silver Eagle Import/Export Company.

The Silver Eagle building was not one of those the Patriot Guard had mined, and the Leatherbacks had found it abandoned. Walnut forced the back door open with casual ease, and they padded cautiously through ranks of scriveners' desks that showed signs of being abandoned in haste. Paper was everywhere, toppled piles scattering and shifting underfoot. Marcus left Walnut in command at ground level and followed Sothe up the back stairs, where a trapdoor let them onto a narrow walk overlooking the shingled roof.

From there, they had a good view. To the south, Marcus could see smoke rising. The Patriot Guard had constructed small barricades at regular intervals, but judging by the volume of musketry he could hear in the distance they weren't making a strong effort to defend them. *It's all part of the trap.* They were falling back slowly, luring Janus and his commanders into pushing into the bomb-lined street. *If we can't stop the Penitent, she'll burn them all to ashes.*

Just ahead, in the crossroads, a small squad of Patriot Guards was gathered around a bonfire of stacked logs. It was just starting to catch, fire licking up from the straw beneath it, a column of white smoke rising into the sky to match the pink-gray powder smoke at the other end of the Green Road. Marcus counted twenty guards—not a strong force, considering the importance of the operation. *Unless Sothe has her information wrong.*

As though reading his thoughts, Sothe said, "I think Maurisk is keeping the involvement of the Penitent Damned as quiet as he can. He won't want more eyes here than he needs."

"So where is she?" Marcus said.

"Coming."

"You're sure?"

Sothe's lip quirked, but without humor. "People don't lie to me. At least not for very long."

She unslung the rifle from her back and started loading it, working hard with the ramrod to jam the tight-fitting ball down the barrel. Once it was prepared to her satisfaction, she propped it on the thin railing that protected the roof walk, sighting on the crossroads and the bonfire.

If she's wrong, we're all in deep shit. It was a lot of trust to place in a self-admitted ex-Concordat agent. But Raesinia's faith in Sothe was implicit. *And we don't have a lot of other choices.*

"I'll head down, then. In case you miss."

"I won't miss," Sothe said, not looking up. "But be ready in case one shot isn't enough. I'll join you when I can."

When Marcus returned to ground level, the Leatherbacks were ready. The Silver Eagle building had one large double door and several smaller entrances, and teams were stationed next to each, prepared to rush the crossroads. Those who had muskets waited beside the old-fashioned leaded glass windows. Marcus doubted any of them would qualify as a marksman, so it didn't matter much that the range was long enough that accurate shooting was going to be difficult.

Walnut, who seemed to have assumed the position of second in command, met Marcus at the stairwell. Marcus found himself half expecting a salute.

"We're ready," the big man said. "The grenade team is by the doors."

"Make sure the musketeers know that they should only fire one volley," Marcus said. "Otherwise they'll be as dangerous to us as the Patriots."

Walnut nodded and moved off, whispering a few words

to the men and women crouched by the windows. Marcus took a position by a glass pane less distorted than most, offering a reasonably clear view of the crossroads. Beside him, a plump older woman he wouldn't have been surprised to find selling him flour and vegetables clutched a musket in sweaty hands.

Outside, a carriage pulled up beside the bonfire, driven by another sash-wearing Patriot Guard. The door opened, and there she was—an old woman, cloaked against the autumn chill, walking with the aid of a cane. She descended one step at a time, carefully, but none of the soldiers offered to help her. The Patriot Guards obviously knew something about who she was, in fact, because they began to drift discreetly away, keeping as much distance between themselves and the sorceress as duty would allow.

Marcus found himself holding his breath. *One shot. One good shot and this is over.* The old woman reached the ground and walked, slowly, toward the growing bonfire. *What is she waiting for? So the—*

Fire leapt upward with a roar, streaming off the bonfire and swirling around the old woman like a glowing ribbon. An instant after, Marcus heard the *crack* of a rifle, and saw something hit the burning, twisting flames with a shower of sparks. The old woman didn't even flinch, merely raised one hand, and bolts of fire slashed upward at the roof of the Silver Eagle.

"Oh, *fuck*," someone said.

"Saints and martyrs."

"It's a demon. A demon!"

Several of the Leatherbacks were frantically making the sign of the double circle. *Give them any longer, and they'll run for it.* He couldn't blame them—fighting Patriots was one thing, and demons were quite another. *We can't give them time to think.*

"Go!" he roared. "Now! Grenadiers, hit that woman with everything you have!"

Walnut, musket looking toylike in his enormous hands, swung the butt of the weapon into the glass of a window. It shattered, and he aimed through the gap and pulled the trigger, smoke boiling out of the lock and around the other Leatherbacks. To Marcus' surprise, one of the Patriot Guards toppled.

That was enough to get the rest of them moving. A man old enough to be Marcus' father pushed the double doors open and charged with a yell, waving a sword that looked older than he was. A girl younger than Andy followed, a butcher knife in each hand. More glass shattered, and an irregular volley of musketry veiled the face of the Silver Eagle building in smoke. Balls found a few more of the startled Patriots, while sparks flew from the whirling fire defending the Penitent Damned woman.

Walnut tossed his musket aside and hefted a long iron-banded staff, following the main group out through the double doors. Marcus, falling in beside him, drew his sword and added his voice to the others. It was pointless to try and exercise command of a crowd like this once battle had been joined—they would fight, or they would run, and there was very little he could do in either event. *Besides, what orders are left to give?*

The Patriot Guards took a moment to recover from their surprise, and another few moments to shoulder their muskets, in which time the attackers had covered much of the distance. When they fired, they were at close range, though still evidently rattled. Leatherbacks in the front line pitched over or crashed to the ground as though they'd tripped, moaning or screaming or lying still and silent. Marcus saw the rest were moving too quickly to falter, though, and clearly the Patriots agreed. As one man, they turned to run, but only those farthest from the Silver Eagle building got the chance. Leatherbacks and Dock-women swarmed over the rest, clubbing and stabbing.

The old woman, whose attention had been focused on the roof, lowered her gaze to deal with the more immediate threat. She spread her fingers, and tendrils of flame licked out like whips, igniting anyone they touched as though the attackers had been doused in lamp oil. The woman who'd been standing beside Marcus screamed as she went up like a torch, dancing like a mad, blazing marionette until she collapsed, still burning. Farther forward, one of the grenadiers was hit, and her satchel exploded with a thunderous roar, spraying blood and bits of flesh in all directions.

That seemed to give the old woman pause, and the fire curled about her like a snake wrapping her in burning coils. One of the grenadiers, a gawky blond boy, dug one of the makeshift bombs out of his satchel and threw it. The fiery snake snapped out, intercepting the projectile in midair, and the powder burst blasted the snake's head into a thousand gobbets of flame that sprayed in every direction.

The woman took a step back as Walnut and one of Jane's girls skidded to a halt and hurled their own grenades, her fire again flicking out to catch the bombs. It caught one, but the blast scattered it badly enough that the second grenade reached the ropes of flame coiled around the Penitent Damned, detonating mere feet from her. Fire sprayed like liquid, raining down across the crossroads in a shower of white-hot droplets, and Marcus' view of the old woman was obscured by the cloud of powder smoke.

It won't finish her, he thought. Raesinia had nearly hit her with a powder barrel, back in the warehouse, and that hadn't been enough. *Someone has to go over and drive a knife in her heart, just to be sure.*

"Marcus!" a girl's voice shouted. "The seedies are coming!"

Marcus spun. Coming up the street from the south was a mob of militia, a hundred or more, some of them already grimed with powder smoke. *They must have been in the fighting already.* Marcus' Leatherbacks, staggered by the Penitent Damned's supernatural assault, hesitated in the face of this new threat, and Marcus could feel them teetering on the brink of flight. *Damn.*

There was exactly one option open to him to prevent this from becoming a massacre. He gestured desperately with his sword at the cloud of smoke.

"Walnut, make *sure* she's down." Marcus wasn't certain the big man heard him over the shouts of the charging militia, but there was no more time. He raised his own voice to a hoarse roar. "Everyone else, *follow me!*"

He slashed his sword down and started to run, straight at the oncoming mass of seedies. It was, he thought, a throwback to an earlier era, when the primary role of a commander was to be the man who literally led the way. He wanted to look over his shoulder, to make sure they were *actually* following, but that would make his doubt visible. In any event, it was too late. *If they're not following, this is going to be a really short charge . . .*

Pistol shots sounded from behind him, and seedies in the front rank went down. Marcus gritted his teeth and focused on the man directly in front of him, a thin, wiry type with a scraggly beard. He carried a cudgel, which he waved over his head in an impressive but impractical fashion.

Marcus timed his move carefully, slowing his headlong run and pulling up short before he collided with the thin man. The seedie hadn't been expecting that, and his club was already coming down in an arc that took it over Marcus' head. Marcus let the man's wrist bounce off his shoulder and thrust, the seedie's momentum doing most of the work of driving him onto the blade. The man just behind him, a larger fellow in a long flapping coat, stumbled to an awkward halt and tried to bring his spear to bear; Marcus jabbed with his off hand, breaking the seedie's nose with a *crunch* and buying him enough time to let the dying man slide off his blade. The spearman, one hand clutching at his face, thrust vaguely in Marcus' direction, and Marcus sidestepped and lopped off his hand at the wrist.

He left the crippled seedie to scream and tried to look around. The Leatherbacks had followed, enough of them at least, and the two groups had collided in a general melee that bore little resemblance to any kind of organized military action. Small groups fought back to back for a few moments before the press tore them apart, the battle dissolving into a confusion of individual duels. Marcus watched a teenage girl fire a pistol full in the face of a huge, bearded man, then charge another seedie with a butcher knife, ramming it past his frantic parries to open a huge gash in his thigh. She spun, triumphant, only to find a spearman thrusting his weapon into her ribs. When she opened her mouth to scream, only bubbling blood emerged.

A housewife still in her apron kicked a seedie's feet from under him and put a dagger in his eye, as neatly as if she were dispatching a chicken for the pot. An older man, screaming the battle cry of some defunct regiment, charged with ancient sword in hand, but tripped over the prone body of a seedie and went sprawling. Two other seedies immediately set about him with clubs, blood flying. A scared-looking boy crawled through the fighting, leaving a trail of blood from one leg, but when a seedie bent to finish him off, his victim surged back to his feet and buried a knife in the attacker's throat.

Marcus, with his sword and his uniform, was evidently not a tempting target. The seedies gave ground rather than face him, and he cut down two men from behind when companions who'd been watching their backs fled. Another man came at him with a spear, which Marcus barely dodged, slamming the hilt of his sword down on the seedie's hand as it went past. The man dropped his weapon and stumbled back, cursing.

Something dropped from the second story of the Silver Eagle building, a lithe black shape that landed in a crouch behind the mass of seedies. Two men nearby turned and raised their weapons, and steel flashed yellow-gold in the light of the bonfire. They both spun away, spraying blood into the dirt, and Sothe got to her feet with a long knife in each hand.

Marcus watched her fight with something like awe. In the army, personal close-quarters fighting skill had never been a priority, and those officers who *had* trained extensively with a sword had done so in the elaborately formal styles of official dueling. He'd seen Sothe fight once before, in the confusion at Ohnlei, but he hadn't fully appreciated her skill. She didn't *fight* the seedies so much as *dismantle* them, twisting and cutting through the press, moving on before her victims had time to topple. It was like watching

a master craftsman at work, every motion neat and efficient, with no wasted energy or missed opportunities.

It wasn't long before the seedies became aware of this
new threat to their rear by the screams of the men Sothe
left in her wake. A few turned to confront her, and were
duly dispatched in showers of gore. The rest of them broke,
scattering back from the terrifying assault and the continued efforts of the Leatherbacks. A ragged cheer went
up from Marcus' troops, who waved their makeshift weapons in the air and shouted curses at the retreating backs
of the militia.

Sothe flicked each blade once, painting patterns of
blood in the dirt, and returned them to their sheaths. She
looked a little singed, and blisters were rising on one side
of her face, but if they pained her she gave no sign as she
nodded to Marcus.

"Apologies for the delay," she said. "The stairs caught
fire."

"You—" Marcus' throat was dry. "That was . . ."

Sothe tensed, hands dropping back to the hilts of her
weapons. A crackling roar of flames drowned out the
cheers of victory, and Marcus felt a hot rush of air against
his back. He spun to find the flames of the bonfire rising
high into the air, with a dark silhouette in the center of
them, her arms spread as though in benediction. Coils of
fire outlined a dark, skeletal mass that might once have
been a large man. Then the woman slashed her hand, and
the flaming tendrils pulled in opposite directions, tearing
the charred flesh in two and scattering blazing bones
across the dirt.

The cheers turned rapidly to screams. This was too
much, even for the staunchest of the Leatherbacks. Marcus
shouted to be heard over them, voice ragged.

"Grenadiers! Go after her! Everyone else take cover!"

He wasn't certain how many heard, or how many were
left after the confusion of the melee. As whips of flame
came down, igniting everyone they touched, the Leatherbacks ran for the protection of the buildings on either side

of the street. Men and women screamed as they blazed up like effigies, flailing until the fire consumed them. Here and there, a stray grenade exploded with a roar.

"This way," Sothe said, and Marcus followed her back toward the Silver Eagle building. He ducked as a fiery lash scythed overhead, touching a middle-aged woman who was headed down the street with her arms pumping determinedly. She must have been one of the grenadiers, because she exploded violently at the kiss of the fire, scattering the dirt with shards of metal and bits of gore. Marcus dove through one of the smashed windows and huddled behind the wall, Sothe vaulting past balletically to land beside him.

"Someone has to get word to Andy," Marcus said. "The grenades aren't going to be able to stop that thing."

"I sent someone on my way down," Sothe said. "She should be on her way."

Marcus watched the twisting fire demon and felt his certainty draining away. *Saints and martyrs. I'm not sure* anything *can stop that thing.* No Leatherbacks remained standing in the open, but Marcus could see a few who'd taken cover in the buildings or amid fallen debris. The demon seemed to be taking its time now, pausing for a few moments before sending a lance of flame punching against a window frame. Screams rose from the other side.

"It'll just pick us off," he muttered. "Fuck, fuck, *fuck.*"

"Back door's open," Sothe said. "We could retreat."

Then all this will have been for nothing, and thousands of men will burn. "We'll have to hope Andy's team will be enough. But they'll need cover to get set up."

Sothe nodded. "I'll do what I can." She looked down at him, for once meeting his eyes. Marcus wasn't sure what it was he was seeing in her impassive face. *Resignation? Regret?* "If I don't make it, Raesinia is your responsibility."

"I—"

She didn't wait for an answer. Sothe vaulted the shattered window frame, cartwheeled, and came up with a knife in hand, whipping it into the heart of the bonfire. The fire spiraled inward, like a closing flower, all the tendrils feeding a ball of blue-white heat that screamed like a kettle about to burst. Something flashed at the center of it, and Marcus saw that at least part of the knife had struck home, leaving a long cut across the old woman's withered cheek.

The single point of fire burst apart, a hundred bolts of flame lashing the ground where Sothe had been standing. She was already on the move, running a zigzag pattern across the packed, bloody earth of the square, one step ahead of the fire that left smoking craters in her wake.

I can't just watch this. Sothe was fast, but she'd slip eventually. Marcus searched among the bodies lying where Leatherbacks and seedies had met until he found one that wore a grenadiers' brown satchel. He gauged the distance, tensed, and hurled himself back through the broken window just as Sothe let another knife fly. This time, the ball of flame formed farther from the Penitent Damned, and molten, broken fragments of blade flew apart in all direction, like tiny shooting stars. Whips of flame lashed out at Sothe, a blazing squid trying to swat an elusive fly.

Marcus reached the dead grenadier and rolled her over, pulling two battered tin spheres out of the brown satchel. He left one on the ground and hefted the other, winding up and putting all his weight into the throw to reach the old woman where she floated in the heart of the bonfire. It flew a bit wide, but a bolt of flame lashed out at it in what seemed like an automatic reaction, and the blast of the powder blew chunks of liquid fire across the square. The other tendrils paused in the pursuit of Sothe long enough for the assassin to throw a pair of knives at once, which caused the bonfire itself to dim as the flame gathered into a single ball big enough to intercept both.

She can't attack and defend herself at the same time, Marcus realized. He grabbed the second grenade and started running, an instant before a long whip of flame slammed down where he'd been standing. There was the *hiss* of charring meat, and weak screams from the wounded nearby. Marcus pounded up toward the corner of the Silver Eagle building, keeping one eye on the old woman. When she'd gathered herself for another strike, he hurled the grenade, a wild throw that her tentacles nonetheless snapped out of the air.

Up ahead, Marcus heard a shout and the clatter of something on wheels. Moments later, Andy and her team came into view, dragging what looked like a handcart with a pair of tubes and a handle mounted on top.

It had been Cora who located the firefighting engine, moldering in some forgotten warehouse. It was a simple thing, really—just two canvas hoses, and a long-handled pump between them with space for four men to work it. Marcus suspected it dated back to the construction of Newtown—the Rationalists had loved engines and machines of all kinds—which made it more than eighty years old. But it worked, or at least it worked once they'd cleaned and oiled it and chiseled off some of the rust.

Some of Andy's team were doubtless taken aback by the rearing, roaring fire demon, but they'd practiced too many times to let it shake them. One of the young women jumped off the little cart and grabbed the end of a hose, running north to the foot of the Grand Span. The riverbank was only a few feet below, and she threw the weighted nozzle as far as she could. It went into the water with a splash, the hose going taut as the current dragged it downstream.

Two teenage boys took the other hose out of its tight coil, dumped it on the dirt, and got the nozzle ready. The rest of the crew, with Andy looking on, got on the pump and started working it furiously back and forth.

It would take time, of course. Marcus looked for another dead grenadier, and spotted one lying against the Silver Eagle building, back the way he'd come. He reversed direction, narrowly avoiding a tendril whipping down to swat him like an insect, and scrambled back away from Andy's team with a spray of bloody dirt from his boots. Sothe threw another knife—*to think I wondered if she was bringing too many*—and the old woman blocked it with another teakettle screech. She slammed one tentacle down to the left of Sothe, missing her by yards, but the assassin had to skid to a stop as the flame blazed upward, elongating into a wall of white-hot fury. Sothe turned to run the other way, but a second tendril cut her off, trapping her against one wall of a building between two blazing infernos. Two more tendrils rose above the bonfires, ready to come down and smash this elusive opponent once and for all.

Marcus hurled his grenade in a low arc, as though he were bowling on a lawn. It bounced across the dirt and directly into one of the walls of flames, where it exploded with a roar and a blossom of smoke. As before, the blast of the bomb seemed to scatter the supernatural fire of the Penitent Damned like water. Sothe reacted fast, flipping sideways through the smoke of the grenade and across the remnants of the wall of flame. She came out the other side, smoke clinging to her, her black silks smoldering. But she was still on her feet, twisting to throw yet another blade at the old woman in the center of the bonfire.

A trickle had begun to leak from the end of the hose, expanding rapidly into a steady stream of river water. One of the boys tightened the valve, squeezing the stream into a high-pressure spray, while the other struggled to direct it upward. It hit the base of the bonfire with a *hiss* like hot metal quenching, throwing up a vast cloud of steam.

The old woman screamed, or the fire screamed—at this point, it was hard to tell the difference. All her flames contracted again and lashed out at the firefighting engine. The lance of fire hit the boy manning the hose and punched *through* him, leaving him pinioned for a moment on a spear of white-hot energy. It twisted up from there to slash across the women operating the pump, who dove for cover. One wasn't fast enough, and the fire hit her with a physical impact, tossing her into the air like a blazing, shrieking meteor.

The single fire tendril, shedding the flame corpse of the boy, reared up to smash the engine itself to flinders. A knife whipped out of the darkness and struck home, burying itself to the hilt in the Penitent Damned's back, but she didn't appear to notice. Marcus, with a shout, hurled another grenade, aiming for where the great tendril joined the bonfire. When it detonated, the flames scattered, raining down across Andy and her crew like a sudden squall from the depths of hell.

"Andy, hit her again!" Marcus hefted his last grenade as the tendril re-formed.

Andy ran to grab the head of the hose, now drooling water into the dirt, and the young women returned to the pump. Marcus was amazed at the fortitude of the refugees, not even professional soldiers, confronting something they couldn't understand and willing to stand to their posts. The stream gained pressure again, raining down on the bonfire, the hiss of steam rising to a roar.

The tendril of flame licked out again, but not toward the firefighting engine. Instead it came directly at Marcus, determined to finish off this interference before dealing with the real threat. Reflexively, Marcus hurled his weapon, and the blazing whip intercepted it only a few feet away from him. He managed to squeeze his eyes shut before the world went white, and the roar of the bomb drowned out even the scream and crackle of the fire.

He never quite passed out, but several moments went by before he was entirely aware of himself again, lying in the glass and rubble in front of the Silver Eagle building. Even through closed eyelids, the bomb had left glowing afterimages, and he blinked them away and struggled to sit upright.

The bonfire was dying, shrinking and melting like an ice sculpture in the desert sun. Strands of fire curved inward, struggling to form the white-hot ball of flame, but they hissed into steam as soon as they met the powerful torrent of river water. Andy played the hose over the Penitent Damned, the fire below her, and the scorched earth that surrounded them, creating a muddy lake in the center of the crossroads. In a few moments, the once-towering inferno was reduced to a nimbus of flame surrounding the old woman, who sank, blackened and smoking, among the wrecked logs that had started the flames. Andy kept the water on her until the last flickers died.

Marcus tried to stand, failed, and sat back down heavily. He was surprised to find himself in a quite extraordinary amount of pain. Looking down, he saw a six-inch-wide chunk of tin plating—part of the shell of one of the grenades—

embedded in the meat of his left thigh, blood soaking a widening black circle in his uniform trousers. He tested the shard with a finger, and the slightest pressure on it brought stars to the edges of his vision and involuntary tears to his eyes.

Marcus had been wounded before, sometimes seriously. But he had never had a foreign object sticking out of him like this, and just the sight of it made his gorge rise. He looked up, swallowing hard, and found Andy and Sothe hurrying in his direction. All around the crossroads, Leatherbacks were picking themselves up and stumbling numbly toward the remains of the fire. Wounded men and women of both sides were praying, swearing, and shouting for help.

"Marcus!" Andy said. "Are you—oh, saints and fucking martyrs."

"I was . . . a little too close to that last one." Marcus tried for a sardonic smile, but the pain made it tight around the edges. His breath came fast. "The demon. Dead?"

Sothe knelt beside him, pushing his hands away and gently touching the flesh around the wound. Even this made Marcus want to scream, and he averted his eyes and stared up at Andy, who was making a similar effort to focus only on his face.

"It—she—is dead," Andy said. "Yes. There was nothing left in the ashes but a skeleton."

"Did you—"

"I pulled its skull off and crushed it," Sothe said. "Just to be sure."

"How many of ours—*aaaah*, damn it!"

"Sorry." Sothe shook her head. "The good news is you're not going to bleed to death right away. The bad news is this needs a cutter, or else you *will* bleed to death if we try to pull it out."

"I have to . . ." Marcus closed his eyes, then opened them hurriedly when darkness threatened to close in on him. "Janus. Have to tell Janus they have Raesinia."

"We shouldn't move him," Sothe said, her voice ringing and distant.

"How about just into the building?" Andy said. "If we get the worst of the wounded in there, we can hunker down and wait. The Patriots are planning to fall back past here, so Janus' troops should be right behind them."

"Anyone who can still walk should get out of the way," Sothe said. "Just in case."

"Right." Andy stood. "I'll find a couple more volunteers to move people, and we'll start with him. Just stay calm, Marcus. We'll take care of you."

Andy ran off, shouting at someone nearby. Sothe stayed where she was, looking down at Marcus.

"You saved my life," she said eventually.

"I did?" Marcus was having trouble remembering. "Yeah. I guess I did. But you've saved mine, more than once. We're hardly even."

"I . . ." Sothe shook her head. "No. I suppose we're not even."

"I would . . . very much like to pass out now," Marcus said.

Something that was nearly a smile crossed Sothe's face. "We'll take care of things here. Don't worry."

Marcus nodded and closed his eyes. He was aware of someone catching him as he slumped backward, and then unconsciousness rolled over him like a numbing blanket.

CHAPTER TWENTY-SIX

RAESINIA

There were no proper cells in the Hotel Ancerre, so at first they'd locked Raesinia in a wine cupboard. Empty racks lined the walls, with just about enough room between them for her to sit cross-legged. She'd done that for a while, concentrating on her breathing and the feeling of the binding tidying up the last of her wounds. The front of her shirt was still heavy with drying blood, and she smelled like a butcher shop.

Eventually, a couple of Patriot Guards opened the door and grabbed her roughly by the arms. They dragged her into the corridor, where Ionkovo was waiting, a thin smile on his face. Under his watchful gaze, the Patriots frog-marched Raesinia through the halls to the door of what looked like a guest room, which had been hastily fitted with an iron bar and a padlock. Inside, it was spartan, with a single bed, a table, and a high window too small to fit through. Probably intended for a guest's servant, Raesinia guessed. There was a basin full of water, though, and she filled a cup from it and drank greedily.

"You'll remain here for a little while," Ionkovo said. "Until we can arrange safe passage out of the city. Then you'll be coming with me to visit His Eminence the Pontifex of the Black."

"Mmm." Raesinia held up one hand as she finished gulping her water. "I'm sure that will be edifying for everyone."

The Penitent stared at her for a moment. "You've lost, you know."

"Probably." Raesinia set the glass down and looked back at him steadily.

"Your general's army will burn in the streets. Even if Maurisk falls, the mob will tear down whoever puts himself in his place, eventually. We will recover the Thousand Names, and you will be our guest at Elysium for the remainder of your days."

"I hope you're prepared to put up with me for quite some time, then."

"Was it worth it? You could have spared Vordan all of this."

"By becoming Orlanko's puppet? Marrying some Borel?"

Ionkovo shrugged. "You'd hardly be the first monarch not to interest herself in affairs of state, nor even the first Orboan. Certainly not the first to despise her spouse. Would that have been such a bad life, in the end? You claim to love your countrymen, but all you've brought them is chaos and death."

"And freedom from the rule of people like you."

"Those who bear demons?"

"Self-righteous hypocrites."

The Penitent actually laughed. "I doubt any nation anywhere will ever rid itself of those."

He was probably right, of course. Raesinia sat on the bed with a sigh and plucked at the sodden neckline of her shirt. "So, what do you want from me? Don't you have a war to run?"

"I wanted to ask you something. I don't expect you'll answer, but please remember I gave you this opportunity."

"What?"

"The man who saved you from Twist. The creature of sand and darkness. Who is he?"

Raesinia laughed. "There are many things I wouldn't

tell you, just on principle, but that's one I honestly don't know. I'd like to ask him a few questions myself."

"We'll see." Ionkovo cocked his head. "My colleague the Liar has a technique for extracting information from an unwilling subject. Thus far, it's been invariably fatal for the person involved, so I'm curious to see what will happen in your case."

"I look forward to it," Raesinia said. "I'm sure it'll be exquisitely painful."

"I hope you maintain that bravado when you're locked in Elysium," Ionkovo said, opening the door. "It's sure to amuse the pontifex."

"Don't worry on that score. My friends tell me I'm incorrigible."

The door slammed shut. A moment later, she heard the bar dragged close, and the heavy *snick* of the lock.

Raesinia stood up and took a deep breath. Being snide to Ionkovo was one thing; something about his thin-lipped smile made her want to smash his face in with a brick every time she saw it. *But he may be right that things aren't looking good.*

She hoped that Marcus had escaped—Ionkovo would have gloated if they'd captured or killed him. If he was still free, he and Sothe and the others would try to stop the firestorm in the Docks, and hopefully save Janus' army. If they succeeded, that meant she had some chance of getting out of here, assuming the attackers could reach the Hotel Ancerre before Ionkovo found a way to smuggle her out of the city. *That's a lot of ifs.*

On the other hand, if Marcus had failed and Janus was defeated, it was very likely the Black Priests would carry her off into an eternal imprisonment. *It sounds like something out of a fairy tale.* What it sounded like, actually, was something she'd rather die than suffer, but she didn't even have that final option.

It had been a long time since Raesinia felt fear on her own account. She was used to fearing for those around her, fearing, especially, that they would feel compelled to sacrifice in order to "save" her, trying to rescue a life that had been lost years ago. *At least Marcus and Sothe know the truth. Not that it will stop them from trying something stupid.*

She closed her eyes for a moment and rubbed her fingers against her temples. *All right. Enough feeling sorry for myself. First things first.*

First of all, she stripped, throwing the ruined, bloody shirt into the corner. Her trousers were only spotted with blood, and would probably serve. There was a washcloth beside the basin, and after filling her glass again she set about using the rest of the water to get herself clean. *Cleaner*, anyway. Once she'd gotten rid of the worst of the bloodstains and rinsed her hands in the now-pink water, she put her trousers back on and stripped the sheet off the bed to wear like a cloak.

That accomplished, she made a thorough search of the room, in case there was something useful she'd missed. All this turned up was a copy of the *Wisdoms* bound in soft leather, forgotten under the bed by some pious butler. Raesinia leafed through a few pages at random, then decided she wasn't in the mood for theological study and left the book on the bed.

She was making a second circuit, paying particular attention to the wallpaper in case there was a loose bit of plaster somewhere, when the door lock clicked open. She turned, clutching her makeshift garment at the neck, and tried to put on a queenly manner. The door opened to reveal Maurisk, dressed in his usual severe blacks and grays, wearing an embroidered sash indicating his position as a deputy with extra embellishments to show his position in the Directory as well. Two Patriot Guards with muskets flanked him, but he stepped through the door and waved them away.

"Lock it," he said. "We're not to be disturbed."

The guards saluted, and the door slammed. Maurisk stared at Raesinia, rage boiling in his eyes. He was swaying slightly, she noted. *Is he drunk?*

"It's generally considered proper to bow to your queen," Raesinia said.

Maurisk's lip twisted into a snarl. He crossed the room

in two quick steps, grabbed the edges of the sheet, and tore it away from her shoulder, exposing her breast. She felt his eyes on her, and her throat went thick.

"I never thought you were the sort," she managed, letting the sheet fall away completely. She resisted the urge to cover herself with her hands. Being dressed and undressed by servants her whole life had left Raesinia with very little modesty on her own account, but being half-naked in front of Maurisk made her feel small and vulnerable. She stood up straighter and looked him in the eye. "Well?"

He reached out with his left hand, resting it on her shoulder. Her skin crawled, but she remained still. *A step closer, and I can go for his eyes.*

Maurisk's other hand emerged from his pocket, holding a long, thin blade. Raesinia barely had time to flinch before he struck, punching the tip of the knife into the soft skin under her breast, angled upward to slice through the lung and find her heart.

Her insides went thick and stiff. Blood bubbled to her lips with her next breath, running down her chin. Maurisk jerked his weapon free, and Raesinia took a shuffling step backward, sitting down heavily on the edge of the bed as her legs turned to jelly. The binding was already at work, drawing the rent closed and tingling all along the dagger's path, but with her heart stilled her muscles refused to respond for the moment. She slumped backward, arms spread, staring at the ceiling.

Maurisk waited, blood dripping from the tip of his dagger. It was less than a minute before Raesinia shuddered, coughing out a mouthful of blood and then sucking in a deep breath. She raised her head, blood and spit dribbling from the corner of her mouth.

"Is that it?" she rasped. "Are you satisfied?"

Maurisk nodded, not taking his eyes off her. Wearily, Raesinia rolled off the bed and staggered back to the basin, spitting into it several times before washing her mouth out with water from the cup. She took the soiled washcloth and wiped it across her lips, then cleaned herself where he'd stabbed her. She could feel him staring at where the wound had been, where the skin was now smooth and unbroken. Satisfied she wasn't going to drip blood all over herself, she picked up the sheet again, winding it around her chest this time before tying it off. *Harder to grab, and it leaves my arms free.*

"Ionkovo told me . . . what you were," Maurisk said. There was a slight slur to his words, too, but his eyes were clear. "I had to see for myself."

"A demon," Raesinia said. "A monster. I know."

"There was never any double, that night on the Vendre." That was the story she'd used, to explain her "death" at the hands of the traitor Faro. "That was you. He shot you in the head and you pulled him off the wall."

"I might quibble with the order of events, but yes. We landed on a bunch of very sharp rocks. If it's any consolation to you, it hurt quite a bit."

"How long have you been like this?"

"Years," Raesinia said. "You get used to it."

"Years." Anger and bitterness were strong in the Directory President's voice. "Since before you met us. Our little club in the back of the Blue Mask, playing at revolution."

"I was never playing at it. Neither was Ben. Neither were you."

"*I* was risking my life. So was Ben, so was Faro, so was *Cora*. What the hell were you risking? A spanking?" Maurisk shook his head. "What the fuck did you get out of it? Was it really just a game?"

"Of course not," Raesinia said. "My *father* was dying, Maurisk. When he died, Orlanko would have declared a regency and taken the throne for himself. I didn't want to spend my life married to some Borel, with Vordan back under the Sworn Church's boot."

"So you came to us. A bunch of ignorant little pawns, to be used up and discarded when they were no longer useful." He grinned viciously. "I'm so sorry everything hasn't gone according to plan."

"It was going fine, until you hijacked the Deputies-General for yourself." Raesinia crossed her arms. "It was your bomb in the square. Don't deny it."

"Not much use in denying it now," Maurisk said, with strange cheer. "Not much use in anything anymore. I just told a fucking witch to burn down half my city. Goddamned Janus bet Vhalnich just won't give up, will he? *Fuck*."

"You know it's over for you," Raesinia said. "If Janus wins, you'll end up on your own Spike. If he loses, then it's the Black Priests who'll be running things, whether they keep you on as a puppet or not. You've sold them Vordan, and for what? A few favors? Getting rid of anyone who got in your way?"

"For *peace*." Maurisk slammed his hand against the wall, leaving a dent in the plaster. "The Church will make peace, the Borelgai and the emperor stop the war. Vordan needs peace, provide that, no matter how many battles he wins, but Ionkovo can." He steadied himself and took a deep breath. "All he wanted was you, some Khandarai trinket, and Janus himself. It seemed like a good bargain. Still does, from where I stand."

The hell of it was, she couldn't entirely say he was wrong. *Except*... "Assuming Ionkovo keeps his promises. Once he has what he wants, what's to stop the Church from taking over?" and Vhalnich offer us. "You would rather have a better chance of the beat Borel and Murnsk for you, is it? All those kind thrown in?" Maurisk Only get one life apiece. really think this madness goes that far." That hit a little too close to home. Raesinia looked and said nothing. But that's not much of a risk risk shook his head, rapping on the door with exag- the lock clicked open, he turned to hear said, "Dr. caution. As interested Morton?" Raesin

Maurisk shrugged. "I believe he's interested in hearing about the *subjective* experience of the victims of the Spike. He's already hard at work designing an improved model. If there's time, perhaps you'll have a chance to assist him with his experiments."

"I'm sure his improvements will be a consolation when they're strapping *you* down," Raesinia spit.

Maurisk snorted. The guards outside opened the door, and he brushed past them without a word, leaving them to close and lock it again.

Raesinia sat down on the bed, arms crossed over her chest. She could still feel where Maurisk's dagger had gone in, a residual tingle of the binding at work.

How much worse could the Spike be, really? She closed her eyes, and tried not to think about it.

Sometime later, she was roused from her solitary contemplation by a rapping at her window.

The Patriot Guard had been busy, rushing up and down the corridors and shouting at one another. The walls muffled the sound too much for Raesinia to understand what they were saying, but for Raesinia to understand what they were saying, and she guessed as clear that *something* was happening, and anything wasn't good. She took this as a hopeful sign — anything that worried the Patriots was a positive step.

The sound at the window, she'd stood on tiptoes to prised her, she'd discovered the room was hotel. So she might have a rolled a small, the top of the, Heart suddenly pounding, Raesini the window, pushing went over to the could see out.

Nothing unusual was visible. It was sun already sliding toward the end of day. The window faced northwest, so North Bank and the Fairy C ed.

Raesinia frowned, then gave a shrug. *No harm in a little fresh air, at any rate.*

She pulled the latch and swung the pane outward. It was tiny, perhaps four inches by six, so there was no question of squeezing through it. But the sound of the city flooded in, and Raesinia was surprised to find she could hear the guns, flat *thuds* carrying across the river from who knew where. It was oddly comforting. *Janus is still fighting. It's not over yet.*

Something stung her cheek, then scraped across her nose. She put a hand up, and came away with a few grains of colorful sand nestled in her palm. At the same time, she felt a familiar pain bloom in her head. *Oh.*

Raesinia jumped down from the box and backed away from the window, and sand rushed into the room in a torrent, rattling against the glass and swirling over the carpet to form a miniature whirlwind. In the center of the maelstrom, the sand mounded up to form a man-sized shape; then the wind died away and the sand fell to the floor, revealing the masked figure who'd rescued her, Feor, and Marcus from the giant Penitent Damned.

"I was wondering what had happened to you," Raesinia said. "I thought you were keeping me safe from Ionkovo?"

"I did not expect you to run into his arms," the man said, then tilted his head, expressionless mask gleaming dully in the lamplight. "Also, over water my power is . . . limited."

"That makes sense. You'd turn to mud." Raesinia sat back down on the bed. "Won't Ionkovo know you're here?"

"He is otherwise engaged at the moment. Janus appears to have thwarted his trap, and the Army of the East is pushing into the city."

Something tight in Raesinia's chest relaxed, just a fraction. "Marcus and the others did it, then."

The man shrugged, sand cascading from the creases of his clothes. "I thought I would take the opportunity to speak to you."

"All right. Do you have a name?"

"Once I was called Jaffa-dan-Iln. Now I am Malik-dan-Belial. The Steel Ghost, in your tongue."

"I think Marcus may have mentioned that. You're Khandarai, I take it? What are you doing here?"

The Ghost paused, as though considering. Eventually, he said, "I was part of a . . . religious order, of sorts. A very old tradition, who guarded the knowledge of *naath*—you would say, sorcery—against the day when it might be needed. Safeguarding the Thousand Names was one of our primary responsibilities."

"Until Janus turned up?" Raesinia guessed.

"Vhalnich only took advantage of our weakness," the Ghost said. "We had grown . . . complacent. Safe, hidden on the sacred hill among the other religious traditions. When the Redeemers turned the city against us, most of our order was lost in the carnage. We knew—our leader knew—that weakened as we were, our enemies would come sooner or later to take the treasure they had always coveted."

"Your enemies. The Priests of the Black?"

"Yes. The *abh-naathem*, those who pervert the *naath*. The Penitent Damned, as they call themselves. We expected their agents, but we did not expect Vhalnich, who sought the archive for himself."

"Not for himself." Janus had explained his reasons to her. "He was working for my father. I have a . . . a *naath*, a demon, and my father wanted a way to free me from it. He asked Janus to find one, and Janus thought the Thousand Names might have a clue."

"No," the Ghost said, the word ringing oddly through his steel mask. "That is not the whole of the truth. Vhalnich has some other purpose, I am certain."

"Then why are you helping us?"

The Ghost sighed, an oddly human gesture. It would be easy to forget, Raesinia thought, that there was a man under the implacable mask.

"I am the last of my order," he said. "Our leader, who bore the *naath* I now carry, passed it down to me, along with as much of her knowledge as she was able to. She was too weak to do what was required. So I have come here alone, and I must walk a knife's edge. If the Thousand

Names is taken by the *abh-naathem*, it may mean the end of the world."

Raesinia gave a startled laugh. "The end of the *world*? I mean, I'm sure the Church would love to get its hands on more spells, but . . ." She trailed off, under the implacable blank stare. "You're serious?"

"Yes."

"How is that possible?"

"I cannot speak further."

"Because your religion forbids it?"

"Because I do not trust you," the Ghost said bluntly. "The *abh-naathem* cannot be permitted to have the Names. But Vhalnich has some purpose of his own that I do not understand, and you are his ally. Revealing too much may create an equal catastrophe."

"I *am* the queen, you know." She gestured around the tiny room, as though to acknowledge the irony of this claim under the circumstances. "Janus works for me, not the other way around."

The blank mask tipped inquisitively to one side. "Are you certain?"

There was the sound of heavy boots in the corridor outside.

"Ionkovo has returned," the Ghost said. "Or his allies have sensed me. I regret that I cannot assist you to escape."

"I'll survive. I haven't got much of a choice."

Sand whirled around the Ghost again, rising into a miniature maelstrom. Over the sound, he said, "Be wary of Vhalnich. He plans deep."

The wind rose, sand cascading into the air and flowing out through the window like a tub draining. Raesinia got up and stood on the little trunk as the last of it whirled away and the door opened to admit a burly Patriot Guard.

"What are you doing?" he said, looking around the room suspiciously.

Raesinia gave him her best innocent smile. "Just getting some fresh air."

In the distance, she could still hear the sound of guns.

WINTER

"The cutter says Marcus is awake," Cyte said.

Winter had to stop herself from looking up at the sun for the hundredth time. It was nearly touching the horizon, and the light was changing to the liquid gold of late afternoon. *Another hour or so, and it'll be dark.* A night battle in the city streets could be catastrophic, with no way to guard against sudden ambushes or accidental encounters with friendly troops. Once darkness fell, she would have little choice but to order her troops into a defensive position and wait for morning. *Giving them that much longer to dig in.*

"How is he?" she said.

"He's lost some blood, and he won't be on his feet anytime soon. But they say the wound should heal clean if it doesn't fester." Cyte hesitated. "He was asking for you. Pretty urgently, I understand."

Winter turned north, where the Grand Span stretched across to the looming bulk of the Island. There were no soldiers on the bridge itself—the Patriots had put it under howitzer fire as soon as the Girls' Own captured the near end, and in spite of Captain Archer's efforts, shells still rose every few minutes to burst on the bridge in gouts of smoke and flame or crash hissing into the river. The Royals had crossed an hour earlier, sprinting in groups after each thundering blast, and the artillery had followed them, cannoneers whipping their teams into a frenzy. Archer's howitzers, still on the near side of the river, had pounded the opposite foot of the bridge in preparation for their arrival.

So far, things were going well. The Royals had assaulted the enemy at the base of the bridge and sent them running, though they'd paid a fearful cost in lives advancing across the open ground. Archer's guns had blunted an attempted counterattack, and Winter had fed troops from the first regiment of Janus' promised reinforcements across as quickly as possible to bolster the bridgehead. Before long, Sevran was advancing again, but his pace was maddeningly slow. On the Green Road, the Patriots had given way easily under pressure, but now they dug in their heels tenaciously, defending barricaded positions with artillery in support.

Rather than waste men in costly assaults, Sevran brought up his own guns to blast the defenders out before advancing. Winter approved, but the strategy was burning daylight fast. The Girls' Own, recovering from their earlier exertions on the Green Road, would be next over the bridge, and once they were there Winter would have to either order an all-out assault and accept the losses or face the reality of a night strung out in the streets of Vordan City under fire. Neither prospect was appealing.

"What was the last word from Sevran?" Winter said.

"Still attacking the barricade a block south of Farus' Triumph. He said he's nearly through, but that there's guns covering the Triumph on all sides. We're going to need more artillery, or else we'll have to work our way around."

Either would take more time than they had left. *Damn.* Winter grimaced. "I can spare a few minutes for Marcus while we're waiting."

The wounded were being cared for in a building that bore the sign of the Silver Eagle, which had apparently been a nest of paper pushers. Winter's soldiers had cleared the desks out of the way and laid bedrolls on the floor, where the cutters worked with scalpels and bone saws amid the usual mix of screams, moans, and prayer. Very few of the patients were from the Girls' Own, who had so far gotten off lightly; the majority were Patriots or militia, along with some Royals who'd staggered back from the bridgehead under their own power. There were also some civilians, who'd been discovered alongside the wounded militia. Both groups had a great many burn victims, including some corpses that had been reduced to charred skeletons, but since none of the buildings had caught fire, the cutters were at a loss to explain why. *Perhaps Marcus can shed some light on the subject.*

A row of offices had been mostly appropriated for surgeries, but Cyte led her to one on the end, where Marcus was lying on a bedroll. The desk that had been in the center of the room had been pushed to one side, and a teenage girl in a blue army jacket sat on it, looking worried. Beside Marcus, sitting cross-legged, was an older woman in tight-fitting black, speckled with blood and ashes. Bobby, waiting at the door, saluted Winter and stepped aside to let her in.

Marcus still wore his uniform, but one leg of his trousers had been cut away and his thigh was swathed in bandages. He was propped up on a pillow, looking a bit gray but undoubtedly conscious.

Seeing him again, especially like this, was strange. Throughout the Khandarai campaign, and even during the fighting around the revolution, Marcus had been Janus' right hand, far above Winter in authority. In her ranker days, she'd thought of the senior officers in the same way the Khandarai thought about their gods, as inexplicable, capricious beings whose notice was to be avoided if at all possible.

Now, though, the eagles on her shoulders matched his, though he was still nominally her superior by seniority. But he had no troops under his command, and his wounded, exhausted state made Winter look at him with new eyes. He was just a man, tired and in pain. *He always was.* That was the secret that the officers conspired to keep the rankers; you gave orders, because it was your *job* to give orders, but it didn't actually mean you knew any better. *We're all just doing the best we can, under the circumstances.*

He looked back at her, and she wondered if the change in their relative status had given him any matching revelations. If it had, he didn't voice them. Instead he glanced at the open door and coughed.

"It's good to see you, Colonel Ihernglass."

"Likewise, Colonel d'Ivoire."

"I need to speak to you privately, if possible." He raised one eyebrow slightly, in what was probably an attempt at subtlety. "It concerns . . . the matter of the Desoltai temple."

Magic, in other words. *The Thousand Names.* Winter nodded at Bobby, who shut the door.

"I think you know Lieutenant Forester, from the

Colonials," she said. "This is Lieutenant Cytomandiclea. They were both involved in an attempt on my life by the Penitent Damned several weeks ago, and I brought them up to speed on . . . related matters." Winter looked at the two women beside Marcus. "I assume the same is true of your companions—wait." The girl's face had finally clicked. "Andy?"

Andy stared at Winter uncomprehending for a moment, and then her eyes went wide. "Oh. *Oh!* You're—" She cut off, uncertain. "You're *Winter.*"

"What are you doing here? I thought you were wounded at Midvale."

"Once I healed up, the Preacher sent me to help Marcus." Andy leaned forward eagerly. "Are the others still with you? Is Jane here?"

"Most of them are here," Winter said, fighting not to show a stab of pain in her face. "They're camped out up the road a bit." Looking at the other woman, Winter realized that she recognized her as well, from their desperate venture under the Vendre. "And you're . . . Rose, was it?"

"Sothe is my real name," the woman said. "I work for the queen."

"She's . . ." Marcus gestured vaguely, trying to find an appropriate description.

"I've seen her work," Winter said.

"They both know what's going on," Marcus said. "The Penitent Damned are working with Maurisk, or else they're running the show entirely. They tried to steal the Thousand Names, and we stopped them for now, but Raesinia got herself captured in the process. We have to get her back before they can get her out of the city."

"Why would they want to get her out of the city?" Winter said. "If they use her as a hostage—"

"She carries a demon that makes her unable to die," Sothe said. "The Penitent Damned want to drag her back to Elysium."

"Ah," Winter said, digesting this rather large revelation.

"Are your troops going to reach the Hotel Ancerre before nightfall?" Marcus said.

Winter shook her head. "I doubt it. They're holding on like ticks over there. We're going to have to dig in and hold through the night, I think. In the morning Janus can bring up more artillery and tear the Island down around their ears if he has to."

She'd made her decision, she realized, sometime in the last few minutes. An all-out rush for the hotel might work, but the odds were against it, and it would certainly cost more lives than she was prepared to spend on an outside chance.

"By morning, they'll have her well away," Sothe said. She glanced at Marcus. "I'm going to get her. By myself, if I have to."

"How?" Winter said. "The Patriots have turned Farus' Triumph into a killing ground, and the surrounding streets are barricaded."

"I'll find a way through," Sothe said, but there was something about her tone that sounded less than confident.

"Even if you do," Andy said, "those Penitent Damned are probably in there, right? The monster who tried to kill Marcus, and the one you fought."

"And Ionkovo," Marcus said. "She's right. You won't have a chance against them alone." He looked up at Winter. "Is there any chance you could sneak a force through? Just enough to get into the hotel and out again. Maybe by the river—"

Winter shook her head. "They've got spotters on the shore." They'd sent small boats out earlier, hoping to find a spot to land a company and outflank the barricades, only to draw fire from the rooftops.

"After dark," Sothe said, "a small group might be able to sneak across the Triumph."

"They'd have to be fools not to put lanterns up—"

"I know a way in," Cyte said.

Everyone paused and looked at her, and she shrank a little, then took a deep breath.

"There's a tunnel," she said. "Under the Triumph. It runs from the south side to the north side, right under the fountain. It's just about big enough for one person at a time. They use it to do maintenance on the pipes. It comes up by the back wall of the Ancerre."

Sothe frowned. "I've never heard of such a thing."

"Not many have. The contract for maintaining the fountain has been with the same firm for the last fifty years, and they're pretty closemouthed about it."

"So how do *you* know?" Andy said.

"The Wastrel Prince, the second son of Farus the Fifth, used to use it to sneak his mistresses into the Ancerre and past his father's guards." Cyte's cheeks colored a little. "I wrote a paper about it, back at the University."

"Is it still there?" Marcus said. "That was decades ago."

"The entrance is, anyway," Cyte said. "I went and found it. It's locked, but it wouldn't be hard to break open."

Marcus caught Winter's eye, and she nodded slowly.

"It's worth a shot," she said. "I'll put together a team from the Girls' Own."

Sothe straightened up and squared her shoulders. "I'll get ready, then."

"Me, too." Andy hopped down from the desk and stretched.

"You don't have to go—" Marcus began.

"If you're going to fight the Penitent Damned, better to have as many people who know what a Penitent Damned *is* as you can get, right?" Andy grinned. "Besides, I missed most of the fight against that old witch. I still owe these fucking Penitent Damned for Hayver."

"I wish I could join you," Marcus said. "But I don't think I'd be very useful at this point."

"You need rest." Winter waved the others toward the door. "Start getting the team ready. I'll be with you in a few moments."

When they were alone, Winter looked down at Marcus. She'd gotten some odd reports from her scouts, and a few pieces were finally falling into place. The picture they formed made her stomach churn.

"It was a Penitent Damned you fought here, wasn't it?" *All those charred skeletons.* They'd wondered if the

Patriots had been drenching civilians in oil and burning them alive. "Some sort of fire demon."

Marcus gave a weary nod. "They set caches of flash powder in the buildings."

"We found them," Winter said. Her mind leapt ahead, full of racing flames. "So when we advanced—"

"The demon would turn the whole district into a firestorm," Marcus said.

"Saints and martyrs." Winter sucked in a breath, goose bumps rising at the thought of how close they'd come to total disaster. And there had been a *lot* of bodies in the street . . .

"All volunteers," Marcus said, reading her expression. "Docks people, refugees. Men and women. Raesinia and I asked them to do it." He smiled weakly. "Couldn't just let them cook you, could we?"

"I . . ." Winter found herself flushing, and coughed. "'Thank you' hardly seems adequate. A lot of men and women owe you and your volunteers their lives."

"Just what I had to do," Marcus said. His eyes were red, and heavy with fatigue. "Listen. Help Raesinia. *Please.* As soon as you can." His hand clenched into a fist, twisting the bedsheet. "She can't die, but she can still hurt. If they get her away from the city . . ."

"We'll find her," Winter said.

"Thank you." Marcus let out a long breath, his fingers relaxing. He put on a small smile. "The eagles look good on you."

Winter touched the gold insignia of rank on her shoulders. "They're heavier than I expected."

His smile broadened a little. "Always."

"Get some sleep," Winter said, straightening. "When Janus gets here, tell him I've gone on ahead."

Cyte and Bobby were waiting for her outside the door, and she gestured them into the empty office next door. Winter closed the door and kept her voice low.

"I'm going," she said. "You know I have to."

"It's going to be hard to explain to anyone who doesn't

know about . . . all this," Cyte said. "What are you going to tell Abby?"

"I'm going to try and avoid her. Bobby, are you in for this? We could certainly use your help."

Bobby nodded, looking down at her hands. Winter frowned, then turned to Cyte.

"You're staying behind." Cyte opened her mouth to object, but Winter cut her off. "Please don't argue. I'm leaving you in command here."

"In *command*?" Cyte's eyes went wide. "That's ridiculous. What about Abby and Sevran?"

"They've got their own problems to deal with. All you need to do is keep sending troops across as they come up and start digging in. Janus will be here in an hour or so, and he'll take over. I want you here to fill him in."

Cyte hesitated, but she could see the logic. "Be careful. We need you."

"I'll do my best." Winter smiled, but it took an effort. "Can you go and ask Abby to put together maybe half a dozen people she'd want in a street fight? Make sure they're well armed, too."

"Yes, sir!" Cyte saluted and hurried out, shutting the door behind her. Winter turned to Bobby, and there was a long pause.

"Are you all right?" she said. "You were pretty quiet in there."

"Sorry," Bobby said. "I was just . . . thinking. I'd got it into my head that this would be over soon. Once we got rid of Maurisk, maybe. But when you started talking about the Penitent Damned, I thought, this is never going to be over, is it? Not for us."

She was staring down at her hand, the one she'd used to stop a sword that would have cut Winter in two. She wore a tight black glove now, but underneath it Winter knew the flesh was white and glittering, like polished marble.

On impulse, Winter stepped forward and wrapped her arms around the girl. It was the first time they'd been so close since that night at the fire in Khandar, and she half expected Bobby to pull away, but she only rested her head gently on Winter's shoulder.

"It won't," Winter said. "You're right. But whatever happens, I promise I'll be there with you."

"I . . ." Bobby's voice was thick. "John talks about what he wants to do, when the war is over."

"Go see him," Winter said. "We've got a little time."

Bobby pulled away, wiping her eyes, and nodded. She caught something in Winter's expression and said, "We'll find Jane when this is over. I know we will. And she'll—"

Winter forced another smile. "I know. Go on."

CHAPTER TWENTY-SEVEN

WINTER

In the end, there were nine of them. Winter, Bobby, Sothe, and Andy, plus a sergeant and four rankers from the Girls' Own. The sergeant, whose name was Maura, was a tall, impressively built woman whom Winter vaguely recognized as one of the Docks people from the days of the old Leatherbacks. In addition to the pair of pistols and saber that they all wore, she carried a long wooden staff, with which she was apparently formidable. Winter was surprised to find two of the Deslandai recruits, Joanna and Barley, among those Abby had picked to go with them.

"They were keen to help," Maura said, her voice surprisingly high for such a large frame. "And I saw them get into some tight fighting in the woods at Jirdos. When Jo hits someone, down they go. And Barely knows what she's doing with those knives."

Winter blinked, a little confused. "I thought your name was—"

"They call me Barely," the slight woman said, with a faint sigh.

"Because she's barely there," Maura said. "Get it?"

"Is it a problem?" Winter said, trying

"You might as well join in. No stopp
point, sir."

The other two rankers, Jenna and Vicky, Winter had never met. The idea that there were women under her command that she'd never *met*, whose names she'd never even heard, filled her with a momentary guilt, but she shoved it aside. They were both Vordanai, who'd volunteered after the declaration of war. Jenna was a Docks woman, about Winter's age, with prematurely gray hair tied up in a coiled braid. Vicky was a Northsider, daughter of a successful livery stable owner, who'd run away to join the army as soon as she heard the Girls' Own was recruiting. They both offered Winter crisp salutes, but the expression on their faces made her uncomfortable. It was the look of women meeting a legend. *When did I become a legend?*

They waited at the foot of the bridge, as the sun slid past the horizon, until a couple of howitzer shells went past, both splashing noisily into the river. Then, with Sothe in the lead, they ran, sprinting across the cracked flagstones of the Grand Span. Here and there, corpses dotted the bridge, unlucky soldiers who'd been caught in the blasts. Winter kept her head down and her mind on her footing. The bridge was nearly a quarter of a mile long, and she was pleased to note she wasn't the only one breathing hard by the time they reached the cover of the buildings on the other side. *Sothe and Bobby look like they could keep running all day, though.*

The entrance was right where Cyte had said it would be, in an alley behind a row of cafés. Most of them had metal trapdoors leading down to their basements, where new stock could be moved in, and the tunnel entrance looked identical to all the others, secured by a battered padlock. Sothe opened this ~~~~ a pair of slim wires and a few moments' work, and ~~~~ as relieved to see that they had the right pla~~~~ a café basement, a ladder led down int~~~~

Andy had brou~~~~, and she handed ~~~~ to Sothe an~~~~ ~~~~ onto her back. She'd ~~~~ stuffed with something ~~~~ she hadn't mentioned it ~~~~ ging the ladder one-handed, and Andy brought up the rear with the lantern dangling from her straps.

The shaft went down farther than Winter had expected, a good thirty feet, before ending on a slimy stone floor. The light of the lanterns revealed a tiny passage, with a large iron pipe fitted to its ceiling. Cyte hadn't exaggerated the close quarters—there was room for one person to walk, bent nearly double at the waist, and that was all. By the time Winter reached the bottom of the ladder, Sothe was already well along, and there was nothing to do but follow.

This was the first potential hurdle. If somehow the Patriots *did* know about the tunnel, it would have been child's play to block it, or arrange an ambush at the other end. They were nearly helpless in such tight quarters, and Winter had her heart in her throat all the way through. She counted steps, to reassure herself that the tunnel had to end *somewhere*. At one point the light showed an open space above her, and she guessed they were under the statue at the center of the square. *Halfway through.* Above them, guns boomed and grumbled, barely audible through the intervening earth.

"I've found the ladder," Sothe said sometime later. "I'm going up." As Winter reached the bottom and started to climb, there was a sharp, metallic noise from above. "Had to break the lock," Sothe reported. "The top's clear."

One by one, they emerged from another trapdoor disguised as a basement access, this time behind the imposing brickwork bulk of the Hotel Ancerre. Joanna, Winter noted, climbed out of the tunnel on distinctly shaky legs, and Barley, right behind her, took her hand and squeezed it tight.

"Are you all right?" Winter said.

The big woman nodded, mutely, breathing deep.

"She's not good with tight spaces," Barley said. "There was this time back when we were kids—"

Joanna slashed her hand in a clear gesture of negation. Barley shrugged.

"She'll be okay," she said. "Just give her a minute."

"That's the kitchen door over there," Sothe said. "I'll

go in first. The rest of you come through when I give the word."

The others all looked to Winter, who nodded. Having seen Sothe in action under the Vendre, she was happy to let her take the lead. They pressed themselves against the wall, four to either side, while Sothe eased the door open and ghosted through. A few moments later, they heard her voice.

"Everyone stay quiet! The rest of you, come in."

Winter opened the door. The hotel kitchens were vast, but apparently underused—only one of the three hearths was burning, and most of the long wooden tables were piled with dirty cookware and other debris no one had gotten around to cleaning up. Four women in dirty linen stood by a tub of foamy water, brushes in hand. They were all staring at a swinging double door, where Sothe was standing. She had her arm around the neck of a man in hotel livery, a bloody knife held tight against his throat. Her other hand held a pistol, aimed at the closest of the women. At her side, another man wearing a Patriot Guard sash was still twitching as blood from the slash across his throat puddled on the floor.

"Don't hurt him!" one of the women shouted, letting her brush fall into the tub. "Please, we—"

"Quiet!" Sothe hadn't discussed her plan beforehand, but Winter felt she got the gist. She kept her voice low. "Nobody's getting hurt if you don't make a fuss."

"We're not with the Patriot Guard," one of the other women said as the rest of Winter's group filed into the room and shut the door behind them. "We just work here, I swear."

"I know. Cooperate, and we'll let you go."

"We'll have to tie them up," Sothe said. "Just in case."

"They didn't give *us* any choice," the man she was holding said. "The boss just told us they were moving in—"

"Prisoners," Sothe interrupted. "Where do they keep the prisoners?"

There was a moment of silence, broken by a crackle

from the hearth. Then one of the women, hesitant, volunteered, "There's no prisoners here. No cells or nothing."

Winter's throat went tight, but Sothe shook her head.

"Maurisk wouldn't let her out of his sight. He's here, isn't he? The Directory President?"

"On the sixth floor," the man said. "We're not allowed up there anymore. We just drop meals off with the soldiers."

"That has to be it, then," Winter said.

"Is there a way up that isn't guarded?" Sothe said.

"We use the back stairs," one of the women said. "But there's a guard, day and night."

"Only one?" Sothe said

The woman nodded.

"I'll handle him," Sothe said curtly. "Winter, get the others tied up and gagged. I won't be long." She removed her blade from the man's throat and said, "Show me the way. If you shout, this is going into your kidney."

He nodded frantically, very pale, and they disappeared through the swinging doors. Winter looked at the four women, and smiled apologetically.

"Sorry," she said. "But we really can't just leave you."

The one who'd spoken first looked at the others, swallowed, and sighed. "I suppose you can't, can you?"

Bobby and Andy handled the binding, using kitchen twine. Even if no one found them, Winter thought, it wouldn't be *that* hard to work loose. They'd just finished gagging the women when Sothe reappeared, still leading her charge at knifepoint. Bobby bound him as well, and set him beside the hearth with the others.

"The stairway's clear," Sothe said, "for the moment." She bent to satisfy herself that the Patriot lying in the doorway was dead, then wiped her knife on his clothes and sheathed it. "I think we can get up to the sixth-floor landing,"

"Lead the way."

Winter gestured the others over, and they crept after Sothe, single file. Winter didn't ordinarily think of herself as noisy, but she felt like a clumsy child in too-large boots following behind Sothe, who seemed to prowl down the drab service corridors without even disturbing the air. They turned a corner, passed another closed door, and reached a switchback staircase, narrow and windowless. Another man in a Patriot Guard sash lay propped against the wall, a dark stain spread across his chest.

"I don't know how long we've got until shift change," Sothe said, her tone implying that this ignorance was a personal failure. "So we'll have to hurry."

Fortunately, there were closed doors separating the back stairs from the hotel proper at every level above the first, and they climbed without sighting any more Patriots. Winter was more worried about running into a servant, but the place seemed deserted. *Most of them have probably run off.* It was strange to be in the headquarters of the enemy, with her own army outside grinding inevitably closer.

Though the sound of the guns had grown more infrequent, she noticed. With night falling, Cyte would be giving orders to dig in and hold until morning.

Six stories up, they were faced with another door. Conveniently, it came equipped with a small peephole, and Sothe peered through it, then gestured for Winter to do likewise.

It looked as though the door was disguised as part of the wall, the better to conceal the presence of servants from the eminent guests. Directly ahead, the main stairs curved upward, gaudy in red carpet and gilt carved banisters. Two Patriots with bayonetted muskets waited at the top, perhaps twenty feet away. To the left, closed double doors presumably led to the grand suite that occupied most of this level, with four more sash-wearing guards standing in front of them.

"Six," Winter said.

"And who knows how many more down below or through the doors," Sothe said. "We're not going to be able to take them all out quietly."

"All right," Winter said, taking a deep breath. "This is ⸱⸱ turns into a fight, then."

⸱n take the two on the stairs," Sothe said.

Winter nodded. "Sergeant?"

"Sir?" Maura said softly.

"Take Jenna and Vicky and follow Sothe. Grab the muskets if you can. Once we start making noise, they'll try and come up the main stairs, but you'll have a good shot and plenty of cover. Keep them back as long as you can."

"Yessir."

"Joanna and Barley, you're with Andy, Bobby, and me. We'll give the guards on the left a pistol volley, then take out anyone still standing."

"Got it, sir," Barley said.

"Okay." Winter put her hand on the door latch and pressed until she felt it click. She drew a pistol with her other hand. "Ready? Three, two, one—"

She slammed her shoulder into the door, throwing it wide, and charged through, clearing the way for the rest. Sothe surged past her, one arm a blur as she threw a knife. It caught one of the Patriots by the stairs in the throat, and he staggered backward, gurgling. His companion gave a shout and lowered his musket, but Sothe had already crossed the distance between them, putting one hand on the barrel and jerking it up before he pulled the trigger. The weapon roared, the ball *pocking* into the plaster ceiling, and the recoil jerked it out of the guard's hands and sent it clattering down the staircase. Sothe drove the heel of her palm into his jaw with a *crunch*, slamming him back against the wall, and had another knife out to finish him before he could catch his breath.

Winter transferred her pistol from her left hand to her right, fetching up against the banister at the top of the stairs and steadying her aim. She sighted carefully—ten yards, not a hard shot—and pulled the trigger. The Patriots were just starting to react, lowering their muskets, and her shot caught one in the chest, driving him against the doors. To Winter's left, more pistols *cracked*, and one of the Patriots dropped his weapon and clutched at his shoulder. Splintery holes appeared in the door where the balls went wide.

She was already moving, dropping her pistol and drawing her sword as she charged through the thin smoke. A musket roared, a deeper sound than the pistol's report, and she flinched but kept moving. The other Patriot set his weapon, bayonet glinting and ready to skewer her, but she spun to one side, dodging the point, and aimed a cut at his head. He was fast enough to get his musket up to parry, her saber leaving a notch in the wooden stock, but Joanna was right behind her, slamming a big fist into the man's gut and then catching him in the back of the head with her elbow as he doubled over. Andy and Bobby, both with swords drawn, came at the other guard, who swung his bayonet wildly from one to the other as they went to opposite sides. He made a wild lunge in Andy's direction, which she deflected easily, while Bobby cut the guard down from behind.

"Get clear of the doors!" Winter said, stepping to the edge of the corridor. The others obeyed, and a moment later there was an explosion of musketry from inside. Big chunks of wooden paneling exploded outward as musket balls punched through the flimsy wood, spraying the corridor with splinters.

"Bobby, open it!" Winter shouted. "Maura, hold here as long as you can, then fall back toward us. Sothe—"

Sothe was already running toward them. Bobby stepped in front of the still-smoking doors and applied her shoulder where they met. Winter had no idea if they were locked or not, but it didn't make any difference; the latch practically exploded out of the wood, and Bobby stumbled through, Joanna and Barley following her with pistols drawn.

The room beyond was a broad foyer, with a big table in the center and a cluster of armchairs at one end. Two doors led off on one side, and three on the other. Of more immediate interest than the sumptuous decor were the six Patriot Guards who'd just fired the wild volley through the door. The two rankers fired their pistols, reflexively, but the shots went wide; Winter, leaning around the door aimed more carefully and put a ball into the fore ne of the Patriots just as the others worked up age for a bayonet charge.

Joanna and Barley, on the left, worked as a well-practiced team as three of the guards closed in. The big woman took the front, waiting until the last moment to dodge the bayonets. She managed to get out of the way of two of them, while the third ripped a narrow cut along her ribs. As this last attack went past, though, she grabbed his weapon and pulled him forward and off-balance. Barley surged out from behind her, opened the Patriot's stomach with one slash of her long knife, and then ducked under the next man's attempt to brain her with a musket butt. She sliced the back of his leg to the bone, jumped under him as he stumbled, and rammed her blade to the hilt in the chest of the third man as he recovered from his lunge.

Winter's opponent, a scared-looking young man, seemed less than fully committed to his attack, and danced backward from his thrust as soon as she feinted at his eyes. She ignored him for a moment, turning to cut down a more energetic guard who was trying to skewer Bobby while she drew her sword. He fell with a cry, and Winter spun back to face the timid boy, only to find a knife sprouting from his throat as if by magic. The musket fell from his nerveless fingers, and he slumped against the wall and slid slowly to the floor. Sothe, coming up behind Winter, had another small knife in her hand.

"More of them coming up the stairs," she said. "I jammed the door to the back steps, and Maura's trying to hold them. But we have to work fast." As she spoke, the roar of muskets and the lighter bark of pistols came from behind them, along with frantic shouting from below.

Winter pointed. One door, on the far right, had a crudely installed bar and padlock on the outside. "If she's here, she's in there—"

The door opposite opened, and Winter felt Infernivore stirring in the pit of her mind as a figure almost twice her height squeezed through the doorway. He was dressed, as he had been dressed the last time she saw him, all in black, with a glittering obsidian facemask. As he stepped forward, two more men, similarly attired, came out behind him, sheltering behind his protective bulk. One was the young man Winter had fought in Desland, and the other was the older man with the long white fingernails. It was the latter who spoke, his Vordanai flavored with a strong Murnskai accent.

"You're bolder than I gave you credit for, Ihernglass," he said. "We sensed you the moment you arrived, of course, and your objective was not hard to guess. I expected to have to hunt you down, but you've kindly delivered yourself exactly where you're wanted."

"You're awfully bold, for someone who was running for his life the last time we met," Winter said, working hard to keep her breathing steady. Her demon thrashed and roared, a caged animal scenting food. *Three Penitent Damned.* She swallowed hard. *If I can just manage to touch them . . .* "We're here for the queen. Stand aside."

"You had the advantage last time of being an unknown factor," the man said. "This time I believe we *quite* understand each other. I will make you a counterproposal. Surrender, and your companions will be permitted to leave."

"I—" Winter began.

"He's stalling," Sothe spit. At the same time, she whipped the blade in her hand in a perfect end-over-end throw that would have ended right between the old man's eyes. Even as the knife left her hand, though, the younger Penitent was pulling his companion to one side, so the blade bit into the wallpaper and stuck there, quivering.

Sothe, who'd apparently expected this, was already drawing two longer knives from her belt. The huge Penitent Damned took a step forward, floor shaking under his tread, and grabbed the big table in both hands. He lifted it high, swinging it down like an oversized club to batter Winter, Sothe, and Bobby into the wall. Bobby, though, caught the other edge of the table in her hands and stopped it cold, the *smack* of wood on flesh audible through the growing firefight in the hallway. She and the Penitent strained, and the wood groaned and popped for a moment before shattering with a noise like a musket shot in a spectacular shower of splinters.

As if this had been the starting gun, the other two

Penitent Damned came forward, one on each side of their giant colleague. Joanna stepped forward to meet the old man, jabbing at his face with a quick punch, but the Penitent was deceptively fast. He let the blow whistle past his head and brought his fingers up and around Joanna's arm, curved nails slipping through flesh as easily as if it were cream. The big woman opened her mouth in a soundless scream as the old man ducked closer for a killing blow, then danced back hurriedly as Barley slid between them, knife slashing at his head.

The giant tore off a piece of the table to use as a club and swung it at Bobby, who ducked the blow and grabbed for the huge man's arm. This time, though, the Penitent seemed determined not to be drawn into a clinch. He gave ground, swinging again, and when Bobby tried to step around the club landed a backhand to the ribs that connected with a *crunch* of breaking bone. Bobby staggered backward, but didn't fall, and the giant came at her. Andy, who'd retrieved one of the dropped muskets, drove it into the Penitent Damned's side as he went past, but he ignored the wound as though it were a flea bite.

Sothe met the third Penitent Damned head-on, a blade in each hand to match his. The two of them seemed to erupt into a flurry of steel, nearly too fast for the eye to follow. But that wasn't quite right, Winter thought. Sothe was fast, faster than Winter would have believed possible, until she seemed to have four arms and four blades instead of two. But the young man was always a half step ahead of her, twisting so that every strike missed him by fractions of an inch, his own blows intercepting Sothe's and leaving long draw-cuts on the meat of her arms. He ducked under an overhand slash and brought his blade up into a gutting move that Sothe avoided only by a frantic parry and step backward.

Winter, sword out, stepped up beside the woman in black, and they exchanged the briefest of glances. That was enough—Winter went right, and Sothe went left. While Winter couldn't match Sothe's speed, the greater reach of her weapon gave her an advantage, and her empty hand could be just as dangerous. This Penitent Damned had barely escaped Infernivore before, in Desland, and he was not eager to repeat the experience. He went on the defensive, even with his uncanny agility, ducking and dodging and only occasionally finding space for his own blades to lick out. But however they tried to press their advantage, he remained out of reach. Small cuts blossomed on Winter's sword arm and a slash across Sothe's shoulder dripped blood, while their opponent remained unscathed.

Bobby, still looking woozy, stepped away from the heavy blows of her opponent, giving ground. Her foot came down on the outflung hand of one of the dead Patriots, and she stumbled forward, as though throwing herself into the Penitent's embrace. He swung a roundhouse at her head, which she avoided by dropping to her knees. The Penitent Damned raised his fists, then roared as Andy darted forward again, sinking her bayonet into the small of his back. He grabbed the weapon from her in one hand, snapped it in half between his fingers, and hurled it aside, then turned his attention back to Bobby.

Bobby, making use of that moment of distraction, had grabbed the giant's ankle. Her hands barely closed around it, but she squeezed hard, with all the supernatural power of Feor's magic in her grip. Something broke with a *snap*, and the giant wobbled. He brought his great fist down between Bobby's shoulder blades with another bone-breaking sound, but Bobby hung on grimly, grinding broken chunks of his ankle between her fingers.

Barley, though skilled with her knives, was no Sothe. Her furious assault had driven the Penitent Damned back, but the old man had more agility than he'd let on. He blocked a cut aimed at his head and let his nails trace paths along her forearm, scoring bloody trails through her skin. Barley screamed, dropping one of her knives, and the Penitent closed his hand around her wrist and swung her into the wall, her head cracking hard enough to leave a dent in the plaster. He raised his fingers to her face, then spun, warned by some movement in the air behind him.

Joanna was back on her feet, one arm sheathed in red, breathing heavily. The old priest feinted at her wounded side, other hand ready to slash when she dodged, but the big woman simply bulled through the attack. His nails cut deep into her side, slicing through skin and muscle and grating against bone, but she kept coming, swinging a balled fist hard into his face. Blood sprayed from his nose as it broke, and he staggered back in time to get a round-house punch to the side of the head that sent him sprawling to the floor on top of one of the Patriot corpses.

Winter's opponent, backward against the wall, spun away from Sothe and left himself open to her sword. She lunged, almost instinctively, and realized too late that the move was a feint. He was already sliding away, and her saber slid through the wallpaper and the plaster under-neath to strike a wooden beam and stick hard. One of his knives was already coming up toward her wrist, and only by hurriedly releasing her sword did she manage to avoid losing a hand. She backed up, pawing for another weapon, as Sothe stepped in front of her.

A change had come over the black-clad assassin. Her fighting, which earlier had approached ragged desperation, had regained the icy calm with which she'd dispatched the Patriot Guard. Her moves were careful and precise, none of them close to striking home, but keeping the Penitent on the defensive and backing away. As the pair of them passed her, Winter was astonished to see the Sothe had her *eyes* closed, hands moving as if by pure instinct in the complex dance of blades.

The Penitent took one more step back, setting himself up for an attack, and his foot came down on the barrel of a fallen musket. Sothe's eyes snapped open, and she bulled forward, accepting a long cut across her back to drive both her knives toward the young man's face. He stepped backward, and the musket shifted underneath him—not much, but enough to put him off-balance, and he stumbled backward into Winter, who wrapped her arms around his midsection.

Not getting away this *time.* She held him tight, as though in an embrace, and slipped Infernivore's leash. The demon surged out of her and into the Penitent, furious with frustrated appetite. There was a moment of conflict as the two creatures warred, but only a moment. Then Infernivore was rushing back into her, fattened by its kill. Winter felt the young man sag against her. His face was a mask of blood, streams of it running from his eyes like tears. When she let him go, he fell limply to the floor.

That left the giant. He'd pried Bobby's hands free of his ankle, and one of her arms dangled obscenely, bent backward at the elbow. He raised her into the air, gripping her by the shoulders, and though she landed blows from her good arm with all her supernatural strength behind it, his grip didn't falter. Winter thought for a moment that Bobby would be torn in half, like a sheet of paper, and she didn't think even Feor's *naath* would let her recover from *that*—

Then the giant dropped her, spinning as best he could with one leg crippled. The brown satchel Andy had been carrying hung from his back, pinned there by a saber that Andy had driven into his flesh for half its length. The young ranker was backing away, a pistol already in her hand, as the giant spun in place, trying to reach the weapon that impaled him.

"Everybody *down*!" Andy screamed.

Bobby, one arm dangling, threw herself away from the giant. Winter and Sothe dove for the floor, and Joanna covered Barley with her body. Andy fired, and Winter heard the *ting* of metal on metal as the ball struck the sack she'd attached to the huge priest. Then there was a *thump*, a sound so loud it reverberated in her breastbone and behind her eyes, and a wash of heat that frizzled her eyebrows.

Slowly, Winter unfolded herself and looked around. The giant was still standing, but his right arm and shoulder were simply gone, and ribs emerged from the bloody, smoking mass of his flesh like dead plants from winter soil. His black face mask had been shredded, as had the skin underneath, and both hung from his skull in torn rags.

And yet he wouldn't die. *Couldn't* die, maybe. As Winter watched, he turned, torn muscles moving visibly in one leg where they'd been laid bare. One of his eyes was gone, the socket leaking vile, gory fluid, but the other stared down at her with a bright, mad glare. His remaining hand scrabbled weakly on the floor for something he could swing.

Winter's ears were still ringing, and the world tilted wildly around her, but she stepped forward and put her hand against the giant's chest. She felt the demon inside her surge at the proximity to one of its fellows, felt its boundless hunger, and she willed it down through her arm and into the Penitent Damned. *One more time.* The two demons met, and tangled about each other, but again the contest was a brief one. Infernivore, the demon that consumed its own kind, spread through the other demon like a drop of blood spreading into clear water, rapidly converting the other's substance into more of itself. When there was nothing left of the giant's demon, Infernivore surged back through the huge man's body and into Winter's hand, diving once more into the darkest recesses of her soul. The huge priest blinked once, and then his eye rolled back into his head and his massive form sprawled in the wreckage of the table and lay still.

What followed was not silence, since the firefight at the other end of the hall continued, but it was relative stillness. Winter's ears still rang with the force of the blast, and tiny nicks and scrapes she hadn't been aware of were starting to make themselves known all over her body. Andy raised her head from where she'd crouched against the wall, and Bobby, her broken arm already working again, pressed herself up from the scorched floor. Joanna had been closest to the blast, and the back of her uniform was torn and bleeding from shrapnel, but she managed to get shakily to her feet.

"Everyone . . ." Winter paused. "Okay" seemed like a stretch, considering. "Still alive?"

Joanna pointed urgently to Barley, who was still lying against the wall. Winter hurried over, then noticed the old man, lying nearby where Joanna had laid him out, was still breathing.

"Bobby!" Winter pointed. "Skewer him if he moves."

Bobby nodded, retrieving a musket and leveling it at the Penitent. While Winter knelt beside Barley, Andy went to Joanna, whose arm was still dripping a steady patter of crimson onto the floor.

"I'll get this door open," Sothe said, bending to examine the lock.

Blood trickled from a cut on Barley's scalp, and Winter probed it delicately with her fingers. The wound was gory, but not deep, and the skull beneath seemed intact.

"I think she'll be okay," she said to Joanna as Andy bound up the big woman's wounded arm. "Nothing broken. We'll get her to the cutters once we get out of here—"

"Colonel!" The scream came from the hallway. "Colonel, they're coming!"

"Balls of the *fucking* Beast," Winter swore, turning back to the doorway. One of the rankers, Vicky, had her hands beneath Sergeant Maura's armpits, dragging her toward the doorway and leaving a darker stain on the red carpet in her wake. A blue-uniformed body lay motionless amid a cloud of powder smoke at the top of the stairs, and the clatter of booted feet mixed with victorious shouts as the Patriot Guards ascended.

"Joanna, watch the old man!" Winter said. "Bobby, Andy, load these muskets!" She grabbed one of the dead Patriots' weapons herself, pulled a handful of cartridges from the corpse's belt pouch, and tore one open with her teeth. It had been a long time since Winter had gone through the manual of arms, but her muscles remembered the movements—powder in the lock, close it up, the rest down the barrel, spit the ball after it, ram the whole mess home with the rod. Raise the weapon to your shoulder—

A dozen Patriots had made it to the top of the stairs, and from the sound of it more were coming. Winter leveled the weapon and fired, and a man in the middle of the group went down. The rest dove for cover, stopping behind the banister or throwing themselves flat. One fired, and Winter heard the ball go wide. The rest, it seemed, hadn't reloaded before their triumphant charge, and struggled awkwardly with their too-long weapons.

Andy fired as well, raising splinters from the banister. Winter turned to Bobby and held out a hand, and the girl passed a loaded weapon.

"Get some of those chairs," Winter said. "We have to barricade the doors."

Bobby nodded and ran to the back of the room. Winter aimed and fired at one man who'd gotten up, missing but sending him diving back to the floor. Before the rest recovered their courage, she ran to the front of the foyer and closed the double doors just after Vicky dragged Maura across the threshold. By themselves, the doors didn't offer much of a barrier, splintered with holes as they were, but Bobby arrived soon after carrying a heavy leather armchair. Andy dragged another one into place, and they went back for more. Vicky manhandled the wounded sergeant out of the way.

"Winter!" Sothe said from where she was standing by the unconscious Penitent Damned. "I need to get Raesinia out."

And then what? Both stairways were on the other side of the now-barricaded door. *The window, maybe?* They were on the sixth floor, but it wasn't far to the neighboring building. *We might be able to jump for it . . .*

"Go!" Winter said. "Joanna, can you keep a sword to this bastard's throat?"

Joanna nodded, a vicious grin on her face. She patted Barley and drew her blade, shifting it awkwardly to her unwounded arm. Sothe bent back to the padlock as Andy and Bobby piled another pair of armchairs against the door.

"You," Winter heard Andy remark to Bobby as they went back for the last two, "are a lot tougher than you look."

"Got it," Sothe said. The door swung open.

Winter had only seen the Queen of Vordan on state occasions, in formal mourning dress. She hadn't really expected to find her imprisoned in a voluminous gown, but she certainly hadn't pictured this: a short, slight young woman, in boyish trousers, bare-shouldered, with a bedsheet tied around her torso. Sothe dropped to one knee, head down.

"Hi," Raesinia said. "What kept you?"

"We ran into some . . . difficulties." Sothe kept her head down. "I'm sorry. I should never have—"

"Done what I told you to do?" Raesinia said, grinning.

"Yes." Sothe looked up, and Winter wasn't sure what was more shocking, the tears gleaming in her eyes or the smile on her face. "I should never, ever have done that."

Raesinia extended a hand to her servant and pulled her up, then wrapped her arms around her. When they finally stepped apart, she seemed to notice the carnage in the room beyond for the first time.

"Oh," she said. "I heard the fighting, but I didn't realize . . ." She took a deep breath and looked at Winter. "You're in command?"

Winter wasn't sure if she was supposed to salute or not. She settled on a bow. "Yes, Your Majesty. Colonel Winter Ihernglass."

Once before, outside the Vendre, she'd felt Infernivore stir in Raesinia's presence. Glutted with two meals, it nonetheless shifted uneasily now. Winter wondered if there was a limit to its hunger, and resolved not to touch the queen if she could possibly help it. She *thought* she could restrain the demon, but no sense taking chances.

"Are your people all right?" Raesinia looked over the scattered, dismembered corpses, showing none of the squeamishness Winter might have expected from the gently born. "It looks like a bomb went off in here."

"That's more or less what happened. We lost one on the stairway, and—" Winter looked at Vicky, who was standing beside the slumped sergeant. The ranker shook her head, tears cutting through the powder-grime that coated her face. "Two. Everyone else should live, if we can get out of here."

Raesinia was silent for a moment, her jaw set, then let out a breath. "Any plans for that?"

RAESINIA

Two more, dead for my sake. More sacrifices for a life that isn't even real. Raesinia fought down her feelings and kept her face impassive.

Winter looked uncomfortable. "Not . . . yet. There's about twenty Patriots on the other side of that door."

They were already shoving at it, though the heavy arm-chairs shifted only slightly. Raesinia could hear fists pound-ing on the wood and raised voices from the other side.

"What about Maurisk?" Raesinia said. "Have you found him?"

Winter shook her head. Sothe quickly opened both doors on the side of the room where Raesinia's cell had been, revealing quarters for another servant and a water closet, both empty. The open door the Penitent Damned had come in by led to a dining room, and a quick glance proved this also to be unoccupied. *That leaves one.*

Sothe put her hand on the latch, but Raesinia waved her aside.

"Your Majesty—" Sothe began.

"We both know that if he's sitting in there with a pistol, it's better if I open the door," Raesinia said. "Stay back a bit, just in case."

She thumbed the latch and pushed the door open. Inside was an office, richly furnished in gleaming hard-wood and gilt, bookshelves lined with matched sets of leather-bound volumes. Directly in front of the door, a prim-looking young man stood with a small sword in hand, waiting in a painfully erect stance right out of a fencing salon. Behind a vast desk, slumped over in his chair, sat a nearly empty wine bottle

jangling fre... Kellerman and ...

"It's . . ." The young man blinked, and the sword quivered. "It's, um, the queen. I think."

"Ah. You may as well stand down, then."

"Sir," Kellerman said, looking over Raes...

"They've slaughtered the guards—"

"Stand down," Maurisk said, a hint of st... his tone. He raised the bottle to hi... then let it fall on the carpet with...

I hadn't expected to see you li...

"Whereas I must admit I was hopin
the sort," Raesinia said. She stepped
man lowered his sword and moved out
risk's bleary eyes focused on her. "I'm a
disappoint Dr. Sarton."

Maurisk barked a laugh. "He'll get his
another. Executioners and grave diggers a
ners of every war."

"Charming." She gestured at the doc
Get up."

He frowned. "Why?"

"Quite a few of your Patriot Guards are ou
going to tell them what you told Kellerman.

"Why would I do that?" Maurisk straig
though his head still lolled slightly. "Perhaps
take my chances when they break in."

"If it comes to that, you haven't got any chanc
sinia said. "I'm offering you a bargain, and it's c
for the next few minutes. Either tell your people
down, right now, or die, right now. Not imprisonm
a trial, no second chances." Raesinia leaned closer
borrow a knife from Sothe and drive it into your f
eye. Get it?"

He was silent for a moment, sizing her up. Kellerr
sword came up again, until Raesinia glanced in his d
tion, at which point he became so flustered
the thing entirely.

"You know I'll do it," Raes. after all, I'd
be returning the favor."

"I believe I stabbed you in the heart," Ma
mured. "Which, as Dr. Sarton tells us, is the seat
sensation, and thus produces a painless death."

"We can compare notes afterward," Rae
"But I'm certain you're going to disappoin
said, a his lips and tippe ump. "You

Winter looked uncomfortable. "Not . . . yet. There's about twenty Patriots on the other side of that door."

They were already shoving at it, though the heavy armchairs shifted only slightly. Raesinia could hear fists pounding on the wood and raised voices from the other side.

"What about Maurisk?" Raesinia said. "Have you found him?"

Winter shook her head. Sothe quickly opened both doors on the side of the room where Raesinia's cell had been, revealing quarters for another servant and a water closet, both empty. The open door the Penitent Damned had come in by led to a dining room, and a quick glance proved this also to be unoccupied. *That leaves one.*

Sothe put her hand on the latch, but Raesinia waved her aside.

"Your Majesty—" Sothe began.

"We both know that if he's sitting in there with a pistol, it's better if I open the door," Raesinia said. "Stay back a bit, just in case."

She thumbed the latch and pushed the door open. Inside was an office, richly furnished in gleaming hardwood and gilt, bookshelves lined with matched sets of leather-bound volumes. Directly in front of the door, a prim-looking young man stood with a small sword in hand, waiting in a painfully erect stance right out of a fencing salon. Behind a vast desk, slumped over in his chair, sat the President of the Directory, a nearly empty wine bottle dangling from one hand.

"Who is it, Kellerman?" Maurisk said without raising his head.

"It's . . ." The young man blinked, and the tip of his sword quivered. "It's, um, the queen. I think."

"Ah. You may as well stand down, then."

"Sir," Kellerman said, looking over Raesinia's head. "They've slaughtered the guards—"

"Stand down," Maurisk said, a hint of steel entering his tone. He raised the bottle to his lips and tipped it back, then let it fall on the carpet with a thump. "Your Majesty. I hadn't expected to see you like this."

"Whereas I must admit I was hoping for something of the sort," Raesinia said. She stepped forward as Kellerman lowered his sword and moved out of the way. Maurisk's bleary eyes focused on her. "I'm afraid I'll have to disappoint Dr. Sarton."

Maurisk barked a laugh. "He'll get his fill, one way or another. Executioners and grave diggers are the real winners of every war."

"Charming." She gestured at the door. "Come on. Get up."

He frowned. "Why?"

"Quite a few of your Patriot Guards are outside. You're going to tell them what you told Kellerman. It's over."

"Why would I do that?" Maurisk straightened up, though his head still lolled slightly. "Perhaps I'd rather take my chances when they break in."

"If it comes to that, you haven't *got* any chances," Raesinia said. "I'm offering you a bargain, and it's only good for the next few minutes. Either tell your people to stand down, right now, or die, right now. Not imprisonment, not a trial, no second chances." Raesinia leaned closer. "I will borrow a knife from Sothe and drive it into your fucking eye. Get it?"

He was silent for a moment, sizing her up. Kellerman's sword came up again, until Raesinia glanced in his direction, at which point he became so flustered he dropped the thing entirely.

"You know I'll do it," Raesinia said. "After all, I'd only be returning the favor."

"I believe I stabbed you in the heart," Maurisk murmured. "Which, as Dr. Sarton tells us, is the seat of all sensation, and thus produces a painless death."

"We can compare notes afterward," Raesinia said. "But I'm certain you're going to disappoint me and take the other option."

"I am, am I?" Maurisk said. "Why is that?"

"Because you're a coward," Raesinia said bluntly. "You always were. You were happy to write speeches and print pamphlets, while Faro and Ben and I did anything the least bit dangerous. Then, when you finally had a chance to enact your beloved principles, you ignored them the moment they were a threat to your position."

"I had a fucking war to fight," Maurisk said, voice slurring a bit. "That doesn't get me any credit?"

"Not with me. I don't blame you for hating me. You have every right to that. I might hate me, in your position. But you made it about more than just me." Raesinia lowered her voice. "There was a young woman, standing next to me, the day of the executions. Just in the wrong place at the wrong time. I had to pull her son off her body." He'd grow up without a mother. *Nobody deserves that.* Another victim, another life ruined by standing too close to Raesinia Orboan.

"—you made it about *everyone*—" Maurisk was saying, but Raesinia was suddenly tired of the game. It had felt good, coming in here and having her say, but in the end it didn't matter. *It certainly won't do Claudia and Emil any good.*

"Enough," she cut him off. "We're done here. Are you going to call them off, or do I need to find a knife?"

Maurisk met her eyes for a moment longer, then looked away.

"Zacaros? Zacaros, are you out there?"

The pounding on the door stopped, and after a pause a deep voice answered, "President Maurisk?"

"You and your men are to stand down. Lay down your arms and leave the hotel. Send messages to the rest of the Guard. The fighting is over."

"You can't be serious!" Zacaros sounded almost frantic. "If they've got a blade to your throat, then I'll have no choice but to assume command."

"The queen and I have reached an . . . accord. We will negotiate with General Vhalnich. It's *over*."

"The queen?" Raesinia could hear muttering among the troops outside, and she raised her voice.

"I'm here. And President Maurisk is right. The time for fighting is done."

That seemed to tip the balance. The majority of the Patriot Guard, Raesinia guessed, didn't know about Maurisk's attempts on her life, any more than they knew about the alliance with the Penitent Damned. As far as they were concerned, they were still fighting in defense of the queen and legitimate authority against a rebellious general.

She could almost hear the wheels turning in Zacaros' head, even from the other side of the door. If he chose to ignore Maurisk's orders and killed everyone present, he could take power for himself, but there was no way to be sure his soldiers wouldn't balk at orders to silence their own monarch. And if the queen was determined to stop the fighting—

There was no way out, no solution except obedience that led anywhere good. Still, Raesinia held her breath for a moment.

"Understood," Zacaros said. "Lay down your weapons, men. I'll pass the command to the others." He hesitated. "There's still some fighting between our men and the rebels. May I have permission to raise a flag of truce?"

"Go ahead. Tell them thank you, and that they can go home."

Raesinia doubted he would go *that* far, but it didn't matter. Morning would bring Janus' troops into the city in numbers too great to be resisted. *It's good enough.* She turned to Winter.

"I'd be grateful, Colonel, if your soldiers might unblock the door. And, Sothe, it might be best if you took the president somewhere quiet until things calm down."

"Gladly," Sothe growled, and took a grip on Maurisk's arm, pulling him toward Raesinia's old cell.

Two of the rankers went to work moving the chairs they'd shoved in front of the door. Raesinia noticed for the first time that Andy was among the soldiers who'd come to her rescue when the girl paused in front of her on the way to help them.

"Marcus told me you'd be all right," Andy said. "I don't know if I really believed him. I saw—I thought I saw—"

"It's a long story," Raesinia said, patting her on the shoulder. "But I'm fine. I'm glad you're here."

"I . . ." Andy bowed her head. "Thank you, Your Majesty."

Another ranker, a big woman with her arm bound up in bandages, tugged on Winter's sleeve for attention. She gestured at one wall, where a man in a black obsidian mask lay slumped over. He was sitting up now, groggy, flexing his fingers. His nails were an inch long, and sheathed in blood, as though he'd dipped his fingers in red paint.

Winter reached down and pulled the mask off while the ranker kept her bayonet leveled at the man's throat. Underneath, the Penitent Damned looked ordinary enough, an older man with thinning hair and an angular Murnskai cast to his features. He blinked, looked up at them, and sighed.

"What's your name?" Winter said. "I know you speak Vordanai."

He nodded. "In Elysium, they called me the Liar."

Raesinia raised an eyebrow. "They must not have liked you very much."

"What were you doing here?" Winter said.

"The Lord's business," the Liar said. "Retrieving the Thousand Names. Killing Ihernglass and his master for the crime of sorcery, and bringing you back to Elysium for the same reason."

"Sorcery," Raesinia said bitterly. "You say that like I made a choice."

"Sin is always a choice." The Liar leaned his head back against the wall. "I chose it because I knew it was how I could do the most good for my fellow men, even if it meant an eternity of damnation for me. All the Penitent Damned—"

"Save your self-flagellating theology for someone who cares," Raesinia snapped. "Where is Ionkovo?" At a glance from Winter, she said, "He's the leader, or seemed to be. I didn't see him out there."

"Shade is furthering the cause of the Almighty in his own way." The Liar looked from one of them to the other. "You think you've won, don't you? Because you defeated us in this little battle. The game is larger than that. Your precious general will not save Vordan, not if you persist in this madness. What will you have left when he falls? Only surrender to the Almighty can save you in the end."

"Janus will want to speak with him," Raesinia said. "We'll have to tie his hands—"

"I think not." The Liar took a deep breath and said in a clear voice, *"Ahdon ivahnt vi, ignahta sempria."*

Then, before anyone could make a move to stop him, he brought his hand up, long nails slashing cleanly through the skin of his own throat. Blood gushed forth, and his next breath was a choking gurgle. His head slumped back against the wall, eyes wide and staring at something beyond the walls.

"This," Winter said to the world in general, "is why I hate fanatics. First the Redeemers, now these lunatics. What is wrong with people?"

"You should get back to Janus," Raesinia said. "He needs to know what happened here."

Winter looked at the dead Penitent Damned, and gave a slow nod.

CHAPTER TWENTY-EIGHT

WINTER

At Raesinia's insistence, Sothe accompanied Winter downstairs, in case any Patriot Guards had ignored their commander's orders and wanted to fight to the last. They took the servants' passage, back toward the kitchen, narrow and switchbacking.

"All right," Winter said as Sothe peered suspiciously around another bend and then waved her forward. "I have to ask."

"Hmm?" Sothe said. Her sleeves were damp with blood where the Penitent Damned had cut her, but she didn't seem to notice.

"When you were fighting the Penitent, at the end. You had your *eyes closed*."

"Oh." Sothe pulled up short, looking uncharacteristically embarrassed. "You saw that?"

Winter nodded, and Sothe sighed and ran a hand through her hair.

"I was . . . guessing, really. His style was predictable, the same responses to my moves every time. So I could get away with closing my eyes for a few seconds, as long as I kept the initiative. Any longer than that and he would have killed me."

"But why?"

"I was playing a hunch. The way he moved—it was like he could see what I was going to do before I did it. But when he had to fight you as well, I noticed he wasn't as fast when he was looking the other way. I think he had a . . . power—a demon, I suppose—that let him . . . *see* better? Or see more detail." Sothe frowned. "I don't understand magic. But I guessed that he wasn't looking into the future or seeing into my mind, just reading cues from my body. Everyone has them, little motions, no matter how hard you try not to. The eyes are critical. I knew he was backing toward bad footing, but he would be able to read that from my eyes, so for a few seconds . . ."

Winter stared at her, and Sothe just shrugged.

"I had no idea if it would work. But I couldn't beat him any other way, so I thought it was worth a try."

"That's . . ." Winter shook her head. "Someday you're going to have to tell me where you learned to fight like that."

"It's a long story," Sothe muttered.

In the kitchens, the servants they'd bound were still there, huddled together in a corner. Winter left Sothe to cut them free and went around to the stables, where she commandeered a horse and tackle. She rode back through the lines, the guns abruptly silenced as the news rippled out from the hotel. It outpaced her, racing through the embattled city faster than fire, spreading on the wind in shouts and joyous exclamations. The details were lost as it went, as usual, but the gist remained: the fighting was over. Winter heard men from the Army of the East crowing over their triumph, or cursing that their commanders had called a halt before final victory. Even the latter, though, seemed relieved that the prospect of a confusing, drawn-out battle in darkness had been averted, and already the camps were taking on an air of celebration in spite of the best efforts of suspicious officers.

The Silver Eagle building was abuzz with activity when she reined in outside, slipped out of the saddle, and left the horse with an astonished aide. Girls' Own soldiers stood on guard by the doors, but they were talking excitedly to one another rather than watching the street, and Winter had to cough before they recognized her.

"Sir!" one ranker said, and offered an astonished salute, while the other hurriedly opened the door.

"Is the general here?"

"Yes, sir," the woman said. "And Captain Giforte wants to speak with you."

Abby had, in fact, sighted Winter already, and was on her way across the floor, threading past the rows of wounded. She looked mad enough to chew lead shot, and Winter took an involuntary step backward.

"Hello," Abby growled, "*sir*. Would you come with me, please?"

"I need to see Janus," Winter said.

"He's been asking for you." Winter hurried after Abby as she stalked away. In a low voice, the captain said, "When you asked me to put together a team for a special operation, you didn't tell me *you* would be going along."

"I figured you'd object," Winter said.

"Damn right I'd object," Abby said. "You are the *colonel* of this regiment, not a goddamned ranker. You're not supposed to go sneaking through tunnels behind enemy lines."

"Sorry. It's hard to explain."

"You're going to have to explain it to Janus," Abby said.

This was actually something of a relief, since Janus would at least understand the reason she'd had to go along. *I'm the one who carries the Infernivore. I couldn't send people up against the Penitent Damned and stay behind.* The demon seemed more active than usual, stirring around in the back of her mind, like a twitching muscle she couldn't actually pin down to a spot on her body. *Maybe getting something to eat got it excited.*

"We rescued the queen," Winter said as they climbed the stairs to the less crowded second story of the building. "And captured the President of the Directory. I hope that counts for something?"

"It might." A smile broke through Abby's stormy expression. "That's for the general to decide."

"Captain!" someone shouted from below. "Captain Giforte!"

"Duty calls," Abby said. "Janus is using the office at the end of the hall. When you're done, I'm going to want a *full* account, so be ready."

The second story was mostly offices, separated from one another by thin partitions. For the most part, they were dark and silent, but lamps glowed at the end of one corridor, and Winter could see a musket-bearing sentry waiting in front of the door. It was good to see that Janus was taking his own security seriously, even in friendly territory. Winter walked over, and the guard, a woman she knew vaguely, offered a salute.

"Sir," she said. "I'm sorry, but the general has instructed me to admit no one."

"He wanted to see me as soon as possible," Winter said. "Can you tell him I'm here?"

"I have specific orders he's not to be disturbed, sir." The sentry looked nervous, which Winter supposed was understandable. *It's never easy to say no to your commanding officer.* She put on what she hoped was a reassuring smile.

"It's all right. I'll wait, then." The door to the next office over stood open, and through it Winter could see a pair of heavy leather armchairs. All the weariness of the past few hours seemed to descend on her at once, and her legs felt as sturdy as cooked noodles. "I'll be in here. Let me know when he's ready."

The sentry looked as though she was about to object, but kept silent. Winter sat down, gratefully, in one of the chairs, sinking into the overstuffed leather cushions. Cuts and bruises all over her body were making themselves felt. *A bath,* she decided. *I need a bath.* She held up her arm, where blood had matted her sleeve. *And maybe a few stitches. I think Abby has the right idea. No more leading from the front . . .*

She leaned back, head bumping against the back wall of the office. As she did, she realized she could hear voices from the next office over, muffled but audible.

". . . is it that you want?" That was Janus. Winter

straightened up, not wanting to eavesdrop, but the next voice froze her in her seat. Even through the wall, it was intimately familiar.

"I want you to let Winter go."

Jane.

"Let her go?" Janus said. "I wasn't aware I was keeping Colonel Ihernglass against her will."

Jane snorted. "Neither is she. That's how you get to people. You get into their heads, make them think going along with you is their own idea. I've been watching it happen to my girls."

"I don't suppose you're willing to consider that they follow me because they believe I'm doing the right thing?"

"They follow you because you've got them all twisted up," Jane said. "You're a clever fucker, no doubt about that. But you can't have Winter."

Winter pushed the chair closer to the wall, all thoughts of propriety abandoned. *Jane's here? How could Abby not have told me?*

The answer came to her a moment later, sending a chill down her spine. *Abby doesn't know.* She remembered, belatedly, the name of the sentry—a woman named Coin, who'd been one of Jane's Leatherbacks, and had followed her with a loyalty that was closer to worship. *I always thought it was strange she didn't leave with Jane and the others. But it can't just be her.* There must be others among the Girls' Own loyal to Jane, who'd stayed deliberately to wait for an opportunity to . . . *what?*

"The fact remains," Janus was saying, "I don't believe Colonel Ihernglass would leave the regiment if you asked her to."

"Right," Jane said. "You've got your claws in too deep. That's why you're going to *order* her to do it. Tell her it's over, that you don't need her anymore. Get her away from the army, and I'll take care of the rest. Once she's seeing clearly again, she'll thank me."

"I would be extremely reluctant to lose an officer of her talents—"

"You've got the city," Jane said, a pleading note entering her voice. "You could declare yourself king, if that's what you want. You don't need her anymore."

"There's more to it than that. You know, I believe, what she did in Khandar."

"The demon?" Jane sounded as though she wanted to spit. "I know."

"The Black Priests will not let her go."

"That's what *she* told me. But we only have your word for that, don't we? Maybe the Black Priests only care about her because she's working with *you*." Jane paused. "Anyway, whatever it is, we can handle it. We did fine in Desland, no thanks to you."

"So you want me to do this out of the goodness of my heart?" Janus said. "Or is it the pistol that's supposed to convince me?"

Oh, Balls of the fucking *Beast*, Winter thought. She pushed herself out of her chair, weariness falling away under a tide of adrenaline. Out in the corridor, Coin was still waiting in front of Janus' office, looking more nervous than ever.

"Sir," she said, "he's still—"

"I know," Winter said. "I realized I've got some notes I should collect. I'll be back in a moment."

She strode confidently down the corridor, around the corner, and then sprinted to the main stairs. The second floor was mostly deserted, but a pair of rankers were coming down the steps, talking to each other and laughing. Winter grabbed one of them by the arm.

"Hey—uh, sir?" The startled woman froze, and her companion awkwardly saluted. "What's wrong?"

"Go and find Abby," Winter hissed. "Tell her to bring a half dozen people up to Janus' office. *Now*. And quietly, no shouting."

"Sir—"

"Just go!" Winter let go and turned around, heading back up the corridor. She forced herself to slow down as she turned the corner, walking back toward Coin at a nonchalant pace.

"Sir," the young woman said at her approach, "perhaps you'd rather wait downstairs, and I'll send for you—"

Winter kept coming, and Coin's eyes went wide a moment too late as she realized her commander wasn't going to stop. She moved to lower her musket, but Winter was too close, stepping beside her and driving a low, fast punch into her gut. All the air went out of the sentry with a grunt, and she dropped writhing to the floor when Winter slipped past her.

She tested the latch on the door and found it unlocked. Very slowly, Winter eased it open a fraction and applied her eye to the gap.

Janus was standing behind a big desk at the far end of the room, hands spread on top of its leather blotter. Jane was in the corner, the pistol in her hand trained on his chest, hammer cocked. Her red hair was matted, and her uniform soiled by several days' worth of sweat, but the sight of her made Winter want to break down and cry.

Jane, June, what the fuck are you doing?

"You'll write the order," Jane said. "Then you'll stay here until I've shown it to Winter and we're well away. Then you're welcome to do whatever the fuck you want, as long as you stay away from us."

Coin was stirring, fumbling for her musket. Winter kicked her in the side of the head, took a deep breath, and pushed the door open. Jane's pistol swung around, reflexively, as she entered, and Winter braced herself for the shot. It didn't come.

"Fuck!" Jane said, rapidly moving to cover Janus again. "Saints and martyrs, I nearly fucking shot you. How did you get in? I told Coin—"

"Jane, what the hell are you doing?" Winter said.

"Rescuing you," Jane said. "Again."

"Colonel—" Janus began, but Jane interrupted him with a snarl.

"One more word out of you and I'll shoot," she said. "I'm tired of you manipulating her."

"This is insane." Winter let the door close and stepped

away from it, moving slowly. "What do you think holding a pistol on Janus is going to accomplish?"

"What's insane is what he's done to you. He's been using you, all this time, and you *thank* him for it. He got you involved in all this, he put a *demon* in your head, and in return you'll follow him anywhere." Her lip twisted in a snarl. "I don't know how he does it, but it ends now, if I have to end it myself."

"Put it down, Jane."

"What has he done for you?" Jane said. "What has he done for any of us but asked us to sacrifice, over and over—"

"Janus has saved my life, more than once," Winter said. "We all would have died in the desert without him—"

"You wouldn't have *been* in the desert without him! *None* of this would have happened without him!" There were tears in Jane's eyes. "We were finally making it work. Those years after Mrs. Wilmore's were bad, but we were finally making it work, and then this *fuck* comes along and turns everything over. And now my girls are marching into cannon-fire and getting their fucking arms and legs hacked off with dull knives, and they all still *thank* him for it."

"That was my fault," Winter said. She took another step forward, raising her hands. "I was the one who came to the Leatherbacks."

"Because he sent you there! You think he gave a fuck about you, or me, or any of the others? He *needed* us, so he used you to get what he wanted."

"You were the one who got them to volunteer," Winter snapped. It wasn't the right thing to say, it wasn't helpful, but she couldn't stop herself.

"Because he had his hooks in me, too," Jane said. "It took me a long time to see my way clear. But I'm out now, and you will be, too." Her voice dropped, nearly to a whisper. "Come with me, Winter. Away from this, away from the army, away from everything. Just you and me, like it was always supposed to be. Please. *Please.*"

It felt as if something in Winter's chest was tearing itself apart. "I can't," she whispered. "You know I can't."

"I love you, Winter. More than anything. *Please.*"

"I . . ." Winter's throat was too thick to speak.

Jane, pistol still trained on Janus, was looking at Winter, and Winter saw her eyes harden. She looked the way she'd looked the night they captured Bloody Cecil, when Winter had stopped her from executing her prisoner by a hair's breadth. *Mad Jane.*

"Fuck," she said under her breath. "All right. New plan. I'll kill this fucker and we'll get you out of here until whatever he did to you wears off."

"Jane, no."

"Why not?" Jane's voice was high now, tinged with hysteria. "He's a traitor, isn't he? I saw the government's declaration, all official. I'd be a hero."

Winter took a long step forward, placing herself in front of the desk, squarely in Jane's line of fire. Jane's eyes, brilliant green, locked on hers, and the hand holding the pistol trembled. There was a long moment of silence.

"Why?" Jane whispered. "Why would you go so far for him?"

"Because I have a responsibility to the people in my regiment. The rest of the army. Everyone. We *need* him. Vordan needs him."

"You never believed that 'glorious death for king and country' bullshit," Jane said. "We used to laugh about it at the Prison, reading those old books! It was *Vordan* that put us there. It was the *Crown* that signed off on my 'marriage' to Ganhide, signed me up for getting fucked by the stinking brute every night. You want to know the kind of things he did to me?"

"You killed him, didn't you?" Winter felt she was seeing Jane with new eyes.

"Of course I fucking killed him," Jane said. "I burned him alive and I laughed while I did it. Then I went back to Mrs. Wilmore's and slit the old bitch's throat like the fucking pig she was. If I'd had my way I would have had them raped over and over, once for each little girl they sold to some old bastard—"

"Jane, stop." Winter could feel tears in her eyes. "Please."

"Don't take the high road with me," Jane said. "You killed your Sergeant Davis, didn't you? And God knows how many others, the people you're 'responsible' for, you send them to die when Janus gives the order, don't you? Don't you dare moralize at me."

"Just . . . stop."

"If it were me, I'd give it all up," Jane said. "You know that, don't you? I'd give up everything for you."

"I know." Winter struggled to breathe. "But I can't."

There was a pause. In the silence, Winter could hear boots pounding down the corridor, voices raised in alarm. Jane's hand shook, the barrel of the pistol wavering.

"I should have known," Jane said. "If you loved me the way I love you, you would have killed Ganhide when I fucking told you to."

The door burst open. Jane's finger jerked on the trigger.

Twice before, Winter had stared down the barrel of a pistol and known she was going to die. The first time, in Khandar, it had been the incompetence of Davis' cronies that had saved her. The second time, under the Vendre, it had been Sothe. This time—

—the hammer came down, spraying sparks—

—the powder in the pan ignited, hissing into smoke—

—and that was all. *Flash in the pan.*

Dumb luck.

She sank to her knees, her vision blurred with tears. As the guards rushed into the room and Janus shouted orders, all she could hear was the distant sound of Jane's hysterical laughter.

CHAPTER TWENTY-NINE

RAESINIA

With the Hotel Ancerre occupied by Janus' troops, Sothe had commandeered a suite at the Grand for the queen, hastily "returned" from her exile in the country. It was the same hotel where she'd once looked out on the Exchange and watched Cora ruin one of the mightiest Borelgai banking houses with little more than a rumor and the magic voice of Danton Aurenne. Neither the food nor the service was up to the standards of those days, the war having obviously taken its toll, but at least there was plenty of wine.

Organizing the Army of the East to control the city and guard against potential counterattacks by Directory diehards had taken most of a day, which had given Raesinia time to send to Ohnlei for some of her old things. It meant that she could at least greet Janus looking like the queen instead of a boyish revolutionary. She'd chosen a dress a bit less severe than those she'd favored earlier, still mourning black in memory of her late father, but accented with silver and a hint of lace. Sothe, her bandages carefully hidden beneath her own elegant attire, had helped her put it on without comment.

Now, waiting in the dining room beside the vast, bare table, she felt suddenly nervous. Janus had never given her reason to suspect he was anything but a devoted servant of the crown, but the fact was that he was in a position to do exactly as he pleased, at least for a while.

There was a deferential rap at the door, and a hotel footman announced, "Your Majesty, General Vhalnich has arrived."

"Let him in," Raesinia said.

To her surprise, Janus was alone, without the usual string of guards and aides. He wore his dress uniform, Vordanai blue with a cape of Mierantai crimson, a thin sword on his hip. The footman, resplendent in the uniform of the Grand, came in just behind him.

"Do you require anything, Your Majesty?" the servant said.

"No," Raesinia said. "See that we're not disturbed."

"Of course."

The footman bowed and withdrew. At Raesinia's gesture, Janus crossed the foyer to stand before her in the dining room. He also bowed, very low, his cape draped wide.

"Your Majesty," he said. "I can't tell you how good it is to see you in good health."

She searched his face for the slightest hint of a smirk, and found nothing. He, of all people, knew that her health was not an issue.

"And you, General," Raesinia said. "Please, sit. I apologize for my lack of hospitality, but I thought we should speak in private."

They were alone in the huge suite. Sothe had herded all the servants out hours ago, then departed herself to double-check Janus' security arrangements. Mierantai guards prowled the halls, and blue-uniformed soldiers from the Army of the East stood watch at the doors and in the stairways.

"A break from being constantly assaulted with hors d'oeuvers is just the thing," Janus said, taking the chair opposite her. "Everyone in Vordan seems to want to invite me to a feast. I sometimes feel like they're fattening me up for the slaughter."

"They're grateful," Raesinia said. "*I* am grateful. I'll

say that officially, of course, but I want you to know that I mean it personally as well. You and your army saved the city from Maurisk and the Black Priests, and saved *me* from God only knows what fate."

"Colonel d'Ivoire and Colonel Ihernglass had a great deal to do with the latter," Janus said. "Frankly, I arrived too late to be much good."

"I'll convey my thanks to them, too, of course." She cocked her head. "You'll be able to retrieve the Thousand Names?"

"Oh yes. The river is barely ten yards deep at that point, and steel tablets won't drift in the current. It shouldn't take long to haul them out again."

"That's good." Raesinia paused, trying to decide how to raise the main issue. Her indecision must have shown on her face, because a quick smile flickered across Janus' features, like summer lightning.

"You want to know what I'm going to do with Vordan City," he said, "now that I've got it."

"The thought had crossed my mind," Raesinia said, obscurely relieved. In a way, it was freeing to be so helpless. She had no army, no loyal followers, nothing to match the thousands of soldiers who would march at Janus' command. *But march where?*

"The Deputies General is in chaos now that the Directory has been arrested," she went on. "Maurisk locked up most of the Ministry of War, and now they've been let free, but nobody seems to know what to do with themselves." Giles Durenne had been one of the Spike's last victims. His second in command, Captain Robert Englise, was trying to keep the basic logistical apparatus of the army running, but it seemed like an uphill battle.

"The situation is confused," Janus agreed. "I think that, just now, the country needs a strong hand to guide it."

This is it, then. The end of the Orboan dynasty, the moment where Janus elevated himself from general to king. *I wonder what he'll do with me.*

"I . . . don't disagree," she said cautiously. "But . . ."

"Let me speak plainly, Your Majesty." Janus put his

hands on the table. "I will not take the throne. Not only would it be against every oath I have sworn, as an officer and a nobleman, but I don't *want* it." He gestured down at his uniform. "War is where my talent and interests lie. Once peace returns, I wish to . . . withdraw."

Raesinia blinked. "Then what are you going to do?"

"What I swore an oath to your father to do. What I told you I would do, before the revolution." He smiled again, there and gone in an instant. "I am going to win the war and make you the queen your father would have wanted you to be."

MARCUS

There was a knock at the door. Marcus put down the paper he'd been reading—a rather lurid account of the battle of Jirdos, from one of the newly reopened presses—and pushed himself up a little higher in bed. His thigh throbbed abominably with every movement, and the skin *itched* under the wool bandages, which was almost worse.

"Yes?" he said.

"I wondered," came Janus' voice, "if you might spare a few moments."

"Oh! Come in, sir."

The door opened, and the general entered. Marcus was mildly surprised to see that he was in the dress uniform he'd worn to Cabinet meetings before the revolution.

He saluted, as best he could from his seated position, and said, "Sorry that I can't stand to attention, sir, but—"

Janus waved a hand airily. "Enough of that. How are you feeling?"

"Not quite as bad as I was." He'd nearly bitten through the gag when the surgeon extracted the metal fragment from his thigh. "Doctor-Professor Haartgen says that if the wound was going to fester, it would have done it by now, so I'll probably keep the leg. He says I may come out of it with a bit of a limp, but considering the circumstances I'd count myself lucky."

"I'm glad to hear it."

Janus pulled a chair across the room and set it beside the bed, then sat, careful not to tangle his cloak or the decorative sword at his side. They were back at the University, something Marcus couldn't but find a little disconcerting given what had happened, but Haartgen had insisted that the facilities were superior. He had to admit it was more comfortable than his cot in the converted office building that housed most of the other casualties, although the vast, echoing emptiness of the halls attested to how few of its residents had returned.

"It's good to see you, sir," Marcus said.

"Likewise," Janus said. "I'm sorry I couldn't come sooner, but matters have been . . . unsettled, as I'm sure you can imagine. I can't stay long, I'm afraid."

"I understand, sir." Marcus had been getting the news in bits and pieces of gossip and hysterical broadsheet articles, but he'd pieced together the gist. "I believe congratulations are in order."

"I suppose they are. I'm due at the Deputies-General in an hour, where they're going to vote on . . . well, the forms are complicated. The legal scholars were up all night going through the precedents."

"They're putting you in charge," Marcus said.

"More or less." Janus lowered his head, hands in his lap. "The Directory is officially dissolved. The queen and I have had negotiations . . ."

He trailed off. Marcus frowned.

"Is something wrong, sir?"

"I didn't come here to discourse on politics," Janus said. "I wanted . . . I felt that I ought to apologize. I believe I have done poorly by you."

"Sir?" Marcus shook his head. "If anything, I'm the one who should be apologizing. You left me here to protect the queen and the Thousand Names, and I lost them both."

"I left you with an impossible task," Janus said. "I had hoped that secrecy would be sufficient to protect the Names, but in retrospect it seems obvious that the Priests of the Black would have more than ordinary means of gathering information. With the forces at your disposal, I could hardly expect you to stand up to the Penitent Damned."

Marcus shook his head, not sure what to say. In the privacy of his own skull, he'd entertained similar thoughts, but he found he couldn't voice them, not to Janus.

"And yet," the general went on, "you did stand up to them. I have heard the story of your attack on the fire demon, and seen the bombs the Patriot Guard planted. Thousands of my soldiers owe you their lives."

"I had a lot of help," Marcus said. "It was Raesinia—that is, the queen—who really took charge. And Sothe, Andy, and the others made it work. The Leatherbacks and the refugees." He swallowed. "A lot of good people died there."

"A great many people have died," Janus said, "both good and bad, to get us this far. But we are not finished yet."

"We're still at war," Marcus said.

"I expect the Hamveltai will sue for peace, and the rest of the League will follow. They were always the least committed to the fight, and with Antova and Desland in our hands their ability to attack us is crippled. The queen will, I expect, offer generous terms. But Borel and Murnsk are still unbloodied, and the emperor in particular has barely begun to exert his strength." Janus paused. "But that is not the heart of it. The queen tells me you know her secret."

Marcus nodded. "She carries a demon."

"The Thousand Names may eventually provide a key to help solving that problem. But the Priests of the Black will not make peace, not now. They know we have the Names, and they know a demonic presence sits on the throne of Vordan. A faith cannot be destroyed with cannonballs."

"So how do we beat them?"

"We must go to Elysium," Janus said. "We must break their power at the source, or we will never have peace."

"Elysium." Marcus stared. "You're—of course you're serious. You're always serious. But—"

"I know the objections," Janus said, holding up a hand. "Elysium is deep in Imperial Murnsk, surrounded by the armies of the emperor and a sea of hostile fanatics. It is a fortress-city that has never been taken, even during the

Demon Wars, when the Church was young. And it is full of *things* like the one you fought on the Green Road."

"That about sums it up, yes," Marcus said. "So how do we get there?"

A brief smile crossed Janus' face. "The same way we get anywhere else, Colonel. One step at a time." His eyes sparkled, but his expression became serious again. "I wanted to ask if you were with me. After what happened here, no one would blame you for wanting to be out of it, least of all me. I could arrange an easy post somewhere, or a comfortable retirement, whichever you'd prefer."

"I . . ." Marcus shook his head.

He'd always considered himself loyal to crown and country, but it had been a vague, distant thing, buried under more pressing concerns. In Khandar, he'd fought for nothing more or less than survival, against what often seemed to be impossible odds. He'd followed Janus home, and when the revolution broke out he'd been mostly driven by a sense of duty to the men under his command, the Armsmen who'd become his responsibility.

Now Janus was willing to declare those responsibilities at an end. But while country had become vaguer than ever—Marcus wasn't certain what Vordan really meant anymore—*queen* had taken on a personal solidity. She wasn't some abstract ideal, a monarch whose honor his oaths obligated him to defend. She was a short, pretty woman with a quick smile, who wore ridiculous boyish trousers whenever she got the chance, never listened to advice when she ought to, and felt the pain of everyone who got hurt trying to protect her like a spear in her own heart. She'd been forced into this world, the world of demons and Penitent Damned, and for the crime of survival the Black Priests wanted to lock her away forever.

He wanted to protect her. But the best place to do that was on the battlefield.

"I'm with you, sir," he said. *As though that was ever in question.* He wondered if Janus knew what he was going to say before he said it, whether he asked only for form's sake. "May I ask one favor, though?"

"Of course," the general said.

"No more skulking on street corners, please. Just give me a command in the field. A battalion of good men." Marcus waved his hands, a gesture intended to encompass the whole city around them. "I've had enough of this kind of war."

"I think I can do considerably better than a battalion," Janus said. "The army will soon enter winter quarters, which will provide a welcome respite and a chance for reorganization. I'll find you a place deserving of your talents."

"Thank you, sir."

"Again, it's the least I can do."

"Have you had any word of Alek Giforte, or the Preacher?"

"I'm glad to be able to say they're both well. Captain Giforte took his men deep into the forest and managed to elude the Patriot Guard pursuit, though he asked me to express his regret that he wasn't able to provide more help. Captain Vahkerson was still awaiting trial for treason when we liberated the Directory prison. Apparently, there was something of a backlog."

"I'm glad to hear it, sir. They were both of considerable assistance."

Janus nodded and got to his feet, straightening his cloak so it fell neatly around his sword. "Well. I have a ceremony to attend, and you need to rest. I'll give your regards to the queen. She asks after you often, by the way."

"Please thank her for me." Marcus hesitated. "For . . . everything."

"I will." Janus turned away, red cloak billowing neatly behind him.

RAESINIA

The Deputies-General had spared no expense. In part, Raesinia guessed, this was to disguise their own impotence. With the Directory dissolved, the Patriot Guard disbanded, and the mob still enthralled by their heroic general, the legislature was helpless to resist Janus' demands, and they knew it. To reassure themselves of their own importance, they'd gone into a frenzy of pomp and ceremony. Artisans had descended on the Sworn Cathedral, mending, replacing, and polishing, until every inch of woodwork gleamed and every carven saint seemed ready to spring to life.

The great and powerful were streaming back into the capital now that the fighting was done, eager to get back to the business of suckling at the national teat. Carriages were lined up four deep in the square outside the Cathedral, and soldiers of the Army of the East formed a human fence that kept the mobs at bay. The royal procession, however, was waved past the lines of those waiting to disembark, and the driver brought the coach to a halt in front of the main doors, in a space kept empty by a pair of women in blue uniforms. A female captain waited between them while another young ranker fetched a set of cushioned steps to enable Raesinia to get down without jumping.

"Your Majesty," the captain said, saluting.

"Captain," Raesinia said.

"May I say how honored I am that you requested the services of our battalion as your escort?"

"It seems only fitting," Raesinia said. "Is Colonel Ihernglass here?"

"I'm afraid not, Your Majesty," the captain said, frowning for a moment. "The colonel is . . . resting."

"Understandable. May I ask your name, then?"

"Captain Abigail Giforte, Your Majesty." She saluted again, then extended a hand. "If you'll follow me?"

The two rankers fell into step behind them as they went inside. More soldiers had cordoned off a path, but beyond them, the cream of Vordanai society had gathered to gawk at their young queen. Raesinia found herself falling back into her old habits, walking with neatly upright posture and eyes carefully avoiding meeting anyone's gaze, as her old tutors had taught her. *Give them a chance to stare. That's what you're here for. Don't send any signals that you don't* mean *to send*. It had been drilled into her until it was unconscious instinct.

"You serve under Colonel Ihernglass, then?" Raesinia said as they walked at a dignified pace down the long hallway.

"Yes, Your Majesty. I command the Girls' Own—that is, the First Battalion of the Third Regiment of the Line."

"I owe your men—your soldiers, I mean—a great deal."

The captain dipped her head. "They'll be honored to hear it, Your Majesty."

The great arch was before them, and beyond it the main hall. The last time Raesinia had been here, it was a wreck, but the Deputies-General had refurbished its meeting place and left very little trace of its original sacred purpose. Two long, tiered benches lining the walls provided seats for the actual deputies, while a visitors' gallery occupied the space where the altar and pulpit had once stood. Between them was the speaker's rostrum, a polished wooden podium set atop a marble plinth with room for five or six people to stand. Sothe was already there, along with four more women soldiers. Raesinia's head of household curtsied as she approached, and whispered in Raesinia's ear as she passed.

"I've been over every inch of this place, in case you're worried."

"No bombs this time?" Raesinia said, equally quietly.

"Nothing but a few rats."

At Raesinia's request, the soldiers standing beside her on the rostrum were the four who'd survived the raid on the Hotel Ancerre. Andy, stiff as a board, looked close to panic as the attention of the room focused on them. Joanna, one arm still wrapped in bandages, seemed to take the scrutiny in stride, but she kept stealing glances at her smaller companion—Barely or Barley, Raesinia wasn't certain which and couldn't figure out a polite way to ask—who had a bandage wrapped around her head like a crown. Vicky, the last, wore an elegantly tailored dress uniform complete with gilded sword with an expression of severe embarrassment.

The new President of the Deputies-General was an octogenarian Free Priest from Essyle, a jolly if somewhat forgetful old boy whose greatest feature was that, as a complete nonentity, he was regarded by all parties as a safe choice. He tottered up to the rostrum now, bowed deeply before Raesinia, and straightened up again with only a little difficulty. Once installed behind the podium, he cleared his throat, and in a creaky voice said, "I declare the one hundred and eighteenth session of the Deputies-General of the Kingdom of Vordan open."

There was more, something about procedures and minutes, but it was drowned under a rising cheer. Deputies on both sides of the aisle got to their feet, applauding for Raesinia, or for themselves, or for Vordan in general. The president kept talking, regardless of the fact that no one could hear him, and the crowd had only begun to fall silent when he finished his long preamble.

"As our first item of business," the president said, "our esteemed monarch, Queen Raesinia Orboan, has come to make an address. Your Majesty?"

"Thank you," Raesinia said. Sothe, efficient as ever, discreetly pushed a cushioned step behind the podium so Raesinia would be able to stand at something like the correct height. Raesinia took her perch and looked out at the sea of faces, the deputies in their bleachers and the balconies full of onlookers, the hall full of those who hadn't been able to cadge a seat. And, beyond them, the nation, waiting for the broadsheets that would spread her words across hundreds of miles.

It's a good thing, she thought, *I don't get stage fright.* She pried her hands, carefully, away from where they had taken a death grip on the edges of the podium, and began her speech.

It was a good speech—not her very best work, but as a speaker Raesinia was no Danton Aurenne. The marvelous acoustics of the Cathedral carried her voice to every corner of the vast room and muted the buzz of conversation in the crowd. She thanked the deputies for their efforts, which brought another round of applause, and thanked the dead and wounded soldiers for their sacrifice, which was met by an appropriately solemn silence. She trotted out the required platitudes about hoping for peace and prosperity—*was there ever a ruler who wished for ruin and disaster?*—while maintaining a will to resist aggression.

She was following a script, and the audience nodded along, like connoisseurs of the theater at a well-remembered play, following every nuance of this particular performance. She said things because it would be remarked on if she *didn't* say them. Her mind ran ahead, to the end of the speech, where the only substance lay. Most of the audience knew what was going to happen, or had guessed, but she had to say the words to make it real. *Like I was a magician,* she thought, and had to work hard not to giggle.

"The events of the past few months," she said, working up to the peroration, "have made it clear that the military of Vordan requires a single guiding hand, a single will to forge it into a sword aimed at the hearts of those who threaten our kingdom. There must be no more accusations of treason, no more feuding generals. My father, if he were alive, would have taken on the task himself."

When he had, Raesinia reflected, it was a disaster. Her father had been a great man, and a brave one, but he'd never had the talent for the battlefield.

"But this is a new age," she went on. "Vordan has a constitution, and true power is vested in the ultimate sovereign, the people, as represented by their deputies in this assembly. The monarch should not command the nations' armies, lest she be tempted to ignore the will of the elected representatives. Yet we also must not stray down the path of the Directory and bring the iron fist of military discipline to civilian affairs.

"I have taken the answer from history. The ancient republics of the Old Coast were wise in this, as in so much else. When war or disaster threatened, they would appoint a single leader best able to deal with the problem, men who would step aside when the crisis was past. Today, I ask the Deputies-General to follow their example, and to name Count General Janus bet Vhalnich Mieran the First Consul of the Kingdom of Vordan!"

Not bad, she thought, as the applause began. The bit about the constitution—which still did not technically exist, in anything but the broadest outline—had been certain to play well with the men largely responsible for it. Emphasizing the limits of the new post, rather than its vast powers, made it more acceptable in a city so recently out from under the bloody hand of a tyrant.

The title "consul" had been Raesinia's suggestion. It carried the weight of history, the connotations of great men who worked selflessly for their republic and then stepped aside. And the truth was that Vordan needed Janus, with practically unlimited authority, if it was going to stand a chance once the vast, slow-moving legions of Murnsk were brought to bear and while Borel continued its stranglehold on the coasts.

Now Janus himself appeared, immaculate in army blue and the red of his home county. He was escorted up the aisle between the deputies by four men of the Mierantai Volunteers, with red uniforms and long rifles on their shoulders. They stopped, standing rigidly at attention, and saluted, while Janus took a few more steps forward and then sank to one knee.

"Count Mieran," Raesinia said. "If the Deputies-General does grant my request, will you serve in the post of consul for as long as the emergency requires?"

"I will, Your Majesty," Janus said, his normally soft voice ringing throughout the hall.

"And do you swear, on your sacred honor, to exercise the powers granted to you only in defense of Vordan and its interests?"

"I swear, Your Majesty."

"And do you swear that on the successful conclusion of the war, you will relinquish your office, and submit yours to the orders of this assembly, where all authority rightfully resides?"

"I swear, Your Majesty."

"Then I submit my proposal to the Deputies-General," Raesinia said, turning to the president. "I request a vote."

She stepped back, and the old man took the podium again, going through the motions. The vote was more or less a formality, of course. Even if Janus' troops hadn't occupied the city, the streets wouldn't have stood for anything less than their hero being put in charge of the nation's armies. The deputies had tasted the mob's wrath once before, for failing to put Janus in command, and she doubted any of them wanted to try it again.

Looking down at him, though, Raesinia felt suddenly uncertain. This was the right thing to do, the only thing she could have done, but there was a sudden, awful sense that she'd stepped over a cliff without looking down. Janus stared up at her, gray eyes huge and luminous, and the briefest of smiles flashed across his face.

Be wary of Vhalnich, the Ghost had said. *He plans deep.*

EPILOGUE

SHADE

Adam Ionkovo pulled himself out of a shadow when the guard turned her back, landing on the flagstones with the slightest rasp of leather on stone. The woman, in a blue army uniform with a musket on her shoulder, was still looking toward the stairs, listening to a muted conversation from the guardroom above.

They were in the cells under the Guardhouse, former headquarters of the Armsmen, which Janus' Army of the East had taken over for important prisoners. One level down, Maurisk and the rest of the Directory languished, along with a few other "traitors" who'd been rounded up or surrendered themselves. This level was unused, except for this single cell, with its single prisoner.

It was also only a few floors away from where Ionkovo himself had been "imprisoned" while he was playing his little game with d'Ivoire. The irony was not lost on the Penitent Damned.

He had chosen his moment carefully. The *infernai*, the desert creature who served the Beast, had dogged his every step the past few days, especially when he came anywhere near either Vhalnich or the queen. The sand-thing couldn't keep Ionkovo from slipping away, but he couldn't hurt it, either. A stalemate, which the Penitent found intensely frustrating. But tonight, with both the queen and Vhalnich at the Sworn Cathedral, he was betting that the *infernai* would be there, too, giving him at least temporary freedom of action in other matters.

A few steps, and he was behind the guard. His right arm slipped up and over her shoulder, then down across her throat to stifle her cry, while his left slid a knife from its sheath and slipped it gently between her ribs. She bucked and twitched against him for a moment, then stilled, and he held her for a moment longer before withdrawing the blade and letting the corpse slip to the floor. He cleaned the weapon on her shirt, sheathed it, and took the keys from her belt.

The door had a small, barred window, and through it he could see the prisoner was awake. Jane Verity's red hair was a tangle, her clothes in tatters. Her green eyes were bright, though red streaks suggested she'd been crying.

The closest lamp was several yards away, leaving the corridor thick with nice, dark shadows. Ionkovo slipped into one, submerging like a diver going underwater only to resurface a few feet away, inside the cell. He stepped out of a shadow on the wall, and Jane backed away, eyes widening.

"You're one of *them*," she said. "The Penitent Damned."

"I am," Ionkovo said. He wasn't wearing his mask, but there wasn't much point in denying his identity now. "You can call me Shade, if you like."

"Are you here to kill me?" Her eyes went briefly to the door, and he realized she'd seen him kill the guard.

He shook his head. "I'm afraid we have need of you. Winter Ihernglass is an object of great curiosity to the pontifex, and I am assured that you know her best of all." *And,* he thought to himself, *we need to salvage* something *out of this debacle.* If you couldn't win a battle, the next best thing was to acquire advantages that might help you win the next time.

"I'm not going to tell you anything," Jane spit. She grinned, savagely, and spread her hands. "If that's what you want, you might as well kill me now. If you can."

"I don't doubt your resolve," Ionkovo said. "If my colleague the Liar were here, we could do this in situ, but I'm afraid he is inconveniently deceased. Thus, in order to get what I need, I will have to take you with me."

"I'm not going anywhere with you, either—"

Ionkovo could move very fast when he had to. He'd drawn another knife, a tiny, thin one, little more than a needle, and held it flat against his side while they spoke. Now he whipped it across the cell, sinking it into Jane's neck just above her collar. She slapped at the little blade, knocking it away and leaving only a tiny cut. When she looked back at him, perplexed, he could see the toxin was already taking effect. Her pupils widened, and she swayed on her feet.

"What . . . ," she managed before collapsing in a boneless heap.

"Something we use at Elysium," he said. "Transporting the demonically possessed can be hazardous, so we've developed a few useful techniques for handling prisoners. Sleep now."

Ionkovo waited another count of fifty, until he was sure Jane's eyes were closed and her breathing was slow and regular. Then he lifted her onto his shoulder, with some difficulty, and concentrated hard.

He couldn't bring other people with him into the shadows if they were awake; he suspected their will interfered with the clarity he needed for the process. With a great effort, he could force the door open wide enough to admit himself and an unconscious companion, though even a short trip would leave him drained and gasping. These days, he took care to drug his would-be passengers thoroughly. Once a young boy he'd been carrying had awoken while on the other side of the shadow, and the results had been unsettling, even to one like Ionkovo, who was hardened by years of service.

But Jane was out cold, and would be for some hours. Ionkovo exerted his will and drew aside the veil, stepping out the way he had come. He took the keys with him. It wasn't strictly necessary, but their absence, with the murdered guard, would make it look as if Jane had somehow escaped on her own. That would cause a bit of consternation, he judged.

Every little bit helps. He grinned to himself, slipping through the endless dark.

DJANGO WEXLER

THE GUNS OF EMPIRE
A Shadow Campaigns Novel

After their shattering defeats at the hands of brilliant General Janus bet Vhalnich, the powers that oppose Vordan have called all sides to the negotiating table in hope of securing an end to the war. Queen Raesinia is anxious to see the return of peace, but Janus insists that any peace with the implacable Sworn Church of Elysium is doomed to fail. For their Priests of the Black, there can be no truce with heretics and demons they seek to destroy, and the war is to the death.

Soldiers Marcus d'Ivoire and Winter Ihernglass find themselves caught between their general and their queen. Now each must decide which leader truly commands their loyalty—and what price they might pay for final victory.

And in the depths of Elysium, a malign force is rising—and defeating it might mean making sacrifices beyond anything they have ever imagined.

R0229

ALSO AVAILABLE FROM

DJANGO WEXLER

THE SHADOW OF ELYSIUM
An e-book novella set in the world of the
Shadow Campaigns series.

Bound and tied, guarded day and night, Abraham has been
stolen from his village, from the arms of the man he loved.
He is being sent to the fortress-city of Elysium to serve a
dark and ancient order, the Priests of the Black. They have
discovered the secret he kept all his life: that inside him
dwells a demon that allows him to heal…and to kill.

But Abraham is not alone. A young woman named Alex,
similarly possessed, rides with him. And as a bond grows
between them, they begin to wonder if they can turn the
demons that have damned them into their salvation.

Praise for the Shadow Campaigns Novels

"Highly entertaining."
—*New York Times* bestselling author Anthony Ryan

Available wherever e-books are sold
or at penguin.com

R0203

Want to connect with fellow science fiction and fantasy fans?

For news on all your favorite Ace and Roc authors, sneak peeks into the newest releases, book giveaways, and much more—

"Like" and Follow Ace and Roc Books!

facebook.com/AceRocBooks
twitter.com/AceRocBooks